Girls' Night In

4

Praise for previous books in the *Girls' Night In* series:

'An entertaining and witty anthology by contemporary female novelists' – *The Times*

'The latest literary phenomenon' – *The Sunday Telegraph*

'An inspirational volume' – *Marie Claire*

'An enchanting and insightful collection featuring anyone who's anyone' – *Elle*

'The perfect girls' night in' – *Vogue*

'A stellar collection and a fundraising phenomenon' – *The Age*

'This funny and feisty collection of womens' short stories has girl power written all over it' – *The Mirror*

www.girlsnightin.info

Girls' Night In

4

Edited by
Jessica Adams,
Maggie Alderson,
Nick Earls &
Imogen Edwards-Jones

PENGUIN BOOKS

PENGUIN BOOKS

Published by the Penguin Group
Penguin Group (Australia)
250 Camberwell Road, Camberwell, Victoria 3124, Australia
(a division of Pearson Australia Group Pty Ltd)
Penguin Group (USA) Inc.
375 Hudson Street, New York, New York 10014, USA
Penguin Group (Canada)
90 Eglinton Avenue East, Suite 700, Toronto, ON M4P 2Y3, Canada
(a division of Pearson Penguin Canada Inc.)
Penguin Books Ltd
80 Strand, London WC2R 0RL, England
Penguin Ireland
25 St Stephen's Green, Dublin 2, Ireland
(a division of Penguin Books Ltd)
Penguin Books India Pvt Ltd
11 Community Centre, Panchsheel Park, New Delhi – 110 017, India
Penguin Group (NZ)
Cnr Airborne and Rosedale Roads, Albany, Auckland, New Zealand
(a division of Pearson New Zealand Ltd)
Penguin Books (South Africa) (Pty) Ltd
24 Sturdee Avenue, Rosebank, Johannesburg 2196, South Africa

Penguin Books Ltd, Registered Offices: 80 Strand, London WC2R 0RL, England

First published by Penguin Group (Australia), a division of Pearson Australia Group Pty Ltd, 2005

1 3 5 7 9 10 8 6 4 2

Cover and text design by Jay Ryves © Penguin Group (Australia)
Illustrations by Anna Johnson
Typeset in Galliard by Post Pre-press Group, Brisbane, Queensland
Printed and bound in Australia by McPherson's Printing Group, Maryborough, Victoria

National Library of Australia
Cataloguing-in-Publication data:

  Girls' night in 4.

  ISBN 0 14 300379.8.

  1. Short stories, English. 2. Short stories, Australian.
  I. Adams, Jessica.

823.01.08

www.penguin.com.au

Contents

Wendy Harmer

Foreword

You can sometimes lose sight of the big wide world on a girls' night in.

Start to focus on what you don't have. A lover for instance – sitting on the other end of the couch, or lying in the bed next to you, or perhaps crammed up one end of a bath full of marshmallow-scented bubbles with their toes tickling your elbows. An object of desire who's looking at you from under thick lashes and thinking, 'I hope she puts down that bloody book soon so I can kiss her.'

You can think about all the things you wish you were doing. Maybe watching a handsome barman putting the final flourish of a pink paper umbrella in a tall, tantalising cocktail. Dancing in a nightclub, heaving in an exciting, sweaty chaos of light and sound.

You can think of all the places you'd rather be. Tripping along the Champs Élysées past the shop windows, swinging a beaded handbag the exact shade of your newly polished toenails. Strolling along a pale slice of beach framed with palm trees and bathed in the light of a tropical moon.

But these few paragraphs at the front of this book are to remind you that right now, as you sit reading in a peaceful place, you are the envy of most of the women on the planet.

For so many of the world's women a girls' night in is a prison sentence. For all the women labouring until the early hours under a single light globe embroidering scraps of silk with calloused fingers; the women huddled in corners with weeping children, singing lullabies to cover the sound of approaching gunfire; the women lying in despair on hard beds in brothels waiting for their next anonymous customer; the women who can't sleep for hunger or for the terror of watching a baby dying of disease in front of them – for all these women what you are doing right now is almost beyond imagining.

You should know that by buying this book you are helping War Child and No Strings to alleviate the suffering of women and children throughout the world.

And, as you read, with every page count your blessings.

With every word make a wish for a peaceful girls' night in for every woman, everywhere. Be thankful for the simple, rare pleasure of just holding this book in your hand.

With love,
Wendy Harmer

From the editors

Thank you to all the people who have made the
Girls' Night In series work so well:

The fantastic authors who've generously contributed
the wonderful stories that make up this book.

Our amazing Australian editor, Susan McLeish, and
our publisher, Julie Gibbs, at Penguin Australia. Our
wonderful UK editor, Katie Espiner, plus Lynn Drewe
and all at HarperCollins. Farrin Jacobs at Red Dress
Ink USA and Andrea Crozier at Penguin Canada.

Our founding agent in Australia, Fiona Inglis, plus
our queen of contracts, Tara Wynne, and all at Curtis
Brown Australia.

Our esteemed English agent, Jonathan Lloyd, plus Camilla Goslett, Alice Lutyens and all at Curtis Brown UK. Eugenie Furniss at William Morris. Our American agent, Laura Dail, and our founding American agent, Deborah Schneider.

Rebecca Lamoin and all at War Child Australia. Julian Carerra and all at War Child UK. Johnie McGlade and all at No Strings.

Our energetic American editors, Chris Manby, Carole Matthews and Sarah Mlynowski, and our founding American editor, Lauren Henderson. Our founding editor, Fiona Walker.

James Williams, for the website.
(Take a look at www.girlsnightin.info)

And, above all, you, whoever you are, for buying this book and helping to make a difference.

Jessica Adams
Maggie Alderson
Nick Earls
Imogen Edwards-Jones

War Child

War Child is an agency dedicated to helping children in war zones around the world. War Child believes that children should never be the victims of armed conflict. Since War Child began in 1993, we have worked in areas such as Afghanistan, Democratic Republic of Congo, Sudan, Bosnia, Kosovo and the Solomon Islands.

In Afghanistan, War Child's mobile bakery in Herat made more than five million breads for displaced people. Since establishing the bakery, War Child's work in Afghanistan has included the building of a kindergarten in Herat for 500 children aged between 6 months and 6 years. These children now have an opportunity to meet and make friends with other children and to start their education.

War Child joined with other agencies to rehabilitate the children's hospital in Nasiriyah, Iraq after it was damaged by battle and looting in 2003. We are currently focused on rehabilitating two drop-in centres in Iraq (in Nasiriyah and Basrah) to provide a safe space for vulnerable children and assist them to access education, skills and training. As well as providing emergency relief and working with communities to develop sustainable projects in areas such as education and agriculture, War Child is very concerned about the rights of children in conflict-affected areas. Recently, War Child was involved in negotiating the release of children from detention centres in Herat.

War Child Australia
War Child Australia has been operating since 2002. We are an all-volunteer team that works hard to keep our costs low so that as much of the money we raise as possible is spent on the work that helps improve the lives of children affected by war. War Child Australia operates as part of the international War Child team, as well as being involved in the development and support of specific projects.

Tractor in Afghanistan
Ten hectares of land were donated to War Child to implement a farm project to provide food and employment for widowed mothers, their children and women living in poverty. A greenhouse and a well were constructed on the farm and wheelbarrows and cleaning equipment were supplied and an irrigation system was developed. In early 2004 a request came to War Child to assist with the purchase of a tractor to increase the output of the farm. War Child Australia donated funds that purchased a second-hand Russian tractor and trailer of a kind that is easily sourced and maintained in Herat. Since the tractor was delivered

a variety of crops have been harvested including green peppers, okra, honeydew melons, tomatoes, aubergines, wheat, cotton and spring onions.

Stationery in Afghanistan

Funding from War Child Australia allowed the purchase of 1400 notebooks, 1000 sets of coloured pencils, over 3000 story books and a large selection of educational toys to assist children in their education and learning. The items were distributed by War Child Australia's aid worker, Joanna Francis, to children in the four orphanages and three kindergartens in Herat city and the orphanages in the western provinces of Ghor, Badghis and Farah. A total of 2850 children received books, pencils and toys as part of the program.

Solomon Islands

In early 2004 War Child Australia, together with the Rotary Club of Brisbane Planetarium and 14 Australian children's book publishers, sent more than 5000 new books to schools throughout the Solomon Islands. The books were distributed in the Solomon Islands by the Rotary Club of Honiara. As part of the project, a set of Encyclopaedia Britannica reference books was donated to the National Library in Honiara.

If you would like to find out more information about War Child please visit www.warchild.org.au

No Strings

Miss Piggy, Fozzie Bear and the Muppets are household names, but in 2003 long-time Muppet designer and producer, Michael K. Frith, and his wife and puppeteer, Kathryn Mullen, decided to use their years of Muppet expertise and experience to do something more serious.

Their idea was to teach children affected by war about the dangers of unexploded landmines using live puppetry and video. And with help from staff and volunteers drawn from some of the world's best known aid agencies – including War Child, GOAL and HAAD – No Strings was born.

Their first project is a landmine awareness video for children in Afghanistan, created in partnership with OMAR (Organisation of Mine Clearance and Afghan Rehabilitation) – and money raised from the sale of *Girls' Night In 4* will fund completion and distribution of the first 40-minute video, which is being translated into the two main languages of Afghanistan. UNICEF have already agreed to field test the video, and No Strings hopes to distribute it throughout local schools, television stations and cinemas.

As more money comes in from *Girls' Night In 4*, further projects will follow – including HIV awareness videos for Africa.

To see photographs of the No Strings puppets, and recent press coverage in *The New York Times* and *The Independent* please visit www.nostrings.org.uk

Thank you from everyone at No Strings for buying *Girls' Night In 4*. Although No Strings has had massive support so far, it is still very new – and exists on a tiny budget. Contributions from *Girls' Night In 4* will help to get the charity off the ground.

Jessica Adams

Heaven Knows I'm Miserable Now

Halfway through Justin Rushcroft's funeral (1970–2005), his ex-girlfriend Jo McGee (1975–present) realised that she had left her mobile phone on. Worse, the offending phone (and it really was offending as it vibrated and flashed pink at incoming calls) was now playing a jaunty version of the Austin Powers theme.

'Shit, bugger, shit!' Jo hissed, as she scrambled in her handbag for it.

On the other side of the church, Justin Rushcroft's other ex-girlfriend, Philippa Earl (1969–present), crossed her legs and smiled. She was glad she had gone all the way to London to buy a new black suit. It only made Jo's leather jacket look even cheaper than it actually was.

While the congregation kneeled to pray for Justin's soul, Philippa kept one eye open and shot a careful look at Jo's feet. As she expected – Jo was wearing her habitual fake tan and trainers. In the middle of autumn.

'As one of Brighton's most familiar broadcasting voices,

and one of its best-loved DJs, it is no surprise to see so many of Justin's fans, as well as his family and friends, here today,' boomed the priest.

What fans? Philippa thought, as she failed to see anyone who wasn't a relative of Justin's or one of his former shags. In fact, she realised, for the entire time she had managed the station where Justin worked she had never seen a single fan.

Occasionally, a mad woman from Wivelsfield posted used cat food cans to Justin, requesting that he sign them and send them back, but apart from her – nothing.

In her peripheral vision Philippa could see another of Justin's ex-girlfriends. She was a blonde, too (they were all blondes – when it came to women, Justin was like some low-rent version of Rod Stewart), but shorter, and – frankly – much fatter than any of them.

Her name was Kate Tickell, and she had been their summer temp at the radio station. Why was the bloody woman crying so much? Philippa thought. She knew for a fact that Justin had viewed her strictly as the most casual of all his casual sexual conquests. Nothing more, Philippa thought contemptuously, nothing less.

Kate Tickell, meanwhile, was sobbing so hard that she was now down to her last scrunched-up tissue, and reduced to wiping her nose on her hand. All she could think about, as she stared at Justin's coffin, was the fact that she had given up her job at the radio station for him – the best job she'd ever had in her life. God was a bastard, Kate decided. She had sacrificed her whole summer for Justin waiting, every single day, for him to return phone messages and for emails that never came.

And now look, Kate thought, as she blew her nose After all that effort, the insensitive wanker had gone and died anyway.

Was it just her, Kate wondered, or did funerals make everyone think about the most inappropriate things? Wiping her eyes, she stared fixedly at the coffin and tried, unsuccessfully, to stop herself remembering the way Justin had always yodelled, Sound of Music style, at the point of orgasm. And then there was his bottom, she remembered. It had looked exactly like her grandmother's balding hearth rug.

Back on the other side of the church Jo triple-checked that her phone was switched off, then shoved a cinnamon Tic Tac into her mouth, and tried to concentrate on the priest, and Justin's coffin, in that order. The whole Austin Powers theme song/flashing phone experience had been completely humiliating. She had never received so many filthy looks in her entire life.

She looked down at her feet, noticed that her fake tan stopped in a line above her ankles, then looked up again – and saw that her trainers were filthy as well.

While everyone else was praying for Justin again, Jo shot a surreptitious look at Philippa. As she expected, she was wearing a black designer suit to match her black designer handbag. And a string of pearls. If only Philippa had worn a hat as well, Jo thought savagely, the magic transformation from station scrubber to Jackie Onassis would have been complete.

Jo decided that she hated her, as she had seldom hated any other woman, and she wanted to ring up one of her friends right now and bitch about her – for the duration of the funeral, if necessary.

Even if Philippa hadn't been her boss, Jo thought, she still would have loathed her. Even if she hadn't stood between her and Justin, she still would have despised her.

While the congregation tackled another hymn, Jo wondered idly if she could ever work her way up from announcer to station manager and take Philippa's job. It suddenly seemed like the best idea she had ever had.

It wouldn't be too hard to supersede Philippa, Jo decided. The woman knew nothing about working in radio – even less about music.

Jo remembered a Christmas playlist Philippa had suggested at a staff meeting last December. It had consisted of 'Agadoo' by Black Lace, The Gypsy Kings, Kylie, Britney, various other people whose names ended in ie or ey, a fat bloke who had won *Pop Idol*, Phil Collins, Cher and Classics on 45.

Bloody Philippa had never even heard of The Clash, Jo thought in disgust, but she had still worn some ripped designer T-shirt bearing their name to last year's Christmas party.

Then Jo looked at Kate Tickell, and realised that not only was she openly sobbing, she was also out of tissues.

And for what? Jo thought. Justin Rushcroft had been nothing more than a womanising wally-brain, with buttocks like the less accessible parts of the Amazon jungle. And the noise he used to make when he came! It was like listening to Julie Andrews stuck on some remote Swiss mountain peak.

Jo wondered if everyone else thought inappropriate things about the dead at funerals – then decided they didn't, and it was probably just her.

She had to thank Justin for one thing, Jo realised, and that was the drivetime slot he had just left vacant. She couldn't wait to get her hands on it.

'Justin was also a popular member of his local cricket team,' the priest droned, while his family wondered why, if Justin had been so popular with his fellow cricketers, none of them had bothered turning up.

Above the sound of the church organ Philippa heard Kate Tickell still sobbing, and flinched. It was the most extraordinary noise, she thought. Like someone having their sinuses cleared with a dredger.

Was it just her, she pondered, or did everyone else think sinful thoughts at funerals? A memory of Justin, pumping away on top of her, yodelling his way to a climax, with his bottom rotating in front of her eyes like two rollers in a car-wash, drifted into her mind.

Stop it! Philippa censured herself. *Stop it!* But as the hymn rolled on, all she could hear was the unmistakeable, high-pitched, undeniably Julie Andrews-influenced 'Hee Ho! Hee Ho!' of her former boyfriend's sexual crisis.

I'll never, ever see Justin again, Kate thought miserably, as she rubbed her eyes and stared at the altar. This is my last chance to see him, for all time. And he got me pregnant too. Even if we did only do it three times. And I loved him – much, much more than anyone else here did. At that moment, Kate wished she'd had his baby after all.

She remembered her long and lonely day at the abortion clinic in London, and put her face in her hands. This was hell, she decided. It was bad enough to have lost Justin's baby. But to lose him as well? For the second time that morning Kate decided she hated God.

She didn't care if Justin had mucked her around. She didn't care if he'd had a photograph of one ex-girlfriend above his bed, and another in his glove box. She didn't care that he never called her, or that he behaved exactly like one of the depressing example men in *Men Are From Mars, Women Are From Venus.*

She didn't even care, she decided, that Justin had said mean things about her weight when they were in the shower together. At that moment, as Justin lay dead in his coffin, Kate Tickell decided that she could forgive him almost everything, if only he would come back.

Then another mobile phone rang, from the other side of the church, this time playing the theme song from 'The Simpsons'.

'For God's sake!' someone tutted. And then, at last, the funeral was over.

Much later, when the coffin had been taken to the crematorium, Kate Tickell made a decision.

'Hello,' she said, walking up to Philippa, who was inspecting the wreaths.

'Oh. Hello Kate.'

'I'm sorry I made such a fool of myself in church. And after all, Justin was your boyfriend. Not mine. I don't know why I got so upset. I'm sorry. Let me buy you a drink,' Kate whispered.

Philippa sighed. Had she sacked her, or had Kate resigned, in the end after all those sick days? She couldn't remember.

'Just go home, Kate,' she told her.

'I can't.'

'Justin's gone now. Move on.'

'I can't. And I don't like it when people say move on. Why don't you come and have a drink at Heaven with me? I'm the night manager there, now. I can have anything I want from behind the bar.'

'But it's three o'clock in the afternoon!' Philippa was shocked.

'Bollinger, Moet. Whatever you want. And get Jo to come too.'

'What?'

'Ask Jo. She likes Heaven. I see her in there sometimes. I'm sure she'd like a drink with us.'

'What's bloody Jo McGee got to do with it?'

Then they both realised Justin's mother had moved closer and was unashamedly eavesdropping.

'That's a nice idea,' she said, squeezing Kate's arm.

'Well, it's just an idea,' Kate shrugged.

'Well, I think it's lovely,' Justin's mother agreed. 'All you girls, together, having a wake. I'm sure Justin would have liked it. Oh – Jo!' she spotted her by the chapel and waved enthusiastically. 'Jo! Come over here! The girls are going for a drink!'

'What?' Jo mouthed, feigning ignorance.

'Drink!' Justin's mother mimed.

'Aah,' she said, when Jo came over at last, in her muddy trainers. 'Aaah. Look at all you girls! I think I'm going to cry again. Justin never had a chance to get married, you see. He died too young. Never had a chance to have a baby.'

Except Justin's mother was wrong about that, Jo thought, as the three women said their farewells to her, and headed for Philippa's car. Kate Tickell had been through an abortion, and everyone at the station – except Justin, of course – had guessed it.

Under grey Brighton skies, in jet black jackets (Prada, Top Shop and Monsoon) the three women drove to Heaven in Philippa's company car.

'I've got to be back at the station by five,' Jo said, as she and Kate walked into the club, ahead of Philippa.

'Well, I'll get the champagne out now, then,' Kate said.

'Oh,' Jo cheered up, as she noticed the jukebox in the corner. 'And I might put a song on.'

Music, she thought. Music and alcohol. As opposed to hymns and Holy Communion. That's what she needed right now. She had been brought up as a Catholic, but all church services gave her the creeps.

She put money in the jukebox, and sniffed the air – the place stank of stale beer, vomit, ashtrays and piss.

'I'd forgotten how awful Heaven is,' she told Philippa, once she had arrived, and Kate had gone to the loo. 'Look at those clouds they've painted on the ceiling. And the *jukebox*. It's themed. Every song's got heaven in the title.'

'Oh yes,' nodded Philippa, as 'Heaven Knows I'm Miserable Now' began booming through the speakers. 'There's that song by The Cure.'

'It's The Smiths, actually.'

'No, it's The Cure.'

'It's the bloody Smiths.'

'No, I'm sure it's that man with the big eyebrows and the mad brother. The one who married Gwyneth Paltrow.'

'God, Philippa. You don't have a bloody clue, do you?'

As Kate came back, carrying two bottles of champagne and three glasses, they saw him.

'Justin! Oh my god. Justin.'

At the end of the table, still in his old jeans and white T-shirt, Justin Rushcroft – looking translucent, but otherwise well – smiled, and waggled his fingers in greeting.

'Shit!' said Jo.

'No!' said Philippa. 'No, no!'

'I've decided to stay here,' Justin explained, looking up at the ceiling with its painted angels and plaster harps. 'In Heaven.'

'But you shouldn't even be here,' Jo said, once she could breathe.

'Why not?'

'Because this is a club,' she said. 'And because if you stay here you'll be – haunting it.'

'Oh, Justin,' Kate sighed. 'You've come back. I prayed you would.'

Philippa spoke.

'Are we dreaming?' she asked her ex-boyfriend.

'Nope.'

'Has someone put something in my drink?' she confronted Jo.

'Wrong again,' Justin smiled.

Then, at last, Jo spoke.

'Justin,' she said quietly, 'since you had the accident. Since you – how shall I put it – *died*. Well. Have you actually tried to get into the real heaven?'

'Oh, come on!' Justin made a face at her.

'Well, have you? I mean, what are you actually doing here?'

'Boring,' Justin said. 'Next question.'

'I bet he has tried to get into Heaven.' Philippa glanced at Jo and Kate. 'I bet he has tried to get in – his name's not even on the door.'

'Crap!' Justin cut her off.

Then suddenly every light in the club blew and The Smiths ground to a halt on the jukebox.

'Aaargh!' yelled Jo as Justin laughed at her and the mirror ball above her head started spinning wildly.

'How do you like the dark, Jo?' he baited her. 'You were always afraid of the dark, weren't you?'

'You remind me of something,' Jo said to him, defiantly taking a swig of champagne, while Kate found some candles.

'What's that?' Justin grinned.

'My niece's Captain Nemo night-light. You should see yourself, Justin. You've gone pale green.'

Despite herself – she tried very hard not to find anything Jo said funny – Philippa laughed. Then she steeled herself to look at Justin properly.

He had died in a car crash, coked out of his brain, and gone straight through the steering wheel. Now there wasn't a mark on him. She wondered, vaguely, if his buttocks were still like a front doormat as well, and stopped herself, in case Justin could also read minds, as well as affect electricity.

'I heard that!' Justin smirked.

Jo got up from the table and sank to her knees on the floorboards, clasping her hands in prayer.

'What on earth are you doing?' Philippa asked her.

'Our father who art in heaven,' Jo recited, then she went blank. 'Oh God. Does anyone know the rest? Something about bread. Trespasses, bread, kingdom come. Bollocks.'

Then her champagne glass flew off the table and smashed on the floor.

'Jo!' Philippa screamed. 'Make him stop it!'

'No, let me try,' Kate insisted. 'I can stop you,' she turned to Justin. 'Because I can help you go to heaven. And I know I can do that – because I love you.'

'What?' Justin looked horrified.

Slowly and carefully Jo got up from the floor.

'I've remembered why I stopped going to Mass now,' she said. 'It's the pain.'

'Don't pray for me.' Justin swore at Kate as she got down on her knees.

'It's the best thing,' she said.

'Oh well. While you're down there—'

'I love you,' Kate smiled. 'Even when you say things like that.'

'Crap,' Justin said. 'You hate me as much as she does,' he pointed at Jo. 'And her!' he added, pointing at Philippa.

'We don't hate you,' Philippa interrupted. 'Or at least, I don't hate you. Not properly. I just forced myself to think of you as a bastard so I could get over you.'

Then she put her champagne down, and kneeled on the floor next to Kate.

'Come on, Jo,' she beckoned her over.

'Our father who art in heaven,' Philippa began.

'Hallowed be thy name,' Jo added.

'Thy kingdom come,' Kate remembered, suddenly. 'Thy will be done.'

'Whatever,' Justin shrugged. 'You have to believe in it, if it's going to work. And none of you,' he said triumphantly, 'believe it!'

'Go to the light,' Philippa heard herself saying. Was she repeating something she had seen in *Poltergeist*? Or was it *The Sixth Sense*?

'Yes!' Jo seized on her words. 'Go to the light, Justin.'

She wished she had never stopped going to Mass, she thought. She wished she had never stopped believing. If only she'd kept it up, she realised, it might not be quite so dark in here now. Without lights or candles, Heaven felt more like hell.

Then –

They all saw him at once, suddenly appearing in a flood of light – a tall, grey-haired man, in a knitted cardigan and tie, with his hand on Justin's shoulder.

'Oh no,' Justin said. 'Dad.'

'I've not been able to get through to you before,' the tall man said, in a Northern accent.

'I'm dead, Dad.'

'I know,' his father shrugged. 'Though we don't call it dead over here. We call it your second innings.'

'Really?' Justin said.

The blinding white light in Heaven appeared as the electricity suddenly came back on, and Talking Heads replaced The Smiths on the jukebox.

'Bloody hell!' Justin complained, shielding his eyes. 'It's so bright!'

'You're just halfway to heaven,' his father said. 'Keep going.'

Then Justin's own light began to fade and started merging with something so powerful that neither Kate nor Philippa nor Jo could look any more.

'Goodbye Justin,' Philippa said, as she watched his father take him.

'I love you!' Kate shouted.

'Have fun!' Jo said, then realised how stupid this sounded, as if she had just been farewelling him to Ibiza.

The three women got up off the floor, as David Byrne sang a song about heaven being a place where nothing ever happens, followed by Hot Chocolate singing a song about heaven being in the back seat of their Cadillac, and Tavares singing a song about heaven missing an angel.

'Wait for it,' said Jo, as the jukebox jumped from song to song. 'Any minute now, we'll get Led Zeppelin.'

'It's stuck,' said Philippa. 'It needs a repair man.'

'There!' Jo punched the air, as 'Stairway to Heaven' replaced Tavares.

'Maybe Justin's stuck in there,' Philippa said hopefully.

'It's divine punishment if he is,' Jo smiled. 'Imagine being trapped between "Stairway to Heaven" and bloody Tavares for the rest of eternity.'

'Ha!' Philippa laughed, feeling strangely pleased with herself as she finally understood one of Jo's music jokes.

'Any chance of getting my job back?' Kate asked her half an hour later, as they opened their third bottle of Bollinger.

'Of course!' Philippa promised, swaying slightly under the mirror ball. 'Besides, Kate, neither Jo nor I can let you work in Heaven any more. It's pure hell.'

Cecelia Ahern

The End

Let me tell you what this story is about before I get into the finer details. That way you can decide whether you want to read it or not. Let this first page be my synopsis. First of all, let me tell you what this story is *not*. This is not an 'and they all lived happily ever after' story. It's not about life-long friendships and the importance of female relationships. There are no scenes of ladies whispering and sharing stories over cups of coffee and plates of cream cakes they swore to themselves and their weekly weight watchers class they wouldn't eat. Drunken giggles over cocktails do nothing to dry the tears or save the day in this story.

What if I told you that this story won't warm the cockles of your heart; that it won't give you hope, or cause you to blame escaping tears on the sun cream as you lie by the pool reading it? What if I told you that the girl doesn't get the guy in the end?

Knowing exactly how it ends, do you still want to read on? Well, it's not like we don't venture into things without knowing the end, is it? We watch *Colombo* knowing his misguided representation of himself as a foolish old man will help him solve the case. We know Renée Zellweger decides that she will be the one to go with Tom Cruise and the fish in *Jerry Maguire* every single time we watch it. Tom Hanks always sees Meg Ryan at the end of *Sleepless in Seattle*. James Bond always gets the girl. In *EastEnders*, every once happy marriage will end in death, destruction or despair. We read books knowing that the character will blatantly and predictably fall in love with the guy as soon as his name is first mentioned . . . but we still watch them and read them. There's no twist in my story. I genuinely mean it when I say it: I do not live happily ever after with the love of my life, or anyone else for that matter.

It was my counsellor's idea for me to write this story. 'Try to keep an air of positiveness,' she kept telling me. 'The idea for this is to enable you to see the hopefulness of your situation.' Well, this is my fifth draft and I've yet to be enlightened. 'End it on a happy note,' she kept saying as her forehead wrinkled in concern while she read and reread my attempts. This is my last attempt. If she doesn't like it she knows what she can do with it. I hate writing; it bores me, but these days it passes the time. I'm taking her advice though; I'm ending this story on a happy note. I'm ending it at the beginning.

I'll tell you, just as I told her, that my reason for doing so is because it's always beginnings that are best.

Like when you're starving and it feels like you've been cooking dinner for hours: the smell is tickling your taste buds, making your mouth water, and it teases you until you take that first bite, that first beautiful bite that makes you feel like giggling ridiculously over the joy of having food in your mouth. You can't beat the first relaxing slide into a warm bath filled with bubbles, before the bubbles fade and the water gets cold; or your first steps outside in a new pair of shoes before they decide to cut the feet off you. The first night out in a new outfit that makes you feel half the size, shiny and new before you wash it, the newness fades, and it becomes just another item in your wardrobe that you've worn fifty times. The first half hour of a movie when you're trying to figure out what's going on and you haven't been let down by the end yet. The half an hour of work after your lunch break, when you feel maybe you have just enough energy to make it through the day. The first few minutes of conversation after bumping into someone you haven't seen for years, before you run out of things to say and mutual acquaintances to talk about. The first time you see the man of your dreams, the first time your stomach flips, the first time your eyes meet, the first time he acknowledges your existence in the world.

The first kiss on a first date with a first love.

At the beginning, things are special, new, exciting, innocent, untouched and unspoiled by experience or boredom. And so it's there that my story will end, for that is when my heart sat high in my chest like a helium-filled balloon. That is when my eyes were big, bright, innocently wide and as green as a traffic light all ready to go, go, go. Life was fresh and full of hope.

And so I begin this story with the end.

The End

Feeling desolate, I looked around the empty wardrobes, doors wide open, displaying stray hangers and deserted shelves as though taunting me. It wasn't supposed to end this way. What had only moments ago been a room overflowing with sound and tension, with pleas and desperate begging for him not to leave, with sobs and squeals, wails and shouts coming from both sides, was now a chamber of silence. Bags had been thrown around, violently unzipped. Drawers were pulled open, clothes dumped into sacks, drawers were banged shut, and zips made ripping sounds as they closed. More desperate begging.

Hands reaching out and pleading to be held, hearts refusing, tears falling. An hour of mass confusion, neverending shouts, boots heavily banging down the stairs, keys clanging on the hall table as they were left behind, front door banging. Then silence. Stunned silence.

The room held its breath, waited for the front door to open, for the softer surrendered sound of boots on the stairs to gradually become louder, for the bag to be flung on the ground, unzipped, drawers opened, to be filled and closed again.

But there was no sound. The door couldn't open; the keys had been left behind. I slowly sat on the edge of the unmade bed, breath still held, hands in my lap, looking around at a room that had lost all familiarity, with a heart that felt like the dark mahogany wardrobe. Open wide, exposed and empty.

And then the sobs began. Quiet whimpering sounds that reminded me of when I was five years old, when I had fallen off my bicycle all alone and away from the safe boundaries of my home. The sobs I heard in the bedroom were the frightened sobs that escaped me as a child running home sore and scared and desperate for the familiar arms of my mother to catch me, save me and soften my tears. The only arms now were my own wrapped protectively around my body. My heart was alone, my pain and problems my own. And then panic set in.

Feelings of regret, gasps for breath in a heaving chest. Hours of panic were spent dialling furiously, redialling, leaving tearful messages on an answering machine that felt as little as its owner. There were moments of hope, moments of despair, lights at the end of tunnels shone, flickered and extinguished themselves as I fell back on the bed, the fight running out of me. I'd lost track of time, the bright room had turned to darkness. The sun had been replaced by the moon that had turned its back on me and guided people in the other direction. The sheets were wet from crying and the phone sat waiting to be called to duty in my hand, and the pillow still clung to his smell just as my heart clung to his love. He was gone. I untensed the muscles in my body and I breathed.

It was not supposed to end like this.

And so I won't let it.

The Middle

Oh sweet joy, the joy of falling in love, of being in love. Those first few years of being in love, they were only the beginning. Twenty phone calls a day just to hear his voice, sex every night until the early hours of the morning, ignoring friends, favouring nights in curled up on the couch instead of going out, eating so much you both put weight on, supporting one another at family do's, catching roving eyes as they studied one another in secret, existing only in the world to be with them, seeing your future, your babies in their eyes, becoming a part of someone else spiritually, mentally, sexually, emotionally.

Nothing lasts forever they say. I didn't fall in love with anyone else, nor did he. I've no dramatic story of walking in on him, in our bedroom with the skinny girl next door. I've no story to tell you of how I was romanced by someone else, chased and showered with gifts until I gave in and began an affair. You see, I couldn't *see* anyone but him, and I know he couldn't see anyone else but me. Maybe the dramatic stories would have been better, better than the very fact that nobody and nothing, living in a state of lovelessness and heartbreak, seemed more appealing to him than me?

We had one too many Indian takeaways on the couch together, had one too many arguments about emptying the dishwasher, I piled on one too many pounds, he refused one too many nights out with his friends, we went one too many nights falling asleep without making love and went one too many mornings waking up late, grabbing a quick coffee and running out of the door without saying I love you.

You see, it's all that stuff at the beginning that's important. The stuff that you do naturally. The surprise presents, the random kisses, the words of caring advice. Then you get lazy, take your eye off the ball and before you know it you've moved to the middle stage of your relationship and are one step closer to the end. But you don't think about all that at the time. When it's happening you're happy enough living in the rut you've carelessly walked yourself straight into.

You have fights. You say things you definitely mean but afterwards pretend you don't. You forgive each other and move on, but you never *really* forget the words that are spoken. The last fight we had was the one about who burned the new expensive frying pan, that's the one that ended it. It stopped being about the frying pan after the first two minutes. It was about how I never listened, how his family intruded, about the fact he always left his dirty laundry on the floor and not in the basket, about how our sex life was non-existent, how we never did anything of substance together, how crap his sense of humour was, how horrible a person I was, how he didn't love me any-more. Little things like that . . .

This fight lasted for days, I knew I hadn't burned the frying pan, he 'could bet his life' on the fact he hadn't even used it over that week and 'of course he didn't seeing as I was the one who did the cooking around here', which according to him was 'an admission to burning the pan'. Years of a wonderful relationship had turned to that? He went out both nights that weekend and so did I. It was like a competition to see who could come home the latest, who could ring the least, who could be gone for the long-est amount of time without contact, who could go the longest without calling all their friends, family and police, sick with worry. When you train yourself not to care, the heart listens.

One night I stayed out all night without telling him where I'd gone. I even turned my phone off. I was being childish; I was only staying in a friend's house, awake all night turning my phone on and off, checking for messages. Waiting for the really frantic one that would send me flying home and into his arms. I was waiting for the desperate calls, to hear I love you, to hear the sound of a man in love wanting to hang onto the best thing that had ever happened to him. As proof, as a sign that there was something worth holding onto. No such phone call came. That night taught us something. That I had stooped that low and that he hadn't cared or worried like he should have.

We had an argument and he left. He left and I chased.

You know those moments at the end of movies when people announce their undying love in front of a gasping crowd? When there's music, a perfect speech, and then he smiles at you with tears in his eyes, throws his arms around your neck and everyone applauds, feeling as happy about the end result as you are? Well, imagine if that didn't happen. Imagine he says no, there's an awkward silence, a few nervous laughs and people slowly break away. He turns away from you and you're left there with a red face, cringing and wishing you'd never made that speech, taken part in the car chase, spent the money on flowers and declared your love in the middle of a busy shopping street at lunch hour.

Well, where do you go from there? That's something the movies never tell you. And not only is the moment embarrassing, it's heartbreaking. It's the moment when your best friend, the person who said they would love you forever, stops seeing you as the person they want and need to protect. So much so that they can say no to you in front of the gathering crowd. It's the moment that you realise absolutely everything you shared is lost because those eyes didn't look at you like they should have and once did. They were the eyes of an embarrassed stranger shrugging off the begging words of an old lover.

Faces looks different when the love is gone. They begin to look just how everyone else sees them, without the light, the sparkle – just another face. And the moment they walk away, it's as though the fact you know they sneeze seven times exactly at a quarter past ten every morning means nothing. Like your knowledge of their allergy to ginger and their penchant for dancing around in their underwear to Bruce Springsteen isn't enough to hold you together. The little things you loved so much about a person become the little things they are suddenly embarrassed you know. All that while you're walking away in that awkward, uncomfortable silence.

When you return home feeling foolish and angry to a house that's being emptied you begin to wish all those dark thoughts away. I began to wish that we were still together and feeling miserable rather than having to go through goodbyes. He still felt part of me, I was still his, I was his best friend and he was mine. Yet there was just the minor detail of not actually being *in* love with one another and the fact that any other kind of relationship just wasn't possible. I begged and pleaded, he cried and shouted, until our voices were hoarse and our faces were tearstained.

Feeling desolate, I looked around the empty wardrobe with its doors wide open, displaying stray hangers and deserted shelves as though taunting me. It wasn't supposed to end this way.

The Beginning

He used to get the same bus as me. He got on one stop after me and got off one stop before. I thought he was gorgeous from the very first day I spotted him outside after wiping the condensation from the upstairs window of the bus. It was dark, cold, raining, seven o'clock in the morning in November. In front of me a man slept with his head against the cold vibrating glass, the woman beside me read a steamy page of a romance novel, probably the cause of the fogged up windows. There was the smell of morning breath and morning bodies on the stuffy bus. It was quiet, no one spoke, all that was audible were the faint sounds of music and voices from the earphones of Walkmans.

He rose from that staircase like an angel entering the gates of heaven. His hair was soaking, his nose red, droplets of rain ran down his cheeks and his clothes were drenched. He wobbled down the aisle of the moving bus sleepily, trying to make his way to the only free seat. He didn't see me that day. He didn't see me for the first two weeks but I got clever, moving to the seat by the staircase where I knew he would see me. Then I took to keeping my bag on the chair beside me so no one could sit down, and only moving it when he arrived at the top of the stairs.

Eventually he saw me. A few weeks later he smiled; a few weeks on he said something; a few weeks later I responded. Then he took to sitting beside me every morning, sharing knowing looks, secret jokes, secret smiles. He saved me from the drunken man who tried to maul me every Thursday morning. I saved him from the girl who sang along loudly with her Walkman on Wednesday evenings.

Eventually, on the way home on a sunny Friday evening in May, he stayed on an extra stop, got off the bus with me and asked me to go for a drink with him. Two months later I was in love, falling out of bed at the last minute and running with him to the same bus stop most mornings. Sleeping on his shoulder all the way to work, hearing him say he had never loved anyone else in his life as he loved me, believing him when he said he would never fall out of love with me, that I was the most beautiful and wonderful woman he had ever met. When you're in love you believe everything. We shared kisses that meant something, hearts that fluttered, fingers that clasped, and footsteps that bounced.

Oh sweet joy, the joy of falling in love, of being in love. Those first few years of being in love, they were only the beginning.

Shalini Akhil

Not Really a Party Girl

Straight from the get-go, he made it plainly obvious what he was after. He didn't try and hide it, to stuff it into something else the way he snuck his Y-fronts in with her washing sometimes. No spoonful of sugar, no 'here comes the aeroplane'. He just out and said it. And that's when Kitty knew the honeymoon was definitely over.

'Would you mind making yourself scarce this evening? The threesome's beginning to look more like a ninesome and we don't want to have to confine ourselves to my bedroom.'

Having to evacuate on short notice was one of the downsides of sharing a house with a socially hyperactive Yogalates instructor. There were several upsides, obviously – he could make a passable chai latte from scratch, he knew at least a million different things to do with tofu and he was very easy on the eye, especially first thing in the morning. Kitty was one of those 'waking up is hard to do' people, but even she had to concede that seeing him emerge from the shower in a cloud of steam (towel tucked taut around his waist, chest slick and hairless, abs shining like honey) wasn't too bad a way to greet the day. Yes, *definite* upside. Though having known him for as long as she had, Kitty was quite satisfied to look, not touch – what lust for life you'd think he might have lost with his no caffeine/no nicotine/no alcohol lifestyle, he more than made up for with his voracious passion for nudey-rudey twister with invitation-only groups of people almost as beautiful as himself.

When she'd first met Heath (that was his actual name), Kitty had felt that 'Oh My God, you're just too stunning for words' explosion in the pit of her stomach. She'd answered an ad in the local papers seeking a 'free-thinking housemate who already had their own life'. Desperate to get out of her living arrangement (back in with Mum and Dad after yet another holiday sponsored by Visa), she might have gone a bit overboard with the non-interventionist angle at the interview. Despite her inner eruptions she flicked her hair about a lot and acted as if she hadn't noticed how gorgeous Heath was. Kitty had opened the conversation by telling him she didn't have much time to chat as she had a party to get to (it was eleven in the morning). Just before she left, Kitty looked him dead in the eyes and asked if he had any objections to recreational drug use. Before the end of the week she was packing up boxes and redirecting mail.

Obviously, all of that was in the past. Like some old married couple, they'd each decided to ignore the other's flaws and just get on with it. They made ground rules – clean up after yourself, always make sure there's milk in the fridge, kitchen implements and appliances are sacred, thus must be used for their intended purposes only, you know, the usual. The difference now was that Kitty no longer spent nights awake in her bed agonising over whether or not he liked, you know, *like*-liked, her. She was honestly no longer curious or (not even just a teeny bit) put out by the fact that Heath never even *considered* inviting her to one of his 'beautiful-people-off-their-faces-and-in-the-nuddy' parties. Like the ad he'd placed (and she'd answered) had said, Kitty already had her own life. Anyway, Kitty's ideal nude-by-invitation parties were not flashy events, and generally involved only one other person (though she could fully understand Heath's need to have free rein of the rest of the house if he wanted it). So she flipped open her phone and dialled backup.

'Jane?'

'Shoot!'

'You free tonight?'

'As a bird. What's the plan?'

'Dirty Martinis?'

'Sold.'

'And can I crash at yours after?'

'He's having an orgy again, isn't he?'

'See you at Fracas in an hour.'

Jane waved and nodded at a waiter as Kitty slid into the chair opposite her.

'I pre-ordered.' Her eyes shone as she leaned across the table, all conspiratorial.

'That boy is in-*satiable*! How many this time?'

'Oh Jesus, I don't know!' Kitty laughed. The Martinis

arrived in record time, even for this place. 'I don't really want to know. Though *you*, on the other hand, sound like . . .'

'Like what?'

'Like you wouldn't have turned down an invite yourself!'

'Oh! No, no, *no*, darling! Not with *him* there!' Jane shuddered dramatically and shook her head, sending her shiny dark curls cascading about her shoulders. 'It's just the whole . . . thing.' Her eyelashes fluttered, Monroe-esque. 'I find it . . . in*trig*uing!'

'Hmmm. I'm sure it's not all hard bodies and tanned skin.'

'How do you know? Does he *tell* you about them?'

'No way! It's hardly brunch-time conversation!' Unlike Jane's, Kitty's shudder was involuntary. 'No, I've read about parties like that.'

'Oh, I know, so have I.' Jane sucked the pimento out of an olive. 'But is that all we're destined to do? Read about it?'

Kitty took a sip of her Martini and tried to imagine herself back at the flat, in the thick of it – *Left foot, Green! Right hand, boobie!* She guffawed, shaking her head. 'You know what, for the moment, I'm happy with being a reader.'

'Well, maybe *you* are.' Jane paused theatrically, sweeping the room with her gaze, drawing multiple appreciative responses. 'But one day . . .'

'One day maybe,' Kitty cut in hastily. 'But tonight . . .' she raised her glass, and just as Jane raised hers in response, a smiling waiter materialised at their table.

'Martinis!' they chorused, clinking.

Despite its name, Bar Fracas was one of the most laid-back places in the city. Kitty and Jane had stumbled upon it post after-work drinks one Friday. Their 'stay out or go home?' dilemma dissolved as soon as they walked through Bar Fracas's heavy, weathered-wood double doors. Despite the narrowness of the alleyway it sat on, the candlelit interior room stretched back forever – or at least it seemed to, what with the back wall being mirrored from floor to ceiling. Kitty and Jane had stayed till closing, sampling the many delights of the extensive Martini list; they'd been regulars ever since. Though it still had an air of exclusivity about it, the patronage of Bar Fracas had changed somewhat in the year since that first enchanted evening.

Tonight it seemed inhabited by different strains of the kind of guy Kitty and Jane continued to avoid at office parties and industry booze 'n' schmooze do's. Long-sleeved business shirts with no ties; the 'kinda corporate' look that so many call-centre phone monkeys got away with these days. Cheap-suited, cheap-scented men about as credible as their corporate-buzzword lucky-dip business titles. There was a smattering of fashionable metrosexual types; the ones that over-compensate for their fragile 'pink logo T-shirt/over fake-tan/try-hard Beckham mohawk hairdo' look with overly macho annunciation. Kitty would have loved to have slunk over to one of them, rest her hand on a toned, hairless bicep; lean in, her plump lower lip millimetres away from an achingly delectable earlobe, and say huskily, 'It's spelt "t-a". It's pronounced "tah", not "t-auu-gh", you tool.'

Anyway, Kitty had bigger fish to fry. She'd been getting

appreciative looks from some potential across the bar. He wore a dark suit, a crisp white shirt and the faintest hint of a five o'clock shadow. *Would that make it half-past two?* When he had a waiter deliver them a fifty-dollar drink card with a note on a serviette ('Won't be presumptuous enough to send over drinks – please accept the next round on me.'), Jane was absolutely beside herself.

'Oh, which one is he?'

'I'll tell you if you behave!' Kitty pinned Jane to her seat with a stern look. Jane pouted, nodding solemnly.

'I'll be good, I promise.'

'Okay. Over at the bar. Dark suit. Superman jaw.'

Jane scanned the bar. 'Oh, him!' she smiled demurely and waggled her fingers.

'He's not bad at all! And,' she leaned in, 'pretty smart not to send us actual drinks. Shows he's trustworthy.'

'Or maybe it just shows he's just had a lot of practice?'

Jane rolled her eyes. 'Oh, come on. He could've been beastly. But he's not! So what are you waiting for? Go on over there!'

'How's my face?'

Jane did a quick inspection – lips, eyes, hair. 'All present and correct. Now, off you go!'

Kitty could feel his eyes on her as she made her way to him. She waited till she was next to him before she let him look into her eyes. He smiled a slow smile, the whiteness of his teeth set off beautifully against his sun-kissed skin.

'I wanted to thank you for the drink card.'

'Absolutely my pleasure.' He straightened, extending a hand. 'Robert. Pleased to finally meet you.'

'Kitty.' She curtsied. His smile widening, he bowed

slightly before leaning against the bar again. His eyes were her favourite kind – pale, pale blue and locked on her.

'I hope you didn't find my approach too generic. I knew the minute I laid eyes on you that I wanted to buy you a drink.' His gaze washed over her, cool as a midnight skinny dip. 'I also knew that a man like me could never presume to know what a woman like you would want.'

'Very perceptive. What do you do?'

'I'm in the entertainment industry.'

'How intriguing.'

'It's mainly a pain in the ass.'

Kitty shrugged. 'What isn't, eventually?'

He laughed. 'You're a woman of few words. You must be a writer.'

'For the moment, I'm happy with being a reader.' Kitty's eyes traced a lingering path across his torso, coming to rest again on his smiling lips. She leaned in and pressed her smooth cheek against his rough one, arching her back slightly, briefly searing herself on his heat. 'Thanks again. See you later.'

Kitty could feel his eyes on her as she turned and wove her way back to her table. And that was that. She'd planted the seed, and now she'd sit back and watch it take root.

Kitty and Jane were like two queens perched high on their barstool thrones as the evening unfurled. The fifty-dollar drink card never ran out, no matter how deep into the cocktail list they delved; sipping and laughing, they granted audiences to only the most beautiful of the men who approached them. If they didn't amuse them sufficiently, the girls would dismiss them with a flick of their wrists, and summon the next batch to step up to the plate. Robert surveyed the auditions from his spot at the bar, returning the smiles and waves the girls occasionally cast in his direction.

Jane was paying particular attention to one of the metrosexual brigade – she had a soft spot for well-groomed types who bordered on the effeminate. Her boy of choice was making it plainly obvious that if she kept this up her attentions wouldn't go unrewarded. As happy as she was for Jane, Kitty was growing a little tired of watching her flirt with metro-boy. Maybe it was time to leave them to it? If only she could go home . . .

'Hello, Angel. You're looking a little world-weary.'

'Oh, Robert! Yeah, a little.' Kitty tried not to puke as Jane and metro-boy locked lips yet again. 'You know what they say, two's company,' she sighed, turning to face Robert. As soon as her eyes fixed on his pale, pale blue stare, it was clear; there was nothing else to be done. He turned and strode towards the door, and Kitty quickly gathered her things and followed him out.

She found him holding open a cab door, waiting for her. She walked straight up to him and pushed him gently, forcing him to take a step backwards, down to the street between the cab and the kerb. The height of the kerb brought their faces to the same level. Robert smirked.

'Get in, you big bully.'

'Where are we going?'

'It's a surprise.'

He slid into the cab after her. As she twisted around to find her seatbelt, she felt a hand squeeze at her knee, then it began creeping up her thigh. She gave it a short, sharp slap.

'No groping on the first date!'

Robert rubbed his hand where Kitty had slapped it. 'Who said this was a date?'

'Well, you're taking me out, aren't you?'

'I guess I am . . .'

'Where are we going?'

'Are you sure you want to know?' Robert frowned. 'It'd be quite a surprise . . .'

'Oh! Don't tell me, don't tell me!' Kitty squealed, clapping her hands and bouncing in her seat. 'Give me a little hint, then?'

'I had to call ahead to let them know I was bringing someone.'

'Oh! Is it, like, an entertainment industry "do"?' Kitty was breathless at Robert's smile. 'An awards ceremony?'

Robert's eyes twinkled. 'I guess you could say it's *like* an entertainment industry "do". But no more hints!' He straightened his tie and put on a serious air. 'I will say this, it's a pretty exclusive event. You should be flattered I've asked you along.'

'Really? Will there be famous people there?'

'You never know your luck in the big city.' Robert winked.

Kitty could barely contain her excitement. If he were smoking a cigar, if the cab were a private limo, he could have been her very own Mr Big – Robert was about as boring a name as John, after all. And he was whisking her away to a high-society private party at some swank, secret location – and when they first met, he'd thought she was a writer! It was meant to be. Kitty reached across and took Robert's hand in her own.

'I hope I didn't hurt you before,' she cooed. 'Would you like me to kiss it better?'

'Abso-fucking-lutely.'

Kitty had no idea where they were going. As the cab zoomed and tooted its way across town, she and Robert wrestled in the back seat. It was mainly Kitty's fault, really. She couldn't make up her mind what she wanted. She wrenched his hands from and to her body as they made out furiously in the back of the cab, frantic as a couple of teenagers. He towered over her, even when seated. It took them a while to realise the cab had come to a halt. The cabbie sat silent in the driver's seat, watching them through the rear-view mirror. When Kitty finally noticed him looking, she was so surprised she nearly bit Robert's tongue off.

Robert paid the cabbie while Kitty hastily repaired the damage. She didn't want their in-cab entertainment to be obvious the minute she entered the room. A quick slick of lip gloss, a light sweep of bronzer, a spritz behind each ear, her hair was tousled but that was the style. Satisfied with her make-up, Kitty straightened her clothing and looked out the window. It was then that she noticed. That tree. That park. That block of flats . . .

Robert opened her door and offered her his hand.

'*Mademoiselle, après vous.*' He stepped back and made a sweeping gesture toward a house. 'Your party awaits.'

Hang on . . .

He was gesturing toward *her* house.

'Thank you, Robert.' Kitty smiled graciously. 'But you know what?'

'What?'

Kitty slammed the cab door shut. 'I'm not really a party girl.'

She tapped the cabbie on the shoulder. He started the engine, and they drove off. Just before they took a right at the end of the street, Kitty looked back; Robert was still standing on the nature strip in front of her house staring after the cab. Kitty couldn't help it, she laughed and laughed. The cabbie eyed her suspiciously through the rear-view mirror.

'Where to, Miss?'

'Gimme a sec,' Kitty said, wiping the tears from her eyes. She flipped open her phone and dialled backup.

'Jane?'

'Shoot!'

Maggie Alderson
Are You Ready Boots?

'Dang diddy dang diddy dang diddy dang . . .' I sang to myself as I zipped the boot up to my knee, the soft black leather stretching to hug my calf. I got up and looked at myself in the full-length mirror.

'Nancy Sinatra, eat your heart out,' I said to my reflection. 'These boots were made for me.' I couldn't believe my luck. Not only were those killer boots fifty per cent off in the Barneys shoe department sale, they were even my size. And they weren't just boots – they were actual Manolos. Here I was in New York city shopping just like Carrie. Sex was the word for it – and for these very high-heeled, very black, very pointy boots. Boots so high and black and pointy indeed, that all I could do after admiring myself in the mirror was to turn round to my pal Spencer and growl.

'Grrrrrrr,' I said, copping a vamp pose with my boot leg forward, my teeth bared.

'Good Lord in the foothills, Miss Lulu,' said Spencer in

his hilarious southern accent – real, he had come to New York from Charleston when he was seventeen. 'You are such a true minx in those boots, I swear I am quite afraid of you.'

Now totally overexcited – Spencer always had that effect on me, not unassisted by the second bottle of Cristal he had insisted on ordering at lunch – I asked the nearest sales assistant for the other boot.

I zipped it on and set off stalking up and down the shoe department, working those heels like Ru Paul.

'These boots were made for strutting,' I sang to Spencer.

'Yes, Maam,' he agreed. 'So why don't you just strut right off and pay for them? It is nearly the cocktail hour and Spencer is one thirsty boy.'

I was still admiring the boots – while the sensible side of my brain tried to reason with the champagne-fuddled one, which was insisting they were a bargain – when my other great New York pal, Betty, came shuffling over in a pair of red patent mules, which were clearly three sizes too big for her. She looked like a little girl dressing up in Mummy's clothes.

'What do you think of these?' she asked us. 'They're only $95, down from $400.'

'They'd be real nice on The Hulk,' said Spencer.

'If only the size had gone down along with the price they'd be great on you,' I added. 'But look, check out these boots. Aren't they totally perfect?'

'Wow,' said Betty, momentarily distracted from the tantalising bargains on her own feet – she was famous in our crowd for never paying the full price for anything; it was like a religion with her – 'Those are so hot. They look great on you. How much are they?'

'Who cares?' I answered, strutting around a bit more. 'They make me feel like a Bond girl, I totally have to have them.' I finally came to a halt in front of the full-length mirror again, where I was quite mesmerised by how good I thought the boots made me look. They seemed to lengthen and slenderise my legs. They made me look browner. They made me look richer. Kinder. More intelligent. I felt like I had won the shoe lottery.

'These are the boots I'm going to be wearing when I meet my husband,' I proclaimed.

And they were. Kind of.

I didn't wear my kinky boots – as Spencer had dubbed them – for six months after I bought them. Even though they were real Manolos and truly beautiful and half price in the sale, I felt so sick and ashamed about how much I had spent on them – money I could ill afford after blowing two months' rent money on that four-day trip to New York – I couldn't bear to look at them, let alone wear them.

They were still in the Barneys carrier bag, which I had brought home in my suitcase as a style souvenir, stuffed under my bed.

And that's where they stayed until one dreary winter Sunday evening when Spencer was over in London for one of his hectic visits and called up to tell me I was coming out with him and six of his favourite boy pals that night to the launch of a new restaurant.

'But it's Sunday, Spencer,' I whined at him. 'We went out last night, we went to brunch today and an exhibition and we're having drinks again tomorrow. It's not like I haven't seen you and it's not like you have no one else to go with. You've got your usual posse of pooftas lined up, haven't you? Why do you need me?'

There was silence on the other end of the phone. A loud silence I knew all too well from the three years I had shared a flat with Spencer, before he had moved back to the States. He could say more just breathing than most people could put over with RADA coaching and a Hollywood script.

'Spencerrrrrr,' I pleaded, stretching out on my sofa. 'It's already past seven, it's a school night, it's drizzling, I'm knackered, my hair's dirty and I have nothing to wear. Nothing.'

'I'll pick you up at eight, Missie Lulu,' said Spencer firmly. He paused, then continued. 'Why don't you wear those kinky boots you bought in Barneys that time? They made you look like a trailer-park Honor Blackman. I like that look on you.'

As always with Spencer, who had a personality so charismatic he could have set up his own evangelical TV ministry, I did what I was told. I put the pointy boots on and standing in front of my mirror wearing nothing but them and my undies, I had to say they looked pretty damned good.

Inspired by their sex-kitten appeal, I backcombed my filthy hair and tied it up into a Bardot-esque high ponytail, with my fringe falling over one eye. Then I threw open my wardrobe and raked through the hangers for something good enough to wear with my special boots.

Almost immediately I found the perfect thing: a vintage Pucci-esque (that is, psychedelic bri-nylon from a charity shop) mini caftan. I slipped it over my head and felt immediately compelled to dance the pony with myself. It was a great look, but I couldn't hack it.

Apart from anything else, the restaurant was in Mayfair and the nylon mini was definitely not a West End look. So I played it safe with a classic black shift dress and some Jackie O–style ropes of pearls, with my kinky boots as a wicked statement at foot level. I pouted at my reflection one more time and ran downstairs.

It was the usual night out with Spencer and his merry men. Hilarious laughter, totally unnecessary nastiness about everyone else there and far too much to drink.

I was on my way to the loo after about five glasses of champagne in half an hour when I first spotted Charlie. You couldn't miss him. He was seriously handsome with a great tan and floppy blond hair, and wearing a beautiful suit. He was standing alone in a corner of the restaurant and as I passed I could feel him checking me out.

When I came out of the ladies', he was still there, still incredibly handsome, still – incredibly – alone and still look-ing at me. And I could tell by that look that he definitely wasn't gay. He wasn't admiring my dress or my French manicure. He was admiring me. I felt a bit giddy.

I went back to the boys, but found it less easy to con-centrate on their antics, even though Spencer had cranked himself up into his most evil mood and was now doing impersonations of people simultaneously as they walked by. It was hysterical, but my gaze kept returning to the mystery man in the corner. Still there. Still gorgeous. Still alone.

I'm sure it was the boots that made me do it, because I can't remember my brain actually forming the thought, but suddenly my feet were on their way over to where Mr Cutie Dream Man was standing.

'Hi,' I said, when I got there. 'You've been standing alone for ages. I've come to keep you company.'

His broad smile revealed perfect white teeth as he held out his hand to me. His eyes were a very pale blue.

'Great,' he said. 'I was hoping you would. I'm Charlie March-Edwards. How do you do?'

Well, I did very well and from that moment on we did very well together. That first fated encounter led to a drink after the party – Spencer and the boys hardly even acknowledged my departure, as they had spotted a group of Argentinean polo players in the corner – and a chaste kiss as he dropped me home.

From that we moved on to a couple of dinner dates, a walk in the park, an exhibition, a movie and finally into a relationship. A boyfriend. I really had a boyfriend. A good-looking boyfriend with a really good job in the City. He even had a Porsche. He was the full 99 with a Flake, sprinkles and raspberry sauce. Amazing.

Even more amazing, Charlie seemed to understand how it all worked. He was very cuddly, always rang me when he said he would and after a few weeks of seeing a lot of each other he said the words every single woman most dreams of hearing.

'I want to be your boyfriend, Lulu, your proper boyfriend. Are you cool with that? Will you be my girlfriend? Will you come and meet my parents? I've told them all about you.'

I smiled like a watermelon.

Needless to say Spencer didn't approve.

'I don't know, Miss Lulu,' he said, when I rang to tell him about the weekend with Charlie's parents at their beautiful house in Berkshire.

I was furious and gave him a taste of his own silence routine, until he continued.

'See, honey, I know all you girls think you want to marry stockbrokers and live in Chelsea and drive around in cars like trucks with two little tow-headed kids in back, and I do grant that Charles is way over on the handsome side of pretty, but are you sure he isn't just an insy-winsy bit straight for you? That's straight as in dull, darlin'. You know, boring?'

'You're just jealous,' I said.

I couldn't believe Spencer wasn't happy I'd found the perfect man. He had always been trying to set me up with people before, but I figured he just didn't like the fact that I had found Charlie all on my own.

But while I was furious with Spencer at the top level of my brain, I soon began to wonder if he hadn't planted a tiny seed of doubt at a lower level. I started to notice little things about Charlie that hadn't bothered me before.

For one thing, he told jokes. He didn't *crack* jokes like Spencer and I did – off-the-cuff, spur-of-the-moment one-liners. He repeated formulated jokes people had told him. And some of them were a little bit sexist and a little bit racist. I tried to dismiss it as one little fault in an otherwise perfect package, but then other things started to annoy me too.

Like the skiing stories and the anecdotes about his so wild (so not) days at school. We'd both left school over ten years earlier, but Charlie was still talking about it. And then there were his friends, most of whom he had known since he was at that stupid snobby school, with their own repertoires of offensive jokes and unhilarious skiing and drinking stories.

So the doubts were there, but they were only small annoyances in an otherwise glorious scenario and Charlie didn't seem to have any such problems with me. He was truly a loving and affectionate man, and his parents seemed to like me too. So I wasn't really surprised when he asked me to marry him.

Okay, so it wasn't the most original proposal – he took me away for the weekend to our favourite country house hotel and went down on one knee beneath the rose arbour – but it was still thrilling. And it was a huge diamond. I accepted.

We went back to our room, called his parents and mine with the good news, made love with the ardour appropriate to the occasion and then started to get dressed for dinner.

I'd had such a strong inkling that the big question was going to be popped that weekend I had packed the kinky boots and the shift dress and pearls I'd been wearing the night we met, as a bit of fun. I thought it would be rather witty to put them on and see if Charlie noticed.

He did.

'Oh no,' he said, coming out of the bathroom with a towel around his firm, brown waist. 'You're not wearing those awful boots, are you? I hate those boots.'

I was too stunned to speak. Charlie continued. 'Please

don't spoil this special night by wearing them, Lulu darling,' he said. 'They're so tarty. They nearly put me off you the night we met. They're chav boots. I was so relieved when you never wore them again. They're really common.'

I looked at him and for the first time saw right through the dashing handsome exterior, to the bigoted bore inside. Spencer had been right. Charlie was a handsome ass.

As he opened the wardrobe to get out his Savile Row suit, lined with cyclamen pink, his Paul Smith shirt and his Hermes tie, I folded my arms and looked down at my kinky boots. They were so great.

'Are you ready boots?' I said to them. 'Start walking.'

Lisa Armstrong

The Common Touch

I owe everything to Clare.

I've always made that absolutely clear whenever journalists ask. I think it pays to be scrupulously honest in these situations, don't you? As scrupulously honest as these situations allow.

And it's true. I don't have any illusions about it. Without Clare I could have been stacking shelves in Morrisons, or trapped in some piss-soaked lift with four snot-faced brats and a crack habit. It's my common touch apparently. It was always going to be all or nothing with me.

The funny thing about the common touch is that it's bloody rare. Or it is in my line of work. Tony Blair had it when he first came on the show, flirting with Clare, flirting with the viewers, flirting with his mug of tea. I'd made that tea, but I take no credit. He'd have flirted with Simon if hadn't been for the Christian vote.

Kate Moss has it. She could sell halitosis to a dentist. It's not actually about being common. It's about accessible classiness, apparently – and I'm going by the focus groups here. It's about reaching out from the screen to grab the nation by the goolies just as it's sitting down to a lunch of cut-price baked beans and sliced white bread that tastes like the foam inside one of those bargain kids' duvets from Woollies – and giving them a bit of easily digested glamour to drizzle on top.

Or that's what Gil, our producer, always said. 'Know why the opposition's sinking without a trace?' he would crow every time the new viewing figures for *Lunch With Simon and Clare* came in. 'Cos that Miss Frigidaire on the other side looks like she's got a poker shoved up her Elle Macpherson's. All right, so she's going out with a soap star and she's always at the right parties. But viewers can't take that much glamour at one o'clock in the afternoon. They want to see a bit of humanity.'

Then he would rake his fingers through his transplant in mock sympathy for the losers running the other side and chuckle. 'They thought they'd pulled off such a coup getting that skinny cow to present, but all it's done is rub the public's noses in precisely how scummy their lives are.'

Clare had the common touch. The battle with the weight. The bad hair months. The procession of pictures in all those celebrity magazines showing her so-called misguided wardrobe choices. I don't know how the witches on those magazines sleep at night. How would they feel if their every tiny ripple of cellulite and wrinkle got blown up like soufflé on the cover of their rags?

But Clare was brilliant. She'd worked out exactly how to turn the taunts to her advantage. I've sometimes wondered whether the flicky haircuts and the harsh shade of newsreader chrome blond that made her pale, crumpled, face look like a pummelled grapefruit were deliberate. It wasn't as if she couldn't afford to go to the best salons – or get a tan and some Botox, come to that. I bet it was part of the game plan, like the mascara that smudged whenever one of the callers got halfway emotional. Jesus, it's been thirty years since the first breakthroughs at Maybelline.

She's much cleverer and more sophisticated than anyone's ever given her credit for. You try sitting at the other end of those endless bleeding-heart calls while three cameras slice away your flesh to get at the sincerity and see what it does to your Magdalene College education. Not that anyone knew about the degree, apart from Gil, and possibly Simon. I didn't even know about it for a while. Clare had a problem with elitism.

She had no problem with sincerity, however. Politicians would kill for that brand of sincerity. And I include Tony Blair – I saw the way he stared at her that time. Clare thought he was flirting and the menopausal flush that spread from her chins (she was going through one of her heavy phases) right up to her freshly bleached roots made it onto the front pages of all the tabloids the next day. For the first time I understood why she never bothered with fake tan.

The *Sun* called her a Clare Babe and said it wasn't surprising that she and Tony had such chemistry. The fashion editor of the *Mirror* concluded that despite, or maybe because of, the occasional dodgy outfit and puffy ankles, Clare was every man's ideal woman.

No one can deny she was good. Every viewer who ever called in to talk about their botched hysterectomy, their obese teenagers and their balding, farting, shiftless pets would get the same sympathetic, owly smile and watery, hazel-eyed nod of sympathy. At the end, the caller would give a satisfied little snivel and then nine times out of ten they'd say something like 'By the way, Clare, I saw you at those awards the other night and those so-called fashion critics don't know what they're talking about. You looked gorgeous'.

And Simon? Simon would look at Clare adoringly, fidget with his Paul Smith shirt collar and nod. Though once, halfway through a particularly harrowing call from a woman who'd had the wrong kidney removed, the camera caught him picking his cuticles.

All right, so I'm exaggerating about the crack and the crappy supermarket job. It wasn't as if I'd grown up on a sink estate, as my step-dad points out with monotonous regularity on the increasingly rare – thank God – occasions the family gets together. Maybe not. But the pinched, miserable, plywood '70s cul de sac we grew up in – rusting Austin Allegro in the garage, nylon fitted sheets on the bed – wasn't exactly a gas either. And it doesn't even make good copy. You realise these things after a while. It's part of the job. You name a publication and I can tailor good copy to suit it. If a tabloid asks how much I value Clare's friendship, I say something like 'I'd give my right ovary to save her'. Usually gets a laugh from the hack at the other end of the phone, and it always makes it into the paper. If it's *In Style* I say something like 'I love her so much, I'd let her have the last Prada dress in the shop'. Prada? That's a laugh. It doesn't have the common touch, you see. And it goes without saying that it wouldn't fit her.

Personally I don't know why they're still so obsessed

with Clare and me. I'd like them to just drop the whole thing and start afresh.

Starting afresh was exactly what I did the first day I walked into Clare's dressing room. She didn't share with Simon because she said his pathological untidiness made her nervous, but really, as I discovered later, it was because she wanted to listen to classical music – and I'm not just talking Mozart and the *Schindler's List* music, but serious, headache-inducing stuff – and he wanted to listen to Dido.

Just getting to that room was a triumph. I almost didn't get the application in on time. The pathetic printer in the library had been out of order and the closing sign had already been flipped round in the post office. But I'd pleaded with the hatchet-faced drone locking the door, spun him a story about this being a once-in-a-lifetime chance, batted my admittedly sparse lashes, and said he wouldn't want me to end up on the scrap heap of society for the sake of two minutes, would he?

I couldn't have been the most qualified for the job. Working in a kennels doesn't give you an obvious edge when it comes to being a PA for one of the country's most successful TV presenters. But I'd been really good at typing and secretarial skills at school. And I was excellent at shovelling shit.

Simon wasn't the only one mystified by his wife's choice. But he was the only one I overheard vocalising his dismay.

'Christ, Clare, you could have got someone a bit more . . . presentable.'

There was a pause. Clare had one of those smiles you

could hear through a closed door. I could hear it now. 'Whom are we going to be presenting her to?' she asked eventually, in her neutral, TV Personality of the Year accent. 'She's our invisible backup. No one who matters is ever going to see her. She's . . . stolid. She'll organise us. And she'll sort out your dressing room. I wouldn't be surprised if she doesn't stumble across a few dead bodies in there. We don't need Julia Roberts for that.' She laughed. 'Honestly, how a man can emerge from such squalor looking so immaculate I'll never know.'

'You're the one with skeletons,' sulked Simon. 'I don't think I can stand having her galumphing round my dressing room.'

'Don't be petulant,' Clare soothed, in her missing-kidney tone. She lowered her voice. 'I told you, Simon, no more miniskirts.'

'Christ, not if she's the one wearing one. On that, my precious, we can both agree.'

I was a bit lardy in those days. Simon's comments were like oil off a whale's back. They don't ever mean much when men say them because half of them secretly fantasise about chubby chasing. But I didn't lose weight for them. I did it because Clare's comments about me being stolid – God, what a Cambridge sort of word – had made me break down and weep.

After a year or so the weight had dropped off. The gruelling hours. And God knows there were enough diet experts on the show to make Clare's excess poundage look like a wilful act of stubbornness.

I worked like a demon. I wasn't going back to those kennels ever again. I sorted out Clare's schedule, helped with her scripts, found her a hairdresser who could do stylish and accessible, and when she went into hospital for her hysterectomy – cue a six-page exclusive in the *Sun*, a huge boost in viewing figures and a mega publishing deal for the rights to her *Life Without a Womb* book – I moved on to Simon's bombsite.

I looked a lot better by then. It wasn't just the weight. You only had to study Clare to see what didn't work. Simon's kindled interest – inviting me round to cook supper while Clare was in hospital – was simply confirmation of what I already knew. I wasn't interested in him, though. He was as transparent as the sheer bronzer he sometimes wore on air. As for his skeletons, everyone already knew about his weakness for leggy blondes in miniskirts. I was far more interested in digging up Clare's. It would take me another two years.

I couldn't believe it when I finally found out about Clare and Gil. They'd been at it for years, apparently. And no one knew. Not even Simon. What a joke. All that synthetic sympathy in the press for Clare every time Simon was caught out with another blonde and all the time she was having it off with a toupee. I suppose they got turned on by each other's Oxbridge qualifications. But I'll hand it to them, they were careful. I only found out myself after I'd followed her out of the office one night – I'd become a bit obsessed with her at that point. I felt betrayed, frankly. It was like being in a really bad car crash. By then I'd become everything to her. I bought her CDs, filled in her medical records, chose her company car, advised her about her underwear, booked her theatre tickets and holidays and told her which magazines to read and which to avoid that week. We were friends. She owed me trust at least.

I won't pretend I didn't feel betrayed. Still, it's no excuse for sleeping with Simon. But he certainly wasn't worth working up a guilt complex about – too worried about rumpling his Paul Smith suits. In a way I was doing Clare a favour – better a meaningless screw with me than a fling that might turn into something with one of his miniskirted blondes. Not that it ever would. I know the press could never understand what he was doing with a mumsy-looking sack like Clare, but the point about Simon was that all he wanted was a mummy. When he went miniskirt chasing, he was just temporarily looking for a younger mummy.

I'd been on *Lunch With Simon and Clare* about four and a half years when the unthinkable happened. The ratings began to slip, gradually at first. But within a year, like an old whore desperate for new tricks, it was down on its knees. They all rushed around – Gil, Clare, Simon and the executives, manic smiles plastered across their disintegrating faces, trying an increasingly desperate roster of gimmicks and competitions. I had to put them out of their misery. It was so obvious – to anyone under thirty. I went to see Gil one day and told him straight that the public had grown up. They didn't want blowsy-looking sympathy. And that clichéd old formula of having some frumpy woman in need of a facelift, flanked by a too-smooth-by-far bloke who could be her son didn't begin to intrigue. Nor was it any good having some geriatric male presenter slumped on a sofa next to some twenty-year-old bimbo. The public wanted a self-possessed presenter with long legs, a glamorous lifestyle and a date of birth this side of the Crimean War. That's why those losers on the other side were trouncing us. The funny thing is, I think he was taking it on board when Clare walked in.

Shortly after that I was moved to the TV production company's new shopping channel. I didn't get a say in this, you understand. I didn't even see Clare for three weeks after I got the letter. She was back in hospital. With a cancer scare, would you believe? When I finally confronted her she pulled that bleary-eyed mascara thing on me, told me how much she'd miss me but that she couldn't hold me back any longer. She was becoming too dependent on me for our own good and that this was a once-in-a-lifetime opportunity for me.

Call me ungrateful, but flogging crap to the bedridden, the brain-addled and the insomniacs struck me as being barely one step up from serving up poor man's Kennomeat in the kennels. It was hardly as if I was one of those desperate-to-be-on-TV-at-any-price girls who hung around outside the offices with their CVs all day. I didn't even want to be a presenter. I just wanted to help Clare. But I did it. I sold anti-wrinkle potions that didn't make a blind bit of difference; creams that purported to banish 'dirty eye-lid syndrome'; gels that got rid of 'puffy finger problems'; and exercise machines that were bigger than the average ground floor and were never likely to be unpacked from their excessive, planet-destroying packaging. I encouraged women to thrash their credit cards, smash their fat, and convinced them they had problems they'd never previously dreamed of. I was brilliant. And Clare never once bothered to watch me. She didn't send me so much as a postcard when I got Cable Presenter of the Year. She didn't even return my call.

It was an act of kindness really when I tipped off one of the tabloids about her and Gil. By then I'd stepped down as a presenter and got what I really wanted, which was the producer's job. As for *Lunch with Simon and Clare*, it had been languishing in the ratings gutter for so long that the press had stopped bothering even to mock it. It wasn't worth the column inches. I got them more press that week than they'd had in the past two years.

I got rid of Gil and Simon when they brought me back to the station. They were just pathetic camp old caricatures. I kept Clare on though, in a five-minute weekly agony aunt slot. I put that skinny cow in as presenter, gave her a clothing allowance that was bigger than Clare's new salary and put it about that she might be a dyke.

Clare and Simon divorced – I think Simon's breakdown on a reality celebrity show was the last straw for Clare. I understand he's got some kind of one-man act on cruise ships now, which should suit him perfectly. They didn't have kids so you can't feel too sorry for them. And that was another myth – that they were desperate to have babies, when the reality was Clare didn't feel like sharing her job with children.

'Times have changed,' I told the shareholders and crew at the first annual meeting after I'd taken over the running of the new lunchtime format. Not that they could complain after the ratings I'd just delivered. 'I'm very grateful to the previous generation,' I said as I flashed my newly whitened teeth at the room. 'I know they felt they were doing the right thing, hiding their bushel under a populist light. Feeling the nation's pain, and sharing their flab. But it's not like that any more. A presenter, even a daytime presenter, doesn't have to pretend to be less intelligent than they really are. Or more . . .' – I looked across at Clare and forced her to meet my eyes – '. . . stolid.' I shook my head. 'What a waste.' And for a moment I meant it. I owe everything to Clare. Perhaps that's why I despise her.

Tilly Bagshawe

Dog Lover

The irony is that I've always thought of myself as a dog
lover.

No, really. Even as a kid, I was crazy about them. Dogs,
I mean. Particularly Chihuahuas, funnily enough. That's
partly why I took the job in the first place. Well, that and
the enormous salary, the guest house in Beverly Hills and
the free use of the boss's Bentley Continental on weekends. But it was mostly the dog.

I can remember the advertisement now, word for word.
I can even remember the taste of the big, delicious, gooey
slab of carrot cake I was eating at The Coffee Bean as I
read it (a cake that, by the way, I gave a good twenty per
cent of to the cute little Bichon Frise tethered to the table
leg next to me. I hate to see dogs tethered, don't you? No?
Well, I do. Because whatever anybody says, I have always,
ALWAYS loved dogs. If you don't believe me ask . . . well,
ask whoever you like. Because what happened was *totally*
out of character for me, I assure you – totally).

Where was I? Oh, yes, the advertisement. 'Housekeeper required,' it said. 'To provide domestic assistance for single lady in early sixties. $50 000 p.a., including guest house accommodation and use of car. No kids. One dog. Only animal-lovers need apply.'

Well, I mean, it was written for me, wasn't it?

Written. For. Me.

I called up then and there, right from the coffee shop. It was a bit awkward if you must know, because the Bichon Frise had thrown up, poor little mite. Apparently she was allergic to sugar, but I mean, really, how was I supposed to know that? The guy who owned her was *extremely* rude to me, as a matter of fact. I can give you a description of him if you like? No? Well, I *will* tell you that he was cursing and yelling so much I had trouble concentrating on the call. I ask you! Some people!

Anyhoo, long story short, I called and I got an interview for the very next morning.

What was that? Was that the first time I met Mrs Andrews? Well of course it was, silly! Never seen the woman in my life until that moment. Of course, now I wish I'd never seen her at all. Amazing how *wrong* you can be about someone on a first impression, isn't it? I mean some people think that, just because I'm a little heavy, I have no self-control! How ridiculous is that? Let me tell you, just because someone battles with their weight, that's no reason to make assumptions about . . . hmm? Oh, yes, sorry. Mrs Andrews.

Well, I met her at the house and she seemed like a nice enough lady. A little quiet, perhaps. Softly spoken. Very well dressed. You know, genteel. Not all Beverly Hills–y with one of those stretched-out surgery faces and too much make-up and jewellery. She asked me a bunch of questions. Just regular stuff, you know, my background, references, experience I'd had with dogs, that sort of thing. And then she had the maid bring him in.

Nebuchadnezzar.

On a red velvet pillow.

Wearing a crown.

You probably think I'm exaggerating, but I swear to you on my departed mother's grave, God rest her soul, that was exactly what happened. A *tiny* little Chihuahua, not much bigger than a jumbo avocado. On a pillow! With a crown!!

Of course, I know what you're going to say: Why didn't I get out then and there? Go on. Say it. 'Why didn't you get out then and there, Mrs McIntyre?' I mean, if the writing was on the wall . . . But you know what I say to that, Detective? *Hindsight is 20/20!* That's what I say. *Hindsight is* . . . Oh, well, all right. There's no need to lose your temper. If you'd just let me finish without interrupting all the time . . . OH YES YOU ARE, YOUNG MAN! . . . I'd get to the point a mighty sight quicker.

So anyway, in comes Neb. (You'll understand I couldn't keep calling him Nebuchadnezzar, although Mrs A insisted upon it whenever she was around. Poor woman. She loved him, but she was obsessed. *Obsessed!* I mean, I ask you. What kind of a name is that to saddle a dog with? Thank the Lord the woman never had children, that's what I say. Oh she did? A daughter? That's funny. She never mentioned her. Oh well, my mistake, Detective, I stand corrected!)

So at first I felt sorry for him. For the *dog*. Do try to

keep up, Detective. Truly, I did, I actually pitied him. With that ridiculous crown squashing his little ears. Oh, and he had leg warmers on. Did I mention that already? Little pink leg warmers shot through with silver thread. He looked like a kid from *Fame*. Did you ever see that show? With Leroy, the dancer? He's dead now, you know, poor man. Aids. Turned out to be one of those, you know, doo-dahs. Fairies. Anyway Neb reminded me of Leroy. Except, obviously, he was a dog. And as far as I know he'd never taken a modern dance class, although knowing what I know now, nothing would surprise me!

I think she picked the leg warmers up at Chateau Marmutt. Do you know that place? On third? No? Well, I do. When I think of the hours, not to mention the *thousands* of dollars, she had me spend in that store. Two words for you, Detective: *Emotional Torture*. Write that down, would you? I want it on record: what I suffered in that job was *abuse*. I swear to God, if I saw that place now, I think I'd have a panic attack. Little doggy sweaters and diamond collars and silver nail clippers and Lord knows what else they have in there. It's a crazy world we live in, Detective. A crazy, crazy world. Not everyone's as nice and normal as you and me.

So, needless to say, I took the job. If I hadn't I wouldn't be sitting here now, talking to you, now would I? I took the job and the next morning I arrived and I'd barely finished unpacking in the guest house . . . have you seen Mrs A's guest house by the way?

Guest House? Doll's house, more like!

I should have sued her then and there for false advertising, but you know what I always say. That's right! *Hindsight is 20/20.* Now, I grant you, I may be a smidgen over my ideal weight – oh! Detective, here, have some more water! Did something go down the wrong way? – but honestly, Calista Flockhart McBeal would have had a tough time squeezing into that so-called Queen Size bed. Queen of the dwarves maybe! Queen Ant! Queen . . . oh, right. My statement.

So anyway, I'd barely finished unpacking when Mrs A came over and handed me my 'List of Duties'.

Oh, look, you have it right there in your hand. How funny! Is that Exhibit A? Ha ha ha! Exhibit A, like on Court TV, geddit? What was that? It *is* exhibit A? Oh. Dear. Well, take a look at it would you, and you'll see my point.

3 a.m.:
Check on Nebuchadnezzar. If his doggie blanket has slipped, re-cover him gently. Make sure room temperature is set to a constant sixty-eight degrees.

6 a.m.:
Check Nebuchadnezzar again. If he stirs, see if he wants to go pee-pee. I prefer him to use his tray, but if he wants to go outside, make sure he's wearing his cashmere wrap. The blue one.

8 a.m.:
Breakfast. Please follow the menu cards provided. If Nebuchadnezzar is reluctant to eat, taste a few mouthfuls yourself first to reassure him. Make sure you do this on all fours or he may take fright.

It goes on for eight pages. Eight pages! Look. The last entry isn't until midnight.

12 midnight:
Insert Chihuahua womb-sounds CD into player. This helps Nebuchadnezzar sleep soundly through the night.

Womb sounds? Can you imagine, Detective?

At first I thought it was a joke. I mean all these doggie duties were on top of my regular work as a housekeeper, you understand. But Mrs A looked deadly serious.

Hmmm? No, no, I didn't say anything about it at the time. Well she was my new employer, wasn't she? I wanted to make a good impression. And, like I say, at first I felt sorry for Neb. I thought perhaps if I stayed, I could help him, have him lead a more normal, carefree dog's life. Because, you know, I have always, ALWAYS loved dogs, whatever anybody might tell you. But of course, all that was before I got to know him. Before I found out first-hand what an evil, Machiavellian little *snake* he was.

And still is.

Oh, yes! You may look surprised, Detective. But he planned all this, you know.

Who? What do you mean *who*? Neb, of course.

Indeed I am serious! Don't you watch Court TV? *Hmmm.* Well, perhaps you should. If you *did*, you'd know that the first question every good detective asks himself is: *Who stood to gain the most from the crime?*

Go on. Ask it. Ask that question!

See? Am I right or am I right? There you have it! You have your prime suspect right there.

Yes, I am aware that he's a dog. There's really no need to take that patronising tone with me. I don't mean to be rude, Detective, but *wake up and smell the coffee*, would you? Don't you see? That's exactly what he *wants* you to think. Poor, cute little Chihuahua, wouldn't hurt a fly! Butter wouldn't melt, that's what you're thinking, isn't it?

Isn't it?

I suppose I can't blame you for being sceptical. He had me fooled at first too. So much so that I actually figured I could *help* him – *ha!* That's why I took Mrs A's list with a pinch of salt. I suppose I thought that I'd be on my own with Neb for much of the day, and she wouldn't know the difference if I took him to Toy-Breeds-Yoga or out for a walk in the park. Plus, she wasn't hauling her bony ass out of bed at 3 a.m. every night to check on the dog, was she? So how would she know if I did? And yes, if truth be told, maybe I was also thinking about the money. Fifty thousand is a good salary after all. Okay, yes, and a little bit about the Bentley too. Maybe. I wanted to drive it by the Coffee Bean at the weekend, you see, and put one over on that dreadful, abusive little man with the Bichon Frise.

Who's allergic to sugar now, asshole!!

But I digress. I'm not a vengeful person, Detective, as you know. Nobody can accuse me of that. No, no. Neb's welfare, at that time, was my main concern.

Anyhoo, long story short, for the first couple of months everything worked out just fine. I stuck to the parts of the list that seemed most important. I gave the dog the specially imported Foie Gras and the truffle oil, just as Mrs A asked. I made endless, and I mean *endless*, trips to Chateau Marmutt for all his little accessories. I even brushed his teeth for him, morning and night, with the tiny silver brush she'd had specially made at Fred Leighton. And believe you me, Detective, that is *humiliating,* even for a dog lover like me: sticking your hand into its mouth and pulling out all the leftover pieces of pate and whatnot? *Eeeugh!*

But what can I say? Neb was the woman's life, her reason for living, her *world.* And I tried to respect that, Detective, truly I did. Within reason.

No, any complaints the old lady had about me at that time were nothing to do with the dog. I'm sorry? Oh, well, it was nothing really. A silly misunderstanding. Those little things, foibles, what have you, that always come to the surface when one starts a new working relationship. What *exactly?* Well, if you must know, she complained – and I mean this is quite ridiculous, there was no basis for it whatsoever – but she complained that I talked too much. *Me!* Can you *imagine*, Detective?

Well, yes, I suppose if you're going to be literal, she did say that once. That I was driving her to suicide. With my constant prattle, yes. But you know, it was said in a very *light-hearted* way. It's really not at all what you're implying . . .

Gosh, now you're *really* blowing this up out of all pro-portion. No, I'm not denying it as such. She *may*, in the heat of the moment, have threatened to sack me. And make me homeless, yes. But she wouldn't have *done* it, Detective. Don't you see? Mrs A and I got on like a house on fire! Two peas in a pod, we were! And we would have carried on that way, for years and years, I'm convinced, if it hadn't been for Neb stirring the pot with his evil, pink leg-warmered paws.

It all started going wrong when she brought in the pet psychologist. You see, I'd started to introduce a little discipline into Neb's life, and he didn't like it one bit. Not that I was cruel, you understand. Far from it. But when I saw him, just minutes after we'd got home from walkies, deliberately lower his little ass over my brand new Victoria's Secret pink mohair slippers . . . Oh yes, he shat in them, Detective. Cool as a cucumber, looking right at me. It was quite deliberate, I can assure you. Well when he did that, I told him 'no!' in a firm voice and I smacked him on the butt. In fact, I wouldn't even say it was a smack. You can cross that out. CROSS IT OUT! It was a tap. It was nothing, really. But *boy* did he not like that! I saw a different side to him from then on, Detective, yes indeedy. And things went from bad to worse.

Whenever Mrs A was around he would ham it up, moping and rolling his eyes, cowering whenever I came near him as if I were about to hit him. I mean *me*, Detective. Me, who has ALWAYS loved dogs. Especially Chihuahuas! Neb as good as told the old lady that I was abusing him! Well, no, obviously he couldn't speak. That would be ridiculous. He's a *dog*. But he didn't have to, did he? His eyes, his evil, scheming little eyes – they said it all.

Anyway, in the end Mrs A hired Dr Maxton, an animal shrink, to take a look at him. Dr Doolittle I called him. You know why? Because he *did little*! Geddit? In fact, scratch that. He did *nothing*. Dr Doonothing! Neb had him twisted around his little manicured paws from day one. He'd be right as rain, playing with his so-called friends down at Tumblepups. (I say 'so-called' because there was no loyalty there, Detective. None whatsoever. Neb didn't understand the meaning of the word friendship. *Uh uh*. He was rotten, rotten to the core!) But then he'd come home, take one look at Dr Doonothing, and start sulking and whining like someone forgot to give him his Prozac.

And the shrink fell for it! Not that I blame him entirely. Neb gave an Oscar-winning performance. Forget Leroy from Fame. He was Laurence Olivier! He was Marlon Brando! (Before he got fat, obviously. Poor man. People are so quick to judge heavier citizens, Detective. In the old days it was blacks and Jews and doo-dahs, but now it's the plus-sized that have become America's pariahs. Let's face it, that has a lot to do with me being here right now, doesn't it? If someone has to be blamed, it may as well be the fat woman, right? RIGHT?)

Sorry. It's just sometimes, the *injustice* of it all . . . What? Yes. Yes, after that Mrs A did let me go. *Uh huh*, yes, on the doctor's recommendation, although of course legally she couldn't give that as the *only* reason.

The other reasons? Oh, I can't remember, Detective. Some trumped-up nonsense about me talking too much – I mean, *please* – and skimping on my agreed duties. Well, yes, if you're going to get literal about it I did cut back on The List a little, but who wouldn't? And as for what she said about pilfering petty cash and taking the Bentley during the week without permission, well that was outrageous. Totally groundless.

Sorry? The mid-week episode at the Coffee Bean? Oh, you mean the assault charge? Yes, yes, yes, but that got dropped. It was all a silly misunderstanding, I can assure you. No, it was Neb who got me fired, Neb who turned her against me.

That was why I had to act.

Don't you see? I had no choice.

I got the arsenic off the Internet, believe it or not. Amazing thing, the Internet. Have you ever been on, Detective? Ever *surfed the web*? See, I've got all the lingo! I can show you if you like. It's a wonder! You can buy just about anything you want there nowadays: fancy Christmas gifts, furniture, intimate feminine apparel, lethal poisons. But I was very careful. I only bought a small dose – enough to kill a household pet, they said – and a little bit extra, to make doubly sure I got the job done cleanly. I wouldn't have wanted to leave him suffering you see, Detective. I'm not a cruel person. But I couldn't just let him think he'd gotten away with it, could I? When we start letting animals lord it over us, it's a slippery slope, isn't it? I had to take a stand.

But then . . . then . . . oh, Detective, it's all so *horrible*! And it's all Neb's fault. He could smell the poison somehow, I'm sure of it. And he stepped back and took his chance. He seized the moment.

How was I supposed to know she'd get down on her hands and knees and taste his food?

Or that she already had a weak heart?

And why, why in the name of Jesus did she go and eat all of it?

Anyway, Detective, I think I've said enough. Like I said, I don't really want to say anything about this until my lawyer gets here. But you are *terribly* easy to talk to. I feel we really connected on some level. Don't you?

All I *will* say is that this whole idea that I was taking my revenge on poor, dear Mrs Andrews is absolute codswallop. It was Neb! It was all Neb! He's the one who should be in here calling his lawyer, not me.

You do realise that she left him everything, don't you? The house, the car, the art collection? Oh yes. Nebuchad-nezzar cleaned up.

It all worked out exactly the way he planned it.

Faith Bleasdale

The Taming of the Playboy

It was more than unbelievable. When my mother called me to tell me that my brother, Tim, was getting married, I thought it was some sort of joke. Because Tim had always said marriage was for mugs. He said that all women wanted to tie men down, but he was cleverer than most men, and wouldn't be trapped. He said he was dedicated to being a playboy.

He was a man who ran away from commitment the way the rabbit runs away from the dogs on a greyhound track. He even moved to Singapore to get away from one poor girl (well he was offered a good job there, but the timing was a bit suspect). I told my mum that she must be wrong, and I hung up on her to get the news straight from his mouth.

'Yes,' Tim said. 'It's true, and I can't wait.' While I was shocked into silence, he then went on to extol the virtues of his bride to be, Angela. She was beautiful, intelligent, very caring, sweet, and he spoke about her with such pride in his voice that I wanted to know where my real brother was.

The engagement was not going to be a long one, which again surprised me. My 'real' brother would have waited at least a year to see if he got bored, or if someone better came along. But no, they were getting married in a couple of months. In Singapore.

As we prepared to fly out there (my parents and I were staying for a month leading up to the wedding), an official engagement photograph arrived. Grinning inanely, Angela and Tim were wearing matching outfits, and had their arms around each other. This wasn't like my brother; he ruthlessly mocked people who did things like that. My mother thought it was lovely and showed everyone she knew; my father commented on how gorgeous Angela was. And she was. But still, nothing was as it should have been. I felt that I was in my own twilight zone.

I actually felt bitter about the whole situation. The way Tim had always been so cynical about relationships and love had ruined every relationship I'd ever had. Or so I believed. For some reason I attracted men like my brother. Every man I dated followed the same path. Didn't call on time, let me chase them (I was verging on becoming the world's best stalker), didn't believe in romance, stood me up on various occasions and then completed my humiliation by callously dumping me. Honestly, every one. And their behaviour mirrored my brother's. I suppose I could have taken comfort in the fact that now my brother was settling down, there was hope for me. But I wasn't feeling like taking comfort, I was feeling betrayed.

Tim had been in Singapore for just under a year and

because of work I hadn't visited him yet. So, despite the fact I wasn't keen on the reason for going, I was looking forward to it.

When we arrived, Tim met us, alone. He looked like my brother, and as he kissed my cheek and told me that I looked haggard, he even sounded like my brother. Tim explained that Angela felt that it was important that he had some time alone with us before we met her. My parents thought that this was the most considerate thing they'd ever heard.

After the twelve-hour almost sleepless flight, wedged in between my mother and father like a child, I was too tired to ask him all I wanted to know. My interrogation would have to wait.

Tim lived in a condo. It was a brand new, tall, skyscraper-type thing. It reminded me of those TV shows set in the future. In London my brother had lived in a bachelor pad. It was sparse, messy and looked about as inviting as his dirty laundry. I knew he'd probably have cleaned up for our coming but as he opened the door and ushered us in, I wasn't prepared for what we faced. Apart from the fact that the apartment was huge, stunning, all marble floors and dark teak furniture, there were fresh flowers everywhere, a number of plants were thriving and warm-coloured pictures decorated the walls. There were even cushions, for goodness' sake.

A tour of the place proved that this wasn't the only room that had been made delightful. I knew who the culprit was, and it wasn't Tim. I know by now you probably think me slightly evil, but I was just confused and displaced. My brother lived in a flat that I would live in. Actually he lived in a flat I could only aspire to live in.

'I suppose that this is what happens when you live with a woman,' I said. My mother gave me a dirty look; I must have sounded surly.

'I don't live with a woman,' Tim replied.

'But . . . Angela?' I asked, confused.

'No, she lives with her parents. It's not appropriate for her to move in until we're married.' My mother actually cried and hugged him. I almost cried, but for a completely different reason.

We freshened up, had some coffee, and waited for Angela to appear. My mother was keener than ever, my father was pretty excited and Tim was more enthusiastic than I'd ever seen him. I was the only normal member of my family, although I was probably the only person in the world who saw it like that.

Angela arrived. My mother immediately pounced on her. More tears and kisses and hugs. My father was slightly more formal and shook her hand. I gave her a half-hearted hug; Tim gave me a dirty look which I very much ignored.

'I'm so glad to meet you all,' she said. In a flash she was part of our family. My mother immediately started talking to her about wedding plans. Flowers, dresses, bridesmaids, cars. Then Angela formally asked me, as her future sister, if I'd be one of her bridesmaids. Luckily everyone else was too busy gushing to notice my ingratitude.

As the time wore on, it became clear that this was no joke. My brother treated Angela like a princess. He couldn't stop staring at her, touching her, and he was constantly making sure she was all right. If I wasn't so evil, I would have said that there was no doubt that they were in love.

But I still didn't understand. Angela was nice enough, and she was gorgeous, but I still couldn't quite get why my brother had changed his entire personality for this woman. And you might think that I'm exaggerating, but as soon as he had his first girlfriend, my brother had been all about breaking hearts. It took up so much of his time that he didn't really have an awful lot else going on.

So in between jetlag, having fittings for my bridesmaid dress (dusky pink, and although it wasn't ugly, it definitely wasn't me), watching my parents literally fawn over Angela, like a detective I tried to work out for myself what was going on. Luckily as Angela didn't live with Tim, I had plenty of opportunities to confront him about it. Unluckily I chose a time when I'd had a little too much to drink.

'What do you see in her?' I demanded. I was slurring as I waved my glass of wine around precariously in his pristine apartment.

'What do you mean?' my mother replied, diving and snatching the glass from my hand.

'She's not that special,' I said, which wasn't nice, I know. My mother called me wicked, then she wondered where she'd gone wrong with me, and finally demanded that I become more like Angela. My brother refused to speak to me. My father's eyes were full of disappointment.

Of course, it was Angela who healed the threatened rift. Apparently she ever so reasonably told my brother that it was hard for me, as I'd never met her before, learning they were getting married. In fact she used the word overwhelming. It was also Angela who said that she would take my parents to see her parents while Tim and I spent some time alone. My hatred for this perfect being grew.

Especially as she'd replaced me as number one daughter in the eyes of my parents.

Tim took me to a bar. He ordered cocktails and he asked me what my problem was.

'It's not that I don't like her. I mean what's not to like,' I started. 'But Tim, it's just not you. You went down on bended knee, and you told me that you'd never do that. You've known her five minutes, Tim, try to understand why I'm so confused.' I was almost in tears. I felt as if everything I knew as certain had suddenly been taken away from me, leaving me with foundations that were very shaky.

'Becks, I fell in love. It's that simple.' He didn't even choke when he said the 'L' word.

'But you don't even believe in love,' I argued.

'I do now. Listen, sis, I met her and I just knew. Well, I didn't, but after dating her for a month I did. She's everything I want in a woman and I didn't want to let her get away.' My brother had never really opened up to me before, something else that had changed. He poured his heart out and I began, reluctantly, to understand.

He met Angela through a work event (they both work in banking). She bumped into him; he fancied her and started chatting her up. Before he knew it they were dating. So far, so my brother. But they quickly discovered that they had everything in common. She liked to look good; he liked her to look good. She loved to cook; he loved to eat. She loved football, and kept him supplied with beer whenever they watched it. She was great fun and enjoyed going out with his friends, who were all incredibly jealous of him, and she never minded if he wanted to go out with the boys on his own. She was compliant in most things he wanted, but not all. She made it clear early on that cohabitation wasn't on the cards. She told him that her respect for her parents prevented her from doing that. He liked that she was old-fashioned and had values. In fact, he confided after a few more cocktails, she was a virgin until they got engaged. And who wouldn't want to marry a virgin? he asked. I had no idea.

It all began to make sense. My brother had fallen in love with a sweet, innocent girl who wanted to take care of him in the old-fashioned way. To such an extent that they'd decided that she was going to give up work when they were married, so she could concentrate on being a good wife. Well, with all that on offer I probably would have married her too.

As my brother got drunk, he made it clear that he was one lucky bastard, to have got everything he could possibly want in a woman, and very importantly know that no one else had had it before him. So, my brother hadn't actually changed as much as I thought. His life with Angela would be better and I didn't doubt that he loved her, but had she not been this subservient little thing, then there was no way he'd be getting married. He was pretty much marrying a very attractive doormat.

I almost felt sorry for her after that. I was much nicer. We bonded over shopping (she wouldn't buy anything unless she was sure that Tim would approve) and lunch and finally I showed an interest in the wedding plans. Still being a little evil, I even tried to teach her about feminism, but she thought that it was a joke. I'm sure I saw her look at her huge diamond rock and then at me with pity as I told her about equality. I still wasn't in love with the idea of Tim getting married. I certainly panicked at the idea that in order for me to get married I've have to be like Angela, but I decided to accept things for what they were. Even my single status. Although that didn't detract my mother from trying to ascertain which of Tim's friends were single and which wouldn't mind a strong-minded woman like me. Apparently none of them, was the answer. So then she decided that if I didn't talk when introduced to them, I might be in with a chance. Her behaviour was like something out of an Austen novel.

Despite this, I began to enjoy my holiday and Singapore. It was incredibly hot, and I was immune to the humidity. My brother's condo complex boasted a swimming pool which I sat next to quite happily for hours on end. Angela had given up work by now, but refused to tan, apparently it's not a popular look in Singapore. I carried on regardless, although my mother fretted that a tan might make me even more unlikely to find a mate.

While Tim was at work I reverted to being a child and went sightseeing with my parents. We went to the zoo, the bird-park, out to the man-made beaches of the east coast, museums, and when we weren't sightseeing we helped out with wedding plans. Well, my mother did; I sat by the pool. Sometimes Angela joined us, and the bond between her and my parents grew.

Jealousy is a bad thing, we all know that, but it's also quite natural. So where I'd spent a week or so making an effort and being almost happy about the wedding, now I wasn't. Angela was like this dream girl. She made me look bad even when I wasn't being. My mother criticised the way I dressed (ten-year-old sarong and plastic yellow flip-flops mainly), my hair, the fact that I didn't wear enough make-up, everything about the way I looked. My personality didn't escape either. My sarcasm made me highly unattractive; I didn't smile enough; my humour was too base; no man would ever want me unless I learnt to be less opinionated. Throughout these attacks, no one stood up for me. Except for me, of course. I was getting to the stage where I just wanted the wedding to be over and for my life to resume some normality. I began to think that Singapore was putting spells on people and I wanted to escape before it got me too.

The wedding day arrived. I donned my dusky pink amidst extreme excitement at Angela's parents' apartment. The other three bridesmaids, two friends and a cousin, were all giggling as our hair and make-up was expertly applied. The other bridesmaids were all beautiful and slim, and although I was only a size ten I felt frumpy next to them. My mother obviously felt the same. She looked incredibly worried for my prospects.

I have to admit to feeling a lump in my throat when Angela was ready. Her white satin dress (which in all fairness she almost had a right to wear) was so incredible. She looked breathtaking. Even my evil side couldn't find fault. And as everyone was so nervous and excited, I got caught up in the middle of it.

In Singapore you have to go to the Registry of Marriage. They'd done that bit already so they were in fact legally married, but it was official and unromantic, according to Angela, so this was their blessing, which was treated as their proper wedding. It was held in the grounds of a lovely hotel, and was beautiful. It went without a hitch. My brother stood there, tall, handsome and proud and I actually shed a tear – whether out of happiness or sadness I'm unsure. Afterwards we had champagne outside while the photographs, which were the horribly cheesy kind, as all wedding photos seem to be, were taken. But Tim didn't seem to mind as he picked Angela up and fed her champagne and they stood looking lovingly into each other's eyes by the flowers.

Finally, the heat got to us so we were allowed to head inside for the air-conditioned reception. The food was wonderful, the speeches mercifully short, and the drink flowing. Although my mother told me that I really ought not to eat and definitely not drink if I had any chance of finding a man.

I didn't. I met Tim's new friends who were politely disinterested in me. I re-met his friends from the UK who didn't bother with politeness as they'd known me most of my life. My mother looked so upset that at one point I'm sure she was trying to persuade a waiter to ask me to dance.

I sat in the corner getting drunk as I watched my brother dancing with his bride. The other bridesmaids dancing with his friends. Angela's friends dancing with the rest of his friends. Even my mother had decided to ignore me. I'm sure I heard her tell one of Angela's family members she had no idea who I was. So I sat in the corner with a bottle of champagne and a very bruised ego.

A woman around my age came and sat next to me. She smiled shyly and introduced herself as one of Angela's cousins, Sasha. I gave her some of my champagne and wondered why she wasn't dancing.

'I'm tired. It's been fun, but I needed to rest. You're Tim's sister aren't you?'

'Yes, Becky. How come we haven't met before?'

'Angela and me, well we aren't very close any more. It's a bit tricky.' She turned red and I became very interested. I plied my victim with more champagne and did the same to myself. Finally I was ready to interrogate.

'Why aren't you close? It seems that everyone loves Angela.' I hoped I didn't sound bitter.

'Oh, they do. Too much. She stole a boyfriend from me when I was twenty-five and she was just eighteen. It broke my heart. I wouldn't have come today but my parents made me.' She turned redder. Emboldened, I refilled her glass and looked sympathetic.

'That's awful. But she was young.'

'No, it's not that. I shouldn't tell you.'

'Please do.' I was almost begging. There was a long pause.

'She is a bitch.' Wait. I stared at my new friend incredulously. I indicated that she should carry on, and she hesitated for just a second before she did so. 'She always has been. She manipulates men and chews them up. I know you wouldn't believe it to look at her but . . .'

'You must be talking about someone else. Angela's compliant, that's what my brother says. And she cooks for him, and takes care of him.'

'Of course she does. She met him and decided that she was going to marry him. That's what she did. She knows that a way to a man's heart is through his stomach – and his ego.'

'Are you saying that it's an act?'

'Well, yes. She hates football but is always boasting about how you can hook many men by saying you like it. And she hated her job, so she told Tim that it would be better for him if she quit.'

'Are you telling me that my new sister-in-law knew what she was doing with my brother?'

'Oh yes, she knew about his reputation with women, my other cousin told me, you know, the bridesmaid. Well, she did her research and she presented herself to him, with the goal of today in mind.'

'You mean my brother, who thought that he was the clever one by marrying her, has been played.'

'Don't get me wrong, I think they'll be happy enough. Apparently she's very good in bed.' Sasha turned bright red; I stared open-mouthed.

'But she didn't sleep with my brother until they were engaged. She was a . . .' the penny fell from a great height.

'She told him she was a virgin. I know, but it's not true. She's clever.'

'My brother thinks she was a virgin, thinks she isn't going to cause him any trouble, thinks he's got a doormat, but all the time she was in control? She tamed the playboy?'

'Yes.' I was stunned; astonished. I stood up. My legs were slightly wobbly, either through the drink or the shock. 'Are you going to tell him?' she asked. I thought of my brother, how happy he was, of my upset, of my loveless life, of my future.

'No bloody way. I'm going to get some lessons.'

Yasmin Boland

What Angels Do . . .

Based on a true story

'Lavender mohair' sounds exotic. It looks it too, when cut in the right way, say, as a minidress on a tall, slim woman's body.

That was Rose that afternoon. Her long, bare legs glistened a little, varnished with sweat and grime from the Manhattan streets she'd been pounding all day going from one museum or gallery to another. She sat in her seat on the Q Train L, exhausted and wary. Yesterday, she'd brought her digital camera along with her on the subway, but she'd barely had the courage to take a single shot. Her fellow commuters hadn't looked in the mood to be snapped by an out-of-towner. The passengers seated around her tonight looked even less likely to allow such behaviour without a fuss. So she sat in her lavender mohair minidress, which was creeping a little too high up her thighs, aware her breasts were jiggling with the rhythm of

80

the train, unable to do anything about anything.

Like heat radiating, she felt the grubby stare of a dirty little man dressed in a soiled, crumpled brown suit. He regarded her like a piece of meat he was searing with his eyes. He traced from her feet, pupils dilating at the tip of her pointy black shoes, up her calves to her knees, lingering on the splash of ketchup dropped from that afternoon's hot dog, up over her thighs to her breasts, flickering briefly to her face and back to her cleavage.

Rose remembered she had a copy of the *New York Times* in her bag and took it out to use as camouflage, opening it wide to block his view. She could smell his body odour as she turned her interest to the newspaper, to an article about the fate of the elephants that saved people during the Boxing Day tsunami. She stared at the accompanying picture. A smiling Sri Lankan boy who'd been hauled to safety via a lift from an elephant. Barely a teenager. Much of his appeal lay in his round brown eyes which seemed to expect fun. His bone structure was perfection. Shiny, young dark skin over emerging cheekbones. The caption said the boy's name was Gobu.

Rose idly tapped a finger on her large silver belt buckle, tugging her hemline down. The dirty little brown man now seemed to be rubbing his crotch as he stared her in the face. Slowly but surely. She'd almost forgotten about the perils of the New York subway. This was the most daring dress she'd worn in her time here, for sure. Men who'd never spoken to her before on her art course had said hello today. One had even complimented her butt. She had decided never to wear the dress during the day again. Way too risqué. What had she been thinking?

She looked up at the station. Union Square.

Rose barely registered the fact that she didn't remember the name of that station from her previous subway trips home and instead lost herself in the photo again, dissecting the shapes of Gobu's face. He exuded an aura as strong as the dirty brown man's over-ripe odour. Gobu glowed as the man reeked. The man now had his hand down his pants for all to see. Rose looked away, back to the newspaper, trying to immerse herself in the tsunami story. It was a glorious feel-good front-page story. Amid fears of further interest-rate rises and the murder of a family of five in San Fran, Gobu glowed. As you would too, most likely, if an elephant had saved you and your family from the torrent of death. The strangest thing was that no one had seen the elephant before the tsunami and no one had seen him since.

'I believe the elephant was an angel,' Gobu had told the reporter. 'Angels come in all shapes and sizes.'

Rose tried to imagine how she would paint Gobu. These days she painted monuments. Pictures of monuments sold; indeed her newest hand-painted cards had paid for this week's wonderful, if self-indulgent, art-history course in New York. Painting flesh and blood was less her thing these days, but monuments have faces too . . .

The train slowed, then jolted to a halt. Rose craned her neck, now recognising neither the station nor the platform. The doors were slammed shut and she realised she was the only person in the carriage wearing a lavender mohair mini-dress with a large silver buckle. For sure, only she showed this much thigh and cleavage.

The little man in the brown suit peeled his sweaty self

off the seat. He moved one seat closer. A youth whose face appeared untouched by either compassion or smarts raised one eyebrow as he watched the manoeuvre. Rose glanced across too. A large woman with groceries on her lap avoided her gaze. The dirty brown man moved another seat towards Rose as the train jolted again, trying and failing to get moving once more. The crush of humanity jammed in the subway seemed to mingle into one foul stench as it pushed its way up Rose's nose. Funny how they said people smelled like animals. Rose had never smelled an animal that stank like this.

Rose reached into her handbag for her subway map and quickly confirmed her suspicions. This line was wrong. She shouldn't be here. Especially not dressed like this. She gripped her handbag to her stomach, remembering the wad of cash inside. She'd planned to use it to buy paints today, but hadn't got to the art shop in time. Camera. Passport. Credit cards. The smell of the dirty brown man was now up her nose. The youth with the raised eyebrow curled his upper lip. The lady with the groceries started banging on the window. 'Hey, you motherfuckers! Get this damn shit train moving. There's a woman about to get in trouble in here.' She heaved herself out of her seat and marched heavily up the aisle to the other end of the carriage, leaving Rose feeling like her lavender mohair dress had fallen away to reveal her nakedness.

'Dear God, please help me.'

Rose knew faces, knew their creases and shadows and folds. Chiaroscuro. She also believed she knew human nature and could see into it via someone's face. She had a fundamental belief that at least 50 per cent of people were inherently good. There were at least twenty-five people in this carriage. That meant 12.5 possible good people.

These days Rose lived in Paris. Well, wouldn't you, if you were an artist with long slim legs and you could? Live there. The cards she painted were of the Arc de Triomphe, the Jardin de Tuileries, the Pont des Arts at sunset, thronged with people. She had, however, grown up in New Jersey. Not too far away from the Boss's shore but still close enough to realise in a New York minute that she was headed for trouble. A slow rising terror crept up on her.

'Hey. Slut . . .' The dirty brown man hissed at her.

Someone will help me, she told herself. I will ask someone to escort me upstairs to a taxi. She eyed a big guy with a body like a fridge standing to her left. For a second, as the train started back to life, the light from the carriage ceiling hit the window behind him, momentarily framing his head. He stood firm as the train jerked into forwards motion. They were moving again.

'Think you're too good for me?' The dirty little man was acting like she was ignoring him, as if they'd met and Rose had rejected him. So she did ignore him. She stood up, and arranged her fine features, her blue eyes, her turned-up nose and kind lips into a smile as the big guy looked her way.

'Excuse me, sir.' He felt familiar. 'I took the wrong train and now I have to go upstairs and get a taxi. Would you mind accompanying me?'

'Oh yes, Ma'm'selle.'

What had alerted him to her French connection? She loved his smile.

'May I take your arm?' His deep voice resonated through her.

She loved that he proffered his arm, too. In fact, if there was one thing she loved in a man it was a gentlemanly elbow to hold. They waited for the doors to open at the next station.

'This way, Ma'm'selle.'

Stepping out without a backwards glance at her fellow passengers, they headed through the crowds. She was aware of the stares around her. It wasn't just Rose who grocked how out of place she was. The big guy kept his arm firmly in place for her, guiding her past a mad woman who was yelling to anyone who would listen about having no money to buy her kids dinner, past the kid in the hood who looked like he'd come straight from Central Casting for Menacing Homeboys, past a dozen dirty little brown men who smirked at her and looked quizzically at the angel of a man who just kept going, leading her through the turnstiles and up the stairs towards daylight.

Outside on the kerb a taxi came screeching to a halt, as if it had been ordered just for Rose. A Puerto Rican guy jumped out, took one look at her creamy thighs and started shaking his head, yelling at her. 'What the hell do you think you're doing here? Are you crazy, lady?'

'I took the wrong train.'

'Well, believe me – it's your lucky day. Hop in. I'll take you home.'

Relieved, Rose turned to thank her kindly escort with a smile. But the pavement was empty. Unwilling to stand around trying to work out how a man built like a fridge could disappear into thin air, Rose got into the taxi, praying the driver would take her home without any further dramas.

Her heart pounded as they drove through the city. Strangely, they hit no lights and the traffic seemed to part for them, so they had an unobstructed and speedy ride. It was only as they arrived outside her apartment that Rose realised the cab's meter wasn't running. When she asked the driver how much she owed him, he winked. 'No charge today, sweetheart.'

Rose looked at him in wonder. 'Huh?' She had been preparing to give him a massive tip.

The taxi driver smiled at the confusion on her face and slammed the car into gear. 'Like the little boy said, Rose – all shapes and sizes,' he added with a grin, before driving off.

Elizabeth Buchan

Kindness

At Rome airport, Sable Farrer climbed into a coach labelled 'Euro Culture 'n' Fun Ltd'. She was dressed in her customary muted way – a matching knitted caramel-coloured sweater and skirt which could have been elegant, but on Sable looked dull and lumpy. Already, it felt far too hot.

As usual, she kept her head down. This was, in part, due to her terror of being noticed but, as she had grown older, in part a deepening desire not to look at things too closely. The world did not, in her view, bear too much close examination. Nevertheless, she knew perfectly well that several pairs of inquisitive, speculative eyes would be sizing her up.

She manhandled her hand luggage awkwardly to the back of the coach and slipped into an empty double seat. 'I wish more than anything I was not on this bus,' she thought. 'I wish I was not in Rome.' Above all, Sable wished she was not scheduled to endure a week in the company of strangers. Yet, in a moment of uncharacteristic impulse, and on a depressing winter's day in the office where she worked as a billing clerk for a utility firm, this was precisely what she had chosen to do and, furthermore, *paid* for. Why? Outside had been rain-lashed, her stomach has been a little bilious and she had discovered the pamphlet advertising the trip in her in-tray. She remembered its thin, glossy texture as she held it between her fingers. *We promise you marvellous things*, it seemed to say.

The coach jerked forward and Sable clutched at her tote bag which had toppled over. A woman in the opposite seat reached over to help and said: 'I had no idea it would be so much warmer than home. It's only April, after all.'

Sable waited for the woman's gaze to fixate on the lower part of her face which she knew from thirty-five years of experience would take approximately ten seconds. (She could see *What happened to her?* slide like news-tape across the mind of any observers.) Sable almost never satisfied their curiosity. It was nobody's business but her own as to what had turned her mouth from the pretty childish pink bow which it had once been, into the twisted thing that marred her adult face. Equally, since she had no family, not even a cousin, there was no one who could supply chatty asides such as '*Of course, Mary was heartbroken by what happened*' or '*It was just one of those things*' or any other interesting nuggets of information to anyone who was interested. As far as most people were concerned, Sable was a blank sheet. Puzzling, but definitely blank. That was the way she preferred it and, occasionally, when someone proved too curious, too invasive with their questions, she could be quite ferocious in her rejection. A psychologist might have concluded that Sable was allowing a trick

of fate to cut her off from full participation in recipro-
cal relationships. Sable would have replied, 'It's none of
your business. No one has the right to know what goes on
inside me.'

The woman opposite looked taken aback at the lack of
response and Sable made an effort. 'Yes, it is surprising'
(which was not the case, for they were in Italy). She pitched
her tone to suggest she was willing to be polite but had
no interest in continuing the conversation. It was a neutral
tone, as neutral as Sable had schooled herself to appear.
Rebuffed, the woman settled back into her seat and concentrated on the view.

It was early evening. The traffic clogged the roads and
progress was inch by inch. 'To your right is an example of
cypressa sempervirens, the Italian cypress . . .' droned the
tour guide, who had introduced himself as Paddy, 'the
man on whom you must rely'. In the becalmed coach,
Sable stared hard at a slender, green exclamation mark of
a tree which had been planted on a roundabout. Didn't
'sempervirens' mean 'to live forever'? This did not strike
her as a welcome proposition.

In the foyer of the Merry Bacchus Hotel, a bald modern
building so ugly Sable felt like crying out in protest, Paddy
issued them with instructions, including the exhortation
to appear at seven-thirty sharp for dinner. As she hoped,
no one spoke to Sable as she hauled her luggage up to the
tenth floor and into a room from which all individuality
had been carefully – and successfully – planned out. She
swept back the curtains from the plate glass window, sat
down on her bed and watched the traffic roar up the Via
Aurelia, which snaked past on the way into Rome's centre.

With a bit of luck, she could contrive not to speak to any-one much for the entire trip. After that, she would return home to the flat on the housing estate and the office in the utilities firm, and drop back into her routine and out of sight.

The following morning, Sable ate breakfast with her eyes fixed on the sugar bowl in the centre of the table. She must have counted the packets in it at least ten times. Her silence and hunched shoulders did not go unnoticed and when the group assembled (many of them breathing out the fumes of strange coffee overlarded with toothpaste) for the morning's outing, Paddy drew her aside and asked, 'Is everything in order?' Sable now riveted her gaze on Paddy's feet, which were shod in suede lace-ups, the kind she considered that only cads wore. 'Everything's fine,' she replied. 'Quite fine.' Paddy was too harassed to take it further. He had done his duty and moved swiftly on to question a fit-looking couple dressed in matching green shorts and Polo T-shirts.

Very quickly, it became apparent that Euro Culture 'n' Fun was a tour company that believed in quantity as opposed to quality. To this end, it floated the sights of Rome as fast as possible past its clients, so neatly captive in the coach. The itinerary was rapid and furious. 'To your right,' Paddy crooned through the microphone, 'is the Palatine Hill, home of the Roman emperors.' He threw in the additional sop. 'Up ahead is the Colosseum.'

'Can you tell us about the gladiators?' A man three rows ahead was curious. 'Do you know any details?'

'Yup, that's where the gladiators fought,' said Paddy.

This, clearly, was to be the sum total of information

that he was going to grant the group and, with a blare of its horn, the coach accelerated. What the Colosseum was, or had been, was left to private conjecture.

In this manner, Rome slid past in a blur . . . the Pantheon, Piazza Navona, St Peter's, the Tiber: colours, shapes and smells melting into one another, nothing distinct, nothing sharp – much as Sable, on her bad days, hoped that her own life would pass. In fact, was passing. *Soon I'll be thirty-six, then forty, then forty-five . . . and it will all be over.* In this respect, the holiday suited her very well.

'Day Three,' declared Paddy, on day three, 'is our villa day, ladies and gentlemen. We take a break from the city in order to enjoy the delights of the country around the capital.' He herded them onto the coach and they were driven up into the hills at Tivoli. Formerly an ancient playground for wealthy Romans, the town scrambled up the slope, offering a cool summer retreat from the baking plain and relief from the stew and swelter of the streets. Later, in the sixteenth century, it provided a playground for the rich (and no doubt spoilt) cardinal who had built the Villa D'Este and laid out its fabled garden.

Still, concluded Sable, intrigued despite herself by the beautiful sight-lines of the garden that was constructed on several levels and by the ingeniousness of the fountains, the cardinal had possessed great taste. And she wondered more than a little about a man of God who had been so enamoured of the good things of this world that he had devoted such energy to them. Surely the cardinal should have been concentrating on the next?

Perhaps it was fatigue, perhaps it was the rebellion of the over-shepherded, but the group displayed a tendency to fragment and wander in different directions. 'Over here,' cried Paddy more than once. 'Over *here*.' Under her unsuitable jersey jumper and skirt, Sable felt the sweat force its way from her armpits down her body. It was so warm, hot even, and the smell of jasmine mingling with dust and new growth was so very invasive. Its sweetness, its suggestion of heat and languor, were unsettling. Sable's nerve endings were quivering with feelings and yearnings with which she was unfamiliar, and for which she had no explanation.

She made her way to one of the larger fountains, sat down on the marble lip which surrounded the pool and willed herself to think of nothing very much. It was cool here and, if she remained quite still, she could imagine herself merging into the background of green box and oleander. Merging so completely until she, too, turned into a shade from the past, like those men and women who used to walk up and down these paths in their rich, colourful garments, talking and laughing, plotting and planning. If that happened, if Sable faded into nothing, became merely a memory, then everything would be over: all the grief and boredom and disappointment of being what she was. *Why am I thinking like this*? But she knew why. If Sable was truthful, if she dug right down into the dark of her subconscious and looked properly at the mysteries which lurked there, she would find anger. *I am angry that I have not been bolder and braver about myself.*

Sometimes, in her better moments, she planned to make changes. Of course she did. 'One day,' she promised herself, 'I will take myself by the scruff of the neck, give myself a good shake. Instead of looking at a glass and perceiving it as half empty, I will declare it half full.'

That would be a sensible, positive attitude to life.

Then (ran her fantasies) a new Sable would emerge: a bright, confident woman who would say things such as *My mouth? I never think about it.*

'I'd say, Dora, that she's had plastic surgery . . .' said a voice, and continued with a triumphant inflection, '*which went wrong.*' It was a rich voice, full of humour and dark velvety tones. If one had to describe it with a metaphor, this voice was a fruitcake stuffed with cherries and raisins.

Sable stiffened.

'Rubbish, Margaret. She doesn't look the type. Still, you can never tell.' This second voice lilted: it ran like a stream, light-hearted and almost girlish.

Haven't you seen the ads in the magazines? You can have your bottom rebuilt Dora, if you wish. If you are prepared to pay enough.'

'My bottom?' said Margaret. 'They'd have a job.'

'Girls nowadays don't know if they're supposed to be mothers or that Jo-Lo person. I pity them. Very confusing. Paddy says you can't get a word out of her.'

'Plastic surgery,' said Margaret. 'I wonder what she asked for? Lips like my settee?'

'It doesn't matter what she asked for, it's what she got that's the problem.'

Sable turned her head in order to identify the speakers. But she already had a suspicion. And, yes, it was the two women who always bagged the front seats on the coach. They wore brightly coloured cotton shirts and trousers in which they seemed completely comfortable, and big straw hats. They had capacious handbags, and guidebooks that they read out to each other. On the return to the Merry

Bacchus the previous evening, they had led the coach party in a group sing-song, '*We're all going on a summer holiday*.' They had sung the words with gusto, and swayed from side to side, and Dora had seized the microphone in order to whip up a response from the rest. 'Come on,' she admonished, looking straight at Sable on her back seat. 'Everyone join in.'

It went without saying that this Dora and her friend Margaret were talking about her. Or rather, the mouth – Sable had reached the stage when she could no longer think of it as 'her' mouth, for it had a life of its own. This discreet, separate existence to which Sable played host was an insoluble conundrum for, wherever and whenever she strove to make herself as inconspicuous as possible, she found herself continually thrust into the spotlight of speculation.

This is what Sable imagined.

No, not imagined. At work, on a station platform, queuing for tickets at the cinema, she knew the disaster of her face always triggered speculation. But why was the urge so strong for explanations in people? For her part, she had no interest as to why Mrs Watson next door was seen frequently stuffing empty whisky bottles into the refuse bin. Or in the rumour that her boss, Damien, was probably having an affair with his assistant. It was no one's business but theirs, and Sable respected the boundaries. Grief and love were private. Feelings were private, and not to be shared. Everyone was alone. Everyone was an island. And that was that.

But she knew, she well knew, that she *was* an object of pity, conjecture, malice even. On those better-moment days, she wondered if she might be – just – developing a sense of humour about the subject. But on the cold, despairing days, she shook with rage and humiliation at the way these chatterers and speculators helped themselves to her story without her permission *and got it wrong.*

The two women moved in the direction of where Sable was perched. Their shirts were loose and bright, so *appropriate* in the sunlight. Their cheeks and arms were sheened with sweat, their feet sensibly shod. They were making no concessions towards beauty or fashion and they wore smiles of complete enjoyment.

Margaret transferred her capacious bag from one shoulder to the other, and plumped down on the rim of the fountain. Dora followed suit, and they sat closely together, with the closeness of friends who knew each other through and through and she heard: 'You'd better ask her Dora, then we can sort it out. *Was it plastic surgery?*'

Sable looked down at her reflection in the water. Somehow (a trick of the refraction?) the scar was not so obvious and a watery portrait of a woman with large and rather beautiful eyes stared back at her. *A bold, bright confident person?*

All around, the warmth was insistent and the sweet scents of spring and growth beguiled.

She opened her mouth and from it issued words which had rarely been uttered. 'If you must know,' she said, 'it was my mother.'

The two women whipped round and Sable had the satisfaction of witnessing the colour storm into their cheeks.

'Yes,' she continued. 'My mother was a failed actress but she liked to keep her hand in. She was demonstrating to my father just what Lady Macbeth should have done with the knife and, unfortunately, I was in the way. It must have been a vicious swipe, but I was too young to judge.'

'Oh,' said Dora.

Margaret was quite silent. Red, but silent.

'She died not long after,' added Sable.

Dora's hand flew to her own mouth. 'What a terrible story.'

'It's funny,' said Sable, 'how wrong you can get things.'

More silence.

'I didn't ask for it,' said Sable, who was experiencing an extraordinary sensation. Inside her, a tap was gushing forth, rather like the fountain behind her, and she wondered how on earth she was going to stop it. 'And for your information, I have had two operations to put it right, but it won't *go* right, and I am stuck with it.' She looked down at the water. 'People think they can talk about it, as if they owned my problem. But they don't.'

It was Margaret who collected herself first. 'No, they don't,' she said. 'And, even if they did, they have other things to think about.'

'*You* were talking about me.'

'We were,' Margaret moved closer to Sable, plump and determined, but, on closer inspection, a kind-looking woman. 'But only because you've let your mouth spoil your looks.'

And Sable heard herself exclaim, '*What* looks?'

She felt the weight of the other woman's good intentions and flinched. She hated that more than anything: kindliness bestowed as a duty, as a form of moral obligation.

But Margaret appeared bent on an instant crusade: to put Sable right. 'You've got it wrong, love,' she said. 'Now that I look properly, I can hardly see anything noticeable. Anyway, you should look up. Then we can see your eyes.'

She took Sable by the arm and made her turn round to face the fountain, which was composed of several marble figures – a god, a couple of nymphs, a flying dolphin – over which the water arced and flowed.

Attended by a few loyal stragglers, Paddy came into view. 'Over here . . . now this fountain has been extensively restored . . .' He paused, gesticulated irritably in the direction of the three women, and then moved on. 'Over here . . .'

'*Do* look up, love,' insisted Margaret, in the voice which dripped plums and satiny warmth. Sable considered flight. She considered flinging herself into the fountain. But actually what Sable did was to raise her eyes. 'Go on, take a look,' said Margaret. 'See that little nymph.'

As Paddy had pointed out, the cracks and repairs to the figures were obvious. They were particularly marked on the face of the smaller nymph, who crouched at the feet of the god bearing a triton. Whereas her larger sister was untouched and glowed with a frozen, somewhat cruel, beauty, this one's nose had crumbled, and a chunk had fallen out of her chin. Her face was half-shielded from the onlookers and yet, thought Sable, and yet the expression on the marble features was of a quiet, and secret, humour. *Too bad*, that expression said. *I don't mind. I have what I have. I know what I know.*

Sable stood between Dora and Margaret, feeling their solid bodies press against hers. A living, breathing solidarity.

'Isn't she pretty?' said Margaret. 'Much prettier than the other one.'

Dora captured Sable's hand and patted it. 'Why don't you join us?' she invited. 'We're going to have an ice-cream at the cafe.'

Sable felt the sun beat down on her neck, smelled the sharp spicy smell of the hedge, heard the splash of the water. She shaded her eyes and looked down the avenue at the solid outlines of the box hedge, the softer tracings of the olive trees and, behind them, the villa, and they registered so vividly and clearly that it was as if they had sprung into focus for the first time.

'We're not the only ones who were wrong,' added Dora. 'Don't you think?'

And, then, something happened. Sable felt her mouth stretch in a novel fashion. The muscles in her lips were tight and unwilling and unpractised but, eventually, they yielded. 'Perhaps you're right,' she agreed, and the smile she directed at Dora and Margaret held the beginnings of an unfamiliar and novel joy.

Meg Cabot

Party Planner

To: All Employees of the *New York Journal*
Fr: Charity Webber <charity.webber@thenyjournal.com>
Re: Company Holiday Party

Just a reminder that all departments will close at 4:30 p.m. today so that employees can get an early start on their holiday merrymaking. We hope to see all of you at Les Hautes Manger (57th and Madison) for cocktails and hors d'oeuvres (not to mention entertainment by the nationally acclaimed Magical Madrigals) from 4:30 to 8:00 p.m. All you need to bring is your holiday cheer!

Charity Webber
New York Journal Events Coordinator

To: Charity Webber <charity.webber@thenyjournal.com>
Fr: Natasha Roberts <natasha.roberts@thenyjournal.com>
Re: Holiday Party

Char—

How in the hell did you get old 'Pinchpenny' Peter

Hargrave to shell out the bucks for a swank shindig at a top restaurant like Les Hautes Manger? Last year's Christmas party was in the Senior Staff Dining Room, where the refreshments consisted of nonalcoholic eggnog and pigs-in-a-blanket. Now suddenly we're having Cosmos and salmon tartare someplace where ties and jackets are required? What gives?

Did you talk the guys in tech support into diverting funds from office supplies into the events budget again? Char, don't you remember what happened last time you did that? You ended up spending five Saturday nights in a row watching *Robot Wars* with the likes of Danny 'When's the last time you updated your software' Carmichael. Do I need to remind you that Danny volunteered to *marry* you when you had too many rum and Diet Cokes and were bewailing the fact that there are no good men left out there? I believe he said that the two of you could live in his mother's basement in Long Island until he'd saved up enough to get his own place . . .

Didn't you swear to me then that you would never again exceed your departmental budget? *Didn't you?*

Just wondering,

Nat

To: Natasha Roberts <natasha.roberts@thenyjournal.com>
Fr: Charity Webber <charity.webber@thenyjournal.com>
Re: Holiday Party

Shut up! I told you never to mention the *Robot Wars* incident to me again. That was *years* ago.

Well, okay, two years ago. Still, don't you think I've learned my lesson?

Besides, sometimes I think I did the wrong thing, turning Danny down. He would have made an excellent husband. I mean, at least if I ever needed my hard drive defragmented, I'd know who to ask.

And I hear his mother is a great cook.

In any case, it wasn't 'Pinchpenny' Peter Hargrave's idea to have the party at Les Hautes Manger. It was his nephew Andrew's idea. You know Andrew's taken over day-to-day operations since his uncle's bypass surgery. Everybody's saying Mr H is going to announce his retire-ment after New Year's, and that Andrew will be taking over as the new chief exec.

I just hope nothing goes wrong tonight. It'd be just my luck to screw up my first party under the new chief exec. I really want to make a good first impression on the new boss . . .

Although I don't see what was so bad with last year's party. I happen to like pigs-in-a-blanket.

Oh my gosh! An e-mail from the soon-to-be new CEO himself! Gotta go—
Char

To: Charity Webber <charity.webber@thenyjournal.com>
Fr: Andrew Hargrave <andrew.hargrave@thenyjournal.com>
Re: Tonight

Just a quick note to let you know how much I appreci-ate the great job you've done planning this year's holiday party. I know it must have been a lot more difficult for you to set up than in previous years when the event was held in the Senior Staff Dining Room.

But I think having the party off-site will be a real morale

booster for the staff, who certainly deserve it after all the hard work they've put in this year, outselling the *Chronicle* for the first time in the *Journal*'s history. Les Hautes Manger is one of the best restaurants in New York and I'm hoping the staff will appreciate it, as well.

I look forward to meeting you tonight. I've heard nothing but great things about you from my uncle, and am glad I can count on you to provide a memorable and smooth-running event for our hardworking staff.

Andrew Hargrave

To: Natasha Roberts <natasha.roberts@thenyjournal.com>
Fr: Charity Webber <charity.webber@thenyjournal.com>
Re: Holiday Party

AAAAAAAAAAAAAHHHHHHHHHHHH! He's counting on me to provide a memorable and smooth-running event for our hardworking staff! He's looking forward to meeting me! What if I screw up??? What if I make a bad first impression?

Oh, God, why me????

C

To: Charity Webber <charity.webber@thenyjournal.com>
Fr: Natasha Roberts <natasha.roberts@thenyjournal.com>
Re: Holiday Party

What could go wrong, you schmo? You've only done a million of these things since you started working in this godforsaken hellhole. So what's the problem?

And how could you make a bad first impression? You know perfectly well everybody loves you. They can't help it, you're one of those types. You know, all bubbly. What are you worried about?

Oh, wait a minute . . . This doesn't have anything to do with the fact that you and Andrew Hargrave have already MET, does it? Didn't you run into him once last month, down at the newsstand? Oh my God, I remember now: You were buying Skittles, and so was he, and the two of you laughed about it, but you were too nervous to introduce yourself because he was so tall and cute and single and had a really nice butt, or something, so you ran away?

Is THAT where all this worry about making a good impression is coming from? Because you're warm for his form?

Nat

To: Natasha Roberts <natasha.roberts@thenyjournal.com>
Fr: Charity Webber <charity.webber@thenyjournal.com>
Re: SHUT UP

SHUT UP SHUT UP SHUT UP

This has nothing to do with that. Well, not the butt part. He's just REALLY cute. And nice. And he likes Skittles! Who else do you know who likes Skittles? I mean, besides me? No one!

Oh, God, this party just HAS to go well . . .

I have to write him back and I want my response to sound witty and professional yet breezy and casual. But now all I can think about is his butt. Thanks a lot.

C

To: Charity Webber <charity.webber@thenyjournal.com>
Fr: Natasha Roberts <natasha.roberts@thenyjournal.com>
Re: No, YOU shut up

Hee hee.
Nat

To: Andrew Hargrave <andrew.hargrave@thenyjournal.com>
Fr: Charity Webber <charity.webber@thenyjournal.com>
Re: Tonight

Dear Mr Hargrave,
Thank you so much for your note. Please don't worry at all about the party tonight. I'm sure it's going to go well. The staff at Les Hautes Manger seem eminently professional, and almost everyone here at the paper is delighted that we won't be having pigs-in-a-blanket again this year.

Looking forward to meeting you as well,
Charity Webber
Events Coordinator

To: Charity Webber <charity.webber@thenyjournal.com>
Fr: Andrew Hargrave <andrew.hargrave@thenyjournal.com>
Re: Tonight

Glad to hear it! And please, call me Andrew. See you tonight!
A

To: Natasha Roberts <natasha.roberts@thenyjournal.com>
Fr: Charity Webber <charity.webber@thenyjournal.com>
Re: No, YOU shut up

ANDREW!!!! HE SAID FOR ME TO CALL HIM ANDREW!!!!!!!

Oh my God, maybe this evening is going to turn out fine after all . . . Maybe Andrew and I will meet at the party and our hands will touch as we both reach for the same Cosmo, and he'll gaze into my eyes and realise I'm the Skittles girl from the newsstand downstairs, and it will be like we can see into each other's souls!!! And he'll ask me to go on a carriage ride with him in Central Park and afterward we'll go back to his penthouse and make sweet tender love and then he'll ask me to marry him and we'll move to Westchester and have three kids and have big bowls of Skittles in EVERY ROOM . . .

To: Charity Webber <charity.webber@thenyjournal.com>
Fr: Natasha Roberts <natasha.roberts@thenyjournal.com>
Re: No, YOU shut up

You do realise that the scenario you just described is this bizarre mixture of *Maid in Manhattan* and *Willy Wonka and the Chocolate Factory*, don't you? But far be it from me to rain on your parade.
Nat

To: Natasha Roberts <natasha.roberts@thenyjournal.com>
Fr: Charity Webber <charity.webber@thenyjournal.com>
Re: No, YOU shut up

A girl can dream, can't she???
Oh, God, things just HAVE to go well tonight!!!!!!!

To: Charity Webber <charity.webber@thenyjournal.com>
Fr: Frank Leonard <frank.leonard@thenyjournal.com>
Re: Holiday Party

Ms Webber,

The guys down here in Shipping and Receiving want to know if they have to dress up for this thing tonight or not. Are they gonna get thrown out of this place if they don't have ties on? 'Cause I looked it up in *Zagat* and it's one of those capital-letter places. And I know they usually like you to wear ties at those capital-letter places. So maybe I should run out and buy a bunch of ties? Can I expense that, do you think? Let me know.

Frank Leonard
Scheduling Manager

To: Frank Leonard <frank.leonard@thenyjournal.com>
Fr: Charity Webber <charity.webber@thenyjournal.com>
Re: Holiday Party

Don't worry about buying ties for your guys, Frank. We are renting the entire restaurant for the evening, so there shouldn't be any complaints about the dress code. Tell your guys to come as they are. All they need to bring is their jingle balls!

Charity Webber
Events Coordinator

To: Frank Leonard <frank.leonard@thenyjournal.com>
Fr: Charity Webber <charity.webber@thenyjournal.com>
Re: Holiday Party

Obviously, I meant jingle bells, not balls. Please ask your staff to stop faxing me their interpretations of what jingle

balls might look like. Although they are amusing, they have offended some members of my staff.
Charity

To: Charity Webber <charity.webber@thenyjournal.com>
Fr: Antoine Dessange <adessange@leshautes.com>
Re: Event Tonight

Cher Mademoiselle,

I don't know what you may have been told by our events hostess Chantelle, but there is no possible way I can provide salmon tartare for three hundred. There is a nationwide salmon shortage due to a recent act of sabotage by the People for the Ethical Treatment of Aquatic Life. They broke into the salmon farm from which our restaurant receives its supply, and released all of the fish there back into the wild! Attempts to recapture the escaped salmon have been in vain, and it will be weeks before the farm can hope to replenish its stock.

In the meantime, there will be no salmon on our menu. We could, if you wish, substitute crab-stuffed mushroom caps for the tartare. However, this will significantly increase the cost of tonight's event.

Please let me know as soon as possible what you would like us to do.
I remain, as always, yours faithfully,
Antoine Dessange
Manager, Les Hautes Manger

To: Charity Webber <charity.webber@thenyjournal.com>
Fr: Cara Powalski <cara.powalski@thenyjournal.com>
Re: Party Tonight

Dear Ms Webber,

Hello, it's Cara from the lobby reception desk. I know you are probably busy planning the big party and all, but I was wondering if you could tell me whether or not Bobby Hancock down in Shipping and Receiving had RSVP'd. Because if he RSVP'd yes, I just want you to know that I have a restraining order against him and he's not allowed to come within five hundred feet of me. So unless this restaurant is big enough that he can stay five hundred feet from me I want you to know that I will be obliged to call the police if he shows up. Please call me if this is a problem.

Sincerely,

Cara

To: Charity Webber <charity.webber@thenyjournal.com>
Fr: Bobby Hancock <robert.hancock@thenyjournal.com>
Re: Cara Powalski

Dear Ms Webber,

Cara told me she e-mailed you about us and I just want to make sure you know that whatever she told you is lies. She doesn't have a restraining order against me – her ex-husband does. I'm not allowed to go within five hundred feet of the guy because of an unfortunate incident involving his eye, which got in the way of my fist last month.

But the judge didn't say anything about me hanging around Cara.

So I'll be at the party tonight, wearing my jingle balls, just like you said to.
Bobby

To: Natasha Roberts <natasha.roberts@thenyjournal.com>
Fr: Charity Webber <charity.webber@thenyjournal.com>
Re: Where ARE you????

I hate everyone. Why aren't you picking up?

To: Charity Webber <charity.webber@thenyjournal.com>
Fr: Bernice Walters <bernice.walters@thenyjournal.com>
Re: Tonight's Party

Dear Ms Webber,

Hello, I don't think we've actually met, but my name is Bernice and I work in ad circulation. I just wanted to let you know that I have a severe shellfish allergy. If I so much as smell crab, lobster or shrimp meat, I go into anaphylactic shock. I do hope you aren't planning on serving anything at tonight's event that contains shellfish. I've noticed that it tends to spoil the holiday mood when I go into convulsions.

Although I do carry an epi stick with me just in case. If you should happen to see me grab my throat and collapse, would you kindly remove it from my purse and stab me in the thigh with it?
Many thanks,
Bernice Walters
Ad Circ

To: Charity Webber <charity.webber@thenyjournal.com>
Fr: Sol Harper <s.harper@madrigalmagic.com>
Re: Tonight

Just a quick note to let you know that the singers you requested for this evening's event are running a little late due to the traffic in and around the Holland Tunnel. Apparently everybody and his brother decided to drive into the city today to see the tree at Rockefeller Centre.

But never fear, they'll be there on time, gridlock alert or not. Nothing can keep OUR knights and fair ladies from 'wassail'ing the house!

Sol

Manager, Madrigal Magic

****Don't hire a DJ for your next party. Let our medieval madrigals 'wassail' you with traditional song in traditional medieval costume! 'Simply the best madrigals this side of the Rocky Mountains!' – *New York Chronicle*****

To: Natasha Roberts <natasha.roberts@thenyjournal.com>
Fr: Charity Webber <charity.webber@thenyjournal.com>
Re: Killing self now

Not that you care, obviously, or you'd have e'd me back by now.

To: Charity Webber <charity.webber@thenyjournal.com>
Fr: Daniel Carmichael <daniel.carmichael@thenyjournal.com>
Re: Party Tonight

Hey, Char! Just wanted to let you know me and the guys up here in tech support are really excited about the party tonight. We hear it's at a real happening place. I think it's a real good choice for a company holiday party. According to *Zagat*, it's the kind of place where a lot of marriage proposals take place because it's so romantic. I just hope I don't get too carried away by the romance in the air and propose to anyone! Especially since my grandma left me her two-carat diamond cocktail ring and I just happen to have it in my pocket *right now*.

See you at the party.
Danny

To: Charity Webber <charity.webber@thenyjournal.com>
Fr: Antoine Dessange <adessange@leshautes.com>
Re: Event Tonight

Cher Mademoiselle,
It pains me to have to inform you that despite the unusually warm weather, the back garden will not be open for use by your guests, due to the fact that at lunch today the fountain there was vandalised by members of the Yardley Middle School French Club, who poured a box of Mr Bubble into it when their teacher wasn't looking.

As the garden area is the only place in the restaurant where diners may legally smoke under New York City law, any members of your party who wish to indulge will now have to do so in front of the restaurant. I hope this will not be an inconvenience.

I remain, as always, yours faithfully,
Antoine Dessange
Manager, Les Hautes Manger

To: Natasha Roberts <natasha.roberts@thenyjournal.com>
Fr: Charity Webber <charity.webber@thenyjournal.com>
Re: Still killing self

I don't know where you are, but I just thought I'd let you know that I'm leaving for the restaurant now. If you want to hook up later – you know, like after the party – you'll be able to find me floating in the Hudson . . . if the concrete block I plan on tying to my ankle fails to do its job, I mean.

This party is going to be a complete disaster. Andrew Hargrave's first official act as CEO is undoubtedly going to be to fire me for organising such a completely screwed-up event. There's zero chance now that we'll ever get married and move to Westchester to raise little bitty Skittles-lovers. I should have known it was all just a pipe dream.

Goodbye, cruel world.

Char

To: Charity Webber <charity.webber@thenyjournal.com>
Fr: Natasha Roberts <natasha.roberts@thenyjournal.com>
Re: I'm so sorry!!!!!

I was in an art meeting. They just let me out. Have you left yet? I tried to call and just got your voice mail. I hope you check your Blackberry.

I'll be there in ten minutes. Don't start drinking! Remember how you nearly became Mrs Danny Carmichael after all those rum and Diet Cokes? We don't want a repeat performance of that, now, do we? Especially if you're saving yourself for Andrew Hargrave, aka Mr Skittles.

See you soon.

Nat

To: Andrew Hargrave <andrew.hargrave@thenyjournal.com>
Fr: Peter Hargrave <peter.hargrave@thenyjournal.com>
Re: Holiday Party

What's this I hear about your having the annual holiday party at some restaurant? What's wrong with the Senior Staff Dining Room? We always had a good time there. The staff really seemed to like the pigs-in-a-blanket.

I hope you know what you're doing. Those boys down in Shipping and Receiving have a tendency to go a little nuts when there's an open bar.

Peter

To: Peter Hargrave <peter.hargrave@thenyjournal.com>
Fr: Andrew Hargrave <andrew.hargrave@thenyjournal.com>
Re: Holiday Party

Don't worry, Uncle Pete. Charity Webber has it all under control. That girl's a real firecracker, just like you said. Well, not that I've gotten a chance to meet her, yet. But I'm leaving for the party now. And don't worry about the boys in Shipping and Receiving. With Charity in charge, I can't imagine anything could possibly go wrong.

Andrew

New York Journal Employee Incident Report

Name/Title of Reporter: Carl Hopkins, Security Officer

Date/Time of Incident: Thursday, 5:30 p.m.

Place of Incident: Company Holiday Party

Les Hautes Manger Restaurant

57th and Madison

Persons Involved in Incident:

Robert Hancock, Shipping and Receiving, aged 29
Cara Powalski, Reception, aged 26
Fred Powalski, Security Officer, aged 29
Nature of Incident:
Security Officer F. Powalski, on door duty at company holiday party per the request of C. Webber, Event Organiser, asked R. Hancock what he was doing at company holiday party.

R. Hancock said he was enjoying the company holiday party, as was his right as an employee.

S.O. Powalski stated that R. Hancock had no right to be at company holiday party, as S.O. Powalski has restraining order against him.

R. Hancock said if S.O. Powalski doesn't like it, why doesn't *he* leave?

S.O. Powalski replied because he was on duty and could not leave, but R. Hancock was under no such obligation.

R. Hancock refused to leave.

S.O. Powalski attempted to physically remove R. Hancock from the party.

R. Hancock punched S.O. Powalski in the face.

C. Powalski begged them to stop fighting and not to embarrass her in front of her co-workers.

S.O. Powalski threw R. Hancock through plate-glass window.

Follow-up: New York Police Department alerted, arrived, arrested R. Hancock, S.O. Powalski.

To: Charity Webber <charity.webber@thenyjournal.com>
Fr: Sol Harper <s.harper@madrigalmagic.com>
Re: Last Night

Dear Ms Webber,

The Magical Madrigals are a group of musical professionals who are not in the habit of being groped, but that's what they tell me happened at your party last evening. Suggestive comments were made to both the flautist and harpist, and one of my singers says she was frequently implored to 'take it all off', apparently in reference to her kirtle, which some guests appeared to mistake for a chastity belt.

I'm afraid I will be unable to offer the services of the Magical Madrigals at any future events at your company. You should be aware that my lute player is considering filing a sexual harassment suit against your firm.

Sol

Manager, Madrigal Magic

****Don't hire a DJ for your next party. Let our medieval madrigals 'wassail' you with traditional song in traditional medieval costume! 'Simply the best madrigals this side of the Rocky Mountains!' – *New York Chronicle* ****

To: Charity Webber <charity.webber@thenyjournal.com>
Fr: Antoine Dessange <adessange@leshautes.com>
Re: Event Last Night

Cher Mademoiselle,

Please note that, in addition to the cost of food and beverage, I must add a damage fee of $1,560.47 for repair and replacement of the plate-glass window, $532.67 for replacement of one of our art deco wall sconces and $267.53 for re-grouting the tiles in the back-garden fountain, which were loosened when a number of your guests felt compelled to leap into the water.

Additionally, I would like to mention that Les Hautes Manger will no longer be available for private parties of any size. Please remove our card from your Rolodex.

I remain, as always, faithfully yours,

Antoine Dessange

Manager, Les Hautes Manger

To: Charity Webber <charity.webber@thenyjournal.com>
Fr: Bernice Walters <bernice.walters@thenyjournal.com>
Re: Many Thanks

I just wanted to say thanks one last time for giving me that shot last night. I had no idea that was crab meat inside those mushroom caps! They were delicious. It was almost worth going into shock for. That is one good restaurant.

Thanks again,

Much love,

Bernice

To: Charity Webber <charity.webber@thenyjournal.com>
Fr: Daniel Carmichael <daniel.carmichael@thenyjournal.com>
Re: Last Night

Listen, I know after the fight and the arrest and that fat lady going into shock and all, you had a few drinks, and maybe weren't quite feeling like your normal self last night. So I just thought I'd ask one more time:

Are you SURE you don't want to marry me? Because the offer still stands. My mom even promised to move her circular-saw collection out of the basement if we do decide to tie the old knot.

What was that you kept saying about Skittles, anyway?
Danny

To: Charity Webber <charity.webber@thenyjournal.com>
Fr: Frank Leonard <frank.leonard@thenyjournal.com>
Re: Holiday Party

Just wanted to say thanks from me and all the boys for
inviting us to such a swell soiree last night. We took a vote,
and we all agree – it was the best office holiday party any
of us has ever been to!

And I'm sure you'll be interested to know – in the
drinking contest between us and Budget, well, we won!
Bet they can't wait for a rematch next year!

By the way, we all think you look real good wet.

Well, thanks again!
Frank
and all the guys in Shipping and Receiving
Ringing their Jingle Balls

To: Charity Webber <charity.webber@thenyjournal.com>
Fr: Cara Powalski <cara.powalski@thenyjournal.com>
Re: Last Night

Dear Ms Webber,
I hope you know that you've ruined my life. My Bobby's
in jail, and it's all YOUR fault! Why didn't you look at the
last names of the officers Security sent down to guard the
doors at the party? Couldn't you have guessed that Fred
Powalski is my ex?
Thanks for nothing,
Cara

To: Andrew Hargrave <andrew.hargrave@thenyjournal.com>
Fr: Peter Hargrave <peter.hargrave@thenyjournal.com>
Re: Holiday Party

What's this I hear about a brawl at the party last night? And an arrest? And people making lewd suggestions to Christmas carollers? And someone stripping naked and jumping into a fountain? Is this really the kind of behaviour we want to encourage at our company holiday parties?

I sincerely hope you plan on doing something about all of this, Andrew.
Peter

To: Peter Hargrave <peter.hargrave@thenyjournal.com>
Fr: Andrew Hargrave <andrew.hargrave@thenyjournal.com>
Re: Holiday Party

Don't worry, Uncle Pete. I'm on it.
Andrew

To: Charity Webber <charity.webber@thenyjournal.com>
Fr: Natasha Roberts <natasha.roberts@thenyjournal.com>
Re: Last Night

Oh my God, are you all right? You look TERRIBLE. How many drinks did you have, anyway? I TOLD you to stay away from that bar.

Although I can't really say I blame you. If that had been MY party, I'd have had a few, too. Could you BELIEVE all that?

Though the topper, if you ask me, was you jumping into that fountain.
Nat

To: Natasha Roberts <natasha.roberts@thenyjournal.com>
Fr: Charity Webber <charity.webber@thenyjournal.com>
Re: Last Night

WHY ARE YOU TRYING TO TORTURE ME????? My head is POUNDING. I could hardly WALK this morning. And you're teasing me about jumping into some fountain?

Nat, my CAREER is probably over. I'm probably going to be FIRED today. Someone at my party got THROWN THROUGH A PLATE-GLASS WINDOW, and then arrested. Somebody else went into anaphylactic shock. One of the Magical Madrigals smacked a wall sconce with her pointy cone hat trying to get away from some pervert in Accounting, and now the company has to pay to replace it – not to mention the sexual harassment suit, if she sues us.

And who knew so many of our fellow employees were alcoholics! The Budget department alone drank, if my esti-mates are correct, a thousand dollars' worth of call liquor.

And to top it all off, apparently I only just avoided becoming Mrs Danny Carmichael again.

PLEASE, do not torture me about some nonexistent dip in Les Hautes Manger's back-garden fountain. You don't have to. My reality is quite bad enough.
Char

To: Charity Webber <charity.webber@thenyjournal.com>
Fr: Natasha Roberts <natasha.roberts@thenyjournal.com>
Re: Last Night

Char, I'm not trying to torture you, I swear. Last night, you DID jump into the fountain. And a number of our colleagues immediately followed suit, particularly the guys from Shipping and Receiving.

I can't believe you don't remember. I TRIED to get you out, I swear. But Char, that's not even the worst part:

When I tried to reason with you, telling you it was too cold to go swimming, and that you were getting your clothes all wet, you said, 'Well, I'll just take them off, then,' and started unbuttoning your blouse . . .

. . . right as Andrew Hargrave came outside to introduce himself.

Please, please don't shoot the messenger.

Nat

To: Natasha Roberts <natasha.roberts@thenyjournal.com>
Fr: Charity Webber <charity.webber@thenyjournal.com>
Re: Last Night

I DID NOT!!!! YOU ARE LYING!!!! I DID NOT DO ANY OF THOSE THINGS!!! I DID NOT JUMP INTO THE FOUNTAIN! I DID NOT TAKE OFF MY TOP!!!

AND ANDREW HARGRAVE DID NOT WALK OUT JUST AS I WAS DOING SO!!!!!

Please tell me you're making this up. Please. I'm begging you.

To: Charity Webber <charity.webber@thenyjournal.com>
Fr: Natasha Roberts <natasha.roberts@thenyjournal.com>
Re: Last Night

Sorry, Char. But it's the truth. Thank God you were wearing a bra.

If it's any comfort to you, it looks as if those spin classes you've been taking at the Y have really been paying off.

Nat

To: Natasha Roberts <natasha.roberts@thenyjournal.com>
Fr: Charity Webber <charity.webber@thenyjournal.com>
Re: Last Night

NOOOOOOOOOOOOOOOOOOOOO!!!!!!!!!!!!

Oh my God. It's all coming back to me now. After Bobby Hancock went through that window, I grabbed a drink off the first tray that passed by me – a Cosmo, I think. I must have had six or seven more as the evening went on . . . Those bubbles. They just looked so inviting . . .

WHAT DO I DO NOW???? He's going to fire me!!! What choice does he have? Oh God, Nat!!! WHAT SHOULD I DO????

To: Charity Webber <charity.webber@thenyjournal.com>
Fr: Natasha Roberts <natasha.roberts@thenyjournal.com>
Re: Last Night

Might I suggest grovelling?

To: Andrew Hargrave <andrew.hargrave@thenyjournal.com>
Fr: Charity Webber <charity.webber@thenyjournal.com>
Re: Last Night

Dear Mr Hargrave,

I just want to apologise for the appalling way that I behaved last night. I want to assure you that I am normally much more levelheaded than my actions last night might have had led you to believe. I will admit to having been slightly unnerved by a few things that occurred during the course of the party last evening, and for that reason may have imbibed more than I'm used to. I just want to make it clear that what happened last night in the fountain behind the restaurant was a complete anomaly, and will never happen again.

And I would also like to say, on behalf of my fellow staff members, whose behaviour last night you might also have found somewhat uncircumspect, that we've all been under a lot of stress this year, and I think they really, really appreciated the effort and expense you exerted on their behalf, and were only letting off a little steam.

I will perfectly understand, however, if under the circumstances, you feel you cannot keep me in your employ, and will tender my resignation at once.

Very sincerely yours,

Charity Webber

Events Organiser.

To: Charity Webber <charity.webber@thenyjournal.com>
Fr: Andrew Hargrave <andrew.hargrave@thenyjournal.com>
Re: Last Night

Dear Charity,

You're kidding me, right? That was one of the best parties I've ever been to! And exactly the kind of shot in the arm this company needed. And I'm not the only one who thinks so. People around here can't seem to stop talking about what a great time they had. That fight breaking out – not to mention you saving that lady, the one who went into convulsions – were definite highlights.

But your jumping into that fountain was a stroke of genius. Who knew cavorting in foam could be such a bonding experience? Departments that were barely civil to each other all year were actually having fun together – exactly what I've been trying to achieve since I started working here! After all the money my uncle spent on expensive corporate retreats and management seminars, you proved that all we needed to come together as a company was a fountain and a box of Mr Bubble.

By the way, I realised last night that – though you probably don't remember it – we've actually met once before. I ran into you some time ago down at the newsstand. We were both buying, of all things, bags of Skittles. I tried to get your name then, but you disappeared, and I thought I'd never see you again. Although admittedly you were wearing considerably more clothing then than you were last night, I recognised you right away: I never forget the face of a fellow Skittles fan. We're a dying breed.

If you have time next week, maybe we could have lunch? I believe there's a party or two in my future that I'm going to need your help planning.

Andrew

Jill A. Davis

New York

My boss is a nightmare. She resembles every gym teacher I've ever had.

Anyway, this is my first day on the job – my very first day on the job. She calls me into her office. It's time for the traditional welcome-aboard speech. The if-you-need-anything-just-ask speech. I know that my assigned response is to reiterate how excited I am to be here at *IT* magazine. *IT*'s such an honour to make so little yet work so hard.

Instead, the boss has a warning for me: 'Anne, you need to spiff it up,' she says.

'Excuse me?' I say.

'Your blazer. It's not pressed,' she says.

Okay, admittedly, not the welcome I was expecting.

She takes a deep breath, annoyed that I haven't coughed up an excuse or apology.

'You represent us. Me. This magazine,' she says.

'In my cubicle . . .' I say.

'And in your cubicle you'll stay – dressed like that,' says Carly.

It's a fine cubicle. I've got no complaints about the cubicle. But I think the implied demotion is what's troubling me. All based on a slightly creased jacket?

'What if we need to send you to interview someone? We simply couldn't. Not dressed like that,' she says.

I didn't sleep in it, for fuck's sake.

'Point taken,' I say. 'Thank you for bringing it to my attention.'

I dart for the door in completely humiliation. Her voice grabs me before I reach it.

'There's more,' she says, followed by a very long pause, which gives me time to slowly turn and face my tormentor.

'The hair . . .' she says.

'The hair,' I repeat. I use a knowing tone, indicating I know exactly what she is talking about. We are conspirators in this recognition of disgrace. Except – I do not know what 'the hair' means.

Is there hair on my blazer? Are we discussing leg hair? Is 'the hair' possibly a nickname for one of our co-workers who I've yet to meet? The hair on my head? Could we be talking about the hair on my head? I've never discussed hair of any kind with any boss – so I know not of what hair she speaks. Besides, and this is the chilling part: Today is a very good hair day for me – not that I've ever been the type to borrow pop moronic phrases like 'good hair day' but in the situation I think it applies.

'Who does your hair?' she says in a voice that suggests she might be considering filing a restraining order against him so he can do no more harm.

'Who does *your* hair?' I ask.

Carly scribbles the name Fabian on a piece of paper along with a phone number. At lunchtime, I trot off and spend $150 on a haircut I can't afford. And now . . . I look like a gym teacher, too.

New York is harder than I thought it would be. And New York is easier than I thought it would be.

After lunch I go to the ladies' room to check out the new haircut for the, well, let's be conservative and call it the fifth time. The other women from the lifestyle department pack into the bathroom waiting patiently to puke up their lunch. This is the female version of the shoeshine line. They just shoot the breeze, read newspapers and file their nails until it's their turn to heave.

They all dress the same. Wear the same perfume. And they're all named something deriving from the name Elizabeth: Liz, Lisbeth, Beth, Betsy, Lizzie, Liza, Eliza, Bizzy.

They drop to their knees at the altar of thinness and heave up their lattes and salads. If you're going to heave it up – why not go to town and have spaghetti with meatballs?

You can never overestimate the importance of being thin in New York City. And the Elizabeths are no slackers. When it comes to blowing lunch, these women rule.

When I'm at my desk, I can hear the sounds. The disgusting puking sounds. But by midafternoon, it's white noise. The noise of my new landscape. There is a rhythm to it.

If the Elizabeths harnessed all of the energy they spend in pursuit of inexpensive frozen margaritas and 'cute boys', they would own the magazine. And in a way, they already own the world. This shiny corner of it. I guess I should be grateful that they haven't confused pretty with capable, though I think they could get away with it.

Tuesday

I've spent the better part of today doing exactly what I did on day one: writing lame blurbs under photographs of glamorous parties.

I use words like *pensive, sultry, myopic* . . . The Elizabeths describe dresses as fun, and sassy, and 'this season's must have' clogs . . . clutch . . . jumpsuit.

I've decided I may begin smoking out of sheer boredom. If you're a smoker, you get a break every few hours and you get to go stand out on Fifth Avenue and inhale carcinogens with other disgusting people who smoke. *Any* club is better than no club, right?

Someone said they saw Andy Rooney almost get hit by a car today. I'll never see stuff like that sitting all the way up here.

The good news is that earlier I looked through the Yellow Pages and I found three hypnotists. Would they be willing to hypnotise me and use the power of suggestion to get me to start smoking? Two said no. One said, 'Yes, for forty dollars.'

Did I mention that since getting my new haircut, I'm the darling of *IT* magazine? I find popularity unsettling and hope it will soon pass. And then I will get to long for it and crave it.

The gym teacher could not be nicer to me. But maybe that's all part of her diabolical plan.

It's after lunch – congratulate me. Thanks to the wonderful world of hypnosis, I'm now a smoker. After all of the hocus-pocus I immediately walked over to Nat Sherman's and bought some mint cigarettes and the most adorablicious (actual word invented by one of the Elizabeths to describe a dress that wasn't just adorable, and not just delicious but a happy marriage of the two) sterling-silver pocket ashtray. If I'd known about the cute little ashtrays I'd have started smoking years ago. I feel like a coma victim, waking up to discover she'd squandered the most precious years of her life.

Anyway, I started smoking my mint cigarettes on the way back to the office and the cutest boy in the cutest starter suit said: You know each one of those cancer sticks will take seven minutes off of your life. So cute, but sooo stupid!

The seven minutes is a reference to the amount of time it takes to smoke a cigarette, bonehead.

'Let's talk about it over dinner,' he says.

'As long as there's a smoking section,' I say.

I know what you're thinking. What? She's meeting men on the street now? Forgive me, a smoker who looks like a gym teacher hasn't the luxury of playing hard to get.

After smoking all those cigarettes I threw up. Apparently smoking is like exercising. You need to approach it sensibly. I never should have smoked an entire pack. But they really are like yummy chocolates. Have just one?

How can you! My heaving put me in good favour with the Elizabeths. They believe I am a convert to their eating disorder.

Wednesday

I've got some great news! Or, in Elizabeth-speak, funtabulous news! Carly aka the cow liked the piece I wrote about being hypnotised to smoke. Thought it was clever. She said to make some small changes and then it's a go.

I called home and my father said it was terrific news. And says the ashtray and the hypnotist are both tax deductible. If that's how it works, perhaps my next project will be a gals' guide to top-shelf liquors.

When the issue hits the stands my father says he plans to buy up every copy. They don't sell *IT* magazine back home. But it was nice of him to say. I am picturing my byline. Anne S. Wheeland (the woman who has no one to share her joy with but her parents).

You know how everyone says New Yorkers are nuts? Well, at dinner Henry didn't seem so nuts. Then he let it slip that he was born in Hoboken.

He took me to his 'club' because it's the only place left in New York to smoke, he says. I told him we didn't really have to go somewhere that allowed smoking. He insisted. He said it was the polite thing to do.

Back home the men are polite, too. But they're different. They could be falling in love with another woman and still tell you that they love you. They're dangerous men. And I always did fall for the dangerous ones.

I keep remembering when I left last Saturday. Her voice. I hear it perfectly.

'No stunts,' she said. 'Problems are patient, they'll be waiting for you when you come home.' The screen door slammed behind me. I threw my suitcase into the back of the taxi. I looked up at the house for a moment. I memorised my mother's silhouette in the doorway. My father glanced up from his drink, and the TV, and waved.

'I love you,' I said. And then I promised myself I'd never go back. Not to them, and not to him.

No stunts, mother said. No stunts. I cannot travel far enough away from that voice. I want to cry when I think of her saying that to me. One bad decision and I am a person who pulls 'stunts'.

Thursday

Today the piece was typeset. Fourteen column inches! Now I am absolutely certain I will die before the next issue hits the newsstands.

I've been alive a little more than two decades and I have done nothing. I would like to have my obituary set in 78-point type, to take up a lot of room and make it look as if I actually *did* something while I was here. Except, there's no one in my life who likes me enough to get that creative on my behalf. How sad.

Everyone pads obituaries. It's a well-known fact. It's done every day. So and so was a lifelong member of the Kiwanis Club . . . Yeah, yeah. Sure. Sure. Who's going to check?

I have lunch with Carly and the publisher, Samuel Manley. Hell of a name for any man to have to live up to each and every day. But I can't focus on that because I'm obsessed with what seems like must have been a mix-up, in that I was invited to this lunch at all. But I didn't mention it, and neither did they. We were all in cahoots and too embarrassed to bring the mistake to centre stage.

'Most new employees are too intimidated to touch the computer the entire first week they start working here,' Mr Manley says. 'And you, Anne, on your second day write a column that we will feature in our next issue. That, my dear – sorry, that, Anne, is why we are having this celebratory lunch.'

Good cover-up, I'm thinking.

'Wait,' I say. 'You mean I could have done *nothing* – for a few *weeks*?'

He laughs. I used to be able to make Nick laugh, too.

'Carly says great things about you,' he says.

'Thank you, Mr Manley. I could not be more grateful to you, Carly and *IT* magazine,' I say. 'Truly, I mean this. As you are aware, it has long been a dream of mine to work for your magazine. When I say "long" I mean since September 1997 when your fine example of gloss was launched.'

They laugh. I'm not exactly sure why. And it's all sort of true. When the magazine was first published I had a subscription. And I read it not for its content, but for its massive number of typos, which was really something of a marvel.

Anyway, the Elizabeths – they all hate me now. I didn't even have a chance to hate them. They seemed okay to me. I mean, okay enough to have coffee with now and then. Okay enough to see a movie with.

When I got to work this morning there was a package waiting for me. Inside was a gold pen from my father. 'Dear Anne, The keeper of words wise and sweet, be true in verse and heart. Love, Dad.' It was so warm and melodic and it reminded me that he is one of those dangerous men. Sometimes I'm just sure you never really know anyone.

Friday

The entire city smells of trash. Carly assures me it's only this smelly in the summer. I feel like my lungs are being coated with toxic dust. Like my organs need to be vacuumed. I imagine my blood is thick and sticky with bugs and germs just stagnating in it. And when I blow my nose, black soot comes out.

I got my first paycheck today. Depressing! I'll never be able to afford rent and cigarettes. I still have some money left from my work at the newspaper. But I didn't want to spend that money just yet. That's my run-away-from-the-world, don't-ever-call-home money.

On my lunch break I sat on the steps of the public library with the concrete lions. Every other man who walked by looked like Nick. And it made me want to go home. Not home actually, but to be someplace familiar. To be in a car and know where I am going. To drive by and see Mrs Hathaway's white house, and see her balancing on tiptoe, hoisting a watering can over her head and drenching the hanging geraniums on her porch.

Good news. Carly just called me into her office. She promoted me to general assignment writer. Gave me a raise. I'm happy to report that my allegiance to smoking has been renewed.

'Don't let them bother you,' she says. 'They're just parking here until they get married. They're too worried about breaking away from the pack.'

I wanted to tell her I am just like them. I'm terrified of not being liked – but if I tell her, maybe she won't like me.

The next thing I know, Carly and Manley and I are sitting, eating thirty-dollar hamburgers at the 21 Club. And then, a fourth person joins us. Carly's husband, James. Apparently she doesn't wear a ring for fear the street goons will cut her fingers off or something.

'Isn't it more about not letting people know you aren't really married to your job?' I say.

That silences the table. What's wrong with me?

'So, Anne, I hear you're on some kind of meteoric rise at the magazine,' James says. 'How is it that you came to New York?'

'James,' I say, 'it's no big secret. There are these tin things nowadays called buses.'

There is no polite way to tell this kind man, or anyone else, the truth. My unfaithful husband. The mental hospital. The hairdryer incident. The good thing about the bin, I could have explained, was not having to decide what to wear every day. But it never got that far. I should have stayed long enough to acquire a charming story or two.

Mr Manley . . . it's so depressing that I think of him as Mr Manley and that I come from a backward place where women call men mister . . . even if he's only ten years (a guess) older.

He stared at me. Those big brown eyes. They were just focused right on me throughout the whole meal. Perhaps he instinctively knew he was dining with an outpatient and was being careful not to let the knives out of his sight. To use a ninth-grade description, it felt as though he was eavesdropping on my soul.

'Knock it off,' I say.

He smiles.

Carly blushes. James blushes. And of course, I just about die.

Saturday

I didn't get up until noon. Went shopping for a nice big heavy ashtray for my new office . . . newest office.

I bought blinds for the windows in my apartment. The poor guy across the street will have to buy a TV or something now. The phone rang six different times. I was happy not to answer it. It allowed me to imagine who it could have been.

Sunday

I can't help but think about Nick. Uninvited, he has a way of creeping across my thoughts. Then I looked at the date on the newspaper. Today is our first wedding anniversary. And there is something sad about Sundays anyway.

There's someone out there for everyone. But what if there is only *one* someone for everyone? What if I was meant to live in my hometown with a dishonest man?

There are things to run away from. And there are things to confront. Nick was someone to run from, and for a day or two maybe I thought I was going crazy. And I did attempt to check myself into the state hospital, but when they tried to take my hair dryer away, I snapped out of it. It turns out that in many cases mental hospitals are for people who can't afford a few days at Canyon Ranch.

I was staring at the hair dryer. Contemplating.

'Why would you take this away?' I asked the intake nurse.

'You might try to injure yourself with it,' she said.

'It's a hair dryer . . .' I said.

'You could hang yourself. Scald yourself. Electrocute yourself,' the nurse said, bored, and then she continued in greater detail.

'I could have done those things at home with any number of objects,' I said. 'Besides, I'm no engineer. I couldn't figure out half of the things you just described.'

'Maybe you need a drink, not a hospital,' she said.

We went and had a beer during her break. That's when I decided to move to New York. I was always afraid to move to New York. Now I had nothing to fear. I'd already made the biggest mistake of my life.

The day before I left for Manhattan, Nick called. My mother handed me the phone. She wore a hopeful look. Her happiness makes me want to do things that don't ensure my happiness. Perhaps reconciliation was not out of the question, her eyes said. Maybe New York City *was* out of the question.

'Hello, Nick,' I said.

'I don't know what to say,' he said.

Sure, sure. Turn my life ass-over-teakettle and then call me and try to get me to do all the talking and make you feel okay.

'You deserved better,' he said. It sounded like a question. You deserved better . . . I'm not even sure I did. After all, I married a man who had a tattoo of Sylvester the Cat on his thigh. A permanent child. I run toward red flags.

Of course, it's not Nick who I can't forgive. And it's not Nick I need to prove something to.

Henry calls. Just in time. Yes, I'm free, I tell him. Dinner at Da Silvano? Yes, sounds great.

Replacing one drug with another is no way to live one's life. I know that. But he's cute, and today is my first wedding anniversary. The menu will count as paper.

Barbie (Barry) Divola

Wing Woman

We talk on the way there in the cab because we've never met, and we have to get to know each other a little bit before we arrive. Then we walk in and both start scoping the place. The clock has started ticking, and I'm on $30 an hour.

'What about her?' I ask.

'Her?' he asks me in a horrified voice, as if I've pointed out a bush pig.

'Not your type?'

He makes a snorting sound through his nose. The girl is pretty. She has shoulder-length brown hair that flicks up at the ends. I wish my hair would do that. And she's wearing a simple black dress with spaghetti straps. She doesn't use much make-up because she obviously doesn't need to.

'Not enough of a glamour for me,' he says, just a little bit too loudly for my liking.

But I just smile and shrug. Did I mention I'm being paid $30 an hour?

We keep looking and furtively sip our drinks.

'What about her?' I ask.

'The blonde in the mini?'

I nod.

He sizes her up. 'Yep,' he says. 'Yep, yep, yep.'

He reminds me of a small, randy dog. She reminds me of that slutty pop star who wears ugh boots and carries a small, randy dog around with her everywhere. They could be perfect for each other.

'Okay, give me three minutes, then break in.'

I sashay over to the bar. She's talking to two other girls who are dressed almost identically, their jeans cut low, their tits challenging the seams of their tight halter-tops. All three appear to be talking at once and moving their hands like small propellers. It looks like they're preparing for take-off.

'Oh my god?' I say. Even though this is not a question, my voice goes up at the end, because this type of girl understands that dialect. 'Is that from Cheeky Tiger?'

I know her bag is from Cheeky Tiger. I know the answer to just about every question I ask. It's part of the job.

'It is!' she shrieks. 'God! I only bought this last weekend! And these bitches haven't even said anything about it yet!'

She likes speaking in exclamation marks. The other two girls have either recently had botox injections, or they don't mind being called bitches, because their expressions don't change.

'Well, it's fabulous, and I'm jealous,' I tell her. 'I just love it. I'm Katie, by the way.' That's not my name, by the way. She tells me her name's Jenny. But then I find out it's not Jenny.

'That's Jenni with an "i",' she clarifies. 'My parents were hopeless hippies.'

And I bet she dots the 'i' with a heart, too. I've only got a couple of minutes before Brad (not his real name) will walk over, so I keep the conversation going and try to pick up on hooks. I call them hooks because they're little bits of information I can use to link things up and make connections with my client. I find out that Jenni is twenty-four years old, she lives in a share house in the inner city, she's working as a PA at a recruiting firm, and . . . bingo . . . she wants to get into advertising. The timing is almost perfect.

'Oh, you should talk to my friend Brad!' I say. 'He's in here somewhere but I lost him on the dance floor. He works in advertising.'

'Is he your boyfriend?'

'No. He's a friend of my boyfriend.' This is my favourite line. I should trademark it. It lets them know that this guy is a friend of mine (so it's more non-threatening when he turns up) and I'm with someone else (so I pose no threat if she likes what she sees).

Thirty seconds later Brad walks over. He's arching an eyebrow and I feel like slapping him. It looks ridiculous.

'Brad!' I squeal. 'Where have you been, you naughty boy?'

'I thought you told me to wait until . . .'

Jesus! The guy is a moron. I cut him off before he gives the whole game away.

'Brad! Meet Jenni. Jenni with an "i". She was just telling me she's interested in getting into advertising and I was telling her about you.'

And off we go. Brad has got pretty much no idea when

it comes to talking to women. But he's got that rugby, ex–private school, chambray shirt thing going on. Personally those kinds of guys make me either yawn or gag, but you wouldn't believe the number of women that seem to find them attractive. So he talks way too much about his job, brags a bit about how much money he makes, and – does he have no idea at all? – is about to go into some detail about his car.

By this point I'm meant to nod a lot, smile a lot and, if things are going well, quietly fade out of the conversation and leave them to it. But too often I find that I have to quickly intercept a client's foot before it becomes lodged in his mouth. I make a few quick saves (why has he started talking about his mother?) and things get back on track long enough for me to excuse myself and disappear for a quick ciggie on the balcony.

I come back no more than ten minutes later, just in time to see Jenni giving Brad her phone number. He's got me for two full hours, so we have to keep circulating. We go to another bar and then a club, and he collects four numbers, one of which he immediately throws into a bin on our way out.

'She was like that *Seinfeld* episode,' he explains.

'Which one?'

'You know, the one where Jerry goes out with that woman who looks like a babe in a certain light, but in another light looks like a real dog.'

Charming. I smile the kind of smile you smile if you're in a lift and slowly realise that someone has just farted. It's just after midnight and we're waiting at a cab rank.

'So, Kathy . . .'

'Katie.'

'Sorry?'

'Katie. My name's Katie.'

'Yeah, yeah. So, Katie . . . am I coming back to your place?'

'It's against the rules,' I say. 'And even if it wasn't, I have a boyfriend.'

I don't actually have a boyfriend. But you can't be rude. They've hired you. So instead of saying 'Not if you were the last man on earth, you sad, pompous dickhead', or simply employing a swift kick to the groin area, it's safer to stick with the boyfriend excuse.

'Your loss,' he mumbles, shrugging his shoulders.

'Nice to meet you, and good luck,' I say as my cab arrives. As soon as the cab pulls away I feel like crying. But I never do. Well, almost never. But I always wait until I get back to the flat.

So, that's a Friday night in the life of a wing woman.

In the beginning, there was the wing man. He's the guy who accompanies his buddy to a bar and acts as the decoy. Women often hang around in twos, and the thinking goes that one will be stunning and the other one, well, won't be. The main man zones in on the woman he wants to chat up (and hopefully sleep with) while the wing man keeps the other one occupied, buying her drinks and feigning interest in every single thing she says. This is sometimes called 'diving on the grenade', as if it's making the ultimate sacrifice for your brother soldier.

The company I work for, The Buddy System, has a fleet of wing women who accompany men to bars and clubs. The thinking goes that women more readily speak to a stranger if she's a woman. So the wing woman breaks the ice first, and then her 'friend' arrives and he's got instant entry into the conversation without having to worry about the nerve-racking approach, possible pick-up lines and withering rejection. If a wing woman is doing her job properly, it's like picking up without looking like picking up.

I don't tell many people that I work for The Buddy System. I mean, it's not like it defines me as a person. It's a Friday or Saturday night once a week. Maybe a mid-week appointment every now and then, but that's only $20 an hour. I work in a bookshop during the day. And I'm trying to be an artist. That's what I really want to do. I'm doing stencil stuff with women's faces and words in the background at the moment, getting a bunch of paintings together for a group exhibition in three months' time. I actually did one called 'Wing Woman' a few weeks ago – it's a close-up of a girl's worried face and surrounding her, almost crowding her out of the picture, are all these terrible pick-up lines.

I'm not a great advertisement for The Buddy System, even though I'm good at what I do. My longest relationship lasted eighteen months. And that ended five years ago, when I was twenty-seven. It really worried me for a while, and I took a dive. I went on anti-depressants, but they just flattened everything out and made me feel fuzzy around the edges, like I didn't have an outline. I know people like to take drugs for exactly that feeling, but it freaked me out, so after six months I stopped taking them.

I can't remember the last date I went on. Actually that's a lie. I remember it really well. The last date I went on, right before the entree arrived, the guy reached into his pocket, pulled out a card and handed it to me. I thought, who the hell hands you a business card on a date?

But it wasn't a business card.

Now I wish it was.

Instead it was a 'Get Out Of This Date Free Card'. In small print it said 'We try to guarantee date satisfaction, but if at any point you feel it isn't working and you would rather terminate the date, hand over this card. No questions asked.' This guy had printed these out especially. He seemed to think this was charming and wry rather than totally creepy. And I was being kind just now in quoting what the card said – he actually misspelt guarantee and terminate.

Of course, I didn't use the card. He obviously knew that I wouldn't. That was the whole point of the thing, I'm sure. I did, however, screen my calls for the next month, and built up quite a collection of his smarmy messages. He was persistent, that card-carrying freak.

Most of the time when I meet guys – when I'm not being a wing woman, but a regular woman – it's like a tug of war. Straightaway I can feel them trying to drag me this way and that way. There's this whole push and pull thing going on. Some of them are just too obvious for words. I've got to the point now where I can even see the really good charmers working the angles. I've hardly ever met a man who doesn't disappoint me. I can think of two if I think really hard about it. And one of them is dead now.

Which reminds me, I have a framed picture of Morrissey in my bedroom. I was obsessed with The Smiths when I was a teenager. The obsession (and the picture) faded slightly over the years, but the picture's still there. I thought those lyrics in 'How Soon Is Now?' were the saddest, most naked words about loneliness ever written. It's that song about a guy who goes to a nightclub because he's desperate to meet someone, but when he gets there he stands on his own all night. And he leaves and goes home. And he cries. And he wants to die.

I know, it sounds kind of melodramatic when I say it now, but somehow when Morrissey sings it and Johnny Marr's playing that shuddering guitar behind it . . . well, there's none of those stupid images about empty streets or tears from heaven or the sun setting in someone's eyes or crap like that. It just says exactly what happens in some-one's night that makes them feel like punching a wall and crying into their pillow and quietly, angrily, under their breath, saying 'fuck . . . fuck . . . fuck . . .' It's very mat-ter of fact, but tragic. It's almost like it's just ripped from someone's diary. Maybe it was.

Anyway, I started dating young guys for a while a couple of years ago. It seemed that guys my own age were mar-ried or gay or arseholes or, in the case of an English guy called James, all three. So I tried picking up guys ten years younger than me. It wasn't that difficult, which was good for my ego at the time. The sex was sometimes good. The conversation was always woeful. It didn't last too long. Here's the final conversation with the final young guy:

'Is that your boyfriend?'

'Where?'

'In the picture.'

'Are you serious?'

'Yeah.'

'You honestly don't know who that is?'

'Why would I know who he is?'

'You've never heard of Morrissey?'

'The singer dude?'

'Er, yeah. The singer dude.'

'That's not him.'

'Yes it is.'

'The dude that died?'

'The dude's not—Morrissey is not dead.'

'Yeah, he is.'

'He's not as popular as he used to be, but he's definitely not dead.'

'Sure he's dead. But that picture doesn't look anything like him. He had a beard and shit.'

'A beard? Who on earth are you talking about?'

'Jim Morrissey. The dude in The Doors, right?'

And he was one of the brighter ones. So, no more young dudes.

Last year I shared a flat with Mitch, who called himself a graphic designer, a profession that he just managed to fit into his hectic schedule as a full-time surfer, pot smoker and womaniser. The flat was huge. The flat was on the beach. The flat was cheap. The only downside was the flat came with Mitch, whose parents owned it.

It was a real education living with Mitch. He specialised in what he called the 'come here/go away' method of sexual conquest. I swear this worked for him every time. I was there for many of these performances.

He'd meet a girl at a bar or a club somewhere, chat her

up and get her phone number. Then he'd call the next day. It was always the next day, because he knew that guys usually waited at least three days, and maybe even weeks before calling, if they called at all. So he'd call and say he'd like to see her again, and naturally she'd be flattered, because no one expects to be called the next day.

They'd meet up for a drink or maybe a bite to eat, and then he'd say, 'Hey, you want to rent a DVD and we can hang out at my place? My flatmate's home, but she's cool.'

And who could say no to Mr Call You The Next Day? So they'd come back to our place, where I would often be, because as you know, I'm going through my extended non-dating phase. And he'd ask if I wanted to watch the movie too, because that showed that he was a good guy who didn't necessarily want to pounce on this girl and tear off her underwear with his teeth as soon as he got her through the front door. So we'd watch the film. And then we'd have another drink and a chat. And that's when it would happen.

He'd wait for her to say something he could latch onto. It could be anything. I swear, once this gorgeous redhead, who could have been a model, said 'I just don't get Quentin Tarantino. All that violence is really unnecessary.'

And Mitch just stared at her. There was a ten-second silence. Then he broke it.

'Jesus H. Christ,' he said. 'You cannot say that kind of shit in this house. You just can't.'

She looked at him.

She looked at me.

I looked at her.

She looked back at him.

He looked at the floor.

It was like a Mexican stand-off with vodka and tonics instead of guns. More silence. Then he sighed, shook his head, looked kind of disappointed.

'Look, I'm going to bed,' he said. He got up, padded off down the hallway, and we heard the sound of his bedroom door opening, then closing.

This particular girl lasted fifteen more minutes, which was a bit of a record. I'd sometimes see them dangling for less than sixty seconds before scampering down the hallway, quietly knocking on his bedroom door, and soon enough there'd be the unmistakeable sound of two people having sex.

'Women just can't let something go,' Mitch explained to me once. 'You put them off balance in some way, and they have to get things back to the way they were. It's just the way they're wired. Fortunately.'

And you people wonder why I'm cynical about relationships.

Now I live with Johnny Bravo. He's a strange, skinny black cat. I was watching a re-run of *The Brady Bunch* the day he walked into my life. It was the episode where Greg becomes a pop star named Johnny Bravo. He jumped through the open lounge room window – the cat, not Greg Brady – then slunk across the floor, looked straight at me, and just fell over on his side and fell asleep. He's been here ever since. I don't want to live with people any more. They kind of shit me, to be honest. In fact, even if I met the perfect guy, I'd have to think for a long, long time before agreeing to move in with him. I mean, there's not a lot of candidates lining up for that particular job right now, but still.

I know, I know. How can I be a wing woman when I've got this attitude? Well, I hide it, and I'm a good actor. When I applied for the job, here's what it said on the website: 'Are you a people person? Do you like matchmaking your friends? Are you the life of the party? Can you strike up a conversation with absolutely anyone? Do others just seem to gravitate towards you when you're in a group? Then we want you! At The Buddy System (TM) we pay great money for all those great personality traits that you have! It sounds like you're a great woman. But we'll turn you into something even greater! A wing woman!'

When I sussed out the kind of money they were paying, and did a little digging to make sure they weren't some sort of prostitute recruiting agency, I signed up. I mean, you're just putting on a performance for a couple of hours, and the audience is usually pretty drunk. How hard could it be? I knew I could kill them every night.

I am wing woman, hear me roar.

I go to the movies by myself all the time. Marissa thought that was the saddest thing she'd ever heard in her life.

'That is the saddest thing I have ever heard in my life,' she said.

'It's not sad at all. I actually prefer it.'

'But there's no one to talk to about the movie after it's over.'

'Exactly.'

'But . . . that's the best part of going to the movies.'

'Not for me. I hate that part. I like coming out of the

cinema and going for a walk and thinking about the film and maybe sitting in a cafe for a while, and then going home.'

'You are seriously weird.'

'Whatever. I think everyone else is seriously weird.'

Marissa is kind of my best friend. I say kind of, because we're actually very different and we're not really coming from the same place a lot of the time, but there's something complementary about our relationship. She's been with the same guy for five years. They got engaged eighteen months ago. She was really excited, but the wedding date has already shifted twice in that time and I smell a rat. Not that I've ever told her that.

The boyfriend is a musician. Say no more, right? His band is actually pretty well known – not super famous, but if I told you the name of his group you would probably have heard of them if you've got your ear anywhere near the ground. Anyway, he's on tour a lot, and I don't know, I just reckon you don't have to be Einstein to figure out what happens in the twenty-two and a half hours each day that he's not on stage. But that's exactly the kind of thing I can't talk to Marissa about.

Of course, she doesn't get my working as a wing woman at all.

'Isn't it basically deceiving people?' she asked me when I first told her.

'Well, not really,' I told her. 'We're not ripping anyone off. I'm just making it easier for guys to approach women, that's all.'

'Yeah, but it's under false pretences.'

'How is it any more of a false pretence than a guy

making up a whole lot of stuff when he's chatting up someone just to make himself look better than he actually is? I mean, come on, Marissa, at least 50 per cent of what goes on between men and women – on both sides – is a game anyway.'

She gave me what I've come to know as the 'Marissa look'; pursed lips, eyes rolled over to one side. 'All I'm saying is, I think it's a bit sad that this is what it's come to in the world of dating. No offence, but I'm glad I'm not out there any more.'

And she wonders why I like going to the movies by myself.

Actually, I haven't been completely honest with Marissa. Or with you. I am seeing someone at the moment. He's forty-nine years old. And he's married. It's complicated. But when isn't it complicated? And really, it's not nearly as complicated as some of the relationships I've been involved in. Weirdly, I met him when I was working as a wing woman one night. I'd just set up this nervous journalist with a legal secretary (common hook: both were into sailing) and was taking a ciggie break on the balcony of The Dive Bar.

'You're one of those women, aren't you?' He was a little behind me, to the right, and I had to turn a bit to see if he was actually talking to me. There were a few people out there smoking.

'You talking to me?' I asked.

'You doing Robert De Niro impressions?'

And I laughed. Not a forced laugh. A real one. It was actually a good line, and I didn't hear many of those.

'So, are you?'

'Am I what?'

'One of those women.'

'It depends on what you mean by one of those women, dear sir.'

I don't know where the dear sir came from. But The Dive Bar was the last stop of the night, I'd had three drinks and I was feeling a bit frisky. And I kind of liked the way he was talking to me.

'I don't know what they're called. But I was watching you before in the bar, and that was an Oscar-winning perform-ance. You're one of those women that guys hire to make it easier to meet girls. You're one of them, aren't you?'

'I can neither confirm or deny, but I'll leave it up to your imagination.'

'I have to warn you that I have a very strong imagination.'

'I bet you do. I can almost see the little wheels whirring around, with tiny mice running inside them.'

I swear, I never, ever talk like this. It was like we were in the middle of a Woody Allen movie – a good old one from the seventies, not the crappy stuff he's been churning out for the last couple of decades. All it needed was a park bench and the Brooklyn Bridge in the background and I could have been Diane Keaton.

Well, la-di-da, I thought to myself. La-di-da.

'My name's Ray, by the way.'

'Hi Ray, I'm Katie. I mean, sorry, I'm not Katie.'

And then, for the first time in a long time, I told some-one in a bar my real name.

Stella Duffy

Siren Songs

Ryan moved into the basement apartment with a heavy suitcase and a heavier heart. And the clasp on his suitcase was broken. And the clasp on his heart was broken, shattered, wide open, looted, empty. When Ryan moved into the basement apartment he was running away from a broken heart. A slow, loping run, limping run, with no home, job or car. Never a great idea for your beloved girlfriend to have an affair with your boss. The new apartment was cold, dark, dingy and not a little damp. It suited his mood, suited his budget, suited him. The bedroom had a small bed. Double certainly, but small double, semidouble. As if the bed itself knew what a mess Ryan and Theresa had made of things and kept its edges tight to remind him of where he had once been, the expansive stretch of past love. And where he was now.

Where Ryan was now was as bad as it had ever been. There had been other breakups of course, Ryan was a grown man, he'd broken hearts, mended his own, broken again. But this one was different. He had loved Theresa, really-properly-always. Love with plans, love with photo albums full of future possibilities, love made concrete by announced desire. Loved her still. And she had loved him, too. But not enough. Just not enough. Not enough to wait while he worked too late, not enough to stay quiet when he shouted, open when he closed, faithful when he played first. Ryan had played first, but Theresa played better. Ryan lost. His fling was a one-night forget-me-quick, hers was his boss and a fast twist of lust into relationship-maybe into thank-you-goodbye. Goodbye Ryan, hello new life.

Ryan did not blame Theresa, he blamed himself and his past experiences and his present ex-boss and the too-grand future he had planned for her in the lovely big apartment with the lovely big rent. The plans and hoping and maybes and mistakes first tempted and then overtook them both. Ryan believed in the future and Theresa was swamped by it. Either one could have been left out in the cold, in this case it was Ryan. Cold in damp sheets and small apartment and no natural sunlight and tear-stained – yes, they were, he checked again, surprising himself – tear-stained pillows. Saltwater outlines on a faded lemon yellow that desperately needed the wash-and-fold his new street corner announced so proudly. And they'd get it, too, these depression-comfortable sheets – once Ryan could make it back up the basement steps into the world. From where he lay now a decade didn't seem too long to hide. He lost some weight, bought some takeaway food, felt sorry for himself and listened to late-night talk shows. He followed the pattern. Waited it out. Morning becomes misery, becomes night and then another day, almost a week and, eventually, even the saddest man needs a bath.

Ryan stumbled his bleary, too-much-sleep, too-little-rest, too-little-Theresa way through the narrow apartment. Touched grimy walls, glared at barred windows, crossed small rooms with inefficient lighting. But then he came to the bathroom. The Bathroom. A reason to take the place at his lowest, when the bathroom looked like a nice spot for razor blades and self-pity. Ryan checked out just two apartments before he moved into this one. The other was lighter and brighter but only had a shower, a power shower in a body-size cubicle. Good size, it would take even his boy-hulk bulk, but Ryan needed more. Needed to stretch into his pain, luxuriate in his sadness. And while heartbreak was pounding in his chest, Ryan's prime solace was the picture of himself in a bath of red. Theresa's constant tears washing his drained body. It was a tacky image to be sure, a nasty one, bitter and resentful and 'You'll be sorry when I'm gone'. Entirely childish, utterly juvenile, ludicrously self-pitying.

It worked for Ryan. He paid the deposit.

The glorious used-to-be-a-bedroom bathroom, highest window in the apartment, brightest room in the gloom. Bath with fat claw feet, hot and cold taps of shiniest chrome, towered over by an incongruously inappropriate gold shower attachment, smooth new enamel to hold his cold back and broad feet. A long, wide coffin of a bath, big enough for his big man's frame, deep enough to drown the grief. Maybe. Picture rail and intricate cornices and swirling whirl of centre ceiling rose, peeling and pock-marked but still lovely, fading grand. Set high into the flaking plaster of the wall was a grille. An old-fashioned cast-iron grille; painted gold, picked out, perfect. The ex-owner had started to renovate the whole place, got as far as the bathroom plaster, the golden grille, and stopped. Dead. Heart attack while painting the ceiling. One corner remained saved from his endeavours, nicotine-stained from the bath-smoking incumbents of years gone by. Ryan liked it, the possibility of staining. Considered taking up smoking. And then decided death-by-cancer would take too long. And he couldn't count on Theresa to rush back to him in a flurry of Florence Nightingale pity. (Though pity would do. Love had been great, but right now, ordinary old pity would do just fine.)

The first time he managed to get out of bed, away from the takeaway cartons, the television, the radio, the box-set DVDs and a wailing Lou Reed on a self-solace sound track (Ryan was in mourning, he hadn't stopped being a boy), he ran himself a bath, poured a beer and poured his protesting body into the welcoming water. Ryan was still picturing stones in his pockets and blades on his wrists, heavy stones, long vertical cuts, slow expiration. He had loved her. So very much. But he'd known nothing and the truth had all been proved to him in the end. Love's not enough, he wasn't enough, siren songs only last as long as the mermaid keeps her hair. Theresa had her hair cut a week before she dumped him. He thought it was for her new job. Seven days later he knew it was for her new man. James was a good boss, but he did have this thing about small women in sharp suits with short haircuts. Theresa had been wearing suits for a couple of months, lost a little weight, tightened up her act, her arse. Ryan noticed the clothes, the body, he read the signs, he just didn't know they weren't for him. The hieroglyphs of Theresa, road maps to a new desire.

There he was, in the bath with blades on his mind, but the water was hot and his skin was beginning to crinkle and in the comfort of the beautiful room, the only beautiful room, he thought – for the first time that week, for the first time since – that he just might make it through. Through this night anyway. And of course, truthfully, he wasn't going to cut his wrists. Not really, not even slightly scratch in actress-poetess-girlie style. He was just picturing escape from heartbreak and the possibility of Theresa running her hands through his hair in the hospital, in the coffin. Just the possibility of her hands in his hair. Ryan likes his hair. Theresa loved it. Maybe he should cut it off and send it to her. She could make a rope of his hair and climb back to him. If she wanted to. She didn't want to. Theresa on his mind, in his hair. Theresa on his hands, time on his hands, nothing to do but think of her.

And then the singing started. Soft singing, girl-voice singing, slight held-under, under the breath, under the weather, under the water, coming from somewhere that was not this room but close. Coming through the steamy air, the curled damp hair, and into his waterlogged ears. Coming into him. At first Ryan thought it was from next door. Another dank basement on either side of his, one more out back across the thin courtyard, too. But it was three in the morning. And the left-hand basement was a copy shop and the right-hand one a chiropodist. No reason for middle-night singing in either of them. Across the courtyard then. Past the rubbish bins, over the stacked empty boxes, around the safety-conscious bars and through the dirty glass. But although the window was high and bright it was also closed. Shut tight against the nameless terrors that inhabited his broken break-in sleep without Theresa. And this voice was floating in, not muffled through walls or glass, but echoing almost, amplified. And gorgeous. So very gorgeous. Just notes initially and then the mutation into song, recognisable song. Peggy Lee's 'Black Coffee'. Slow-drip accompaniment from the now-cold hot tap. Gravelly Nico 'Chelsea Girls', Ryan soft-soaping his straining arms. Water turning cold and dead-skin scummy to Minnie Ripperton 'Loving You'. And finally, letting the plug out and the water drain away from his folds and crevices while a voice-cracking last-line Judy Garland saluted 'Somewhere Over the Rainbow'. Torch-song temptress singing out the lyrics of Ryan's broken heart.

Ryan dried his wrinkled skin and touched the steam-dripping walls of the bathroom. Reached up to the golden grille. The grille that ran the height of all four apartments this old house had become. The grille that was letting in the voice. The voice that woke him up.

Ryan went to bed. Slept soundly. Arose with his alarm clock. (Midday, no point in pushing too far too soon.) Ate breakfast. (Dry cereal. Sour milk.) Tidied the apartment. (Shifted boxes and bags, some of them actually into the rubbish bin.) And, with a cup of coffee in hand, made a place for himself on the low wall opposite his building. He waited three hours. Buses passed him and trucks passed him, policemen talking into radios at their shoulders passed him. Schoolchildren passed him shouting and screaming at each other, entirely oblivious to Ryan's presence, his twenty years on their thirteen making him both invisible and blind. Deaf, too. An old man passed him. Stopped, turned, wanted to chat. The weather – warm for this time of year; the streets – dirty, noisy, not like they used to be; young women – always the same. Ryan did not want to converse, did not want to be distracted from his purpose. So he nodded and smiled. Agreed to the warmth, shrugged off the noise, and couldn't help but agree about the women. The conversation took fifteen minutes, at most. In that time Ryan looked at the man maybe twice. But the man didn't think him rude. He thought him normal. The man was old after all. Didn't get many full-face chats any-more. Nannies passed with squawling babies in buggies. Dog walkers passed, pulled on by the lure of another thin city tree, the perfect lamppost. And one cat, strolling in the sunshine, glanced up at the sitting man and walked off smirking. Tail high in the air, intimate knowledge of Ryan's futile quest plain and simple. And laughable. Ryan knew it was laughable. But still, at least he was laughing.

At six in the evening, as the sun was starting to go down behind the building opposite, with a red–orange glint bat-tering his eyes, a woman rounded the corner. She was young. Very young he thought. Too young to be living alone, surely? Scrabbling for keys in the bottom of her bag she walked right past him, turned abruptly, looked left and then right, crossed the road and walked up the steps to the door that led into the thin shared hallway and then the dark staircase to all three of the apartments above his. On her back she carried a backpack. In her backpack she carried a sleeping baby. The girl didn't look as if she sang lullabies. Not often. And he'd heard no crying baby through the grille. He watched the lights go on in the front room of the top-floor apartment, her blinds fall down the window, crossed her off his list. Shame. Too young, too mothering. Nice legs though.

He waited until midnight. It was time for dinner, supper, hot chocolate, bed. No one else came. The young mother turned off her lights. The other apartments stayed empty and dark. He was cold, late-spring day turned into crisp still-winter night. The woman in the top apartment needed to be careful of her window boxes. This hint of frost wouldn't do her geraniums any good. He could tell her that, when he found her, if he found her, if she sang the songs. He crossed the road and let himself into the hallway. Looked at the nondescript names on their postboxes. Wondered which and who and went downstairs to the darker dark.

Ryan turned on every light in the apartment and ran a long bath, made a fat sandwich of almost-stale bread and definitely stale cheese (cleaning was one thing, proper shopping was definitely a distant second on the getting-better list) and lowered his chilled body into deep water, sandwich hand careful to stay dry. And just when he'd finished the first mouthful, a door upstairs opened and closed. Then footsteps, more muffled. Another door. A third. He waited. Swallowed silently, chewed without noise, saliva working slowly on the wheat-dairy paste, teeth soft on his tongue. And then, again the water was cold, the food done, his arms just lifting water-heavy body from the bath, he heard it again. Singing through the grille, slow voice through the steam. Billie Holiday tonight. A roaring Aretha Franklin. And surprise finale theme tune to *The Brady Bunch*.

Sweet voice nudged harsh voice twisted slow and smooth into comedy turn. He leaped even farther then. Wet hand reaching to the grille, stronger determination to find her. Bed, and alarm set for 6:00 a.m. Maybe she worked late, left early. He would, too. Theresa was there, in his bed, in his head. But she wasn't hurting just now. Or not so much anyway. He must remember to buy some bread.

For a full week Ryan follows the same pattern. Gets up early, runs to the closest shop, buys three sandwiches, takes up his post opposite the house. The young mother comes and goes. Smiles at him at first and then gives up when he doesn't smile back, when his gaze is too concentrated past her, on the steps, on the windows, up and down the street. The old man passes very morning and every afternoon. Each time a new weather platitude, a new women truism. Ryan thinks he should be writing these down. The old man is clearly an expert in the ways of women, in the pain of women, the agony of women-and-men. Ryan changes his daily shifts by two hours each time. In twelve days he will have covered all the hours, twice. There are two other occupants of the house. One of them is the singer. He will find her. Theresa is fading. Still there, still scarring, but fading anyway. There is something else to think about, something else to listen to. It does help. Just as they always say so. Just as the old man says. She left him a message yesterday morning, Theresa. And he only played it back five times. It was just a message, some boxes he'd left behind, when he planned to pick them up. She had nothing more to say to him. Even Ryan, even now, knew it didn't need playing more than five times.

And in the night, when he hasn't yet found the other two, caught the other two, followed their path from the door to hallway to specificity of individual window, while all he still knows for sure is the young, young mother, at night Ryan listens to the songs. Every night a new repertoire. Deborah Harry, Liza Minnelli, Patti Smith, Sophie Tucker, Nina Simone. A parade of lovelies echoing down the grille and into his steamy bathroom, through the mist to his eyes and ears, nose and mouth, breathing them in with the taste of his own wet skin, soapsuds body, music soothing the savage beast in his broken breast. Ryan is really very clean. His mother would be proud. (She never much liked Theresa.)

The following Sunday, his eyes switching from one end of his street to the other, the old man just passed ('Never trust a pretty woman in high heels, either she'll trip up or you will'), about to start on his cinnamon bagel, he sees the door open on the other side of the street. The door to his maybe. A woman comes out. Middle-aged, middle-dressed, middle face between smile and scowl until she checks out the sky – it is sunny, she turns to smile. She is dressed to run. Locks the door behind her. (She has a key! She is one of them!) Makes a few cursory stretches, jogs down the steps, up again, down, stretch and away to the west end of the street. Ryan notes the time. Twenty minutes later she is back. Red-faced, puffing hard, she is not running fast now, did not start off fast either, a slight lean to the left, lazy – or unaware – technique, bad shoes maybe, she stops at the steps. Sits, catches her breath. She takes off her shoes, removes a stone from one, replaces the sticky insole in the other. Runs fingers through her hair, red fingers, red face, faded red hair. She is his mother's age maybe. Ryan has a young mother, but she is his mother's age all the same. He is both disappointed and comforted. If she is the singer, then they are lullabies. Not the young mother lullabies to the wailing baby, but this older woman's lullabies to him. And they work. He is soothed. Would sleep in the bath but for the cooling water. She wipes sweat from her forehead. She is not beautiful, or particularly strong. She does not look like the singer of the songs. He watches her go inside and some minutes later he follows. In the hallway, before descending the dark stairs to the basement (a lightbulb to replace, time to do it now, time and inclination) he catches the scent of her in the air. Woman older than him and more parental than him and sweatier than him and under all that a touch of the perfume she must have worn yesterday, last night. A stroke of the perfume she will wear again, proud to have been out and sweating, pleased with her slow progress toward firmness from age, flushed through with the pumping blood. Ryan scents all this in the hallway. And is happy to think of something not himself. Not Theresa. Brand new.

Then the songs change again. Britney and Whitney and Christine and Lavigne and other song lines he doesn't know the name of but knows what they look like, what they all look like, MTV ladies of the night, little bodies and lithe bodies with low pants or high skirts and bare midriffs, flashing splashing breasts beneath wide mouths with good smiles. They are up-tempo these songs and they don't soothe him any more, but they do excite him, awaken him a little, remind him of what else and possibility and – when they rail and rant and proclaim and damn (mostly men,

mostly boys, mostly life) – Ryan is reminded he is not the
only one. The identification with sixteen-year-old girls
may be a little unusual, but he is not the only one. He
is glad to be joined in his suffering-into-ordinary. Glad
to have companionship in his ordinary-back-to-life. And,
given the choice, he feels happier shouting along with the
Lolitas than looking on with the old men. Ryan has never
done letch very well. Naked and wet, he is all too aware of
his own vulnerability.

Ryan decides the third woman must be her. The She.
The Singer. The One. Of course, either of the other two
might be the singer, but he just can't see it. Not the young
mother, tired as she seems to be from the baby and the college books she carries in and out every day. He knows they
are college books. He has stopped and asked her. Helped
her with them once, when the baby was screaming and she
couldn't find her keys, and then another time, too, when it
was raining, summer rain, hot rain, and she needed to get
the baby and her shopping and her books all inside at once.
She asked him then if he was always going to sit on the
low wall opposite the house. If he didn't get bored. And
Ryan wondered before he answered, what it must look like,
him there, every day. How to answer her question without
sounding insane. Or frightening. He told her that it was
dark in the basement flat. He wanted to be outdoors. And
she nodded, agreed. She used the fire escape herself quite
often. Not that it was very safe. Not that she'd ever let the
baby out there. But she needed to see the light sometimes,
have it fall direct on her skin. And then she went upstairs.
Grateful for his help with the books and the baby. And he
smiled, realising he'd told her the truth.

It couldn't be the older woman, either, his singer. Not that she didn't have a good voice. He'd heard her as she ran. She was getting better at running, faster, a cleaner stride. After the first few times listening to her own panting, she decided music would be easier and played tapes to keep herself going. Show tunes mostly. He heard her coming round the corner. Of course, she had the slightly out-of-tune twist that comes from only hearing the sound in your ears and not your own voice as well; even then though, he knew she could sing. But she was a high, very soft, sweet soprano. Quite breathy. Perfectly nice but not strong. And the siren who sang down into his bath time did so with a low growl, a full-throated roar, a fierce, passionate woman's voice. This older lady was sweet, but she wasn't the one. She nodded at him now, as she had started to do when she got back to the house, wiped her brow, loosed the pull of her shoelaces. He heard the click of her tape recorder and the *42nd Street* tap-skip-hum as she made her way up the steps.

Ryan nearly missed Carmella the first time. He'd almost given up waiting. Was worried about what it looked like to be sitting there day after day. Was worried that the old man thought he was a fixture, that Ryan himself was a fixture like the old man. Was worried he needed to get a job. The redundancy package that left him without Theresa and without an apartment only left him with three months of feeling sorry for himself as well. And he'd wallowed through the first and now sat through another. He needed her to be the one. And, just as he was thinking now might be the right time to get up from the wall and walk to the shop and buy a newspaper, look for a job, there she was. Tall and slim and gorgeous. She'd been singing it last night, 'Girl from Ipanema' in her swinging gait. Walking slowly down the stairs from her apartment, out of the gloom of the hallway to the glass of the front door. She stopped to check her mailbox. Long perfect nails, each one pretty pink. And Ryan knew this was her, she, the one, his singing angel. He started to get up from the wall, he didn't know what he would say but he knew he had to say it, must make a move, he'd lost Theresa, this wouldn't, couldn't happen again. She opened the door, he had his foot on the bottom step, she pulled the door back, he was looking up, she down, brown eyes met blue eyes, she smiled, he smiled, he started up, she started down. And kept coming, she fell on the second of five steps. Ryan decided it was meant to be. She fell into his arms, they tumbled to the pavement, arms and legs, hands and feet. When he sat up she was leaning against him, his right hand holding her left shoe. She smiled again.

'How kind. If you wouldn't mind?'

And he knelt to replace the shoe and knew with startling clarity that this time, this one, this vision . . . was a man. A beautiful, tall, delicious, perfect, angelic . . . man. Ryan replaced the size-ten shoe and looked up.

'You may stand. If you wish.'

He did. Both.

'I'm Carmella. I live on the second floor. I'm a singer.'

'Yes.'

'I have to go. I'm sorry. I have a show.'

'Yes.'

'Thank you so much.'

She walked away. Ryan called after her, 'No. Thank

you.' Except that he didn't. When he opened his mouth there was no sound. She had stolen his sounds. And then Ryan laughed and gave in. Maybe the dream woman was not waiting for him on the other side of the grille. Maybe she wasn't really there. But she has woken him anyway.

That night Ryan lies in the bath and waits for his siren. She comes through the mist, singing of dreams and awakening. Of perfect men and wonderful women. The next day, waiting by the doorstep at the appropriate time for the appropriate woman, Ryan asks each one of them out. He asks the young woman to breakfast – on the way to the nursery, via the park, then quick to college.

'Thanks, I'm really busy, but . . . yeah. Okay. Thanks. Anyway.'

The older woman agrees to lunch. An hour – and then another half – grabbed from the office, damn them, why not, why shouldn't she, after all?

'I'm never late back. Who'd have thought? Late back? Me!'

And then with Carmella to dinner. In her high heels and short skirt and no need to catch when they fall.

The young mother is delighted and charmed and astonished to be treated as anything other than Jessie's mum. The older woman is delighted and charmed and astonished to be treated to anything by a younger man of Ryan's age. And Carmella who is Colin is delighted and charmed and astonished to be treated generously by such an obviously good-looking, obviously straight man. (And it's such a long time since Ryan thought of himself as good-looking that he too is astonished, charmed, delighted.)

There is eating and drinking. They are nice, good to do.

There is music and singing. Of course, there is singing. Time passes. Because it does. Ryan feels better. Because he can. Life goes on. It cannot go back. The baby grows, the young woman takes on another year at college. The older woman enters a six-kilometre fun run. It takes her ninety-eight minutes to complete the course and Ryan waits for her at the finish line. Carmella gets another gig, a better show, learns a whole new repertoire. And buys a new wig, lovely shoes. Ryan gets a job, one he thinks he might like, where the office is high above the street and floor-to-ceiling windows let in the light missing from his home. He begins to date again: good dates and inappropriate dates and wildly misjudged dates. And then the right one comes along when he isn't even looking, when he has a paper to be worked on this minute, before lunch, right now. Passes his desk. Stops for a chat. Stays for coffee. Ryan has met another woman. Carmella sings into the night. A right woman, a good woman. Carmella sings clean through the morning. And Ryan tries harder and the new woman tries harder and it works. Carmella tries out her opera routine, segues into slow ballad, then fast rock, hint of lullaby calm. Ryan and the new woman are giving it a chance. For now, for as long as it can, for as long as they will. As is the way of these things.

And, in the basement apartment with the deep claw-foot bath and the sound of possibility echoing down the golden grille, Ryan and his new love, Chantal, bathe happily ever after. More or less.

Nick(ola) Earls

Ladies' Night at the Underwood Pet Hospital

Perhaps boredom runs in the family. My mother was bored and decided that might be fixed if she dragged my father to a five-star Thai spa where she could take classes that would teach her how to carve a carrot into something that looked like a rose. I was bored and decided I had to meet the guy next door.

My parents were gone for a month, so I agreed to move into their place to look after their high-maintenance, sleek black cat Arabella and to try to keep at least a few of their plants alive. I gave no guarantees about the plants; my mother gave detailed written instructions.

'It's not that I don't trust you, Sally,' she said, 'but I've grown used to some of these plants.'

She had the instructions printed out and in a plastic sleeve before I had even told her there were no guarantees. 'I'm twenty-eight,' I wanted to tell her. 'I'm twenty-eight and promoted from weather presenter to newsreader for the summer, so stop treating me like I'm ten and just accept I have no affinity with plants.' She gave me the sheet of Arabella instructions, which annoyed me since I'm great with cats, and started talking me through her appliances.

And then she told me about the guy next door. He was house-sitting for his parents too. They had left on Boxing Day to grey-nomad their way around Australia, and he had moved in to look after their place while he was writing up his PhD thesis in marine biology. I thought of the last scientist I knew, and he dressed like the eighties, walked like a Thunderbird and had wing-nut ears – not that there's anything wrong with that – and I didn't hold out much hope for the neighbour.

Not that neighbours are about hope, and not that I'm shallow when it comes to Thunderbirds who have ears like satellite dishes built onto the sides of their head, but . . . my luck hadn't been great lately. I had been single since the last series of *I'm a Celebrity Get Me Out of Here* was shot at the Gold Coast, and my line-producer boyfriend had decided to 'console' one of the cast's evicted busty East-Ender slapper non-celebs by taking her for long, lingering handholding-type walks on the beach.

He took about two days to go from 'Aussie mystery man' in the UK tabloids to 'line producer Dan Chappell' in the *Sunday Mail* – same grainy photo, next to one of the two of us at a theatre opening night with the caption 'Dan and Sally in happier times'.

I later read that it started in the spa at the Palazzo Versace, when she tried to teach him something about some English game called 'bobbing for apples'.

'Honestly,' my mother said when she called me about it.

'That's a children's game involving actual apples. They've spoiled it for everyone now.'

Among all the conversations you hope never to have with your mother, top of the list would have to be the one about the ways used to describe the blow job a slapper gave your boyfriend in a spa.

But I had put that behind me, handled it with dignity and the support of the station publicist, and moved on. Moved on, as it turned out, to co-hosting the news for summer. 'This will be a year to focus on your career' my horoscope said, and I was sure it was right.

Then I saw the PhD guy, and wished I had paid more attention to my mother's briefing. But I'm sure she completely omitted to tell me that he was no Thunderbird, that he jogged early in the morning and then peeled off his singlet in the front yard, that he sat on the back verandah late at night with his guitar playing Paul Kelly songs.

And she certainly didn't tell me that he did that to the silent accompaniment of me sitting watching TV, singing along in my head and sending him a telepathic message that went, 'Watch my news, watch my news'.

Arabella the cat had ceased to fascinate me with her extreme neediness, most of my friends were out of town for the holidays and the PhD guy drifted around the edges of my world without even knowing it, looking better and better as the days went by.

I wanted to meet him, but in one of those natural unhurried ways that kept everyone's dignity intact. Nothing too overtly staged, nothing embarrassing, nothing that could end up in 'Q Confidential' in the *Courier-Mail* if it all went wrong. But I wanted one of those natural unhurried ways to come along right now.

I was completely charming on the news. I'm sure I read each intro in a way that told him that he was welcome at my door, but I saw him less if anything. He was putting in far too many hours on that PhD for my liking. What was I supposed to do? Coincidentally take up morning jogging, straight after the *Sunday Mail* had done a piece on my regular tae bo workouts? Find my primary school recorder in my parents' spare room and start playing 'Annie's Song' on their back verandah late at night?

'I'm on TV,' I kept thinking. 'You're supposed to want me. I get mail, you know. From people who want me.' Okay, the word 'people' should actually read 'creepy old man who writes in limericks' but, on a technical level, it is mail.

Two weeks passed. It was far too late to go over and knock on his door out of simple, uncluttered neighbour-liness. No, I needed a plan. And freeloading, annoying Arabella gave it to me. The next night, when I wasn't back at the station doing updates, I picked Arabella up from the rug, and moved with the silence of a commando, out the back door, down the steps and across the garden. The PhD guy, meanwhile, was singing 'To Her Door'. He was taunting me, surely.

I held Arabella up to the top of the fence, but she grabbed at it with her front paws and started to kick. I pushed, she hissed. I pushed, she tumbled over the fence and into the garden next door. I snuck back inside, I checked in the hall mirror that all was as it should be – I was going for the 'newsreader relaxing at home' look, which takes a good half-hour more than it actually takes to be a newsreader relaxing at home – and I picked up my keys and went out the door.

I walked to the neighbours', mentally practising my 'I think our cat might have jumped over the fence' line until it clearly went, 'I'm into Paul Kelly too and you need to invite me in for a drink right now'. I was most of the way up their front steps when it all went wrong. Wrong with the mad barking of a dog, the yowling and hissing of a cat, the thump of a guitar hitting the verandah, and feet running down the back steps. Arabella howled, the dog howled, the PhD guy shouted, 'Get back, get off her.'

I ran down the steps and around the side of the house. There were monsterias and ferns, and one of my Birkenstocks – which should have sent just the right signal – caught on a hose and sent me tumbling into the tan bark. I yanked them both off and stumbled around into the yard, where the PhD guy was holding a small dog in his arms and Arabella was lying on the grass. He turned when he heard me and his shirt front was dark with blood (or, as it turned out, urine, since the dog had been caught rather badly by surprise).

'I think our cat might have jumped over the fence,' I said, rather alluringly, since it was too well rehearsed not to be the first thing that came to mind. A piece of tan bark fell out of my hair.

'Are you insane?' he said, which was not a good start. 'You pushed it. I saw you.'

'No, no,' I said, and then, 'No,' again, because of course I had pushed it, but he wasn't supposed to see.

'You pushed it with both hands.'

'I was trying to stop it.'

'It was trying to stop you.'

'Oh my god, Arabella,' I said, with something of a wail, as if I'd just noticed her. 'What's this dog done to you? I told you not to come next door.'

Why had my mother never told me there was a dog? Why wasn't that printed out and slipped into a goddamn plastic sleeve somewhere?

I kneeled down and Arabella looked up at me, her eyes full of fear and dog saliva. I picked her up and she went limp. She panted and oozed blood messily on my arm from a head wound.

'I'm Sally,' I said. 'I'm minding my parents' place next door while they're away.'

'Right,' he said. 'Right. I'm doing something simi-lar. I've got to get Charlotte to a vet, I think. She's been pretty badly cut up.' He turned and walked to the bottom of the back steps before stopping again. 'It's the second of January. It's ten o'clock at night on the second of January. What's going to be open?'

'We can find somewhere,' I said. 'I'm sure we can.'

Okay, so it wasn't the plan, but we were back on some kind of track. We were working together now. Arabella yowled weakly as I walked towards the PhD guy and Charlotte.

'Um, Brendan,' he said. 'I'm Brendan.' Then he walked up the steps and led the way into the house.

We called Charlotte's vet and got an answering machine with an emergency number that turned out to be the after-hours pet hospital at Underwood.

'Where's that?' Brendan said, and I told him. 'It's a long way. Distant southside. I'll drive.'

He said, 'Oh,' and looked hesitant. I'm sure he was trying to remember the moment when we'd agreed to go together.

I went home with Arabella and found her cage and put her into it along with her favourite blanket. It took me much longer to find my Paul Kelly CDs, and then to choose one, but by the time I backed the car out 'Under the Sun' was playing at a respectful volume. Arabella's cage was behind my seat, and Brendan got in the front with Charlotte wrapped in a towel. She growled, Arabella yowled. It was a bad, bad idea taking the two of them in the same car, but there was no way we were changing the plan now.

'So, you're a marine biologist?' I said as we drove along Coronation Drive and he said, 'Yes. I think there's blood soaking through the towel.' He manoeuvred Charlotte and looked underneath her. 'Yes, it's blood.'

I turned the music up; he continued to fail to notice it.

He wiped his hand on the corner of the towel and said, 'What the hell were you doing pushing the cat over the fence?'

'I love this album,' I said. 'I love it. I think it's one of his best.'

He stared at me, and then looked back at Charlotte.

'Are you navigating?' I said. 'This could all go to shit if you don't get the navigation right.'

'As opposed to already, you mean.'

Charlotte panted, Arabella yowled, Brendan had a point but I wouldn't concede it.

'So, you're a marine biologist?' I said, and he said, 'Yes, still.'

He wasn't liking me quite enough so far.

'You're not from Brisbane though?'

'No.' He looked at the blood on his hand, made comforting noises down towards Charlotte. 'I've been working on Heron Island, but my family's from Port Macquarie. My parents moved here a few years ago.' He turned the map light on and worked out where we were on the freeway. 'It'll be the exit just before Ikea, I think.'

He navigated us flawlessly to the pet hospital and we pulled up outside the door in the near empty car park. The waiting room was large and bright and lino-floored, and we rang the bell at the desk. For the first time, I got a good look at Charlotte, a well-cared-for spaniel with blood oozing through her white and ginger hair. She was blinking, panting, distressed. Why couldn't I just have gone to the door and introduced myself?

The vet came out from a back room and introduced himself as Alasdair. He was pale and ginger-haired, and thirtyish, and he spoke with a thick Glaswegian accent.

'I'm Sally,' I said, and shook his hand.

And he said, 'Of course you are, Sally, it's you who tells me what the weather's like at the beach on my days off. And you're doing the news now too, I've noticed. Very nice.'

'You know each other?' Brendan said, just not getting it, and Alasdair gave a laugh and said, 'No, I'm just a viewer. A fan.'

He blushed and took us through to an examination room. Arabella hissed and scratched him when he took her out of her cage. Charlotte barked in response.

'I could put you in separate rooms,' he said, 'but I can tell they're going to fight me whether I do that or not.

I think they'll turn out to be okay, but they're going to need sedation for me to take a proper look at them.'

So we sat in the waiting room, Brendan and I, and we watched midnight pass on the wall clock and we tried to read ancient copies of *National Geographic*.

'Suddenly,' he said, 'I notice the smell of dog urine.' He picked some dried blood off his wrist and looked down at his shirt. 'I really hadn't expected that I'd be seeing midnight under bright fluoro lighting with dog piss down my front.'

'Sorry.'

'It was just an observation.' He picked off more blood. 'Admit you did it. Admit you pushed the cat over.'

'I pushed the cat over.'

'Ha,' he said, finally the winner.

'I pushed the cat over because I thought it would be nice to meet you. I didn't know you had a dog. I thought I'd just come to the door and say—'

'I think our cat might have jumped over the fence . . . I think you did say it.' He looked at me, and then looked back at the heartworm poster on the wall. 'You wanted to meet me?' He smirked.

The door to the back room opened again.

'Come through,' Alasdair said. 'It hasn't exactly been the ideal night out for these two young ladies, but they'll both be okay.'

We followed him into a room that was much bigger than I'd expected, with bandaged animals in cages all along one side and three operating tables. Arabella and Charlotte were on two of them, partly shaved and wide-eyed and dopey.

'It's the sedation,' Alasdair said. 'It makes them a bit dissociated, but they should be all right to go home and sleep it off.'

Guilt hit me again as I looked at them, slumped and stitched up. I patted Arabella, who looked up at me with huge, unseeing pupils and then dropped her head onto the table with a clunk. Brendan was bending over patting Charlotte and getting the same kind of response.

'Hey Charlie,' he was saying quietly. 'It'll all be okay.'

Alasdair introduced me to the three vet nurses, who each shook my hand. He introduced me to some of the other animals in cages and told me what had brought them in. He went across the room to fetch a specimen jar that contained an air rifle pellet he had removed from under the chin of a large ginger cat. They handed me a drowsy Arabella so that they could take a photo for their noticeboard.

'How lucky is it that you're not the one with the urine and blood all over your shirt?' Brendan said, and he made them take a shot of the two of us, each holding a wounded pet. 'Now, let's have a big TV smile,' he said to me.

He wrote down his e-mail address so that they could send it to him. Alasdair told me he thought the air rifle pellet would make a good animal cruelty story for the news. Or the large number of dogs injured running away from New Year's Eve fireworks – that'd make a good story too. I said I'd put it to the news director.

We went back out the front to pay, and I handed my credit card over to one of the nurses and said, 'It can all go on that.'

Five hundred dollars later, we were on our way out with our drugged-out pets and our bottles of antibiotics.

There was peace in the car on the way home. Arabella moved around in her cage but kept slumping to the floor, Charlotte looked out at the streetlights with big eyes and no comprehension.

'I've been wanting to meet you for the past few weeks,' Brendan said. 'I've been emailing my parents – who will love the picture, by the way, once I can assure them that Charlotte's actually okay – and fortunately *your* proud parents talk about you all the time, apparently. So, it was easy to find out quite a bit about you.' He started humming Paul Kelly's 'To Her Door', and then laughed. 'You make me feel very subtle.' He patted Charlotte's head and smoothed out one of her ears along her towel. 'We might have to watch these two, don't you think? How about we set up some bowls of water and a couple of trays of pet litter and open some wine? I've just found my parents' cellar, and they've been keeping some of those elderly reds for far too long, I'm sure.'

Imogen Edwards-Jones
A Blast from the Past

Claire takes the train to London to get away from her husband. It's eight months since they got married and quite frankly things have become a little dull. After all the excitement of the wedding, with the dress, the presents, the party and all that lovely attention, married life is turning into something of a letdown. Living in the countryside, away from all her friends, the great big happy ending isn't quite as great or as big or as happy as she'd expected.

No one had warned her that the first year of marriage was not a bed of elegantly sprinkled rose petals. In fact, none of her friends had ever really actually discussed marriage beyond the altar very much at all. Viewed as an end in itself, something to aspire to, along with a flat stomach, size ten jeans and a Balenciaga handbag, marriage was just another one of those things one had to tick off on your lifetime achievement board.

In fact, the only marriage that Claire had witnessed up close and personally was that of her parents. Three decades of quiet compromise and disappointment, it ended in the most banal and passion-less of solutions – an amicable divorce – when Claire was 25 years old. And as Claire sits in her country cottage in the middle of nowhere, she can't help but think that this is exactly where she is headed. All she really has to look forward to is thirty years of domestic drudgery, peppered with occasional bouts of polite sex with her less than dynamic husband, Howard.

So last Thursday when she saw Jefferson's name, hidden in there, amongst a group email sent by an old friend, it was like a lifesaving bolt from the blue. And Claire grabbed it with both hands.

You see, Jefferson represents everything that Howard is not. Jefferson was her ex-boyfriend from years back and he was glamorous, he was intelligent, he was drop-dead handsome, he was American, good in bed, wild, hedonistic, tanned, toned and totally reminded her of her youth. Not that Claire is at all old, mind you. She is 32. But let's just say that in the recent past, catalogues have become much more interesting, and cropped-tops from Top Shop are increasingly out of bounds.

It took her all of ten seconds to reply. Her tone was flirtatious, racy and let's be honest here, for a recently married woman, it was rather forward.

– Jeff, darling! It's been a long, long time. Still as sexy as ever? Still playing the guitar? Still travelling the world? Still got that little tattoo? Still single? Wld love to hear from you. Love Claire.

She held her breath for a second before she sent it. What

if Jefferson didn't reply? What if he didn't remember who she was? What was she thinking? She smiled. Of course he would. Jeff was one of the great loves of her life. He was one of those boyfriends who, were it not for circumstances beyond both of their control, would be with her right now. He was one of those significant lovers that Claire tended to talk about, when she was sharing with girlfriends, drunk, at 2 a.m. And the mere idea of him put a spring in her stride. She pressed send and sat back in her chair.

That night when Howard came home from the coalface of estate agenting, he found his wife was unusually chatty. She'd had a bath, washed her hair, and put some make-up on. She was altogether different from the tracksuit-wearing, monosyllabic woman he normally returned to. She'd even done some cooking. Not the sort of Nigella cooking that he craved and that she'd produced in the early days of their relationship, but she had cut open a few sauce bags and jazzed up chicken breast in his honour, and he was pleased.

Well, Claire had become a little difficult of late. She had changed from the carefree soignée girl about town that he'd married into this rather tetchy, grumpy, withdrawn woman who could barely be bothered to speak to him when he came home. Howard had been so worried about the change in her, he'd spoken to his mother about it from work. He always spoke to his mother when he was concerned about things. She always gave such great advice. His mother had originally suggested that Claire might be pregnant, and when he said that there was no chance of that, his mother suggested that he give her a wide berth. 'The first year of marriage is difficult,' she warned. 'There are lots of teething problems. Particularly for a girl who had a career and a life in London, before moving to the country. Give her some space and she'll find her feet.'

So Howard had been giving Claire space. Plenty of space. So much space, in fact, that they hadn't had sex in six weeks. As a result Claire was under the impression that her husband no longer fancied her, and Howard thought that he was being a caring, sharing new man.

However, that night, after their chicken supper, Howard thought that perhaps Claire might have had enough space and suggested that they get an early night. But Claire politely refused, saying she had a few emails to send.

Sitting in the darkness, her husband asleep next door, Claire hoped against hope that her ex-lover had replied. She stared at the screen as the computer dialled up a message from her sister, a spam selling her Viagra, an invitation from her old boss. And then, there it was – Jefferson Allen's reply.

Hey there sexy!!!!!!! – long time no hear – definitely still single, still paying the guitar, still got the tats, am coming over 2 ur neck of the woods nxt wk, poss record contract, u still there? U still got great tits? JA.

Claire could hardly contain herself. Jefferson's response was so quick, so funny, and so flirtatious. He'd always been such a laugh. He'd always been so entertaining. And he was coming over next week. Claire leant forward on the desk and smiled. She ran her hands through her blond hair and looked down at her own cleavage. She did still have rather nice breasts. Round and pert and rather under-wired, she'd always been quite proud of them. She was pleased that he remembered them too. But then he would, wouldn't he? They were meant to be together. So he would remember every inch of her, as she remembered every inch of him. His dark hair. His blue eyes. The way his lips curled when he smiled. His smooth back. His long, strong legs. She'd lost count the number of times she'd lain in bed at night and imagined it all, poised above her, on the point of penetration. She curled a strand of blond hair around her finger and bit the end of her nail. And he was still single.

J – can't believe u r coming over here nxt wk. Of course I'm still in town. Where else wld I be? Let's meet up? C. ps tits still great.

It took another flurry of flirty emails for Claire and Jefferson to finalise the rendezvous. It was hard for Claire to keep the arrangements from husband. She had to get up early to make sure he didn't check their shared email before she'd the chance to delete the messages. And she had to go to bed late to ensure the same. Howard thought that her behaviour and sudden computer interest was a little erratic, but nothing dramatically out of the ordinary. However, the tension in the house was something else. Claire's temper was even shorter than usual. She seemed to be sighing out loud a lot. And she was overly critical of everything he did. The way he brushed his teeth seemed to annoy her. The way he blew his nose. The way he ate. The way he laughed. The way his socks never quite made it into the laundry basket. In short all his little old habits that she used to find endearing, now apparently got right up her nose. So when she suggested she wanted to see a girlfriend in London, and that she planned to spend the night, Howard was only too pleased for her to go.

Sitting on the train, looking out of the window, Claire's heart is racing. Her hands are clammy, her top lip is moist and her desire is mounting with each mile travelled. She hasn't felt this excited since her wedding day. There is only an hour to go before she sees Jefferson again. Will he be the same? Will he still fancy her? It's taken ten years for their great love to be reunited. All she has to do is keep herself together for a little while longer.

She exhales through her mouth, trying to relieve some of the tension, and looks at her reflection in the glass. Perhaps she should lengthen her bra straps? She's pulled them so short and pushed her breasts up so high, she can practically lick her own cleavage. She tweaks the collar of her white silk shirt and undoes another button. Now is not the time to be subtle, she thinks. Jeff has got to realise immediately what he has missed out on. She takes out her handbag and starts to rattle around inside for her compact. Her mobile rings.

'Hello?' she answers.

'Hi. It's . . . me.'

'Who?' she asks.

'Me? Howard? Your husband?' he says.

'Oh, Howard,' she stutters. 'Sorry. I was miles away.'

'You sound it,' he replies. 'Um, I was just calling to wish you a great evening. I hope you have a wonderful time and I can't wait to hear all about it. Oh, and send my love to Sue.'

'Right,' says Claire, fighting the hot wave of guilt that suddenly engulfs her. 'Will do.'

'Love you,' says Howard.

'Um, thanks,' is all Claire can manage in reply.

She hangs up, just as the train pulls into Marylebone Station. The fuss, confusion and rush for a taxi fortunately prevent her from dwelling on her lies and duplicity all that much. And by the time she is in the back of the cab, on her way to Duke's Hotel, the anticipation and the adrenaline more than take over. Pulling up outside the hotel, Claire checks her appearance for one last time. The tight black pencil skirt, the sheer black stockings and high black shoes, teamed with the white silk shirt, all go to make up the slim sexy secretary that she is after. She smooths down her hair, adds some extra lip-gloss and, finally, removes her wedding ring, popping the gold band and diamond solitaire engagement ring into her handbag.

She is the requisite ten minutes late as she walks into the quiet, panelled bar. It smells of tradition and old cigars. She searches the leather-padded armchairs. There's a fat bald bloke in the corner. Is that him? She looks confused. There's a couple talking. A man in a suit. A woman on her own, staring expectantly at the door. Where is he?

'Claire!' comes a familiar voice with a Boston brogue. She turns around to find Jefferson sitting in the corner. Her heart stops, her mouth goes dry, her heart is racing . . . He is . . . Oh? A little shorter than she remembers. Dressed in jeans, with a blue jacket and a white T-shirt, he's thicker-set, older, with more lines, less hair and round horn-rimmed specs.

'Jeff!' she exclaims, making a step backwards as she takes it all in. 'You look . . . exactly the same,' she lies.

'So do you,' he lies right back.

'How great to see you.' She leans in and kisses him. Even his skin smells different.

'God, it's great to see you too,' he grins. His bright, white heavy orthodontised teeth haven't changed at all. 'So how have you been? Still working hard?'

'Absolutely,' she lies again, perching down next to him. 'I've had such a busy day in the office.'

'Well, you need a drink,' he says. 'Waiter!' He clicks his fingers. Claire blushes slightly. A charming white-jacketed waiter approaches. 'A martini for the lady,' says Jeff. 'And another one for me.'

Jeff and Claire sit there, eating peanuts, drinking their incredibly strong cocktails, searching for topics of conversation. Claire shifts uncomfortably, Jeff laughs too loudly, as a ten-year gap yawns before them. He tells her about his music career, omitting the fact that it is still going nowhere. She fills him in on her stunning rise through her legal firm, not mentioning that she gave it all up to get married and move to the country.

They order another drink. Claire cracks open her first packet of cigarettes in six years. She keeps staring down at her left hand; her wedding-ring finger looks rudely naked and vulnerable. She drinks some more vodka. They resort to talking about old times. Claire leans forward, pushing her breasts together. Her lips are wet with booze.

'God,' she drawls. 'Do you remember when we made love in that little hotel in Paris and you covered me with bits of chocolate?'

'No,' laughs Jeff, leaning in. 'Did I really?'

'Yeah,' says Claire. 'You licked them off, crumb by crumb.'

'Really?' says Jeff, smiling away. 'I don't remember that at all!'

'How about when we were on holiday in Spain?' suggests Claire.

'Oh,' he replies. 'That was great.'

'And we drank all that Sangria . . .'

'Oh yeah,' he nods.

'And we made love on the beach . . .'

'Yeah,' he nods.

'And we swam naked until dawn . . .'

'Did we?' he grins. 'God . . . you've got a great memory.' He laughs.

'I have,' smiles Claire. 'So many great memories.'

'We've got plenty of those,' says Jeff. He leans over and starts to run his hand up and down Claire's leg. The feeling is electrifying. She can hardly move, breathe or concentrate. 'You do look really great, you know, Claire,' he mumbles, looking directly into her eyes. 'Just like I expected . . .'

Claire's stomach lurches, all the old familiar feelings come flooding back. She and Jefferson were always made for each other.

'Why did you never ask me to marry you?' she says suddenly. 'Why did you never ask me to run away with you? Back to the States?'

'What?' he says, his face falling with confusion. He snaps back into his chair, withdrawing his hand. 'Ask you to marry me? Why would I do that?'

'Because we're soul mates.'

'We had a fling.'

'Because you love me.'

'It was just sex.'

'Sorry?' says Claire. The colour drains from her cheeks as she begins to feel sick.

'Yeah,' he says. 'Sex,' he repeats. 'That's what I always loved about you. We had great sex but with no commitment. Don't tell me you didn't get that?'

'Well . . .' Claire struggles. She looks around in her handbag for another cigarette.

'That's one of the things that I loved most about you,' continues Jeff; he rubs his hands together, warming to his theme. 'You were so strong, so independent, clever and sexy and we did it like rabbits all over Europe. Happy days,' he smiles. 'You were one of the best flings I ever had.'

'Fling,' repeats Claire.

'Yeah,' he nods. 'I have no idea where you get this marriage thing from. It was the last thing on my mind.' He starts to laugh. 'You're not marriage material, Claire. You're far too filthy.' He grins and gives her thigh a squeeze. 'What are you thinking?'

'You're right,' says Claire, getting out of her chair and draining her glass. 'What am I thinking? Listen,' she says. 'It was nice to see you. Rekindle an old fling, that sort of thing, but I'm afraid I've got to go.'

'What?' says Jeff, sounding a bit surprised. 'I thought we might . . . You know . . . for old time's sake.'

'Well, you thought wrong,' says Claire. 'I'm afraid I have a train to catch and husband to see.'

'You do?'

'I do.'

'Someone married you?'

'They did.'

'Well, he's a brave fellow.'

'I know,' smiles Claire. 'It's just a shame it's taken me this long to realise it.'

Claire calls Howard a few times from the train but there is no reply at the house. She wishes she'd listened more this morning when he was saying goodbye, because then at least she might have an idea where he might be. She calls again from the cab but still there is no response. His mobile is switched off. Maybe he is working late? If only she could remember.

Letting herself back into the cottage, Claire suddenly shivers. The air is remarkably cold. Turning on the lights, she looks around the sitting room and it all looks a bit bare. Have they been robbed? There are bits and pieces missing. Empty shelves, missing objects. She runs upstairs to the check on the computer. It is still there, purring away in the darkness. She turns on the light, the window is open and there are reams and reams of curling paper blowing in the wind. As she walks across the room to the close the window she looks down at the paper on the floor. 'Of course, I'm single!' she reads. 'My tits are still great!' 'I can't wait to see you.' 'It'll be just like old times.' 'Remember the night of chocolate chips?' The sentences swirl around her feet. Claire cups her own cheeks in horror and slowly sinks to the floor. The full extent of her undoing slowly dawns on her. She had never totally deleted the emails. Tears of self-pity crawl down her face, she looks up at the desk and there, stuck to the screen is a note, written in neat controlled script, and it says: 'You're a liar and cheat. I want a divorce.'

Michaela (Mike) Gayle

Victoria's Secret

'Dan?' says my girlfriend, Liz, as we sit down to eat dinner round at her place.

'Mmmm,' I reply, with a fork full of pasta in Lloyd Grossman's tomato and chilli sauce hovering just inches from my lips.

'Do you know what it is the day after tomorrow?'

'Mmmmm.' The pasta is now mere millimetres from its destination.

'So what day is it?'

'It's Saturday,' I tell her as the tip of my tongue flicks against the end of the fork, sending my taste buds into a paroxysm of delight. 'The weekend.'

'But it's not just any Saturday, is it?'

'Isn't it?' I move the fork away from my mouth. I need to concentrate.

Liz punches me playfully but firmly on the shoulder – as if to say 'I know you're only joking but you can take a joke too far'.

'It's my birthday,' says Liz.

'I know.' Relieved, I reposition the forkful of pasta again.

'I'm just checking that you hadn't forgotten.'

'That,' I say, smiling at both Liz and my pasta, 'would be impossible.' And with that I open my mouth and shovel in the forkful of pasta.

In the ten months that Liz and I have been together she has reminded me of the date of her birthday on an almost weekly basis. Any chance at all to shoehorn it into the conversation and she practically leaps at the opportunity. I don't mind too much because in the time that we have been together I have come to the conclusion that I love her a great deal. The problem I have, however, isn't about remembering when her birthday is, it's this: what do I get her? In the last ten months I'm pretty sure that I've thought about every single present under the sun. Small presents, big presents, home-made presents, sexy presents, edible presents, and even presents that will last a lifetime. And while all of these presents seem fine on the surface, I know deep down that Liz will somehow manage to find fault with all of them, because she's like that. To Liz, an innocent box of chocolates isn't just a box of chocolates, it's '. . . a cellulite time bomb waiting to be released on my thighs'. For most normal people vouchers for treatments at a beauty spa might be a way of saying 'You deserve a bit of pampering', but when they're a gift from me to Liz apparently they mean 'You look hideous! Get some work done!' And quite how a promise of a weekend in Barcelona could be interpreted as 'an excuse to ogle women with a better tan than me' I'll never understand.

Thanks to the little Liz-voice that now lives in my head, over the past few months I've managed to reject parachuting lessons: 'What, are you trying to kill me?'; posh new shoes: 'Why don't you just come out with it and tell me how much you hate all the rest of my footwear?'; perfume: 'What made you buy that particular brand? Is it one your ex-girlfriend used to wear?' and a whole multitude of gifts that any normal woman would've been grateful for. But of course, Liz *isn't* normal. She's the very definition of the word 'neurotic'. And 'mad', and 'slightly unhinged'.

With less than a month to go until her birthday I realised I was all out of ideas, so one night when she was round at mine watching telly I asked her outright: 'Liz, this is driving me mad trying to work out what to get you. So, just tell me, what do you want for your birthday?'

With a smile on her face, the like of which I'd never seen before, she turned to me and whispered in my ear, 'Underwear. Because it reminds me of . . . you know . . .'

'Of course,' I'd replied sadly. 'But are you sure?'

'Yes,' she'd smiled. 'I'm one hundred per cent sure.'

On the face of it Liz's request made perfect sense. Why? Because Liz loves underwear. Sometimes I think she loves it more than life itself. She's always said that good underwear can make her feel special. How could I not want to buy her something that made her feel special? I wanted her to feel special all the time. But if there was one thing I really did not want to do, buy Liz underwear was it. I didn't want to do it. Not if I could help it. Why? Because the last few times I've bought girlfriends underwear have resulted in a whole lot of trouble. The kind of trouble that can turn a man's world upside down.

This time, I told myself, *I can't just crumble. I have to be strong-willed*.

It's late the following evening and all I want to do is go home, have something to eat and fall asleep in front of the TV. My knees are killing me, I've had a terrible day at work and rather than being in the car on the way home I'm in a high street department store, skulking around the women's lingerie department in search of the perfect bra and matching knickers. To say I was scared would be something of an understatement. I was terrified. To a man, the lingerie section of a department store is a bit like the moon. While we know it exists we're also aware that it's best not to go there without the aid of breathing apparatus. And yet here I am, the only man on the moon, and I'm in desperate need of oxygen.

It's hard to concentrate around all this underwear. It's as if I'm drowning in a sea of B cups and C cups and double-D cups. And what a way to go! Engulfed in a deluge of frills and lace. *How do women concentrate in a place like this?* I ask myself. And then the answer comes back: *They concentrate by not being men*. I have to stop and touch the corners of my mouth several times to make sure that I'm not drooling. I feeling like I'm sticking out like the proverbial sore thumb but all the women around barely notice me. Thankfully it's as if I'm invisible. They all have a look of extreme determination about them. They are in Bra and Pants World – a dimension of the universe where men don't exist and where underwear isn't merely about base seduction, but rather about celebrating the feminine form in all its glory. And so as they pick up bras and scrutinise them carefully with all the analytical skills of a scientist in a laboratory they ask themselves the question: will this be the underwear that finally makes me feel like the woman I want to be?

Following the women's lead, I gingerly pick up a black lacy uplift bra with matching thong and hold it up to the light. As women's underwear goes it looks nice. I could easily imagine Liz in it. But then again as a man I could easily imagine Liz in any of the underwear in this store. I'm not that fussy. And so it soon becomes clear as I continue to hold the underwear aloft that I have no idea what it is that I'm looking for – I am just a man, alone, standing in the lingerie department of a high street department store staring at women's underwear. Surely, I think to myself, it must be just a matter of moments before someone calls the store's security guards to have me escorted off the premises.

Just as I'm about to throw down the underwear and run for my life a woman enters my line of vision and approaches me. She's wearing the department store's pale grey uniform. Her name badge reads: Victoria. She has jet black hair, a clear complexion, and smiling eyes. She is also very attractive.

Not again, I tell myself. *I knew this was a bad idea. I knew it. I can't let it happen again.*

But before I can do anything this monster in Mac eyeliner is upon me.

'Hello,' she says. 'I'm Victoria. I was just wondering if I could help you at all. You seem a little bit bewildered.'

'I'm looking for a bra,' I tell her and then after a moment I add: 'And some pants,' and then after that I add: 'They're not for me. They're for a woman.'

'Your partner?' she asks.

I nod as though I have momentarily lost the power of speech.

'Well, she's more of a girlfriend than a partner,' I say eventually.

'And what kind of thing does your girlfriend like?'

I take a moment to mentally scan through Liz's underwear drawer.

'Not red,' I reply. 'It's too tarty apparently. Not white or cream because it's too boring. And nothing with a pattern because she doesn't like patterns.'

'So that's all the things she doesn't like,' says Victoria, smiling gently. 'What about the things that she does like?'

'Well, she likes lacy-type stuff I think . . . you know, stuff that looks pretty . . . oh and she loves stuff that utilises new technology . . . you know the type of thing . . . materials that stretch or breathe . . . oh, and she likes underwear in black . . . of course . . . oh, and pastelly colours too.'

'Right, then,' says Victoria, grinning. 'Let's go and find your girlfriend some underwear.'

Together Victoria and I roam the rails of underwear. Some things I dismiss because they're not right, some things she dismisses because she thinks they're not right, but then finally we come across what we both agree is the perfect set of underwear. It's a lilac bra (with lacy detailing and excellent support both front and rear) and matching knickers (high cut on the leg which apparently is more flattering, yet more lacy detailing and extra support in the form of a new elastic fabric first designed for use by the crew members of an early US space shuttle mission).

'These are perfect,' I tell her. 'How much are they?'

Victoria repeats a figure large enough to make my eyes water.

'Is that too much?'

'No,' I reply, trying to steady my voice. 'Liz is worth it. I'll take them now, shall I?'

Victoria laughs. 'Well, you haven't actually told me what size your girlfriend is.'

'I have no idea,' I reply.

'None at all?'

I shake my head.

'Maybe you should leave buying them until you do know,' says Victoria.

I feel woozy at the thought of having to come back here.

'Well . . .' I begin, holding the bra and pants set up to Victoria, '. . . if the truth be told she's probably about your size.'

Victoria laughs sweetly – it sounds like summer – and then flicks through the rail skilfully. 'Well, that'll be size 10 knickers and a 32C bra then.'

I swallow hard and nod. 'I suppose it must be.'

'Right then,' says Victoria, 'let's get these paid for.'

At the till I hand over my credit card and Victoria says casually: 'She's a lucky woman, your girlfriend. What did she do to get a nice guy like you?'

I pause, lost in my own thoughts until the silence is broken by the sound of the credit card receipt churning out of the machine.

'Could you just check the amount and sign there?' asks Victoria.

As I sign I say: 'It's a long story.'

'What is?' says Victoria.

'How Liz and I got together.'

Victoria smiles warmly. 'Well, I get off work in ten minutes, so perhaps you can explain it to me then over a drink or two?'

'I'd love to go for a drink,' I tell her. 'But I'd prefer to keep the story of Liz and me a secret for just a little longer if you don't mind.'

'Fine,' says Victoria softly. 'I like a man with a little bit of mystery.'

It's a Saturday morning and today is Liz's thirty-first birthday. The two of us are sitting on the sofa round at her house while she opens all the presents she received from her friends and family last night when we all went for a drink. So far she has had chocolates from her friend Kate, vouchers for a beauty spa from her brother Ben and a weekend break in Barcelona for two from her mum and dad. She tells me she loves every single one of her presents and right there and then I come to the conclusion that I will never understand her.

'I've saved the best till last,' says Liz, picking up my present. 'Can I guess what it is?'

'Liz, you don't need to guess,' I tell her. 'You know what it is because you told me what to buy.'

'But you did ask,' she sniffs.

'Okay . . .' I say sarcastically, '. . . well guess away then, Sherlock.'

There's a brief pause while we teeter on the brink of a fully blown argument. It could go either way, but I can see in her eyes that she's deciding against it and her annoyance soon dissipates.

'I'm guessing it's underwear,' says Liz, laughing.

'I'm guessing you're right,' I reply and with that she starts tearing at the wrapping paper.

'Oh Dan!' says Liz excitedly, as she holds up the underwear in the air. 'They're wonderful . . .' She pauses and looks at the label, '. . . and they must have cost you a fortune. Did you choose them yourself?'

I swallowed hard. 'Not exactly.'

'What do you mean 'not exactly'?'

'I had some help.'

'You had some help choosing *my* underwear? Who from?'

'Victoria,' I reply.

'Who is Victoria?'

'She's the assistant in the lingerie department who helped me choose your underwear.'

Liz's face falls.

'And the thing is Liz, Victoria and I have kind of fallen in love.'

It's six months later and I'm sitting on the sofa round at my new girlfriend Victoria's house.

'Dan?' says Victoria.

'Mmmm,' I reply.

'Do you know what day it is the day after tomorrow?'

'Mmmmm.'

'So what day is it?'

'It's Saturday,' I tell her. 'The weekend.'

'But it's not just any Saturday is it?'

'Isn't it?'

Victoria punches me playfully but firmly on the shoulder – as if to say 'I know you're only joking but you can take a joke too far'.

'It's my birthday,' says Victoria.

'I know.'

'I'm just checking that you hadn't forgotten.'

'That,' I say smiling, 'would be impossible.' I pause and then ask her the big question – the same big question that I'd asked all my recent ex-girlfriends (Stephanie from Knickerbox, Eliza from Anne Summers, Tracy from Rigby and Peller, Shannon from Agent Provocateur and Belinda from the Calvin Klein underwear counter at Selfridges): 'What would you like for your birthday?'

She turns and whispers in my ear: 'Underwear. It reminds me of . . . you know . . .'

'I know . . .' I reply. 'I know. But you work in an underwear shop. Why do you lot always need me to buy it for you? That's what I'd like to know.'

Victoria laughs and smiles to herself and then finally she says: 'I guess that's just my little secret.'

Emily Giffin

A Thing of Beauty

My manicurist, Betty, who doubles as a numerologist, has just informed me that I need to make some changes in my life. 'Three changes, to be exact,' she says as she massages lavender oil on my cuticles. She glances up at the low stucco ceiling of her salon as if to ponder further. 'And you should make these changes within six days.'

Normally, I don't put much stock in Betty's chatter. I am a pragmatic person, a Senser and Thinker on the Myers-Briggs scale. But I am long overdue for some upheaval in my life. Either that, or I should fill the prescription for Prozac that has been tucked into my date planner for months. I've always believed that drugs should be a last resort, so I take Betty's advice and opt for a rapid-fire trifecta: in the next six days, I cut off my long hair, resign from a job I loathe and break up with Peter, my boyfriend of nearly four years. In that order. Afterwards, I consider that the haircut should have followed the breakup because Peter likes my hair short. It seems to add needless insult to injury. Still, I'm pretty sure he will get over me quickly.

I call my best friend Kate and inform her I have some news that is too big to share over the phone. We meet at Prohibition, our favourite bar on the Upper West Side. 'What do you think?' I ask, pointing to my new pixie cut.

'I think you look fabulous!' she says, grinning. 'Congratulations on leaving the nineties – and your 'Rachel-Friends' cut behind. It was about time.'

'Thanks,' I say, ignoring the back-handedness of her compliment. 'Doesn't it make me look artsy?'

'You're an actuary dating an actuary,' Kate says as the bartender pours our chardonnay. 'Nothing can make you look artsy.'

'Not any more I'm not,' I say, beaming. I can hardly contain myself. I can't remember the last time I shocked Kate. Or anyone else for that matter.

'Nina,' she says with a worried glance. 'What do you mean by "not any more"?'

I announce that in addition to my Jean Louis David hair special, I also quit my job and dumped Peter. Normally I eschew the term *dump*, but it adds a nice, dramatic flourish in this instance. Kate is a defence attorney, trained never to look startled, but there she is, mouth agape for several seconds before calling my actions rash and imprudent – two things I have never been accused of being. I smile, wearing the adjectives as a badge of honour.

'How foolish,' Kate says, shaking her head and taking a sip of wine. 'What in the world came over you?'

'Betty told me I needed to make three changes. So . . . job, Peter, hair,' I say, ticking the items off on my fingers.

Kate rolls her eyes and takes a larger gulp of wine.

'I can't believe you quit a high-paying job and ended a four-year relationship because of that wack job,' she says.

I shrug, run my fingers through my spiky hair and tell her that I feel liberated.

'Being single and unemployed is not the same thing as being liberated,' Kate snaps back.

'I hated my job almost as much as I hated dating Peter,' I say.

It is an overstatement – at least the part about Peter – but I am on a roll.

'You should have held out for the ring,' Kate says, admiring her own recently acquired diamond. 'Peter was right on the brink of proposing. He just asked me again what kind you liked best.'

I shoot Kate a dubious look. She knows full well that it has been nearly a year since I clipped the photo of a cushion-cut diamond ring from *Town & Country* and gave it to Kate to give to him, along with my ring size. Plenty of time to find a jeweller in the diamond district and come up with a somewhat original proposal idea. Hell, he even had enough time to concoct one worthy of a *Vows* feature story in *The New York Times*.

'You never even gave him an ultimatum. Some of the worthiest bachelors need an ultimatum,' Kate says, obviously thinking of her own fiancé and the end-of-the-year deadline she had issued only a few months ago. 'It's almost like a ritual. Part of a modern-day mating dance.'

'I don't believe in ultimatums,' I say.

'Ultimatums aren't part of a belief system,' Kate shoots back. 'It's like saying "I don't believe in compromise". Or "I don't believe in sticking up for myself".'

I disagree with Kate's premise but have learned not to argue with her. She can debate circles around me. Instead, I just say, 'Peter didn't want to marry me. And deep down, I didn't want to marry him.'

'I hope you know what you're doing,' Kate says. She then adds, 'You're thirty-four. You don't have to be an actuary to know that your odds of finding someone in your child-bearing years are rapidly decreasing . . . It's not the time to look for Prince Charming. Just Prince Charming Enough. And Peter could be really charming when he wanted to be.'

I would have held the comments about my age against her, but I know she has my best interest at heart. She only wants us both to get married, have babies, and move to the same neighbourhood in Westchester. Now I have gone and ruined her plans that began years ago when Kate met Peter and his friend David at a wine-tasting course. After targeting the taller, more outgoing of the pals for herself, she insisted on setting me up with the other. 'You and Peter are a match made in heaven,' she kept saying, after her first successful soiree with David. 'You're both petite Jewish actuaries.'

Describing a man as petite would be a death knell for most girls, but I kept an open mind and went on the blind date, discovering that even with heels, Peter cleared me by a good inch. He was also well-mannered, somewhat funny and very articulate. So we kept dating. Kate, who by this time was spending every night with David, began her chatter of our suburban future. I told her not to get ahead of herself. 'The jury is still out on this one,' I said.

But as the weeks passed, I had to admit that Peter and

I were very compatible. We both enjoyed reading autobiographies, watching *The NewsHour with Jim Lehrer*, and doing crossword puzzles. We both preferred the mountains to the beach, cats to dogs, and tea to coffee. We even liked our thermostat at the same temperature: 69 in the winter, 72 in the summer. The most significant thing we shared, however, was the depth of our feelings for one other. We liked each other *a lot* – the word love even surfaced on occasion – but we weren't crazy about each other. There were no passionate embraces, longing gazes, or romantic love letters. We could go more than a couple of days without talking, and neither of us seemed to feel much of a void. Which in the end was the real reason I never issued an ultimatum. I was afraid that Peter just might follow through, and that I might get caught up in the moment and say yes. I didn't like to think of what would come next, of how I might feel walking down the aisle on my wedding day. And every day after that.

I tell Kate some of this now, but I can tell she's too upset to really listen. Instead she finishes her wine and orders another glass. Then she calls David on her cell and asks him in a loud voice if he's heard the tragic news.

The next morning, I return to Betty's salon under the ruse of a chipped nail. In truth, I want to ask her what to do next. I pose the question, and she pauses before telling me to 'seek beauty.'

'What do you think I'm doing here in a nail salon?'

She ignores my quip and says again, 'Seek beauty.'

Later that day I buy a newspaper and check the want ads. I think of Betty's advice and find two jobs that fit the bill – a receptionist position at the Elite modelling agency and an opening at Milly's Floral Designs. As a five-foot-two, slightly pear-shaped ex-actuary, I decide that the job at Elite might not be the best for my self-esteem. So I go and apply for the flower job. Milly and I hit it off, and I am hired on the spot.

When I give Kate the report over brunch at our neighbourhood diner, she shakes her head and mumbles something about all of the tests I passed to become an actuary. 'It's such a waste,' she says, slathering her toast with grape jelly. Then she reminds me of the ferns in my kitchen that I under-watered, and how I had replaced them with artificial ones.

'Actually I *over*-watered those ferns,' I say. 'And, anyway, if I could pass those tests, surely I can learn about flowers.'

'But why flowers?' she asks, exasperation creeping into her voice.

I strike a noble pose and say, 'Flowers are at the heart of every human drama. Births, funerals, and every milestone in between. I want to hear the stories, and I want to create arrangements worthy of the people who share them.'

Kate desperately doesn't want to admit it, but I can tell she's impressed by my reason. I have even impressed myself.

I start my new job the following Monday, and right away I love it. Milly's flower shop is located in the heart of Murray Hill, one of my favourite neighbourhoods in the city due to its lack of tourist attractions or major shopping appeal. It feels quiet, more like Brooklyn than Manhattan.

Milly is an older woman with a young spirit. She wears brightly-collared tunics and speaks in a sing-songy voice. Everything about her is sunny. Her only other employee is an overtly gay Mexican named Hector who boasts of how he swam across the Rio Grande to come to America. He tells me he got caught and sent back to Mexico the first two times, but made it on the third. I tell him I am impressed, and he says he has a lot more stories where that one came from.

When we aren't busy, Milly, Hector and I play gin, listen to the radio and sit around and chat. Often we talk about relationships and love. Milly has been married to Dennis, a retired fireman, for thirty-six years. They never had children, only basset hounds, but she says her life has always felt complete. Hector, too, is in a long-time relationship with a man named Chuck, the head chef at an Italian restaurant in Tribeca. He and Chuck are planning to marry in Kauai this winter. I tell him that Chuck does not sound like a gay man's name and he laughs. Milly and Hector both think I'm funny, even when I'm not trying to be. I realise that nobody laughed much at my last job, and certainly not at my jokes. When I think of my old sterile cube and my stiff ex-colleagues, I feel giddy with my good fortune. I catch myself humming as I keep the books, sweep the back workroom, and run to answer the phone.

In addition to my office duties, Milly and Hector teach me about a whole new world of flowers – a world of colour, form and texture. I learn their tools and techniques – how to coax poppies open, hydrate the hollow stems of amaryllis and strip the thorns from roses. One day, when I create a fan-shaped arrangement of apricot calla lilies and golden holly berries, Milly calls me a natural.

The thing that I enjoy most about my job, though, is our customers. I am in charge of taking the flower orders and transcribing the notes that will accompany them. I discover that virtually no one can refrain from giving me significant background about their order. 'My friend had a baby girl today!' one caller gushes. 'She's my very best friend in the world – and she tried for years to get pregnant – so I want something really special. What do you suggest?' Or 'I just met the girl of my dreams. She's amazing. Would two dozen roses scare you off?' Or 'My daughter finally passed the bar. Three tries it took her – just like John Kennedy, Jr. Only your grandest arrangement will suffice for this miracle!' I take my time with every customer, savouring the stories as I consult with Milly and Hector to select the perfect flowers for every occasion.

Then there is Byron Skydell. He is our sole regular customer who resists what seems to be human nature by never offering an explanation or any detail. He also comes into the shop rather than placing his orders by phone. My guess is that he works nearby, somewhere in Midtown. He wears handsome navy suits, carries an old-school leather briefcase, and has a mysterious, dignified air. Milly and Hector tell me that he has come in about once a week for the past two years, ordering flowers for his wife, Ellen. He always takes his time looking around before making a decision and then writes his own notes. He is left-handed, and as he writes, my gaze always falls on his slim, gold wedding band.

One day when Byron comes into the shop, he places an

order for pink begonias. I busy myself with a stack of paper near the cash register, but out of the corner of my eye, I watch him remove an elegant silver pen from his jacket pocket, write a note on his own monogrammed stationery and carefully tuck the flap in on the envelope.

He hands it to me and says, 'The usual address, please.'

I nod, feeling oddly nervous. 'Thank you, Mr Skydell.'

'Thank *you*,' Byron says. His voice is a rich baritone, reminding me of Tom Brokaw. As he turns to leave, I admire the way his chestnut-brown hair curls at the nape of his neck. I glance down at the envelope and cannot control my impulse to read the card. His handwriting is distinguished yet romantic, reminding me of one of the signatures on The Declaration of Independence. He has written one sentence: *You looked so lovely in pink last night that I thought you might enjoy these.*

My heart beats double time. To think that a man such as this really exists! I wonder if perhaps Byron has a brother, preferably an identical twin. I can't help comparing him to Peter, who only sent me flowers once – red roses and baby's breath along with a computer-printed card that read: *Happy Valentine's Day. Love, Peter.* At the time, I felt grateful, almost moved. I proudly displayed the vase, conspicuously shaking the packet of powdered flower food into the water. Now, in comparison to Byron's begonias, Peter's predictable red roses seem as lacklustre as our relationship was.

When I next see Betty for a manicure, I confess to having peeked at Byron's card.

'Do you have a crush?' she asks me.

'No,' I say a bit too emphatically. 'It's just that Byron

gives me faith that someone is out there. Someone who will love me the way he loves his wife.'

Betty beams and tells me that she thinks I will find such a man very soon.

'When?' I ask her.

'Soon,' she says, filing my pinky nail into her trademark squared oval. 'And I'm feeling a strong nine vibe – so that likely means September will bring him to you.'

Later I tell Kate of Betty's prediction. Kate misses the point and demands to know how I'm affording manicures on my new salary. I remind her that I saved plenty of money in my former life. 'Peter and I seldom went out. Remember?' I say, thinking of all of our lifeless nights on the couch.

She frowns and says, 'Speaking of Peter, I saw him yesterday. He and David went to look at tuxedos for our wedding, and we all had lunch afterwards. He said to tell you hello.'

'Well. Give him my best,' I say, meaning it. Then I silently make a wish for Peter to meet his Ellen. To feel inspired to send her flowers on days other than Valentine's. To feel inspired by something as small as the colour pink.

The summer passes quickly as I fall into a new rhythm – one that feels pleasant and honest and real. I am alone, but have never felt less lonely or more hopeful. All the while, my crush on Byron evolves into a small obsession. I think of him every night as I crawl into bed, imagining him with Ellen, bringing her a cup of herbal tea or smoothing her dark hair away from her ivory skin. I am holding out for something that special.

Then, one sweltering day in late August, a troubling thing

happens which upsets the delicate balance emerging in my life. Hector is delivering a funeral arrangement to a church in his neighbourhood when he decides to swing by his apartment to surprise Chuck, who has the day off. Apparently, Chuck's personal trainer also has the day off because Hector discovers the two in bed together. Hector is beside himself with grief, but his anguish quickly gives way to a deep bitterness. He says he no longer believes in true love, and nothing Milly and I say can persuade him otherwise.

Bizarrely enough, I sense a shift in our orders around this same time. Specifically, I notice a marked increase in apology arrangements – flowers sent to wives, along with cards reading: *I'm so sorry* or *Please forgive me.* The male callers clear their throats and sheepishly admit that they are in the 'doghouse.' Hector assumes the worst – that they, too, were caught red-handed.

'Dirty cheaters,' he growls as he snips stems with a vengeance.

I struggle to find a more benign explanation. 'Maybe they just forgot to take out the trash,' I say. But I can't help picturing leggy mistresses wearing crimson lipstick and too much Poison perfume.

'The heat makes people do crazy things,' Milly says. 'They'll come to their senses.'

Hector grumbles as he continues to flip through the order book, pointing out an influx of our regular, married customers sending flowers to women other than their wives. The cards read: *Thanks for last night* and *Thinking of you.* These orders are harder to defend so I don't even try. Instead, I remind Hector of Byron.

Hector looks at me for a long time and then says, 'Byron

probably cheats on Ellen, too. He's just smart enough to use another florist for his ho.'

I meet Kate for sushi later that night. When I tell her of our unfaithful clientele, she sighs and says, 'That's the thing about Peter. He would *never* have cheated on you.'

I tell her that I aspire to more than the lack of infidelity in my relationship, but as I dip my tuna roll in soy sauce, I wonder if perhaps a faithful, steady man *is* a benchmark worth striving for. Maybe Byron is too rare a creature to bank on. For the first time, I picture Peter with another woman, and my stomach hurts just a little.

The next day I ask Milly how she knew Dennis was 'the One.'

'There was no particular thing,' she says as she trims the stems of red geraniums.

'But there were fireworks, right?' I ask.

She thinks for a moment and then says no, there were never fireworks with Dennis. Just a quiet, mutual respect for one another. I must look disappointed because she says not everyone needs the earth to shift to be happy. She calls it a misguided conception of today's youth.

Hector nods vigorously. 'I had sparks with Chuck. Look what that got me.'

I find myself thinking of the quiet, mutual respect I had with Peter. My worry deepens. Even Betty's prediction, which she has steadfastly maintained all summer, doesn't console me.

Byron returns to the shop a short time after that. He smiles at me and then says hello.

'Hello,' I say, feeling a shiver of excitement. 'What can I get you today, Mr Skydell?'

He glances around the store and then points to a white marble bowl on the shelf behind me. 'I'd like that bowl filled with lilac delphiniums, purple cornflowers and starlight roses. Those are the silvery lavender ones, right?'

'Yes,' I say, feeing myself blush. I remember that Milly once told me that the colour purple is enigmatic – intense and reserved all at once. She also said that it symbolizes the first flicker of love. 'That's a fine choice . . . I will make sure that your arrangement is beautiful, Mr Skydell.'

'Byron,' he says.

'Byron,' I repeat nervously.

'And what is your name?' he asks softly.

'Nina . . . Nina Lipman,' I say.

He leans in a bit and says, even more softly, 'Well. You have a nice day, Nina Lipman.'

Our eyes lock for a long second. Then he turns to leave. I feel guilt and pleasure knot in my chest. After the front door chimes have stilled, Hector shouts from the back room, 'He's a *married* man, ya know!'

'I *know* that. I wasn't flirting with him,' I yell back, although I'm not so sure that is true. My face is hot, and I have just filed his order in the wrong folder.

That night when I return home I am startled by the sight of a white bowl perched on my doorman's stand filled with lilac delphiniums, purple cornflowers and luminous starlight roses. It is my arrangement, the one I spent over two hours creating.

'For you, Nina,' my doorman says, pointing toward

them. 'A nice gentleman dropped them off for you. And I must say, those roses smell deee-licious!'

I bite my lip and rip open the card, silently reading Byron's words: *Please have dinner with me.* I picture his sapphire eyes and my heart gallops. But the thrill quickly gives way to a rush of shame and then loss. The ideal of Byron is gone, and so is my hope of finding someone like him. Even worse, I feel a profound sadness for Ellen. She is married to someone much more deadly than a beer-guzzling, ball-scratching ne'er-do-well. Byron is lulling her into a false sense of happiness. I will not succumb to his charm, but some day Byron will find a way to break Ellen's heart.

That night I have several glasses of wine and fall asleep on my couch. I dream that Byron and I are walking through a field of lavender when he suddenly drops to one knee and says he has something very important to ask me. As he removes a ring from his pocket, his face morphs into Peter's. I awaken in tears, feeling compelled to either call Peter or confront Byron. I decide on the latter, embarrassed that I have memorised his address. If Ellen answers the door, I will simply give her the flowers, say they are from Byron.

I shower, dress in a simple black suit and find my way to the Skydells' townhouse on West Seventy-fourth. My hands are clammy as I ring the doorbell. As I wait, I can feel myself losing courage, hoping that Byron has already left for the day. I ring the bell again, and this time I hear brisk footsteps. An attractive, grey-haired woman opens the door. She smiles expectantly.

'Is Ellen home?' I ask as I spot a black-and-white photo

of a much younger Byron on the hall table. My stomach lurches.

'I'm Ellen,' she says.

'Oh. Hi . . . uh . . . how do you know Byron?' I stammer, thinking that surely the woman standing before me is too old to be his wife.

'I'm his mother . . . And who are you?' she asks. Her expression is placid and curious.

'I . . . I work at the flower shop,' I say.

'Nina,' she says.

It is a statement, not a question, but I still nod in response. Then I think of Byron's wedding band and ask, 'Who is his wife then?'

Ellen's smile fades. 'She and my grandson died in a car accident three years ago.'

'Oh . . . I'm so sorry,' I murmur. 'I didn't know.'

'Byron is very private,' she says.

'Oh,' I say. 'I mean . . . yes, he seems that way.'

She pauses and then says, 'You folks at Milly's have helped him so much. At first I thought he was sending me flowers for my sake. And they did help fill a void for me . . . But I also think the flowers have helped him heal. Life can be bleak, but we must continue to look for beauty.' Her voice trails off.

'Yes. Milly's flowers *are* beautiful,' I say quietly, glancing down at the bowl full of flowers which I am foolishly holding against one hip.

'I'm not just talking about the flowers,' Ellen says.

I give her a quizzical look, and she reaches out, squeezing my free hand.

I realise I am on the verge of tears so I look down and say, 'So Byron's not here then?'

She shakes her head. 'No, but would you like to come in? I just made some coffee.'

'No, thank you,' I say. 'I . . . I really should go.'

I wish Ellen a good day and escape back to the street. My head is spinning as I wonder what she will tell Byron, whether I should come clean with my assumption. I find my cell phone in my purse and consider calling Kate to arrange an after-work drink – or Betty to schedule a manicure. But for once, I realise I don't need any advice or predictions. I am sure of what to do and what I hope will happen next.

It is a brisk September day, and I decide to walk to work, rather than take the subway. The blocks pass in a blur as I make my way across the park, down Fifth Avenue and over to the flower shop. I think about love and loss. I think about friendship and passion and all the hues in between. I think of Kate and David. Hector and Chuck. Milly and Dennis. Of how different people need different things to be happy. I think of my own breakup with Peter, and how no matter what happens from here, I know I have done the right thing. I think of Byron – his rich voice, loopy handwriting, shy smile. Mostly, though, I just walk, taking my time and occasionally lowering my face to smell my roses.

Kristin Gore

Stray

I've never been on a plane I didn't assume was going to crash. Even on the smoothest flights, I still manage at least one moment of sheer, liver-gripping terror – one moment of complete certainty of imminent doom. I have yet to be in an actual plane crash, though I generally average a couple of flights a day. I'm a flight attendant, or stewardess if you prefer, which I do. Few join me in this preference. Most people consider it a politically incorrect term. I consider it a spiritually satisfying one. The Bible instructs us to be good stewards of the earth in a passage that's particularly popular with environmental groups. The Bible talks a lot about mankind, and makes it clear that my gender came from a rib, so when it talks about stewards, I can't help but think it's addressing men. And if I were a man, I'd be a steward of the earth. And probably gay. As things stand, I'm a stewardess. A stewardess with a fear of flying.

I realise I'm a throwback, but I'm a sucker for the 'ess' suffix in general. To me, Meryl Streep is not a phenomenal actor, she's a stunningly talented actress. Similarly, Audrey Niffenegger is an engaging authoress. And the fact that I stole a pack of Big League Bubblegum Chew from the Rite-Aid when I was eleven didn't make me a burglar, but a burglaress. I suppose I'm still a burglaress, though I'm no longer practising.

I'm non-practising when it comes to a lot of things, actually. I'm a non-practising exerciser, a non-practising inventor, a non-practising genius. When I was younger, I was a non-practising child prodigy. The brilliance of the 'non-practising' adjective impressed me from the moment I first came across it. It allowed one to declare oneself something and then never have to actually back it up, since that would be against one's beliefs. I *am* this, but I choose not to demonstrate it, so you'll just have to take my word for it. Genius. Like me. Non-practising.

One might think a non-practising genius like myself would find another job that didn't panic me several times a day, but I don't feel qualified for anything else. I got into stewardessing because of a fascination with the tiny little liquor bottles available on planes and in hotel mini-bars. These perfect little vessels never fail to soothe me. I stare at them and feel happy that not everything is forced to grow up. I decided early on that I wanted to be near them.

The hotel industry was slow to respond to my over-tures, but the airline snatched me and my largely fictional resume right up. I soon realised I was a naturally talented stewardess and felt less guilty that I may have been hired thanks to false claims of extensive hot air balloon work. I am disturbingly good at fake-smiling when I feel like crap, which is the single most important skill a steward-ess can possess. That, and the self-restraint not to ram the knees of obnoxious passengers with the beverage cart. So far I've made the cart assaults seem like lawsuit-proof acci-dents. Micro-turbulence is a trusty alibi.

One of the perks of being a professional stewardess for a major airline is that I get to fly for free whenever I want. I appreciate this benefit, though I've never taken advan-tage of it. I won't set foot on a plane unless contractually obligated to do so. No, flying is much, much too risky, which is why I'm presently driving the eighteen hours back to my hometown. I know the statistics about driv-ing being more dangerous than flying, but I don't believe them. I think they're perpetuated by the airlines attempt-ing to drum up more business, just like I suspect the movie *Attack of the Killer Tomatoes* might have been funded by the Pickle Lobby.

I've asked if I can cash in all the free flights I'm not taking for some other kind of perk, like use of the stair car during holiday house-decorating season or free massages at the Shiatsu Stall in terminal A, but my requests have thus far been denied. I plan to continue pestering HR, because those massages are worth fighting for.

I could certainly use one of them now. I sense the famil-iar stiffness in my neck settling in for a long stay as I pilot my banged-up Dodge Neon down the back roads I prefer to the highway. A learner's-permit driver sideswiped my car months ago, leaving me with a handicapped passenger door that can only be opened from the outside and a per-sistent case of whiplash.

I try to self-administer a quick neck rub and am suddenly

reminded of a ghost story I heard when I was younger, back in the non-practising prodigy days. It was about a woman who always wore a ribbon around her neck. Her husband repeatedly asked her why but she refused to tell him. Finally, when she was a very old lady, she told him to go ahead and untie the ribbon. He did, and her head fell off. This story had haunted me when I was little, and to this day I'm very wary of women wearing chokers.

I glance over at the passenger seat to check on Grant. Or rather, to check on Grant's ashes, which are resting in a slightly mangled plastic Elmo doll that used to be one of his favourite chew toys. It's made of some sort of canine teeth-cleaning material that he'd really flipped for. He'd loved holding it down with one paw and leveraging his lean torso into an optimal chewing position, turning his tail into a thumping metronome. If they made human dental products that exciting, no one would ever have cavities. Grant had been a large, happy, loyal dog and I never imagined he would be insubstantial enough to fit inside one of his little toys. He didn't even fill it all the way up.

I blink a few times and wonder what my aunt and uncle are doing. Most likely, my uncle is setting up one of his elaborate Dominos exhibits in the room that used to be my bedroom, before he and my aunt garage-sold all my childhood possessions to make more space for themselves. And when I say Dominos, I'm not referring to the small plastic rectangles people arrange to cascade in spotted waterfalls. I'm talking about the pizza boxes. My uncle eats a small Domino's pizza every day and then glues the empty boxes together to construct various sculptures.

He started doing this soon after I came to live with

them. I've heard that the Domino's Corporation owners give tons of money to anti-choice groups and I've suspected my uncle's sculptures are more political than he lets on, but I've never had the energy to investigate.

My aunt, I feel sure, is asleep. That's what she does when she isn't taking pills. She hasn't always been like this. Just for the last twenty years. I sigh and remember the phone call that had led to an earlier eighteen-hour drive to pick Grant up in the first place.

'We're going to put him down. He's old and it's for the best.'

'Is he sick?'

'No. But we're sick of taking care of him.'

I'd got in the car half an hour later. Grant had lived three more years under my care before dying on his own terms.

Were there some meaningful place to scatter Grant's ashes that didn't involve a trip home, I gladly would have pounced on it the way he used to pounce on the mail the instant it slid through the slot. Wrestling it away from him before he managed to shred anything important was always an adrenalin-pumping project. But for better or for worse, there was only one place where Grant could rest in peace – the ravine behind my aunt and uncle's house.

Grant and I had escaped to the ravine every day of our lives together in that house, no matter the weather. It was our refuge – our land of magic and intrigue. Anyone observing would have seen a sad little kid and a dog not fitting in together, but we saw ourselves as world-weary adventurers ever determined to plot one more mission. Grant was the copilot, my Chewbacca. I, obviously, was

Han Solo. We were devastatingly significant, whether or not anyone else realised it at the time. Often the fate of the universe rested in our hands.

The summer I turned nine, my aunt and uncle toyed with the idea of clearing out the ravine and putting down Astroturf. When I heard about this scheme, I screamed for seventeen minutes and thirteen seconds. I knew the exact duration because I used my mom's old watch that I'd started wearing to measure it. After minute fourteen, my aunt and uncle just left the house. That's how they tended to deal with difficult things. But they never brought up Astroturf again.

Sometimes I feel like screaming for extended periods of time on plane flights. Not in response to obnoxious passengers – I handle them with cart rams and practised ignoring – but in reaction to repetition. Instead of telling people the same useless lines about their seat buckles and flotation devices, I often feel like screaming. Or actually like high-pitched shrieking, à la Yoko Ono, but I never go through with it. I mentally add non-practising artist to my résumé.

The only part of the standard stewardess recitation that I attach any sort of significance to is the part about the emergency exits, because I think one of the instructions is philosophically profound. I infuse my voice with subtle but palpable reverence whenever I utter the line: 'Bear in mind that the nearest exit may be behind you.' How true. To me, the words are poetic and wise. And tragic, because in real life I can't go back to those exits.

Approximately every third flight, I fantasise about jumping out of the plane. My neighbour told me when

I was younger that falling through clouds makes a person go blind. I'd been suspicious of this claim but never had the chance to prove it wrong. Doing so is one motivation for jumping, but the stronger one is the shock value. No one would ever expect it. People would be so surprised. I therefore find the prospect almost overwhelmingly tempting. If opening the door mid-flight and leaping out wouldn't endanger the lives of my fellow passengers, I might consider it. But I know that it would and therefore can't in good conscience seriously fantasise about it. Maybe jumping off a building would be a better bet, if I could ensure that no passers-by would be landed on. The building would need to be tall enough for clouds.

I don't consider myself suicidal, just fundamentally bored. But maybe that's occasionally the same thing.

And when I think about jumping, I think about my aunt and uncle. My guardians. I suspect they'd be surprised, and sad, and probably annoyed to have to deal with the aftermath. Would they even deal with it? Or might they just leave it to someone else?

I sneeze violently and wonder whether I'm allergic to Grant's ashes. Or to his absence. I've never had any problems with live dogs, but dead ones are a previously untested allergen. In general, they shouldn't be too difficult to avoid.

My aunt and uncle had never liked the idea of Grant. They warned me that I didn't know how hard it could be to take care of another living thing and did everything to dissuade me from adopting him, short of forbidding it. They told me I'd regret it, that I'd grow to resent him, that I'd be driven crazy by the demands of his simply existing.

I listened to them, knowing they were really talking about me, and reminded them that my parents had promised me a puppy before their accident. They sighed and shut up.

As I think about these people who never chose to have me, it begins to rain regularly, then unreasonably. I have to pull over because I can't see anything except my windscreen wipers drowning. I'm annoyed, but also pleased that nature is still capable of such sabotage. I'm happy we haven't completely won, and I feel like this sentiment elevates me to the ranks of enlightened stewardesses.

When the river of rain finally slows and I can discern actual individual drops again, I hear barking. I look quickly at the Elmo urn, but Grant remains in ashes, which shouldn't surprise me but does. The barking is close and ostensibly part of the land of the living. I stretch myself up to look further over the steering wheel and see a three-legged dog engaged in a fierce face-off with my car's right tyre. My money's on the tyre. The dog must be a stray, since I know from previous drives that there's no one and nothing around for miles. I purposely drive this stretch of back road *because* it's lonely and abandoned – I don't feel like either of us has to put on any airs.

But just as I've begun to empathise with the loner life this three-legged dog must lead, I spot a dishevelled man limping out of the trees towards my car. He whistles to the dog as he stares at me through the windscreen. He's completely soaked.

I stare back at him. He jerks a hitchhiker's thumb but doesn't smile or soften his expression in any way. I feel like he's double-daring me to be crazy enough to pick him up. I consider the options. He could either kill me or make the drive much more interesting. Or both. On the other hand, I could just drive away and stay alive and bored. I roll down the window.

'Where are you headed?'

'End of the rainbow.'

'Is that off Route 9?'

He glares at me for a moment before nudging his dog towards the passenger door. I open the glove compartment and carefully place the Elmo urn full of Grant inside. The man opens the door and climbs in, getting the seat wet and muddy. His dog takes care of the floor.

'What's your name?' I ask. I should at least know his name.

'Tall,' he answers.

He's not really that tall, but I notice he has enormous feet. Maybe he'd been born with them and his parents had made assumptions. I wonder if they're still alive, worrying about him. I put the car in gear and ease back onto the bumpy road.

'And that guy?' I nod to the dog.

'L. Like the letter.'

L is pretty cute, in a mangy and wild sort of way. For the first time, I notice a bedraggled ribbon tied around his neck. It might have been red or blue once, but it looks as though it's been the colour of damp, dirty fur for a long while. I wonder where this pair has been.

'How'd he lose his leg?' I ask.

'Accident,' Tall answers. 'Wrong place at the wrong time.'

'Mmmm. People say timing is everything.'

'What people?'

His tone is unmistakeably challenging. And paranoid? I wonder if he battles imaginary enemies. I wonder if the metal flashlight in the pocket of my door could be an effective weapon.

'Um . . . I don't know. My mom. My mom always said timing is everything.'

I glance sideways at him to see how he takes this. His forehead appears deep in thought, though his eyes look dull and dead.

'What's your dad say?'

'I don't know. He agreed, I guess.'

Tall breathes in and out in loud, irregular gasps, before sneezing raucously. I feel the spray on my arm and grow nauseous. When Tall speaks again, he speaks slowly in a low voice, drawing out each word.

'Do you love your parents? Would you die for them?'

I continue steering with my right hand and close my left one around the flashlight, testing its weight. I'm left-handed, like my father.

'My parents passed away when I was young,' I reply, trying to keep my voice even. 'My aunt and uncle raised me. As much as they bothered to, at least,' I can't help but add.

'What's that mean? What'd they do to you?'

He's confrontational again. It's getting dark and the rain is still battering the windscreen. I wish it would stop so I could just see a little better. Maybe the back roads weren't such a fantastic plan.

'They didn't do anything to me. Which was the problem. They never seemed to want to deal with me.'

Tall bursts into gravelly laughter. I hold my breath,

waiting to hear what's so funny. I wonder if it's the gleeful thought of my imminent strangling.

'Maybe *you* were bad timing.'

Lightning flashes overhead and I mentally review what I'm supposed to do if it strikes the car. We can survive it, as long as we don't touch anything metal. Grant's collar is metal, and I've strung it around my neck with even more metal. It felt better to put it against my skin than away in some box. The flashlight in my hand is metal too. I fake-smile at Tall.

'Maybe I was.'

He seems mollified. He slides his neck around in a reptilian stretch.

'Got anything to drink?'

I do. I have a backpack full of tiny liquor. I don't drink, but I'm always encouraging others to partake so I can have the empties. I like filling the little bottles up with things I think are better for them. Tall is having none of it.

'I meant water.'

He sounds angry and offended. I don't have any water, which I tell him. Buying water depresses me. It should be free and available, like air and love.

'We'll have to stop then. L is dehydrated.'

Tall says this defiantly with a smack of his gums, like he's challenging me to argue with a toothless maniac. L doesn't look particularly dehydrated. He's curled up beneath the glove compartment, snoring the stuffy snores of flat-faced dogs.

'I'll find some place when we make it back to the highway.'

I sneak a sideways glance at Tall and am alarmed to see

that his face has twisted into a menacing sneer. Behind him, the side of the road drops off into a steep, rocky ravine.

'Stop now,' he hisses abruptly. 'You don't have a choice, YOU'RE GOING TO STOP NOW.'

He's reaching into his coat for something. A knife or a rope. I am instantly hot with the panic that comes with sheer, liver-gripping terror. I think about Grant in the glove compartment and wish he were in the passenger seat instead. I open my mouth to finally start screaming.

Suddenly, I remember the passenger door is broken and can only be opened from the outside. My panic flees. I feel calm, practically giddy. I break into a real smile as I curl my fingers tighter around the flashlight. It's all I can do to keep from giggling. I glance down at L and know I won't have to throw Grant's toys away after all. The ribbon's coming off though. I'll give him a nice chain collar instead.

I take a long, deep, free breath. As of right now, I'm a non-practising victim. Tall is the one who's trapped, not me. Though he hasn't been told yet, his only exit is behind him.

As the adrenaline courses through me I catch a split-second glimpse of Tall's weapon: a soggy packet of cigarettes. The truth is, people have been killed for less.

Anita Heiss

The Hens' Night

At 5 p.m. the alarm on my mobile rang loudly, waking me from my catnap in preparation for the hens' night ahead. Both Liza and I had been dreading the thought of participating in the outdated, socially embarrassing, have-to-get-pissed-to-have-a-good-time event that we were obligated to attend as part of the process of our friend Melanie marrying her Mr Right.

Before I even got off the bed I began to coin a mantra that would hopefully see me through the night and have me wake the next morning without a hangover. If the same mantra could also help me find a new love interest that might even lead to him being my *own* Mr Right, then that'd be even better.

I smiled with the realisation that perhaps going on a hens' night mightn't be that bad after all. Perhaps sixteen women having a good time would attract a few guys having a good time, and among those few guys, just *perhaps*, my Mr Right might be. Yes, it was possible that the hens' night would be a great evening after all.

But I needed to keep my options open. Even though Liza had mentioned the possibility of setting me up with a new guy from her office that she hadn't *actually* met yet, and might *not* be single, or *straight* for that matter, he was still a potential date, and that meant he was still a chance at least of being my Mr Right, as were all the other men I hadn't yet had the opportunity to meet. No, I definitely didn't want to put all my unfertilised eggs in one basket. My mantra became: I have many eggs and many baskets.

I showered, shaved my legs, curled my lashes and plucked one or two annoying hairs from my chin, noting that I really needed to get my oestrogen levels checked. I put on my lucky bra and knickers that I only wore on 'special occasions', donned a slinky black dress, straightened my hair, ran some blood-red lipstick across my lips and dabbed a little glitter on the arch of my brow. All within an hour.

I cruised over to Liza's place at Bondi, where she had a jug of sangria waiting on the balcony. After ten years of friendship she knew how to impress me, but I noted to myself that she'd been drinking a lot lately after being on the wagon for nearly two years. She had been really pissed one night after a really big session at Kitty O'Sheas. So out of control she lunged over the front seat of the cab on the way home and asked the driver if she could cut the fare out with him. I thought it was hysterical, and the cabbie loved the offer, but Liza beat herself up for days afterwards whenever she had a flashback. She rarely drank much after that night, and never booked a Legion Cab again either. She really was an all or nothing kinda girl.

'So what's the deal with a hens' night, anyway?' I asked, knowing she, who was a fount of all knowledge, would have an answer.

'Well, someone at work told me that the hens' night is meant to replace the old tradition of the kitchen tea. So you either do one or the other I reckon. Get presents for your kitchen or go out with your girlfriends.' Liza was also very matter-of-fact about most things. I put it down to her training as a lawyer.

'Don't tell me we were meant to get her a present for this as well?'

'No, we just pay for her dinner.'

'Thank God. This whole wedding gig's costing me a fortune. You know, engagement present, kitchen tea, wedding present, outfit, hair, nails and, of course, we're going to have to stay overnight, what with the wedding happening out west.'

'You say it with such venom, Alice, it's only past Penrith.'

'Yeah well, my own fucken wedding won't cost this much, I'm sure.'

'Tell me about it. We should book a motel soon, too. Are you taking a partner?' Liza asked between sucking the alcohol-soaked fruit out of her already empty glass and struggling to reach the jug for another refill.

'I live in hope. There's still time before Christmas to meet someone, maybe even New Year's Eve. Else, it might have to be you!' As soon as I said it, it reminded me of a conversation I had with Mum the day before. She desperately wanted me to admit to being a lesbian simply because I wasn't married and didn't have a man in my life. The only thing I would admit to was that it was easier to organise a date with my female friends than blokes. At least Liza liked to eat, shop, drink (well, a bit more now) and would commit to an outing a couple of weeks ahead. Men rarely did that. But did Liza, like Mum, think I was a lesbian too? I was getting paranoid. I tried to keep the conversation going without referring to her as my 'date'.

'What about you then, you got someone for the wedding?'

'Mum said a woman she works with has a son who's just come back from studying in the States and –' before she finished the sentence she started jumping up and down spilling her third glass of sangria over herself and waving her hands about in the air. 'I forgot, I forgot! My cousin Marco has just arrived from Sorrento. He's here for a couple of years working with my uncle's exporting business. He's gorgeous, Al, you'd love him. The most beautiful green eyes you have ever seen, and tall, with the most beautiful head of hair and olive skin. No lie, if he weren't my cousin I'd be taking him myself. I'm sure he'd love to go with you. Do you want me to ask him?' She was so excited, and he sounded lovely, which made it harder when I said, 'Liza, remember my friend Jane?'

'No, why?' she answered, confused.

'No, you wouldn't, because she's not talking to me any more. I went out with her cousin for a couple of months and when I realised he was into some really kinky shit I dumped him. She never spoke to me again and wouldn't even listen to my reasons why. So, I don't even want to risk losing my friendship with you.' I watched her body language to see what she was thinking, and wondered briefly if that sounded lesbian-like.

'First of all, that wouldn't happen to us, and secondly, I'm sure Marco's not into kinky shit. He might look like an Italian Stallion, Alice, but he's a good Catholic boy, the ripe old age of twenty-nine.' Did she really think that Catholic boys weren't into kinky shit? What about all those hideous priests? But I let it go as she tried to convince me to take up the Marco offer.

'Anyway, you can't just take one bad experience with Jane-the-Pain and not at least try again.' Liza was very persistent and making sense, but it wasn't just one example and I was compelled to remind her.

'Okay, what about when you tried to set me up with your Uncle Tony and we went out for dinner. He took me to the restaurant where he and your aunt used to go and she was there with her new man. It was a bloody nightmare. I looked like a hooker, she looked like she was with a twenty-year-old gigolo. I really think we should leave *your* family out of *my* search for Mr Right. We might even meet someone tonight if we don't look like a herd of pathetic henning housewives.'

'You're right, Alice. Anyway, we can always coordinate our clothes and take each other to Melanie's wedding, you know I make the perfect date, eh?'

Oh my God, was she teasing me now? Did she think I was a lesbian and was having a go at me by calling me her 'date'? I was becoming obsessed with perceived mixed lesbian messages, sending them and receiving them. Liza had no idea of the mental turmoil she was part of in my head.

We toasted each other, the hens' night, a possible New Year's pash and the upcoming wedding as we looked out over her balcony to the block of flats behind us. It was enough simply knowing that Bondi Beach was somewhere out there.

While elegantly slurping down Liza's 'special sangria' that lent itself to the strong side, I was relieved to learn that the night's henning was going to happen a little closer to home, not Parramatta as was previously planned. Apparently a few hensters from the east and the north-east didn't fancy doing the M4, M5 or M2 trip so Melanie agreed to a venue change. Capitan Torres in Liverpool Street (hence Liza's choice of pre-dinner drinks) and then on to the Bristol Arms for some serious seventies and eighties retro sounds. The night was already looking better than it was an hour before. The warm glow in my cheeks was a bonus, especially since I'd left home in such a rush I'd forgotten to put any blush on.

A short time later we were eating garlic prawns and potatoes, squid in ink and the best paella ever, even though Liza and I spent more time arguing over how it was actually pronounced than eating it. Like the frightening experience at the kitchen tea the week before, we were all given name tags to wear. 'The Bride', 'Chief Bridesmaid', 'The Bridesmaid', 'The Mother of the Bride' and so on. I was grateful that 'Granny of the Groom' wasn't there this time, as I was still processing having watched her pin the penis on the spunk at the kitchen tea. Mine and Liza's tags simply had our names. We consoled ourselves with the fact that at least if we got lost or speechless, other people would know who we were. We were tempted to write our address on them as well for worst-case scenarios and we could just get in a cab and point to our tags, but decided against it.

'I won't be getting in a cab drunk tonight anyway, Alice.' Liza gargled and spoke through the sangria adamantly.

There was giggling and chatter and some pretty crappy jokes being told to the left and right of me. All noise stopped though when the Bride's 'Maid to Be' (her name tag said) mentioned that her hens' night was going to be in eighteen months' time and she was planning on taking her henners abseiling in the mountains.

'What the hell are we doing here, Liza?' I couldn't believe how it was that we'd managed to be among these women.

'Even Melanie can't possibly fit in here,' Liza whispered in my ear.

'Ab-fucken-sailing?' I slurred back in hers. 'How does pre-wedding freedom-ending socialising with your girl-friends translate into ab-fucken-sailing?'

'You tell me. I know you're supposed to do something *daring* on your hens' night, but I was thinking about going a little crazy at a strip show rather than going crazy rock climbing'. And Liza and I are off on a tangent about our own final-night-of-freedom party plans.

To my complete surprise Liza admitted that she wanted to do the male strip show 'Bad Boys Afloat' for her hens' night. I can't say the thought *totally* repulsed me. Seri-ously, I think it's good for women, whatever age, to be reminded of that animal urge to just jump a complete stranger in a leopard-print G-string. Not that I'd actually do it myself, of course. But I think it's completely normal to think about doing it.

'Pity most of the dancers are gay,' I thought I should tell her in case she didn't already know. She was a little naïve that way, having obsessed over a gay guy for six months before she realised he was batting for the other team.

After a few unflattering comments about male strippers wearing mesh tops Liza dared me to come up with something more innovative for my hens' night. And even though I was on a mission to meet Mr Right I didn't really want the whole process that led to the final walk down the aisle and the happily every after.

'Liza, I am a little older than you.' I could hear the lack of fun in my voice as I prefaced my desired hens' night schedule to her. Liza was twenty-five and doing her first year at the Aboriginal Legal Service and had only just left home. I was twenty-eight and had been renting a gorgeous place in Coogee for four years.

'And I have done the 'Bad Boys Afloat' gig more than once . . . okay, five times. And I'm not the least bit interested in abseiling or going to the Lone Star Tavern at Parramatta as part of my wedding preparations either.'

'Yeah, okay, I get the picture, big noter. What do you want to do then? Have a girls' night in with pizza and a DVD?'

'Perhaps. Buuuuuut, if someone *happened* to order a stripper I wouldn't be the least bit offended.' Liza took the hint and I could see her making a mental note. I wasn't *that* much older than her, and definitely no more conservative. Okay, so I'd never made a pass at a cab driver before, but other than that we were equal in the having fun stakes.

Then, just as I was trying to catch the attention of a very sexy waiter to order another jug of sangria that only Liza and I were drinking, an ugly pink cake arrived at the table.

'That is the aarrrrgllliieessst-looking attempt at a cake I've ever seen,' Liza slurred loudly, not realising the cook was 'The Bride's Cousin' sitting immediately to her left. Silence almost strangled the table and 'The Bride's Cousin' threw a deathly look at my friend. I tried to break the tension with a petty statement. 'Looks better than any cake I've ever made', to which I received a look of appreciation from 'The Bride's Cousin', but Liza, who was really pissed by then, burst into laughter and fell off her chair. I was tempted to leave her down on the floor, but helped her up, just so that I could find out what was so funny.

'You've never cooked a fucken cake in your life. So my arse looks better than any of your so-called cakes . . .' She was swearing, which wasn't like her at all. I couldn't help laughing, and recognised that it had been a long time since she let all her inhibitions down. I made a mental note that I had better strap her into her seatbelt in the cab on the way home.

We all got a piece of the ugly pink cake and a big cheer went up for the cook, who'd bitten into the piece with a ring in it. Melanie jumped to her feet.

'Tradition says that the hen that gets the piece with the ring in it is the next to get married.' And the table went up with a roar for 'The Bride's Cousin'.

'Riiiiigggged, rriiiigggged,' Liza belched across the table while pointing her empty glass at 'The Bride's Cousin'. 'She planted the ring in there and she knew which piece had it. That doesn't count. Re-draw! I want a re-draw.'

As the others just whispered and tried to ignore Liza's claims, I tried to appease her with more sangria while explaining to her that she wasn't at a chook raffle at the

RSL, and that we couldn't do a re-draw as most people had eaten their cake.

'You should've got that ring. You want to get married, don't you? Why aren't you upset? If 'Mrs New Carpet' can get married, then why the hell can't you or I? This sux.' Liza had given the hostess of the kitchen tea the title of Mrs New Carpet because none of us were allowed to go upstairs to use the toilet unless we took our shoes off because she'd just got new carpet.

Of course, Liza was right. If a woman who won't let you wear shoes to pee could scoop a husband, then why couldn't we? I tried not to think about it for longer than ten seconds and focused on eating the leftover fruit at the bottom of the sangria jug, becoming increasingly aware of how drunk I was as I shoved my entire hand into the jug to get the last piece of apple.

The bill came and Liza and I threw in a few extra dollars before anyone could comment that we drank more than the rest of the table. Surely they understood that the only thing between making them all seem like complete losers and being just bearable was the three litres of grog we'd each drunk.

Turning right out of Liverpool Street into Sussex Street, Melanie led the way. My vision was blurry, very blurry, and I was staggering slightly, not wanting to hook arms with Liza because I was paranoid that everyone thought I was a lesbian. And even though I couldn't really focus my sangria-pickled eyes, I could make out a huge bag being wrestled with at the front of the group. I wasn't sure what was being pulled out of it, but all the women were struggling with bright wispy things, trying to put them on their heads. The penny finally dropped – they were tiny little pseudo wedding veils. And one by one they were being fitted by Melanie, who was already wearing a metre-long white one. All the others were smaller fluorescent pink ones. The plastic bag made its way to the back of the group to Liza and me. I was sure I was thinking to myself, but realised halfway through the sentence that my words were actually coming out of my mouth. I said, 'No way am I putting on some fucken pink tulle mini-veil because someone else is getting married.'

Liza was just saying over and over again, 'No way, no way, no way.'

As luck would have it, the bag reached us empty. For some unexplained but much appreciated reason, they were two mini-veils short. Liza and I roared with laughter as all the others felt bad for us, finding reasons why they shouldn't part with their veils for us. We both said with sincere gratefulness, 'No, no, we'd never ask you to do that.' And God knows we wouldn't.

Before we knew it we'd paid our $20 entry fee to the club and elbowed our way to the bar.

'More wine?' Liza shouted over Katrina and the Waves, not even waiting for my answer. She grabbed the bottle by the neck, left the ice bucket on the bar and headed towards the first of the three dance floors. Lots of bodies were 'Knock, knock, knocking on wood', bopping along to some of the coolest music from the seventies. I loved it.

The evening became more of a haze the later it got, as smoke mixed with testosterone and body odour and more wine and a few tequila shots. Liza and I just staggered between floors minus the other henners. Before long I had some young gun gyrating against me with a sleazy, cheesy grin, singing 'Don't rock the boat, rock the boat baby . . .' and I immediately felt seasick.

'Time to go.' Liza tugged at my arm and within seconds we were out the front door and walking barefoot along Sussex Street arguing because Liza refused to get in one of numerous Legion cabs that were vacant.

Lauren Henderson

Dating the Enemy

We treat the people we want to love like adversaries.

'You can't trust what people say any more,' says my friend David.

'Everyone knows now what people want to hear. We all know exactly how to show the socially acceptable sides of ourselves. Don't listen to what they say. Watch what they do. They can't disguise that.'

David gave me that advice when I first moved to New York. I thought he sounded as paranoid as a character from a horror film telling the others how to spot the aliens. But he was right. We're fighting for our emotional lives. Guides to dating rules might as well be called Lao-tzu's *Art of War*. As soon as you let down your guard they knife you. Then you crawl back to your friends to have your wounds licked while they analyse where you went wrong and what was going through your attacker's head, with the finely honed skills of thirty-somethings who have already paid extortionate amounts to have their sensitive psyches probed by Upper East Side analysts.

We dress in grey and black and khaki. Combat trousers, big sweaters, bags strapped across our chests so that our hands are free to defend ourselves. The bare minimum of make-up. Big ugly rubber-soled shoes, in which we can run away from trouble. Our one sign of frivolity is the occasional bright, lace-trimmed, thermal vest. And pretty underwear, seen, alas, mostly by ourselves. We are urban survivors, striding across concrete pavements, ducking and weaving to avoid being elbowed by passing strangers who think we're in their path, dodging cycle deliverymen riding the wrong way down one-way streets, navigating through subway systems and a network of late-night bars where we drink too many martinis and smoke too many cigarettes to forget the last person who looked as if they could be the one and turned out to be a liar on a quick break from their ex.

We spend a fortune on cabs.

Case study one: Paola goes out for a drink with friends and bumps into a guy she nearly had a fling with at a work conference a few months ago. They fooled around but she didn't actually sleep with him because they're on the same work network. He's younger than she is and lower down the pecking order – she was nervous of the gossip. By not actually having sex with him she could keep her options open.

All good excuses. Actually she was scared.

So now here is he again, keen, handsome, attentive and making it clear that he still wants to sleep with her. A sure thing. And, from the fooling around, she assumes that the sex will be excellent. But she's out with a couple of people from work, and they know him. No way is she going to let down her guard, show that she wants to take him home, with the danger that it won't work out and that word will get around: it might make her vulnerable. What if he only wants her for sex? If they were both going in the same direction at the end of the night they could share a cab; but they aren't. So she lets it go. He asks her to ring him. She says she will. She won't. It's too close to home. Think of the risks.

We are perpetually sensitised to possibility. Phrases of cheap music run through our heads; we're always at the stage where they're meaningful. Even the most banal lyrics seem directly applicable to our current tortured situation.

'If only you were here tonight
I know that we could make it right . . .'

We would die rather than confess to liking the singers; our images demand that we listen to the latest hip bootleg remix, not trashy sentimental pop.

Case study two: Laura's the only one of our fighting unit in a relationship. She loves Skip and he loves her. He keeps asking her to marry him. They met four years ago and spent the first few months fucking each other's brains out. Laura ate like a horse and lost five pounds. After a year they decided to move in together. Both of them were ecstatic. The first night they spent in their new apartment, Skip rolled over with his back to her and said that he was really tired. That was it. They've hardly had sex since.

She tried to talk to him about it but every time he had

a different excuse. He was stressed at work, he'd overdone it at the gym, now that they were living together they were going to have to get used to not having sex every single night. Gradually the excuses faded away, to be replaced by what turned out to be a manifesto. Why did sex matter that much anyway? Surely what mattered was how much they loved each other. Most people had much less sex than they boasted about, after all. They were just another normal couple. Laura shouldn't get so worked up about this. Hadn't she heard the story about the jar full of coins?

And every so often he would have sex with her, when he sensed that the strain of celibacy was becoming unbearable. The night before last had been one of those times.

'Pity fuck,' says Phil.

'Relationship-maintenance fuck,' I correct.

'Well, no. The trouble is,' Laura says helplessly, 'is that it was *good*. You know what I mean? It wasn't a let's-get-this-over-with-so-she-can't-complain-for-another-few-months fuck. It was like the old times. That's the thing. Nothing's changed. And that just makes it worse. I mean, he can still do it like that, so why doesn't he?'

'Would you have preferred it to be perfunctory and loveless?' David enquires.

'"You're going through the motions but you don't really care",' Paola sings, a snippet of an old song that's just been covered and remixed within an inch of its life and is enjoying a brief heyday in the charts, the original singer long forgotten.

'No, he did care, he does care,' Laura says miserably. 'And yeah, I would much rather the sex was crap. At least I could say, okay, that side of things is over, and deal with it. But when it's that good, it's like he's keeping me on a string. Doling out something from time to time just so I keep from starving completely.'

'You do have that I-had-good-sex-recently glow,' David observes.

'Yeah, what's your problem, bitch?' I say jokingly. 'You had great sex the night before last! That's probably more recent than anyone round this table!'

Laura shoots me a foul look. But so does everyone else.

'What's the jar-full-of-coins thing?' Phil asks.

Three of us start to speak at once. David makes it through.

'That if you put a coin in a jar for each time you have sex the first year in a marriage, and take one out every time out you have sex after that, the jar'll still have coins in it when you die.'

'Whoa,' Phil says. 'That's why I'm never getting married.'

This is a complete bluff, a moment of machismo. Phil would love more than anything to get married. We all know this so well that no one bothers to call him on it.

'Look,' Paola says to Laura, her voice sober. Clearly she has decided to be the voice of reason. 'It'll never get much better. You've got two choices – leave him or have affairs. I think you should have affairs. Bet he never asks questions. Shit, he'll probably be grateful.'

'Well-concealed commitment issues,' says David, grave as a doctor diagnosing a fatal disease. 'That's a tough one.'

'Maybe he's depressed,' says Phil. 'That's the first thing to make a guy lose his woody. The trouble is, even the new anti-depressants don't exactly up your libido.'

We all look at Phil.

'Yeah,' he says. 'But you know, the thing is, I don't care! I'm so happy on my Prozac right now I don't care if I ever get laid again!'

We all edge back in the booth like vampires who have just spotted a clove of garlic in the middle of the table.

'We'll do that one later,' Paola decides. 'Right now we're still on Laura.'

'I'm scared of rocking the boat,' Laura says. 'The rest of the time it's so perfect. And maybe if we get married it'll get better.'

We all laugh sardonically. Laura has talked about this problem enough times that we are allowed to find this amusing.

'What makes you think that?' David looks weary. We have all had this conversation with her, over and over again. 'If moving in together fucked up the sex, then marriage'll be ten times worse.'

'But it's so perfect in every other way,' Laura repeats hopelessly. 'I mean, I don't have to tell you guys that.'

We all know and love Skip. He's funny, sweet and dealt very well with the trial-by-fire of meeting Laura's friends. He has a good job that he enjoys and is good-looking without being so unnecessarily handsome that other women hit on him all the time or are automatically hostile to his girlfriend. He's easygoing, not a slob, and obviously adores Laura. Your ideal man. As a gay best friend.

'What happens if I do leave him?' Laura is so scared by the thought she can barely get the words out. 'Back on the street again, out there in dating hell . . .' She shivers. 'No offence, you guys . . .'

We shrug to show that none has been taken.

'You all know what I went through before I met Skip. I honestly don't think I can do that again. My God, I'll be single for the rest of my life.'

Laura doesn't actually say it; she knows we'd shoot her down. But we can see her thinking it. Better a stable relationship with a guy who loves her, the social certainties of being in a couple, the end to loneliness, than our nocturnal, bar-crawling existence, our latest reports from the war front.

I can't blame her.

'Is he getting it anywhere else?' asks Phil. Prozac has not managed to suppress his cynicism.

This is the first time anyone has put this question to Laura. She looks shell-shocked.

We don't know how to advise Laura, or anyone with long-term relationship problems. No one does, apart from our shrinks. Long-term relationships require patience, compromise and faith, and we are familiar with none of the above. Indeed, we see them all as signs of weakness.

'I hung on, hoping she'd change,' one of us will say feebly, and the others will expel their breath in tight hisses from clenched teeth, like the last puffs of a milk frother making cappuccino. In our world, you never hang on. You explain that the person's behaviour is unacceptable, that they have breached your tolerance limit, that you value yourself too much to put up with their latest sin of omission or commission, and you move on, head held high. Your friends applaud: you have done the right thing.

We are terrified of being like our parents, either trapped

in unhappy marriages or undergoing bloody, prolonged divorces. We all remember what those felt like, our limbs strapped to four horses all running in different directions. Even now, we are barely managing to put the pieces together again, with the help of the aforementioned expensive therapists. No way are any of us getting into that kind of mess ourselves. Our parents' pathetic excuses for the misery we went through are still vivid to us. The lesson we have learned is never put up with anything. Any signs of trouble and we're out of there.

We are all desperate to be in love. But we are more desperate to hide it. So for pride's sake, we pretend, to ourselves and others, that it's all about sex instead.

I'm waiting for Ivan to call. It's been a week now and my stomach is processing food faster than I can eat it. I'm chain-smoking and ringing my friends constantly to discuss what might have gone wrong on the date that would mean he wouldn't want to see me again.

'Go to bed with someone else,' says David. 'It's perfect. You distract yourself and then, when he does call, you can be really cool.'

'What, just go and pick some guy up in the bar on the corner?' I say sarcastically.

'You must know someone . . . What about that guy you were seeing a couple of months ago?'

'Seamus?'

'He was really into you, wasn't he?'

'Yeah,' I say smugly. 'Took him ages to stop calling.'

'And the sex was good, wasn't it?'

'Great,' I confirm. 'It was the conversation that was the problem.'

'Well, that's perfect!' David says enthusiastically. 'Call him up right now and tell him to come over because you need to get laid. If a woman I'd been seeing gave me a call like that I'd be ecstatic. Even if I was busy, or dating someone else, I'd be ecstatic.'

'Wouldn't you think I was a slut?' I ask.

David is my, and many other women's, Official Man. We touch base with him to see what men are really thinking. The trouble is that he tells us.

'No way. I'd be hugely flattered and I wouldn't be able to stop thinking about you. So ring him.'

'Oh, David,' I whine. 'I can't. He's only just stopped calling. It would be cruel. It would give him false hope.'

The mere thought of seeing Seamus again – reading that happiness in his eyes, his pleasure at seeing me – makes me feel horribly guilty.

'Bullshit. Just be straight with him. Tell him you don't want to date him but the sex was fabulous and you want to get laid.'

'You'd never do something like that yourself,' I say. 'It's all very well advising other people to do it.'

Silence. My phone beeps.

'David, I have another call, hold on—'

I switch over. It's Paola. I tell her I'll call her back.

'Was it Ivan?' David says.

'No,' I say.

We observe a moment's silence, as if in mourning.

'Anyway, I feel really bad about the way I treated Seamus,' I say.

I do feel bad. But also, shameful though it is to admit it, I am cheered up just a little by the knowledge that, while I am pining for Ivan, someone else is doing the same for me. 'Here I am complaining about Ivan not ringing, just disappearing like this –'

'You don't know that,' says David, automatically re-assuring. 'He might just be busy at work. You know, girl time is very different from boy time.'

'– and that's exactly what I did to Seamus.'

'You haven't had sex with Ivan yet.'

'Well, that makes what I did to Seamus even worse. I never returned his calls. I was a real bitch. And now I'm whining about someone doing that to me. I don't deserve Ivan to ring me back.'

'Hey.' David's voice sharpens. 'It's all tactics. Remember that. You didn't promise Seamus anything, did you?'

It's a rhetorical question: he knows the answer already.

'So there's no guilt,' he continues. 'You didn't break any promises.'

'I could at least have told him what was going on.'

David sounds weary now.

'Forget the conscience,' he says. 'That isn't how it works. You know that.'

Our pockets are full of matchboxes from bars we can't even remember, hangouts we have been swept along to at three in the morning by groups of people we don't know that well. It's not so much that we think if we stay out till dawn we might finally stumble across The One, bleary-eyed and blinking, like us, in the daylight; no, we want to postpone the moment of going home alone to our single-bedroom apartments until we're too drunk or tired, or both, to be anything but grateful that there are no witnesses waiting up to see the state in which we stagger through the front door, throwing our keys clumsily at the hall table and missing.

We are in our thirties. We all earn plenty of money and have only ourselves to spend it on. We are very spoilt. We know we're spoilt, but it doesn't make us feel any better.

Paola's on a radical diet. She's decided that she needs to lose ten pounds. Paola probably does need to lose ten pounds, but we're worried about her reasons – she's frantic to get a steady boyfriend – and her methods, which are frighteningly drastic. All she's eaten for the last three weeks are meal-substitute bars and the occasional piece of fruit. And she's taken up circuit training.

'Her body is just not up to this,' Laura says. 'I mean, think of the shock to the system!'

'Not as much of a shock as it would be if she gave up drinking,' I say.

We exchange a glance. This is the trouble. The one vice Paola is allowing herself is alcohol. She's drinking as much as ever, only now with much less in her stomach to soak it up. As if to compensate for the deprivation through which she's putting herself, she eats her meal bar and then comes out with us to consume the same amount of cocktails that she did when she was still packing away heaped platefuls of comfort food. Every night we have to practically mop her up off the floor and pour her into a cab.

The reason Paola doesn't have a boyfriend is that she gets off with men practically as soon as she meets them.

She hasn't been on a first date in the last couple of years that didn't end, at least, with a tongue-sandwich fumble in the back of a cab. Mostly, this city being a brutal arena in which women who give away too much too soon are seen as weak, the men never call her again. But sometimes they do. In which case she decides that they must be desperate. Why would they want a fat girl otherwise?

Paola isn't fat by any standards but the near-anorexic ones of this city. One would think that the legions of men who keep asking her out would eventually convince her that she's attractive, but it doesn't seem to work that way. Instead, the way she behaves toward them creates a self-fulfilling prophecy.

'She blames everything on her weight because it's easier that way,' Laura says.

I agree. 'But if she loses it, what's her excuse going to be?'

'That's the problem,' Laura says darkly. 'I'm sure that's why she's getting so drunk.'

'Fear of not having anything to hide behind.'

'Exactly.'

'Oh, fuck,' I say selfishly. I have enough to deal with right now without the prospect of a hundred-and-twenty-pound Paola in deep existential crisis.

Case study three: Ivan seemed perfect. A friend of a friend, highly recommended. Attentive, funny, sweet, caring, good job, nice apartment. Someone older than me, stable, a rock in high seas. For every question I ask about him he asks ten about me. It's wonderful. He rings me regularly. We're making plans for the next few weeks. Then nothing. Two weeks later, I finally get a phone call telling me that he's hooked up with an ex-girlfriend; they'd had problems that they've now resolved. And – the clincher – she's madly in love with him.

'He's trying to set up a competition between the two of you,' says David.

'What's this madly-in-love thing?' says Laura. 'What are you supposed to say – I love you more? You've only known him a few weeks!'

'You should have said – "What are you really telling me?"' says my therapist. 'Think more about your own emotions and less about his.'

'What's his emotional history?' says Paola. 'Has he been married? Lived with anyone? For how long? What do you mean, you didn't ask him? You've always got to find that out! If a guy's hitting forty and he's never been married or lived with anyone, he has serious issues to resolve.'

I realise that I am very, very tired. I go to bed instead of hitting the bars with my posse and I sleep for twelve hours straight. I don't feel that much better in the morning but at least I don't have a hangover. Maybe this is a new start.

Yesterday I was walking down Fifth Avenue, listening to my iPod, when a wash of peace flooded through me. I felt invisible, or at least transparent. I wanted to open my arms wide and stand there, letting people walk through me as if I were a ghost. It was wonderful. Does that mean I don't care any more? That would be such a relief.

'Typical of you to have a Zen breakthrough on the middle of Fifth Avenue,' Laura says.

'I know!' I say. 'And I wasn't even outside Gucci!'

'What does your shrink think about it?' she says.

'I haven't told her yet,' I admit. 'I'm keeping it to myself.'

And as I say this, I realise how good it feels. Maybe I shouldn't even have told Laura. David, Laura, Paola, Phil – we're each other's safety net, and everyone outside is the enemy. And now I wonder how much it's actually helping. Perhaps I should start keeping more things to myself. I don't know if it would help, but it might be worth trying.

Something has to change, after all. Maybe I'll start with this.

Wendy Holden

Hello Sailor

He was loud and red-faced with small, suspicious eyes. He looked boorish – the sort who farted in bed and routinely belittled women. He had an unattractive body – that solid, thick-necked, wide-calfed build of a man predisposed to fat but who keeps it off with sweaty and straining exercise. It was horribly easy to imagine him in a pair of smelly black Lycra cycling shorts.

Nevertheless, I looked at him and knew that he was everything I had been searching for. He was The One. The One I would marry. My husband. And the reason I knew this was because he had the perfect wife.

It had taken me a while to spot her. I have to admit that, by the time I did, I was close to despair. The whole exercise seemed about to prove fruitless. The night I sat down to the right of the captain at his table, I was convinced I'd wasted thousands of pounds of my savings for no return at all.

The captain chattered merrily away, doing his 'cheer

up the poor single woman on board' routine. Which was understandable, given how miserable I must have looked. Though the captain may well have been interested for other reasons – I keep myself in pretty good order and manage to turn heads in the street a good decade after most women my age have bade their last building-site wolf-whistle a long-distant goodbye. Not that builders are my target audience exactly. Or ships' captains, come to that. What I'm after is serious money, and while there was obviously plenty of it on board, it was being guarded by the most ferocious set of spouses I'd yet come across.

'. . . and of course tomorrow we arrive at Buenos Aires, which is great fun, a simply marvellous place . . .' As he banged on in a well-practised undertone, the captain was eyeing up the point at which the two sides of my Diane von Furstenberg wrap parted over my upper thigh. I've always had good legs, thanks to being a dancer all those years. And it was also thanks to being a dancer that I got involved in all this in the first place.

I almost didn't, mind you. I was desperate not to do the cruise-ship job when my agent first suggested it. Dancing on cruise ships was the naff lowest of the low – at that time I still entertained hopes of *Swan Lake* at Covent Garden, or, failing that, *Chicago* in the West End at the very least. When I told this to my agent, Moira, a no-nonsense Cockney, she clearly decided she had had enough of my fancy ways. 'Darlin', there ain't no nice way to say this, but you ain't no Margot Fonteyn. I'm not even sure you're *Strictly Come Dancin'*.' Being told that, despite being a professional dancer of many years' standing, I didn't even come up to television amateur standards was a sobering moment. I took the cruise-ship job. It was on a vessel labouring under the moniker *Cornucopia II* (wasn't ruining one ship with a name like that enough?) which was going along the coastline of the south of France.

I hate sailing, it makes me feel sick, and cruises are particularly grim. All that trapped humanity endlessly milling about low-ceilinged lounges carpeted in swirling orange and edged with trestle tables bearing platters of poached salmon. There seemed to be the most amazing quantity of said fish on board this ship. It was obviously meant to be a symbol of luxury, but it made me feel ill every time I passed it.

The gig, if anything, made me feel worse. It was an excruciating twenties-style variety show with the toe-curling title *What Ho!* The purpose of it was to encourage the saddoes on board to persist in the fantasy that they were Bright Young Things from the great days of luxury cruising. What they in fact were was lumpy businessmen from the East Midlands and their dim wives. It would have been funny were it not so pathetic – the sight, night after night, of large-tummied natives of Nottingham turning out in sequinned headbands and white tie and tails and waving fat legs around to the charleston. And that was just the blokes.

Afterwards, I chatted to some of the punters in the bar. I can't say I particularly wanted to, but there was sod-all else going on. One chap, whose name was David, was actually rather nice. It turned out he hated cruises as much as I did and had only agreed to this one after a year-long lobbying campaign by his wife, Rita. 'That's her over there,' he said without enthusiasm, pointing to a generously-proportioned woman whose tight silver sequinned dress only increased her resemblance to a vast and over-made-up herring.

David and I ordered a few more drinks and found we got on increasingly well. For example, we both liked Indian food, Agatha Christie novels and going to Italy on holiday. After that first meeting, we rather got into the habit of a chat in the bar after the show. There was no agenda, at least not from my point of view. I knew that David was rich – he owned some massive DIY business that was apparently going great guns. But I can't say I cared. I feel about Destroy It Yourself much the same as I feel about poached salmon and dancing in Twenties spectaculars called *What Ho!*

Then, one day, something quite bizarre happened. The *Cornucopia II* dropped anchor at Beaulieu-sur-Mer where, apparently as a result of the intense heat, Rita had a heart attack and dropped dead.

Naturally we were all terribly shocked. There was no show that night as a mark of respect, and of course no David in the bar. I can't say I was expecting ever to see him again when, two days after Rita snuffed it, I was called to the ship's telephone. It was David on the line.

Of course, I expressed my sincere condolences. And I did feel sympathetic, I really did, especially to the sequin industry of the East Midlands, who probably didn't get an acreage like that to cover every day of the week. 'Well, it's very kind of you to say so,' David said. 'And I do appreciate it. But the truth is that Rita and I, well, we were friends and all that, but to be honest, some of the zing had gone out of our marriage.' He went on in this vein for a while until I realised what he was getting at. He wanted to ask me out just as soon as I got back on dry land.

Reader, I married him. A couple of dates on terra firma made me realise that, while DIY bored me to tears, I could get very interested in the money it made. David lived in a vast nouveau mansion with a butler and three Rollers in the garage, and was quite obviously stinking rich. We had a luxury honeymoon in Porto Ercole, eating Indian take-aways and reading Agatha Christie until our eyes popped out. And for a couple of years all was well, until I real-ised the age gap – twenty-six years – was about to become more of an issue. I decided to bail out before the Parkin-son's started. I divorced him for unreasonable behaviour (his obsession with Derby County football club came in very handy here) and, thanks to the toughest lawyer I could lay my wallet on, walked off with a good portion of David's dosh.

The thing was, as I realised shortly afterwards, it wasn't enough. I was rich, but not super-rich. I'd been used to limos taking me everywhere, or the company helicopter. Once or twice I'd even been on private jets. Admittedly I had a flat in London and an old rectory crawling with wisteria as part of the divorce deal. But it wasn't the same. What I needed, I decided, was another rich husband.

As I had no idea where else to look for one, I went back to where I had struck lucky before. A cruise.

Unfortunately, in the years since we'd last met, the good ship *Cornucopia II* had run into some bad luck – and a ferry – in the Bay of Biscay. She had been so badly damaged, she'd had to be scrapped. I shed a sentimental tear for those swirly-carpeted lounges and cast around for a replacement. Eventually, leafing through some Saturday supplement, I noticed a double-page ad for a cruise of the Dalmatian Coast on board the *Princess Persephone*. Bingo! The Dalmatian Coast, I knew, was the new Riviera. Everyone who thought they were anyone, which admittedly usually meant that they were not, would be down there this summer.

Within minutes I had booked my stateroom and hoped there would be a footloose millionaire or two on board.

When, at the appointed hour, I rocked on board with the old Louis Vuitton, I could see that there were plenty. Thanks to my marriage to David, I'd spent enough time with rich men bored with their wives to be able to spot the breed a mile off. The problem was the wives.

Obviously sensing the possibility that their husbands might hare off at any moment, they were all but sitting on them. No doubt that was why they had chosen a cruise holiday; there was nowhere for their menfolk to run. Nowhere for any of us to run, which was a shame. The *Princess Persephone* made the *Cornucopia II* look elegantly understated. The lounges were vaster, the carpets even more whirly. There were even more platters of poached salmon, and after dinner the staff handed round small plates containing huge and sickly Belgian chocolates. To cap it all, the on-board show was rock-and-roll themed and called *Gee Whizz!*

I decided to bide my time. I made the corner stool at the copper-lined cocktail bar my headquarters and sat there sipping martinis and reading Agatha Christie. Eventually, as I had hoped, a fish slipped enquiringly into my net.

And a pretty big fish, too. His name was Nigel, he was from Aylesbury, and he was neither the most handsome nor the ugliest on board. But he was the richest. I'd worked this out already by observing that he and his wife had dined with the captain more than anyone else, and had noted from the passenger list that they had the biggest stateroom of all, some sort of duplex penthouse somewhere up front. Nigel told me, with marked lack of enthusiasm, that it even had its own swimming pool.

We got on well. I was slightly disappointed to learn he was even keener on football than David had been, but as he was obviously considerably richer (his company was one of those faceless mega ones owning several household names), I was prepared to make allowances. David's Derby obsession even came in useful – I was able to trot out some of the terminology I'd picked up. This electrified Nigel, who swiftly became smitten. 'My wife hates football,' he lamented. 'It bores her to tears.'

I had initially been encouraged by Nigel's much-aired dislike of his wife. The problem was that she was unlikely to remove herself from the scene. Maureen, for that was her name, not only looked like an ox, but was apparently as strong as one. I questioned her husband carefully about her health and was disappointed to learn that the only way she might drop dead in the street was if somebody shot her. And tempting though that was, subtle it wasn't.

'I'm not sure my wife understands me,' Nigel moodily shovelled peanuts into his mouth. 'I wish she'd stop eating and lose some weight. The way she stuffs those chocolates down every night, even after she's had cheese and pudding . . .' Blah blah blah, it went on.

I yawned and sipped my martini. This would be music to my ears, except that it had by now become obvious that Nigel would not be leaving his wife unless his wife left him first. He was quite clearly terrified of her, which was understandable. So I was hardly listening to what he was saying when something, I'm not sure what, made me tune in. 'Tell you what, though,' Nigel was gesturing at the peanuts. 'These are about the only things she doesn't eat. Kill her if she did, they would.'

I spluttered into my martini, but managed to regain my composure. It was vital not to seem too interested. So I pretended to be only half listening as I hung on Nigel's every word while he described Maureen's vulnerability to anaphylactic shock.

I lay in my stateroom that night plotting. By morning, I had come up with the answer. The simplest and most effective thing to do would be to slip a peanut into the base of one of the big white after-dinner chocolates I'd noticed Maureen was particularly fond of guzzling. It was so simple it was like something out of an Agatha Christie novel, which perhaps it was. I'd read enough of them, after all.

The plot went like clockwork. I saved a white chocolate the night before (no mean feat considering how popular they were), and spiked it in my stateroom during the afternoon. 'There you go, my little friend,' I told the tiny piece of peanut as I poked it into the bottom of the chocolate. After dinner, I joined Maureen and Nigel's group. The women all looked at me suspiciously, which was quite right, except it was because I was half their size rather than because they thought I was about to bump one of them off. I pretended to knock over the plate of chocolates and slipped the adulterated one out of my bag as I gathered the rest up from the floor. I handed the plate to Maureen, waited until I saw her fat, shiny, bejewelled fingers hovering over it, then quickly slipped away.

I was glad I missed the crucial moment. According to witnesses it was not a pretty sight. And unfortunately Maureen was not the only victim; the ship's patissier, who had, for Maureen's benefit, been making all his chocolates nut-free, was arrested on manslaughter charges. But these things happen; collateral damage, as they said during the first Gulf War. And it worked, anyway. After a suitable pause, Nigel and I were married and no one, least of all my new husband, suspected a thing.

Unfortunately, as with David, I got fed up with him pretty fast. Nigel didn't even have David's interest in reading; all the books in his nouveau mansions (two in all) were bought by the yard and, when opened, contained blank pages. He evidently didn't expect anyone else he knew to read either. So we divorced and I got another good settlement, but not as good as the first, because Nigel was wilier with money and had hired a lawyer so sharp you could cut yourself just passing him. So, moneywise, I was back to square two again. And as I obviously needed more, it was back to high-seas piracy.

Which is where you find me now. On a cruise of the Baltic states with what seemed like the entire population of Glasgow. Posh end, obviously.

He was loud and red-faced with small, suspicious eyes.

He looked boorish – the sort who might fart in bed and who routinely belittled women. He had an unattractive body – that solid, thick-necked, wide-calfed build of a man predisposed to fat but who keeps it off with sweaty and straining exercise. It was horribly easy to imagine him in a pair of smelly black Lycra cycling shorts.

Nevertheless, I looked at him and knew that he was everything I had been searching for. He was The One. The One I would marry. My husband. And the reason I knew this was because he had the perfect wife.

Well, that and the fact he'd been giving me the glad-eye in the bar as well. We'd even exchanged a few words and I was able to trot out my football knowledge again – he was a Rangers fan. We also, it turned out, had a mutual passion for *Dalziel and Pascoe* – well, he did. I had no idea if it was a department store or a brand of brown sauce, but I played along until I learned it was a TV program; one, moreover, that the ship's DVD library had copies of. Obviously *D & P* fans were a well-established part of the customer base.

But if the conditions were ripe, the wife was even more so. We'd slipped into conversation earlier – side by side on the loungers with aspirational striped cushions that lined the ship's swimming pool. She was, as usual, a whale in human clothes, like those pictures of dogs playing snooker in tailcoats that one of my husbands – I forget which – used to be so fond of. I'd asked her what she liked about being on board and she'd stretched in a wobbly sort of way and said it was the sky at night.

'The sky at night?' I'd echoed. All that suggested to me was Patrick Moore.

'Ooh yes,' crooned Susie, as I'd learnt she was called. 'I'm the romantic type, I am.'

Aren't you just, I thought, taking in the size-million navy swimming costume under her bathrobe. It looked as if it had been constructed in the same place as the boat.

'Not that Fergus understands that, of course,' she sighed, referring to the husband. 'He's not very romantic. He never wanders around the deck alone in the middle of the night like I do.'

It was as if someone had plugged me straight into the National Grid. I forced myself with all my might not to sit bolt upright and yell '*Eureka!*'

But I didn't, of course. I lay back and listened as Susie described how she plodded alone, at two or three in the morning, around the dark, deserted and potentially very dangerous deck. Her favourite place for star-watching was where they stored the buoys at the front of the ship. 'Pitch black and empty. No one can even hear you if you yell,' she smiled at me.

And no one will, I thought, as I smiled back at her.

Anna Johnson

Princess Goes Down

The sun was rising like a sour lemon over the corner of Bleecker and Bowery.

A forty-seven-year-old Latin/jazz percussionist with silver sideburns and a matching tongue had recently planted a baby in my belly and was now leaving for Brazil. I should have been horrified but secretly I was relieved. Serge had a thirteen-year-old son in Bahia and a love history more tangled and stained than a vintage macramé bikini. I think his first ex-wife actually made macramé bikinis in Costa Rica, back in '73.

Thinking about his love life made me think of the first time I opened *One Hundred Years of Solitude* by Gabriel García Márquez in the school library. I had wept, intimidated by the knot of names in the family tree. Those names had made me feel so freckled and bland.

Mesmerised by his storytelling, I now knew the list of Serge's lovers like the names of the saints: Soula, Meera, Indra, Federica, Magdalena, Isabel and one simply known as Sol. And jealously I cherished every special flaw in each one's character. Those tactless details he had bothered to impart to me in bed, with an arched brow of warning. Serge had the most flaws of all but the most rational terms to justify them. Infidelity was his cosmic obligation.

'I am the subject of universal freedom and the servant of pleasure,' he would spout, with one hand on the stem of a wine glass and the other on his balls. Utter bullshit, but very convincing when your hair is tattooed to damp sheets. He put the 'man' into manifesto and I was his pale page inscribed. It was true that the very worst men made good lovers – no, great ones – and out of all of them, it was Serge who convinced me I was occupying an alternate moral universe. A place where babies blossom seasonally like mangoes and men can stay out all night if they came home smelling like beach sand and orchids.

I withstood Serge like a romantic curse and, like all spells, he had his season. When winter was approaching he always found a pretext to spirit off to somewhere sweaty with no telephone. Family trouble. A mural to paint. The need to send blank postcards smudged with blood and pollen. Some ex-wife with a name that ended in aaaaah.

Serge had a way. Or at least he had his way and, now, he was on his way. I was going to miss the smell of him, the dry grain of his tongue on the nape of my neck as he lied to me in Spanish, the late-night beat of drums coming from the foot of the bed and the way he sprinkled red dried herbs on every food from porridge to trout. It would be good to find someone to pay the rent and finally clean the bathtub. I had little other choice.

'Sky Dove,' he would say to me, doing up his thick brown

plaited belt (a gesture he seemed to enact almost hourly), 'Sky Dove, today we paint the kitchen the colour of the roof of a church I once saw in Uruguay. Cielo blue. Heaven kissed. With tiny stars of real gold leaf.' We often got lost in projects like that. Blowing the rent money on plaster or tassels or lengths of chipped tile. The kitchen remained half-painted. We lay down on the flat wooden bed of the table to admire it and fell to making inevitable love. Nameless red spices had been imprinted on my spine as Giancarlo was conceived. Looking up at a half-finished sky.

Three months later I was desolate yet optimistic. Like a stick-on star half peeling and barely adhered. Then, ten minutes before he was due to leave, Serge picked up the ringing phone and handed it straight to me. There was something disappointing and predictable in his gesture. The man who never answered the phone, opened the mail, posed for happy snaps or spoke before midday was leaving.

The receiver slid into my hand like a revolver, a cold crisp voice spoke my name as if it were both a demand and a question.

'Manon?' the voice barked imperiously.

'Yes?'

'My name is Lucy Staunton-Jones. Call me Jonesy, every-one does. I am so terribly relieved you are *there*. I am the senior style writer at *Claude*, and I need a writer to swap lives with me for a month. Major style feature. Uptown/downtown. Working title "Princess Goes Down".' She spoke in point form and I scrambled to make mental notes. 'Cosima Cosgrove Smythe told me that you are the perfect candidate. I need someone very –' she finally paused for breath, 'specific.'

I lifted a bare grainy foot off the kitchen floor and placed it slowly down again to gain balance. Good old Cosima, I thought. She was my only uptown friend, and she had seen fit to present me for the prime experiment: the cultural transplantation specimen number one. I hadn't worked in seventeen weeks so I immediately put one hand on my hip; a phone confidence secret.

'The story is about radical life changes. And clothes,' Lucy continued. 'It's aspirational. Reality. Fashion. Food. Sex. Values. Beauty. The *gamut*.'

I had always hated that word and bit my bottom lip to silence a sigh.

'By shifting down to your loft I'll be doing it *all* the Bohemian way. Your way,' she paused for about ten seconds, then said silkily, 'Cosima says you *are* downtown in a bottle.'

I gazed out the window at a large hunk of unidentified sodden tissue and rag floating in a small pond of scum that was bathed in a pool of light in the gutter directly below my kitchen window. The Bowery looked bruised by centuries of footprints and filth.

'Thank you,' I managed to reply without too much seething resentment.

'Shall we meet?' she asked, as my hand fell away from my hip.

'Yeah, Lucy. I mean, yes.'

Just as I began to scratch down the address of the Pierre Hotel the front door closed as swiftly as my mouth. Serge always knew when to make his silent escape.

When I reached the Pierre Hotel, the carpet underneath my feet felt like the spongy undergrowth in a fierce trip, when the floor beneath you becomes a layer cake with innersprings. The Rotunda Tea Room was up some dainty little steps, so shallow that I tripped going upstairs. An ingrained habit.

Inside, three women sat on discreetly spaced cushioned banquettes. Each one had subtle blond highlights, aggressive Italian handbags and an abstracted, expectant smile. One was flicking her nails impatiently on the tablecloth. That had to be her.

'Manon,' she purred.

For a second the room froze and I wondered what the waiter and the other two honeyed blondes were thinking. Perhaps they saw an emergency psychic, flown in from New Orleans for a pre-marital crisis reading. Or perhaps they thought I was Lucy's mad long-lost sister, the one who had blown her trust fund on cat food, amethysts and opium. It was my own stupid fault for wearing three different shades of vermilion – looking like a human blood clot. Who wears vintage velvet above 14th Street in Manhattan except Lexington Avenue tarot readers? If class is colour-coded then I was 'handwash and lie flat' and Lucy Staunton-Jones was 'dryclean only'. I folded my broken nails into my palms.

Lucy leapt up, embraced me in a cloud of Je Reviens, praised my mottled velvets and began her speech.

'Yes! Bohemia! God, Manon, if you aren't just *It*! Now, this is our brief. Our readers and naturally, *moi*, can ski, speak French and waltz backward in heels but I doubt they've ever ridden the subway or carried a plain plastic shopping bag stamped with I HEART NY.'

I struggled to empathise.

'The true Princess still delegates *everything*, including grating the parmesan onto handmade pasta. In fact,' her voice dropped an octave, 'the real pedigree girls are so smooth they'd delegate blow jobs if they could. Anything sticky or manual,' she half-whispered, 'just doesn't come into it.'

My mind was moving rapidly from truffle pasta to fellatio. I knew I was floating far above my sustainable altitude, and was way, way out of my depth. Lucy pressed on. 'Our readers need someone like you. They need your help to find the *real* underground New York, to live a *richer*, more *textured* life.'

'And to help the precariously thin summer issue?' I interrupted cynically.

'Oh yes, of course, Manon, we all want to see tiaras in the mud! But no, my concept is *waaaayy* more sophisticated than shoving Paris Hilton into an ugly sweatshirt and putting her behind some neon-lit checkout at Walmart. No, what I want is to *Reaalllllly. Live. Like.* You. And to love it.'

'Slumming it?' I asked hoarsely.

'No, Manon, it's an even exchange. You get to live on Fifth Avenue in my apartment for the length of the assignment, with complete access to my dermatologist, my limo man, the manicurist, the personal trainer, the hairdresser, a dog walker, my astrologer, my plastic surgeon, my tanning consultant, my Reiki guy, my dietician and, well, the boyfriend is optional.'

The round hushed room began to spin like a sickly sugar-dusted carousel. I had always suspected journalism to be one of the lost arts of prostitution, but now, it seemed, I was being asked to sell my shabby but resolutely authentic life in exchange for a by-line and the chance to sleep between ironed Frette sheets. New York is nothing if not Faustian.

Lucy's face clouded.

'Don't you want to come uptown?'

'Yes, but –'

'But what, Manon?' She wagged a slyly beckoning index finger complete with a massive topaz cocktail ring above the teacups.

'But,' I cleared my voice, trying to sound ethical and calm, 'how can I be the high priestess of Bohemia if I am seen in public with a small dog?'

'Dogs,' she corrected softly.

'Yes, dogs and doormen and soft wig-like hair and cashmere beige pastels and all that other young Republican drag?'

'Well,' Lucy managed stiffly, 'we need to initiate you too. Ying/Yang. Vintage/Chanel. Visible roots/invisible tan line. We love the contrast and besides, in this particular scenario you have the upper hand, you get to be the Aunty Mame of Nolita, challenging my spoilt little readers to meet the challenge of Bohemian style on a budget, while we get to woo you with a bit of tradition, straighten those seams, polish you up. It's Pygmalion in reverse.'

'Or backward in heels?' I asked meekly.

'Exactly!' Lucy smiled with a flourish and snapped her fingers for the bill.

Heading back downtown on the R train I felt like Persephone plunging back down into Hades to grab a few frocks and re-emerge into the light. And I felt like a terrible traitor.

The plastic bohemian. Bohemian. God, how I had come to detest that word. Smeared on anything with a ruffle. Attributed to people with dark hair and kohled eyes. A euphemism for women who didn't iron. Made seasonally fashionable by the wearing of eggplant-coloured cheesecloth. I felt branded by the word, yet so unworthy of it.

Back in 1917, the artist Baroness von Freytag-Loringhoven had walked through Washington Square in an old fur studded with celluloid kewpie dolls, with her shaven head painted bright vermilion. She fashioned a bra out of severed tin-can lids and was frequently arrested for obscenity. I had never been arrested for anything; was I going to get arrested? That would be too easy. Uptown, *everything* felt like a transgression, except blatant displays of surgery and shopping. No one had their own biological nose. No one seemed to have lint, squints or a definable chronological age. It was troubling. But fascinating.

Packing for Fifth Avenue, I checked the answering machine, the post box and the cool space under my pillow. Nothing. I closed my eyes tight to see if Serge was sending psychic waves from Brazil to his unborn son. But all I could see was the image of his bare brown behind plunging into sea-foam-and-jasmine-scented thighs. Damn, if I was defecting without him.

I tried to concentrate on the job at hand. Lucy was expecting some kind of Edie Sedgewick epiphany upon arriving at the Bowery. God knows she was probably sneaking her housekeeper and a crate of Rigaud candles into the joint, but I had my pride. For theatrical impact I slung some handcuffs and a copy of De Sade's *Justine* on the night table. I washed the kitchen floor with rose oil

and put three bottles of Prosecco, some ricotta and a pun-
net of fresh strawberries in the fridge. Take-out menus,
a large box of incense, some Chelsea art invitations, the
business card for tango night at La Belle Époque dance
hall (where I met Serge), a half-used metro card and my
almond oil-soaked membership card to the Russian baths
on 10th Street were arranged on the kitchen table like a
contrived map of the soul. With a flourish I hung my best
red satin dress from a beam in the centre of the loft. If she
couldn't get laid, frayed or seriously pregnant in that, she
was sub-mediocre, below contempt. A debutante.

I thought about Marianne Faithfull packing for a trip
to Tunisia in 1968, stoned on acid, cruising through cus-
toms with nothing but a silk batik, a conch shell and a
volume of Aubrey Beardsley. With this rock icon in mind
I stuffed two big pink Schiaparelli hatboxes with the following priceless possessions: Serge's Panama hat, a lime
green suspender belt from Fredericks of Hollywood, a
faux leopard raincoat, a lacquer box full of fat 'Anna Sui'
black eyeliner pencils, a tin lunchbox full of morbidly
sexy French perfumes, a volume of *Les Fleurs du Mal*, a
Bonnie and Clyde-style beret, Opium-scented incense,
a framed portrait of Rudolph Valentino, a length of all-
purpose, violet-dyed 1920s lace (windows need lingerie),
some gold dancing shoes, two Captain Beefheart CDs and
one Edith Piaf, a knot of vintage dresses and a fistful of
Victorian mourning jewellery to show them I wasn't just
about kitsch. Oh, my passport, and a chipped floral tea-
cup stuffed with my last three muslin pouches of Russian
Kusmi tea. I was ready to emigrate.

The doorman at 1267 Fifth Avenue grimaced. Attempting sweeping footsteps I adopted the hauteur of a woman with a massive freshwater pearl lodged in her knickers and an ice-cube in her mouth and headed for the lifts.

In the elevator I realised the zip on my Earl Jeans was down and my mascara was smudged. A man with school-boy hair and a cashmere coat bounded into the tight space as the lift doors were closing and almost laughed in my face. Perhaps it was my cocktail hat and veil. Or my quick grab for the zip.

'Going up?' he asked sarcastically.

'Perhaps just this once,' I mock drawled.

On the eighth floor we both got out. His door was across the hall from mine and he smelt like freshly cut green grass or freshly minted C notes, I couldn't decide. Hating him as I fumbled with the keys, I was shocked to hear him speak again.

'Knock,' he said straight-faced, 'if you need some sugar.'

'Or spice?' I mumbled and immediately thought of Serge's strange taste in food.

As autumn dusk fell each evening night uptown Manhattan looked like a fairytale with small children in velvet coats running after nannies and small dogs dotting the street like scatter cushions. After a hard day of being buffed, squeezed, plucked, bleached, teased, tousled and massaged, I would come home to the 'maison' and toss Mouche the Pomeranian and my tatty vermilion velvet coat on the massive sleigh bed. It became a silent ritual to press my achy growing breasts against the tall French windows that overlooked Central Park.

Jonesy and her editors didn't blanch when I told them I was now four months pregnant.

'How Bohemian!' they all chimed in a mix of open pity and awe, and I muddled on. Growing accustomed to Lucy's retinue of minders, buffers and polishers, I began to get the ineffable glow of the professionally groomed. Even my nose seemed to be shrinking. To her credit, Jonesy and her miniature Chow 'Saigon' claimed to love the Bowery.

'*J'adore* Chinatown and all those weird rhinoceros-horn apothecary shops, darling!' she would gush through mouthfuls of glazed doughnuts at Dean and Deluca, some eight blocks north. I didn't care if she cheated. She had braved a tattoo parlour, sucked a bass player's face at The Bowery Ballroom and held a séance at my kitchen table in my best red dress. I was doing time for three dollars a word in her satin cage, but my nights were growing longer.

By week three Serge sent a parcel: a brown paper box containing a terracotta roof tile, a fragment of Brazilian cotton bedding (unstained) and four green mosaic squares. His short handwritten poem said something about a house near the sea shaped like a shell or a woman's bottom. It was hard to translate. On Friday nights I took to retiring early with Mouche curled at the base of the big bed, embalmed in the hushed blandness of luxury. Until my final Friday when it all came down.

I decided that simply being Jonesy made for a pretty dull tale. Standing around at the Metropolitan Opera judging fake bakes from real Positano tans, ogling Hope Atherton's dusted gold leather cowboy boots at the Frick ball, going for endless power strolls around the reservoir with women whose ponytails bounced in tandem, trying to swear less, tolerating the odd night when Jonesy's man took me to 'Swifty's' and made shabby jokes about his pregnant mistress. I began to palpably long for the sound of garbage trucks or bongo drums at the foot of the bed. I wanted the taste of sin on the tip of my tongue: hash cookies and black coffee laced with whisky – or something simple, like a midnight film in an empty cinema.

Slamming the mahogany door behind me, I escaped the Palace and ran, as free and silent as a subway rat. I made for the lifts wearing a mean lipstick pout, Lucy Staunton-Jones's silk raincoat, a pair of vermilion velvet mules, pyjama pants and a black Italian lace bra. I pressed 'down'.

He got in. The man from the apartment across the hall. We had three weeks of meaningless banter to our credit. I liked to pretend he was Spencer Tracey, with abs. Seeing him made me the human *bon mot* machine. I straightened my *soine* and summoned a line. Yet before I could say anything at all, he had pushed me against the wood panelling and thrust his soft, freshly shaven face into my stolen bra. Oh dear.

I could feel his tongue sliding across my clavicle as I lifted one red velvet shoe up onto the button marked 'close'. His fingers traced across my belly with a sensitive sweep and buried themselves in a knot of Italian silk between my legs as his mouth kept pressing with wet explosions on my breasts. Words cannot . . .

Kiss a pregnant woman's nipple at the right moment and she is likely to feel a rush of flame course from the tip of the aureole to the core of her clitoris in about seven seconds. Oxytocin is the name of the hormone that makes this happen, but the man across the hall didn't know that and I didn't bother to explain. I was barely showing.

With my back against the jammed lift door I buried his head between my pale, freckled thighs and dragged one slender red heel onto the shoulder of his cashmere coat. Looking down I saw his sandy clean hair shaking like a wheat field in a gale force or a Ralph Lauren commercial. Looking up I saw the small security camera in the corner of the lift, unblinking as a shark's eye.

Back in Lucy's sleigh bed he finally told me his name, Jasper Jefferson Dodge (the Third), and I told him he was kissing a grand imposter. The 'maison', the pyjamas, the heels and even the dog were on loan – the baby was real, and so were the wild scratch marks I had carved down the side of his sinuous torso.

We had the savage love that only strangers can seize, half remorseful, half mad with the alien freshness of lust. His skin tasted like cinnamon ice-cream. The hair under his arms was flaxen pale. He also had the good sense not to talk too much between mouthfuls of hip-bone, nipple and fingertip.

As the sun came up I felt a familiar swirling in the pit of my stomach. Jasper was sprawled across the crumpled storm of Frette with a pair of sticky apricot silk knickers crushed in his left fist. The phone rang.

It was Serge, the man who never called, and his voice beamed across the sheets like a searchlight.

'Hola, Sky Dove,' he said in a gravel whisper. Down the crackled line he told me he had built a small house on the beach and it would be ready in three weeks, his Daddy casa, his big surprise.

Guilt was not the word for it. Suddenly the room looked

horribly bright. Mouche looked appalled. I put one hand over Jasper's widening mouth and the other on my subtly swollen belly, I hummed a favourite song I only ever sing in bed, then murmured 'Adios' to Serge, and let the phone slip to the silk Aubusson rug.

Six hours later, the Co-op board were calling an emergency meeting. Lucy had been threatened with eviction. *The New York Post* had the video (I had forgotten to tip the doorman) and the entire editorial board at *Claude* wanted *every* detail. My walk of shame from marble lobby to yellow taxi cab was more of a skid. My only vestiges of defiance were Jonesy's massive sunglasses and my bouncing bouffant hair, stiff with product.

Jasper Jefferson-Hodge-Podge-the Third was the upper east side's most coveted bachelor. An old tennis buddy of Gwyneth's, a pin-up on the gym lockers at Spence, and also the hottest ticket in Palm Beach. He was a catch the size of a silver-skinned marlin, girls with names like Paige and Anna-Maria Cristalle jammed Jonesy's answering machine begging to know if he had left his boxers behind. I had my apricot knickers but I didn't have his number.

Lucy was at my old half-broken kitchen table the next morning with three papers, fresh lattes and a box of Krispy Kreme doughnuts. She was smiling like a lottery winner.

'Do you know what a *New York Post* headline is worth?' she bleated. 'Do you know what a headline with the name of *Claude* magazine neatly tucked beneath it is worth?' She was dancing across the dirty floorboards. 'Manon! You are so *money* right now. Darling, you're the slut that saved the day! The naughtiest girl in school! The most notorious bump on the Bowery! This,' she said pointing to the front page that screamed PRINCE CHARMING GETS DOWN, 'is your own personal miraculous conception. ABC want you to have your own show. *Vanity Fair* want the exclusive. Liz Smith won't leave me alone. And *Claude* are talking about a regular style column. Do you know what it all means?'

'One word,' I replied bloodlessly. 'Prostitution. Lucy, I took this job because I was broke, pregnant and elegantly, if perpetually, desperate. I emptied the treasures of my boudoir on your boardroom table. I trailed your tribe of trust-fund brats from Canal Street to Union Square in an attempt to stop them wearing beige slingbacks with tweed trousers. I was imprisoned in your plush but sterile apartment like a beatnik guinea pig, then, out of sheer and inevitable frustration, I blew my passionate, if admittedly tenuous non-existent relationship, on a blond man whose last name rhymes with 'stodge'!'

Lucy bit into a glazed doughnut.

'However,' I added, 'if I take up those offers, I'm going to lose something no amount of money can buy.'

'Which is?'

'Privacy! Glorious anonymity. The freedom to leave the house, un-ironed and invisible. The faceless, gritty, glamour of Bohemian oblivion. I feel more low rent than bloody Courtney Love! Now please leave my charmingly dilapidated loft and let me sit here with my foetus and the remains of my conscience and *think*.'

Lucy took it well. People who are money can have their diva moments. No doubt she was already memorising the grand finale of her story.

I sat on a Moroccan footstool and wept like a fool.

The New York Observer doesn't make it to Bahia – and fortunately, Serge does not read newspapers from this century; by the time he called, I already had his air ticket in the mail.

'Sky Dove,' he growled softly. 'When will you fly to me? I need to place my hand on your belly and sing to Juan Carlito.'

It was such a soothing vision. Fresh mango pulp on our chins and the jealous eyes of all the ex-wives on my rosy belly. The baby was three months away, but already I felt he had been exposed to so many toxins: TV producers, newspaper gossip, pedigree dog hair, Howard Stern saying my name in the same breath as Paris Hilton. I choked for a reply.

'Serge, I am not Brazilian. I burn like a sausage in the sun. I am not Holly Go-Lightly, I swear like a bush pig and can barely walk in heels. In the course of two months I've been up and down and over and out . . . And . . . and . . . I just don't know the real turtle soup from the mock any more!' I was wailing now, and I knew I had lost him. Our relationship was never that verbal. I promised to send him a photo of my belly, and a telegram in one week. As I hung up the phone the doorbell rang. It was Jasper in a cashmere polo shirt, grasping a massive bouquet of Lincoln roses. Vermilion. My personal *bête noir*.

'Manon!' He leaned through the doorframe like a schoolboy and reached for the sash on my kimono. 'I am not ashamed of anything! The Co-op kicked me out and I never felt more free. I came here to thank you for taking me down. Downtown, that is.'

'You're moving?'

'Yes. I am looking for a space in Tribeca. I need air. I need life. I think I need you.'

Golden, and suddenly a touch tarnished, Jasper Jefferson Dodge seemed exalted, invigorated by danger and scandal, and the physical closeness of a naked, pear-shaped, tear-stained woman in a half-open kimono.

I had never seen anything weirder in my life: a grown man with so little life experience. He spoke in a cool rush of clipped confessions. He was thirty-three had never been to the Bowery. Never tongue raped a pregnant woman in an elevator. Never really loved a brunette with her own biological nose. Never listened to Muddy Waters. Never had to explain himself to his mother or face the censure of people as gilded as himself. The more he grinned like an escaped convict, the more caged I felt. Freedom seemed so new to him, such a novelty. It was something he simply hadn't considered. Looking at him, it was easy to imagine the luxury he could graft onto my sepia-toned existence: a subscription to the opera, a suitcase of French chiffon maternity dresses, summers in Capri, a loft in Tribeca, some semblance of fidelity and a latte machine from Rome. Perhaps even, given time, a small turquoise box from Tiffany with a pristine white satin ribbon. Convention in the palm of my hand.

I ran to fling open the windows. God, how easily I could have been corrupted. Thank God I still loved the unfinished sky painted on the kitchen wall – it never looked more vast than in that moment. The clouds looked like question marks. My favourite shape in the universe.

I left Jasper facing the window, as he watched the light

drain from the sky over Bleecker and Bowery. I made another pot of coffee, smoothed the lacy tablecloth with the flat of my hand, put the vermilion roses in an old cut-glass vase and put on Edith Piaf. Very, very loud.

Belinda Jones

One Mother of a Hangover

I don't know how often you get drunk with your mother but last night was a first for me. I wouldn't say we were three sheets to the wind but we were at least two and a pillowcase.

The occasion was her sixtieth birthday and though I expected tears, I didn't expect them to be great chugging, puffy-eyed, snotty-nosed affairs. I also didn't expect them to be mine.

Originally we'd planned for her to escape the gusty chills of cliffside Devon and enjoy a week of winter sun at my pad in Los Angeles but as her arrival approached it dawned on me that, with the possible exception of Copacabana beach in Brazil, there could be no worse place on earth to embrace becoming a senior citizen. It's no myth that LA is overrun with flawless twentysomethings gussied to the max even at the mall just in case today is the day they get discovered; and what kind of message would it send her that everyone over forty is botoxed to robotic blankness and fifty-pluses look like they're pushing their faces through a sheet of cellophane? Hardly the poster city for growing old gracefully. I decided there must be a neighbouring locale that could offer an OAP a little TLC and consulted my road atlas . . . We'd already exhausted the coastal communities on previous visits and I wasn't sure either of us were street-savvy enough for Compton. And then I spied Palm Springs.

I'd only visited fleetingly a few years back but I recalled it being rife with liver-spotted wrinklies and boutiques selling those sequinned baseball hats favoured by eccentrics vrooming around on motorised wheelchairs. Surely my mum would feel like a young, sleek gazelle by comparison? I checked the logistics – just two hours' drive, easily navigable (bomb along the 10 freeway, then wiggle a bit on the 111) and a whole ten degrees hotter than Hollywood – we had a winner!

As we pelted along the freeway ignoring the lure of the outlet stores I casually peppered my conversation with mentions of Marcus. It was such a novelty for me to have a boyfriend, I couldn't help but show off a little. Now she could yap about Greg all she liked and I wouldn't feel left-out and unloved like I'd always done before. (Greg is mum's boyfriend of ten years. I definitely consider it a blessing that I've been out of the country for the majority of their relationship because that man gets on my very last nerve – he always hums when I talk as if to say, 'Not interested in anything you have to say! You don't exist! Na-na-na!' And though he's sickenly attentive to my mum, he's never once asked about my video production company or what it's like to live in a country without Marmite. I pretend to be interested in his world, couldn't he at least extend the same courtesy to me?) So there I was, primed to match her slushy anecdote for slushy anecdote but she just didn't give me the opportunity. Just once I wanted to be able to say, '*Oh I know, Marcus does that!*' But no . . .

As we joined the privileged few in the car pool lane I wondered if maybe she was uncomfortable with the fact that I've finally found myself a man. I've heard that those closest to you are often resistant to change, even when it's for the best. People get so used to you being one way – in my case pitifully single – that when you can no longer be labelled as such they are almost at a loss for how to view you. There certainly seemed to be an unfamiliar awkward-ness, as if she didn't quite know how to respond to me as half of a couple. Not that we'd ever talked much about relationships prior to this, mostly because I'm never in one. I told myself it could just be jet lag making her seem distant and vague. Or maybe she was a little uneasy at the prospect of saying farewell to her fifties? That was probably it.

'Look ma, we're nearly there – see the wind turbines?' I tried to bring her glazed expression into focus by pointing out row upon row of rotating white blades on mile-high poles.

'We've got those on Dartmoor now,' she observed as I wrestled to steady the car against the sudden buffeting breeze. 'But the locals say they ruin the aesthetics of the landscape and want them removed.'

I understand their concern but to me they are so starkly graceful they actually enhance the view, at least set against this desert mountain range.

'So, this is Palm Springs.' Mum chivvied herself into a state of interest as we merged onto the main drag of Palm Canyon Drive. 'I've heard of it like I've heard of Key West but I don't really know anything about it. What's it most famous for?'

I censored my 'Rich retirees!' response and instead said, 'Let me see – Sonny Bono was once mayor, U2 shot their Joshua Tree video here and Bob Hope, Howard Keel and Frank Sinatra were all former residents. Basically it's considered a chi-chi resort oasis, though I'd say its heyday was in the fifties . . .'

Right on cue, we're cruised by a silver-finned convertible Imperial and a cream '56 Chevy with a gleaming copper dashboard.

'I feel like we're in *Grease*!' she giggles, looking if not like a teenager, at the very least like Olivia Newton-John playing one.

So far, so good!

We continued on past innumerable restaurants offering patio dining and a gift shop selling comical granny statuettes including one draw-dropper quipping 'You're never too old for a booty call!' and then we came to a halt at the lights. There a man shuffled in front of us leaning heavily on his walker and breathing wheezily through a nose clip of plastic tubing which dangled for yards about his person. I joked that this was Palm Springs' version of iPod wires but judging from the mortified look on my mum's face I'd gone too far, inadvertently scaring her with what might lie ahead for her. Mercifully our hotel was definitely more hip than hip-replacement – The Viceroy bills itself as 'Dramatic glamour under the sun' and the lobby alone provided a visual spritzing with its striking black-and-white décor zapped with acid yellow accents. I snuck a look back at my mother reclining on the pinstripe chaise while I checked in and was delighted to see her eyes widen as she took in the zebra-skin rug on the marble floor, the lacquered white of the bar beyond and the skinny plaster greyhounds guarding each balcony.

Minutes later we were gasping in unison as we stepped into the living room of Suite 304: wall-to-wall striped carpet in ridges of charcoal and ivory, a chequered sofa you could stretch out on in stilts, white walls stencilled with black panels, a vast yellow enamel chandelier, a white gloss urn, a laminated TV cabinet, a wall of mirrors . . .

Mum sat in one of the high-backed canary-yellow Regency chairs and told me she felt like Alice in Wonderland.

I felt triumphant! Alice was, what, twelve? That was forty-eight years lopped off and we hadn't even unpacked yet!

Having admired the theatrical curtains framing the bath and twisted our necks at the off-kilter bedroom (ornate ceiling rose at the head of the bed and black-and-white potato-print wallpaper on the ceiling), we had planned to while away the afternoon lolling beside one of the three pools before getting dollied up for a night on the town. But then it started to rain.

'Oh no!' We were both appalled. There's something about rain and our family – it just seems so conducive to tears. I chose to distract her with her birthday card. (Well, the clock had just struck four, which meant it was midnight in England.)

'Happy sixtieth, Ma! You're finally grown-up!' I teased as I handed her the hot-pink envelope.

'That I am,' she said, sounding serious for a second before perking up as she read the words I'd transcribed from a recent Round Robin email and surrounded in glitter.

'Life should not be a journey to the grave with the intention of arriving safely in an attractive and well-preserved body but rather to skid in sideways, margarita in one hand, chocolate in the other, body thoroughly used up, totally worn out and screaming "WOO HOO! – What a Ride!"'

She gave me a big hug and whooped, 'The cocktails are on me!'

Now that was unexpected. Not her offer to pay but her eagerness to imbibe before dark. I'd only ever seen my mum a teeny bit tipsy at Christmas, but there she was downing a Frozen Bikini so fast she was in danger of getting brain freeze. I told myself this was celebratory abandon but as her second empty glass hit the mirrored surface of the side table I realised it was Dutch courage:

'I've left Greg,' she blurted, wiping a stray dribble of peach vodka from her chin.

'*What?*' I balked. 'When?'

'Six weeks ago. Six weeks today in fact. Let's have another drink!'

I was totally thrown: I'd wanted to match her in the man department, not better her. Suddenly I felt extremely unbalanced.

'Why didn't you tell me before?' I wavered uncertainly as she reached for the cocktail menu.

'I didn't want you worrying about me coping on my own, and besides you were so happy with Marcus, no one wants to hear of a breakup when you're in the honeymoon period of a new relationship.'

The honeymoon period? I wanted to query that senti-ment straight off but I was distracted by further questions.

'Why? What happened?'

'Oh, you know how relationships are . . .'

'Not really,' I confessed. 'It seems awfully out-of-the-blue. When did you realise it was going wrong?'

'About four years ago.'

'*Four years?*' I squawked. 'You've been miserable for four years?' Amidst the shock I also felt shame – I couldn't believe I didn't even notice anything was wrong. 'Why didn't you say something before?' I complained.

'Well, you've never liked him, I didn't think you'd want to hear it.'

'Are you kidding? I would have loved to have heard all the bad stuff!'

She laughed and took my hand. 'It's okay. It's all in the past now.'

She was clearly keen to proceed with dialling room serv-ice but I wasn't finding it so easy to move on. 'So what was it specifically?' I persisted.

She set down the phone and sighed. 'You really want to know?'

I nodded.

'Where to begin? The constant nit-picking and critiqu-ing he tried to pass off as friendly teasing. The running commentary on everything I ate, his constant reminding that he didn't want 'a fat woman on his arm'. The way his frustrations at his own shortcomings spilled over into impatience with me. His unpredictable mood changes. How off-hand he was to my friends. I think he wanted them to feel unwelcome so they'd stop visiting. And they did. I'd visit them but then he'd ask me so many questions it felt like an interrogation . . .'

As she spoke all I could think was: *Marcus does that. And that. And that.*

The horrible sinking feeling got worse as I listened to her saying how often she felt judged or controlled or simply wrong; and a small, long-ignored voice inside me said, 'That's just how I feel.'

'But enough of my wallowing!' she jumped to her feet. 'I think we may as well order dinner while we're at it. I know we said we'd paint the town scarlet but it's bucketing out there. Wouldn't it be cosier if we had a nice girls' night in?'

I was so dazed listening to her place the order for monkfish with picoline olive, saffron seafood risotto with manchego cheese and a dessert of Valrhona chocolate soufflé (whatever would Greg say?!) that when my phone rang I answered without thinking.

'Baby?'

Oh no. I closed my eyes in dismay. It was Marcus.

'I've been waiting for your call.' He sounded instantly petulant. 'You said you were going to ring to let me know you arrived safely.'

'Sorry about that. Mum and I got chatting and—' I curbed what was about to become a rambling apology. 'We are here and we are safe.'

'Do you miss me?'

'Yes, of course,' I replied, checking myself too late. Did I even have a say in what I felt any more or was I merely programmed to respond in the appropriate way?

'You know if I left now I could be there in time to join you for dinner.'

'Actually we've already ordered something, we didn't stop for lunch, so –'

'You realise your mum will probably be asleep by 7 p.m. after that long flight. What will you do then?'

Was he worried I wouldn't be able to amuse myself, or worried I'd go out and pick myself up a sugar grand-daddy?

'I'll be fine,' I told him.

'Okay, well then in that case I'll probably go out with Grant.'

He waited for my reaction but I gave none.

'I don't know though, you know he's on a bit of a pick-up binge at the moment, ever since he broke up with Carly. He'll probably want to go to the Saddle Ranch . . .'

Was this a threat of some kind? Was he trying to provoke me with the prospect of loose women astride a mechanical bull? For some reason I simply didn't care.

'Well, you have fun! Don't you go leading him astray!'

'A-all right,' he faltered. 'Well, call me before you go to sleep. Let me know everything is okay.'

'Right.' I wanted to say 'I'll let you know if the air con is too cold or the water is too hot or the towels are too rough or the bed is too firm or the alarm is too loud so you can make it all right for me cos I'm so helpless and incapable myself'. But I didn't.

'Okay baby, I love you.'

'Speak to you later!' I tried to hurry my goodbye out but he was too swift, whining 'Aren't you going to say you love me too?'

I squirmed inside and out. I'd parroted the phrase enough times, why was it sticking in my throat now? Was it because I didn't want my mother to hear me lying?

'Sorry, the reception isn't good in here, let me try out outside . . .' I slid open the patio door and stepped onto the terrace. 'That's better,' I faked as my insides contorted. 'I love you!'

'I love you more!'

I wasn't going to argue with that. As I closed the phone I came to the sick realisation that every conversation with Marcus left me feeling peeved or patronised or simply awry in some way. Was I really so desperate to have a boyfriend that I'd convinced myself I was happy with him? For a few minutes I stood and watched the rain. And a couple braving the downpour to get to the jacuzzi. They were laughing as they sank into the steaming water and I thought, *I don't remember the last time I laughed with Marcus.* I knew if he was here now he'd be too concerned about the bacteria in the bubbles or getting concussion from a falling grapefruit off the overhanging tree to enjoy himself.

I returned to the room to find my mother holding up two bottles of wine – a Lapis Luna chardonnay for me and a Dynamite merlot for her. 'Well, a glass wasn't going to be enough . . .' She patted the sofa cushion next to her. 'Are you all right, darling?' she asked as she poured, then tutted: 'This is exactly why I didn't tell you before. I knew you'd get upset . . .'

'It's not just that—'

Again my phone rang.

What now? I was ready to cut the power but the display read Out of Area and I was waiting for a business call from New York, so I answered.

'Hello?'

'Charlotte?'

'*Oh my God, it's Greg!*' I mouthed frantically at my mum.

It was very clear from her responding mime that there was no way she was going to talk to him.

'Um, she's busy right now Greg, can I take a message?' What is it about being English that makes you be polite long after it's ceased to be necessary?

'I just wanted to wish her a happy birthday—'

'Okay, lovely, will do.'

'Look, just put her on.'

'What?'

'I know you girls are up to your usual conspiracy shit,' he spat. 'Put Anna on the phone now.'

He had me reeling, amazed that he thought bullying would be an effective tactic. 'No!' I scoffed – the cheek of the man!

'Charlotte!' he growled.

'*Grrreg!*' I mirrored his threatening tone.

My mother started to look vexed. I may not be able to be strong for myself but I can be for her.

'Look,' I began before he could say another word. 'My mother has already said everything to you that needs to be said. Now she's here with me. Please respect our time together.' I took a breath. 'And don't call her again. Ever.'

With that I clicked the phone closed.

'Oh my God, you were brilliant!' Mum leapt to her feet, spinning me around in a giddy dance.

I couldn't believe it either. Where did that steel come from? For the past six months I'd been feeling so weak and ineffectual . . .

'Bloody idiot's been badgering me every five minutes, let's see if you did the trick and I can finally get some peace!'

The pair of us sat down and stared at the little silver Sony Eriksson. Two women, desperate for the phone not to ring. Now there's a turnaround.

'Oh, put the telly on!' Mum finally broke the silence. 'Let's think about something else until the food arrives!'

I snuggled beside her as we watched Oscar-winner Jamie Foxx being quizzed about his bachelor status, the interviewer implying that perhaps at thirty-seven he should be settling down.

'You are currently single, are you not?'

He smiled, didn't look in the least bit concerned or apologetic and whispered, *'Single deluxe!'*

Was that a pang of envy I just experienced?

'I don't think he's going to ring,' I ventured as my mum began to channel-hop.

'Neither do I,' she confirmed happily.

'Ma, will you do the same for me?' I scrabbled up onto my haunches and turned to face her. 'Will you tell Marcus I don't want to speak to him again? *Ever!*'

'What?' she looked stunned.

'Please!'

'What's going on? I thought you were happy?'

'I was just pretending. I mean I've tried so hard but it just doesn't feel right. Hearing you talk about Greg . . . I don't want to wait another God knows how many years before I get the chance to escape!'

'Escape? Is it that bad?'

I nodded.

'Then you should definitely talk to him.'

'I can't!' I wailed. 'I've tried so many times . . .' Suddenly I'm blubbering and I can't seem to stop. My body is shuddering as the tears of frustration and disappointment and sadness flood out of me.

'Oh, Charlotte darling, why didn't you tell me this is how you were feeling?'

I heaved a juddery sigh. 'Same reason as you, I suppose – I didn't want you to worry. Didn't want you thinking I wasn't capable of having a relationship.' I oozed and sniffed some more. 'When I first told you about Marcus you sounded so relieved that I finally had someone of my own . . .'

'Oh, gosh, if there's one thing looking sixty in the eye has taught me, it's that life's too short to waste a single heartbeat on the wrong man.' She takes my chin in her palm. 'If I had a single birthday wish it would be that you don't have to wait till you're claiming your pension to get wise to that fact.'

'I just don't want to be thirty-five and single again!' My fears elbowed their way to the fore.

'Try being single at sixty!' my mother countered.

'Actually, in this town I think you've got the edge!'

My mother laughed. 'You could be right there!'

I sighed again. 'Coming here has made me realise Marcus is not a man I want to grow old with.'

'Then don't put it off any longer.'

As mum slid the phone over to me I experienced a surge nerves. 'Can't you do it for me, please?' I implored her.

'He's got to hear it from you first or he'll never accept it.'

'What if you pretended to be me?' I blustered, grasping as straws. 'Everyone says we sound so alike on the phone . . .'

I looked pleadingly into her eyes until she succumbed with a brow-beaten sigh. 'What's his number?'

I was shaking as I waited for him to pick up. I couldn't believe the time had finally come, that within minutes I might actually be free!

'Marcus?' My mum held the phone so I could hear.

'Baby! Heyyy, I knew you'd call. Are you feeling a little needy? Are you missing your boy?' His voice was so condescending, almost like he was willing me to be weak and dependent.

'Listen,' my mum began. But before she could get to word two I grabbed the phone.

'Marcus, it's Charlotte,' I tried to stop my voice from quavering as I blurted, 'I'm sorry to have to do this on the phone but I no longer want to be in a relationship with you.'

There, I said it! I didn't think I had it in me but I did it anyway!

First there was incredulity. Then anger. Then begging.

'I don't want to lose you!' he whimpered.

'I don't want to lose me either, that's why I have to do this.' I stood strong.

Then came the abuse, which just confirmed my decision. And then tears, which came too late. And then the calm after the storm . . .

The next morning, after my first full night's sleep in months, we awoke to blinding sunshine. The promise of a poolside breakfast had me pogo-ing out of bed and into the shower, where I tried to soap my armpits with a bar of white chocolate. Turns out ma had been getting up to drunken mischief after I'd conked out, switching the toiletries for items from the minibar. Ahhh, so the reason the shampoo wasn't frothing was that it was in fact vodka.

'If you'd used beer that actually might have done my hair some good!' I yelled from the tub.

'I was going to swap the crème de menthe and the mouthwash but I don't suppose anyone would notice the difference!' She stuck her head around the door. 'You nearly ready? I'm starving!'

You've got to love a hotel that sneaks a spirit onto the breakfast menu – there can be no more discreet and yet decadent a way to garner a little 'hair of the dog' for your hangover than ordering a platter of buttermilk pancakes soaked in raspberry cognac. I tucked in with vigour – all this time I was so dreading finishing with Marcus but I think I must have used up all my anxiety prior to doing the deed. Now I just feel relieved. Detoxified even. There's something about telling the truth that is so purifying. Not to mention rejuvenating – Mum looks easily ten years younger as she stretches out on one of the yellow-and-white candy-striped sunloungers set with matching towel scrolls.

I recline beside her, counting three types of palm tree around us – one spindly skyscraper resembling one of those dusters with extendable handles, one twelve-footer with what looks like a soft green scarf wound around its giraffe-like neck and another stumpier variety with ruffs of brown bark. All set against a forever blue of sky. I inhale deeply and smile to myself. I mean, look at us – the pool is all ours. We've got no schedule to meet and only ourselves to please and we're sipping on crushed ice doused with citrus and mint freshly plucked from the hotel gardens.

Now if this ain't the definition of single deluxe I don't know what is!

Nicola Kraus & Emma McLaughlin

Cinderella Gets a Brazilian

Without fail, the Big Night Out only seems to present itself when you have insane deadlines, have not eaten, drunk anything uncaffeinated, showered, exhaled, or even peed in minimally forty-eight hours. When you are living on fumes until you can collapse (coat still on and remote in hand) with a big 'whumph' in your long-neglected apartment. When you have been getting from minute to pressure-filled minute fantasising about flannel pyjamas and Chinese take-out, not about shivering atop three-inch heels by a drafty window in a jam-packed bar. When there is not so much as an ounce of small talk to be had from your little, tuckered-out self.

When you are just plain shot to shit.

As your boss screams for you and the copy machine simultaneously implodes, it is, of course, at this exact moment that your perkiest friend, whose perfectly relaxing job has got her 'positively bored to sobs', calls to remind you about so-and-so's mid-week cocktails. While a billowing cloud of errant toner transforms you into a chimney sweep, Perky wants to know if you're wearing your hair up, if you want to 'duck out' early and get matching pedicures, if you are as b-o-r-e-d as she is. And you are overcome in a lightning flash of pure, murderous rage. You want to reach through the phone and drag Perky all the way through the wire, morph her into your sweaty, toner-stained, hunched-over-the-broken-copy-machine self and scream, 'WHAT?!'

Instead, tears welling, you attempt to extricate yourself gracefully. 'I have to go to the bathroom. I'm thirsty. My feet hurt. My contacts are rolling back into my brain.'

But Perky knows exactly how to get you, knows it is merely a matter of five little words, knows not to waste time dillydallying when she is armed with a spinning gyroscope.

'____ said he'd stop by,' she mentions casually.

BLANK!!!!

As in long-hot-romantic-Labor-Day-weekend-at-Perky's-summer share Blank?

As in 'I'll-call-you-before-your-tan-fades' Blank?

As in has-not-been-at-a-single-party-since and may-have-joined-the-witness-protection-program Blank?!

And you are back. You are in. Fuck the copy machine. Fuck the deadline. Fuck even being employed. You have a mission! NASA has called in your number! The wagons must be circled. Pronto.

Having drawn you wholly under her power, she proceeds to play dumb. 'Yeah, I heard he was stopping by around some dinner thing.'

'Around? What does 'around' mean?! Before?! After?!' You grip the phone, hover over the copier, ready to spring, awaiting the specifics.

'I don't know! *Coooommme ooonnn,* let's sneak out for margaritas! I'm *dying* for a drink, my day has been *soooo* tediously *b-o-r-i –*'

But you are flying out onto the street, your purse still open, a battle plan forming in your head as you elbow your way through tourists and Salvation Army Santas. You look at your watch and try to calculate how to get the biggest grooming bang from your minimal time buck. Because, let's face it, you could be crossing paths with him in less than two hours. Less than two hours to stand before him and look so fucking great that all of New York will be stopped in their fucking tracks.

You get yourself to a nail salon and are momentarily paralysed in front of their price list by the cosmic implications of which services to select. Option A: The He's Just Going To See Me For Five Minutes And Regret His Entire Existence Package – above the neckline, below the ankle (manicure, pedicure, and upper-lip wax). Or Option B: The He's So Overcome By My Smooth Upper Lip That We Have Mad Passionate Almost And I Leave Him At the Height Of It All Regretting His Entire Existence Package (manicure, pedicure, wax everything). Virgin. Whore. Virgin. Whore.

'Wax me! Wax me NOW!'

Your entire body is chafing and violated, screaming against your winter woollen wear, you still haven't eaten, had a glass of water or peed since, like, two days ago. Only sixty minutes to go and there is still dirty hair to contend with, make-up, and the matter of wardrobe. Think, think, think. What to wear to make someone regret his entire existence in the dead of December?

Halfway across Fifth Avenue you take a full moment to look up at the cold evening sky and scowl angrily, like Moses, up at a God who has waited to present you with this opportunity in entirely the wrong season. You waste a good ten minutes on a crowded subway car lost in a nostalgic haze over your summer wardrobe: sexy little sundresses, bare tank tops, strappy sandals. All of which positively scream, '*Trying!*' in the dead of December.

'Fuck.' You startle the businessman hogging the seat beneath you, *The Financial Times* spread to its full width between his relaxed thighs, his stubby legs outstretched. You hate him because it's a pretty safe bet that he has not just waxed his entire body, nor does he have a five-minute window in an eight-hour evening to make someone regret his entire existence. Fucking seated asshole.

Then you are home. You bounce through the apartment on one foot while pulling off your boots. You reach your closet. Hateful, winter woollen, frumpy closet that it is. You stare each other down. Humph.

'By the time I return from my shower I fully expect you to have found at least one borderline fabulous suggestion.' It shrugs.

You are naked in the bathroom, telling your skin to just get over it already, everybody gets waxed, and it needs to stop having a pity party and begging you for aloe. You are not doing aloe tonight. Better yet – how about lemon shower gel, astringent and a brief salt scrub?! It's an S&M fest with you and your skin while you both wrestle in the bathroom to become a supermodel.

You pant back to your closet with a half an hour on the clock, hair wrapped tightly in a towel. You take a deep Tantric breath, say a quick prayer to the long-neglected laundry gods, open your lingerie drawer and let out a sigh of relief as you spot The Bra. The one that practically comes with its own boobs. Then you just need the angora sweater with the deep V that shows the cleavage, which goes perfectly with the red pants. A choir of angels clears its throat – but the red pants are at the cleaners – #%&!! – which leads to the leather skirt, which means the boots, which need to be polished and THERE IS NO FUCKING TIME FOR THAT. So back to the sweater – you consider for a nano-second forgoing clothes from the waist down because that would definitely accomplish the mission. And then, as the last garments fly over your head and onto the coverlet, you remember the black evening pants you got in the Christmas sales last year. And you dig, sweating, on all fours through the back of your dark, dusty, hateful closet until you find them, flattened in their shopping bag between the hamper and the wall.

And then you are in the shower again and your skin just CANNOT BELIEVE that you won't even leave it alone for just one single minute!

Less than sixteen minutes to go, in which ensues a cloud of perfume, a WWF match with your stockings, a make-up job timed for speed, and an attempt to blow-dry your hair by the open oven door to shave off valuable minutes.

And it all comes to a screeching halt on the street below, which has suddenly emptied of its holiday traffic and is tra-versed by a lone delivery man pedalling slowly on his bicycle against the snow. You contemplate throwing his burritos to the sidewalk and leaping in his basket. But he cycles on, oblivious to your desperation. You run in your three-inch heels to the nearest avenue, hopping up and down in oncoming traffic for an empty taxi. Or a clean pickup truck.

A sweet, merciful cab finally pulls up and a guy in a camel-hair coat opens the back door. 'Hey, you goin' uptown?' he asks.

You hop right in, despite the fact that he could be a well-dressed serial killer, because risking death while in pursuit of getting-someone-to-regret-his-entire-existence is noble.

'You looked pretty desperate out there . . .' He heh-hehs, taking advantage of a sharp turn to sidle closer and engage in a bit of holiday cheer: 'Man, red's your colour' or the more strategic 'I bet your boyfriend loves you in red' or, forgoing the niceties, a classic, yet elegant 'Blow me, red girl'.

'Well, umm . . . ,' you reach, 'since I'm a cop I have to wear blue for work and I'm really an autumn, but mostly I'm just a cop. With a gun. A cop with a gun.'

Then he presses even closer and you are beyond grateful to be let out within even a mile of your destination. You hobble like a madwoman through snow-lined streets, any sensation in your feet slowly ebbing as throbbing gives way to tingling gives way to numbness, and, quite possibly, frostbite.

Miraculously, at exactly eight o'clock, you reach the overcrowded apartment. Heart pounding from adrenalin and four flights of stairs, you breathlessly seek out Perky, who you find in the kitchen, rooting through the hostess's cabinets in search of fat-free hot chocolate. You lock her in your tractor beams for The Shakedown.

'Yick! You are so totally sweaty . . .'

'Am I [wheeze] late? Is he [wheeze] here?' Deep breath, take her firmly by her shoulders, 'TELL ME.'

She confesses and tells you you're a 'weirdo'.

You win! You have not missed him! He's ON HIS WAY. The choir of angels belts it out for all they're worth.

Now it's just a matter of waiting, an hour, or two, or six. You get a drink and strategically manoeuvre towards the nuts. Every time the buzzer rings you gulp. Every time the crowd parts you smile. You make hours of agonising chitchat with guests who have had way too much to drink and are way, way too rested.

Disgustingly rested.

Your focus wavers as anecdotes about golf-club memberships and restaurant openings blur. Of course, in your current state, even an actual Beatles reunion concert by the carrot sticks could not hold your attention. Every twenty minutes your adrenalin lags so dangerously low that it hurts to speak, to smile. You take the cheese into the bathroom. Shaky and nauseous with exhaustion, you still haven't had any water, eaten a vegetable or closed your eyes.

'*You* got a promotion? Sorry, that, uh, didn't come out how I meant it.' You are not making friends. An invitation to the July Fourth barbecue is looking more and more like a long shot.

And then it's 1:15. Perky went home. Promotion went home. Barbecue went home. It's down to you and the hostess. In her pyjamas. You have helped clean up to the point of reorganising her spice rack. She is looking at you oddly as she leaves to brush her teeth. You now must hit on her or there will be no other way to explain your behaviour.

You gather your coat where she has left it, not so subtly, by the front door, and let yourself out. Defeated.

You were prepared for every alternative – he could have arrived with a model, a gay lover or a tonsure and you'd have handled it with aplomb, but *this*?! This anticlimactic nothing? Inconceivable!

What kind of a person says he's going to go to a party and then just *doesn't show up*?! That is so like him!

You stand immobilised in the stairwell.

People buy drinks and food based on a number and one can't just say that one's going to attend a party and then just not show up!

You gingerly traverse the icy steps of the brownstone, pausing momentarily to consider a new option.

He doesn't exist!

Which would be so like him just to appear randomly on the earth one weekend a year to brush people's hair off their faces, massage suntan lotion on their backs, whisper unsolicited promises about the future, and then just not call any of them before their tans fade!

'MY TAN HAS FADED!!!'

Dejected, you hail a taxi and head back to your apartment, which looks like an eighties hair band used it as a dressing room. You pull your mangled, frozen feet gingerly out of your salt-stained shoes, peel off your clothes and stand under the hot shower, letting the make-up and styling cream swirl down the drain with your exalted expectations.

You pull on your favourite pyjamas: worn sweatpants, bunny T-shirt, and your dad's old wool socks. Too wound up for bed, you sit down on the floor and slump back against the base of the couch, all adrenalin spent.

And then you are hungry. Oh, man, hungry like a teen-age boy in spring training. You want eggplant parmigiana, a loaf of bread, pie and a glass of whole milk. Maybe a rib-eye steak. You crawl to the fridge. Seltzer, a yoghurt and one furry bagel.

You grab your keys and head down to the deli. You order a roast-beef sandwich and open a bag of potato chips while you're waiting. You're peering into the ice-cream case, your mouth full, when a familiar voice behind you requests a pack of Marlboros.

This is when you're supposed to look up, softy lit by the brightly coloured frozen dairy, glowing in your natural state of beauty, and be struck by how pointless it was to pour yourself into a socially supported dominatrix outfit. By what a bigger person you are. By the revelation that this scruffy, sexy smoker from your past is just another human being with whom you are fully at peace.

But the moment you catch his eye it's that same jolt through your spine of months past. And he smiles lopsid-edly in that way he does, as if he has just remembered the idea of you and likes it. He gives you a 'Hey' and then reaches over to tuck your hair behind your ear. And you are ready to throw down with him right then and there in front of the deli guy. Ready to sacrifice any amount of sleep, hydration, comfort, financial solvency, for one more fuck-ing kiss. And then, as he is asking for your number – the one that 'accidentally got washed' in his jeans pocket by some idiotic roommate – his gaze flickers behind you and you follow it. Straight to the flash of long blond hair lean-ing impatiently from a cab window outside.

And you give him your number without flinching.

Taking it directly from the Heimlich Manoeuvre hotline on the poster behind him.

With a 'cool', he is gone. And maybe someday, if his roommate stays away from his wash, he will call for you and find out exactly how to make someone throw up.

WHICH IS PRETTY GODDAMN CLOSE TO MAD PASSIONATE ALMOST! And even closer to making him regret HIS ENTIRE EXISTENCE! Damn close! And you'll take it! You are running a victory lap around the bagel bin, past the produce, grabbing your roast beef on the way out the door.

And you couldn't have planned it better if you tried.

You are Perseus gloriously gripping the head of Medusa.

You are Alexis with Crystal knocked out cold at your feet.

You are exhausted.

Melanie La'Brooy

Boys' Night Out

Will shook his head in bewilderment for the third time. 'I dunno. I give up. How does it work, Ed?'

'Don't look at me,' Ed said in alarm, unable to tear his gaze away from the phenomenon. 'I don't bloody know.'

'But you're a *physicist*. I thought you understood the laws of nature and the universe.'

'This has nothing to do with universal laws. It's completely unnatural. It's way out of my area of expertise. Why don't you ask Johnno? He's the engineer.'

Hearing his name, Johnno turned and grinned cheerfully at them.

'Oi, Johnno! How does she do it? Are they motorised?'

'Wouldn't have a clue. But give up trying to work it out. Sometimes, my friends, you just have to accept the inexplicable.'

The entire table of men sat entranced, staring at the spectacle of the stripper in front of them. Her routine was choreographed to perfection, her face giving no hint of the anomaly occurring below. Because (despite the laws of nature which dictated that it was an impossibility, a complete lack of motorisation and the absence of contortionist movement) the miracle was irrefutable.

The tassel affixed to each of her breasts was circumscribing perfect circles in completely opposing directions.

There was no denying that the beer was very good. It was cold, imported and plentiful. The food was also well above average pub fare and the service was attentive. And yet . . . Will couldn't help wishing that the waitresses were clothed.

It wasn't political correctness, prudishness or that he found the waitresses unattractive. Quite the opposite in fact. It was simply that the combination of food and sex was an anathema to Will. He abhorred mess. The only ardent desire that the refrigerator scene in *9½ Weeks* and the bit with the butter in *Last Tango in Paris* had aroused in him was a longing for a pair of rubber gloves and a nice, hot frothy bucket of disinfectant. An ex-girlfriend who had once unwisely brought chocolate body paint and a can of whipped cream into the bedroom had politely been given a bowl, a spoon and the flick in that order.

Tonight, however, Will had no choice but to witness this unsanitary juxtaposition of 'Tits & Schnitz', for next week Gus was getting married and the unwritten laws of bucks' nights ordained that after a day spent playing golf, they had to end up at a strip club.

At a nearby table a group of girls, who had just emerged from a pole-dancing class in the private room, were shrieking with laughter and plainly having a fantastically sexually empowered, ironic time. No, Will thought bitterly. Strip clubs weren't what they used to be. Not that he really had any idea what they used to be. But he was pretty sure this wasn't it. Well-lit, completely devoid of tacky furnishings and not a single dirty old man in a raincoat to be seen. But then again, he thought practically, it was summer.

As Will pondered the vexatious question of correct seasonal attire for dirty old men, Johnno sank down into the adjoining seat and nudged him. 'Come on mate, *try* to enjoy yourself. Look at Dante. He's having a good time.'

They observed their good friend Dante, who was wedged right up against the stage. A cigarette clamped between his teeth, he was somehow still managing to whistle while attempting to tuck a twenty-dollar bill into the G-string of the exotic dancer who went by the entirely unoriginal name of Bambi. His task was made more difficult by the fact that Bambi was dipping and sliding up and down the greased pole, like a piece of venison that was particularly anxious to be properly marinated. When he finally managed it, he turned to the boys and executed a triumphant thumbs-up.

'Dante?' Will began, as Dante made his way back to their table.

'Yes, mate.'

'Did you really just say "Phwoar, what a set of knockers"?'

'Yep. Why shouldn't I?'

'Because you have a doctorate from Melbourne University, you speak four languages and I've never heard you say "Phwoar" in any of them. Or "knockers".'

'It's a boys' night,' Dante protested. 'And we're at a strip club. I can't help it if I've come over all blokey.'

'Dante, you're *gay*.'

'So what? Marty's not here.'

'This isn't about your partner and fidelity issues!' said Will, frustrated. 'It's about the fact that you're eyeing off breasts when we all know you're just pretending.'

Dante considered this comment and decided that it was fair. 'Look, try to think of it this way. Remember that time we went to the West Indies versus Sri Lanka test match and you barracked for the Windies?'

'Of course. What does that have to do with anything?'

'Well, you support Australia.'

'Yes, but they weren't playing.'

'Exactly,' Dante said, pleased that Will had caught on so quickly. 'All I'm saying is just because you barrack for a different team occasionally, doesn't mean you want to switch sides.'

'He's got a point,' Johnno said, trying to sound authoritative, as the pretty stripper with the beautiful smile went past their table. He couldn't help thinking wistfully that while he was able to gaze at her long legs, her bare navel and even her breasts to his heart's content, it was proving impossible to catch her eye. 'But anyway, we're here to celebrate Gus's bucks' night and – hey – speaking of the groom, where the hell is he?'

Gus was, at that precise moment, hiding in a toilet cubicle. And as an extra precautionary measure he had chosen the women's toilets. Trembling and sweating, his stomach in a knot of anxiety, he was miserably wondering what in the hell he had gotten himself into. His brief period of sanctuary came to an end when he heard the voice of his best man outside the cubicle door. Will and Gus had been friends since they were ten, so Will hadn't even bothered checking the male toilets first. One of Gus's most comforting traits was a certain predictability.

'You right in there, Gussy?'

'Nope.'

'Wanna talk about it?'

'Nope.'

'Do you want me to send Ed in?' Will paused to belatedly consider the wisdom of offering the services of their friend whose marriage was in crisis.

'Why would I want to talk to Ed rather than you?' asked Gus, puzzled.

'Because he's the only one of us who's married. And I know that he and Jen are having a few problems right now but I thought that if you were having cold feet about getting hitched he might be able to help, seeing as how he's been married for six years.'

'I'm not having second thoughts about *marriage*,' Gus said, outraged. 'I'm hiding in here because I'm terrified of you lot.'

'What in the hell are you talking about? We're your mates.'

When Gus answered, it was in a pained tone. 'Do you remember Ed's bucks' night?'

'You mean when we took him to the paint-ball commando course, dressed him in a rabbit suit and told him to run?'

'No. I mean what happened *after* that.'

'Oh. That.' Will mused for a moment. 'Yeah, Dante probably went a bit far that time. But I swear we're not going to do anything like that to you. And I really don't think that night has anything to do with Ed being in counselling now.'

Gus glared suspiciously at Will through a crack in the toilet door but realising that he didn't really have a choice, he emerged from the cubicle. 'Why do men need these stupid rituals involving sex and degradation on bucks' nights?' he asked plaintively. 'I mean think about it, Will – we're celebrating the fact that I've found the love of my life and we're at a strip show. It just doesn't make sense.'

'It makes complete sense. If sex is intimacy for men then going to a strip show must be a form of romance.'

'Are you honestly trying to tell me that watching some twenty-year-old medical student get her kit off is the same as buying Kellie a bunch of roses?'

'Absolutely. Scientifically proven,' Will said firmly, deciding to change the subject. 'What are the girls up to for the hens' night, then?'

'Going to a strip show.'

'Oh.'

There was a small silence.

'So then how does that work?'

'Shut up, Gus, and get out there.'

'Right.'

Gus and Will arrived back at the table in time to intervene in a heated debate between Johnno and Dante as to whether the line in 'You Can Leave Your Hat On' was 'You give me a reason to live', as Johnno insisted, or 'You need more seasoning in this', a conviction that Dante was prepared to espouse unto his last breath.

'Stop arguing,' Will interrupted, steering Gus firmly back into the centre of things.

'They weren't arguing,' Ed said morosely. 'They were differing.'

'What's the difference?'

'You have to beg to differ. It means that you're starting from a position of submissiveness, which negates the classic male aggression in any argument.' He heaved a despondent sigh. 'Only you can't call it an argument, of course. It's a difference.'

The others eyed him cautiously.

'How is the marriage counselling going, mate?' Johnno asked carefully.

'All right, I guess. Last week we dealt with my inability to identify core emotional responses.'

'What's a core emotional response?'

'Buggered if I know,' said Ed glumly, momentarily lifting his head from his hands. 'We spent so long talking about my identification inabilities that the core emotional response bit sort of got sidelined.'

'A core emotional response is an individual's learned pattern of behaviour,' said Dante airily, tapping his cigarette into the ashtray. 'It's most likely to be your standard reaction to any given situation involving disturbances or intensity of feeling. Which in your case, Ed, is a tendency to put your head in your hands and look glum.'

'How do you *know* this stuff?' asked Johnno in awe.

'Because when we were twelve and you lot were playing footy on the oval during lunchtime, I was realising that I was made differently to all the other boys in my class. Although that may not be completely true. I always had my doubts about Warwick Sedgeman. On 'Foreign Cultures Dress-Up Day' he turned up in a loincloth and gold sandals that laced up to his knees. Claimed he was a Roman legionnaire.'

'How do you know he wasn't?'

'Because Warwick spent the entire day astride Mark Byers. Kept insisting that Mark was his horse. And, as anyone who has seen *Gladiator* would know, legionnaires were foot soldiers. Our history teacher Mr Mathers never corrected him, either. I had my suspicions about him too. *Anyway*, the point of my story is that because I knew I was different in some way from the majority, I spent a lot of time thinking about my feelings.'

'We do know what feelings are, Dante. Gay men don't have a monopoly on emotions.'

'I know that. But you must admit we're more in tune with the traditional female psyche. That's why so many gay men and straight women are great friends. Women love us because gay men are perfect companions in so many ways but ultimately we're unobtainable. It's the classic Madonna/Whore distinction. Or the binary opposition of the Playboy Bunny/Centrefold if you prefer.'

'What *are* you talking about?'

'The Playboy Centrefolds fulfilled the whore role. They were sexually available for male visual consumption. The Playboy Bunnies on the other hand were very strictly supervised, never appeared nude and were completely untouchable.'

'So according to you, you're a Playboy Bunny while Johnno here is Miss December?'

'Pretty much.'

There was a silence and then Ed said hollowly, 'Dante?'

'Yes, mate?'

'You had to bring up rabbit costumes, didn't you?'

'Oh, for heaven's sake. Your bucks' night was six years ago. Let it go. Your problem is that you're taking the wrong approach with Jen. Women like talking things through. Men prefer action. You should be thinking of something to *do* to help the situation.'

Ed had clearly already expended some thought on this tactic because he now said tentatively, 'You know how they say you can relight the spark with a bit of role-play? Well, what I've been thinking about is maybe dressing up for Jen – you know, giving her a fantasy,' he finished, blushing wildly and looking at the floor.

'Do you know what she fantasises about?' asked Will doubtfully.

'She likes black men,' Johnno offered helpfully.

A table of speculative gazes fastened upon him.

'Well, she does,' he said defensively. 'She mentioned it one night when we were watching a Will Smith movie.'

Ed regarded him bleakly. 'Right. So now I just need to be black.'

'Maybe you could get one of those spray-on tans or something?'

'And get it all over the sheets?' Will said, horrified.

Dante shook his head at Will and started ticking off problematic points on his fingers. 'One, you assume that the only place to have sex is in a bed and two, you're worried about the sheets. Your ideal woman, William, would probably have a Chux-lined vagina and think doggie-style means a matching collar and leash. Maybe you should book in for a session with Ed's counsellor.'

Will ignored Dante. 'Why don't you buy a really nice pair of pyjamas? You know – like how women buy sexy lingerie when they want to spice things up.'

Dante started to hyperventilate. 'Pyjamas? *Pyjamas? Spice things up?* What are you – the eighteenth-century Amish Dr John Gray? I can tell you this, Eddie – if you're even *wearing* pyjamas when you're sleeping next to your wife that's where you're going wrong for starters, boyo.'

Up on stage, meanwhile, Daisy, the stripper who had captivated Johnno, was becoming increasingly desperate. She had performed the Peekaboo and the Peruvian Starfish Surprise (the surprise being that you ended up in a Brazilian area), and was now seriously considering unleashing the rarely performed and highly perilous Pandora's Box, in a last-ditch attempt to gain the attention of the group of men sitting directly in front of the stage. The table of girls was no problem; having just spent two hours in a beginners' pole-dancing class, they were fully appreciative of the skill and flexibility needed to perform the routine and were applauding every contortion with enthusiasm.

It was obviously time to pull one of the men up on stage. Her gaze took in the group. Definitely not the one with his head in his hands, she decided. Dante was the best dressed, Will was the handsomest and Johnno had been eyeing her off all night, but it was clearly her duty to single out the bloke wearing a printed T-shirt that read 'Elopement (noun) meaning: Who gives a fuck about matching stationery.'

As Johnno watched enviously, Daisy dragged a reluctant Gus up onto the stage and introduced him to the crowd.

'Cheers,' Gus said feebly, giving a thumbs-up and

feeling increasingly stupid as 'Macho Man' by The Village People started to boom through the speakers.

'You have to choose a character,' Daisy explained hurriedly. 'Do you want to be the Indian, the construction worker or the policeman?'

'Can I be the cowboy?'

'Our budget only runs to three costumes. Hurry up or I'll miss my cue.'

Gus stood obediently still as she hastily fastened a tool belt around his waist and jammed a hard-hat on his head. 'Don't worry, love,' she whispered reassuringly. 'Just stand still and I'll slide up and down and around you a few times and pretend to fiddle with your belt buckle and it'll all be over in a few minutes.'

'You see,' Gus squeaked as Daisy inched her way up his inner thigh. 'The thing is I really, really love my fiancée. She's beautiful and smart and she's never once asked me to go to dancing classes with her.'

Daisy looked up at him sceptically. 'Not even salsa?'

'Nope.'

'Huh. You really have got yourself one in a million.'

'I know,' Gus said proudly. As Daisy gyrated against his buttocks and stuck her tongue in his ear, he couldn't help but think of the way that Kellie's eyes sparkled when she laughed.

'Sweetheart?'

'Yes?' Gus snapped back to the present.

'Just try to relax and look like you're having a good time. It's your bucks' night and I'm a highly qualified professional. And I guarantee that at this very moment your fiancée is being made to eat a banana from the underpants

---

of some steroid-abusing hunk whose head is connected to his torso by a clip-on bow tie in the absence of a neck. It's tradition, and you don't want to mess with tradition, do you?'

Yes I do, thought Gus, flushed with humiliation as he stood awkwardly in the spotlight in front of the cheering – no, *jeering* – crowd.

'Look, try thinking about something else,' Daisy suggested, as she executed a neat back-flip and rested her ankles on his shoulders.

'Um, okay. Is Daisy your real name or is it a stage name?'

'It's a stage name. Stay very still – I'm about to do the double-handed reverse Mongolian Squirrel Grip and I don't want to hurt you – you know how if you want to come up with your porn star name you take the name of your first pet and the name of the first street you lived on?'

'Of course.'

'Well, I would have been Mungo Farts.'

Gus had to bend his neck severely to look her in the eyes, as she was now writhing around his crotch.

'I was nine, Mungo was my ferret and I was never any good at spelling,' she explained. 'We actually lived on Fharts Street. Silent H. For about a year after we moved in, every time the postman came he made an amusing raspberry noise and Mum would go into the bedroom and cry. Then Mungo died and Mum bought a Rottweiler. So,' she continued, raising her voice slightly, as she flipped into a handstand and did something alarming with her hips, 'I used the backup method. You just name yourself after a cartoon character.'

It was true, Gus realised in horror, as he gazed around the room. There was Bambi, all thoughts of her poor mother shot dead by the hunter forgotten, taking a tip from the table of girls. In the corner was Minnie, doing something with a feather boa that Mickey would most certainly not have approved of. And that's when it hit him that he was being rubbed up by a duck. And a duck, moreover, that he had never found attractive in the first place. Gus had peeked at a few unusual websites in his time but cartoon porn was another level of weirdness entirely. He had the horrible feeling that at any moment he might see Elmer Fudd giving Dante a lap dance.

Thankfully the song finally finished and as Daisy executed a triumphant high kick in response to the wild applause, Gus staggered down from the stage, still wearing his tool belt and hard-hat and trying not to think about the potentially erotic subtext of Tweety Bird's insistence that he tawt he taw a puddy-tat.

'So what did you talk about?' Johnno asked jealously, the instant Gus sat down. 'What's she like?'

'She's really nice,' said Gus, wiping his brow. 'She was telling me about the pet ferret called Mungo that she had when she was nine.'

'SHE WHAT?' Dante's head whipped around and he caught Daisy's eye. They held each other's gaze for a long moment and then Dante's voice rang out shrilly across the club. 'Warwick Sedgeman, you old slapper, put down that feather boa and come and say hello to your old classmate.'

'Dante! I thought it was you.'

'Warwick, you look fantastic.'

'Thanks, Dante. Did you enjoy the show?'

'Loved it. Nice work on the double-handed reverse Mongolian Squirrel Grip. So how long have you been Daisy?'

'Oh, Daisy's just a stage name.' Warwick added coyly, 'But I've been Mrs Byers for quite some time now.'

'You're married?' Johnno whimpered, wisely focusing on the legal impediment to his desires, instead of the whole 'Formerly known as Warwick the Roman Legionnaire' revelation.

''Fraid so, sweetheart.' Turning to Dante she whispered, 'It's sad, really. We're just doing our jobs, trying to provide a bit of sexy entertainment, but the men get all romantic and send us flowers and ask us out. Happens all the time. They just can't see the line between sex and romance. *Don't* want to see it if you ask me.'

Dante shook his head in commiseration. 'They're my mates and I love them, but they're bloody hopeless,' he confided. 'No self-esteem, in a mad rush to fall in love and get married, and just can't stop talking about their feelings. One hour with them and even Oprah would want to mainline heroin and shoot up a book club.'

He turned and regarded them affectionately. Johnno was still gazing, helplessly entranced, at Daisy's perfect features. Gus was oblivious to the entire conversation as he posed for a photo so that Kellie could see him in the hard-hat and tool belt. Ed was taking the photo and wondering whether Jen would be impressed if he wore a hard-hat and tool belt *over* a pair of sexy pyjamas, while Will was working up his courage to go and talk to the cute girl with the crisply ironed shirt and neat ponytail who was seated at the pole-dancing-class table.

Dante's gaze followed Will's to the gathering of girls. They were energetically throwing back vodkas, singing at the tops of their voices, dancing on the spot and emitting appreciative whistles as Pocahontas demonstrated the Inverted Teepee pose.

'Women,' Dante said fondly. 'Give 'em some booze, a schnitzel and a strip show and they're happy. They really are so basic.'

Kathy Lette
The Art of Genital Persuasion

When judging penises, it's probably not the most appropriate time to make small talk. That's the only bit of advice I can pass on if you are unsuspectingly called upon to undertake such a task – as was I, one bleak London day when I was abducted to a theatre in Shaftesbury Avenue and told by my best friend that now, once and for all, I would be cured of my 'irrational fear of the phallus'.

Phobias are as common as freckles. Heights, snakes, spiders, commitment, crowds, work . . . Well, I suffered from a phobia which was a little harder to explain away, especially to prospective boyfriends. I was penis-phobic. Successfully brain-washed by the nuns at Our Lady of Mercy All Girls School not to be a 'fallen woman' (the nuns failed to point out that women didn't actually 'fall', but were invariably *pushed*), I'd only seen one or two male appendages in my entire life. And they'd terrified me. Especially during my late teens, when they'd been unsuccessfully prodding and pushing at me in a cold car on some dingy back road accompanied by male cries of 'Is it bloody IN yet?' or 'What are ya? Frigid?' (When will sexologists realise that the problem is not women faking orgasms, but men faking foreplay?)

Did this penis-phobia cramp my style in later life? Well, put it this way – the Pope took to ringing me up for tips on celibacy.

My best friend since kindergarten, Collette Kennedy, on the other hand, was a penis-aholic. If there were a twelve-step program for such cravings she'd be a regular. 'My name is Collette Kennedy and I am addicted to dick. I'm ad-dick-ted!' It was a love of word play that cemented our friendship from day one in kindergarten when she asked me which reptiles were good at maths. I looked at her blankly and kept chewing my braid. 'Adders,' she'd replied.

But it was the reptilian species known as the 'trouser snake' which now sparked her interest. A run-in with a lousy boss, a bad-hair day, a hangover, a rejection by a casting director . . . all could be alleviated by taking the Phallic Cure.

Collette had thespian tendencies. Lesbian tendencies would have been preferable to her rather formal family, but um, sorry, absolutely no chance there. Collette giving up men was as likely as Michael Jackson getting a job in a day nursery. Her main stage roles had been limited to those of 'Buxom Wench Number Two', but she'd been murdered once or twice on *The Bill*, so she had already written her Oscar acceptance speech.

My career choice was the antithesis of Collette's. I, Judith Jenkins, was studying to become a lawyer. Although all I'd experienced so far in my pupillage was subpoena envy. The barrister I worked for gave me nothing more intellectually arduous than menial filing. And he seemed to require an awful lot of papers to be put away under 'x', 'y' and 'z'. Which meant a *lot* of bending over.

'What pins, Jenkins! Let's make the word of the day "legs". Why don't you come back to my pad tonight and we'll spread the word!' had been Friday's sexist comment du jour. Which is why I'd agreed with such alacrity to join Collette for lunch while she judged some competition or other at a theatre in Soho.

Collette was forever telling me to stand up to Rupert Botherington, QC. She maintained that the reason I found men intimidating was because of my penis-phobia. Demystification of the male was her mission. I just hadn't realised it would begin today.

'Oh, goody. I love judging competitions. What sort? Scones? Flowers? Pumpkin carving . . . ?' I chirped as the minicab belched its way through Covent Garden.

It wasn't until we strolled onto the stage that the horror hit me.

'Penises!' I read the promotional poster. 'You want me to judge penises! Are you mad?'

'*Puppetry of the Penis* auditions. It's the cure, Judith. Surely you've heard of these Aussie guys? They perform a kind of genital origami. Anyway, the show is so successful the producers urgently need more puppeteers. And as the producers are all gay, they booked me and some other actresses to judge the boys' performances from a heterosexual point of view. And I took the liberty of signing you up as well.'

'I know I'm training to be a cut-throat lawyer, but this

is taking the term "naked ambition" a little too literally Collette . . . I mean, saints preserve us!'

'And don't give me any of that shy convent shit. You know how I loathe that miserable God with his white beard and wagging finger.'

As Collette dragged me towards the other four female 'judges' already sitting on the panel, my shoes left skid marks visible from outer space. I tried to calm myself. It was all a bit of frivolous fun.

WARNING: These craft ideas are for amateurs. Do try this in your own home . . .

I also made another mental note – kill Collette and sell her internal organs on the Internet.

You see, unlike my best galpal, I'm not all that comfortable with public nudity. I've been to a nudist beach only once, in Greece. Gritting my teeth, I tried to shed my swimsuit and dive-bomb face down onto the towel in one deft movement – which merely resulted in a grazed chin, a cracked rib and a bit of seaweed up my freckle. Mortified, I lay rigid on the sand, fantasising about putting my clothes back *on*. Then, just to be really kinky, I fantasised about other people putting their clothes back on as well! So you can imagine how I felt about an undress rehearsal.

Clipboard in hand, I perched one bottom cheek precariously on my swivel chair. As the twenty or so male job applicants trooped on stage in jeans and T-shirts, I tried to put a positive spin on things. There are, after all, some good things about being nude. First off, you never have to buy anyone a drink – '*I'm sorry. But my money's in my jeans pocket*'.

Nor is it likely anyone will ever steal your barstool. Having a dress code which reads 'clothing optional' also does away with all that boring '*I've got nothing to wear!*' angst.

But then the contenders started to disrobe. Shirts. Shoes. Jeans. As their undergarments came off, I wasn't quite sure where to look. I glanced at my clipboard for help. The score sheet comprised a list of boxes to be ticked.

Facial looks: _____
Body: _____
Appendage: _____
Comedy skills: _____

It was not unlike the kind of questionnaire Collette would hand out to a prospective boyfriend, really. Until I came to the last category, which read, more worryingly:

Tattoos/Piercings/Other : _____

'Other?' I gasped in a piercing whisper. 'What could they possibly mean by *other*?'

What was left of my mind boggled and my heart beat out a drum solo against my Wonderbra. Overcome with timidity, I decided to concentrate on **Personality** and made eye contact only. But eventually, having exhausted questions on stamp collecting and star signs, I had no choice but to slide my eyes slightly southwards . . .

All the applicants had serious 'pecs' appeal. Judging by their muscled physiques, these were '*excuse me while I do the six-hundred metre butterfly, climb two alps and abseil back down for some dressage and parachute formation before lunch*' types. Next to the boxes marked **Body**, the all-female judging panel enthusiastically scribbled their 10/10 scores.

I would have given the candidates a high mark also, except that my hand was shaking so badly I couldn't write. It was palsied with terror, because the time had come to look at the men's actual appendages. I'd heard of clubs for 'Members Only' but auditions for *Puppetry of the Penis* seemed to be taking this motto too seriously. Besides which, it was my lunch hour and I was decidedly worried that what I was about to see might put me right off my baguette. Anxiously and with great hesitation, I lowered my gaze even further.

If *I* was nervous, the candidates were more so. As the female collective gaze lingered on their groins, the men before me deflated faster than pump-up plastic lilos at the end of a beachside holiday.

'At least we know that the art of shrivelry is not dead!' Collette whispered to me. But as the director put the trainee puppeteers through their paces, they all rose heroically to the challenge.

In the next five minutes, the 'wow' factor of party balloons definitely paled into insignificance. The best way to describe the puppetry is to imagine party balloon tricks performed using the penis, testicles and scrotum. The fleshy origami I witnessed included the *Atomic Mushroom*, the *Hamburger*, the *Loch Ness Monster*, the *Windsurfer*, the *Baby Bird*, the *Boomerang* and the *Eiffel Tower*.

'Well, what do you think?' Collette dug her elbow into my ribs.

'The only apt word for such a spectacular performance is "outstanding", really,' I told her breathlessly.

Collette giggled. As did I. Only I couldn't stop. The laughter started to effervesce up in me like champagne. Nervous laughter I suppose, mixed with relief that the 'trouser snake' wasn't the carnivorous, venomous, aggressive creature I'd feared it would be. And my laughter proved contagious. Soon we were all guffawing, judges and job applicants alike.

The barrister I worked for had inveigled me into a drink after work on my first day, only to dragoon me into a lap-dancing club. The atmosphere had been predatory and sinister. Men watched from the shadows in eerie silence as scrawny young women acted out their ersatz sexuality. But this experience was the opposite. With cheery rascality and matter-of-fact humour, the heterosexual men before me were happy to satirise their own sexuality. With not a whiff of baby oil.

'You see?' Collette prodded me again. 'It's nothing more than fear of the unknown. Blokes get to ogle naked women on a daily basis – page three girls in the tabloids, magazine centrefolds, Internet porn, advertising. Naked women are used to sell everything from toothpicks to tractors.'

'The true meaning of "ad nauseam",' I interrupted.

'Exactly! But when it comes to the male appendage, women don't often get to look it in its eye. I figured once you got to scrutinise a few scrotums they'd no longer threaten you. So, what have you gleaned?'

I glanced back at the performers. What I'd gleaned is that penises, like snowflakes, are all different. There's the lean, slinky, kinky ones. The thick, succulent types. The low-slung gunslinger sort. The stubby button mushrooms. The round-heads. The hooded eyes. The meat and two veg, packed-lunch variety. And women like them all. We judges admired every different shape and size. All this male angst over size. It's attitude women are really interested in. Women like a male member which says 'G'day! God, am I glad to see YOU!' And we certainly appreciate one which has been trained to do theatrical tricks for our entertainment. At the end of the auditions we applauded heartily. And the men on stage also looked pretty pleased with the way things had gone.

'Now *that's* what I call a standing ovation,' I told Collette as we left the theatre, hooting with laughter.

That afternoon I strode back into chambers. Rupert Botherington, QC.'s reprimand for being late was compounded by a threat to report me to our Head of Chambers. Except that this warning was followed by a salacious wink and a suggestive purr. 'Of course, you could always calm me down by letting me know just where those legs of yours end . . .'

Instead of wilting, I found myself imagining him naked, his scrotum comically stretched into a windsurfing sail. I then told him that these legs he so admired were now going to walk me to his Head of Chambers and report him for sexual harassment.

Puppetry of the Penis is referred to by the puppeteers as 'the Ancient Australian Art of Genital Origami'. But I prefer to think of it as the Art of Genital Persuasion.

PS: The names in this story have been changed to protect the guilty. The author would also like to add that no animals were harmed in the writing of this story, except for one misogynistic lawyer.

Louise Limerick

The Milk Queen

She could sleep for one hundred years – if the baby would let her. But the baby snuffled and whimpered in her crib, sucking noisily on her tiny pink fist and then kicking her feet in the air. Wendy tossed in frustration on the bed. If she could just snatch some sleep, while the baby wasn't actually howling, she might feel less wretched. Less sore, less teary, less tired. Then, with some sleep to sustain her, she could prepare herself for the afternoon onslaught of visitors, the reception of gifts and good wishes and the inevitable speculation about the looks and nature of her newborn child.

She rolled over onto her side, facing the loosely swaddled bundle that was wriggling in the crib. If only the baby would sleep, she thought. Then it wouldn't be so hard to rest. But the baby hadn't slept all day. Not properly. The baby was three days old and famished. And there was nothing she could do to satiate the child. Her milk wasn't 'in' yet and she had nursed and nursed the baby until her breasts were tender. She'd had enough. She was worn out and desperate for sleep. She pulled the cover over her ears, trying to block out the little sniffles and huffs that her newborn baby made.

There was a story her grandmother used to tell her. One that had been slipping in and out of her mind since the moment of Rose's birth. She had not thought of it since her childhood. The story, as she remembered it, was a strange one, an unusual derivation of *Sleeping Beauty*. And it was called, oddly enough, *The Milk Queen*. She supposed that the story had come back to her through the power of association, a result of her present fixation with the troublesome matter of milk.

As Wendy relaxed into the pillow, the beginning of the story drifted like wood smoke through her mind. *Once upon a time . . .*

Once upon a time, there lived a King and Queen who longed for a baby. Years passed and they gave up hope of ever having a child. Then, one day, the Queen walked into the Forbidden Forest to search for some magic that would help her to conceive. After days of fruitless wandering, she fell asleep among the nettle bushes and, by some curious enchantment, managed to conceive a child . . .

In the crib, Wendy's child rolled her hard round head back and forth, crunched her little pink fists up against her face and cried. Wendy shrugged off the five minutes sleep she'd been able to catch, sat up in her bed, unbuttoned her nightgown and wearily reached for the baby. When she stroked the baby's cheek, the baby turned her head and opened her pink mouth very wide. Seizing the moment, she brought the baby into position and tried to attach the child to her breast. The tiny girl bit down on Wendy's nipple with her hard gums. Wendy's eyes smarted. She could feel the baby sucking and it stung.

When the infant was born, a fragile little Princess, the Queen looked into the child's tiny elfin face and her heart sank. She is a changeling, thought the Queen. An unearthly child.

The Queen gave the infant to the wet nurse. 'Take her away and hide her from the King,' she said. 'No one is ever to look upon this child.'

'As you wish, Your Majesty,' said the wet nurse. And she took the child away and hid her in one of the castle towers.

Wendy slid her little finger into the baby's mouth to break the vacuum suction. The baby screamed and went purple. Wendy looked helplessly down into her daughter's mouth, open wide, like a flower. The baby's little pink tongue trembled with longing. She wanted milk and Wendy's breasts were still empty. Wendy fastened her nightgown, put the baby over her shoulder and pressed the button above the bed to call for the nurse. She hated feeling so desperate and having to ask for help. But she reminded herself that the staff were accustomed to exhausted and emotional mothers. This was day-to-day life in the maternity ward. There were complications in every fairytale here.

'Please!' Wendy said to the efficient woman in the white

uniform who had appeared almost instantly at the door. 'Please, just take her away. Give her a bottle. I don't care. She won't settle. She's not like my other babies were. Besides, I've got no milk for her. And,' she said, her voice beginning to tremble, 'I'm . . . so . . . incredibly . . . tired.'

The nurse inclined her head thoughtfully and clicked her tongue. She took the baby and wrapped her up tightly in the cotton blanket. 'I can see you need some rest. I'll take baby up to the nursery for a few hours and give her some boiled water – enough to take the edge off her thirst. The third day is always the hardest. Mother's exhausted. Baby's agitated. Everyone's waiting for the milk to come in. I shouldn't worry if she seems a bit grumpy. Every baby is different, you know.'

Wendy lay back in her hospital bed and sighed. Yes, it was true. Every baby was different. But how different was this baby going to be? This baby, this tiny girl, was a mystery so far – like the changeling in *The Milk Queen*. And it was hard to ignore the well-meaning comments that friends and relations made about the child. Of course, people couldn't resist making judgments, finding likenesses, and creating expectations for the newborn. It was only human nature and Wendy knew that it was all part of belonging to a family, a community and a tribe. It wouldn't even matter, except . . . Except that this baby wasn't her husband's child.

On the second day of the infant's life, the King was searching for his sceptre in the castle when he came upon the child and her wet nurse in the tower. The infant was so beautiful, with milky skin, like the Queen, and silky

soft hair, that the King adored her at once. And, pre-
suming the newborn infant in the tower to be his own
flesh and blood, he knelt and kissed her tiny fingers. All
might still be well . . .

Now that the baby had gone up to the nursery, the room
was quiet and Wendy felt a little guilty – as if her peace
was not deserved. In the interests of mother–infant bonding, the baby was supposed to be 'rooming in'. And yet,
as Wendy surveyed the bouquets of fresh flowers banked
up along the windowsill, she couldn't help feeling a surge
of relief that the baby was gone. Without the distressing
snuffles and whimpers of the newborn, the room had an
aura of serenity. Finally, she was alone.

She lay on her bed and tried to relax. It would be difficult to fall asleep again. She had lost the urge to sleep, the
sense of immediate heaviness she needed to draw her mind
down from the conscious world. Her thoughts returned
again to the fairytale. She knew that there was a point to
her grandmother's story. That was why she couldn't get
it out of her head. When she was a child the story had
seemed fanciful. But there was something much more
pointed about it now . . .

On the third day of the infant's life the King ordered
that she be removed from her seclusion in the tower.
Against the wishes of the Queen, he set the infant's cra-
dle down beside his throne and bade the wet nurse to
attend to the child.
 The Queen worried that the entire Court would see
the elfin baby lying in the cradle and know her secret.

On her knees, she begged her husband to return the baby to the tower. The King refused and, taking the tiny elfin baby from her wet nurse, he dressed the infant in a silken gown. Then he summoned all the fairies of the Forbidden Forest to come and bless the child.

Wendy sighed. She couldn't remember what happened next in the story. Not exactly. Not word for word. What did it matter? It was only a fairytale. And a weird one as well. She clasped her hands over her soft, swollen belly and tried to drift towards sleep. But sleep was strangely elusive to one so tired. Her breasts hurt. Her bottom hurt. And her middle felt like a huge bowl of unset junket. She worried that she wouldn't be able to grab any sleep before Joanna came to visit that afternoon. Her other friends had already been to visit her that morning, wafting in bright and breezy with gifts and good wishes just like the good fairies in the tale . . .

The fairies arrived at the castle one by one. Each one looked at the infant in the silken gown and saw at once that the child was made of magic. Still, every fairy that visited took pity on the Queen and blessed the infant, giving her human graces . . . intelligence, beauty, charm . . .

Susan was the first to arrive that morning. Always punctual. Always on time. She arrived at the stroke of ten, dropped a small parcel, tastefully wrapped in fine pink tissue paper, in Wendy's lap, and rushed straight over to scoop up the baby and rock her in her arms.

'She's a bit testy today, Susan.'

'Is she? Poor little love,' said Susan pursing her red lips at the baby. 'Don't worry, Wendy. I'm sure she'll have a sunny nature. Just like her dad. She must take after him in some way. She certainly doesn't look much like him, does she? Still, I expect that's a blessing in disguise . . .'

'My milk hasn't come down yet, Susan,' Wendy cut in. 'She's hungry. That's why she's unsettled.'

'Oh, of course!' Susan frowned. She didn't like discussing bodily functions. She sat on the end of Wendy's bed smiling and cooing at the fussy baby while Wendy unwrapped the parcel – a wooden mobile of circus animals painted in brilliant colours and abstract designs.

'Thank you, Susan. It's lovely.'

'I thought it might be . . . stimulating,' Susan said, reaching over to take the mobile from Wendy and jiggle it over the baby. Baby Rose threw her hands back, a classic newborn startle reflex, and cried.

Susan spoke louder, so that Wendy could hear her over the crying baby. 'At birth the human baby has an immense capacity for learning. And your little Rose is clever. See?'

Rose stopped crying and sucked her fist for comfort while Susan held the mobile about thirty centimetres above her eyes.

'Look, how alert she is!' marvelled Susan. 'She's watching the zebra. She's interested in the pattern – now she's got over the surprise.'

Wendy nodded, resisting the urge to grab Rose back and cradle her safe, secure and *under-stimulated* in her arms.

'She's going to be clever, Wendy, I can tell.'

'Clever . . .' mused Wendy. Yes, she'd be pleased if the baby turned out to be clever. Women could do anything these days . . .

Susan gave Rose back to Wendy and attached the mobile to the hand bar that swung out over Wendy's hospital bed.

'You won't be needing to use this, will you?' she asked Wendy, as she spun the mobile around. 'I never used the bar to help me get out of bed when I had Maxine. Bad for the pelvic floor, you know. Besides, you're not infirm, Wendy. You've just given birth!'

Wendy looked meekly at Susan and smiled. She didn't dare tell her that she had been using the bar.

'Well then, I'd better be off,' said Susan briskly as she bustled towards the door. 'Jonathan has a piano lesson at ten-thirty.'

Susan blew a kiss to the baby and, in an instant, she was gone.

Clare had been the next visitor that morning. Tall and thin, she swept into the room while Wendy was bending over Rose, changing her nappy.

'How are you today, Wendy?'

'Fine thanks,' Wendy said, without turning around.

'How are you really?' Clare asked, putting a hand on Wendy's shoulder.

Wendy turned around and looked up at Clare. Clare's golden hair was swept up off her oval face and pinned loosely, in an artful tangle, at the back. A smudge of pale pink lipstick had been hastily applied on her lips and she was wearing a plain T-shirt and a long sea-blue skirt of indeterminate style. The skirt wafted around her ankles and she looked, as always, almost ethereal and effortlessly lovely.

Wendy wished she had put on a fresh nightgown. She had a feeling that the one she was wearing was soiled at the back.

'How are you really?' Clare repeated.

'Fine. Just fine,' Wendy smoothed down her hair. It felt greasy. She'd forgotten to wash it that morning.

'I expect you're a bit sore.'

'Oh, yeah. And Rose is cranky this morning too. You know how it is . . . I'm just hoping this isn't a sign of things to come!' Wendy meant to have a laugh at her own expense but suddenly she didn't find the premonition funny.

Clare smiled and looked behind Wendy at the baby lying in the crib. 'Oh, I nearly forgot!' she said. 'I've a present! I meant to wrap it, but I was in such a rush to get here this morning, that I'm afraid I didn't have time.' She handed Wendy a plain brown bag.

Inside the bag were a small blank canvas and a pot of purple paint.

Wendy looked at the gift. 'Well, thank you, Clare,' she said. 'Is it rude if I ask what it is?'

'Well,' said Clare mysteriously, 'if you just close your eyes for a minute, I'll show you.'

Wendy closed her eyes and listened to Clare moving around the room.

'Hush, hush!' Clare said to the baby. 'There, now. I'll just clean you up . . . Oh, what a performance! What's wrong? That wasn't so bad.'

Wendy opened her eyes and saw Clare comforting Rose.

There on the bed was the little canvas, and, in the middle, was a perfect print of Rose's tiny hand.

'Oh Clare, that's lovely!'

'I thought you'd be pleased. I noticed, on the day she was born, that she had elegant little hands. Such long fingers . . . Very unusual. A baby with hands like that is bound to grow up to be artistic. I shouldn't be surprised if Rose grew up to be a musician or a writer or an artist . . .'

'Artistic? Well, that would be a miracle in our family! But, if her finger paintings demonstrate any artistic potential, I'll bring her to you for lessons. Okay?'

'You're on!' laughed Clare. 'What do you say to art lessons, Rose?' she said, holding the baby up in front of her face. 'Would you like that?'

Rose opened her mouth and howled.

It was nearly three o'clock. Nearly time for afternoon visiting hours. Joanna, the last of her good fairies, would arrive soon. Wendy reached out and picked up the little canvas that Clare had given her and stared at the tiny handprint. She watched Susan's mobile twirling from the iron bar over the bed. Stimulating. Yes, she supposed it was. And now she remembered. Word for word, she remembered the rest of the story. She remembered the sting in the tale.

As the good fairies flitted around the cradle, the King smiled, for the little Princess had been given many virtues. The King did not see the Wicked Fairy standing near the cradle, for she wore a dress as dark as midnight.

'It was by forbidden magic that you conceived this

*child,' the Wicked Fairy accused the Queen. 'The infant
is an elfin child! But, because you bore her, I will give
her a human virtue, just as the other fairies have done.
Mortality is hers. I give it. See! Even now she begins to
wither . . . And, as you have no magic to sustain the life
of this elfin child, I will take her back to the forest to live
with me.'*

'Where's the baby?' asked Joanna, as she sat herself in
the chair at the end of Wendy's bed and anxiously looked
around.

'The nurse took her to the nursery,' Wendy answered.
'She was so hungry and cranky that I couldn't get any rest.
I haven't got any milk yet, you see.'

Joanna looked pained and shook her head pathetically,
as if this shortage of maternal milk was a catastrophe of
epic proportions.

She had made it to the hospital at the end of visiting
hours. At ten to four, she had lumbered in, hot and pink
and covered in perspiration. Now she sat, exhausted, in
the vinyl chair at the end of Wendy's bed, flapping the
edge of her stripy T-shirt in an attempt to create a draft in
the hot, clammy region beneath her large breasts.

'Is the air-conditioning working properly in here?'
Joanna asked.

'I think so.'

'Well, I guess I'm just overheated.'

'Have you been running around a lot?' Wendy asked.

'Yeah, I went to visit Evelyn. I told her about Rosie
being born. I . . . I . . . hope you don't mind,' she added
tentatively.

'Of course I don't. Why should I?' Wendy looked away. Did Joanna sense something? As far as Wendy knew, Evelyn was the only one who had so far guessed the truth about Rose's father. She was like the bad fairy in the story and she had the power, if she wanted to use it out of spite or revenge, to make trouble.

Joanna stood up. 'Would you mind terribly much if I went and saw Rosie in the nursery, Wendy? I can't bear to visit without seeing her. Do you think they will let me nurse her?'

'Sure. They ought to be used to you by now.'

'She's a darling, isn't she? She looks just like a pixie!'

'Yeah, she's special,' Wendy said solemnly. 'But, can I tell you something, Joanna?'

'Of course. You can tell me anything.'

Wendy swallowed, hesitating.

Joanna's face became still and expectant. 'What is it? What do you want me to know?'

Wendy saw the worried look in Joanna's eyes. 'Oh, it's nothing really,' she said, trying to make light of the matter. 'It's probably just third-day blues . . . It's just that I'm at the end of my tether with Rose. Without any milk, I can't seem to comfort her at all. And it's hard to *bond* with a child you can't soothe.'

Wendy felt like crying. Instead she blushed and looked at the floor. 'Harry's . . . I mean, my . . .' She faltered. 'All my other children were so easy to relate to – when they were born.'

'Give yourself a little time, Wendy,' Joanna said softly. 'You're going to love Rosie, once you get to know her. Really you are. You'll see.'

When Joanna left the room, Wendy pressed her face into her pillow and wailed. She knew that hormones made her emotions more extreme. Tomorrow she'd be her practical, reasonable self again but now she needed to have a good cry.

When her crying was done, she stumbled upon a deep and exhausted sleep. She slept for hours. The evening meal that had been delivered to her room went cold on the tray. Visitors were ushered out of the hospital and the lights were dimmed. Dreams formed and dissipated in her mind, drying up like clouds and then gathering again. She sensed, rather than recalled, scenes from the fairytale – images of the Milk Queen running to save her baby from the dark fairy and clutching at the child's silken robes . . .

The Queen cried out in anguish. 'She is mine! Do not take her away!' And with those words, the Queen began to weep a river of milky tears.

Then the smallest of the good fairies, who had hitherto been overlooked, rushed forth. The smallest fairy was not strong enough to break the Wicked Fairy's spell, but she caught some of the Queen's tears in her hand and fed these to the infant. Instantly, the child stopped withering and began to grow.

'Your tears have saved her life,' said the smallest fairy to the Queen. 'You may keep her. But, to stay the Wicked Fairy's spell, you must feed her your tears for as long as you shall live.'

Slowly, sleep and dreams of fairytales left Wendy. Then, in the strange semi-conscious state before waking, she became aware of the steady pull of the umbilical cord that stretched from her bed to her daughter's crib, in the nursery outside her room. Her breasts ached as milk began to swell the glands beneath her skin and, when she opened her eyes, she saw a warm, wet patch spreading across her nightgown and spilling with abandon across the sheet. The milk was in.

Gay Longworth

Girls' Night In

To: Carrie@hotmail.com; Val@aol.com
Subject: Girls' Night In

Hey,
Stocked up on wine and fags. See you at 8. When the kids are asleep.
Can't wait, LOTS OF GOSSIP!!!!
Love Joss

Reply: Joss@BTinternet.co.uk; Val@aol.com
Subject: Girls' Night In

Counting the minutes. Get me out of this hell hole . . .
Kisses and hugs
Carrie
PS still on detox, so I'm bringing vodka and edamame.

Reply: Joss@BTinternet.co.uk; Carrie@hotmail.com
Subject: Girls' Night In

Anything I can bring?
Val xx

Staying in is the new going out. There is no queuing. The chances of having your drink spiked are minimal. And you don't have to pay for a babysitter. Three friends of old decided they would try it on for size. The location was chosen between the ones who had offspring and then narrowed down to the one without the husband. That would be Joss. Joss had two children and had lived alone since her husband had yelled 'I want a divorce' at her in the middle of a drunken row. Sensing an opportunity, she'd kept him to his word. Joss stocked up the fridge with white wine and stomach-lining taramasalata, put her children to bed and pulled out the first cork. Music to a mother's ears. She was in a great mood and looking forward to the evening. She'd lost five pounds, covered her grey and had met a man at work. She was longing to tell the other two about him.

Carrie was the first to ring the doorbell. She arrived carrying a bottle of vodka, some limes and soda. She'd read somewhere that vodka was a cleaner alcohol, and since she was still detoxing, she thought she'd bring her own. There were fewer calories per unit in vodka than wine. Carrie was a fashion and fads kind of girl. She had been blessed with exceptional good looks, but knew it. Her jeans were always skin-tight. Her make-up ever-present. She was that rare breed of blonde, bright and beautiful, with a razor-sharp wit and buckets of sexuality. She was also single. Carrie could be described as a trifle on the high-maintenance side, and had on more than one occasion been referred to as neurotic. But to her friends she was always good value to have around.

Val was the last to arrive. She brought champagne.

There was always something to celebrate in Val's life. Her husband's small business had become a slightly bigger business and had just been sold for a great deal of money. She and their twins were well looked after. Their house in Kensington appeared in magazines and they were currently in negotiations over a large yellow stone manor in Gloucestershire. Very quickly, Val had got used to turning left when she got onto an aeroplane, and no longer thought it strange that the nanny struggled alone in the back with the twins. Val had always been the fulcrum between Joss's moods and Carrie's overly dramatic take on life. She prided herself on her strength of character and her level-headed approach to life. As Joss and Carrie had been her friends since they'd been forced together in a hostile school environment, Val knew they didn't like her for her money.

Val walked in with a bag clinking with goodies from the off-licence. 'I am gagging for a drink,' she announced.

'Hi Val,' said Carrie. 'You look fabulous. You've lost weight?'

'No.'

'I'm sure you have.'

'You say that every time I see you. If you were right, I'd weigh two stone by now. You know I don't diet.'

'Get yourself a drink,' said Joss, kissing Val. 'The bottle is already open.'

Val looked in the fridge. 'I've decided since we're saving ourselves a fortune by staying in, we should have the best at a fraction of the price.' She pulled out a bottle of vintage Bollinger. 'There are two more in the bag. Throw that stuff away, and have this.' She popped the cork. 'I've been looking forward to this all day. The twins have been a nightmare. Ill and grizzly, which I know isn't their fault, but still . . .'

'Me too. I've had a bitch of a day at work,' said Carrie, turning back to the job of squeezing limes. 'You know that presentation I've been working on . . .'

'Yes,' said the other two in unison, anticipating the worst.

'They've only gone and shelved the entire project. Not enough funding, apparently.'

There were communal sighs of sympathy and hugs. The drinks were poured, and they moved out onto the small balcony, where smoking was permitted. Joss had enforced the rule on herself to try and cut her cigarette intake down to one pack a day. No one who knew her thought it odd that the telly was placed in the middle of the room, and angled towards the French window.

'What does that mean with regard to your job?' asked Joss, inhaling deeply and taking a large slug of champagne. Joss was effectively the sole breadwinner of her family. Her soon-to-be-ex-husband was one of those creative types. She had underwritten his lack of talent and vodka habit for years. She'd loyally backed up his stories of 'things in the pipeline', 'scripts being picked up', and 'interest from several parties'. It made her particularly sensitive to Carrie's irregular working patterns.

'They're bastards and don't know what they're talking about.'

Val and Joss looked at each other knowingly. Their beautiful friend would soon be looking for new employment. Her average stay at any one job was eighteen months. Six months of best behaviour. Six months of sliding productivity. Six months of scandal. Followed by the inevitable explosive walkout. Her love life followed much the same pattern, but could be measured in weeks, not months, and sometimes days.

'What about you?' Val asked Joss, coming in from the cold. She couldn't handle listening to Carrie blame the entire management of L'Oreal for the failure of her product. She also liked to deflect the attention away from Carrie, who frankly got enough. Joss on the other hand had a tendency to melt into the background. Val thought of herself as the most stable of the three, and therefore could afford to be considerate. 'What's happening with the divorce?'

'Well he's drinking again, so things are getting worse.'

'Thank God you're out of it,' said Carrie, swigging back the booze.

'I know, but the kids don't see it like that. They want their daddy home.'

'Of course they do, Joss, he never disciplined them. You had to do all that by yourself and then he'd come in, break all the rules and undermine you completely by giving them the things you'd said they couldn't have,' said Val. 'You are very brave and I'm very proud of you.'

Carrie refilled everyone's glasses. Why did the first bottle always go down so quickly? Val went and fetched the second.

'You're not changing your mind, are you?' asked Carrie. Carrie had very much enjoyed having Joss returned from the wasteland of marital life. Her partners in crime were waning and she'd been left having to make do with women she met on the treadmill.

'God no. Actually, I've met someone.'

'What?' asked Carrie. 'Where?'

'That's great,' said Val. 'Tell all.'

'At work. Bring the bottle and I'll tell you the gory details on the balcony.'

'You slaves to nicotine,' said Val, peeling back the foil.

'You'll get pissed and start smoking yourself,' said Joss.

'No I won't. I've stopped doing that.'

Joss and Carrie gave each other knowing looks as the second cork flew into the neighbour's garden.

Carrie couldn't be bothered to go and squeeze more limes and anyway, after two, she was getting acid tummy. She poured the ice into the garden below and filled the tumbler with champagne. Most of Joss's belonging were still in storage and there weren't enough flutes anyway.

'He is younger than me,' said Joss. 'Twenty-six.'

There was simultaneous squealing.

'Lucky girl,' cried Val. 'I'm so jealous.'

'No you're not,' said Joss.

'Okay, I'm not. But I am happy for you.'

'So am I. It's fabulous, you deserve it. So when you say he's at work, like the same building, or the same office?' asked Carrie.

'Ten feet away.'

'Isn't that a bit dangerous?' asked Val.

'Not if you haven't had sex for ten months it isn't,' said Joss. 'And to be honest, things in that department weren't that great at the best of times. I'm like a bitch on heat and I'm powerless to stop it. And he's so star-struck, it's like child's play.'

'It is child's play,' said Val, and they all howled again. 'Have you slept with him yet?'

'No. We're still on a lot of eye contact and naughty sex-texting.'

'Now I am jealous.'

Joss grinned with delight.

'Honey, I've done what you're about to do, and it always, but always, ends in tears,' said Carrie.

'Doesn't stop you doing it again though,' said Val, coming to Carrie's defence.

'Bitch. It's not my fault, men just seem to like me.'

'Well they don't always fancy me, and it's nice to have some attention. The last thing I want is a relationship.'

'I'm just saying be careful,' said Carrie.

'Carrie has a point. You don't take rejection very well.'

They drank in silence for a while. Carrie broke it. 'Do you remember the man who owned the gallery I worked at?'

The three women started laughing again. It had been a disastrous affair from the outset. He was short, pale and ugly. But rich. He wooed Carrie with trips to Paris and expensive bags. After a stay in a posh hotel, Carrie felt a little guilty that she still hadn't put out. So she gave him a blow job in the car on the way back. They got busted by a juggernaut, who gave them a blast of the horn. The boss panicked, accidentally slammed the Porsche into reverse gear and blew the engine. Carrie got the delightful reputation of having given the most expensive blow job in history. When Carrie walked out on her contract, the company let her go. Val and Joss always thought it wasn't, as Carrie had said, because they were frightened of a lawsuit, but because they were so relieved she'd taken her dramatic antics elsewhere. But as always, those dramatic antics made up for the lack of any antics in the lives of the other two. Carrie coloured their lives and gave them something to talk about. When they weren't despairing of her, they were actively encouraging her. The three women laughed and drank and drank some more and talked about all the bad sex they'd ever had. When Joss opened the third bottle of champagne, Val mentioned it would be a good thing if they had something to eat. So the hummus and taramasalata came out of the fridge and sat open, but untouched, on the table. It was way too late for food. Their appetites had been successfully drowned by then.

'Oh sod it,' said Val. 'Can I?' She pulled the pack of Marlboro Lights towards her. Joss and Carrie said nothing. 'It's just been such a stressful day.'

'Looking after the staff can be so tough,' said Carrie.

'Claws,' said Val.

'I'm only joking.'

'I wish I had a husband who paid for the nanny,' said Joss. 'Who am I kidding. I wish I had a husband who paid for a loaf of bread.'

'I wish I had a husband,' said Carrie.

'Then don't shag everyone at work,' said Val, laughing.

'I don't shag everyone at work,' said Carrie.

Joss joined in the tease. 'What about the pass you made at your boss's assistant?' said Joss.

'I didn't know he was gay.'

'He had a penis, that was enough of an incentive. And everyone else in your office is a woman,' said Val, finishing the story.

'At least I go to work,' Joss retorted. 'We can't all file our nails all day.'

'Now who's being bitchy?' said Val.

'You are.'

'No I'm not. You're just being over-sensitive,' said Val. 'We're only teasing. I have to go and have another pee.' Val turned too quickly, glanced off the door and tripped over the step. She lurched forward, but managed to right herself. She held up her glass triumphantly. 'Not a drop spilt.'

'Pisshead,' said Carrie.

'Make a sentence of the following words – pot, kettle, black, calling.' Carrie prodded Joss in the ribs hard in retaliation as Val tottered off to the loo.

'Could the woman get any more patronising? I don't sleep with that many men. My dreadful sister is a million times worse,' said Carrie, pouring out the remnants of the third bottle and swilling it down in one. 'And bring back a bottle, you old tart,' shouted Carrie as an afterthought.

'Takes one to know one,' shouted the disembodied voice of Val. Val and Carrie cackled, then Carrie turned back to Joss.

'She's such a bitch. Why should I say no, if these men want to take me out? You've said yes to the first bloke who's shown any interest.'

'One, the guy is on secondment and two, he is not my boss.'

'You really think I sleep around?'

That wasn't exactly what Joss was trying to say. 'Well . . .' It was a tricky subject. Carrie did seem to get herself into more situations than anyone she'd ever heard of, let alone met. If there was a drama, then Carrie was at the centre of it. Her 'scenes' always dented her prospects. She'd be back to temping any moment and she was one of the brightest people Joss and Val knew.

'Get off the fucking fence for once. Do you think I sleep with too many people?'

'Honestly?'

'Jesus Christ, spit it out . . .'

Joss inhaled deeply. This was dangerous territory. 'Perhaps it would make life easier if you didn't always sleep with someone at work. Then things wouldn't go wrong for you so much.'

'The people I work with are fucking idiots.'

'All of them? In every one of your twelve jobs? There's only one common denominator, hon, and it's you.'

'Christ, you're as bad as Val.'

'Are you still slagging me off?' asked Val, returning with Carrie's bottle of vodka, chopped lime and a glass of ice. 'We've run out of champagne. Vodka, lime and ice?'

'Perfect.'

Val poured the clear spirit unsteadily into the medley of glasses. 'So what were you witches saying I was bad at?'

'Nothing Val, you're practically perfect in every way.' Carrie was beginning to rock from side to side. It was only a small movement, but noticeable to those who knew which signs to look for.

'Anyway, let's change the subject before someone gets out of control.' Joss was trying to defuse the tension, but like the others she was more pissed than she realised and failed to hear the condescending tone in her voice. Val heard it and decided to take over the job of defusing the bomb.

'I agree,' said Val, raising her glass and an eyebrow.

'Down in one, ladies. To our girls' night in. Long may they continue.' They drank their vodka kamikaze-style.

Joss poured again. 'To finally getting laid,' said Joss. 'The ex has the kids for half term, I'm planning to put in a lot of extra hours at work . . .'

'Listen to you. One sniff of attention from a boy, and you get as worthy as Val.'

'I'm not worthy,' insisted Val.

'I am not like Val, and anyway, what's worthy about shagging?' Joss laughed.

'What does *I'm not like Val* mean?' asked Val, turning to Joss. 'I've been supporting you all night.'

'Nothing, Carrie just didn't understand what I was saying as usual.'

'Superior as hell is what Joss means, Val,' said Carrie. 'And now you're doing it,' Carrie pointed a red nail at Joss. 'All because this little bus-boy who is probably after your job is pretending to fancy you.'

'That's not true.'

'You're only in a good mood when a boy fancies you, Joss, which sadly for us isn't very often.'

'Well it would be if I didn't have you throwing yourself at every male who walks in the room.'

'That's bollocks.'

'Calm down, you two,' said Val.

'Fuck off,' snapped Joss. 'You're just as bad, Val, pretending to be the loyal wife, but you draw everyone in. You can't have them, but you don't want anyone else to have them either. You wrap them round your little finger until every boy in the room is eating out of your hand. You've never left any for me.'

'Who is being over-sensitive now?' said Carrie.

'Yes, you should have some water, Joss,' said Val, as she poured more vodka for herself and Carrie. 'You don't drink that much any more. You haven't got the stamina.'

'No, I was married to an alcoholic, remember. Kind of put me off drunken antics.'

'Oooh, sorry we're so immature, madam,' said Carrie, pushing herself up from the sofa by leaning on Val.

'Exactly. If I can't let my hair down with my mates, who can I get drunk with?' said Val. 'I'm always with important people and have to be on my best behaviour.'

'I'm amazed you still condescend to see us,' said Joss. 'Did you hear that? She called us unimportant.' Carrie was zig-zagging her way to the bathroom.

'Don't be so ridiculous,' said Val. 'It was a compliment.'

'I don't like your compliments, they make me feel like shit.'

'That's more to do with you, Joss, than me.'

'Bollocks it is. You love the fact that Carrie and I are all over the place, it makes you feel so much better about yourself, doesn't it? God, I bet you love going back to your stiff of a husband to tell him how utterly neurotic we both are and how very lucky he is that he got someone as rare as you.'

'It's not my fault that I don't have hang-ups like you do,' said Val.

'You're worse, you just pretend to be oh-so-level-headed, but you're as fucked as the rest of us. Where the hell is your emotion? You're like a zombie.'

'Just because I don't go around throwing wobblies doesn't make me a zombie. Now who's trying to make themselves feel better? I refuse to engage with this nonsense.'

'Let's call your fancy boy,' said Carrie, returning from the loo.

'No.'

'Come on. It'll be funny. What's his number?'

'No.'

'Come on!' Carrie grabbed for Joss's phone, knocking over the bottle of vodka, but managing to grab it.

Val started valiantly mopping up the mess. 'Children, children.'

'I said no.'

'Uh-oh, she's going into one of her moods. Everyone duck. Incoming!'

'Piss off,' Joss marched past Val and Carrie, and stormed off towards her bedroom.

'Don't start fucking crying, it's so boring.'

'Look, you mad anorexic bitch,' said Joss, turning wildly on Carrie, 'just because I don't want you to ruin yet another of my dates doesn't make me boring.'

'I'm not anorexic any more!'

'Like fuck you aren't.'

'I'm not!'

'You are!'

'Come on, you two.'

'*Piss off, Val!*' they screamed in unison.

'You're the only anorexic I know who got down to four stone and never gave up the booze. One stick of cucumber isn't eating. You're so fucking obsessed with yourself –'

'You can talk. You wish you were as thin as me, we both know you chuck up in secret. Bad breath kind of gives it away.'

Joss picked up the plastic tub of hummus and threw it at Carrie. It missed.

'You stupid cow.' Carrie picked up the taramasalata and threw it at Joss. She darted sideways. The pink dip hit Val. 'What the hell are you two doing?'

'*Fuck off, Val!*' they shouted, again in unison.

'I'm just trying to help.'

'We don't need your help!'

'I'm not staying here to be insulted,' said Carrie, picking up her coat.

'That's right, run! Run away, like you always do. God forbid you should see something through to the end.'

'At least I'm not desperate enough to marry a drunk midget!'

'At least I'm not a desperate old whore who fucks anything that moves!'

'Come on, you two.'

'WILL YOU JUST FUCK OFF, YOU POMPOUS COW!' shouted Carrie.

'Fine. I will.' Val picked up her coat and marched out. 'You two are absurd.'

'You can fuck off, too,' Joss shouted at Carrie. 'Take your over-exercised arse out of here. Run off to some poor boy who hasn't wised up to how fucking *nuts* you are!'

'I wouldn't stay here if you paid me, you jealous freak,' shouted Carrie, as she picked up her coat and stumbled out.

Joss had slammed the door of her bedroom before Carrie had reached the hall. After three bottles of champagne, one bottle of vodka and no food, silence ruled. The girls' night in was over.

To: Carrie@hotmail.com; Val@aol.com
Subject: The morning after the night before

Hey,

Hope you both got home all right? What the hell happened to the hummus? I've got a stinking hangover, why the hell didn't we eat something? Talk later, lots of love Joss.

Reply: Val@aol.com; Joss@BTinternet.co.uk
Subject: The morning after the night before

Ouch. Can't remember getting home. But what a lovely evening. Same time next week at mine?
Kisses and hugs
Carrie

Reply: Joss@BTinternet.co.uk; Carrie@hotmail.com
Subject: The morning after the night before

Ouch indeed. Perhaps the bottle of vodka wasn't absolutely necessary . . .
Love you both.
Val xx

Mardi McConnochie

Daddy's Girl

'Darling,' choked Mrs Azagury, 'I've got some terrible news.'

Dr Azagury had suffered a massive coronary on the eighth hole of his weekly golf game, and even though his golf partner was a distinguished cardiac physician, nothing could be done to save him. The funeral was to be held in two days' time.

Claudia got off the phone and opened her wardrobe. She would throw some things in a bag and go to the airport and get on the next flight out. But as she stared at the wall of clothes her mind would not function. *Daddy? Funeral?* A wall of skirts, pants, jackets, tops, T-shirts, dresses, shoes, shoes, shoes, handbags, belts, scarves. *Daddy? Dead?* Packing was something she usually enjoyed – what could be more fun than creating a capsule wardrobe? – but now she could not even begin to think. *Funeral. Black.* Not that she had much stuff that *wasn't* black . . . *No time. Got to get to the airport.* She pulled things at random from the wardrobe and threw them on the bed. Collected up a slippery handful of bottles from the bathroom. Stuffed it all into a Louis Vuitton travelling case. And somehow she was out the door and into a cab and on her way to the airport.

Claudia had experienced death before. Family pets. Unlucky kids from school, dying from the strange misadventures of childhood. Grandparents. All of these deaths were tragedies, tragedies of different sizes, but tragedies nonetheless. But none of them had really *touched* her. None of them had punched a hole in the fabric of her world. None of them had torn her free from her moorings so that suddenly she was adrift, terrified and alone.

There was no one at Tullamarine to meet her so she took a cab to the house, and oh God! The terrible familiarity as they drew closer and closer to home! She knew every street, every corner, every house and tree as if they were engraved on her memory. *The way home.* But home would not be the same now. Would never be the same again.

The taxi drew up outside her house. Inside she could see all the lights blazing. She paid the driver and began to walk up the front path.

'Miss? 'Scuse me! Miss!'

She stopped and turned. The driver was making his way round to the boot. 'Your bag?'

She would have walked off without it. She took it from him without a word (too disturbed to make him carry it to the door for her as ordinarily she would have done) and went up the garden path. Dreading the moment when she would have to go into the house and face her mother.

Her mother's friends were everywhere, all tea and

G&Ts, little chicken sandwiches, tears, tissues, flower arranging. The air quivered with the radiation from a thousand mobile-phone calls as her mother's friends called their friends, seeking advice about funeral directors, florists, death etiquette, the name of that wonderful caterer who did Melissa's gallery opening, you remember the one? They were all half-pissed and loving the drama – making shopping lists, rearranging hair appointments, changing lunch plans – and their eyes lit up as they saw her arrive.

'Oh Claudia, I'm so sorry, you must be devastated!' they carolled, one by one, as she moved through them.

'Where's Mum?' she asked.

'She's having a lie-down.'

'But she'll be so pleased to see you.'

Claudia went down the hall and into her parents' room. Her mother was curled on her side, clutching a pillow, crying in a loose, unfocused, medicated way that made Claudia suspect she'd been in this state for some hours already. The sight of her father's dressing-gown, slipping off the end of the bed and onto the floor, suddenly seemed unbearably poignant.

'Mum?'

Her mother's head rolled back from the pillow she was clutching, and the wretchedness in her face sent a stab of panic into Claudia's stomach.

'Oh darling—'

Claudia dropped to the floor and threw her arms around her mother, and cried and cried and cried.

Claudia had never really felt a powerful attachment to her family before. They had brought her up and loved her (and why wouldn't they – everyone loved her) and when the time was right she had turned her back on them and got on with her life. She had moved from Melbourne to Sydney to become a model – it hadn't really worked out, but that wasn't the point. Daddy had wanted her to follow her dream and follow it she had without so much as a backward glance. At the time it had seemed like a healthy and natural thing to do but now, suddenly, it seemed heartless and ungrateful. Ingratitude: it had always seemed like one of those stupid old Victorian values, like prudence or modesty, but now it began to seem desperately important. But this realisation had come too late, of course. The person she should have loved the best was gone, and there would never be another chance for her to let him know how she really felt. Because she hadn't even *known* how she felt until he was no longer there and she became guttingly, flailingly conscious of her loss. Too late, too late.

She discovered the next morning she had forgotten to pack shoes that went with the dress she'd brought, but she could not bring herself to go out and buy some more. *That's* how bad it was.

A lot of people spoke at Dr Azagury's funeral. There were relatives, colleagues, friends, grateful former patients. Mrs Azagury was crying so hard she couldn't speak. She sat with Claudia, holding her hand, while her tearful but curiously expressionless friends dabbed at their eyes with teeny little hankies.

Claudia decided she owed it to her father to say something.

'I'm so lucky,' she quavered, 'to have had the best dad

in the world. He was always so supportive of me in everything I did. Unconditional love, that's what he gave me, and that is so rare these days.' She paused, to collect herself. 'Every step I took in life, he was always there for me. I couldn't have asked for more love and support. He always taught me to have faith in myself and to believe I was a special person. He gave me so much. But the most important thing he taught me was to care for the people around me, and to give the gift of love. If you've got love in your life, you can do anything. I just hope I made you proud, Daddy.'

Her mother sobbed. The crowd clapped. Claudia thought about saying more, but she was too choked up to continue. It wasn't every father, she thought, as she went back to her seat, who had such an amazing daughter.

After the great surge of emotion that was the funeral and the long grief-filled wallow of the wake (the caterer did a wonderful job, she really did) the next day was always going to be a let-down. Claudia woke with a hangover in a house emptied of people but full of wilting flowers.

She sipped black coffee with her mother. It had never been much of a house for breakfast. For a long time, no one said anything.

'What do you want to do today?' Claudia asked.

'I don't know.'

'Is there someone we should call?'

'I don't know.'

'What about the solicitor?'

'The solicitor?'

'Dad had a will, right?'

'I don't know.'

'I'll call him, shall I?'

Her mother nodded limply and said, 'I'm going back to bed.'

Of course there was a will. The life insurance paid off the house, and Mrs Azagury got the superannuation, as well as the income from the investment properties and the stock portfolio.

'Don't I get anything?' Claudia asked.

'I think your father assumed,' the solicitor said, 'that you would be taken care of by your mother.'

'She could live another forty years!' Claudia snapped. 'What am I supposed to do until then?'

Her mother burst into tears. The solicitor sighed.

'Well, it's true,' said Claudia. 'It had to be said.'

Mrs Azagury found it harder and harder to get out of bed in the morning. Everything was too difficult: having a shower, eating lunch, picking up the phone. Claudia bought groceries, opened the mail, paid the bills. It wasn't difficult, but it was not at all how she'd expected things to be. Her father was dead – didn't she deserve some coddling? But no coddling was forthcoming. She had been forced into the unwelcome role of *coddler*.

But she was still partially enthralled by those powerful emotions that had come over her on the first day, and it seemed important that she should be there for her mother – it's what Daddy would have wanted. At first she did it for him, out of a compensatory impulse she didn't bother to examine, but gradually, surprisingly, she found she was almost beginning to enjoy this feeling of being in charge. She *enjoyed* feeling like the capable one as she ordered this and dealt with that, cancelling Dad's magazine subscriptions and fielding calls from people, making decisions, getting things done. Her mother's friends all told her she was an angel and a pillar of strength. No one had ever told her that before and she found herself swelling with pride. She considered moving back to Melbourne permanently and taking charge of her mother's affairs. She pictured herself, the charming daughter, escorting her mother to lunch and taking her to matinees at the ballet. Dear Claudia, everyone would say, such a lovely girl, totally devoted. The more she thought about it the more choked up she got. She knew she had never been a particularly wonderful daughter before, but from now on everything was going to be different. Everyone would be able to see what a wonderful, caring, selfless girl Claudia Azagury really was.

But as the days passed and the shock faded she began to lose patience with her mother. Sure, she'd lost her husband and it was terrible, but did she have to keep going on about it?

'Mum, don't you think it's time you pulled yourself together?' she asked, ten days after the funeral.

Her mother wept and moaned.

'You can't go on like this,' Claudia said. 'I'm not going to be around forever, you know.'

She had given up all thought of escorting her mother to ballet matinees. Her mother moaned louder.

'I think you need closure. To help you move on.'

'Closure?'

'It's time we got rid of Dad's stuff.'

Her mother looked at her through wide, red, wet eyes. 'I can't,' she moaned, and started sobbing.

'Yes, you can,' Claudia said impatiently. *This must be what being a parent is like*, she thought. *Being responsible for things*. She held up the twenty-pack of green garbage bags she'd bought. 'Where do you want to start, his clothes or his study?'

Her mother recoiled from the brutality of the green garbage bags, but Claudia would not be put off. *Someone* had to take charge round here or they'd never be able to move on.

The clothes were a little daunting, so she began with the study. Out went the medical journals and the books of golfing anecdotes. Out went the old sporting trophies and the cricketing memorabilia. Out went the collection of pornographic magazines she found hidden in a drawer of his desk. Out went all the odd little bits and pieces which didn't match the immaculate décor of the rest of the house: the kitsch hula dancers and engraved beer steins and novelty hats. Out, too, went an ashtray Claudia had made in primary school as a gift for Father's Day, back in the days when you could safely assume that most fathers smoked and that an ashtray was not an inappropriate present for a child to give. The thought that her father had kept it all these years made her cry a little, but not enough to keep it.

The clothes were harder. As soon as she opened the wardrobe door she could smell him – the scent of his aftershave, mixed with the smell that was just him. But there was also something so *personal* about clothes, something so intimate and singular. Claudia spent an endless amount of time thinking about her own wardrobe, augmenting it, embellishing it, rearranging it, editing it. Her own wardrobe was like a conversation with the world; it announced who she was, where she was going and what she was doing there, her hopes, her fears, the kind of day she was having, whether she was happy or sad, intimidated or in a killer mood, having a thin day, having a fat day, ready to take on the world or ready to hide. If you knew how to read the wardrobe you would have seen Claudia's soul laid bare. And as Claudia stood in front of her father's wardrobe, armed with her green garbage bags, she knew that the story of her father's life was written here, if you only knew how to read it. The work shirts, the ties, the suits. The sports jackets and polo shirts, the baby-boomer jeans. The diamond-patterned golf jumpers. The tux for weddings. (But he hadn't lived to see his daughter's wedding.) New things just bought, old things he couldn't bear to part with. Things his wife had bought on a whim that he kept solely to please her. A history of his adult life. And the thought that all this history would now be lost forever was almost more than she could bear.

Almost. But at the end of the day they were just old clothes.

'Mother, are you going to help me with this?' she asked.

'I can't, I can't,' her mother moaned, rolling around on the bed like a cat on heat.

Claudia curled her lip in disgust and started to pull the shirts off the hangers.

'There are going to have to be a few changes around here,' her mother announced the following day. To Claudia's surprise she had got up and had a shower, blow-dried her hair and put on proper clothes. She had even made herself a piece of toast. Claudia's efforts to provide closure had clearly had the desired effect, for her mother was up and raring to go.

'What kind of changes?' Claudia asked.

'I can't go on living the kind of lifestyle I'm used to. From now on I'm going to have to be careful.'

'What are you talking about?'

'I'm very young to be a widow, and there's longevity in my family. I don't want to run out of money –'

'Run out? Dad left you squillions! How could you possibly run out?'

'Anything can happen,' Mrs Azagury said. 'From now on I'm going to have to tighten my belt. And so are you.'

Claudia nearly choked on her coffee. 'Me?'

'You know I'll always support you, darling, but I may not be able to help you out quite as much as before.'

Mrs Azagury had been slipping Claudia pocket money on the sly. She clearly had no idea that Mr Azagury had been doing the same thing.

'But Mother!' Claudia shrieked. 'What am I supposed to do for money?'

'You could get a job.'

Claudia couldn't believe what she was hearing. 'What, like you did? You've never lifted a finger in your fucking life!'

'It was different for my generation!' Mrs Azagury snapped. 'We didn't have the opportunities you've had.'

'If Dad was here he'd be rolling over in his grave,' Claudia said, and then burst into tears.

Mrs Azagury looked at her weeping daughter coolly. 'If your father was here we wouldn't be having this discussion.' She took a compact from her handbag and checked her lipstick. 'I'm having lunch with the girls today, if you want to come.'

'I'd rather eat my own vomit.'

'No need to be sulky, Claudia. You should look on this as an opportunity, not a setback. You're a very talented girl, I'm sure you'll think of something.'

Claudia gave her mother a death glare. 'You never loved me,' she said. 'I wish I was dead.'

'Be careful what you wish for, darling,' her mother said.

Claudia flew back to Sydney the next day.

She discovered that the glittering city was a hard place to grieve in. Deep emotions seemed to bounce off those radiant surfaces and blow away across the Pacific. There was a heedless glint to the way the sun shone off the harbour, and the sky was an insensitive shade of deep blue. Even Claudia's beautiful Neutral Bay apartment, with its all-white décor and very expensive harbour glimpses, seemed comfortless. Daddy bought this apartment for her. Daddy wanted her to be safe and secure. But now Daddy was gone and what was to stop her mother evicting her so she could start getting a return on the investment? It was a cold, hard world out there without Daddy to rely on.

Claudia picked up the enormous pile of mail on her floor and found forty-seven catalogues, thirty-three invitations, six credit-card statements, an electricity bill, a phone bill and a gas bill. She kept the invitations and the catalogues and put the rest of the mail in the bin.

Claudia sat on a bar stool and sipped her flirtini, not listening to the chatter of her friends. The bar was filled with beautiful people but all she could see around her was transience. Ahead lay drunkenness and the spoilage of all that pristine beauty, the evening winding down to its shabby close, freshness fading, charm disappearing, a slow descent over days, weeks, months into dissolution and death. The beautiful people would grow old and fat and lose their bloom. The beautiful places would grow boring and shabby or go broke and close down or fill up with awful people from the suburbs and live on as a travesty of their former selves. It was so depressing she could weep. Was there anything to look forward to between now and death? She had tried to use her favourite credit card and it had been declined. Tonight the world seemed a harsh and brutal place and all of human life a bitter joke.

'Claude, you remember Simon, right?'

Claudia focused on the guy who'd joined them. He had red hair and foxy features – she couldn't stand red hair on guys – but he was immaculately dressed and perfectly groomed, and as she leaned over to kiss him she remembered who he was. Although not yet thirty, Simon was the owner of this bar, and several others. Young, cool, rich. Famously one of Sydney's most eligible bachelors – and not just one of those straight-acting gay guys they use to fill out the numbers in the magazines. He was a genuine, heterosexual, good-looking, rich, single guy. And he was looking at her with an expression of unbridled covetousness. All her worries seemed to drop away in an instant as brave new worlds opened up before her. So what if he had red hair? He was rich!

'Of course I do,' she said, and gave him her most bewitching smile.

Monica McInerney

The Long Way Home

Shelley made the age limit for the ten-city *Rave* tour of
Europe by two months and three weeks. The woman in
the travel agency pointed out that fact as she ran her eyes
down the application form.

'You're thirty-four? Nearly thirty-five? Our clients do
tend to be the younger end of the age group. You're sure
you're happy to go ahead? We've other tours with more of
a focus on culture, less on—'

'No, I'm very happy with this one, thanks.' Shelley had
her hand on the brochure on the desk between them as if
she was staking a claim.

The woman lowered her voice. 'They're usually all single, not really into the history side of things. More out for
a good time.'

Shelley dug out a bright smile from somewhere. 'I am,
too, I promise.' A pause. Then her confidence faltered.
'Don't I look like I am?'

The other woman seemed relieved when her phone rang.

At home, on the new sofa in the centre of the living room which still felt nothing like home, even after three months, Shelley leafed through her ticket folder and read the brochure. All the people in the *Rave* photos looked like models. Happy models. Happy and high-on-life models. She'd have to do her best to look like them. She had obviously not dressed casually enough that morning. She pulled her hair out of its current plait. Made a mental note to buy some T-shirts. Decided to wash her jeans a few unnecessary times to fade them. She automatically went to the towel cupboard to get the washing powder when she realised that was where she'd kept it in her old house. In their old house. In her new house, she kept it under the sink.

She'd seen the *Rave* ad on TV the previous week, rung the toll-free number for the brochure and picked out the tour that lasted two weeks and took in ten European cities, finishing with a visit to Edinburgh and the highlands of Scotland. She read the description, fighting her way through the exclamation marks that surrounded the brief eligibility questionnaire. Yes, she was between eighteen and thirty-five. Yes, she was single. As of three months previously. Yes, she was out for a good time. 'Are you looking for carefree days of fun, adventure and romance? We supply three out of three!' the *Rave* copywriter promised.

Travel was the key, Shelley had heard. Lose yourself and find yourself at the same time. She had a different motto in mind. Run, run, run as fast as you can. She couldn't get away from her own life fast enough.

Her taxi was delayed the morning the tour group left. She heard the driver make his excuses about heavy traffic and oil spills but she was too nervous to console him the way she normally would. She needed him to concentrate on his driving and get her there before she changed her mind. She was the last to arrive at the meeting point in the departure area. She knew immediately it was a mistake. She should have got there first. She could have welcomed the others, been someone they came to and wanted to talk to, instead of having to edge in and join the group, feeling left out on the sidelines. She hated being late. She was always the first to arrive anywhere. Harry said it was from being the daughter of a schoolteacher.

They'd been late for the first appointment at the maternity hospital. She'd been fidgeting in her seat, willing the tram to go faster. He'd taken her hand and squeezed it.

'Shell, relax. We're about a minute late, that's all.'

'What if they give our appointment to someone else?'

'Then I'll tie myself to the receptionists' computer until they give us another one. Go on a hunger strike. Hire a brass band and march up and down outside until they see you.'

They'd had to wait another hour in the reception area, for an appointment that lasted less than five minutes. It only took that long to confirm a pregnancy these days. Outside they'd sat on a stone step, in the sunshine, not speaking, just gripping each other's hands and smiling, at each other and at everyone who walked past.

On the plane, a hitch with the seating arrangements meant she was in a different section from the rest of the tour group. She didn't mind. She took every distraction on offer. She watched five movies, one after the other. She ate everything put in front of her. She drank red wine. She left in the earphones when the movies finished, hoping they could block the thoughts.

'Shelley, at least send me emails. Let me know where you'll be.'

She could barely look at him. It hurt too much. *'Harry, there's no point. Please, can't you accept –'*

'An email. Just now and again.'

'It has to be over. We have to make a clean start. Away from each other.' How else could they recover from something like this? It wasn't a normal fight.

London was the first stop. The sky was grey, the weather cool, even though it was spring. They visited Big Ben, took a cruise down the Thames, stood outside Buckingham Palace discussing whether the Queen really was inside.

The guide called her. 'Shelley? Come on, the bus is waiting.'

'Sorry.' She'd been looking at a couple further down the footpath, peering through the gates into the palace like everyone else. The woman was her age. The man was about Harry's age. About their height, too. There was a pram between them. The father's hand kept absently reaching into the pram and stroking his son or daughter's head.

Two nights in Paris. A joke party with everyone wearing berets and an impromptu quiz. The tour guide was good at impromptu activities. Name three famous French people. Shelley couldn't. She could name three French restaurants in Melbourne. She could remember three meals she'd had with Harry in those restaurants, one for their first date, the second when they got engaged. The third for no reason at all.

She could remember telling him in detail about something funny that had happened at work and him interrupting her. *'I love you very much, you know.'*

'You're dropping it into the conversation? Just like that?'

'Just like that. Sorry, go on.'

In Amsterdam she followed the group down the canal paths, through the red-light district, into the clog factory and the cheese shops. The guide was talking but she was remembering different conversations and attempted explanations.

'I don't understand. I get home from work and you tell me it's over. You're moving out. Without even talking about it with me?'

She didn't understand herself. *'I need the space, Harry.'*

'It's not about that, is it?'

It was about the pain she felt every time she looked at him. She was trying to get as far as she could from that, not from him.

Venice. City of love. City of food. The forty members of the tour group took up three long tables in the cheery restaurant. The waiters were friendly. There was no European snobbishness. 'We're worth too much to them,' the guide had whispered to Shelley as they walked in.

'And here for poor tired Shelley who has had a long week and needs to spend the weekend with her feet up being spoiled is a glass of shockingly expensive Italian wine and the speciality

of the house, crostata di pastore, colloquially known as shepherd's pie—'

She needed to remember the bad times, not the good times.

'You're running away, that's what you're doing.'

He was right. She was running away as fast as she could. But she wasn't getting anywhere. Everything that made her feel bad had come with her.

Rome. She wanted to be pinched. She stood in St Peter's Square hopefully. She watched confident, curvy Italian women walk past, watched the promenade – the *passagiata*, the guide told them. The women glanced over their shoulders, knowing they were being watched.

She remembered him walking in and finding her standing side-on in front of the full-length mirror in their bedroom. *'Is it showing yet, do you think?'*

Harry coming up behind her, with a pillow, putting it in front of her, the two of them laughing. *'Now it is. It might be twins.'* Another pillow. *'Triplets, even.'* He grabbed a third pillow.

The guide organised football and basketball matches in Madrid. Shelley didn't play. She sat on a wooden bench back from the park.

'You need to relax. Promise me you won't do anything while I'm away.'

'Sit still for three days? Harry, I'll go mad. And I want to get the room painted while I can still move.'

'It'll wait. I'll do it when I get back.'

'It'll take me less than a day.'

'But should you be doing all that sort of climbing around?'

'I'll be fine.'

She'd been up and down the ladder, moving the chest of drawers, wriggling the cupboard side to side across the floor, wincing at the screeches it made on the floorboards, out to the car, carrying in heavy pots of paint, singing to the radio. She'd felt a twinge, so attuned to every movement in her body. Then another. Then something worse.

It was all over by the time Harry got home, even though he'd left the conference centre the second he heard her voice on the phone.

Hands held in front of a doctor the next day, but this time no smiles.

She'd asked the question. 'Doctor, did I make it happen?'

He was an old doctor. He hadn't looked at her, making notes as he spoke, pulling open a drawer beside him, taking out a fresh prescription pad. 'I can't say. It mightn't have helped.'

Outside, at home, the next day, the day after, the week after, they discussed it, over and over. 'He said it mightn't have helped. He didn't say you killed your own child.'

'But I did. It's what you think, isn't it? You think I killed him.'

'Shell, I don't.'

'That's what you think every time you look at me.' It was what she felt every time she looked at herself in the mirror.

'Shell, I—'

She couldn't listen to the rest. She could see it in his

379

eyes. He didn't want it to be that way, but she knew that's what he thought.

In Munich she came across a carpet shop that wouldn't have looked out of place in Morocco. The rest of the group were in a beer hall. She'd run out of things to say to them, and they had run out of things to say to her. She wanted to tell them that a year ago she would have been different, a year ago she would have loved this. Two years ago she and Harry might have been on a trip like this together. But she couldn't find the words. She hadn't been able to find the right words for anything for three months.

There was a deep red carpet in the front window. It had a purple and green border of flowers and leaves. The longer she looked at it, the more she found hidden in the pattern. It wasn't as beautiful as their rug at home. It was the only thing she had taken with her. The carpet that had been in the hallway of their house. She'd found it in a second-hand shop a week before their wedding. It had come with a spiel from the shop owner, a second-generation Afghan. The patterns signified the future, happiness, growth. She and Harry had made love on it that night. At first on the rug itself but then it had tickled and started to burn and then she'd got the giggles. So he had put a quilt on it. She wasn't fanciful enough to think that's when their baby had been conceived. The timing was wrong. It had been a practice run.

The rug didn't look as good in her new flat. It looked out of place. It didn't quite fit. The edges pushed up against the sides of the hallway.

In Prague the bus driver tried to make a pass at her. He'd had too much wine at dinner.

'Isn't this against the company rules?' she said.

'To hell with the rules. There's something special about you.'

She'd heard him say the same thing to one of the other girls the previous night. For a moment she gave in. This was what she needed. A new experience, the feel of a different body, to cancel out and cover over memories of Harry's body. The bus driver was a good kisser. That made it easy at the start and easy for a little while. It would have been simple to sink into it, to let feeling take over from thinking even for just an hour. To cover the traces. To try and forget about everything. But when his hands strayed beneath her shirt, against her skin, it was like she was burnt. She pushed him away.

'I'm sorry, I can't. I'm married.'

'Come on. No one comes on these tours if they're married.'

'I'm separated, I mean.'

'Then you're not married, are you?'

She still felt married.

Back in London she heard music in shops, from car radios, that reminded her of him. She saw places she'd heard sung about. She imagined Harry seeing them with her. She bought a CD for him. She would send it to him. No, he had the key to her flat, he was keeping an eye on it. He'd insisted. She'd give it to him when they met after she'd got back. A thank you. A farewell present.

'Let me be sad with you. It was my baby too.'

'But you didn't hurt it, like I did.'

'You didn't hurt it. It wasn't the right time for it. We'll try again.'

'We can't. We can't go backwards.'

'Then we'll go forwards. Don't give up on me.'

In Edinburgh there was a free afternoon of shopping time. On the second floor of a large shopping centre she found herself at the entrance to a Mothercare store. She had avoided any babywear shops since it happened. She would leave a shopping centre if she saw on the directory that there was one inside. This one surprised her.

In a basket in front was a collection of pale yellow, pale blue, pale pink and creamy white knitwear. Little booties. Little hats. It came up from deep inside her, the hurt and the anguish and the sorrow and the guilt. There, in a strange city, she cried for the first time. The same woman who was embarrassed if she discovered she'd walked around town with a ladder in her stocking, now standing in public, in the middle of a shopping centre, crying hard. Sobbing. The younger girl inside the store looked shocked. An older woman didn't.

'Come in here with me, pet.'

There was a small room at the back of the store. The woman didn't need to ask. She seemed to know. She handed Shelley a cup of hot tea.

'When did it happen, lovie?'

'Three months ago.'

'How old?'

'He wasn't born yet. I was five months pregnant.'

The woman nodded.

'We thought we were over the danger time. We thought we had nothing to worry about.'

'He was your first child?'

Shelley nodded.

'Is your husband all right?'

A pause. 'We separated.'

'Not for good.'

'It was my fault.'

'It wasn't your fault. It was nobody's fault, not yours, not his. Nobody's. I know.'

Shelley looked at her.

'Five times,' the woman said.

'Five miscarriages?' At the woman's nod. 'Did you ever . . .'

'One daughter, just when I'd given up hope. And she's had five children. I'm supergran. Keep talking to him, pet. Keep loving him. He needs you as much as you need him. The two of you made this baby together, so the two of you have to grieve together. Where is he?'

'At home.'

'Here in Edinburgh?'

'Australia.'

'Go home to him.'

'I'm on a tour.'

'Go home to him.'

'Promise me you'll email. I need to know you're all right. Let me collect you at least.'

She sent it from a crammed Internet cafe. She didn't know if he was picking up his emails regularly. She wasn't due home for another five days. He'd be expecting her to go on to other parts of Scotland. He had the itinerary. He'd said he needed to have it, to know where she was. She could remember everything he had said to her and she could remember everything she had said to him.

Her plane arrived at Melbourne Airport before dawn. The queue was long through passport control, through baggage reclaim, through the double doors out into the airport. Dozens of people were waiting. There was no sign of him. He wasn't in the line of people pressed against the barrier. He wasn't there with a cardboard sign with her name written on it. He wasn't in the group of people near the door having cigarettes, or outside, double-parked in their old Holden station wagon, ready to whisk her away.

He was under the meeting-point sign. He was standing on a rug. Her rug. Their rug.

She was crying as she moved towards him. His arms were open. She moved into them and pressed her face against his chest.

'I'm so sorry, Harry.'

'Welcome home, Shelley.' He didn't say anything else. Not yet. He just held her tighter.

Chris Manby

The Last Man on Earth

Newspapers all over the planet made front-page news of the sorry story of the sudden deaths of Mimi and Leo, the last breeding pair of human beings in captivity. The brilliant scientists at the top research zoo in Outer Mercilon had been trying unsuccessfully for fifteen years to be the first to produce a real human baby. They had gone to great lengths to ensure that breeding conditions were perfect for their charges. They had provided the mating pair with everything they needed to be healthy and happy. The right food – no meat, pure soya for protein (though some geneticists argued that since a modified soya crisis had wiped out most of the earth's population in the late twenty-first century, Mimi and Leo might actually have adapted to need a contaminated food source).

The right environment was important too. A small part of the enclosure had been completely blocked off from the prying eye of the 24-hour CCTV camera, because it had quickly become clear that the human female in particular would absolutely not engage in even the affectionate pre-liminaries of mating if she felt she was being observed. The scientists even had to go so far as to replace the one-way mirror with a proper wall when it became clear that the unusually intelligent female had cottoned onto the trick and was subsequently still inhibited.

But the privacy room was to be the breeding project's downfall, for, while the scientists assumed that their sub-jects were getting down to creating the next generation, the grunts and cries they heard were not in fact the usual inelegant sounds that accompanied human mating, but the sound of the subjects killing each other with the can-dlesticks that some bright spark from the University of Mercilon had suggested would make mating inevitable and successful (he had picked up the tip about using candles for seductive lighting in an article on 'Perfect Seduction Techniques' in the *Cosmopolitan* book from the vast Earth archive).

Doctor Eugynon, the eminent professor who had been leading the breeding project, was distraught. His life's work, gone forever. They tried to rescue the female, who wasn't quite dead when the operative who fed the humans three times a day found her lying in a pool of blood upon the satin sheets of the mating platform. But she seemed to have lost the will to live. She refused food and medica-tion until she too finally faded away. Not even the noxious brown substance the humans called 'Chock-let' could save her this time. Doctor Eugynon considered following the female to wherever it was that humans thought they went after death. He held the candlestick the woman had used to club her mate into unconsciousness in his own third hand and turned it over contemplatively. He went so far as to bash it against his own head a couple of times but it didn't even dent his radiation-resistant silicon-based skin.

He was about to take more constructive suicidal measures with an atom dispersing gun when his assistant, the lovely Doctor Microgynon, with her fetching knee-length tentacles, raced into his office bursting with the news that a human ship had just been sighted outside the planet's atmosphere. A ship that contained at least two carbon-based life forms!

Eugynon shrugged his bony neck-plate. It was probably just another ghost ship infested with the spider-like parasites from Oooo-on Three that had finished off so many of the Earth Alliance Freedom Fighters during the Six-Hundred Years War. They gave a life-force reading very like that of a human child, those Oooo-on critters. The Oooo-on house at the zoo was about as popular as pigeons had been on the original Planet Earth. The last thing Eugynon needed was another pair of those, but he gave his permission for a hunt in any case. And within hours the ship (made of that primitive earth material that was actually affected by a simple magnet!) was dragged in.

And not only did the life forms inside survive the punishing entry into Outer Mercilon atmosphere, but when the flimsy hull of their vessel was opened, the travellers were revealed to be humans after all. Two perfect, tiny humans. All pink and shivering and covered with that disgusting silky hair that felt like entrails to the Mercilonian scientists lucky enough to handle the creatures. Eugynon was delighted.

The two humans (one of each sex, praise the moons!)

were taken straight to the enclosure. The tiny room had been thoroughly cleaned since the death of Mimi and Leo but the new female one still wrinkled her nose in the way that female humans did.

'She can smell the previous female,' Doctor Microgynon suggested. 'Do you think the remaining pheromones will encourage her to mate?'

'We can only hope so,' said Doctor Eugynon, as he crossed about sixteen of his fingers.

'There is blood on the sheets!' hissed Captain Melanie Eve to First Officer Andrew Adams when he finally came round from his concussion on the rock-hard bed.

'Where are we?' he asked.

'Well, I don't think we're in the Earth embassy on Mars,' Eve commented sarcastically. 'What the hell were those things that brought us in here?'

'I don't want to know,' said Adams.

'Looked like some kind of cephalopod to me,' Eve mused. 'And it had to wear breathing apparatus to come inside here, which suggests that their atmosphere isn't friendly to humans and vice versa. We could be on one of the Outer Oooo-ons.'

First Officer Adams paled.

'I've got to speak to their leader,' Eve continued. 'Though I'm not entirely sure that the squid that brought us in here can speak.'

'Well, at least they haven't tried to kill us,' said Adams. 'Look at this food. They're trying to make us comfortable.'

'Or fatten us up!'

Captain Eve hammered on the glasslike substance that

enclosed them. 'Nobody eats this soldier!' she shouted. 'I'm Captain Melanie Eve of Squadron Eleven of the Earth Alliance. I demand to speak to your leader at once!'

Professor Eugynon watched Eve closely from the observation deck. They weren't taking any chances with blind spots in the enclosure this time. Another ten cameras had been fitted. The humans couldn't so much as sniff without him knowing about it.

'What's the female saying?' asked Microgynon. The only human dialect she knew fluently was Chinese – the most popular.

'I think that's a human display of physical strength,' said Eugynon as Captain Eve thumped the glass so hard she set off the breakout detector. 'She's signalling her genetic viability to mate.'

'Aren't they peculiar?' Microgynon mused. Human lovemaking was just so . . . rough. Once again she was glad that, as a Mercilonian, she merely had to flash a few lights along her bony head crest to signal her intentions. Not that Eugynon ever seemed to notice. Just that morning she had twisted her tentacles into a particularly complicated lattice in his honour. Professor Femodene had complimented her on her 'do' but Eugynon, as usual, only had eyes for the revolting sniffling creature he called 'the girl'.

'Are they a mating pair?' Microgynon asked her mentor when it was clear that he wasn't going to be distracted.

'I would say they are,' Eugynon nodded. 'Judging from the heated way in which they are communicating. See, Microgynon, she's touching him now.'

Captain Eve laid her First Officer out with a single punch.

'We're in the sodding Outer Mercilon research zoo, you idiot!' she screamed at him. 'See those two moons? The moons we never fly past??? How did we get here?'

'It's not my fault,' Adams whimpered.

'You were the fucking navigator! I told you to set the coordinates for home via the Oooo-ons, specifically avoiding here. Even a bloody first-year grunt in the military knows that the magnetic forces around Outer Mercilon are irresistible. Even to our best fighter ships. You got us sucked down onto the most hostile planet known to humankind!'

'Hostile atmosphere?' Adams asked helplessly.

'Hostile bloody everything. The Mercilonians used to take package holidays to the Earth colony on Venus to partake in their equivalent of fly-fishing – with the Japanese cosmonaut community taking the place of the rare Scottish sea-trout.'

'I didn't think that was true,' said Adams in horror.

'It was true,' shrieked Eve. 'They only stopped when the Intergalactic Community of The Dark Planets put a conservation order on the Japs. This is deep shit we're in now, lover-boy. Deep shit.'

'They're definitely a mating pair,' said Microgynon proudly, snatching on the one word of their dialect she did know. 'Did you hear her address him as 'love'?'

'What's going to happen?' Adams asked nervously.

'We could be experimented on. We could be dissected. We could even be forced to mate.'

An uncontrollable spark of interest flashed in Andrew Adams' blue eyes.

'Dream on,' said Eve.

'But that wouldn't be so bad, would it? It's quite nice in here. Perhaps we're as precious as Giant Pandas.' Adams reached for an apple. Eve karate-chopped it from his hand before he could get it anywhere near his mouth.

'Are you mad?' she asked him. 'What if it's been drugged?'

'She's preventing him from taking sustenance,' Professor Eugynon observed. 'They're definitely about to mate.'

'How are we going to get out of here?' sighed Captain Eve.

'I don't know,' said Adams.

'Trust me, I didn't intend my question to be anything other than rhetorical,' Eve sighed. She paced the enclosure. 'Why did I let them palm me off with a man for a First Officer?' she murmured to herself. 'Everyone knows a man couldn't navigate himself out of bed in the morning if his girlfriend wasn't pushing him.'

'Your sexist remarks aren't going to help us now,' Adams said petulantly.

'Just go back to thinking with your dick,' said Eve.

Adams' mouth dropped open.

'I mean the memory chip,' Eve clarified impatiently. 'The one implanted in your penis so that the Oooo-on fundamentalist rebels wouldn't find it. Don't you have maps of all the Dark Planets stored on that?'

'I do. But it won't work with my handheld info reader,' he told her. 'I have to insert my penis into the download port on board the ship to access it.'

'Brilliant!' Eve spat. 'Just my luck to get stuck with the

one guy who *can't* just stick his prick into anything and get a result.'

'Blame the Defence Ministry,' he said, trying to raise a smile.

But Eve was not in the mood for joking. She pressed her nose against the wall of the compound and squinted out into the dusk. Outer Mercilon didn't have its own sun. The only light was the feeble glow of a distant star reflected by the two moons that orbited the planet three times every Earth hour.

'See anything?' Adams asked.

'As a matter of fact, I can see our ship,' she told him. 'And there's nothing between us except these glass walls. It doesn't seem to be tethered. If we could just get out of this ridiculous pod. I don't think we sustained too much damage on entry. I loaded fuel to take us all the way back to Florida. We've done half the trip. We should have enough left to effect one more take-off . . .'

Adams looked at her doubtfully. 'If the Mercilonians have got us here as part of a breeding program, there's bound to be heavy security. Wouldn't it be better just to lie back and think of Earth?'

Another slap from Captain Eve landed Adams on his backside in the fruit bowl.

'Send in more fruit!' barked Eugynon to his assistants. 'I don't want anything important to be missing when they finally start to make love.'

The feeding operative carrying the bananas didn't know what hit him. Mimi and Leo had never moved so fast.

Captain Eve ran a swift circle around the confused Merci-lonian with the bedclothes from the mating platform. The operative was blinded by a duvet cover. Adams finished the job off with a swift rugby tackle that took out all six of the operative's knees.

'Stop them!' Eugynon cried when the debacle was relayed to the viewing deck.

But it was too late. Captain Melanie Eve was not top of her class at Air Fleet Training School for nothing. She could get her ship ready for take-off in just under thirty seconds, which was ten seconds less than it would take the average Mercilonian to don breathing apparatus to enter the controlled atmosphere of the human compound. Even if he used all his arms.

As Eugynon slithered into the compound, followed by his assistant Microgynon, Captain Eve put pedal to metal and the deceptively powerful Earth ship blasted through the compound's fine silicon membrane roof. The roof shattered into a snowstorm of needle-sharp splinters that pierced Eugynon's Earthling-encounter suit and sent him scuttling back to the door.

'Foolish Earthlings!' Eugynon wailed. 'If they won't let us help them to regenerate, they'll be extinct within a year!'

Microgynon stole the opportunity to wrap one of her tentacles around his shoulder. 'There, there . . .'

It took almost all their fuel reserves to blast out of Mer-cilon's magnetic atmosphere. They didn't have the fuel to get back to Florida but there was just enough to get them to Van Halen. First Officer Adams was delighted.

Van Halen was a small planet in the Pleiades that had been opened as a holiday resort by the legendary Paris Hilton's great-great-grandson.

'Think you can get us there?' Captain Eve asked her navigator.

'I'll need the maps in my . . .' Adams cast his eyes downwards.

'I won't look,' Eve lied.

Adams unzipped the front of his flight suit and sought out the info download port in the flight desk.

Meanwhile, Captain Eve took off her helmet and shook out her long dark curls. She was still a little breathless from the exertions of getting the ship safely out of Mercilon's orbit. She wondered if Adams really had any idea just how close they had come to disaster.

With the vital connection made between his body and the fighter ship, First Officer Adams was busy at his console, tapping in the coordinates that would get them to the party planet in the Pleiades. Captain Eve looked sidelong at him. He had a rather attractive look of concentration on his handsome, if somewhat bovine, face.

Much as Eve wished she could suppress it, a primitive human reflex tugged at something deep inside her. It was just the adrenalin. She knew that much. And yet . . .

'Hey, Adams,' said Eve, kneading his shoulders with her long, strong fingers. 'Maybe I do fancy starting a breeding program after all.'

Lara Martin

Caramel Kisses

Bethany discovered the job by accident when she was out buying chocolate.

She hadn't been looking for more work but when she'd seen the woman at the counter she'd immediately recognised the symptoms; the thin, downturned lips, the dullness of the eyes and the fingers curled and stiff counting out coins in manic fury.

What choice had there been?

She put another chocolate-covered caramel in her mouth and sucked on it as she pushed the book carefully into place. The sweetness swirled across her tongue and she clicked the hard sweet against her teeth. She picked up another book and flicked it open, inhaling the sharp chemical scent of the ink, then pushed the book reverentially into place. So many books, so many possibilities; her lips curved in secret pleasure and she glanced at the slim woman watching her from the office.

Christina Etherton was unaware of the faint frown on her brow as she stared back through the glass. The head librarian, she was in her early fifties and still attractive. Her blond hair was lightly misted with white and her brown eyes were clear, her skin barely wrinkled, yet since Bethany had come she felt . . . diminished.

The girl was so young. That bright red hair spilling down her back in a river of curls, the pink lips always smiling. Bethany was plump and not really beautiful, but there was such a dazzling brightness about her that Christina felt she had to squint to look at her. She was a firefly in a dim field of books and shelves.

She wondered again why she'd hired her.

Bethany smiled, and Christina smiled back before she realised she didn't want to. Picking up her frown again she went back to her paperwork. She was interrupted a short time later by the dull buzzing of the phone.

'Yes?'

'Mrs Etherton,' Sharon spoke in short bursts. 'It's Mr Etherton. Line two.'

Immediately Christina's heart lurched and she stared at the flashing red light on the phone for several seconds before picking up.

'Steven. What is it?'

Bethany put her hand in her skirt pocket and pulled out another caramel, sucking on it as she wheeled the returns trolley back to the front desk.

'She looks upset.' She tilted her head towards the office. Sharon glanced around, her dark ponytail swinging.

'She's all right.'

Bethany smiled and began filling envelopes with overdue notices.

Sharon was in her late twenties and was covetous of Bethany's hair. Her pert little mouth twitched when she looked at her and her little hands moved quickly from book to book, fixing labels. She reminded Bethany of a sleek brown mouse with her dark eyes and brown skin that was like milk chocolate. Mice made such lovely pets.

'Caramel?' Bethany pulled a few foil-wrapped morsels from her pocket and handed them to Sharon, palm up.

'No thanks,' Sharon replied without looking. 'Don't want to get that stuff on the books.' Her small flat nose wrinkled and she sniffed as she stuck another label carefully on a smooth spine.

Bethany leaned over and placed one brightly wrapped sweet on the counter near her coffee cup. 'Save it for later then.'

'Maybe,' Sharon shrugged and Bethany's smile dimpled her cheeks as she saw the other woman glance at the gleaming pink wrapper. She went back to stuffing envelopes.

'I was thinking of cutting my hair,' Bethany said after a while.

'What?'

'It's too long,' she frowned. 'Maybe shoulder-length like yours would be better, it'd be easier to manage.'

'But why?' Sharon stopped working to look at her. 'It's so –'

'It's really heavy,' Bethany interrupted with a grimace. 'It takes ages to wash.'

'No!' Sharon exclaimed, then, embarrassed, looked away. 'I mean it would be a shame.' She went back to labelling books.

Bethany said nothing for a moment. She looked out over the counter, staring at a young man studying at a desk. He'd been in before, last Thursday and the Thursday before. An idea rustled like the swish of wind through wheat.

'I suppose I could keep it,' she said. Turning, she gave Sharon a dazzlingly bright smile. 'You know, your hair would be lovely curled.'

Sharon looked up tentatively, a reluctant curve tugging at the corner of her mouth. 'You think so?'

Bethany nodded and, unwrapping another caramel, she sucked juicily and smoothed the foil between her fingers. The chocolate coated her teeth as she looked at the young man bent over his book.

'Sharon,' she flicked the wrapper onto the floor, 'what's your favourite book?'

Christina put down the phone and stared at the wall for several minutes.

The murmur of the other women's voices drifted through the thin walls of her office. She looked at the clock. Two forty-three. He'd be here in just under three hours.

She slammed the ledger shut, eyes skitting away from the band of gold on her left hand. There was a lump in her throat trying to get out. She swallowed hard and went out into the library. The lump was in her chest now, growing, squeezing out the air.

'I'll be in the storeroom,' she forced from her lips as she walked quickly past the two women and made for the grey door at the back. Her fingers shook as she separated the key from the rest on the key ring and shoved it into the lock.

The door opened, then swung shut behind her. Standing among the steel racks, she held onto a bracket as the sob tore from her throat, frighteningly loud and echoing in the small room. She put a hand over her mouth, struggling to hold it in. She was so angry she was choking on it. Furious grief clawed at her. Why had she told him? What had possessed her?

Suddenly it felt as though there was nothing solid beneath her at all, just a drop, a dizzying endless drop into uncertainty. She sucked in air and sat down on a dusty box. Her face was hot, her muscles quivered with adrenalin and she wondered why regret was said to taste bitter. It wasn't bitter at all. That made it sound like a sour orange but it wasn't anything near that refined, that tolerable. It was like acid, it ate away at you and this regret had had seven years to fester.

It had been locked up in that place she didn't visit; the vault in her mind where all things went that should never have been, or had never been. Dreams of travel she'd never realised, the hope for a third child, bitter words spoken in fear – and him.

She'd thought she'd buried it deep enough, wrapped up those few days, his laugh, the feel of his fingers on the inside of her thigh, wrapped it in steel and dropped it into the ocean of forgetting. But it had surfaced, seeking the light, clawing at her until she'd let it spill out, unable to contain the monster any more. And it had become so twisted a memory, so despised, that she could hardly even remember his face now. Not that it was important. Betrayal had its own face. She'd seen it on Steven, on herself.

She sat on the box, staring at her shoes, and wished she still smoked.

Bethany laid three caramels on Christina's desk. One for the past, one for the present and another for the future. She looked down at them in satisfaction.

'She won't eat them.' Sharon poked her head in the door behind her. 'She doesn't like sweets.'

'Everyone likes these,' Bethany joined her at the door and put out her hands, accepting the stack of books Sharon handed her. 'They're magic.' She smiled and they walked to the historical reference section.

'It'll be magic if her marriage holds together,' Sharon sniffed and put her load down on a nearby table. 'You should've heard the words her daughter called her the other week.' She shook her head and glanced at the store-room door 'Poor thing. Those girls of hers are a couple of bitches anyway. Ungrateful cows. And him! You'd think he'd forgotten about how much she did for him. You know she supported him while he got his engineering degree.' She shook her head and shoved a book about Henry VIII onto the shelf. 'I'd just started working here then and I'm not surprised she took up with another guy. Her husband was always turning up late, if he turned up at all! Meetings, meetings – and now look what happens.'

'Mmm.' Bethany pushed *The True History of Marie Antoinette* into its slot. 'Love is a mistress that loves to bite,' she said. Sharon paused in her re-shelving and looked at her.

'You're weird, you know?'

Bethany smiled. 'You know what else is weird? You

know that book you told me was your favourite? Well, that young guy that comes in here a lot, you know the one with dark hair that sits near the front desk? He checked it out earlier.'

Sharon frowned. 'Really?'

'Yep.' Bethany nodded

'But guys don't read that book, not normal, non-nerdy guys, anyway.'

'Told you it was weird,' Bethany shrugged and watched from out of the corner of her eye as a slight pink tinge rose on Sharon's brown cheeks.

'Yeah,' Sharon echoed quietly and Bethany smiled.

Later, as she was leaving Bethany made sure the book was tucked in at the very bottom of her bag, under the chocolates.

She left Sharon tidying up some client cards and pushed out through the glass doors. Going down the shallow concrete steps she passed a balding, stocky man in a dark suit. Sadness hovered in the air around him and his pale blue eyes looked beyond her to the swinging doors. The faint smell of expensive aftershave wafted as he went by, climbing the steps two at a time.

Christina's husband. Bethany checked out his rear view. Not bad for over fifty. She turned away and smiled. Reaching into her bag she pulled out the other book she'd taken, a beautiful glossy picture-filled tome about Morocco. Anticipation tingling along her spine, she penned the note and slipped it, with the book, onto the back seat of the car.

Christina came out of the office and stood waiting as he strode up.

LARA MARTIN

She hadn't wanted him to catch her unawares. She felt hollow, unsteady, and when the doors swung shut behind him, guilt punched her hard in the gut.

Dark circles ringed his eyes and his shirt was wrinkled; he probably hadn't even ironed it this morning.

'Chrissy.' He came towards her.

'In my office.' She turned away, wishing he hadn't called her that, and led him quickly to her small cubicle. She could feel Sharon's eyes on her back.

'Sit down.' She closed the door behind him and went to the chair behind her desk, waiting for him to speak.

He sat silently for a moment, staring at the edge of her desk.

'Where are you staying?'

'With friends.'

He nodded. 'I saw the girls. Julie said she was going to come see you.'

Christina felt a little wrench inside. She didn't want to talk about the girls. Not after what they'd said to her.

'What did you come here for, Steven?' She sat back, trying to look relaxed, steady.

'Jesus, Chrissy, what do you think? I want to know why. Why did you –' his lips twisted.

'Why did I sleep with another man?'

'Yes! And why did you tell me? Just like that. I had a crap day at work and when I come home my wife says, honey, seven years ago I fucked another bloke, just thought you'd like to know.'

'Because I couldn't stand keeping it any more!' The anger came back, arrowing up like a swimmer bursting for air. 'I couldn't breathe. And you would never have

402

noticed, Steve, You were always in meetings or bloody conferences.'

'I took you away on weekends'

'When they coincided with some conference,' she retorted.

'You said you enjoyed them.' He flared up at her tone. 'What do you want, Chrissy? I don't understand.' He spread his hands and she flinched at the pain in his eyes. 'I thought you were happy.'

She couldn't look at his shadowed, weary face. The anger leaked out of her.

'I was, mostly,' she shook her head, 'but I wanted . . . I never went anywhere, never did anything, never . . . there were so many things.' How to explain it? She stared at a spot on the wall. 'I don't know. I wanted to go places, something different.' Her head ached with pressure.

He stared at her. 'Jesus, Chrissy, I thought we were going to get old together, we promised . . .' His lips tightened and he looked down at his hands, up at her, around the room.

Now was the time, she thought; if she wanted to plead for another go, to hold the fraying edges of this marriage together, she had to do it now. But she couldn't speak and the silence in the room became a shroud, suffocating her. She looked down at her desk and fingered the bright foil-wrapped sweets someone had left.

Bethany came in to work on Friday morning and noticed Christina had eaten one of the chocolates she'd left on her desk.

Good. It was time, but it had to be big to get this job

done. She checked on Sharon first. She was looking at some records on the computer and switched the screen quickly when she saw Bethany coming.

Bethany smiled and unwrapped the first caramel for the day.

'He definitely took it,' she said, and Sharon turned pink.

'I was checking the overdues,' she said quickly.

'Mmm,' Bethany leaned over conspiratorially, 'he'll be bringing it back next week but I wouldn't mention it, he looked a bit jumpy when he took it. Maybe you should just ask him about films or something, he took out some books about movie making as well.'

Sharon went pinker. 'I have to go get some files,' she said and headed for the bank of cabinets behind the encyclopaedias.

Bethany clicked the caramel against her teeth, and picking up the phone called the delivery company.

The crate arrived just after lunch.

'Mrs Etherton,' Bethany made her voice suitably anxious, 'there's a stack of books arrived and Sharon's busy on the desk, can you show me what to do, please?'

Christina frowned. 'I didn't order any.'

'Well, they're here and there's a proper order with them.' Bethany smiled and Christina sighed and tapped on her keyboard with pale pink nails. 'All right, maybe I did ask for some.' She rose gracefully.

'I told the courier to put them in the storeroom,' Bethany said, walking quickly ahead of her. 'Sharon opened it, so –' She pushed the grey door, holding it open until Christina had come through. 'Here they are.' She indicated the big box full of books. 'What do I do?'

'They're all travel books,' Christina said, scanning the order with some confusion.

'I think there's some of Frances Mayes' new one as well,' Bethany said, digging her hands in the box and pulling out a bundle of paperbacks. The covers gleamed with gold lettering and rustic Tuscan shades. She handed them to Christina.

'And look,' she dug in again, '*Images of Zanzibar.*' She smiled as she forced it on Christina. 'I went there once, you know. You can smell the spice on the wind; cinnamon and cloves.' She closed her eyes and breathed in, smelling again the warm sweetness of the air.

Struggling with the stack of books, Christina looked at her in surprise. 'You don't look old enough.'

'Really?' Bethany grinned. 'What do I do first?'

Pulling treasure after treasure out of the huge box, Bethany kept Christina in the storeroom. Every time the other woman went to leave, Bethany would pull out another glossy-leaved delight and flip it open, letting loose the cerulean blue of a Greek sky against whitewashed walls, or the burnt-sugar sands of the Sahara. Christina would come back, her fingers drifting like feathers across the pages.

By the time they had finished, the floor was littered with glittering chocolate wrappers and there was the palest pink flush on Christina's cheeks.

'You can enter them into the system tomorrow,' she said and Bethany saw that she took the book on Zanzibar with her, cradling it against her chest, as she left the room.

On Saturday Bethany took her time with the new books.

Sharon didn't work weekends so she used the whole

space. She stacked the books up around her on the counter and on chairs, turning the front desk into a sea of exotic cultures and worlds. The few patrons who came in stared at the chaos, but Bethany only smiled and offered them chocolates.

Just on midday, closing time, Bethany found she had worked so slowly that there was still over half the books left to be done and she smiled in contentment as she tapped on the open door of Christina's office.

'Um, I haven't finished. I'm sorry I'm so slow. I didn't really manage to get through enough. There's still heaps left.'

Christina looked at the desk and shook her head, exasperated. 'Bethany, I needed them done for Monday.'

'I know I'm sorry, um, and I can't stay I've, ah –' She gave Christina an apologetic look mixed with just the right hint of embarrassment.

'Oh, it's all right.' Christina waved her away. 'I'll finish them, it won't take me too long. Go on, go home.'

'Thank you,' Bethany smiled and went to fetch her bag.

'I'll see you Monday,' Christina said vaguely, going over to stand in front of the stack of books.

'Here, I'll leave you these.' Bethany dropped a handful of caramels on the bench. 'Good luck, Christina,' she said. The head librarian looked up with a frown to protest against the familiar use of her name but the young woman was gone, the glass doors swinging shut behind her.

With a sigh Christina went around to the other side of the bench and got to work. Barely five minutes later the doors swung open again. Irritated, she looked up; Bethany should have locked them but the sharp words died on her lips as she saw Steven standing there.

'Hi.' His face was guarded, hesitant.

'Steven.'

'I found this in the car.' He held up a book. 'You must have left it there. There's a note from someone asking if you could return it. I brought it in for you.'

'Thanks.' She looked at the title. *Morocco* written in gold under the plastic cover. She took it from him awkwardly. She couldn't remember it, but given the last few weeks – she put it down near the new books.

'New order?' Steven was still standing there.

She nodded, watching him.

'Africa.' He picked up a glossy hardback and flicked through it. 'You always wanted to go there.' He half glanced up at her and something in his look, his stance, made Christina still. A tiny flutter brushed at her heart.

'Yes,' she whispered.

'There's still time.' Steven stopped on a picture of Kenya, of a mountain purple against a dusk sky. 'It's majestic, isn't it?'

Christina swallowed and stepped back a bit. 'Do you want to give me a hand? I've got to get all these books done today.'

He looked at her and smiled and for the first time in years she noticed the flecks of gold in his blue eyes. 'Sure. Where do I start?'

Bethany sealed her resignation letter with a contented sigh, licked a stamp and placed it precisely in the top right-hand corner. She always liked to be precise with all things, that way all things always worked out precisely as she had intended. She turned the envelope over and carefully peeled off one of her signature stickers; she pressed it down on the creamy parchment, her finger running over the gold symbol. She was so glad she'd switched to books; arrows did have their place and had worked well in the past, but they could sometimes be a little off target.

With a happy hum, she unwrapped another caramel and sucking noisily went to find a postbox.

Carole Matthews
Travelling Light

The myth is that Americans don't like to travel. Yet wherever I've been in the world they seem to get there – in droves, usually. Though I hadn't quite expected to see one here for some reason.

'Hi,' he says, looking up from his unpacking.

I just love how casual Americans are. We Brits are so much more self-conscious, reserved, uncomfortable with etiquette. Our brothers across the pond wade in affably without preamble. 'Hello.'

'How are ya?'

'Fine, thank you.' I edge into the small compartment from the corridor of the carriage. Our train is travelling overnight from Gaungzhou to Guilin and I've booked 'soft' class, which means that I get a lovely comfy bunk bed, a little bathroom shared between fifty of us at the end of the carriage and a pair of fluffy blue complimentary slippers from the railway company, whose name is spelled out in Chinese characters, so I can't tell you what it is. It does mean, however, that I get to share with a complete stranger and it looks like this is him. I'd sort of expected to be sharing with another woman, but then I might have learned by this stage of my travels that I should always expect the unexpected. My room-mate is already wearing his complimentary slippers and his are pink and fluffy. As they're intended for tiny Chinese feet, he's cut the toes out of them and is wearing them flip-flop style. I can't help but smile at them.

'Cool, right?' He holds up his peep-toes for my inspection.

'Very.'

Discordant Chinese musak plays, plinky-plonking over the intercom system, and there's no way of turning it off.

'Do you want to be on top or on bottom?' If only the other men in my life had been so direct! 'I'm easy,' he says.

'I'll take the top bunk if that's okay.' I reason that if he's planning to murder me during the night, then at least I have a chance of hearing him clambering up to my eyrie. If I keep one of my boots handy I could whack him on the head before he has the chance to do his dastardly deeds. These are the considerations of a lone female traveller in today's society.

'I'm Kane,' he says. 'Kane Freeman.' I have to say that he doesn't look much like a murder. He look more like one of those surf-dudes – if that's the correct term. We don't have many surf-dudes in England, so I'm having to rely on Hollywood teen movies for my terminology. Anyway, he's wearing surf's-up type clothes, he's got shaggy blond hair that bears some witness to sun damage, a ridiculously golden tan (ditto the hair re sun damage), a freckly but otherwise perfect nose and clear blue eyes that if I were up for being mesmerised would be truly mesmerising.

'Alice.' I shake his hand formally because that's what Brits do.

He grins at me. 'Alice.'

I should point out that I don't feel like an Alice. This was my mother's idea of a sober name for a well-behaved, studious child. She thought that by calling me Alice, I wouldn't climb trees or fall off my bicycle, tie fireworks to my brother's head or try to torture frogs. And, for a while, she was probably right. I have gone through life with a name that I don't feel suits me.

'Well, Ali . . .'

I'm taken aback at the familiarisation of my name. No one calls me Ali. And I suddenly wonder why not.

'. . . shall we crack open a beer? It's going to be a hell of a long night.'

I don't normally drink. Stephen, my fiancé, doesn't like women who drink – or smoke, or wear revealing clothes, or say 'fuck' in public.

Kane wiggles a bottle of beer in my direction.

'Yes, please.' My feet are killing me and my shoulders are aching from the weight of my backpack. I need some-thing to help. 'Beer would be nice.'

My companion snaps off the cap and offers the bottle to me. 'I also have a French baguette and cheese.' His eyes flash with unspoken wickedness.

I barely stop myself from gasping. In mainland China, the rarity of these jewels shouldn't be underestimated. I have been travelling across the country here for three weeks now and have lived on nothing but noodles – prawn noodles, chicken noodles, occasionally beef noodles. Noodles, noodles, noodles and more bloody noodles. Dairy products and bread are as scarce as blue diamonds. He could ask me to perform any dastardly deed he jolly well liked for a quick bite of his baguette.

'Oh, my word.'

He gives a smug smile, knowing that he has me in his grasp. Kane starts to prepare our impromptu picnic while I heave my rucksack onto the top bunk and fuss with settling in for the journey. The small compartment is spic and span. We have a lacy tablecloth on a little shelf by the window which bears a plastic rose in a silver-coloured vase. There are lacy curtains at the window, obscuring the view of the seething mass of humanity at Gaungzhou station. I have never seen anywhere as crowded in my entire life. I inspect the bedding, which is spotless, starched within an inch of its life and embroidered with the same characters as our complimentary footwear.

I put on my slippers, position my boots in case I need them as a weapon and slide down to sit next to Kane on his bed. It feels terribly intimate to be in this situation with someone I've barely been introduced to. Stephen would pass out if he could see me now.

Kane carefully slices the cheese onto the bread. I can feel myself salivating and sink my teeth in gratefully, the minute he hands it over. I can't help it, but I groan with ecstasy. Unless you've been there, you will never imagine how good this tastes.

Kane shows off his set of perfect pearly whites. 'Good, huh?'

'Mmm. Marvellous.'

The train whistle blows and we rattle out of the station, out of the town, leaving the squash of people behind and head into the countryside.

'So?' he mutters through his bread. 'You're travelling alone?'

I like men who are keen-eyed and sharp-witted. 'Yes.' It pains me to have to pause in my eating. 'I'm getting married in a few weeks.' I want him to be absolutely clear from the beginning that I'm not available. I would flash my gorgeous engagement ring – which is a whopper – but I've left it at home in case I got mugged. 'This is my last chance to travel alone.'

Kane frowns. 'Should you want to travel alone if you're getting hitched?'

He isn't the first person to voice this concern. My parents were particularly vocal. As was Stephen.

'I just needed to get away,' I say. 'It was all getting too much. I had to escape. You know how it is.'

'No,' he says. 'I've never gotten close.'

'Oh.' I give a dismissive wave of my hands. 'There are so many things to organise. It's hell.'

'So why are you doing it?'

My French bread nearly falls out of my mouth. Why *am* I doing it? 'My fiancé. Stephen. We've been together for years. Many *happy* years. He felt it was time we settled down.'

'So you're here on a Chinese train with a stranger and he's at home ordering bridal corsages?'

I give a carefree laugh. 'You make it sound a lot worse than it is.'

Kane contemplates that while he chews. 'He must be an understanding man.'

'He's very . . . understanding.' Actually, I'm not sure that Stephen understands me at all.

Kane says nothing. We eat in silence. Try as I might, I can't recapture the joy of my cheese again.

'What about you?'

Kane shrugs. 'I've always been a drifter. I like to see the world. I have no ties, no commitments, no permanent base. I go wherever the wind blows me.'

I can't even begin to imagine what that must feel like. My life is layer-upon-layer of commitment, confinement, duty. I live by timetables, schedules, appointments, mortgage payments. Doesn't everyone?

We finish our meal and the grinning guard comes and checks our tickets and gives us a thermos of hot water for tea. I reciprocate for the bread and cheese by supplying tea bags. We Brits may like to travel the four corners of the globe, but we also like to do it with 'proper' tea.

'Do you work?' Kane asks as he examines his brew suspiciously. Quite frankly, most Americans just don't understand the concept of decent tea so I don't wait for his approval.

'I did. As a radio producer.' I had to resign from my job to take this trip as my employers at Let the Good Times Roll Radio also failed to 'understand' my need to fly – particularly when I've already got two weeks in the Bahamas booked as a honeymoon. Who could possibly want more than that? And yet I do. Is that greedy? Does it make me a bad person? 'I'm taking some time out.' Not necessarily voluntarily. 'I'll look for something else when all the fuss from the wedding has died down.'

'You're using a lot of negative images with reference to your forthcoming nuptials,' Kane observes.

'That sounds terribly Californian, if you don't mind me saying,' I observe back.

He smiles. 'I am from California. I'm allowed.'

At ten o'clock it's lights out on Chinese trains, which reminds me of my time at boarding school. The sudden plunge into darkness curtails our conversation and we scrabble to our bunks, clicking on the faint night lights above our heads. I decide to stay clothed for modesty's sake, but Kane has no such inhibitions. He's wearing battered, baggy shorts and a sleeveless tee-shirt, that bears the faded remains of a logo, now too pale to discern. I'm used to a man who favours pressed chinos and striped shirts and who goes into the bathroom to change. In a moment, Kane is stripped down to his boxer shorts. He's clearly comfortable with his body, and I suspect if I had a body like that, I would be too. I know that I should look away, but I'm afraid to say, I can't. I just can't. He has a tattoo of a dragon high on the broad sweep of his shoulder. I wonder where he had it done and if it hurt him and I find myself thinking that I'd like to trace the outline with my finger.

He turns and smiles up at me. I do hope he's not a mind-reader. 'Sleep tight,' he says and hops into the bunk below me.

I do no such thing. I lie awake looking at the air vent in the ceiling, occasionally peeping out of the lace curtain to the blackness of the paddy fields beyond and watching as, even through the dark hours, we stop at brightly lit stations to let passengers come and go.

The train runs minute-perfect. Stephen would like that part of it. Stephen likes things to be regular. His habits, his meals, his bowels. Sorry, that's not nice of me. You don't need to know that. Even though it's true.

Stephen, on the other hand, wouldn't like the crowds, the smells, the squatty loos – apologies, back to toilet preferences again – the food, the heat, the pollution, the whole damn foreignness of the place. We'll be taking our holidays in the Caribbean from now on with maybe the odd deviation to the Cote d'Azur. We'll stay in five-star hotels, with fluffy towels and spa facilities – some place where we don't have to mix too closely with the locals. We won't even have to trouble ourselves to go to the bar for a drink, it will be brought to us on a tray at our sun-loungers by a smiling waiter. Is this what I want?

I close my eyes and try not to think of anything connected with the wedding. Have you ever felt like everything was crowding in on you? My whole world was becoming smaller and smaller, until I felt like my namesake Alice in Wonderland after she'd drunk the potion and had shrunk to barely ten inches high. I felt I just didn't matter any more, that I had become too tiny to be of consequence. My days were taken up with invitations and flowers and bell-ringers and wedding cars and who the hell was I going to sit next to who? Everyone gets pre-wedding nerves, I was told – time after time. Is that all it is, this nagging feeling? I screw my eyes tighter shut but still sleep eludes me. The stations, towns, miles flash by. I hear the sound of my neighbour's soft snoring from the bunk below. Kane doesn't look like the sort of man who worries if he misses a poo.

Bang on time, the train pulls into Guilin station just after dawn. Kane and I haven't said much to each other this morning. Kane, because he's only just woken up after sleeping like a bear – his words, not mine. Me, because I'm not sure what I want to say.

We pack our rucksacks, bumping into each other in the tiny space as we prepare to leave the train. The doors open and the slow shuffle towards the exit starts. Kane and I make to join it.

'Thanks for the bread and cheese,' I say. 'It's been nice . . .'

'Where are you heading for?' Kane asks.

'Yangshuo.'

'I've been there before,' he informs me. 'It's a blast. I know a great hotel. Want to hang out together?'

I nod, mainly because my brain is urging my mouth to say no.

The Fawlty Towers hotel in Yangshuo is, indeed, a great place. It has showers complete with hot water and clean sheets. And 'hanging out together' also seems to involve sharing a room. Single beds – I'm not that reckless. After spending a night together it seemed churlish to refuse. And it will help keep down the costs. I don't think I'll mention it to Stephen, though. It's another thing he wouldn't understand.

Kane rents bicycles with dodgy brakes and we head out into the countryside, weaving our way through narrow valleys and straggly villages whose houses are still pasted with red-and-gold new-year banners to bring good luck to those inside. Weather-worn mountains moulded by the rain into sugarloaf shapes tower over us. I can't remember last when I was on a bike and I'd forgotten how great the wind in your hair feels as it lifts the strands away from your neck to kiss the humid dampness away. We climb Moon Hill, Kane tugging me up the steep slope by the hand, until we look over the landscape that spawned a thousand paintings – soft, misty mountains, meandering rivers, the pink blush of cherry-blossom trees. I return to Yangshuo feeling achy and strangely liberated – like a dog who's dared to stick its head out of a car window for the first time.

In the Hard Luck Internet Café, I pick up an email from Stephen. 'Hello Alice – the caterers have suggested these canapés.' There is a list of a dozen nibbly-bits, all of which sound perfectly acceptable. 'Shall I give them the go-ahead? Stephen.'

I stare at the picture of Bruce Lee on the wall and wonder if you should be addressing your future wife 'Hello Alice' – particularly when she's been away for nearly three weeks. Shouldn't the word 'love' appear in there somewhere? Perhaps Stephen is beginning to wonder why his future wife has been away for nearly three weeks. There has been a distinct lack of 'I'm missing you'–type emails. But then Stephen is very reserved with his emotions. It's one of the things I love about him. Really, it is. I've never been one for gushy stuff.

I type: 'Dear Stephen. Canapés sound fine.' And then in a rush of guilt or something. 'Missing you. Love Alice.'

As I head back to the hotel, I see Kane sitting outside the Planet China restaurant drinking green tea and Yanjing beer with his feet up on a chair. I've never seen anyone look so laid-back. My stomach lurches when I approach him and it might not be due to the fact I'm back on the noodle diet. How old is Kane, I wonder? The same as me?

Not quite thirty. He is so loose and carefree with his life that it makes me feel older than time itself. I plonk myself down next to him and hear myself sigh wearily.

'You look stressed.'

'I am.'

'Wedding arrangements not going to plan?' Kane grins. I'm sure he doesn't believe that this wedding is ever going to go ahead.

'I've just agreed to the canapés,' I say crisply. 'They're going to be wonderful.'

'Try this.' He hands me a cigarette.

'I didn't know you smoked.' But then there's a lot I don't know about Kane, even though I'm sharing a hotel room with him. I have no idea why I'm taking this, as I don't smoke either. Stephen doesn't like women who . . . oh, you get the gist.

'It's herbal,' he says. 'It will relax you.'

I drag deeply on the cigarette and then the smell hits me. 'Oh, good grief,' I say. 'Do you know what this is?'

Kane grins at me.

'Of course you do.' I take another tentative puff. I'm not a natural law-breaker. 'Is this legal here?' I suspect not. It's making me even less relaxed than I was. I can't do drugs, not even soft ones. Quickly, I hand it back. 'I could end up in prison for twenty-five years.'

Kane fixes me with a wily stare. 'Isn't that where you're headed anyway?'

'I need a drink.' In what sounds to me like passable Mandarin, Kane orders me a steaming glass of jasmine tea and some rough Chinese vodka. I pick my way through the beautiful white blooms, inhaling the fragrance as I sip the tea, spoiling it with the raw cut of the alcohol as I chase it with swigs of vodka. I was going to have jasmine in my wedding bouquet, but now it will always remind me of Kane. And that might not be a good thing.

From Yangshuo we take a plane to Chengdu to see the giant pandas, and I don't want you to read too much into this, but we're already acting like an old married couple. I can't believe how easily I've fallen into step with this man. At the airport Kane looks after the passports while I go and top up on 'western' snacks – potato chips and boiled sweets rather than scorpions on sticks.

The next morning, we join the old grannies in the park doing tai chi, causing great hilarity as we heave our bulky frames alongside the delicate, bird-like movements of the elderly Chinese ladies. Kane causes a particular stir. He laughs as they cluck round him like mother hens and come to touch his spiky blond hair and his bulging biceps, which makes me flush as it's something I've considered doing myself. The old men, some in ageing Maoist uniforms, promenade proudly with their song-birds in cages and a feeling of sadness and oppression settles over me. Without speaking, Kane takes my hand and squeezes. I can feel the edge of my engagement ring cutting into my finger even though I'm not wearing it, but I don't try to pull away.

Kane keeps holding my hand while we travel further into the country to visit the Terracotta Army at Xian. Beautiful, untouchable soldiers, frozen in time, unable to move forward. I cry at the sheer spectacle of it and at other things that I can't even begin to voice. He's still holding it a week later when we hike up to the mist-shrouded peak of Emei Shan and book a simple room in the extraordinary peace of a Buddhist monastery that looks like something out of a film set.

We have dinner in a local cafe with no windows and a tarpaulin roof, lit only by smoky kerosene lamps, the sound of monkeys chattering in the trees high above us. A group of local men play mah-jong boisterously in the corner, each tile slapped down with a challenge and hotly contested. A scraggy cat sits hopefully at my feet. We're the only diners and the waif-like Chinese owner brings us dish after dish of succulent, stir-fried vegetables – aubergine, spring greens, beansprouts, water chestnuts.

Kane has been on the Internet at the monastery. It makes you realise that there's nowhere in the world that can truly be classed as remote any more. It also makes me realise that our time together is coming to an end. He's planning another leg of this trip which will eventually take him round the world. I had always dreamed of travelling the world and I feel a pang of envy that he'll be continuing the rest of his journey without me. He says the surf is good in Australia right now and that he'll probably head out that way. See? I knew my assessment of him was right all along. Do surfers attract groupies? I think they do. And I wonder will he hook up with someone else as easy? Someone less tied, less uptight, less duty-bound.

Kane is adept with his chopsticks while I still handle mine like knitting needles. Give me a plate of chow mein and I could run you up a sweater, no problem. We finish our meal and bask in the warm night air with cups of jasmine tea. He plucks at the plaited friendship bracelet on his wrist and, not for the first time, I contemplate when and how he acquired it. We both look so terribly mellow in this half-light and I wish I could capture this moment forever. Me and Kane cocooned in our own microcosm.

His fingers wander across the table and find mine. 'Just in case you were wondering,' he says gently. 'This brother, sister thing we're doing is taking its toll on me.'

I don't know what to say, so I say nothing.

Kane sighs, his eyes searching mine. 'What I really want is to make love to you.'

'Oh,' I say. 'Okay.'

He looks at me for confirmation and I nod. 'Let's go.'

Kane wraps his arms around me and holds me tightly as we pay the bill and hurry back to the shelter of the monastery. Is it a sin to make love in a monastery? I don't know. I don't want to know. I'm too Catholic by half. I might burn in hell for this at some later stage, but I think it will be worth it. Can something so beautiful be punishable by fire and brimstone? I hope the monks don't mind. I wouldn't like to offend anyone. As I hold onto Kane in the dark, I don't consider that it might be a sin against Stephen. I don't consider anything but the curve of his spine, the strength of his arms and the look of love on his face. And it takes me by surprise, as no one has looked at me with such passion for a long, long time.

We take another overnight train to Beijing, to the Forbidden City. How appropriate. This time we squeeze together in one bunk, making love to the rhythm of the rattling rails, falling asleep in each other's arms.

The pollution in Beijing is worse in the spring, when the sands from the Gobi desert blend with the exhaust fumes of a million ozone-unfriendly cars. The mixture stings your eyes, strips your throat and makes it hard to see too far ahead. A grey veil blocks out the sun, which tries hard to break through but is generally thwarted.

When in China you must do as the Chinese do and we hire sit-up-and-beg bikes again to cycle through the jammed streets to the vast expanse of Tiananmen Square – the symbol of freedom to an oppressed world. We join the throng of Chinese tourists flying kites and are royally ripped off as we buy flimsy paper butterflies from a canny, bow-legged vendor. He could feed his family for a week on what we pay him for a moment's fleeting pleasure, but I begrudge him nothing as our lives are so easy compared to his. It makes me appreciate that I have very little to complain about.

We laugh as we run through the square, trailing our kites behind us, watching them as they duck and dive, playing with the erratic wind. But even then, I notice that my kite is not as exuberant in its swoops and soars as Kane's. It's more hesitant, fearful and it's tearing easily. I trail after him while he takes the lead, clearing a route through the crowd, leaving me to follow behind. And then he holds me close and I forget everything. I forget to hold tightly to my kite and it floats away, bobbing, bobbing on the air, reaching for the hidden sun until it's quite out of sight. Free.

'I love you,' Kane says. But I watch my kite fly away from me.

Email from Stephen. 'Hello Alice – have ordered cars. Think you'll like them. Doctor and Mrs Smythe have said no. Shame. Missing you too. Stephen.' Is it a shame that two people who I don't even know aren't coming to my wedding? Do I really care what car will take me there? I stare at the screen, but can't make my fingers type a reply. Now what do I do?

That night we lie on the bed in our horrible Western-style hotel which has matching bedspreads and curtains and shower gel and shampoo in tiny identical bottles. Already I can feel my other life calling me.

'Have you told him?' Kane asks.

'No,' I say.

'You can't go back,' my lover states. 'You know you can't.'

But I can. And I will. I can't explain this to Kane, but I love Stephen because he's anchored in reality. He understands about pensions, for heaven's sake. He polishes his shoes. He has chosen the wedding limousines. He may not make love to me as if it is the last thing he will ever do in this life. He may not chase life with an insatiable, unquenchable thirst. But Stephen is safe and solid and secure. We'll grow old together. We'll have a joint bank account. I will never feel the same about anyone in my entire life as I do about Kane – never. Not even Stephen. Kane is the sun, the moon and the stars. He is all the things I'm not, but that I would want to be. In a different life. I have never loved anyone more or as hopelessly. But Kane is as flighty as the paper butterfly kites, answering every tug of the breeze. How can you base a future, a whole lifetime, on something as unreliable as that? What would we do? Spend our lives wandering the earth, hand-in-hand, rucksack slung on back? Or would there come a time when I'd want to settle down, to pin the butterfly to the earth, stamp on it, crush it flat? Would I eventually become Kane's Stephen?

We make love and, this time, I feel that it *is* the last thing that I will ever do in my life. Every nerve, fibre, tissue, cell of my body zings with the prospect of life. Beneath him I lose myself, my reason, my mind. I'm part of Kane and he'll always be a part of me. But this excitement would die, wouldn't it? Could we always maintain this intensity, this intimacy? Isn't it better to have loved so hard and so briefly than to watch it sink and vanish from view like the setting sun?

I wake up and reach for Kane, but he's gone. The bed beside me is empty. There's nothing left of my lover but a crumpled imprint in the sheets. I pad to the bathroom and take a shower, concentrating on the chipped tiles so that I won't feel that my heart is having to force itself to keep beating. You can taste devastation – did you know that? I didn't until now. It coats your teeth, tongue and throat and no amount of spearmint mouthwash will get rid of it.

I decide to check out of the hotel, even though my homeward flight isn't until tomorrow. I can't stay here alone. Not now. Slowly, methodically, I pack up my things and take the lift down to reception where I queue for an interminable amount of time behind a party of jocular Americans to pay my bill. I told you. They get everywhere. Inside your undies, inside your heart, inside your soul. Eventually, I reach the desk and hand over my credit card and my key. In return I get a receipt and a business card. The receptionist taps it.

'It was left for you,' he says.

I flip it over and my broken heart flips too. Somehow its jagged edges mesh back together. There's a caricature of a scruffy surfer and in big, bold type – Barney's Surf Shack,

Bondi Beach. Kane has scribbled. 'I'll wait there every day for two weeks.'

But I don't think he'll need to. I know now that there'll be no wedding. No hymns. No white dress. No bridesmaids. Not now. And maybe not ever. But I know that it's the right thing to do. I only hope that Stephen will understand. He deserves more. I shouldn't spend my life with someone I can live with. I should be with someone I can't live without. Wherever that may take me. My pension fund will just have to wait.

I hail a taxi and jump inside. I might just make it.

'Beijing Airport!' I say. 'As quick as you can!' My word, I've always wanted to say that! It doesn't matter that the driver can't even speak English. He must sense my haste as he careens out into the six lanes of traffic, horn blaring. I feel as if I'm swimming in champagne, bubbles rising inside of me.

We pull up outside the terminal building and I race inside. There standing by the check-in desk is an unmistakeable figure. His rucksack is over his shoulder.

He's head and shoulders above everyone else. One blond mop above a sea of black. I run towards him as fast as I can. 'Kane!'

He turns. And when he sees me he smiles.

Anna Maxted

The Marrying Kind

For a short time, Michelle was a hippie. This aberration occurred during college. She wore gypsy skirts, skim-read left-wing newspapers and ate a lot of vegetarian food. Suddenly, it wasn't enough for her to be merely 'in love'. This limp inferior emotion had to be upgraded to 'loved up'. A reference to ecstasy, which I found affected and irritating. Worse, she was suddenly *kooky*. 'Oh! I'm so ditsy!' was the message, even though her sharp eyes, black as currants, assessed you. She proclaimed the wonders of alternative health.

I have to tell you, Michelle couldn't fool me. I'm no expert, but the deal on hippies is that they're *caring*. The entire point of them is that they boo war, they don't overspend on shoes, and they would eat dirt rather than use a Flash Wipe in their kitchen. A Flash Wipe (a disposable cloth infused with a powerful bouquet of poisonous chemicals, to clean household surfaces, and sold, I'm ashamed to say, in packs of fifty) is just typical of this selfish, convenience-obsessed, fast-food age. And Michelle *loved* Flash Wipes. So much more hygienic than an old germ-ridden rag.

Happily, the pose ended the minute she returned from college to her friends in North West London.

'Michelle!' said Helen. 'Where are your . . . clothes?' Boom, that was it. Helen Bradshaw – less a *fashionista* than a fashion-missed-her, despite working for a women's magazine – criticising *her* sense of style. It was important to Michelle to feel superior to Helen. It was how their friendship had survived. Embracing the New Age philoso-phy (peace, love, whales, er, couscous) was another excuse for Michelle to look down on Helen. Helen was a capital-ist (her pay at *Girltime* was dreadful, her crime was she wanted to earn more), and she blew what little cash she had on six-inch heels instead of worthy causes, such as dolphins. But it was impossible, Michelle realised, to look down on someone when they were attired normally and you were wearing dungarees. Jesus, thought Michelle, I look like a freakin' baby.

I can't tell you what a relief it was for Michelle to revert to type. (Intensive grooming, fake leopard-skin tops, big shiny car, Jackie Collins novels, spending money, money, money on little old *moi*). But it's only fair to explain why the ill-starred foray into floor cushions and plates of beans had occurred at all.

Men.

All Michelle had ever wanted, from the time she was a little girl, was to get married. Oh, I know. So very uncool. But true.

And, at college, even though it was 1991, it was

considered – I do loathe this phrase – *right on* to be a hippie. (I think the only alternative was to be a young Margaret Thatcher, and Michelle wasn't interested in posh boys. She knew she wasn't their type. They'd only waste her time. Meanwhile, she noted that both Aaron Levitt and Jonathan Kaplan had stopped shaving and said 'basically' a lot.)

The hippie pose worked at first.

Men gazed at her while she talked. They seemed *interested*. Though if in her as a person or as a body she wasn't sure. Occasionally, it turned out, neither.

The man with whom Michelle professed herself to be 'loved up' was an astrologer named Josh. He had long shiny black hair (Michelle had a suspicion he washed it in lashings of hot water and luxury shampoo every other day, but this was denied) and asked Michelle her birth date. She told him and he whispered, 'Now I can find out all about you. It's like you've given me the key to your house.'

Michelle didn't believe in all that shit, but found it pleasing that Josh *wanted* to find out all about her. Hence, the loved-up nonsense. Sadly, the day after they kissed, they met for lunch, and Michelle said to Josh, 'So, what have you been doing this morning?' Forty minutes later, he finished telling her. Then he sat back, sighed and asked, 'Hmm. And what *else* have I been doing?' The louse didn't even try to put his hand up her skirt.

Michelle left college as she began it, single, and without a degree.

I'm sure you're judging her. Because, despite the fact that any sane person would prefer to live a life rich in love and affection – as opposed to one poor and starved of it – if a woman professes a desire to marry, she is regarded as somehow weak and pathetic. At least, she is in Britain. (Strangely, if you live with a 'partner', that's okay.) Why, only last week I found myself at a table with three authors, all of us cosily discussing our children. It emerged that they all lived with their 'partners'.

'Marriage!' scoffed one. 'I don't understand why anyone *does* that any more!'

Another author thought to check, belatedly, if *I* was married. I imparted the bad news. And Big Mouth – too stupid to understand that marriage is not a wretched constant, but as good or bad as those within it – looked at me as if *I'd* made the faux pas.

Huf. So for obvious reasons, I'm a little touchy about people judging Michelle for wanting to marry.

You have to understand that from the second that she was born, and her mother murmured, 'My beautiful princess,' Michelle was expected to marry. In her parents' circles, it was what people did. And they were happy. If they *must*, they had affairs, but had them discreetly. That way, no one got hurt. At least, not in public. Living together – note, these are the opinions of Mr and Mrs Goldblatt, not me, whatever works for you, *I* say – living together was a nonsense, a nothing, there was no point to it. You lived with a man if you were a cheap girl and he was just using you for sex. (Here, I beg the feeble excuse, 'It's their generation.')

I'm aware, there are other options. They are:

One. Gayness. Fab as it is, homosexuality never occurred to Michelle, and thank goodness because life's tough enough without having to come out to your parents when they're Lewis and Maureen Goldblatt.

Two. Singledom. Michelle was forced to endure single-dom in short bursts and she didn't love it. She had no plans to embrace it long term. She wanted a man to embrace, thanks.

You won't be surprised to hear that once Michelle stopped eating pulses and got a manicure, her wish was soon granted. She met Sammy. If I were being snide, I wouldn't *totally* define Sammy as a man. I happen to be quite close to Michelle's friend Helen Bradshaw, and I know that poor Helen spent a lifetime in dog years listening to Michelle whine about Sammy. Privately, Helen described Sammy as a 'namby-pamby bore'. If that sounds harsh, I prom-ise you that Michelle described him in public as far worse. That boy wouldn't cut his hair without permission from Mummy. They ate at Mummy's on Friday nights where she decently refrained from cutting up her son's food for him. No girlfriend needs an opponent like *that*.

And yet. Michelle dated Sammy for over five years. Admittedly, dating Sammy had compensations for Michelle. She could do whatever the hell she liked. Her parents approved. Everyone presumed it would 'end in marriage'. (A dubious phrase if ever there was.) Also, Michelle liked to be the main attraction. She always made an entrance at par-ties, nails asparkle, cheeks red with blush, hair coiffed and teased till it *pouffed* just so, Diamante black top hugging her food-deprived figure, beaming, gleaming, husking, 'Hello *sweetheart*!' to people whose names she didn't know.

Sammy would arrive a second or two later, dragging his feet, hands deep in his pockets, eyes half-closed, meekly resigned to his inferior status.

He followed her everywhere, and yet he was barely

there. He even spoke as if it didn't matter. His voice was quiet and nasal. I'd call it a drawl except 'drawl' is too go-getting for Sammy. I'd prefer to say 'He talked very slowly'. Truth was, Sammy didn't *have* to go-get. He'd already got. His father was known in certain circles as The Big Bagel. Not because he was round and doughy with a hole where his heart should be – why do we always assume the sinister? – but because he was a sizeable part of the New York bagel business. And as he said at least three times a year, he planned on handing his entire bagel empire to Sammy.

In this, The Big Bagel might have been rash, but he wasn't stupid. He invited Sammy to come to New York, to learn about the business. There would be no trouble obtaining a green card. Anyone would have leapt at the chance. Sammy barely budged off the sofa. That boy certainly preferred to watch life from the side of the pool rather than jump in. He would have happily stayed in his ugly house in Temple Fortune (an indifferent London suburb) watching as much reality television as he could cram in between bed and work (telesales), letting a wife and a family come to *him*, allowing the world to rough and tumble and grow around him until he reached an untenable age and quietly left it.

However, Michelle was present – overseeing a new cleaner – when The Big Bagel rang, and she overheard the conversation. To be honest, she *heard* the conversation, as she had picked up the phone in the bedroom. (Sammy probably thought the click was wax in his ear.)

'Oh my God, we're GOING TO NEW YORK!' she screamed, and threw her arms around him.

Sammy, used to taking the path of least resistance, let Michelle book the tickets on his credit card. Possibly, they had sex that night. Michelle – I trust you'll be discreet – wasn't mad on sex. She disliked men grabbing at her hair. Eleven lovers and (until Sammy, who'd been taught not to grab) not one exception. Also, she hated sweating off her make-up. She had this nasty sensation of the chemicals seeping into her pores, of bouncing up and down with a face like a melting clown. She always worked out in the gym bare-faced. But in the bedroom, there was scant regard for health or hygiene.

Michelle had a ball in New York. She loved the place, she loved the people. They weren't afraid to speak up. They had *energy*. There was so much to do and the shopping was glorious! Unlike in stodgy whey-faced London, no one in New York called you 'boring' for going to the gym. Jesus, you could work out in a freakin' shop window, that was how progressive they were! And the food! So much choice in what not to eat!

Sammy, I apologise, loathed New York. He hated change. He had a horror of exploration. He didn't like speaking to people he hadn't known for at least a year. In London, people didn't expect him to speak because his girlfriend spoke for him. In London, people were *used* to Sammy. They didn't care that he had a dead-end job, it made them feel better about their own meandering career paths. They knew who his father was, they appreciated that Sammy never talked about him – in London we're strange like that, we don't like to be graphically reminded that our friends are richer than us, or will be.

Well. The good people of New York were agog at

Sammy. The guy had, like, *nothing* to say for himself! His father was The BB, he didn't give a damn! What the hell was his problem? Didn't he *want* to succeed? It was all there, laid out for him! Ah, but Michelle! Michelle was *so great*! What a fun girl! Why was she wasting her time with him?

Sammy stuck it out on the Upper East Side for just over two years. Then he fled back home to Mummy, who could at last stop sulking. Truth was, Sammy would always feel he was a disappointment to his father – he wasn't brainy, he wasn't sporty, he wasn't a businessman. And perhaps his father knew that he would always be a disappointment to Sammy for having divorced Sammy's mother. Michelle could hardly reside in The Big Bagel's rent-free apartment without Sammy, so, furious and miserable, she followed him home. And then, shock, horror, she dumped him.

Incredible!

I was delighted for her. But from the way her family reacted, you'd have thought she'd turned down the king of England. I'll pause here to say what a pity that was. For Michelle, now twenty-six (talk about ancient), had not wanted to dump Sammy. She had wanted very much to marry him. Not because she loved him, alas. But because her little clique of friends – not Helen, but Helen was different – were all engaged, or just married. Worse, her younger sister, aged twenty-three, lived in a big white house in Pinner, and she and her husband (a doctor) were expecting their *first freakin' baby*.

Being single made her look like a loser. She knew they all talked about her, pitied her. She was desperate to be part of the pack again, to discuss conservatory furniture.

What My Husband Bought Me, child-friendly areas with good schools – despite that Michelle couldn't think of much worse than being tied to a small person. When they went to Pizza Express for their girls' nights out, Michelle ordered a salad. All the rest tore into Four Cheese This and Pepperoni That – getting grease on their wedding rings – because, it seemed to Michelle, they were loved unconditionally and no longer had to worry about growing grossly obese and having to be rolled downstairs.

(It didn't occur to Michelle that even if her married friends weren't loved unconditionally, their husbands would think twice about divorce, as they were sensible men who did not wish to live in wretched penury for the rest of their days.)

So. For Michelle it was a brave decision. It would have been nice, therefore, if her parents had appreciated this and supported her. One would like to assume they wanted their eldest daughter to be happy. And yet, they made their disapproval unpleasantly plain. Now. To a reasonable soul, the explanation Michelle provided was unassailable. ('Sammy bores me rigid – I can't stand to be in the same room as him, and if he kisses me in that gross, slobbery way of his, I get this, like, *lurch* of revulsion.')

Really. Who could argue with that? You'd have to be some kind of debating champion.

Lewis and Maureen excelled at bridge, which I hardly feel qualifies. And yet, they saw fit to object. They even dragged Jemma (she of the white house and doctor husband) into the fray. The poor girl – not for her the pregnant bloom – she had haemorrhoids and looked like a beach ball. It was hardly fair to force her to 'talk sense' into Michelle. The sisters had never been close, the final insult was that Jemma's normally minuscule bosom had temporarily outswelled Michelle's. There was a feeble attempt to persuade Michelle that the lurch of revulsion might actually be a lurch of excitement. Then Jemma drove home in the Freelander in tears.

So Lewis and Maureen went on the offensive. (Very offensive.) A lot of piffle about being sensible. Good prospects. A nice boy. At your age. Settling down. Look at your sister. Too choosy. On the property ladder. Get a reputation. Other things to consider besides *romance*. Too late. Grandchildren. Even Roberta and Leon's daughter. Did well for herself. People keep asking. *People keep asking!!* Pardon, but I insist on drawing your attention to that one. Of all the cheek! Call themselves parents?! So what if people keep asking? Let them ask! Not that it's any of their goddamn business!

Forgive me. I just find it insufferable that Lewis and Maureen were less bothered about Michelle's *life* than the prying opinions of their neighbours. Why, if this wasn't a free country, they'd have bullied her up the aisle to spend the rest of her days with a man who repulsed her, just so that when Mrs Lily Frosh up the road enquired after their daughter, they'd be able to provide an answer that *they* felt didn't imply failure on their part, that wouldn't have her tutting and shaking her head and whispering to Irene Frankel in synagogue, who would then pass it on up the row to Nina Koffler (the poor rabbi, he might as well have read the sermon to himself) until the whole congregation was aflame with the shocking news that the Goldblatts' eldest girl *still* couldn't find a nice Jewish boy, and what *would* become of her . . . ?

Ha. She met Marcus.

So as you know, I sighed just then but it didn't translate to the page. The reason is . . . well. I have to confess. Michelle and Marcus figured in a previous tale I wrote about Helen, and I'm afraid I wasn't too kind to Michelle. She appeared to be that spiteful, infuriating friend – most women have at least *one* – who a girl hangs on to for no decipherable reason other than masochism. Helen's father died and Michelle didn't call or come to the funeral. When she finally deigned to ring, it was to invite Helen to her birthday 'boogie'. When Helen confronted her about her silence/absence, Michelle told her, frostily, that 'women in my family don't attend funerals'. As Helen rightly observed, this would cause a problem when one of them snuffed it.

Nor did Michelle distinguish herself throughout the rest of Helen's tale. Indeed, from Helen's viewpoint, it seemed that the prime reason Michelle got together with Marcus was to spite *Helen*. Oh boy, is that a bad reason to get together with any man. (Helen's nine-year crush on Marcus, her landlord and flatmate, had recently ended in an excruciatingly awful one-night stand, the consequence of which was mutual loathing.) Helen – who in her defence *was* in the clutch of grief, even if she didn't realise it – was pretty scathing about Michelle from start to finish. At the time, I endorsed every word.

But, gosh. I guess that back then I didn't *know* the details of Michelle's background and upbringing. (A shocking admission from an author, please keep that information from my publisher.) Now that I do, I feel I understand her better, I even *like* her. Feel a little sorry for her. Oh, but she'd hate that. A fine attribute in a person, don't you think? Self-pity in others is so life-sapping, you have to invent a million lies to tell them and it draws the energy out of you like an all-day wedding. Michelle had pride. I think the whingeing about Sammy owed a lot to the fact that Michelle liked to talk about herself.

Ah, well. Back to Marcus. What can I tell you? He was different from Sammy. Certainly, he was more suited to Michelle. Which was good. Marcus was a fitness instructor, ambitious, fit, good body. (His penis was kinda small, so he was lucky that Michelle was no *Sex and the City* Samantha. Michelle was more concerned with the size of his wallet. Not, I hasten to add, that Michelle was a money-grubber. The last thing I want to do is to reinforce a racist stereotype. For one thing, my mother would kill me. My old colleagues on the *Jewish Chronicle* wouldn't be too impressed, either.)

No. Michelle was unpretentious and she didn't see the moral good in pointless struggle. Let's not forget, she'd been schlepping Sammy around for the greater part of a decade, and his idea of a good time was a takeaway eaten on a sofa in front of *Jay and Silent Bob*. But she wanted to be treated nice. She liked luxury, and who doesn't? And it wasn't as if she didn't plan to work herself. She had taken a course and hoped to set up as a freelance beautician. It was a pleasure to find Marcus, who took care of his appearance, who liked to be seen at the finest restaurants (he was yet to be caught *eating* in one) and whose disposable income was at her disposal.

Thus far, they were perfect for each other. I have to admit that Michelle did enjoy needling Helen. Let's put it down to Michelle's own insecurity. Remember, her parents were not the sort we all hanker after – proud and loving no matter what a beast you are. You can imagine that when she was little, they whipped away their approval whenever she was wilful, i.e. disagreed with them. It must have shaken her confidence.

And if your self-opinion is a little wobbly, you're more inclined to care what other people think. Michelle needed Helen to be jealous of her 'catch', and thus reinforce her hope that Marcus was a man worth pinching. (Not that Helen had any real claim, bar having trod in that muddy puddle before Michelle put her foot in it, so to speak.)

Michelle was happy. She enjoyed showing off Marcus to all her married Pinner friends, whose own men were already developing paunches – watching football instead of playing it, eating *two* pepperoni pizzas where their wives confined themselves to merely one – and they admired his triangular torso, despite themselves. (Then they sped home and blew up in a rage at their husband for eating chocolate. A sweet tooth, it was so . . . *unmanly*, and when was the last time you ran on a treadmill?) By a quirk of fate, Marcus was Jewish, so at last her parents gave Michelle some peace, and Rabbi Markovitch was finally able to make himself heard in the synagogue.

And how did Marcus feel about our lovely Michelle? Good news. He was smitten. This for Marcus was unusual because he tended to wander from woman to woman rather like a dog wanders from tree to tree. An exciting new scent would catch his attention and he'd amble off. *Sorry!*

Marcus got away with this impudent habit because as

well as being pleasing on the eye, he wasn't a man who had problems talking. He was witty, acid, and he loved to gossip, particularly about the celebrity clients at his health club. Marcus gave a fine impression of a man who was, as they say, *in the loop*. And in this cynical, media-savvy age, where we no longer believe what we avidly read in the papers, a lot of women found it thrilling to have a boyfriend who literally touched the stars. At first. Eventually, they tired of going out with a big girlie gossip who had the conversational habits of a fishwife. So, Marcus's fickle nature suited both parties.

As for Marcus, he surprised himself at how much he let her get away with. But he was in love. Michelle made him feel *fabulous*. She never made disparaging remarks about his private parts – unlike some women. She never tired of discussing famous people. Secretly, Michelle found his loquaciousness an acquired taste (she was accustomed to autocracy in dialogue), but she adjusted. Then discovered its advantages. As a woman whose dreams were frequently populated by variations on Ben Stiller, Liza Minnelli, Kate Moss and Rob Lowe (nothing kinky, all they ever did was have intimate chats with the dreamer), Michelle was in her element with Marcus.

She was devastated, *devastated*, I tell you, when J. Lo and Ben 'postponed' their wedding. 'But,' she wailed to Marcus, 'they were really in love!' Helen's spoilsport friend Tina tried to tell her it was a publicity ploy with tax breaks but Michelle wouldn't hear of it.

Every Hollywood split, Michelle felt in her heart. She was surprised and a little disappointed in Harrison Ford when he left his wife after all those years to shack up with

Ally McBeal. She still bore a grudge against Jennifer Aniston (Brad and Gwyneth were so good together, why couldn't he see that?). Demi and Bruce, the breakup – *shattering* (but she was holding out for a reconciliation, their relationship was so cordial now), and she'd never *quite* warmed to Cruise & Cruz. The Tom and Nicole arrangement had been so cosy. She couldn't imagine either one asking for a divorce. Did Tom stamp into the bedroom and shout it, 'I wanna DIVOOOORRRCE!' or was it a subdued announcement, sitting down, over coffee. 'Look. I think we should . . .'?

Marcus understood that these people were the landscape of Michelle's emotional life, that she was easily as close to them as to her blood relatives. Closer, probably. And that was fine by him, because he was pretty pally with them, too. It gave them a warm feeling to see in their precious *Hello!* magazine that Steven had invited Gwyneth to his son's bar mitzvah. Bet Jennifer wasn't on the guest list. Their conversations regarding the stars, their choices, their highs and lows, were interminable. Marcus swore that Meg would *never* get over Russell's marriage to that Danielle girl and Michelle agreed. '*Oh!* like, totally, I mean, who *is* she, a freakin' *nobody* . . .' When Michelle prompted Marcus to ask her to marry him, he accepted. Michelle was beautiful, she ate small portions (some women ate like pigs), she was proud of him, his career, she admired his dress sense, she wasn't sexually voracious (so uncouth in a girl). She *was* messy – Marcus was insanely neat – but that was rectified by a cleaner, and she was awed at his instinct for what made a home *home*. His Poggenpohl was dear to him, I'm not being rude here, it's a *super*-exclusive kitchen range, pricey, but so worth it (I'm quoting Marcus as, alas, my own kitchen is cheapy-cheap from a horrid store).

Once the monster diamond ring was secured from Tiffany, and Marcus had recovered from the shock, they held an engagement party – with a modest gift list, at Harrods. Certain people, I'm sad to say, speculated on how long the alliance would last. Laid bets, even. (All the while heartily tucking into the smoked-salmon bagels and fish balls, paid for, of course, by Michelle's suddenly fond parents.) It's human nature to bitch about marriage – fair enough, as it is human nature to bitch about most things – but one or two acquaintances seemed to have a vested interest in its failure.

They murmured amongst themselves, bagel crumbs at the sides of their mouths, that Michelle was, mmm, quite self-obsessed. And so was Marcus. Michelle was, you know, a tad selfish. And so was Marcus. Michelle wasn't what you call, ahem, a great intellectual. Nor was Marcus. Michelle could be so catty. And so could Marcus. Think he'd cheated on her yet? It made you wonder what was missing in these so-called friends' own petty lives to make them so keen for misery to afflict the lives of Michelle and Marcus.

I get confused with the use of irony, but I'm almost certain it was ironic that the only people present at the wedding (besides the bride and groom) who didn't entertain thoughts of imminent disaster, infidelity, divorce and divorce settlements were Lewis and Maureen Goldblatt. Now that their eldest girl was striding up the aisle in an elegant cream princess dress, wearing a tiara encrusted with seed pearls, toward a handsome man who looked only a little scared to see her, they felt that all was right in the world, and always would be.

This, as anyone with half a brain knows, is a highly dangerous assumption. Life can be, as the poets tell us, a right bastard. There is no guarantee of happiness, however special you feel you are. Fate has fickle fingers (whatever the hell that means). Even if you've had more bad luck than other people, and feel you've done your share of suffering, who knows, maybe destiny has it in for you, and is about to heap yet more agony upon your shoulders. God does *not* give you as much as you can carry, often he gives you a great deal more, which is why at least half of us are clinically depressed and on Prozac.

If you're in any way superstitious, the Goldblatts' open satisfaction at the marriage of their eldest daughter was a harbinger of doom.

Not to mention that neither Marcus nor Michelle was a prototype of loveliness, and so one rather feels that they *deserve* to fall flat on their faces.

In addition, what could be more unfashionable than to claim a happy union for this most bourgeois of couples? What could be more unlikely? Marriage, as we're all told till we're sick of hearing it, is a difficult, complex state, often impossible to negotiate, strewn as it is with tripwires and potholes and suspicious dinner receipts in back pockets. What hope for two middling-intelligent, medium-unpleasant people such as Michelle and Marcus?

Well, here's the thing. Fate is not in charge here. *I* am. And I approve of marriage. It's often romantic, optimistic, a beautiful gesture. Also, call me soppy, *I* believe that there's someone for everyone. Marcus is not *my* cup of tea, as we say here, in ye olde Englande. But he was Michelle's. As for Michelle, plainly, she's a pain in the behind. I wouldn't choose her as *my* wife. But Marcus did, and discovered to his surprise that he'd made the right decision. Perhaps it was a fluke. Because really, to assign those two a happy ending is wrong and unfair – there are so many far sweeter, more deserving candidates out there, currently enduring woe after woe.

I confess. At first, I was fully convinced that Marcus would betray Michelle with a client, or that Michelle would embark on a steamy e-mail affair. I was all set to conclude on a note of despair and a stern moral warning. What can I say? I found, like they found, people grow on you.

Sarah Mlynowski

Know It All

My new room-mate, Dee, claims she can see the future.

It's Thursday morning, and she's in the kitchen pouring herself a glass of my OJ. 'You should take an earlier flight to California,' she says, gulping it down.

'Why?' I'm crouched in front of the closet next to the kitchen, already late for work, debating if taking six pairs of shoes on a three-day trip is absurd.

'There's going to be a blackout tonight,' she says. She's wearing pigtails, and the bright pink pyjamas and matching flip-flops she never takes off.

'Yeah? Did they say that on the news?' If I have to, I can probably catch an earlier flight. My mother is swimming in airline points. To cheer me up about the Brahm breakup, she offered me a business-class ticket to visit the world's most perfect – and sadly former – room-mate, Janna, in California for the weekend.

Dee shakes her head no and pours another glass. Does she think orange juice grows on trees? A friend of a friend of a friend, she moved in three weeks ago. She's no Janna, but so far she seems normal.

'It wasn't on the news,' she says. 'I dreamed it.'

'Very funny,' I say, and reluctantly eliminate one of my three pairs of gorgeous but impractical stilettos.

'No, really. I'm a little bit psychic.'

'If you say so.' I turn to her and smile. 'Can you be a little bit psychic? Is that like being a little bit pregnant?'

'I have premonitions,' she says, her lips pursed and serious.

My smile falters. I might have chosen a wacko for a roommate. 'What kind of premonitions?'

She shrugs. 'Random stuff. Usually about things people talk to me about. Like your flight. I dreamed about us watching DVDs on my laptop by candlelight. You were complaining you'd missed your plane. So I'm assuming there'll be a power outage.'

'You dreamed about us watching a movie? Dee, you need to get out more.'

Weirdo.

At a little after four o'clock, I'm lugging my still-stuffed-with-shoes suitcase toward the front door, when the hall lights go out. Did a bulb just pop? A quick check reveals that the microwave clock is blank. No power. Damn. My flight departs in two hours, I'm late and I still need to flag a cab. I lock up, tow my ridiculously massive suitcase to the elevator and press the down button. Two minutes. Five minutes. After ten minutes, I force myself to accept the atrocious truth: the elevator works on electricity. And I have to take the stairs. All twenty-eight flights of them.

Crap.

Since my bag weighs at least four hundred pounds, I can't actually lift it and must instead drag it down each individual stair, controlling the momentum by bumping it against my hip. One, bump; two, bump; three, bump . . . twenty steps per floor. Twenty-eight floors.

Bump.

By the time I get to the lobby, it's 4:52, my arms feel like rubber, and I'm an excellent candidate for a hip replacement. But I have an hour, I can still make it.

Outside I frantically search for a cab. And search. Until I realise the traffic lights aren't working. The entire block has no power. Then, like a patio umbrella in the middle of the desert, a taxi catches my eye. I wave the driver over.

He rolls down his window. 'Where you going?'

'Airport.'

He laughs and drives away.

At six, I lug my bag back to my building. I've missed my one and only chance at business class.

I find Dee home from work, back in her matching pink outfit, in the foetal position on the couch, reading by candlelight. Sweating profusely from my real-life Stairmaster, I spread myself across the carpet like melted peanut butter on toast and remember her premonition about the blackout.

'I told you, I'm psychic,' she says, as though reading my mind. 'And I have a feeling the airports are closed, so your ticket will be reimbursed.'

Yeah, right. I roll my eyes.

'Tell me about the picture in your room,' she says brightly. 'The guy with the messy hair.'

'Brahm?' I'm surprised at how open she is about her snooping. 'He's my ex. We broke up last month.'

'Why?'

Apparently, she's snoopy *and* pushy. 'He wanted to move in when Janna left. I wasn't ready.' I shrug as though it's no big deal.

I recalled the night Brahm and I broke up. We were in my bed and he was kissing my throat, telling me we could use Janna's room as an office or maybe a spare bedroom, why not, we'd been together for two years, he wanted to take the next step, he wanted to live with me, cook with me, clean with me.

I couldn't breathe, as if my room was bursting with hot post-shower steam. I loved him, but was I *in* love with him? I felt a nagging at the back of my throat, like a vitamin you still feel two hours after you've swallowed it.

I loved his short, curly hair that stood up in opposing directions. I loved the way his eyes closed when he laughed. How he ate pickles with everything. Sandwiches, pizza, macaroni and cheese. I loved the way he wrapped my curls around his fingers when we watched TV.

I loved the way he talked about us. For my twenty-fifth birthday, we tried oysters for the first time. I couldn't believe we were supposed to slurp them down without chewing. 'That's how I feel when I'm with you,' he said, grazing my hand across the table. 'Swallowed whole.'

I wanted to feel swallowed whole, too, but I didn't. Yet I knew what he meant. I'd once lost myself entirely to someone, but the object of my devotion informed me he didn't feel the same. I couldn't get out of bed for weeks, until Janna forced me into the shower, turning on the water, telling me that His breaking up with me was the right thing to do if He didn't feel the way I did.

'It must have been hard to let go,' Dee says. Not sure if she's referring to me, Brahm or Him, I don't answer. 'Come,' she adds. 'I rented *Cold Mountain* and *Alfie* and charged my laptop. Let's watch DVDs like we're supposed to.'

I nod, too tired to be freaked out. And anyway, I love Jude Law. He kind of swallows me whole.

The next morning Dee pushes open the bathroom door while I'm brushing my teeth. 'I had a dream last night, but you're not going to like it,' she says. 'It's about the guy we were talking about.'

I spit a gob of toothpaste into the sink. 'Jude?'

'No, your ex. Brahm. I dreamed that he was at a place called Jeremiah's.'

'The store in the Village near his apartment? How'd you know where he shops?'

'I told you, I dreamed it.'

My back tingles, like hundreds of mosquitoes are feasting on my skin. 'And?'

She sits on the toilet. 'It was open even though there's no power. He walked in and bought a flashlight and a jar of pickles.'

The man loves his pickles.

'And then the woman said that in case the pickles made him thirsty he should buy some water. That's why she was there. For some H_2O.'

'The woman? What woman?'

'The woman in line. She was wearing a camel V-neck.

She had straight red hair and a million freckles. And bright green eyes.'

What kind of a sicko is Dee? Did she make this up just to upset me? 'And?'

She lifts her gaze to the ceiling as if she's watching a movie up there. 'They're talking about where they were when the power went off. The guy behind the counter hands him his bag, and Brahm asks the redhead if she wants to join him for a pickle-and-water picnic.'

Maybe she really did dream this. I could have mentioned his pickle obsession in my stair-induced stupor, and she conjured it up in her sleep. 'So what happens next? Am I invited to the wedding?'

She laughs. 'They just met, Shaun. Don't be crazy. She says why not, and they walk to Washington Square Park and sit on a bench and eat their pickles. But they can't keep their eyes off each other. They have this instant connection, you know? Has that ever happened to you?'

'And then?' I ask.

'He asks her out for tonight. Then I woke up.'

My new room-mate is a freak, and I am dismissing her entire freakish dissertation from my mind. I will not give her, or her dream, or the supposed new love of Brahma's life any more thought.

I freak out at noon. What if Dee really is psychic?

I throw my novel on my bedroom floor. She's not psychic. There's no such thing as a third eye. My room-mate is a Wall Street receptionist. She's not Nostradamus.

I'm putting the entire Brahm conversation out of my head.

At one I decide that I, too, need a flashlight. From Jeremiah's. Who knows when the power will come back? I speed-walk since the subways still aren't working. When I push the door open to the store, I see no redheads. Ha.

I wonder what Brahm is doing today. When I spoke to him last night he said that since his office is closed because of the power outage, he'd probably just bum around. He wanted us to hang out, but I told him it wasn't a good idea. I don't want him to get his hopes up.

I know I shouldn't be talking to him past the more-than-friends hour of eleven. But I don't speak to him every night. Just last night, and the night before, and the night . . . oh, crap. Maybe it *is* every night. It's not my fault. He calls me. And we were friends for three years before we started dating, so we can't just *not* talk. His voice makes me feel warm, and safe. And I need an end-of-day phone call to signify bedtime, otherwise I lie in bed all night listening to the cacophony of honking and car alarms that sound like a five-year-old kicking a piano.

I buy my flashlight, but continue wandering around the store, my eyes peeled for Brahm. I don't want him to get his hopes up, but I don't want him to meet someone else. By the time I've combed every aisle at least twice, I'm relaxed. And feeling stupid for showing up. I'm cramming my bagged flashlight into my oversized purse when I hear a woman's voice say, 'Six jugs of water, please.'

Standing at the counter is a redhead in a camel V-neck.

My body starts shivering, like the temperature just dropped thirty degrees. How did Dee know? Did she set this up?

I peer closely at Ms Redhead, about to ask if she's a

friend of Dee's, when through the window I see the familiar messy hair. I leap into action, sprinting out the door before Brahm has the chance to open it. He's wearing his black T-shirt with the white lightning-bolt, the one I once told him is my favourite, the one he wears to death. A smile lights up his face when he sees me.

'Hi,' I say, trying to suppress the shock I feel by keeping myself bleached of expression.

'Shaun,' he says, happily. 'What are you doing here?'

'Buying a flashlight.'

The redhead pays for her water.

'How's your day?' I ask, glancing at her out of the corner of my eye. I hold my breath.

'Not bad. Do you want to hang out in the park for a bit?'

The redhead leaves and I exhale.

Shouldn't lead him on, shouldn't lead him on. 'I can't, I have to get home.'

His face falls. I wave good-bye. As I walk back to my apartment, a weird feeling comes over me, like I've been transported into *The Twilight Zone*. I'm not sure if Dee is psychic, if she set this up, if I just ruined Brahm's life.

Maybe this never even happened. Can I pretend this never happened?

A week later, when the power has been restored and the chance of me finding a free weekend to reschedule my trip to California is pretty much nil, Dee once again barges into the bathroom, clad in her usual pink PJs and matching flip-flops. Instead of pigtails, this time she's wearing her glasses on her head like a hair band. Her third eye, perhaps?

I'm on the toilet, and I'm too tired to yell at her to leave. I was on the phone with Brahm until 3:00 a.m. talking about the weather, TV, how much he misses me. 'Can I help you?' I ask her.

'I had another dream about your ex and the redhead.'

I feel queasy, like I'm on a sailboat in choppy waters. 'What happens?'

'He's on the subway after work, and she's rushing down the stairs on Thirty-third to get on. Brahm spots her running toward the car and, throwing his suitcase between the subway doors before they close, he helps her inside. They share the same pole and feel that connection again. He asks her out.'

'No way.' He wouldn't ask out a random woman on the train.

She shrugs. 'That was my dream. But why didn't they already meet at Jeremiah's?'

I pay special attention to the toilet paper. 'Guess you were wrong.' I don't mention my Jeremiah's intervention in case I screwed up the fate of the universe.

'Guess so.' Perplexed, she exits the bathroom.

Is she for real? Will I miss him if he dates someone else? Will I be able to sleep at night when he no longer calls?

I must stop them from meeting.

At a quarter to five I leave the ad agency where I work to lurk outside the cosmic subway station. At 6:34 I spot the redhead from Jeremiah's. I admire her red slingbacks before stepping directly in her path. 'Excuse me.'

She has a round face, with eyes the colour of the inside of a cucumber. 'Yes?'

Um . . . 'Can you tell me how to get to Central Park?'

'Sure.' She leans in close and gives me directions.

Many follow-up questions later, I thank her and let her disappear down into the station. I wait a few seconds and follow. I peek over the turnstile, and spot her waiting by a bench.

Hurray! She missed Brahm's train. That's it. It's the end of this redhead and Brahm. Mission accomplished. I've altered the fate of the universe. I glance over my shoulder nervously, refusing to feel guilty as I make my way home.

Mmm. Bacon.

On Saturday the aroma of crisping meat awakens me. Funny, I would have pegged Dee as a vegetarian. Being in touch with the earth and all that stuff. What do I know? Maybe she's more of an evil witch. I stretch, and stagger into the kitchen.

'Want some breakfast?' she offers.

'Sounds divine,' I reply, putting my anti-Dee thoughts aside in honour of this splendid meal.

She scoops two eggs out of the pan and slides them onto a plate. Then she makes a smiley face by adding a curved slice of bacon as she asks, 'Can you explain something?'

She's already halfway through a glass of my OJ, but I don't mind, since my meal smells so delicious. 'Sure.'

'Why is it that I had another dream last night about Brahm and the redhead?'

Again? Enough already. 'What happened?' I try to keep my voice steady, as though none of it matters.

'I dreamed that they're at the Astor Place Barnes & Noble and both reach for the last copy of the new Grisham novel.'

'And?'

'They compare Grisham's literary work with his legal thrillers, and she asks him to join her for a coffee.'

'She asks him out?' Getting aggressive, is she?

'What I'm wondering is why I keep dreaming they're meeting for the first time. They should have already met twice by now.'

I shrug. 'Maybe you're not as psychic as you think you are.'

She cracks two more eggs into the frying pan. 'No, that can't be. Have you spoken to Brahm recently? Do you know if they've met?'

I stuff my mouth with bacon so I can't be expected to answer.

'Wait a sec,' she says, mouth widening as if she's about to yawn. 'Did you somehow prevent them from meeting?'

I chew extra slowly. Swallow. Fake chew. Fake swallow. 'Would there be consequences if I did? Is it wrong to mess with the future? I mean, you told me to take an earlier flight to California, right?'

'I'm not entirely sure how it works,' she admits. 'Last week, I dreamed that my sister missed my father's birthday, so I reminded her and she called him.' She shrugs. 'No harm done. No cosmic implications.'

I breathe with relief. I haven't botched the fate of the world. Unless the redhead and Brahm's future offspring would have found a cure for cancer, or invented a flying chair or something. I take another deep breath and confess in a rush, 'I've been stopping their meetings before they could happen.'

She calmly turns over the eggs. 'Why? Didn't you break up with him?'

'Yeah, but the idea of him kissing someone else makes my skin crawl. I can't sit by and let them meet. I just can't.'

She nods. 'Fair enough.'

I arrive at Barnes & Noble a half hour later. After two chai teas and a scone, I spot Ms Redhead browsing in the romance section on the second floor, and I make a mad but hopefully subtle dash over there.

'Hey,' she says. 'Didn't you ask me for directions yesterday?'

Damn, she recognises me. She's going to think I'm a psycho stalker. I *am* a psycho stalker. 'Thanks again.'

'No problem. It's so weird that you're here. The universe must be trying to tell us something.'

I lower my gaze and pick up a book.

'Are you visiting New York?' she asks.

'Me? No.'

'Really? And you needed directions to Central Park?'

Damn. 'Um . . . I have no sense of direction.' Change subject, change subject! 'Do you read a lot?'

'Yeah. Mostly mysteries and romances, I like happy endings.'

'Don't we all.'

'I'm heading to the cafe. Want to join me? I'm Simone.'

Apparently Simone would have asked *anyone* to join her for coffee today. 'Sure. I'm Shaun.'

In the cafe once again, I order another chai and she orders a cappuccino. Even though I want to hate her, I like her. She laughs at my jokes. Asks me about my job. She just moved to the city and wants to meet people. She gives me her business card and tells me to call her.

Thirty minutes later I spot Brahm at the magazine rack. He doesn't see me. Tucked under his arm is the new Grisham novel.

'Operation Stop Brahm and Simone, take four,' Dee says two mornings later, pounding on my door.

'Not again,' I whine.

'They unknowingly sit next to each other at the Union Square movie theatre, and they start chatting.'

I feel sick. Possibly because I had sex with him last night. Okay, I know I shouldn't have, but we were on the phone until two, and he said he missed me and wanted to see me and I thought, Why not? I told him he could come over if he wanted to, and to wear the lightning-bolt shirt, and twenty minutes later he was kissing me. And it felt so nice and safe.

I can't let him meet someone new, I just can't. 'I don't understand, why do they keep meeting?'

'I don't know.'

'What do you mean you don't know? What kind of psychic are you? Eventually it'll stop, right? They can't keep bumping into each other indefinitely, can they?'

'I don't know.'

I need to put an end to this. I search in my purse for Simone's business card and call her. 'Hey, it's Shaun. Your bookstore buddy? Want to catch a book signing tonight?'

'Sure,' she says. 'I was going to see a movie, but a book signing sounds great.'

It's Thursday morning and Dee throws open my door.

I pull the pillow over my head. 'Go away,' I moan.

'He gets out of a cab at 11 p.m. on Houston and Broadway. She gets into it.'

I call him at ten and tell him I'll meet him for a drink. By eleven I'm drunk and under his satin sheets. He plays with my curls and tells me he loves me. I pretend I'm asleep.

On Friday morning Dee wakes me up at six. 'Starbucks. Forty-second and Third. Forty minutes. He spills coffee on her shirt. Go.'

Saturday morning, 10 a.m.

Flip-flop! Flip-flop! Dee stomps from her room to mine and whips open my door. 'I can't take it any more! I can't stand dreaming about Brahm and the redhead continuously. It's driving me crazy!'

What, it's my fault she's psychic? Like I can control what she dreams? I jump out of bed. 'Where are they?'

'Shaun,' she says, 'you have to let go.'

'Tell me where they are.'

She sighs. Loudly. 'They're sitting at a table on the patio of French Roast in the West Village.'

'How are they sitting together if they don't even know each other yet?'

I must look crazed, because Dee says, 'I don't think you should intervene this time.'

'If you didn't want me to intervene, you shouldn't have told me.'

She shakes her head. 'I'm not making your choices for you.'

The phone next to my bed rings and I turn my back to her and snatch it up. 'Hello?'

'It's me,' Brahm says. 'Have you eaten? Want to go for brunch?'

'Sure,' I say slowly, trying to process this phone call. 'Where do you want to go?'

'How about French Roast?'

Huh? 'Sure. Thirty minutes?'

Thirty minutes later, panicked that I'm late, and exhausted from the run, from the week, from these damn interventions, I see Brahm's curly-haired head. He's sitting on the terrace, his face tilted toward the sun. Every few seconds he looks down and eagerly scans the street, searching for me.

He's wearing the lightning-bolt shirt.

And suddenly I remember that I was once a girl who wore my hair up every day for a year because He, the boyfriend before Brahm, remarked in passing that he thought my neck was sexy.

I have to let him go. Have to let him move on. I want him to be with someone else. Someone who feels swallowed whole.

My heart breaks and I flip open my cell. I dial. Slowly.

I know someday I'll feel it again, too. But until then?

Maybe Dee and I'll take a vacation. I'll trade in my business-class ticket for two economy seats to California. Or maybe Vegas. Bet Dee kicks ass at the tables.

She answers on the first ring.

'Simone?' I ask. 'What are you doing for brunch? There's someone I'd like you to meet.'

Santa Montefiore

A Woman of Mystery

When Celestia Somersby moved into Old Lodge, the sleepy, insular village of Westcotton was roused to wakefulness by a blazing curiosity. It wasn't that they hadn't witnessed the arrival of strangers, though, being a small, remote town on the Devonshire coast there was little to entice people, except the odd few who came for the peace; it was because Celestia Somersby was a woman of mystery. 'She's very beautiful,' said Betty Knight, standing back to admire the expanding flower display she was arranging in the nave. Vivien Pratt screwed up her nose and leaned on her broom, surrounded by leaves and twigs from Betty's overenthusiastic creation.

'In a severe way,' she replied with a snort. 'I don't think that black she wears is very becoming. Makes her look pale and drawn. Older, too,' she added and there was an ill-disguised timbre of pleasure in her voice, for she was sixty-five and looked it.

'You can't deny she's elegant, though. I used to wear

long skirts with boots like that when I was young.' said Betty with a sigh.

'It's not your age, dear,' said Vivien, passing her reptilian eyes up and down Betty's squat build. 'It's your girth. You shouldn't indulge so. I'm not this thin by nature but by abstinence, Betty. Jesus taught us that, and he was thin, wasn't he? No cream buns and pies from Ethel's Pantry for him, just the odd fish and crust of bread after the five thousand had troughed.'

'Do you think she's a divorcee?' Betty pulled her stomach in, then let it out with a heave as a wilting lily diverted her attention.

'She wears a ring, you know. I saw it. Though, there's been no sign of a man. Must be divorced, otherwise why would she look so sad?'

'If Cyril gave me a divorce, I wouldn't look sad. I'd be positively gleeful. Thirty years of sitting about like a fat walrus. I'd be more than happy to roll him back into the sea.'

'You'd be lost, dear, have no illusions. That woman's a walking tragedy; you can see it on her face. A smile would do much for that sallow complexion.' Vivien didn't bother to reflect on her own smile, lost long ago with her sense of fun. Slowly she began to sweep.

'She hasn't said so much as a hello to anyone. Just lots of sightings, though no one seems to know what she does or why she's come. There, I think Reverend Jollie will appreciate my effort this week. I do love spring, don't you? Still, she'll come to church on Sunday, I'm sure. We can all get a good look at her then.'

'My dear, if she hasn't had the decency to introduce

herself by Sunday, I shall think her very rude indeed. She shan't be welcome here.'

'That's not for you to say, Vivien. This is God's house.'

'Then I shan't invite her back for tea. She'll know she's caused offence then, won't she.' *And she'll know who calls the shots around here, too.*

By Sunday the whole village was whispering about the enigmatic Celestia Somersby. She had wandered into Agatha Tingle's shop and bought a basket of provisions, infuriating the docile shopkeeper by hiding her features beneath a black sunhat and dark glasses. She had said nothing, just paid, handing the older woman crisp pound notes with long white fingers. Agatha gossiped with Betty and Vivien over tea in Edith's Pantry, dissecting every detail, from the goods she had bought to the strange old fashioned buckle shoes she wore on her feet, while Vivien sipped weak tea and Betty bit into a large slice of chocolate cake. What they didn't know, however, was that Fitzroy Merridale had seen her down on the beach, walking wistfully with her feet in the surf, her long black dress billowing about her ankles, the chiffon scarf tied about her hat flapping like the wings of a bat and that there, in the roaring wind and the crashing of waves, he had lost his heart. It had been a wonderful moment. An awakening from somewhere dull into somewhere bright and full of possibilities.

Since that exquisite sighting, Fitzroy had been able to think of little else but Celestia Somersby. He had sat in the Four Codgers pub and listened to the mutters of speculation. Some said that she was divorced, others that she had murdered her husband. He believed none of it and took pleasure from the fact that she hadn't deigned speak to any of them, because he knew instinctively that she would talk to him. After all, he was one of the few in town her age. Westcotton was an old people's town. He had only moved there to write, having found no inspiration in London. He was also bold. Why, he mused, was it up to her to approach them? Surely as the newcomer *they* should make the gesture and welcome *her* into their midst. He sat in the pew, on the cold hard seat of ancient wood, and looked about him. Agatha, Betty, Vivien, Edith and a gaggle of other grandmothers in feathered hats and pastel dresses. Their husbands fat and weathered or thin and dominated. A few young couples with fidgeting children, following in the deep, stodgy footsteps of their parents. There was nothing for Celestia Somersby here. Why had she come?

When Reverend Jollie stepped into the nave, his long gowns disguising a belly full of Edith's scones, the disappointment that was felt by every member of his congregation caused the very air in the church to drop. Betty glanced warily at her flowers, afraid that the lilies would wilt too, for everyone had expected the first proper sighting of Celestia Somersby. She had not come.

Reverend Jollie was aware of their frustration because it reflected his own. He had indulged in fantasies of a more godly nature than Fitzroy Merridale, envisaging her confessing her sins, of which there were many, onto his chest. He was appalled at his own weakness for since Celestia Somersby had arrived in Westcotton he had wished he were Catholic.

With a heavy sigh he raised his palms to the sky and addressed the sheep in his flock like the good shepherd

that he was. 'Welcome, friends . . .' Just when his enthusiasm was on the point of stalling, the large doors of the
church opened with a deep groan. At once the air was
charged with expectation. Reverend Jollie watched his
congregation turn their heads to face the entrance now
gaping open like the toothless yawn of an old man. Fitzroy
Merridale's heart stopped for a second as did his breath,
both suspended between anticipation and disappointment, as he willed it to be her. He craned his neck past
Cyril Knight's thick shoulders and saw, to his delight, the
slim, hesitant figure he had dreamed about since he saw
her walking barefoot up the beach. She remained there for
what seemed like a very long while, her arms outstretched
on either side, her gloved hands holding the doors open.
She wore black and her white face and neck glowed luminous beneath the veil that was pinned to her hat. Only her
crimson lips and the pink apples of her cheeks retained
their colour. With a purposeful stride she walked up the
aisle, passing the many pairs of eyes that strained for a better view of her face. To Reverend Jollie's astonishment she
knelt before him, for he still stood in front of the altar,
and crossed herself, inclining her head as the Catholics
do. He experienced a frisson of excitement, then let out
a controlled though staggered breath. She smiled a small
but unmistakeable smile, before turning and walking back
down the aisle to a seat at the back. Fitzroy grinned with
admiration. What a cool, confident display that was and
how dignified. He had noticed her slim ankles and the
high heels on those old-fashioned buckled shoes. He wondered what she looked like with her hair down, cascading
over naked shoulders.

Fitzroy wasn't the only man in the church unable to concentrate on the service; even Reverend Jollie flustered over the sermon like an overexcited girl, anticipating communion when she would at last raise her veil and cast her dark eyes to him in submission. He was to be disappointed, however, for although she knelt before him she did not raise her veil or her eyes, which remained lowered and demure.

'Well,' huffed Vivien once the service was over and they were all standing about in the sunshine. 'She might have introduced herself. What does she have to hide, I wonder. I shall not invite her to tea.'

'I don't think she'll mind,' said Betty with a laugh. 'She doesn't look the type for tea. Much too common for her, I suspect, as are we.'

'Oh, for goodness' sake, Betty. You talk such nonsense. Your father might have been a plumber but mine, my dear, was the son of a gentleman.' Betty raised her eyebrows cynically. She knew better than to argue with Vivien Pratt.

Fitzroy had noticed Celestia leave during the blessing and had slipped out behind her. As she walked briskly down the path towards the green he hurried after her. 'Miss Somersby,' he said, catching her up. 'May I introduce myself?' She continued to walk until they were out of sight of the church. Only then did she turn. He was surprised at her small stature, for her charisma gave the impression that she was taller. She did not lift her veil, but he saw her eyes shining behind it. 'My name is Fitzroy Merridale. I want to welcome you to Westcotton.'

'Thank you.' Her voice was soft and deep like brown suede. He noticed she looked around furtively.

'May I accompany you home?' he asked. She nodded and proceeded to walk across the green. 'I don't imagine you know anyone here.'

'That is why I have moved,' she said and her words weighed heavily with significance.

'I see,' he replied, intrigued. 'I hope you don't mind me approaching you. You just seem so . . . alone.'

'I am alone,' she said, then sighed. 'It is nice to talk to someone.' Fitzroy felt his insides flutter as if they were filled with bubbles.

'I'm a bit of a loner myself. I'm trying to write a novel, but it's not really working. I live in a cottage by the sea. I saw you the other day, walking along the beach.' He was sure she smiled beneath her veil. Encouraged, he continued. 'You had taken your shoes off and your feet were in the water. It must have been cold.'

'I didn't notice,' she replied.

'Well, I live near there. It's meant to fill me with inspiration, but I just stare out at a void. You inspired me, though.' She stopped and looked up at him.

'Did I?'

'Yes, you gave me an idea for a story.' He felt himself blush and put his hands in his pockets. 'I've already begun.' She stared at him a long moment, then walked on.

'Why don't you come back for tea?' she said. 'It's not much, but it's home.'

The house was pretty, with tall ceilings and sash windows overlooking a large garden surrounded by lime trees.

Once inside the wall that encircled the property they were entirely alone. Fitzroy followed her into the house. He watched as she took off her hat in front of a gilt mirror in the hall. She unpinned her hair so that it fell in dark waves over her shoulders and down her back. Then she slipped off her gloves and unbuttoned her coat with delicate white fingers. When she turned to him he was struck by the surprisingly pale colour of her eyes. Like water in a tropical sea. Her mouth twisted once again into a small smile and he felt the colour rise in his cheeks. She was more beautiful than he had imagined.

He followed her into the sitting room, where a fire smouldered in the grate. There was a piano upon which large church candles were placed in clusters. The melted wax revealed that they were often lit. 'Do you play?' he asked.

'Of course,' she said and sat down on the stool. As she launched into an emotive solo, her face was suddenly darkened by some unspoken sadness.

'Play something happy,' he asked. She raised those strange pale eyes to him and shook her head.

'I'm afraid I can't play what is not in my heart.'

'Then don't play,' he said impulsively. 'Please don't play if it makes you sad.' Once again she smiled but this time it was the smile one gives in the face of a beautiful sunset. A smile tinged with sorrow. She got up from the stool and walked up to him. The look in her eyes was intense. He turned away.

She raised her hand and ran it down his cheek. 'You're a sensitive man,' she said and then she kissed him. He didn't pull away or question his good fortune, but wrapped her in his arms and pressed his lips to hers. He breathed in the scent of her skin, warm and sweet like the smell of blue-bells, and closed his eyes.

Suddenly she pushed him away. 'You must go!' she said hastily, shaking her head as if ashamed of what had come over her.

'But Celestia!' he pleaded.

'Not here. Not here, Fitzroy. I can't. It's wrong.' She staggered back and leaned against the piano, her hand pressed against her forehead.

'What's wrong? Are you married?'

'No.'

'Are you divorced?'

'No.'

'Are you a widow?'

She stared at him with frightened eyes and hurried into the hall. 'You must go!'

'Will we meet again?'

'There's a cave on the beach, you know the one. I'll meet you there tomorrow at noon. Don't breathe a word to anyone!' Fitzroy promised, then departed. The door closed behind him and he was left bewildered. If she had been mysterious before, she was even more mysterious now.

The following day Fitzroy went down to the beach and waited for her in the cave. He waited and waited but she did not come. When finally he was on the point of leaving she hurried in through the narrow entrance and fell into his arms. 'I'm sorry,' she breathed, kissing him fervently. 'Forgive me!' He did not bother to ask why she was late. He did not care. He had her in his arms and was happy.

The following weeks passed in the same manner. They met in the cave and she was always late. But he had learned to wait for her. They didn't talk much and every time they parted he felt he knew her less than before. In the evenings he went to the Four Codgers and listened to the talk. The rumours had grown. They called her the Black Widow and were certain she had killed her husband. Maybe one, perhaps more. Fitzroy sat smiling to himself. He knew her better than any of them.

At the end of May, when the air was filled with the sugary scent of summer, Fitzroy invited her back to his cottage. 'I want to make love to you,' he said. At first she was hesitant, as if betraying another or breaking a vow, but then overcome with desire she agreed. In the amber light of evening he unburdened her of the black clothes she wore, unwrapping her slowly as if she were a precious gift. Her skin was soft and creamy and blushing with youth. *You are too vibrant a woman to be subdued by black*, he thought as he kissed her flesh. Then he noticed a scar on her chest. It was pale, barely visible. It was the texture that made it stand out. Afraid of wounding her, he said nothing. After they had made love they lay entwined, engulfed by an unsettling mixture of joy and sorrow, as if instinctively aware of the transience of their affair.

Then one night in the Four Codgers, Fitzroy heard them talk of another man. One who came and left her house in a car. He was dark, in his late forties. He never stayed for long. Fitzroy was consumed with jealousy. He marched over to Old Lodge and knocked on the door. When she did not open it he pounded with his fists. 'Who is he?' he bellowed into the night air. Before walking away he noticed a brief flash of light from upstairs and the hasty drawing of a curtain.

The following morning there was a furore on the beach. Policemen and onlookers and dozens of people he did not recognise. When he approached, Vivien Pratt drew him aside. 'Don't,' she said, shaking her head. 'It's that woman. Celestia Somersby. She's dead.'

'Dead?' he gasped, feeling his world unravelling about him.

'Drowned.' Then she hissed. 'They say it's suicide. I don't know. Might have been murder.'

Celestia Somersby, or Jane Hardwick as she was really called, was not buried in Westcotton. Fitzroy found her brother sorting through her things at Old Lodge. 'She was a Londoner at heart,' he said sadly. 'She was once an actress. A good actress too, before the accident. After that she was too frightened of the stage to continue. She turned her life into a drama. Moving from place to place where no one knew her. Where she could be anyone she wanted to be so long as she was playing a role.'

'Why did she kill herself?' Fitzroy asked and the pain must have echoed up from the hollowness in his heart. Her brother looked at him for a long moment, then smiled compassionately.

'She fooled you too, didn't she?' He sighed and picked up her photograph. 'She died, my friend, because she couldn't sustain that bizarre life forever. She wanted to be Celestia but Jane was always one step behind her. I think she preferred to die dramatically than live modestly.'

'But I loved her.'

'No, you didn't. You loved someone who didn't exist. Even she had lost sight of who she really was. But in a way she got what she wanted. A dramatic life and a dramatic death and she will live on as Celestia in your memory and in the memory of the others who gave her their hearts. Only I will remember her as Jane but she never cared much for me. I was a constant reminder of the truth and she cared little for that.'

Liane Moriarty

Mothers' Group

Apparently serial murderers are difficult to pick. If one lives next door to you, you will invariably describe him as, 'Quiet, kept to himself.' You might add 'I did think he was a bit creepy' but that's because you like to think you're a good judge of character. Really, you just find him creepy in hindsight.

So maybe it's not surprising that our first impressions of Sarah weren't especially memorable.

Not that she was a serial murderer.

As far as we *know*. Meaningful eyebrow-twitching all around.

It's twelve years now since we met her and since then our 'Sarah theories' have become increasingly outlandish. But in the beginning, she was just another New Mum. We'd all had our babies in June (seven 'restless, adaptable, eloquent' little Geminis) and this was our first Mothers' Group meeting, organised by the local clinic. We jostled our stiff, shiny new prams into a coffee shop, as righteous and nervy as only first-time mothers can be.

Sarah was tall, with stylish spectacles. I decided she was an intellectual, for no more insightful reason than the spectacles. Her baby, Jessica, slept quietly through the first meeting. Sarah arrived late, left early and didn't say much.

I didn't think she was particularly interesting, to be honest. The other mothers made more of an impression. There was Natasha, who was large and loud, and circulated paper and pen so we could list our names, telephone numbers and food allergies. We forgave her because it was helpful to have a take-charge person, and because her baby, Zak, was breathtakingly ugly.

There were the two Karens. Suburban princesses with silky, tanned arms, jangly bracelets, and baby daughters called Emily wearing denim Pumpkin Patch dresses. The Karens were beside themselves when they discovered this astonishing coincidence. 'What are the odds?' they cried, tossing shiny hair. Actually the odds weren't that long. 'Karen' was popular in the seventies and 'Emily' was in the top ten of girls' names that year. Lack of imagination probably runs in your families, I thought cattily, even while I yearned to be best friends with them.

There was Audrey, a tiny Japanese girl who didn't appear to speak a word of English. She giggled delicately behind her hand whenever you spoke to her, which made you feel stupid and gigantic. Her baby was fat-cheeked and irresistibly kissable. There was Amy, who had twin boys through IVF and a husband called Norm, who was funny and a butcher.

And there was me, so exhausted from lack of sleep, I felt drunk. I was the frightened, fumbling, bumbling new mother. I kept banging my pram into things. Daniel vomited down my back and I knocked over a full glass of apple juice with my elbow. The Karens cleaned me up, soothing and smoothing, while Natasha shouted for the waitress to bring over cloths.

Of course, the first thing we did was share labour stories.

Natasha had a home birth in the spa bath with the help of her three sisters in bikinis, while her husband kept sneaking off to watch the NRL. Karen C.'s waters broke – *flooded!* – during a snooty dinner party. Karen M. nearly popped her Emily out on the hospital driveway, it all happened so fast. She thought labour was a piece of cake. Well of course you do, we said. Amy had the twins by caesarean and her husband Norm dropped the video camera because he was crying so hard when he saw his sons for the first time. Ohhhh, we said. Audrey managed to mime her labour story for us, with lots of face scrunching. We nodded along and got the gist of it.

I trumped them all with my story of how I nearly died having Daniel and my husband was told he might have to choose between me and the baby, which would have been a problem because Nick was so indecisive he wrestled with the 'chicken or beef' choice when he flew. It was good to laugh, even while I got teary, because Nick wouldn't talk about it at all. He still won't, and Dan is starting high school next year! That's men for you. I was telling these women intimate details about my emotions and my body before I even had their names straight.

And Sarah?

What was Sarah's story?

Not one of us can remember. It's possible that she never took her turn and we rudely didn't even notice. We were all so absorbed with spilling our own experiences.

After that first meeting we decided, or to be more accurate, Natasha decreed, that we should meet in parks rather than coffee shops. So that's what we did the following Wednesday. Once again, Sarah's baby slept through the whole morning and Sarah herself seemed perfectly normal. I didn't talk to her much. Apparently she gave Amy an excellent recipe for marinated lamb cutlets which she still uses to this day, and Karen C. remembers her wearing an especially nice top from Portmans and Natasha chatted with her about local politics and the problem with parking outside the chemist. You can see the minute level of detail to which we've analysed this whole thing.

It was at our third get-together that we discovered the truth about Sarah's baby. Once again, we were in the park. I was feeling euphoric because I'd got six hours' sleep the night before, and Daniel was feeding sedately, instead of like a demented vampire. Sarah had gone back to her car to get her sunglasses. We were sitting on picnic rugs in the centre of our horseshoe of parked prams.

Natasha had got Zak off to sleep and was nosily peering around, observing us and our babies.

'We haven't seen Sarah's baby yet,' she commented.

'She's a good sleeper,' said Amy.

Natasha stood up and bent over Sarah's pram. 'Let's have a look at you, Jessica!'

'Don't wake her up,' warned Karen C.

There was silence for a few seconds. An Emily gurgled.

Natasha stumbled back with her hand pressed hard to her mouth. 'Oh, my goodness.'

'What is it?' we asked.

My first thought was that the baby was brutally

deformed. I was already preparing my face not to look shocked so as not to offend Sarah. Amy said afterwards she thought the baby was dead.

'She's—' Natasha seemed lost for words and we already knew her well enough to know that was rare. She looked over to the far side of the park, where Sarah was opening her car door.

'She's, um—'

'*What?*'

'She's not real.'

We stared blankly at her.

What do you mean, she's not *real?*' I asked.

'She's a doll.' Natasha gave a crazed giggle. 'A plastic doll.'

Audrey made a high-pitched sound and held up her son's teddy bear, pointing at it with her eyebrows raised.

'Yes,' said Natasha. 'It's a toy. A toy baby.'

'Oh, stop it,' said Amy. 'You're pulling our legs.'

'Um, I wish I was,' said Natasha. 'Because this is pretty, ah . . . freaky.'

And then we couldn't talk any more because Sarah was back, with her sunglasses on, looking absolutely, utterly normal.

'The sun is warm,' she commented.

'Yes!' we shouted, with deranged enthusiasm. 'Very warm!' We were shocking actresses.

Karen M. struggled to suppress an attack of nervous laughter. Natasha sat back down and massaged her forehead with a fingertip, smiling strangely at the ground. Audrey stared openly at Sarah. Amy busily breastfed a twin, Karen C. busily checked her Emily's nappy and I busily buried my face in Daniel's sweet neck.

Sarah bent over her baby's pram and everybody's eyes flew wildly back and forth. Karen M. looked like she was silently choking to death.

'How often is Jessica feeding?' I asked recklessly.

I felt Natasha's hand on my arm, squeezing.

'I don't really have her in a routine yet,' answered Sarah. 'Oh, it looks like she's awake at last.'

She reached into the pram and lifted out her baby.

We froze. My heart beat double-time and Natasha's fingernails dug painfully into my arm.

For a second I thought, No, no, of course that's a real baby and then, as Sarah turned towards me, I saw the pink-plastic curve of her daughter's face.

Jessica was undoubtedly a doll. A beautiful, lifelike baby doll.

Nobody spoke. Even our babies were quiet. We could hear the distant roar of day-time traffic. A dog's bark. Sarah cradled the doll's head (yellow hair shining synthetically in the sunlight) with loving, motherly nonchalance. I caught a glimpse of glittery blue eyeballs and rigid black eyelashes.

I felt sick and giggly and emotional all at once.

It was Karen C. who broke the silence. She spoke in a high, tense voice. 'She's beautiful, Sarah.'

Natasha's head whipped around to Karen C., who gave a tiny, defiant shrug.

'Thank you,' said Sarah. 'I think so, but I'm biased, of course.'

She patted the doll's back, rocking and jiggling, oblivious to our frenzied, silent squirming.

Natasha took a deep breath and lifted her chin. 'Sarah—'

she began, but Amy interrupted her. 'So, same time, same place next week, do you think?

And we all rushed to answer Amy, trampling over Natasha's voice in our anxiety to avoid hearing Sarah confronted. Natasha subsided, compressing her lips.

For the next half-hour we were stilted and self-conscious, our eyes constantly sliding over to Sarah sitting cross-legged, rocking her doll. I was acutely aware of my own baby's warm soft skin, his blinking eyes, the rise and fall of his tiny chest.

Natasha said afterwards, 'All I could think was, oh my God, what if she starts *breastfeeding* it!'

Finally, Sarah got up and carefully placed the doll back in the pram, as though she'd rocked her off to sleep. Perhaps she had. I felt myself exhale, as if I'd been holding my breath. It was a relief to have the doll out of sight.

It gave me an odd, off-balance feeling observing Sarah in this new light. This nutty new light. Before, I would have said she was saner than me. She *still* seemed more grown-up, more neatly pressed and together than me.

Sarah looked at her watch. 'I'd better be off.'

We waved her goodbye cheerily. You could hear the anticipation in our voices. We were *dying* to talk about her. As she pushed her pram towards her car, we sat in silence, until we simultaneously judged she was far enough away not to hear us, at which point we burst into a delirious babble of 'I nearly died!', 'I nearly fainted!', 'I nearly had a heart attack!' In the excitement, Audrey forgot that we didn't speak Japanese, but it didn't seem to matter, she was obviously saying all the same sorts of things as us. Karen M. finally gave way to a stream of pent-up giggles, and her laughter was so infectious we all caught it. We rocked in unison, gasping for breath, clutching our sides, our faces creased like monkeys'.

And then we realised that Karen M. wasn't laughing any more, she was crying, and she said, 'I bet her baby died,' and she told us that Emily wasn't her first baby. She'd had a son. 'Cot death,' she told us. 'He was three weeks old.'

It was like being slapped across the face. We were silent, watery-eyed with sympathy and shock.

Then Amy said, 'Or maybe Sarah was like me, she couldn't get pregnant, and it's sent her over the edge. After our third go at IVF failed I was diagnosed with clinical depression.'

'Yeah, or maybe,' said Natasha, 'Sarah is a fucking psychopath and we don't want her anywhere near our kids.'

Audrey burst forth into a torrent of Japanese involving a lot of pointing at our babies.

I spoke up. 'Whatever the reason, she needs help. She needs to see a psychiatrist. She probably should be on medication.' I didn't tell them about Mum. I didn't want to be the mental illness expert, and remnants of schoolgirl shame still lingered.

Everyone agreed that Sarah needed help. What we didn't agree on was whether *we* should be the ones to confront her with the truth.

'We can't collude in her fantasy!' said Natasha.

'But I think she knows perfectly well it's a doll,' said Karen M. 'This is just her way of grieving. Why can't we just go along with it for a while?'

'What if her plan is to kidnap one of our babies?' said Natasha.

'I didn't say we'd ask her to *babysit*.'

The conversation went back and forth and voices became edged and it was getting late. In the end we put it to the vote. Natasha and Audrey wanted to confront her. Amy, the Karens and I wanted to wait and see. I admit that a lifetime of avoiding messy emotional confrontation was behind my vote.

When Sarah turned up the following week, it was like a film star had arrived. We were the paparazzi, avidly observing and recording her every move.

Did it add a certain 'frisson' to Mothers' Group? You bet it did.

With elaborate casualness, we took turns asking questions. We learned that she'd worked in publishing before 'Jessica was born', her husband was a town planner, she liked cooking, hated cleaning the shower, ate muesli for breakfast, read thrillers, watched *ER* religiously and didn't get on with her sister-in-law.

Mmmmm. It all added up to just about nothing. Apart from when she was cuddling her plastic doll, Sarah was a perfectly normal, nice, intelligent girl. She kept politely turning the conversational spotlight back onto other people, so we all got to know each other better. It was an enjoyable morning. When she was the first to leave again, we all agreed that it was just . . . inexplicable, really.

It's true you can adapt to anything. As the weeks passed, Sarah and her doll no longer seemed so bizarre. There were surreal moments, of course, like when Sarah asked Karen M. to hold Jessica for a second, but Karen just took the doll with unruffled care.

Once, Sarah was sitting next to me, making Daniel gurgle and grin, playing peek-a-boo with him. Without even thinking, I asked if she'd like a hold. As soon as I'd said it, I regretted it, wondering if I was risking my son's life, but nothing happened. She just cuddled and cooed like any mother or friend.

Once we were talking about who our babies took after, and Amy, without thinking, said to Sarah, 'What about Jessica?' and blushed purple. Sarah said, 'I think she has my eyes.' It was times like those that we remembered: Oh, that's right, she's a lunatic.

Natasha kept saying this is ridiculous, it can't go on forever, what happens when our babies start to *crawl*? It wasn't right and it wasn't fair to Sarah.

Finally, reluctantly, we agreed that next week Natasha would take Sarah aside and have a 'little chat'.

I wonder what would have happened if she'd ever had that little chat.

Because the following week was when it happened.

It was a lovely warm day. Daniel was asleep in his pram, and I was relaxing, tipping my head back, enjoying the sun. A few of the girls had laid their babies out on the picnic rug in an orderly row. There was an Emily, a twin, Natasha's baby, Zak . . . and Jessica. The other babies kicked and clutched at the air and blew bubbles. Jessica stared blindly at the sky, but seemed strangely content.

Sarah's mobile rang and she asked if we could keep an eye on Jessica while she took the call. She walked away so we couldn't hear her conversation.

It all happened so quickly.

None of us even saw the dog coming. Suddenly, it was right there in the middle of us, panting black fur, snarling teeth and the rug caught up in out-of-control paws. We screamed like people on a roller-coaster, a man shouted in the distance and the mothers swooped up their babies to safety. (I will never forget the ferocious expression on sweet little Amy's face.)

But the dog went straight for Jessica.

I didn't even stop to think about what I was doing.

Karen M. and Audrey say they didn't either. We instinctively, ludicrously, threw ourselves on that dog to save Sarah's baby. The dog had Jessica's leg firmly clenched in its jaws and I swear to this day she looked terrified. We tumbled together in a mad tangle of limbs and claws, teeth sinking into my flesh, and then Sarah was there among us, grabbing at our shirts, even our hair, anything to get us away from the dog, shrieking hysterically, 'Stop it! Stop it! *It's only a doll!*'

And then the dog was gone, pulled away by its owner, and I remember sitting there with Jessica safely in my arms, blood dripping, and Sarah sobbing, 'Oh God, oh God.'

I had to get fourteen stitches for bites on both my arms. Audrey had six for a bad one on her leg, and Karen M. had a dramatic scratch down the side of her face. It was Sarah who called the ambulance. She was in a state, dabbing at our wounds, bringing us water and never even looking at her doll. Jessica had lost a leg and was pretty dirty, but was otherwise unharmed.

And then, in all the fuss and hullabaloo, Sarah disappeared.

Apparently she rang the hospital to check if we were okay but that was the last we ever heard of her. The numbers she gave us were disconnected. Nobody could find her. We've tried a few times over the years but no luck.

Personnel File Note
Employee Name: Sarah Harrison

Sarah Harrison was an excellent journalist who filed a number of great comedy pieces for us, but she let us down with 'Mothers' Group', which we had scheduled for the July edition last year. The story involved going 'undercover' as a new mother and attending a mothers' group in the suburbs. The twist was that her baby was a plastic doll. We wanted to see how the women in the group would react. (A 'Candid Camera' sort of practical joke. Her own idea – we thought it was brilliant.) But two days before the deadline, she suddenly quit and refused to submit the story, with comments along the lines of: 'They're my friends and I'm not betraying them.' Last we heard, she had moved o/s and was pregnant. Would probably not recommend employing her again.

I still have Jessica. I cleaned her up, got her a new leg, mended her dress and keep her sitting comfortably on the spare bed. 'Oh, for God's sake, *get rid of it*,' says Natasha each time she visits.

I still keep her, just in case her mother comes back.

Elizabeth Noble

What Goes on Tour . . .

They had been doing this to her all her adult life.

Ever since those first years of training, when they were all sharing a grotty flat in the nurses' quarters in Lambeth. Young, free and single (-ish). Spoiling her fun. Cramping her style.

There'd been that policeman, the one who'd unzipped her dress at the dance, and who'd stumbled back with her to her room. Her three best friends had stood outside and hammered on the door, calling her name, until he'd given up, pulled his trousers back on, and gone home.

And there was that anaesthetist, the tall one with the Tintin hair and the aquamarine eyes. He'd been taking great care of her vital signs until they'd had him bleeped, the bastards, just before the crucial moment.

But not this time. This time was her fortieth birthday, and this time the three of them were not going to stop her.

He was gorgeous. Well, good-looking. In a dumb sort

of way. Swarthy. With the glossy kind of hair that is only a few degrees away from greasy. And a wide nose. Even wider shoulders, and an ass that was undeniably smaller and tighter than hers, which would absolutely rule him out as a lifelong partner, but which made him pretty much perfect for the one-night stand she was utterly determined to have. Because what goes on tour, stays on tour. The T-shirts said so.

They were probably for children, really, the T-shirts. Or emaciated women. Hers particularly was too tight, so that the spangly words were stretched luridly across her bosom and quite hard to read. They had found them in a tacky gift shop on the strip, alongside the birthstone dice and the rip-off designer sunglasses.

This whole trip had been her idea. A fortieth birth-day long weekend in Vegas. With who else but the three women she had known all of her adult life?

She was sick of her adult life. Sick of her immaculate semi, with the beech-effect laminate flooring throughout. It was so bloody safe. Keith was so bloody safe. Reliable, sensible, practical. Yes, she knew how lucky she was to have him. Everyone was always telling her, weren't they? Even her own mother used to say, 'He's been the making of you, has Keith. Lord knows where you'd have ended up without Keith. Who could have asked for a better provider and a better father?'

Well, she wouldn't have. He'd provided laminate floor-ing throughout, hadn't he, and who would dare shoot for more than that? And of course he was a fabulous father. The kids would rather have him than her, truth be told, unless they were ill, or hurt themselves. She might have asked for a better lover, mind you. Not that she discussed that with her mother. Even if she knew it wasn't all Keith's fault that their sex life had been whittled away to a quick fumble every second or third Saturday in the dark between the football and a curry. Usually one of them kept at least one item of clothing on. A pyjama top, or socks. It was hardly the sort of thing to set your pulse racing.

Not that any of her friends' lives were so different. If anything she was a little better off than the others. Angela had those lumpy stepchildren who arrived every Friday night and wedged themselves into her three-piece suite for the entire weekend. Frances spent her whole life at the gym, claiming that she was trying to hold back the years, but really just trying to hold back Malcolm, who was usually breathing lager and cheap cigars all over her. And Trish? Trish had a nice enough husband, who'd laminated the kitchen floor, at least, but she was still working nights at the hospital to pay for it, and for the golfing holidays Bernard always insisted they took, although she didn't know a driver from a wedge.

What the hell was it all about? It wasn't that she wanted to do a Shirley Valentine. Not really. Not never go home. But they were here, right now, weren't they? Now that she was turning forty, she had this tremendous sense of something if not exactly lost, then never actually found. She'd missed something. Not just all those one-night stands she'd been interrupted from, although that was part of it. She'd had a happy life. She'd liked her job, really liked it. She'd had the white wedding and the home, and the husband who didn't cheat on her and brought wages into the house each month and took her out on birthdays and

anniversaries. And the children, the beautiful, rotten children she loved as much as any mother could. And these
friends, who knew her well and loved her anyway. She just
hadn't had an adventure.

This was supposed to be an adventure. And it had been,
a bit. Not having your husband and children made it different, for starters. Doing what you wanted to do, all day.
They'd drunk cocktails with umbrellas, they'd played rou-
lette, they'd wandered around the outlet mall for hours
and lingered in coffee shops, nattering. They'd spent as
long as they wanted getting ready to go out, like they used
to, giggling and drinking wine in their underwear, swap-
ping lipsticks and necklaces. It had been nice.

But an adventure?

It was in the nightclub that her mood had changed.
They had no business being there, of course, not really.
They were too old. They didn't know the songs, and they
didn't know how to dance in that way the kids did, with
one arm waving rhythmically above your head, like you
were doing an impression of an elephant. And all that
bumping and grinding stuff. So they stood awkwardly,
leaning against the mesh of the balcony above the dance-
floor, and watched. You couldn't have talked.

There was a young couple in one corner engaged in
vertical foreplay, oblivious to the gyrating crowd around
them. Their attempts to dance were half-hearted. Her
arms were above her head, fingers clinging on bars, and
he was rubbing himself against her, vaguely in time to the
music. When he came in to kiss her the kisses were deep
and desperate, and they trailed down her neck into the
top of her shirt. Then he would draw back and stare at

her. Open, staring eyes. She couldn't stop staring at them, until Frances pulled at her arm. Trish was miming sleeping actions, and Angela had her arms folded.

They took off their stilettos outside Caesar's Palace and the cold pavement felt wonderful beneath their feet. Her ears were ringing, a little.

'Did you see that couple in the corner?' Trish asked.

The others giggled. 'Filthy little sods!'

She sighed. 'Lucky little sods.'

'What do you mean?' Angela nudged her.

'I mean, it's been seventeen years since I had a first kiss. Seventeen years. Don't you remember how amazing a first kiss is?'

The others were quiet for a moment.

'I do.'

'Me too. Your knees go, don't they? You tingle all over.'

'There's nothing like it.' Even Trish conceded.

They'd stopped now. It was a gorgeous balmy night. Behind them fountains sprang into action in front of one of the big hotels, and overhead the omnipresent helicopters zoomed up and down the strip. It was like nowhere else, this place. Adventures could happen in a place like Las Vegas.

'Supposing you could have a first kiss here. Nothing else. Just a kiss. And no one else would ever know. No one would get hurt. What goes on tour stays on tour. You'd just have that knee-trembling, body-tingling, unbelievable first kiss and then you'd go home. That's it. Would you do it?'

She wasn't looking at the others. They didn't answer straightaway.

'Course not,' Trish was the first. 'I mean, be fair. I'd bloody kill Bernard if he kissed someone else. So, no. It wouldn't be right.'

'I couldn't,' Angela grinned ruefully. 'I know what you mean, but I don't think I could go through with it, not when it came down to it.'

'I wouldn't want to. Can't think of anything worse than being out there on your own again. You're only remembering the first kiss, and how long does that last? A few minutes. Nah,' Angela shook her head dismissively. 'Not worth it.'

That was that, then.

'What about you?'

She shrugged. 'Not much chance of that, hanging around the moral high ground with you lot, is there? It'd be like the bad old days all over again. You know those cartoons where people have good angels on one shoulder, telling them the right thing to do, and devils on the other, pushing them the other way? I've never had a devil. The devil in me has always been outnumbered by you three blinking angels. Spoiling my fun.'

'Don't you pin that on me,' Frances smiled. 'You're forty now, love. You wanna do it, you do it.' They all grinned. 'After all,' and the rest joined in, 'WHAT GOES ON TOUR STAYS ON TOUR . . .'

And the moment passed. They linked arms and started off again towards their hotel. And she almost forgot about the couple in the nightclub.

Until she saw him the next night. He'd been dancing in one of the free shows that played on the casino floor on the hour. He'd come up through the floor, on a platform with five or six others. Topless, in leather trousers, with just a bow tie around his neck. She hadn't been particularly struck by him then. She had never been into that sort of thing. It was silly.

But now he looked different. The leather trousers had been replaced by faded jeans, and the muscles were less defined beneath an old-looking T-shirt. He was drinking deeply from a bottle of beer and watching the next show, smiling. He looked normal. He was more animated, somehow, watching his friends perform, than he had been on stage himself.

She was staggered when he started smiling at her. She told herself that, of course, this was how they all got laid. Turn the sad housewives on with the leather and the dancing, then pick them off one by one when you come off your shift. But she didn't want to believe it. And he was good at making it seem unlikely. Making it seem like she had really hit him like a bolt of lightning in the middle of this cacophony, made his world stand still for a minute. Trish elbowed her. Angela was mouthing 'Sad old woman' at her, and smiling. They turned away, heading towards the bar. They didn't recognise the moment.

The first kiss was just as fabulous as the four of them had acknowledged it was bound to be. The gentle, warm, tentative lips of a thousand novels, the feel of a new hand on the back of your head, a new mouth opening into yours. The show, the crowd, the *Wheel of Fortune* slot machine they were leaning against, all fading away. She almost cried when she felt her knees go. Seventeen years.

'Come with me. We have rooms, round the back.' It was the memory of all the times when she hadn't gone that propelled her round the corner, off the casino floor, away from the gaudy lights and the loud music and into a world of grey corridors. And then they were in his room. The leather trousers were over a chair, and there were photographs on the wall, but he turned the lights down as soon as the door was closed, and was kissing her again, unwrapping her from her clothes with flattering alacrity.

They'd be here in a minute, the three of them. Good job it wouldn't take much longer than that. She felt drunk. She probably was. But it was this, this that was making her feel light-headed. He wanted her. His hands were everywhere, urgent and warm. His kisses landed wherever he could hold her still. She wanted him. It was years since desire had been this sudden, this unexpected. It wasn't Saturday. She almost laughed. It was Wednesday. She hadn't had sex on a Wednesday in a long, long time.

No knocking. They weren't coming to stop her. And he clearly wasn't wearing a pager. Just a suntan, which now that she was close up to it, looked just a little streaky around the armpits; a lascivious smile; and a quite terrifying, wobbling erection. It was unnaturally hot against her thigh.

Still no knocking. They couldn't knock, of course. They didn't know where she was. And she wasn't carrying her phone. She'd put it, defiantly, in the hotel safe with her passport as soon as they'd arrived, so that Keith couldn't bring her down with queries as to the whereabouts of the washing powder or the cooking instructions for shepherd's pie. There was absolutely nothing to stop her going through with it.

She didn't, of course.

If they hadn't shown up outside her door, or paged, or dragged her out of nightclubs, all those years ago, would she have done anything differently? Had she ever had the spirit? Had she spent all those years believing things about herself that weren't true? Was this what she was now, or what she'd always been?

She couldn't do it. Instantly her stomach burned with it, and the other sensations faded away. She couldn't do it. She wasn't fearless, she wasn't lost in a moment, she wasn't a free spirit. Not any more. Not now. And she didn't know whether that was a triumph or a tragedy.

It was hideously embarrassing, extricating herself. He looked momentarily crushed, and she wondered briefly whether he would go hunting again that evening, or just stay there, wondering what was wrong with the English woman who had been led so willingly and stayed so briefly, and who had backed out of his door, half-dressed and muttering apologies. Crying and laughing.

'Where've you been?' Frances asked her. 'Got you a drink in.' Trish was pushing a glass towards her.

Angela looked at her, eyes narrowing. 'You all right? You look like you've been crying.'

She pulled her T-shirt down roughly, and took a long drink. 'Crying? No way.' She winked lasciviously. 'You know me, girls. I've been having a bit of an adventure . . .'

Adele Parks

Wake-up Call

I can't imagine why I'm here. What possessed me to accept an invitation to a college reunion? When the envelope dropped onto my doormat, my first reaction was to put it in the bin. Why would I want to meet up with people that I haven't seen for years? Surely the point is, if we'd wanted to stay in touch we would have.

I graduated ten years ago, and despite popular myth, student years were not the best years of my life. I remember them as a blur of damp accommodation, cheap curries, and a series of broken hearts and essay crises. While I send Christmas cards to about half a dozen old acquaintances, I only really have three true friends from college – one of whom lives in Australia and does something impressive as a management consultant. Another lives in India and does something worthy in a hospital in the Calcutta slums. And then there's Laura. Laura works as a junior copywriter in a small advertising agency, but dreams of writing novels. I'm a temp – a receptionist on my third career break and I dream about a knight in shining amour.

We share a flat and it was Laura who insisted that I attend this reunion.

'You can't not,' she'd argued. 'What else will you be doing that night?'

Which seemed to settle it.

We push open the bar door and I'm hit by beer and cigarette fumes. Laura starts waving to people. I don't actively recognise anyone, although one or two faces are vaguely familiar. We force our way to the bar and buy a bottle of wine. That's my idea, because if we find a table we can offer people a drink when they join us. Laura is insisting on smiling at everyone and she even thinks the name tags are a good idea. Mine's spelled wrong.

'It is you, isn't it?' I recognise Anna Crompton's voice without having to check the tag.

'Wow, Anna, you look wonderful!' says Laura, flinging her arms around Anna. Anna smiles and although she shoots an up-and-down glance at both Laura and me, she doesn't return the compliment. I pass her the bottle of chardonnay and an empty glass and pray for the evening to be over.

'Are you married?' she asks, with all the subtlety of red lacy underwear. Our silence is our confession. Neither Laura nor I are even regularly dating, which suits Laura and horrifies me.

'I got married last summer,' smiles Anna. Which I suppose explains why she's here. She never was one for team events, but she obviously saw this as a good opportunity to gloat. Her recently married state also explains why she is glowing. I try not to resent it.

'Have you seen Sue?' she asks as she looks around the bar. Anna, Laura, Sue and I were not only in the same hall of residence, but we also all did the same course. This should mean we have plenty in common.

'There she is,' says Laura, pointing excitedly towards the door. Sue waves, blows kisses, and then flies towards us. She oozes activity. She always did. Sue is one of those people who always have thousands of friends to see and places to go. I lost touch with Anna because she's a horror to be with: I lost touch with Sue because I didn't have the energy to keep up.

Sue's still striking. If I'm pedantic and draw a distinction between beautiful and attractive, then she's attractive – but quite *especially* so. She's wearing her hair in a silky bob. She has an exquisite face, which she can rely on: enormous brown eyes framed with Bambi lashes, a wide nose and a rose-red, lopsided mouth.

Everyone air-kisses and then settles down.

'I hear you're married now, hey?' says Sue, nudging Anna. This is all the prompting Anna needs. From nowhere she produces wedding photos and starts to give us a blow-by-blow account, from first kiss onwards. I remember when Anna wasn't above going out and getting wrecked, losing her shoes and if not quite flashing her boobs at passers-by, then at least insisting that she can pee standing up. Now, it appears, all she can talk about is matching towels from M&S and the importance of damp-proofing.

It's so depressing. And what's more depressing is that I'd pay a king's ransom to be so blissfully content with domestic dreariness, which makes me ashamed that women chained themselves to railings for me and burnt good underwear.

Laura entertains us with stories about the advertising agency and details her plans for getting her novel published. Her plans have been thwarted on a number of occasions. She regularly receives don't-call-us-we'll-call-you letters from publishing houses and agents. She puts this down to their inability to take risks. One thing can be said for Laura – she certainly isn't a quitter. I drift off as I look out of the window. The sun is doing its best – not exactly shining, more shimmering from time to time, whenever there's a gap in the clouds. I must have drunk too much. I'm feeling maudlin.

'What's up?' asks Laura.

I'm that transparent. I shrug.

'How's the teaching going?' asks Sue, politely.

'Teaching?' I'm confused.

'Didn't you always want to be a teacher?'

God, I'd almost forgotten wanting that. 'Er, never panned out. Couldn't face more exams after I got my degree.'

'Oh.' Sue nods, but she doesn't ask what I do instead.

'Are you seeing anyone at the moment?' asks Anna, but only because she knows the answer.

'I was seeing a lawyer until quite recently,' I comment. 'Didn't work out.'

'Why not?'

I shrug again. The problem is, it's difficult for me to explain *exactly* what went wrong. The difficulties, which must have been obvious to him, are indefinable to me. He'd said he wanted us to finish. That's all he said. Odd, because I'd spent my morning planning mini-breaks in Edinburgh or Prague – somewhere cold, so we'd have to cuddle. Somewhere old, so I could pretend to be cultured.

I'd asked him if he thought things were moving too quickly, if he thought I was commitment-shy. I offered him a range of options, from large-white-wedding to let's-just-be-friends. He didn't comment. We had the most silent breakup *ever*. I can't see him making much of a living as a barrister. His silence was particularly frustrating, because when I met him I was almost overwhelmed by how very interesting, articulate and clever he was. He had an opinion on just about every subject you can imagine, and it *always* impresses and thrills me when people can talk knowledgeably about politics, religion, history, sport – any, or a combination. All I can talk about with any certainty are feelings.

Laura always maintained that the lawyer was a bit overly fond of his own voice. But then she thought the management consultant was too materialistic; the web-designer, too flighty; the estate agent, too manic. Tinker, tailor, soldier, sailor, none of them ever meets her criteria. I think she's too picky. She thinks I'm not picky enough. She's always going on about the fact that I deserve better, '*if only you could see that*'. I tell her the issue is getting other people – male people – to see me *at all*. That's challenge enough. She usually sighs at this point in the discussion and offers to make a cup of tea.

I wonder if the girls can throw any light on the breakup. I reach for the wine and pour myself a generous glass. 'I know that it's mostly my pride that's bruised. He was nice enough but . . .' I leave the sentence unfinished. *Nice enough* is condemnation enough.

'Just physical, then? Good sex?' asks Sue.

'Not even that.' We grin.

I decide against telling her that I can't remember when

I last had good sex. The most I hope for nowadays is an absence of any out-and-out peculiarities: an over-reliance on sex toys, premature ejaculation, ingrowing toenails, hairy backs . . .

'How's Dave?'

Dave is Sue's husband. They met during Fresher's Week and have been together ever since. Thirteen years! The longest relationship I've ever had is four and a half months. Unless you count Karl. But you can't really count Karl, as that only lasted two years because he lives in Germany.

'Fine.' She hesitates and then adds, 'I imagine.'

As she tries to light her fag the match breaks and she throws the box onto the table in a temper. None of us say a word. Laura holds up a lighter. There is so obviously something wrong that you can almost touch it in the air.

Finally she adds, 'We're getting divorced.'

'Divorced?' repeats Laura in astonishment.

'Did he have an affair?' asks Anna, angrily.

I'm too stunned to say anything. Sue shakes her head. She's debating whether old friendships, which have been neglected are still relevant. It could be the distance between us that prompts her to go on.

'Nobody warned me. Nobody told me the important stuff, like why *doesn't* respect, peace and trust always add up to being in love? How can we possibly mistake excitement, passion and lust for love?'

'*You* had an affair,' says Laura, deadpan.

Sue nods and puts her head on the table. Her silky hair falls forward into a puddle of wine. She doesn't seem to notice or, if she's noticed, she doesn't care. I'm fascinated and repelled.

Our intimate party breaks up fairly swiftly after that. Some blokes who studied Geography ask if they can join our table and instead of shunning them as we always did, we eagerly welcome them. None of us want to face the intensity of Sue's confession. We drink a lot and then drunkenly swap telephone numbers, promising to not leave it so long next time

Laura and I treat ourselves to a cab home.

'You're quiet. Did you hate it?' asks Laura.

'I'm glad I went.'

'What, even though your dream of Happily Ever After was blown apart when you heard Sue's news?'

'Especially because of that.'

Laura starts to chat about how grey someone or other is and how lined thingummybob is but how radiant blah blah is. I barely follow. My mind is full of plans. I don't say so, but I plan to get up really early tomorrow morning and get on the Internet to research teacher training places. Because, while it might just be the alcohol giving me a false sense of optimism and a new perspective, I don't think it is. Sue's story, and Anna's too for that matter, didn't depress me, as I'd have expected. They poked and prodded me. Never again will I sit in a room and admit that my only news is that a mute barrister has ditched me. Even a divorce seems more of an achievement than doing nothing at all.

'You didn't mean it when you said we should meet up again, did you?' asks Laura.

'I might have. I think I did.' Laura looks surprised but pleased. 'The thing is, Laura, life is what passes you by when you're waiting for something to happen.'

Laura looks confused. 'Did you read that on a Hallmark card?'

'Probably, but it doesn't mean it's not profound.' Laura looks sceptical so I admit, 'Well, it probably does, but either way I've decided not to wait any longer.'

She doesn't understand but she puts her arm around me anyway. She'll get it. I'll show her. I'll show myself.

Victoria Routledge

The Leading Lady

Etterbeck Women's Institute Hall, one wet night in February

. . . yes, it's absolutely coming down stair-rods, now, isn't it? Where does all this water come from? Still, it means we get a jolly good turnout if it's too wet for the crown green bowls. That's the only explanation I can think of for an attendance like this on a *Crimewatch* night. Goodness me, there must be over twenty ladies here!

Well, perhaps they have come to see you, dear, yes. Who knows? We do have one or two bookworms in our membership. Don't get out much, you know. No fines on large-print books either . . .

Hello? Ladies?

They're not normally this rowdy, Mrs Bannister, I can assure you! I think we may have some interlopers tonight from the sugarcraft society. I don't want to use this bell, but if I have to . . .

Hello? Can I have your attention to the front? Please?

Thank you! Thank you, Mrs Eelbeck! If you've quite . . . Yes,
if you could see my lips moving, it means I *was* talking. Mrs
Granger, could you adjust her hearing aid for her? I don't
think she's quite tuned in to WI FM, if you get my drift.

That's better. I said, that's better, Mrs Eelbeck!

No, I have not had my hair set. Really . . .

May I welcome one and all to our February meeting,
which tonight includes a convening of the Etterbeck
Ladies' book group, and let's extend an especially warm
welcome to our newest member, Mrs Parkinson, who has
recently moved into Audrey Richard's old bungalow. Just
another twenty years to go and you'll be one of the village,
dear! I'm joking, of course.

Yes, I *am*, Mrs Riley!

We're a *very* inclusive group, Mrs Parkinson. We have all
sorts here! As you can see.

Just a few notices before we launch into our literary
appreciation this evening. First of all, let's remember in
our thoughts Audrey Richard. We have decided to donate
the money raised by the Guess the Weight of the Cake raffle to the RSPCA. It's what she would have wanted. (How
heavy was it? Eight pounds ten, Mrs Gore. Yes, I *know*.
The *currants*, apparently.) And let's all bear in mind just
how dangerous aquariums can be when you've got basset
hounds. A lesson there for us all, especially you, Mrs Rick-
etts. Your Tilly . . . still barred from the obedience class, is
she? Well, think on, dear.

(I hope it's all dried out now, Mrs Parkinson? Oh. The
estate agent didn't mention . . . Oh, I see . . . Well, it's
nothing Febreze and a good airing can't nip in the bud, I
dare say.)

Thank you. Now, may I remind everyone that this week's competition is for Oldest Teapot, and will be judged by our guest, Mrs Bannister. After last month's furore over Prettiest Spectacle Case, you're limited to two entries each.

Yes, I'm sorry, only two, Mrs Tyler.

Well, yes, I can see you've brought more than two, but if you put them all out there won't be room for anyone else to . . . Yes, I know your father was the area's top tea importer but that makes you semi-professional, dear, so maybe you shouldn't be entering at all!

Up to you, dear. If you could limit yourself to two . . . Well, I imagine Mrs Bannister is as able to adjudge the age of a teapot as anyone else, unless you'd rather step aside from the competition and judge it yourself . . . ? No? Well, suit yourself.

So, everyone else, if you could place your entries on the competition table, Mrs Bannister's final decision will be made over refreshments. Our hostesses this week are Mrs Granger and Mrs Parkinson. I hope you're prepared to have your sponge examined by experts, Mrs Parkinson! We have been the Rannerthwaite regional WI baking champions four years running! Not that I want you to feel under any pressure!

So, if we could . . . Is someone whistling? Am I hearing things?

Oh, it's Mrs Eelbeck's hearing aid. Mrs Granger, would you . . . ? Just down a little . . . that's much better, thank you. I said thank you, Mrs Eelbeck.

Any volunteers to visit Mayton Institute's spring fair next month as Ambassadors of Friendship? No? We have to send *someone*. No? Anyone? Now, I don't think that's a Christian thing to say, Mrs Tyler. It's a good while since the curd incident. Four years at least. We can't hold it against them for ever! No, I'm serious – we can't. Well, if no one will volunteer, I'll put names in a hat after tea, and I'm afraid it'll be compulsory.

I said nothing about pustules, Mrs Eelbeck. No. No, I didn't. Really, I didn't. Well, why on earth would I? Up a notch, please, if you would, Mrs Granger . . . thank you so much.

Anyway, on to the main business! Now, Mrs Bannister is, as you know, our very own local 'celebrity author', having had three of her 'saga potboilers' published. Some of you may know her as . . . Well, that's what they're referred to in the trade, aren't they, Mrs Bannister? 'Pit-fic'? You prefer regional family epics? I see. Well, they *are* your books, I suppose! Anyhoo, at the request of various members, Mrs Bannister has graciously agreed to lend her professional opinions to our discussion this evening and if, only *if* though, any time remains to us at the end of the meeting, she may answer some questions about writing.

At the *end* of the meeting, if you wouldn't mind, please, ladies.

Now, just to bring Mrs Bannister up to speed – who's minuting? Mrs Andrews? Well, can someone give her a biro, please. We had a very spirited debate about what we should select as our Novel of the Month, and there were one or two members who suggested one of Mrs Bannister's own little potboilers! Yes, really! Well, not so little, I suppose. Quite the doorstops, those books! Do they pay you by the ounce? Only joking! But, anyway, I said how embarrassing it would be for you to hear us picking it to pieces, so –

Or having to listen to compliments, yes, Mrs Tyler, that's true as well, I suppose, though there's no need to suck up to Mrs Bannister! She's going to judge those tea-pots fair and square!

Don't minute that, Mrs Andrews.

As I say, we had a very lively debate, with several intrigu-ing titles being proposed, including my own magnum opus, *The Love That Knew No Bounds*! But as it's still being considered by several top London agents, I decided to plead modesty and hide my light under a bushel. I know, I know – next year perhaps.

(Minute that, Agnes. Thank you.)

So, getting back to the matter in hand, Mrs Bannister, we plumped for Mrs Rance's suggestion, and this month we've all been agog at the adventures of Harry Potter. Some more than others, I would hazard a guess. And the topic that little know-it-all man at the library has sug-gested for us to discuss is, let me just get my spectacles on, is . . . 'The reality of magic: how much magic is there in everyday life?' (How *ridiculous*. He's not running the Open University. Someone should have a word . . .) So! Who'd like to start us off?

Anyone? Don't be shy!

It was quite a long book, yes, Mrs Duckworth. Although length is not necessarily a mark of great penmanship! Well, yes, I suppose it did make it good value, but still . . . Any thoughts on the, er, reality of magic? In everyday life?

Excuse me, but if anyone has questions for Mrs Ban-nister, would you mind directing them through the chair.

Through me, Mrs Eelbeck. Me. Through. Me. Dear. Thank you.

How did she feel when she saw her book in the shops? Well, I imagine she felt very pleased, didn't you, Mrs Bannister? Very pleased and ever-so-slightly humble at the thought of all those people out there reading it and forming judgements about your . . . very distinctive style.

Yes, I enjoyed it too. We all enjoyed it. Didn't we? Of course I've read it, Mrs Eelbeck! *Friend or Family*?

Friend of the Family. My mistake, I beg your pardon. Easy mistake for anyone to make though, the amount of nasty little squabbles there are in it! All that bickering – you'd think they loathed each other!

Yes, well, it *was* an excellent story. A little melodramatic in parts, perhaps, but maybe that's what made it such a hit with the soap opera crowd. I myself felt there was no need for some of the language, but I daresay that's what sells. Yes, Mrs Tyler, I *have* read it, more or less. The first few chapters, at any rate. No offence, Mrs Bannister, but it's not really my cup of tea. I myself lean towards literary fiction. Anyhoo, shall we get back to the . . .

Another question? Well, make it a quick one, Mrs Pattinson. Now, that's a very good question. How *did* you get published, Mrs Bannister? Sorry, dear, that came out badly.

I see.

Mmm.

Well, that's fascinating, but time is against us as always, and I'm sure everyone would like to get back to the matter in hand, which is . . .

Now it's funny that you should bring that up, Mrs

Granger, because that, for myself, was the weakest part of the book. I myself felt that the character of Linda was far from credible. I mean, women like that simply don't exist! What a fishwife! All that bossing and shouting . . . And some of the expressions!

Goodness me, you do seem to have brought a fan club with you, Mrs Bannister. One more question, ladies, because I'm sure there are plenty of people here who spent a great deal of time ploughing through Harry Potter and all those goblins and what-have-you when they could have been getting on with more pressing tasks like editing their son's wedding video. Yes, I am talking about myself here! I know it was last year, but my own writing commitments have taken priority, and believe me, there was a lot of editing to be done on that video. I was far from happy about some of the singing. Not that I'm criticising your organ-playing, Mrs Barber. Well, not much. Ladies! One more question, and that is it.

Where does any writer get their inspiration from? From their imagination, I should think! It's certainly where I get my inspiration from. Mrs Bannister? From real life? Really? As I say, I've never met characters like yours in real life, dear.

I don't think it's necessary to elaborate with an anecdote, no, not even a very amusing one. Well, yes, I hope I can take a joke, but I don't really see . . . Well, no, I hadn't read quite as far as the scene in the church where . . .

. . . where the mother-of-the-groom stops the wedding to –

No.

No, I don't believe you would do something so . . .

Marjorie!

No, Mrs Tyler, I'm not choking. I'm just . . .

Yes, Mrs Granger, that's quite correct, Mrs Bannister is my sister-in-law. There's no need for Mrs Eelbeck to whisper, I can hear her from the front of the hall. I'd hate to hear her shouting.

Sister-in-law, yes. No *blood relation*. No, my middle name is not Linda. I don't know what you all find so amusing.

All right, so I may have *temporarily* stopped the wedding so the vicar could redo the vows with better enunciation, but that's no reason to assume that Linda is based on me! What? Even if she does . . . ? No, I hadn't read that far. And for the record, before anyone asks, I have never asked my mother to change her will, I have never thrown my children out onto the street, although I admit I have come perilously close to changing the locks a few times when our Colleen got her tongue done, and I have never, *ever*, taken my belt off to anyone, buckle end or not!

No, I don't know what happens at the end of the book, Mrs Mattock. I haven't got that far yet. I don't think I want to . . . Oh, should I? Really? Linda gets what? *Where?* Good God . . .

Pass me that orange squash, Mrs Tyler. I think I need it more than you.

Does anyone have anything else they want to ask? No? Good, well, in that case, shall we . . .

Have I ever worked as a dockside daisy? Well, what do *you* think, Mrs Eelbeck?

Mrs Eelbeck, I don't care if you *were* asking Marjorie, I think I have a right to reply. Well, if you don't mind my interrupting, Marjorie, evidently there are people here who *do* have trouble distinguishing fact from fiction, especially now you've planted that thought in their heads. You, for a start.

Yes, I *am* upset. I am absolutely speechless. I am struck *dumb* with shock. I simply don't have words to tell you how very unpleasant I find this. I honestly don't know what to say. Words fail me, Marjorie. After all we've been through with your Arthur! I mean, it's not as though you've not got plenty of material right there in your own front room. Have you been using that, eh? That funny business with the courgettes? And your Barry's leg? Hmm?

You may well blush, lady. And yes, *do* let's continue this conversation somewhere more private. What do you mean, there's something else I should know . . .

Film rights?

Patricia *Routledge*? As in Hyacinth *Bouquet*?

No, I am not 'having an attack', Mrs Granger. I'll have you know this is yoga breathing.

Give me a moment.

(How could you, Marjorie? Now, *Penelope Keith* I could have understood.)

Is there any other business?

Any other *Institute* business? Fine, well – no, save it till the next meeting, Mrs Tyler, please! – in that case I call this meeting closed, and will see you all Tuesday next. Mrs Granger, pick a teapot – that one? Right, fine. Talk to the hand, Mrs Tyler! I said *talk* to the *hand*, Mrs Eelbeck! Yes, I am being rude! Now, Marjorie, the car, if you don't mind. No need to offer lifts, ladies, Mrs Bannister's coming home with me. No, there isn't time for you to tell them about your new book. Even if it is going to be in Tesco's next . . .

'*No Blood Relation*'?

Charming.

The car, Marjorie. Before I say something you might write down.

Allison Rushby

The Temp from Hell

'You have *got* to read this.' Julie tears into the tearoom.

I glance up from what I'm doing. From something I hope, one day, to win a Nobel Prize for – making Mr Downs's coffee. His special Machu Picchu coffee filtered through his special unbleached filter into his special heat-retaining stainless steel mug. Julie is waving a magazine around. 'Read what?'

'Here. This. You've got to read it right now. Come on . . .'

I don't think I've ever seen Julie so excited. Not even when the fireman strip-o-gram was sent to her by mistake instead of to Julie on the fifth floor. That was the day I found out she liked a man in uniform (or should I say *without* uniform).

I abandon my coffee making, take the magazine and begin to read. The article seems to be about some actress who specialises in infiltrating company workplaces and impersonating people.

'Susannah, do I have to get down on my knees and beg for my coffee?'

Julie and I both jump. Mr Downs must have crept down the hallway.

'Sorry.' I put the magazine on the bench top and check to see if the coffee has finished filtering. Almost. 'It's coming.' I watch him as he goes. Three more months. Three more months until I have enough money to buy my round-the-world plane ticket. Three more months till I can tell him I'm out of here.

Julie gives the spot where he'd been standing an evil look. 'That's it. You're *so* doing this.'

'Hmmm?' I open the fridge and begin the search for Mr Downs's milk. His special low-fat, lactose-intolerant, non-genetically modified soy milk. 'Doing what?' I pull the carton out.

'Didn't you read this part?' Julie points to a section of the article. The "Temp from Hell" bit. She comes in and pretends to be a temp. But you feed her information first. About the things your boss would hate and then she plays a cat-and-mouse game with them, seeing how far she can take it. It's brilliant. Come on, Susannah, if there's ever any way you're going to get you-know-who to see what a good you-know-what you are, this is it.'

'You've got to be joking,' I laugh, stirring in Mr Downs's one and a quarter teaspoons of sugar. His special organic raw sugar scented with his special Tahitian vanilla pods. 'For a start, it'd cost a fortune.' There is no answer to this and, after a while, I realise Julie is being far too quiet for Julie. I look up slowly to see a dangerous glint in her eyes. The exact same glint I'd seen when, after the strip to end all strips, she'd asked the fireman if he needed any help carrying his hose back downstairs. 'I can't afford it. I'm supposed to be saving, remember?'

The glint remains.

Julie arranges it all – including the long, long list of Mr Downs's pet hates. 'That's it,' she says as she puts the phone down that afternoon. 'It's all set for next Friday. All we need now is an excuse to get a temp.' We look at each other and I see the glint return. 'Hey, I know . . .'

I soon find myself knocking on my boss's door.

As it turns out, it's quite easy to get a temp. All you have to know is the magic word and, funnily enough, it isn't please . . .

It's gynaecologist.

'Enjoy!' Julie ducks out of her boss's office (who is, luckily, in Singapore for a week), leaving me to peek through the venetian blinds.

And I wait.

The lift doors ping and open at precisely 8:45, as they do every morning, belching out Mr Downs. As he exits, his eyes immediately travel to my desk for the first yell of the day. I can almost see his tiny mind ticking over as he registers that a) I'm not there; b) a temp is meant to be coming in this morning; c) the temp is late; and d) this means he won't be getting his usual morning coffee.

Tick! Tick! I think, as I spot his reaction. Tardiness and caffeine withdrawal down, approximately 3642 pet hates to go.

It's a good ten minutes later when the lift pings again

and a woman breezes into the office. I suck my breath in, almost choking on my Columbine (the shop downstairs was, unfortunately, out of Clinkers).

It can only be the Temp from Hell.

'You Julie?' the woman says loudly to Julie, who is by now working diligently at her desk.

Tick! Mr Downs hates raised voices that might disturb him from his work.

Julie nods at the woman's question and gets a wink in return.

'Right. I'm Cheryl. This me desk then?' She goes over and dumps her gigantic bag on top of it. I clock what 'Cheryl' is wearing. Too-tight faded black jeans, scuffed black sequinned heels and a gaudy pink polyester blouse that is knotted at the waist. Her hair has been teased and hair-sprayed to within an inch of its life and her blue eye-shadow and pink blusher, left over from the seventies, have been applied with a heavy hand. Even the bag is perfect – one of those cheap plastic red-, white- and blue-striped storage bags.

Tick! I think again, knowing this isn't going to go down well. Mr Downs likes his staff to be a bit 'Country Road'. 'Country Road' on a 'Target' budget, that is.

Julie smiles a big smile at Cheryl. 'Make yourself at home.'

'Geez, thanks. Better tell the boss I'm here, eh?'

'Guess so,' Julie says and leans forward over her desk to get a better view.

Cheryl bashes loudly on Mr Downs's office door, opening it before he answers. 'Hi, I'm Cheryl. The temp. Right?'

One of my eyebrows rises involuntarily. I can't see what's happening from my position, but my imagination is running wild. Stapler throwing? Highlighter poisoning? Death by toupee suffocation?

But Cheryl soon closes the door behind her, still alive. 'I reckon that went pretty good,' she says to Julie. 'He wants a coffee and I could do with one meself. What about you, love?'

'Oh, not for me, thanks. But you know how he likes it, don't you?'

Cheryl shrugs and goes over to rummage around for something in her bag. 'Dunno. I'll take a punt. Ah, here we are. International Roast. It was on special this week and coffee's coffee, ain't it?'

'I guess,' Julie says, her grin getting larger by the minute.

A few minutes later, Cheryl barges back into Mr Downs's office. 'Here we go. I've even got two bikkies for you as well, growing boy that you are. Iced Vo-Vos. Sorry they're a bit soggy. I overfilled the mug a bit and it spilled.'

Tick! The Iced Vo-Vos are an especially nice touch – the only biscuits Mr Downs ever lets me buy for the office are the expensive Nonna-rolled pistachio biscotti from the deli two streets away. And only when clients are expected. I wheel my chair as close to the window as possible and wait for the yells. But, again, none come and Cheryl closes the door behind her with a bang, just like before.

'Pretty good boss, I reckon.' She looks at Julie. 'Didn't mind that the Iced Vo-Vos were soggy, even.' She crosses back over to the desk and starts to unload more goodies from her bag. I watch in absolute awe as she starts to line up the items. A full set of trolls – the plastic kind with the long, lurid hair that stands on end. Two picture frames, each holding a picture of a Rottweiler, and then, the *pièce de résistance*, a blue lava lamp, which she sets up, plugs in and turns on.

Tick! I'm not allowed trinkets of any kind on my desk. Mr Downs hates clutter, says it leads to a cluttered mind. As the lava lamp's insides start globbing up and down, I have to admit that this woman is good. Really good.

So good she may even have a Crazy Clark's store card.

Cheryl pulls one last item out of the bag and I crane my neck, trying to get a closer look. It's a make-up bag. A clear make-up bag full of bottles of nail polish. Cheryl lines the gaudy pinks, purples and reds up on top of the desk carefully, inspecting them slowly, picking up one here and there before finally deciding on an absolutely hideous sparkly neon pink. She begins to roll the bottle between her hands. 'Learnt this rolling trick here from me nail technician,' she says to Julie. 'If you shake it, it adds bubbles. Wrecks the polish. And I'm not wrecking me polish. This baby alone cost me $5.95.'

'Wow, $5.95. And I didn't know that about the rolling,' Julie plays along. 'Thanks for the tip.'

'No worries.' Finished rolling, Cheryl opens the bottle and starts painting the nails on her left hand. Halfway through her middle finger, Mr Downs's office door opens. My eyes widen, but Cheryl remains calm. She takes her time over the nail.

'Sorry about this,' she says, looking up at Mr Downs who's now standing in front of her desk. 'But if I don't do it now, they won't dry properly by tonight and Gazza's taking me to the Leagues Club for all you can eat. It's our five-month anniversary and I've gotta look me best for him.'

I watch, a stunned smile on my face, as Mr Downs's mouth opens and closes in disbelief a number of times. After a while, he seems to pull himself together and shakes his head quickly. 'Er, well, hurry up, woman. I'm not paying you to colour-in your nails, you know. File these.' He places some paperwork on the desk.

Cheryl doesn't reply, but looks back down and starts on the next nail. Mr Downs stands on the spot, watching her, waiting for her to say something.

'It's okay, love, you can go now.' Cheryl looks up at him for a second. 'I'll do the filing in two shakes.'

My eyes almost pop out of my head at this one. You can go now? Love? Ouch. There'll be no holding him back now . . .

And, still, I wait . . .

I can't believe it. Instead of throwing a tanty, Mr Downs snorts and, although muttering to himself, makes his way back into his office almost as meekly as the lamb whose tail Cheryl just mentioned.

Julie shoots a look in the direction of her boss's office and hangs her mouth open in surprise.

I know exactly what she means.

The next hour and a half passes uneventfully. Cheryl finishes painting her nails (including a second coat and a clear topcoat) and dallies over the filing, reciting her alphabet every so often. I guess the break from harassing Mr Downs is all part of the act. What had Julie said? Cat and mouse, that was it. I suppose Cheryl has to ease up every now and again so she doesn't get booted out of whichever workplace she's in within the first five minutes.

'Finished.' Cheryl slams the filing cabinet closed, making me jump and Julie look up. 'Hey, Jules, I've been meaning to ask. What is that? That awful whining sound?'

Julie looks confused. 'Sorry?'

'Is it, like . . . music?'

'Ah,' Julie says then, glancing up at the speaker in the corner. 'That's Mr Downs's favourite. It's opera.'

'Right. So how do you change it?'

'Well, I don't. My life wouldn't be worth living if I did. But there's a stereo system in that cabinet over there if *you* want to put something else on.'

I watch in anticipation, chewing my Columbine faster and faster, as Cheryl goes over to the stereo system. Changing Mr Downs's music – this really *would* be a sin.

Cheryl goes back to her bag of tricks to grab something – a CD. She then heads back across the room and sticks it in the stereo, turning the volume way, way up, even before the music starts.

I stop chewing. There is a large ominous pause.

And then, ear-blastingly, the music starts.

Cheryl hotfoots it back to the filing cabinet and tries to look busy. Julie keeps on typing, one eye fixed on Mr Downs's office door.

I lean forward.

'What the hell is going on?' he bursts out, looking first at Cheryl, then at Julie, accusingly.

Cheryl looks up with a smile. 'Thought I'd chuck us on some Barnesey. Liven the place up a bit.'

'I—you—I—turn it off. Immediately,' Mr Downs roars above the music.

'All right, all right,' Cheryl says, getting up and going

over to the stereo. She turns the music off. 'Don't get your knickers in a twist,' she pauses before glancing at him slyly, 'or is it boxers, eh? I bet you're a silk man. Classy.'

Mr Downs stares at Cheryl as if she is, perhaps, a psychopath. His face is pink again and his breath puffing in and out like a bull. 'Which agency are you from?'

'Jo King's.' Cheryl crosses her arms on hearing his question. 'Why? There a problem?'

Mr Downs pauses, looks at the clock, then gives one final snort. 'You could say that.' He eyes Cheryl, who eyes him back. But it's Mr Downs who backs down first. 'Oh, just do your work,' he says, throwing his hands up in defeat. He retreats into his office, slamming the door behind him.

Ha ha ha. I give the air a good punch.

'Must be a John Farnham man.' Cheryl rolls her eyes at Julie when he's gone. 'Right. Time to catch up on me soaps.' She sits back down at the desk, pulls out a magazine and starts reading. I shake my head. Fantastic. There are a million things I can see that need doing. Mr Downs's diary needs updating, new clients need their details added to the database, files need to be pulled out and made ready for his meetings on Monday. If I'd decided that, rather than taking care of these things, it was 'time to catch up on me soaps', Mr Downs would have my head on a stick.

With tomato sauce.

Rather like a Dagwood Dog.

Cheryl reads for ages, every so often letting a chuckle or a sigh and a small comment escape in Julie's direction. 'That Rick, he's a catch, isn't he? Gloria's lucky he waited for her while she was in that coma.' And 'Ooohhh, Hunter better watch out. I'm guessing that's not Serge's bun she's got in the oven there.' After a good hour, Cheryl turns the last page. 'What's the time, love?' she asks Julie.

'Um, twelve-thirty.'

'Crikey. Really? It's getting on. Susannah's due back at one. I'll just pack up me stuff, make us some lunch and then I'll be off.'

'Lunch?' Julie looks at her.

'Yeah. I've been making me own lunch recently since the price of ciggies went up again. I guess I'd better make Downsy some, too. Be a bit rude not to, I reckon.'

I wait in absolute, absolute *agony* for what I know will be Cheryl's final triumph. The minutes pass . . .

Suddenly, the door to the office opens, making me start. Julie ducks inside and runs over, grabbing my arms. 'You have to come out. You can't miss this.'

'But I can't. He'll see me.'

'So?' Julie shakes her head. 'It doesn't matter. You're supposed to be coming back to work now anyway, aren't you? He'll just think you're a bit early. Wait until Cheryl comes back with lunch.' Julie heads back towards the door as I nod.

A few minutes later, Cheryl makes her way from the tearoom carrying a tray. I take my cue and leave the office to go and stand beside Julie's desk. We both stare at the tray as Cheryl passes.

'Is that—' I trail off.

'I think so,' Julie says.

'And—'

'Yep.'

'Oh my God.' We look at each other.

This time, Cheryl doesn't even bother to knock. Balancing the tray on her forearm, she unhooks the door handle with one elbow, then turns and pushes it open with her backside, and enters Mr Downs's office. The door is open as far back as it can go, and Julie and I have the perfect view of Cheryl, Mr Downs and the lunch tray.

'What—?' Mr Downs begins to say, but is cut off by Cheryl, who places the tray on his desk.

'Thought I'd make us some lunch, yeah? Vegemite and cheese on Vita Wheat. It's good for you. A bit of fun, too, you get to squeeze the little worms through like the kiddies do.' As she speaks, she drags another chair over to Mr Downs's desk. 'Usually I'd have a pie, but I'm on a diet. Like I said before, got to look good for my Gazza.' She sits herself down opposite Mr Downs and starts unloading the tray. 'Here you go,' she passes him one of the plates. 'And something to wash it down with,' she passes him a glass. 'Hope you like Fanta.'

Mr Downs takes both the plate and the glass silently, his eyes glazed. It occurs to me that he's in some kind of shock. Either that, or the glue on his toupeed head has chosen this moment to seep through to his brain, leaving him in a chemical haze.

The tray pushed aside, Cheryl tucks into her Vita Wheats, intermittently slurping her Fanta noisily. Halfway through she stops. 'Have you got a permanent job going here?' she looks up.

Mr Downs shakes his head slowly. 'No.' Then, 'Definitely not,' he adds.

Cheryl nods. 'Oh. Pity. It's just that I thought your

usual PA must be leaving. I found an old employment section from the paper in her bin. It had some jobs ringed on it.'

Mr Downs frowns. 'In Susannah's bin?'

Cheryl nods and knocks back the rest of her Fanta. 'Yeah. Thought I'd be perfect.'

Mr Downs stands up suddenly, stumbling as he pushes his chair back.

'What? You going?'

'I . . . forgot. I have a lunch meeting,' he says, stuffing some papers into his briefcase, then scrambling for his jacket.

'Oh. You could have told me,' Cheryl looks up at him, unimpressed, seemingly forgetting the fact that *she* should have told *him*. Touché, I think. 'Wouldn't have had to make lunch for you, then.' She doesn't wait for an answer. 'Well,' she says, getting up and brushing her hands together, raining crumbs onto the desk, 'time for me to push off.' She picks up the tray. 'Nice to meet ya and all that.' Without looking back, she leaves Mr Downs's office for the last time. She whistles as she closes the door and traipses off down the hallway.

Just as we're about to set off down the hall after her, Mr Downs's office door opens once more. His head appears hesitantly and he looks around. 'Susannah!' he says, far more loudly than usual when he spots me. He steps out into the main office.

I stare at his dishevelled appearance. He looks stressed, his tie is askew, sweat stains his collar and papers are sticking out of his briefcase. This is an amazing sight considering he will usually spend a good half-hour preening before he goes out.

'Is she gone?' he says, quietly this time.

'Is who gone, Mr Downs?' I decide to milk the situation for all it's worth.

'The temp. That Cheryl woman,' his eyes dart up and down the hall. He moves over and presses the lift's 'down' button four or five times.

Before I can answer his question, the lift pings and Cheryl reappears behind us, as if from nowhere. 'Oh. You off then? See ya, Downsy. I can call you that, can't I? Downsy?' She skips past me to give him a playful punch on the arm.

He recoils in horror at her touch, backing into the now open lift.

'Was there anything else, Mr Downs?' I ask pleasantly as he hits the back wall and stops. I'd been sure he was going to say something else. He pauses and looks down at the floor beside my desk. No, not at the floor, I realise, following his eyes. At the bin. He's staring at my bin, where Cheryl's left a newspaper casually peeking over the top.

He looks up. 'Er, yes. Monday morning. See me first thing Monday morning. You're, er, doing a good job. I think it's time you had a, er, raise.'

The lift doors close and the three of us stand in silence for quite some time.

It's Cheryl who breaks the silence, with a laugh. 'Well, that's one appointment you'll be remembering to put in his diary.'

'God, Renee, line up for the Oscars, girl! You were amazing!' Julie claps her hands together. I join her in a round of applause, still dazed. I didn't think Mr Downs knew the word 'raise'.

'Thanks.' Cheryl goes over to grab her bag. In seconds,

she pulls a cap out and over her hair, tears off the pink shirt to reveal a plain black singlet, kicks off her heels, pulls the black jeans off, pulls some normal blue jeans on, slips on some leather mules and tissues off the worst of the make-up. The transformation from Cheryl to Renee is complete.

'Wow. You look . . . normal.' I stare. Then I laugh. 'You mean you're not really from hell? I'm shattered.'

Renee laughs. 'I'm too scared to go outside as Cheryl. Who knows? Gazza might ask me out on a date. Sorry about this, but I've got to run. I've got another Temp from Hell at two o'clock. At an advertising agency across town. The boss hates overly religious people, so I've got to try and convince her to join the Moonies.'

'Good luck,' I say.

'No, good luck to *you*. I can see you've got your hands full. Usually we let them in on the joke at the end of the day, but I don't think that's going to work for you, is it? A larger pay cheque might, though.'

'Definitely,' I agree.

Julie nods. 'Yes. And it'll definitely help with all those cocktails you're going to buy me tonight too.'

'Oh, really?'

'Really. Ladies' night?'

I laugh. 'You're on. Though I really do think we should invite Mr Downs. The poor guy could do with a drink after the day he's had.'

Tamara Sheward

I Should've Known

I should've known. Really. Anything calling itself a Beer Festival, well, as *if* there's going to be beer.

This was Russia, and after two months of low-rent rail journeys, gulag accommodation and vodka breakfasts, I was already thinking like a Russian. I knew that 'Express Lane' meant that it took *less* than three hours to be told you've been standing in the wrong queue; that bar signs reading 'No Guns' didn't apply to anyone with gold teeth and expensive leather jackets.

I also knew, after a few early days of frenzied confusion, that every man in Russia was of the expressed opinion that I, with my lumpy coat and strict cosmetic regime of Chap Stick and weekly teeth cleaning, was a hot-to-trot strumpet. Given that most of the native women looked like Milla Jovovich and oozed glamour with every twitch of their sculpted bottoms, I reckoned this pointed to an ingrained yen for the days of agricultural collectivism and all the bawdy, dirt-smeared peasants they could get their hands on.

I guess that's why I agreed to go on a date to the Beer Festival with Sasha. He was the first guy I'd met who hadn't rubbed his fingers together and sleazily murmured, 'Mottle?', the bastardised pronunciation of 'motel' that had initially led me to believe that Slavic men were concerned about my weather-splotched skin. And he was certainly a standout in Sochi, the famous Black Sea resort town where stalkers were more common than sand (in typical Russian fashion, the celebrated beach was covered in ugly, mammoth rocks) and white slave traders were said to be legion. He actually seemed kind of normal.

I should have known. Really.

I first met Sasha after an afternoon watching the glamazons pick their way across Sochi's boulders in the standard local beachwear: leather G-strings and six-inch stilettos. Looking ravishing myself in a pair of ratty Bonds knickers – who packs bathers when they go to Russia? – I'd whiled away breaks in booty-spotting by buying salted fish-heads off the *babooshka* mafiosa (three feet tall, this sly grandma sported both a pathos and a coiffure I couldn't refuse) and getting into a jellyfish fight with two Azerbaijani girls. The Russian word for jellyfish, by the way, is *medusa*, which was exactly what I resembled after getting the writhing, gelatinous bastards stuck in my hair.

Salty and snaky, I decided to walk back to my *gastinitsa*. I'd been cruising for cirrhosis since arriving in this country where spirits were cheaper than soft drink, and I wanted to get to my room before the temptations of Sochi – rowdy, bar-lined boardwalk, booze kiosks, kids drinking paint thinner beneath the ubiquitous Lenin statue – encroached on my plan of spending the night on an outrageously expensive call to my boyfriend in Sydney and chilling out, sober, in the bath. And I figured that looking like a deranged Gorgon would be too much even for the throng of mustachioed men who'd adopted the disconcerting habit of congregating by my hotel, yelling 'Mottle?' every time I scurried past. I would, at last, have a quiet night in.

But this was Russia, where weird – President Putin as sex god, McDonald's as gourmet cuisine – was a way of life and plans were for suckers. Just as I was about to bolt past the bewhiskered brigade to the oasis of my room, a thin, slightly pockmarked guy popped out from behind a flower bush. With an élan I normally wouldn't associate with anyone with a mullet and mandals, he announced that his name was Sasha and that he wished nothing more in life than to take this particular *devooshka* to that night's Sochi Beer Festival. I told him I had a boyfriend in Australia who would wish nothing more than for me *not* to accompany him thither, but he assured me that he would play both escort and chaperone.

'I am good boy,' he said in a manner that made even his mullet look coy. Taking into account said hairdo and thoughts of my beloved, I realised it would be easy for me, also, to be a *very* good girl. Liver notwithstanding, of course.

'Okay,' I said. '*Da!*'

The Russian word for beer is *piva*. It was one of the few shreds of lingo I came equipped with, if only because Mum – a refugee from the Russian/Ukrainian border –

braved her Cold War paranoia enough to stubbornly use it in lieu of the ocker 'beeeeeah'. The only other Russian she busted out was *katashkinapolkie* – shit on a stick – when I asked her too many times what was for tea. Just your average SBS upbringing, really.

But while I didn't know much about the domestic *piva* before my arrival, I certainly knew a lot about it now. Whereas vodka was the official Russian drink, as in *real* drink, *piva* was, as every Russian told me, 'like lemonade'. Everyone, from ranting, homeless Kazaks to eight-year-old girls, drank *piva* everywhere – in the metro, on the church steps, while operating heavy machinery. It was sold at every kiosk and came in a variety of brands ranging from the whimsical ('Old Miller', 'White Bear') to the macho ('Hawk', 'Three Athletes'). I'd settled on the omnipresent Baltika Seven but was looking forward to the Piva Festival where I could step outside my comfort zone. It's woefully indicative when one bases their sense of security on the beer one swills.

'You will be loving this *piva*,' Sasha said as he took my arm an hour later. 'He is big love.'

When he'd made his dramatic appearance earlier, Sasha's English had struck me as far superior to the wide-eyed 'You are kangaroo?!?' type I was used to facing from over-excitable bumpkins on the train. Yet now that I'd showered the *medusa* out of my eyes and ears, Sasha seemed a bit, well, shabby. His linguistic calibre was falling like Yeltsin off the wagon and he'd changed into a red leopard-print shirt and faded denim nuthuggers, lending him the impression of having once played in The Scorpions.

But as he swung me towards the gaily decorated square,

I chastised myself. Who was I to expect everyone to be a polyglot, when the best I could come up with was 'beer' and 'shit on a stick'? And who cared how he dressed? Even I couldn't deny that *Winds of Change* rocked.

'*Piva, nyet.*'

I choked on my cigarette – a not unusual event in a country that flogged yak droppings as Marlboros – and swung around in disbelief. 'What do you mean, no beer? At a beer festival?'

He shrugged in that definitive Russian way: a slow raising of the shoulders and in-sync exaggerated pout. It was like Mel Brooks and the entire cast of *Goodfellas* rolled into one collective national gesture.

'*Piva, nyet,*' he repeated. 'Maybe vodka?'

Of course, there was no vodka either. The Piva Festival, billed as a three-day whopper of non-stop debauchery, had been open for four hours and the crazed boozehounds of Sochi had already drunk it dry. The makeshift beer gardens were sodden and starting to empty. The only people left behind were the craggy-faced *piva* vendors (whom I suspected more than a little of swallowing up their own wares), swaying, singing men and women who were beginning to buckle at the knees. If beer was lemonade, I was going to have to start drinking a lot more Solo.

Sasha twirled tendrils of hair – the 'party-out-the-back' bit – around his fingers and flashed me a look that had zero in common with his erstwhile 'good boy' vow.

'Come,' he said, taking my hand. 'We go new bar.'

I flinched. Hair twiddling? Coquettish eyeballing? Handholding? Sasha was mutating from metalhead to milkmaid and it was freaking me out. My Russian was abysmal, his English appalling, but that didn't mean we had to start speaking the Language of Love.

'Um,' I mumbled, slipping my hand out of his. 'My boyfriend—'

'Is okay! Good boy!' He shot me an artful glance reminiscent of the fishmongers on the beach. 'You love *piva*, *da*?'

I must have had my jaundiced liver stapled to my forehead. I loved *piva*, all right, and now that I'd had a whiff of it – albeit emanating from the drenched clothes of passing drunkards – there was no holding back. Besides, being pissed was a boon for my language skills; if the time came, I could always tell him to rack off in his native tongue.

The bar was posh, so swank that it had a terrace view *and* they gave you free peanuts. But clean glasses and only semi-surly staff or no, the bar had nothing on the traffic below.

'*Adin, dva, tri* . . .' I counted. 'Fifteen Mercedes parked just there! What's going on?'

Sasha made with the shrug. 'Sochi is much Russian mafia. Mafia, work and holiday this town.'

I'd almost figured as much. While I'd often wondered how the Russian race managed to propagate – before morphing into wizened *babooshkii*, most women were at least six foot and, as mentioned, as dishy as a sushi restaurant, while overall, men were squat and somehow tuber-esque – Sochi took things to the extreme: all of the thong-flossing beach bunnies belonged to morbidly obese men with tiny togs and a 'fuck you' attitude that reeked of power. Even discounting the gaggles of *goomahs*,

Sochi was a mere five-hour drug run from Turkey, reason enough to believe we were in prime *organizatsya* territory. Kids ran around in *Brigada* – the homegrown version of *The Sopranos* – T-shirts, and even the dogs looked heavy.

'And you, Sasha.' I turned to him, trying desperately not to flirt. 'You are mafia?'

The Shrug. 'Maybe in future. Now, I am only small in mafia.'

I'll admit right now that I'm pathetic. I'm a sucker. My favourite movie is *The Godfather*. I love the sight of James Gandolfini in a soiled wifebeater and I have three overdue Puzo novels beside me at any one time. Before I moved to Australia and became an ocker yob, I lived in New Jersey – Joisey – where all the girls at my pricey school had dads in 'Waste Management'. I couldn't help it: I was a goner for gangland.

But not for Sasha, I reminded myself sternly. Desperate for a reality check, I peeked over my glass to remind myself that he wasn't Gotti, he was Guns'n'Fuckin'Roses. Besides, I'd accidentally fallen in love back home only months before and couldn't imagine cuckolding my Sydney spunk for anyone, let alone a weaselly wannabe. If I really started to swoon, I'd make a break for my hotel room and think of Michael Corleone until I went blind.

'So, erm,' I said, wishing my voice would stop wavering. 'What work do you do for the mafia?'

He slid his hand onto my knee, then – what else? – shrugged as I firmly slid it off.

'A little this,' he winked. 'A little that.' I sat there with a frozen smile on my face. Damn, I thought. A crim *and* a player. I needed, I thought as the waiter delivered us another four beers, to keep my wits about me. I re-zinged my smile and gulped at my schooner thirstily. It was just like lemonade, right?

I may not have had my lemonade goggles on, but two hours and nine schooners later, I was starting to see things in a different light. I'd decided to stop being afraid of Sasha and his amorous intentions and simply revel in the otherwise harmless company of an underworld figure. It's amazing what soft drink can do for the powers of logic.

It was with this conjecture in mind that I found myself agreeing when Sasha stood up and announced, 'Private *piva* festival is finish. Now, meet friends at *klub* for *koktail*.'

As he paid the bill, and I pocketed the free peanuts, an image from *The Godfather II* – the scene where the nattily dressed gangsters do business over cake and cocktails on a chic Havana rooftop – flashed through my mind, leaving me atingle with expectation. Ice clinking in crystal glasses! Muted power in leisure suits! Cravats! I mourned Sasha's cock-rock ensemble – something a little more Rat Pack would've been nice – but I hardly looked like a saucy gun moll in my jeans and op-shop singlet.

The street, now dark, was still cluttered with luxury cars parked at insouciant angles, and I did my best to avoid lurching sottishly into them. The last thing I needed was to have some jumped-up goons collecting their auto insurance premiums out of my hide. Actually, that's untrue. The last thing I needed was to discover Sasha jimmying his way into a black Merc with ominously tinted windows.

'What the fuck are you doing!' I screamed. 'That is *so* not your car!'

In one swift, catlike manoeuvre, he leapt out, grabbed my flailing arm and drew me into him. 'Is okay,' he cooed in a tone both subdued and stern. 'Friend car. He wants I take it to *klub* for him.'

I narrowed my eyes. 'Oh yeah? *Gde klutch*?' In other words, Where's the goddamn keys, hotshot?

Still concentrating on the door, he let ceremony lapse and offered the merest hint of a shrug as explanation. For a Russian to gesture, sans-histrionics, this had to be serious stuff.

'But—'

He gave a satisfied grunt as the door popped open. 'Come,' he said, glancing around furtively. 'We go, we go. Is okay!'

Since I'd been in Russia, my concept of 'okay' had come to embrace previously insufferable things like fifty-four-hour train trips, offal, and waking up on crowded buses to find hospitable dipsos pouring vodka down my snoring yap. In the hours I'd been with Sasha, 'okay' had mushroomed further to include grand theft auto and acceptance of a truly heinous hairstyle. But however my standards had slid, it was still most definitely *not* okay for his hand to be creeping up my thigh.

'Sasha, *nyet*!' I plucked his hand off my leg and shot him a threatening glance. Being that we were cannonballing through the backstreets of Sochi at 70km/ph, I *hoped* I looked threatening instead of like someone about to poop their strides. Sasha was a passable driver, but we were both shickered and I had a notion that piloting a stolen car didn't exactly inspire caution in the driver. I pinched his wrist and plonked his hand on the steering wheel. Which, incidentally, was pointed directly at an oncoming truck.

'Sashasashasashalookout!' As the high beam hit my eyes, I was struck by the irrational, yet oddly comforting, fact that at least I wasn't going to die in a Lada.

'Okay, okay,' Sasha muttered calmly. His knuckles white, he swung the wheel and veered, within an inch of the truck, out of harm's way. Comparatively speaking, running up a kerb and into an overflowing bin *was* out of harm's way.

'What the hell happened?' I asked as Sasha pried *my* terrified hand off his leg. 'Should I drive? Are you oka—'

He wasn't listening. Reversing clunkily off the kerb, he was already squealing off into the night. I stared at him, maw agape, as we hurtled onwards, his eyes glued to the rear-vision mirror.

'Sasha, the road,' I begged, no longer content with the idea of an opulent demise. 'Watch the road!'

'Mmm,' he said, his eyes darting anxiously behind us. I followed his gaze and noted with some queasiness that a nearly identical car was practically running into our rear bumper. When we swerved, it swerved. When we took an illegal left turn, ibid.

'I think we're being followed,' I whispered, feeling like a doomed two-bit player in a bad Bruckheimer flick.

'Hold,' Sasha grunted, stomping his foot to the floor, cockroach-killer style, until the needle quivered near the 120km/ph mark. 'Is okay. Is okay.'

If his mantra was designed to soothe, I figured he'd better come up with a new one quick smart. Something along the lines of 'Don't worry, we're not really being hunted down by vicious mobsters in a car as fast as this one we just stole. Oh, and I'm not pissed either' would do nicely. But the way we were going – frantically zooming in and out of traffic, screeching around narrow corners and careening down blackened-out lanes – I wasn't sure if even *my* chronic naïveté would take that bait.

The car kept pace for what seemed like a double eternity, its headlights swinging in and out of view like a drunken spotlight. Nothing we did, and certainly not my petrified hollering, could shake them until finally, blissfully, Sasha squealed around a blind corner, killed the lights and drove, as if by remote control, into an open garage.

The garage doors slid down, leaving us in fabulous, felicitous darkness, and I tried to catch my breath and remain utterly silent.

Sasha shifted in his leather seat, turned off the engine and lit a cigarette, the orange glow illuminating the cavernous interior. He smiled graciously through the smoke.

'*Koktail?*'

The bartender was shaking and so was I. Thing was, he was making a jug of martinis and I was cacking my dacks. It wasn't too hard to figure out who had the better look.

Not that anyone would notice. The *klub* was actually a massive, single-storey disco where frantic strobe lights froze the capacity crowd into random, spastic snapshots; a cluster of gorgeous, yet world-weary, women here, an unsmiling knot of low-talking, steadily-drinking men there, all with an air of studied nonchalance. The music was, as expected, crap. Russians were enamoured with cheesy metal and even chintzier love songs, so presumably to save time, they combined the two and put the hideous hybrid to awful Turkish dance beats. Every now and again, a Western pop song would crop up, but any sense of familiarity was dashed by the fact that it was overdubbed in squawking Russian. The cacophony was worsened by the presence of a pokie corner which, despite sitting beneath an innocuous sign reading 'Super Slots', was loudly and gleefully advertised by a looped voiceover as 'Super Sluts!!' This optic onslaught, combined with the near miss at the hands of mysterious but clearly malevolent tailgaters, left me with no choice but to get monstrously hammered.

'*Spaciba.*' The bartender passed me the jug and I turned to Sasha for the necessary roubles. But he had gone, vanished into the crowd. Harumphing, I opened my handbag and riffled through my admittedly full wallet, sheepishly realising I hadn't shelled out a single *kopeck* all night. At first I'd protested, going so far as to wave my wad of dosh in Sasha's face, but had soon settled into a Sugar Daddy routine. *Without* the sugar.

Guzzling determinedly from the pitcher – and just as intently ignoring the fact that the 'martini' tasted like surgical spirits – I pushed through the throngs of neutral-faced revellers until I clapped eyes on Sasha in a dim corner largely ignored by the light show.

'Hey!' I shouted over a particularly revolting local rendition of 'Jenny From the Block', waving the rapidly emptying ewer. '*Koktail* party time!' But even had I been swinging from the disco ball, yodelling in Cantonese, Sasha would not have noticed me. He was deep, *fathoms* deep, in conversation with what appeared to be an authoritative, rather dapper rock ape. About five-foot-four, the well-dressed anthropoid seemed to be bursting out of his suit with inharmonious rolls of fat and ripples of muscle battling for space, and even through the gloom I could see that his face was heavily scarred. This was not, I realised, lowering the jug, a few quieties between mates. This, clearly, was *bizniss*.

I ducked behind a pole and watched them. Sasha was practically nuzzling the apeman now, speaking directly into his ear. He didn't stop talking even when, in a barely discernible motion, he dropped a set of keys into the bulkier man's suit pocket. Feeling their weight, Apeman smiled – an offensive grimace that displayed a mouthful of gold teeth – and disengaged himself from Sasha, giving him an avuncular pat on the cheeks.

'Jesus,' I murmured through a mouthful of methotini. 'Sasha's making his bones.' It was a slight exaggeration: in mafia-speak, 'making one's bones' refers to murder as a means of admission to the mob. As far as I knew, Sasha hadn't killed anything but brain cells, but there was obviously some form of initiation going on. I snuck another peek around the pole. Sasha and Apeman were now facing each other and chatting in a manner less reminiscent of godfather and protégé than a couple of horny frat boys; with a grotesque leer, Apeman was cupping his hands in front of his own well-equipped chest in the classic 'big jugs?' charade. I guffawed into my drink and thanked a rather unsafe bout of fasting at age fourteen that my breasts had never grown out of their training bra. At least I'd be safe from this cretin.

Or not. As I watched with dawning horror, Sasha shook his head and mimed a flat chest before breaking into a sly grin, rubbing his fingers together. She's no boob-bot, he seemed to be saying, but she's loaded.

She? Shit. Me.

You know those bizarre instances when you sneeze, cough and fart simultaneously? What happened next was just like that – disorienting, enervating and just plain weird. In a split second I dropped the jug, Sasha and Apeman spotted me and three heavyset goons burst through the protesting crowd.

Earlier, blinded by fear and beer, I hadn't been able to see the faces of our pursuers, but I had no doubt I was looking at them now. With rabid expressions and ham-like hands reaching into their trouser waistbands, I didn't think these plug-uglies had come to boogie.

In the flash of a strobe, Sasha charged across the room and pinned me to the wall. 'Kiss!' he ordered, pushing his contorted face into mine.

'Get stuffed!' I exclaimed, pushing him away. I have been known to be turned on by quixotic notions of trans-gression, but this was ridiculous. Real-life mobsters were after us and unless we were talking the Liverpool variety, I doubted *they* were in any mood to kiss.

'Kiss!' he cried frantically, nudging his face into mine as the goons raced by. Miraculously, they ignored us, just another couple groping, or in my case, grappling, in the dark.

'They've gone,' I said after an aeon of surreptitious fumbling. 'Get offa me. I'm leaving.'

'Go?'

'*Da*, go. This entire night has been ridiculous! No beer

at a beer festival? Hotwiring cars? Maniacs trying to kill us, not to mention gold teeth – hey!'

Sasha's mouth squashed heavily onto mine with a strength I didn't think possible without being afflicted by lockjaw. 'Love,' he drooled. 'Mottle.'

'Mmmph!' Thrashing wildly, I whipped my head from side to side to avoid his horrible mouth. In a whirl of fury, I spotted Apeman chortling at my futile struggle, before suddenly his eyes lowered in solemn anticipation. Still flapping, I followed his gaze.

In a sparkling example of multi-tasking, Sasha was not only doing a great vacuum impression on my face, he was also pickpocketing me. In a flash, he had my bag open and my passport and wallet in hand. How romantic.

'You fucker!' I screamed, hurling him off me with a hitherto unrealised force. With his ghastly lips still puckered, I yanked my possessions out of his hand and smacked him across the face.

'You are k . . . k . . .' I stammered furiously, whacking him again. '*Katashkinapolkie*!'

Being bitch-whipped and publicly denounced as 'shit on a stick' does not go a long way towards gaining respect from the wiseguys, and I saw Apeman shake his head sadly. As a mobster, Sasha, slack-jawed and slumping, was finished.

I gave him a final, triumphant slap, then turned away, smirking as I marched towards the exit.

He should have known. Really.

Rebecca Sparrow

The Twilight Ritual

She called it our twilight ritual. The nights when we would scramble out of bed at a deliciously forbidden hour and make our way down to the creek. Me dressed in two-sizes-too-big stripy pyjamas. Her dressed in a perpetually crumpled pink satin slip, knotty hair trailing down her back like a creeping vine. We'd meet at her gate and tramp barefoot through the wet grass, mud squelching between our toes and leaving telltale clues to our mission.

She was as obsessed with mermaids as I was with Olivia Newton-John. (I longed for white roller-skating boots and on Saturday afternoons was known to slide around our living room singing slightly skewed *Xanadu* lyrics, much to my brother's disgust.) I respected her. Madly. Deeply. Without question. I mean she was eleven years old, a whole year older than me and, back in 1982, she and I both felt like she was the town's leading authority on mermaids and their likely Samford hangouts.

There were only two rules. Well, three if you included

the rule about me not being allowed to have my chocolate biscuits until afterwards. I had to bring my recorder to play. And I wasn't allowed to tell anyone else about our full-moon escapades. No one. Not Mum and Dad. Not Joe, my younger brother. And definitely not Mrs Lindsay, our Grade Five teacher, who owned five cats, had a simply enormous gap between her front teeth and frequently waxed lyrical about her penchant for fish and chips. Sometimes, during little lunch when I would be staring into my lunch box, questioning my mother's overt fondness for the cheese stick, she would turn and gravely tell me that Mrs Lindsay was the mermaids' Lex Luthor. And I'd nod sagely before suggesting we start a game of BP or TV Times.

And so we'd go to the creek and sit on the same patch of grass and I'd get out my recorder and do my best to play a mermaid-esque type of song – though the reality was that it always sounded more like 'When The Saints Go Marching In' than either of us was ever prepared to admit. And as I huffed and puffed and moved my sausage fingers up and down the holes, she would hum. Or sometimes jump onto the 'Big Rock' and recite what we thought was terribly bohemian poetry. Or better still read *The Bunyip of Berkeley Creek* aloud. Other times she would sing songs about their beautiful hair and hold a mirror over the water; since it was common knowledge that mermaids were slightly, well, vain and couldn't help but grab any opportunity to see themselves.

I'm pretty sure they never came. She would disagree with this, of course. She would say they did come once when I had nodded off. And it's at this point that we'd start to bicker because I could hardly understand why she didn't wake me up. She claims she was too busy asking them important questions about their tails. But I digress.

Thomasina Lamb was, is still, my best friend. Twenty years on, she looks the same as she did back then. Rower's shoulders. A smattering of freckles across her nose that look like they've been drawn on with a felt-tip pen. Shoulder-length blond hair and a slightly rebellious look in her eye. When Thomasina came to my school, Samford State School, at the start of Grade Five, she had a tin pencil case, not the plastic zip-up type like the rest of us. She could raise one eyebrow higher than the other. During maths she could add up sums faster than anyone I had ever seen. And her mum drove a car with a pop-up boot.

Thomasina and her mum Nina were from Byron Bay. So Thomasina had a habit of always looking as if she had just come off the sand, even though the beach was at least an hour's drive away. She had that windswept beachy look, and smelt of salt water and seaweed. Even in winter when she was dressed in a parka and jeans like the rest of us.

From the very start, Thomasina's mum had insisted that I call her Nina. The name Mrs Lamb made her feel oppressed. She was a travel agent, but she said her real calling was as a psychic. But it looked like her duty was to book Greek holidays for people who didn't know where Athens was. I mean, she had responsibilities, bills to pay, right? Right, I'd say, wondering when I could rejoin Thomasina in the backyard, having come indoors for a glass of water, only to find myself trapped into talking to an adult. But, in truth, I liked her. She spoke to me like I was her equal. Not a child. And she was definitely beautiful. Nina wore lots of headscarves and big hoop earrings and once, when she was picking Thomasina up from our house, told my mother to buy me a dog. My mother smiled and laughed and said goodbye and shut the door and wandered away muttering that she'd buy me a dog the day Mrs Lamb started wearing a bra. I thought this sounded imminently promising. Thomasina told me not to hold my breath.

We were as thick as thieves, Thomasina and I. We remained best friends through primary school and during our years together at Mitchelton High. We arranged our uni lectures so that we both had Wednesday afternoons off (me from Journalism, her from Arts). We shared our first flat in Ashgrove and calmed each other's nerves when we started our first jobs. We'd been through boyfriends, retrenchments, dumpings, promotions and Nina's death from breast cancer.

And we still called ourselves 'the mermaids of Samford Creek', even if our twilight ritual eventually had more in common with the pub on a Thursday night than creeks and recorders.

Thomasina is the sister every girl wants. The best friend everyone longs for. Even if she is abominably messy. The aroma of salt water still lingers on her skin.

I miss her.

I miss her. Madly. Deeply. Without question. And she hasn't even gone yet.

It's not like I don't see her. I go in most days. Every day. Sit on her bed. Talk to her about stuff. The fact that Daryl Somers is back on TV. How much we love George's new album. Whether I should be brave enough to ask out a guy from my work. How good it would be to own an

Apple iPod. And also know how to use it. The reasons why I should dye my hair blond for the hell of it.

But it's not the same.

Because now Thom has tumours growing in her right breast. And around her brain. And up her spine. And when the doctors come in to see her they don't charge in with clipboards, talking authoritatively about tests and scans and treatments. Instead their eyes act as apologies as they speak in whispers about Pain Management and Being Comfortable and Doing What They Can.

And it's not the same.

Because she gets tired more easily now. Can't remember conversations. From last week. Or even yesterday. Can't get up to go to the bathroom or comb her hair or grab the box of tissues if the nurses straighten things and move them out of reach. And sometimes, when I first arrive, it's hard to know if today is a good day when we pretend everything is fine and the most important thing to discuss is whether Brad and Jen will reunite. Or. Or a day when the mere mention of me getting a flat tyre or getting shitty with my landlord seems flippant. And thoughtless. And unkind.

Sometimes, when they're readjusting her bedpan and I can feel Thom's humiliation burning through my skin, she turns to me and whispers, 'Fuck this. Let's go to Greece.' And I say, 'God, yeah.' And we laugh conspiratorially. But then she stops laughing – eventually – and just gazes out the window. So I wonder aloud what's on TV.

These days we have a new twilight ritual. Not creeks and recorders. Not pubs and beers. Instead as the sky lights up, I sit on her bed while she drifts into sleep and stroke her hair and read her *Moby-Dick*. Or sometimes recite *The Bunyip of Berkeley Creek*. Or tell her tales about mermaids and chocolate biscuits and a little girl from Byron Bay with knotty hair and freckles. And always, always I remind her that I will miss her. Madly. Deeply. Without question.

Rachael Treasure

From Tarot to Tractors

'Ah,' sighed Eliza. It was so good to be in the country again. So good to see the hawthorn-lined roadway, the lush green grass, and the pretty white chooks clucking out of the way as her zippy red car whizzed past. She hadn't realised she'd hit one until she turned into the farm's pine-flanked drive and pulled up outside Samantha and Jeremy's farmhouse.

'Oh my God!' she said, putting her hand to her mouth as she looked at the meaty mush of feathers stuck to her glossy black bumper bar. 'I can't believe it! I've killed a chook! The poor thing! Oh, how awful. I thought I'd just hit a pothole!'

Her friend Sam surveyed the scene, cradling her three-week-old baby.

'You've turned into such a townie! It's not a chook, you dork. It's a bantam rooster. Annoying little bastard, too.' With her free hand Sam stooped, grabbed a scaly leg and peeled the flattened rooster off the car. 'I'll chuck it in the compost. Hose is over there if you want to squirt the blood off.'

Eliza swallowed and winced as she watched Sam disappear behind the garden shed with babe in one arm and dead rooster swinging from her other hand. Eliza suddenly realised she had spent too long in the city, driving to work on clean concrete, sitting in the air-conditioned boxes of the bank. She had gone soft.

She thought of her farming childhood, remembering the feel of gravel pressing into the soles of her feet and the smell of sheep manure rising up from the grating of the shearing shed. There was no playing in the creek in cut-off jeans these days, no sifting of waterweed through grubby fingers or inhaling the murky smell of frogs' spawn rising up from the pin rushes by the dam. She was all designer clothes and regular foils at the hairdresser to keep her blond hair looking just right.

Eliza sighed and looked up beyond the farmhouse to the craggy mountain where a summer storm was dragging dark clouds across an indigo sky. Beneath her on the river flats, the sun lit up Jeremy's big square hay bales like giant bullions of gold. If only she'd wanted a country bloke. Instead, Eliza had spent the past ten years chasing suits in the city. Weekend trips from Tasmania to Sydney to disrobe young stockbrokers in swish hotel rooms. Lazy weekends spent painting her toenails on yachts belonging to various swanky business-beaus. A ritzy-ditzy, flashy life. A neat, clean, tidy life. A lonely, boring, soulless life, she concluded, as she watched Sam walking towards her. The sun lit up Sam's messy, shiny black hair as she bent to kiss the baby's head. What different paths they'd chosen. Different lives.

Sam had Jeremy, her tall farming fella, and a homestead full of babies, blowflies and home-cooked food. Eliza compared this to her own bland minimalist flat, which she shared with her overweight, overwrought cat.

'I'll hose it later,' Eliza shrugged. 'It's only blood.'

'Could be a bad omen,' Sam said. 'Bring you bad luck. Better do it now.'

'You've always been so superstitious!'

But Sam simply smiled back. Up high, in the limbs of a dark old pine, a cockatoo screeched.

'Ah!' Eliza went on, pointing to the bird. 'Could that be another omen? A sign that I'll get a cock-or-two tonight? On my hot date?'

'I thought we were having a girls' night in?' Sam protested. 'Jeremy's got a big contracting job down the valley. He'll be out till dawn, going round and round on the tractor, so I thought we'd have a few drinks and –'

'I know,' Eliza said guiltily. 'But there's this guy . . . he phoned earlier. He's getting off the plane at nine and we're having a midnight feast at a swanky hotel, if you get my drift. Cock-or-two for sure.'

'Maybe all you'll be getting is a flattened cock!' Sam said. This was typical of Eliza. 'Like the one you just splattered. It's an omen for sure.'

'Good or bad?'

'Who knows,' said Sam, and her words were carried away on the wind.

Poking the slice of lemon that floated in her gin and tonic, Eliza looked around the cosy kitchen. A pendulum clock ticked above an unlit wood heater. Toys were stacked up in the corner. Absently Eliza positioned a pert-breasted Barbie on top of a naked Ken doll. Barbie's long flexible legs creaked at the knees as she straddled Ken.

'Pity he's only got a plastic mound, and not the real tackle,' Sam said as she plonked herself onto the couch, hoisted up her T-shirt and put the baby to her breast. Then she reached for her gin and took a gulp. 'So what's this bloke you're seeing tonight like?'

'Well, he's certainly not like poor Ken here. Far from it,' Eliza said, inspecting the region between Ken's muscular plastic legs. She told herself it was worth driving two hours out of the city to see Sam's new baby before driving two hours back again just to see this man.

'So where are the kids?' she asked, wanting to change the subject, feeling guilty again for putting a man before the needs of her oldest friend.

'Over at Mum's. Just for the night. Thought we could make a night of it, but if you're busy, you're busy.'

'I'm sorry I'm not staying. Really.'

Sam shrugged. She was used to Eliza and her men-frenzies. 'Well? Who is he?'

Eliza set down her drink.

'You know. The usual story. Met him at a conference. He's based in Sydney. Describes himself as an entrepreneur so he can swindle trips to see me fairly often. He's flown down *three* times already.'

'Sounds nice,' said Sam flatly as her baby belched and white breast milk landed with a plop on the wooden floor.

On their second gin, with the baby in bed, the girls headed out to the verandah to relax in the warmth of the summer evening. As they sank into wicker chairs, Sam offered Eliza a Barbecue Shape.

'Sorry there's no cheese platter for you. I haven't had time to go shopping. I thought we'd ring the general store and order a pizza for tea. Noggin, the guy who runs the shop, will drop it off on his way home. Sort of like an informal delivery service. Even if you're not staying I'll still order a big one. Breastfeeding mother and all that. I can treat myself to cold pizza for breakfast.'

'Stop it! You're making me feel guilty again for not staying!'

'No! Don't think like that. Not at all. I'm used to being a tractor-widow. But when Jez is home, he's a legend with the kids.'

'And he's the love of your life.'

'Hate to be one of those a smug married types . . . but yes, we're happy. How about you? Is this Sydney fella the one for you?'

Eliza shrugged and Sam looked at her probingly.

'What?'

'Oh, nothing,' Sam said.

'*What?*' insisted Eliza.

'Nothing really. It's just your track record. You seem to pick the least likely blokes to settle down with. I mean this bloke you're meeting tonight. Is he father material?'

'He most certainly is!' Eliza said, trying not to let the defensiveness creep into her voice. 'He's got two kids. And he loves them dearly.'

'What? Loves them dearly and flying down to shag you?'

'They're separated. He and his wife.'

'Huh!' was all Sam said as she motioned to refill Eliza's glass.

'No. No more, thanks. I'll have to drive back soon. Anyway, who says I want to settle down?'

'Come on,' Sam said with a gleam in her eye. 'I can tell. You're longing for it. Only you don't know it *yet*.'

'Maybe I haven't met the man for me *yet*?'

'You never know, he could be right next door. Tell you what, how about you feed the dogs for me while I order the pizza. There's some wallaby hanging in the meat shed. Then . . . I'll get my tarot cards! We'll see how far off this man of yours is.'

'Oh no!' groaned Eliza. 'You and your bloody witchy ways!'

Eliza walked beyond the green homestead garden into the gold of summer grass. A sudden hot wind lifted dust from the driveway and the seed heads whispered to Eliza as she passed. Fate, she thought, as she gingerly picked up the sinewy wallaby carcasses and walked towards the dogs. She recognised Sam's older collie, Lucy, but all the others were new to her. She'd become so out of touch with her best friend's life. She should come out here more often. It was so beautiful. The sun was now low over the mountain and the dark storm clouds were looming above her. Thunder rumbled and she felt it tremble through her whole body.

'Awesome,' she said to the landscape. She turned and walked back to the house. She should at least indulge Sam and her stupid fortune-telling before she headed off.

'You call *them* tarot cards?' Eliza sceptically flicked through the pack.

'They were free with a copy of *Cosmo* magazine. But they still work,' Sam protested.

'Work? How can someone as practical as you be so "out there" when it comes to this crap?'·

'Oh, ye of little faith. Look around you. Mother Nature speaks to us all the time.' Sam waved her hand gracefully towards the mountains that towered over the valley. Thunder rumbled forth again just as Sam gestured. 'See? She speaks!'

'Sounds more like Mother Nature's got gastro to me.'

Sam shuffled the deck and laid the cards out before her friend.

'Pick four cards,' she said.

Eliza pulled a face and rolled her eyes before tugging out the cards. Despite her bravado, she felt nervous as Sam arranged them face down on the table before her.

But after the reading she sat back in her chair grumbling.

'I will be in a quiet place surrounded by water and dogs? Huh! Ridiculous. That's your life, Sam, not mine. The cards have got confused. If my promotion comes through it doesn't sound like Sydney at all. And where in there does it say untold fortunes?' She stabbed her index finger accusingly at a card.

'Richness will come in other ways. Through the landscape.'

'Great,' Eliza said flatly. 'And the children thing? How do you explain the children? Maybe it's because I'm going to end up in Sydney with his children visiting every second weekend. We can do nice exciting kiddy things.'

'Maybe you'll meet someone else.'

A sudden blast of hot wind picked up the cards and scattered them over the green lawn beneath the verandah.

With the wind came fat drops of rain that smelt better than chocolate as they landed on the warm garden. All Sam and Eliza could do was watch in awe as the summer storm unleashed itself above the tin roof of the homestead. The sound was deafening. The clouds obliterated the sun and darkness shrouded them. Soon, with water splashing up on their bare legs and the wind turning cold, the girls moved inside.

'It's an omen, Eliza. It's an omen,' Sam said as she ran to shut the windows of the house. 'Mother Nature speaks to us.'

A little later, under the shelter of the verandah, they shouted their goodbyes over the din of the storm in an eerie, early darkness. A hug and a kiss and Eliza darted out and leapt into the car, gasping at the stinging coldness of the rain. The engine turned over and she flicked her lights on, capturing the luminous red eyes of a possum nestled in the rafters of the old garage next to the house. But she didn't see them. The rain was so thick on her windscreen, all she could see was a watery blur. She flicked on her windscreen wipers. Nothing. She turned the switch on and off again. Still nothing. She looked out to Sam, who was still standing with her arms wrapped about herself.

'Bugger,' she said as she got out of the car and ran back to her friend. 'My wipers. They won't work.'

'No probs. I'll call Jeremy on the two-way. He'll know what to do.'

Sam picked up the handpiece of the two-way radio that sat on a shelf above the phone in the kitchen.

'Jez, are you on channel?'

Soon his friendly, crackly voice came over the airwaves.

'How's it going, babe? How's Eliza? Over.'

'She's sick of playing with Ken's plastic mound and she wants to get back to town for the real deal. But her wipers won't work. Over.'

'Do her pissers work? Over.'

Sam turned to Eliza. 'Did your pissers work?'

'My *what*?'

'You know. The things that wash your windscreen.'

'I don't know! Mother Nature was pissing so hard on me I didn't think to check. And can't other people hear you on that thing? Do you mind not talking about my sex life in front of the whole valley.'

'She didn't check her pissers, babe. Over,' Sam said.

'Could be the fuse. Drive the car down to the shed, get the fuse out. You'll figure which one. Then look for a black case on the workbench full of spare fuses. Grab one of those. Over.'

'Got it. Thanks. How are you going? Over.'

'Rotten. Bogged up to the eyeballs. Both the ute and the tractor. And it's still belting down. No more harvest for this little black duck for the next few days. Don't reckon I'll get home tonight. I'll have to camp here in the quarters and see you in the morning. Over.'

'No worries, babe. See you then. Over.' And Sam hung up the handpiece.

Eliza could see it really was 'no worries' to Sam. This sort of thing happened all the time round here. Mother Nature clearly ran the place.

'You'd better borrow a coat,' Sam said, handing her a strange-smelling Driza-Bone on the verandah and throwing her a pair of massive gumboots. 'Might pong a bit on the sleeves. I gutted the wallaby in it. Was in a hurry. You know.'

No, thought Eliza, she didn't know. She was a city-slick city chick, with a hot date tonight. As she ducked into the rain again to start her car, she wondered if she'd have time to shower and blow-dry her hair again before the not-so-Ken-doll got off his plane.

Safely back in her car once more, with Sam waving from the verandah, Eliza turned the engine over, flicked on the windscreen wipers, which gave a satisfying swish, and rattled off over the grid and up the now muddy drive. She tooted the horn merrily for good measure.

'Hot date, here I come!'

In the darkness, the massive pines that lined the driveway whirled above her and she could just make out the white blobs of cockatoos battling to stay on the branches as the wind hurled bullets of raindrops at them. She was about to pull onto the highway when she noticed the fuel gauge.

Empty.

Back at the kitchen door, she wailed at Sam, 'I meant to get some at the store on my way here but I was so excited to get back to the country and your place that I forgot!'

Sam looked at her watch and shook her head.

'Too late. It's after seven. The garage is shut. Seven till seven, seven days a week.'

'Are you sure?' begged Eliza, thinking desperately of 'no-plastic-mound-man', who was probably in the departure lounge at this very minute. Thunder rumbled from the inky black sky and more rain lashed down. Eliza knew what Sam and Mother Nature were thinking. Bloody city slickers. Where life is easy and everything is on tap twenty-four hours a day.

'Come on,' Sam said, handing her the coat again. 'Jez has got some unleaded in the shed. In case of people like you.'

'Sorry,' said Eliza, frowning. She realised how selfish she was being. This was Sam's night in. Almost child-free. A chance to catch up with her old mate. And here she was, flitting in for an hour or two before flitting off again for a night of shagging. Eliza pulled on the gumboots, angry at herself.

At the machinery shed, rain zinged in silver sparkles in the bright floodlight that lit up the machinery. The giant machines were parked like sleeping beasts, warm and dry in their cave.

'Hold this,' said Sam, handing Eliza a fuel funnel. Eliza imagined running her petrol-smelling fingers through Suit-man's hair in a couple of hours' time. He'd hate it. Eliza inserted the funnel into the petrol tank as Sam lifted the jerry can up and the fuel glugged out with a heady waft and a gurgle.

'It's kind of sexual, isn't it?' Eliza said, surveying Jeremy's shelves. 'All these male and female bits that fit into one another or screw onto one another. It's a turn-on really. Very macho.'

'Why do you think I fell for Jez? I love a man with diesel on his hands and dust on his boots. A real man. You know.'

'Yep. You picked a beauty. He's a machinery man to the core. So masculine and sexy.'

And suddenly Eliza wished for a machinery man herself. As she screwed the petrol cap back on she longed to know what it was like to kiss a man who didn't smell of the latest scent *pour l'homme*. To feel a rugged jawline, rough with stubble, and have coarse and work-worn hands on her skin. To find a man whose eyes creased with the sun and had not a scrap of vanity in his soul.

'I'd better go. His plane will be halfway here,' she said, almost reluctantly this time. 'Want a lift back up to the house?'

Sam shook her head. 'Nah, I'll walk. I love it when it pours like this.'

The girls hugged, and again Eliza drove off into the wet, dark night.

Her foot hit the brakes hard. At the top of the drive, the little car fishtailed and stopped just short of the giant trunk that lay across her path. Eliza sat breathing heavily, listening to the swish and drag of the wipers. Through the falling rain she watched the headlights capture spindly pine needles swirling madly in the wind. She clutched the steering wheel. That was close. Very close. She sucked in a breath. Shaken, she sat for a time before looking to see if she could drive around the fallen pine tree. But it was completely blocking the drive.

'That's the *third* time,' Sam said, offering Eliza another gin. 'Mother Nature is telling you not to leave here tonight. It's an omen. It's not safe. Three times. It's a message.'

'But my date! My hot juicy date?'

'If you insist, I can get the tractor and the chain and drag the tree out of the way for you. Do you want me to do that? But if you die in a car accident between here and town, don't blame me. You've had enough messages for you to stay.'

'I won't be able to blame you if I'm dead, will I?'

'Don't make jokes. You know what I mean. This is a serious message. You are not meant to leave tonight, Eliza.'

Eliza thought of Sam's baby sleeping in the nursery, who would be awake in just an hour for another feed. Sam had enough on her plate. She didn't need to be out on a night like this hauling a giant tree off her drive, just so she, Eliza, could go and shag some high-flier. She nodded. Sam was right. She should stay.

'Can I use your phone then? Ring him? He's only down here for one night.'

But his phone was switched off. Instead she left a message.

'Oh, stuff him,' she said, slamming the receiver down.

'That's it then,' said Sam. 'It's officially a girls' night in. Let's get cracking!' She began to rummage in the kitchen cupboard and pulled out a breast pump. 'Ta-da!' she said, holding it up proudly.

'What the—?'

'Express milk now, get drunk next, feed baby Mummy's wholesome milk in bottle later. Perfect.' She sat down on the couch and plugged in the pump. Bottle in place, boob in place, the pump set off with a groan and then rhythmically began to suck milk with sounds similar to a dairy.

'My hot night out with a hot-rod has somehow turned into some sick lesbian fantasy,' said Eliza wryly, looking at Sam's plump white breast.

'Get over it. Mother Nature has saved your life.'

'Well, where's my cock-or-two, like she promised?'

Then the phone rang.

'I'll get it,' offered Eliza.

It was Noggin from the shop.

'River's burst its banks so I can't deliver your pizza. Flood's made it over the road in the dip just out of town. Tell Sam I'm sorry 'bout her pizza, but we can't help the weather.'

'No, we certainly can't,' agreed Eliza before she hung up.

'No pizza?' asked Sam, switching to the other breast.

'Nup.'

'Baked beans on your toast then?' Sam asked.

A vision of the midnight room-service feast of oysters and caviar that she would now never eat flashed before Eliza's eyes. Strangely, she felt quite relieved. Sitting with her friend on the couch eating baked beans on toast seemed like the right place to be.

'Shall we light the fire too?' Eliza asked eagerly. 'Make a proper rainy night of it?'

'Yes! And I've taped all the *McLeod's Daughters* episodes. We could watch them . . . perve on Alex Ryan. Oh, to die for!'

'Mmm!' said Eliza suddenly excited. 'And Dave the vet. Just *so* yum.'

'I thought you were into suits?'

'Mother Nature just might have converted me. I like a man who'll take her on. When I think of getting a glimpse of your husband's giant machinery, so . . . so . . . robust – I get the shivers.'

'Oh, you do, you do. I just love a massive tractor.'

'Mmm. Me too. I think, now, me too.'

The gin bottle was empty. They were wheezing and snorting like pigs as they freeze-framed the vet's backside on the TV-screen for the tenth time, when a knock at the door sent them screeching into each other's arms.

'Who the *hell* is that?' said Eliza. 'The tree! How did they get in here? Are you sure it's not a serial killer?'

'I'll get it,' said Sam, who was clearly not frightened by the strange after-hours visit. She flicked on the light and opened the door.

'Pizza delivery!' exclaimed the tall man, setting the box down on the kitchen table. Sam clapped her hands.

'You legend! But how . . . ?'

'Saw Noggin from the shop,' he said. 'I was bringing my tractor back home, so I offered to drop your tucker in. Got the dual wheels on her, so she's high enough to clear the flood. Shifted that tree for you, too. Big bugger. She's got the horsepower to move something that size. Should see the size of the chain I had to use. Lucky I had it handy. Pizza might be a bit cold though.'

The man took off his rain-darkened Akubra hat and shook off his oilskin coat. Eliza took him in. The size of him. The flash of his blue eyes, the bloom of dark stubble over his square handsome jaw. She swallowed. Lightning flashed right outside the door and suddenly all the lights went out and the TV fizzed to black. Thunder roared in Eliza's ears as she sat in the darkness. The image of the handsome man was etched in her mind. Then she heard Sam say, 'Hang on. I'll get the candles.'

As the flames flickered to life, Sam waved the match in Eliza's direction.

'This is my friend Eliza. She's staying the night.'

The man looked straight into Eliza's eyes. Lightning and thunder again. This time in Eliza's heart.

'Weekend,' she said quickly. 'I'm staying the weekend.'

'Looks like I am, too,' he said with a glint in his eye. 'I just heard on the two-way that the river's cut me off from my house. Can't get back there. I've got a couple of kelpies in the tractor that'll need a kennel, too. That's if you don't mind?' he said to Sam.

'Not at all,' she said, smiling knowingly. Then she turned to Eliza. 'This, by the way, is our neighbour, Owen. Owen the omen. A good omen, that is.'

'Pleased to meet you, Owen,' said Eliza, smiling. 'Maybe you could show me your massive tractor later? I love a good tractor.'

Alisa Valdes-Rodriguez

Cat Lady

Teresa looked at her watch again, just to be sure. Gucci, good watch, time and date. Diamonds. January fifteenth. Birthday. Thirty-five, an age not even diamonds could help.

There was a time, twelve years ago, when Teresa believed a Gucci watch and the cool job that allowed a girl to buy it for herself would naturally facilitate a lifestyle that would naturally facilitate the meeting of great guys. Or at least *one* great guy. The kind who read books and might look good helping a child learn to ride a bike. That's all she asked for. But now it looked as if Teresa's mother – absolutely never to be confused with Mother Teresa – had been right all along.

'No mens want a girl so smart, so independent as you, with your expensive car that makes him feel so small,' she had said the last time they met, at Versailles, for some post-Christmas *buñuelos and café con leche*. 'A man wants to be needed, *y tú*, you don't need nobody.'

Teresa's mother had been in Miami since 1960, and still the double-negative thing vexed her, as did the notion of her only daughter, the youngest and unmarried, living on her own, rather than living at home where she could be useful in helping serve her father.

Teresa popped open the white plastic file box beneath her glass-top home-office desk and took out the letter she had written to herself. She often typed such letters on her word processing program, printing them in soothing dark blue ink before folding them into neat squares, tucking them into greeting cards, and sealing them until whatever doomsday she wrote in clean, clear script on the front.

This envelope was marked 'thirty-fifth birthday' and the message inside was simple:

Dear Self:
If you are still single and haven't had one good date in the preceding two years, you must admit the search is over. Get rid of the belly shirts. Toss the miniskirts. Save yourself a future of humiliation and too much make-up and realise one important truth: You are now a cat lady.
With love,
Teresita

When Teresa wrote this to herself, she was only twenty-two, and had never owned a cat. She did not own a cat now, and had never owned a cat in her life. Her mother was from Cuba. And in Cuba, according to her mother, no one in her right mind had cats for pets.

'To kill the mouse, she is fine,' griped Mami. 'To kill

the cock-a-roach, is good. As pet?' Ugly face. 'Filthy. Disgusting. Only an American would have a cat pet.'

Teresa folded the letter and replaced it in the card and envelope. She owned no belly shirts and no miniskirts. She had not owned these even as she wrote the letter to her future self. At her dressiest, she was a Liz Claiborne kind of girl. Otherwise, khakis and oversize shirts were fine. As it so happened, this was precisely the outfit she had on at the moment. Beige pants, black T-shirt, black button-down hanging open on top of that. But make-up? That was another matter. She wore a lot of stuff, more out of ritual and habit than anything else. She walked up her condo stairs to the master bedroom, through to the bathroom, and began dumping her cosmetics one by one into the wastebasket, leaving only a tube of foundation, a blusher and a mascara. A cat lady did not need more than that.

Finished with her task, Teresa observed herself in the mirror. She would have to stop colouring the grey. And no more round-brushing with the blow-dryer to get it straight, no more slicking balm. Cat ladies ought to have bushy hair, she thought. Witch hair. She bent over and shook her head, tugging on it, plumping it with her hands. Upright once more, she looked wilder than she remembered looking in a long while, red in the cheeks and uncontrolled.

'Okay then,' she said to her reflection. 'Let's go get a goddamn cat.'

As Teresa steered her white Volvo sedan through the traffic on Biscayne Boulevard, she thought about how different the words *lady* and *woman* were when paired with the word *cat*.

Cat Lady – crumbs on shirt, hair grease, newspaper stacked in towers inside the house, the same paisley dress for years on end, said dress worn with flat black Easy Spirit shoes.

Cat Woman – slinky, black leather, sex goddess. She felt heat spread in her lower belly and willed it away. She wasn't supposed to feel this any more, was she?

Teresa eyed herself in the rear-view mirror. She did Pilates and ate organic produce, just the sort of activities that invited scorn and ridicule from Mami, who preferred her milk 'normal' and full of damaging hormones. Teresa took good care of herself. She didn't look a day older than twenty-nine. Or was it thirty?

'I'm not ready to be a cat lady,' she whispered to her face. The man driving the car behind her laid on his horn. The light had turned green, and Teresa sat staring at her ageing face. 'Sorry,' she said, though he couldn't hear her. Nervously, she drove on, toward the pet store.

A bell on the door jangled as Teresa opened it and stepped into the shop. The sound of the bell signalled a cageful of parrots to screech and gargle. Teresa looked around, but saw no one.

'Hello?' she called out.

A worker sulked out of a back room and bucked his head in her direction, some sort of pet store–employee greeting. He looked like Harpo Marx, with a big blond Afro. Justin Timberlake, Teresa's mind corrected her. That would be the modern comparison. Harpo Marx? That wasn't even her generation. Not only was she getting old, but her references were older than she was. Pathetic.

'Do you sell cats?' she asked. She tugged her outer

shirt closed, wishing for a large paisley dress to hide in. The worker led her to the back, to a glass wall with rows of cages like drawers of a mausoleum on the other side. Inside each cage was at least one cat, usually two or three. Some were full-grown, most were kittens. All seemed to have cat poop in their fur and sad, scared eyes. They all stared at her, and looked half-dead. Except for one.

A small white cat stared at the lock, intelligent, focused. It swatted at the lock mechanism, squinted its eyes at its failure, and tried again. Failing once more, it stood up and circled its pen. It had no tail. Then it sat again, and swatted from a new angle, ever hopeful. A patient cat. A cat that wanted freedom more than it wanted a human. Teresa identified with it instantly.

'That one,' she said.

'Japanese bobtail,' said the clerk. 'Good choice.'

Mami came for dinner with a birthday cake, and screeched like a parrot at the sight of the cat sitting patiently in Teresa's entryway, staring at the front door.

'What is that *rat* doing here?'

Teresa took her mother's fur wrap – it did not get cold in Miami, ever, but Mami still had to dress for winter – and hung it in the closet. It felt like the cat's fur. The cat stared coldly at them both, incriminating, and padded away toward the litter box in the guest bathroom.

'I'm a cat lady,' Teresa announced. 'Congratulate me.'

'You should have kept Richard,' said Mami, lighting a cigarette. Teresa had asked many times that Mami not smoke here, and many times Mami had completely ignored her.

'Richard?' Teresa asked, feeling dizzy. She sat on the sofa across the living room from her mother and gagged on the smoke and memories. Richard, the asshole. The womaniser. The cheat. The liar.

'Richard.' Mami made a face to indicate she found her daughter retarded.

'I like being a cat lady,' said Teresa. 'Next subject please.'

'He was a good man.'

'I named her Eli, after Grandma,' said Teresa, pointing to the cat who had returned to her post at the front door. Eli stood on her hind legs and with one paw fiddled with the doorknob. Mami blew smoke from her widened nostrils, like the devil, and narrowed her eyes.

'There is a hot place in hell for you,' she hissed.

As if she'd understood, Eli pivoted her head on her neck and stared at Mami. Never had anyone been able to outstare Teresa's mother. But this cat did it. For ten full minutes they glared and glowered, until, at last, Mami broke.

'Filthy creature,' she said, standing to fetch her stole. 'I go now. From now on, we visit on my house, not here on the rat nest.'

In, on. Since 1959 the words had confounded Mami. In Spanish, there was only one: *En*. Life was so much simpler for Mami.

Since bonding over their discomfort with Mami, Eli and Teresa had become friends. Eli slept on Teresa's feet, and in exchange for the physical affection, Teresa scratched behind Eli's ears and fed her something in a fancy pink can that once opened smelled noxious and fish-guts. Why, Teresa wondered, did pet food manufacturers lie like Richard? Eli obviously liked the food, which smelled nothing like the pâté it purported to be, and everything like the mouse-ass and sparrow-trachea it actually was. They lied to appeal to the ones with the money and the power, Teresa realised, sort of like porn directors who told men women enjoyed choking on their snotty fluids.

Teresa began rushing home to see Eli after work. She had never known what it felt like to look forward to a creature with a beating heart cuddling up with her after a long day of crunching numbers and making insincere phone calls. It was heavenly. To thank Eli for her love, Teresa did something the vet begged her not to, and started to let the animal roam free outside. Teresa lived in a quiet part of Coconut Grove, with lots of trees for a cat to climb and few cars to run over her. Eli, ever wishful of freedom, had run far and fast the first day out, unsure whether she would come back. But memories of the mouse-ass food and the ear-scratching overcame her, and ten hours later, she was there, at Teresa's back door, mewing sweetly. After several weeks of this, Eli thought her keeper deserved a thank-you, and so dragged home a half-dead bird for Teresa to kill.

Teresa opened the door with her hair wild and greying, and screamed at the flopping feathered mess on the door-mat. She gripped the front of her paisley dress. 'Oh, Eli, what did you do?'

'Meow,' said Eli. The cat tilted its head and Teresa understood. It was an offering, a token of affection. A Gucci watch, from a cat.

'Eli,' Teresa purred, scooping the cat into her arms and leaving the bird outside to its fate. She shut the door and carried the cat to the pantry for another can of mouse-ass. Teresa shed a tear as she pulled the pop-top. In her life, she'd had exactly three boyfriends. And none had ever been as thoughtful as this cat.

Teresa ate a wedge of cheese for breakfast with artificial-orange drink, because this was the sort of thing cat ladies ate. She tried to read the paper through Eli, who flipped and flopped across the broadsheet like a showgirl. Normally, Teresa cared less about what was in any section of the paper other than business, which pertained to her job. But today, the metro section wrote of a cat lady who'd died and left 341 cats homeless. The city was going to exterminate them all if people didn't rescue them. Three hundred cats! Teresa chewed her cheese and observed Eli.

'You know what your problem is?' she asked the cat. 'You're a loner. You need friends.'

Teresa had never been to an animal shelter before, and the sight and smell of the place made her want to cry. Hundreds of wet eyes stared at her, begging. Take me. She approached the counter and informed the volunteer that she could take home two of the cats left behind by the cat lady. The volunteer eyed Teresa's paisley dress with suspicion.

'Sorry, ma'am,' she said. 'Another . . . lady beat you to it. They're all gone.'

Teresa felt tears of envy sting her eyes. 'But I only wanted another cat.' One of *her* cats, thought Teresa. The cat lady's cats.

'We have plenty of cats,' said the volunteer. 'But if you want *free* cats, you should go to the beach. The city's rounding up all the strays under the boardwalks, to kill them.' She leaned forward. 'I can tell you love cats,' said the volunteer. 'Save them.'

Because Teresa expected to crawl beneath the boardwalk with the cat trap the volunteer at the shelter had loaned her, she did not wear the paisley dress to the beach. She wore a flirty pink velour J. Lo jogging suit she had promised herself she'd get rid of now that she was the same age as the singer/actress. It was the only exercise outfit she had left, and she wore it with white sneakers stained with pink mouse-ass splatters.

Teresa followed the volunteer's instructions and waited beneath the boardwalk, in the sand, listening to the people walking up above. They had no idea there was a society of felines down below, hundreds of them, going about their lives. The strays were skinny and wiry and wanted nothing to do with Teresa, no matter how many times she clicked her tongue gently at them. *It's like when the old Cuban men do that to me*, she thought. *I don't look at them.*

Teresa decided to stop trying to degrade the animals, and simply sat in silence. That is when she realised she was not alone among cats. Not twenty feet away, partially obscured by a wooden support beam, sat a man. She saw his toes first, then his knees, then his beer bottle. He was balding, but no less cute for it. At first she thought he might be homeless, and her blood ran cold. But then she saw the Old Navy T-shirt and trendy carpenter jeans in a dark blue colour that indicated they were new. He also wore fashionable eyeglasses, and bracelets. No ring. Why was she still checking for that, especially here, under a bridge? His beer bottle dripped condensation, indicating it was cold, and had likely come from the ice chest he sat on. Seeing her, he smiled and tilted the beer bottle her way. Cats swirled around him, unafraid. They knew him, and liked him. He talked to the cats, touched them gently. He applied some sort of salve to the cut ear of one of the creatures, and forced pink liquid Teresa now recognised as cat antibiotic into another's mouth. He cleared his throat. And waved. Friendly. He looked comfortable here, as if he were sitting at a cafe table.

'Javier,' he said. 'Nice to meet you.'

He had a beautiful smile.

'I'm Teresa, the cat lady,' she said sullenly. Javier stood and opened the chest. He took out another beer and offered it to Teresa, laughing. He looked her up and down as she politely took the bottle.

'More like cat woman,' he said.

Teresa blushed. 'I'm thirty-five,' she said, as if this explained something.

'I'm forty,' he said.

'Oh,' she said, surprised. 'You don't look, I mean, the jeans and all.'

He continued to smile. 'It's too bad the city wants to kill them,' he said.

'Horrible,' she agreed. She watched the cats rub against his new jeans. 'They seem to like you,' she said.

'I'm a vet,' he said.

'What war?' she asked. If he was forty, it would have to be, what? The Gulf War or something.

He laughed, but she hadn't meant it as a joke. Then she got it. He was a *vet*. As in *veterinarian*.

'I've always loved animals,' he said.

'Me too,' she lied. Then she decided that cat ladies didn't need to lie to impress men, because cat ladies no longer concerned themselves with men.

'No,' she said. 'That's not true. I've never had a pet until this year. I wasn't allowed.'

'Wasn't allowed?' he asked.

'My mom,' Teresa said with a sigh. 'There were lots of things. No sneakers, no bike riding. No pop music.'

'She sounds like my mom,' he said.

'Really?' Teresa's heart fluttered again, against her will. He nodded kindly and she continued to speak. 'I'm collecting cats because I swore to myself I would if I got this old and was still single.'

He looked into her eyes for a brief moment, and looked away, blushing a little and smiling to himself. 'Thus, the "cat lady" thing,' he said.

'Right,' she said.

He chuckled to himself, and felt for lumps or something beneath the chin of one of the cats. 'You don't dress like a cat lady,' he said. 'I know lots of cat ladies, trust me. Bread and butter of my business.'

'No, I *do*!' she cried. 'I usually do. I have this paisley dress I got at a thrift store. It's quite stained, with a frayed hem. It's perfect. Just today I didn't.'

'You look nice today,' he said. 'You shouldn't dress like a cat lady.'

'But I'm getting old,' she said. 'Cats love you no matter what you wear, unconditionally.'

'That shows how little you know about cats,' he said. 'A real cat lady would never say something so misguided. Cats prefer cashmere.'

Misguided. He was literate. Her heart beat faster yet. Did he say *cashmere*?

'So,' he said to Teresa without looking at her. 'How many cats do you have now?'

'One,' she said.

He laughed, then apologised. 'One? That's nothing. You have to have at least a hundred to qualify as a bona fide cat lady,' he said.

'Why do you think I'm *here*?'

'These guys are feral,' he said. 'They'll never be happy as housecats, unless you take the kittens. That's what I'd suggest. The older ones are wild as raccoons.'

Teresa watched the cats roll and play. 'They seem tame around *you*,' she said.

He grinned, winked and raised one eyebrow. 'I'm the cat whisperer,' he said.

Cat whisperer? *Super*-literate.

'What do you whisper to them?' she asked.

'Ancient Cuban secret,' he said with an exaggerated Cuban–Spanish accent. He was Cuban? There *was* a God.

'You seem cheerful for a guy who knows his little friends are going to die,' she said.

'It's called denial,' he said simply.

Denial? Super-literate, cute, smart – and up to date on psychobabble? Amazing.

Before she knew it, Teresa had blurted her thought into the air: 'Why aren't you *married*?'

'Who says I'm not married?' He looked surprised.

'You don't wear a ring.' He must be gay, she thought.

He looked at his hand. 'No, I don't wear a ring.'

'Gay?' she asked. He threw his head back and laughed loud enough to scare a few cats away.

'Not quite,' he said. 'I *was* married. She . . . was killed.'

'Yikes. Sorry.'

For a moment, Teresa wondered if *he* had killed his wife, and whether to scream now, run later, or run now, scream later.

He shrugged. 'It was five years ago. Drunk driver.'

He looked at her again, and smiled. He didn't look dangerous. He looked nice. Huggable. She didn't know if he meant the wife had been a drunk driver, or that a drunk driver had killed her; now was not the right time to ask, she decided. She noticed a book next to the cooler, a popular nonfiction hardcover about a political subject she agreed with.

'I'm sorry,' she said again. *For thinking you were a murderer.* 'About your wife.'

'Don't be. It wasn't your fault.'

'Good book,' she said, changing the subject. She wondered if he had ever taught a child to ride a bike, and decided a cat woman would simply ask. She did.

He laughed again, a laugh like bells ringing. 'I have a son. He's ten. I helped him learn to ride a bike, yes. You ask a lot of probing personal questions for a dried-up spinster,' he added.

'Cat lady,' she corrected him.

He shook his head. 'Nah,' he said. 'Far as I'm concerned, you're ninety-nine cats short.'

Teresa thought of Eli, and wondered how she'd adjust to a sibling. Not well, she imagined.

Javier cleared his throat again, and Teresa saw him blush.

'Listen,' he said. 'I don't usually meet girls here, but – you want to go get a bite to eat or something?'

Teresa nodded, almost too quickly. She felt the heat in her lower belly again and wondered if it was possible for a woman of thirty-five to go into heat.

Mami had always wanted Teresa to marry a doctor. A real doctor, not a cat doctor. But given her age and disposition, Javier would have to do. He wasn't even from a real Cuban-exile family, either. He was a Marielito, and *prieto*. But that's how it was with Teresa. You told her one thing, and she did the opposite, just to spite you.

Mami pulled her legs closer to her, scrunched up in her seat. Dogs everywhere! And cats. And birds. Whoever heard of a wedding open to animals? Teresa had lost her mind. And the wedding announcement in the *Herald*? It had Teresa's picture, but not her name. Instead of her name, it said 'Cat Lady', and instead of Javier's name, it said 'Pet Saviour'. They were crazy. They thought it was the funniest thing in the world. How crazy? So crazy that between them they now had nine cats, six dogs and God only knew how many hamsters, fish and birds. And something called a pig that didn't look like a pig. It looked like a rat.

'What is that thing they have in the cage?' she asked Papi.

'What?' Papi was distracted with shooting off a dog that insisted on sniffing his crotch.

'That thing, the furry thing they call a pig.'

'Guinea pig,' he said.

'Why would they want such a thing?' Mami wailed, dabbing her eyes with a tissue. A few of her daughter's new friends looked over from across the church and smiled, thinking Mami was crying in happiness for her daughter. She was in truth crying because her daughter was insane.

'Thank God they're too old to have children,' Mami whispered to Papi.

He did not answer, but rather stared at a woman with a snake slithering across her breasts. Who were these people?

'Did you hear me?' she chided, slapping his arm.

'I heard you,' said Papi. 'She's going to have children. She's not too old yet. Now be quiet. Your daughter's wedding is about to start.'

Louise Voss

Best Served Cold

Clive prised open his eyes at 4:30 p.m., squinting from the slits between his matted lashes. His shift at the restaurant started in less than an hour, three different-colour tube lines north of where he lay, queasy and fed up.

He climbed out of bed and gingerly reached for the uniform – black trousers, white shirt – he'd discarded at seven that morning, feeling the sickening memory of whisky pressing behind his eyeballs. He'd have to iron the shirt, or he'd be fired, but the trousers should be okay. That had been some session. Him and Burt, one of the sous-chefs. Surely they hadn't talked about Lisa for six hours solid? Or rather, Clive had ranted and Burt listened. How dare she dump him after two weeks? What was wrong with her? He'd only asked for that other woman's phone number, that was all . . .

'I've got a boyfriend,' the woman had said smugly, and it turned out that Lisa had been looming in the background the whole time, with the woman's bill on a little silver tray, and a face that would pickle walnuts.

Cursing Lisa, his job, and his hangover, Clive managed to dress, iron the shirt, and simultaneously pee and comb his hair, in fifteen minutes flat. A voice in his head nagged him with the same boring persistence as his headache: why are you bothering? It's only a crappy job. Let her have the hassle of finding a replacement for you. Ditch the bitch (he forgot, temporarily, that it was in fact he himself who had been ditched).

It was a shame, because Lisa was very pretty. She had four different shades of blond in her long stripy hair, which matched the colours of the restaurant's wooden floor exactly. After their first proper date, Clive had asked her if she'd had it done intentionally that way, but she just laughed, not answering. He'd concluded that she had.

In the end, Clive decided that trying to find a new job would be too much like hard work, so he hunched his arms into a thick woollen jacket, and took a last look in the mirror.

Clive's mirror was purposely not full-length, so that he could admire the beauty of his sharp planed face, amber eyes, and black hair, without having to dwell on another part of his anatomy: his exceptionally bandy legs. Clive *hated* his legs. They were cartoon legs, worse than chicken legs, humiliatingly puny and grotesquely bowed. 'John Wayne' was his nickname at school, and not because he was a handsome burly cowboy. That was the main problem with being a waiter – too many opportunities for punters to look at his legs. If only desk jobs weren't so boring, he'd have gone for one like a shot.

Clive's restaurant (or rather, the restaurant of which his ex-girlfriend was assistant manager) was an upscale,

modern eatery, identical in ambience and menu to count-
less others in London. It was all halogen spotlights and
roasted sea bass, couscous, fennel fritters and coulis, and
frequented by hordes of beautiful, rich women – which,
for Clive, was the biggest perk of the job.

He made it his mission to see how many propositions he
could attract in one night. When he and Lisa started going
out, it became even more of a challenge to see if he could
still pull. He'd managed it twice before she caught him out.

'Birds,' he said to his reflection in disgust. 'They're so
damn clingy.'

After gulping down a carton of strawberry milk, Clive
slouched off to the tube. He didn't feel at all well. In fact,
his right leg seemed to be dragging very slightly, and he
hoped he wasn't about to have a heart attack.

At 5:34, four minutes late, he was pushing open the
heavy glass doors of Richmond's Place and heading for
the kitchen.

'Where's Burt?' Clive called over the top of the servery
to another of the sous-chefs, Mick. Mick was all right,
apart from the fact that he was always moaning about his
constipation. Clive had absolutely no patience with people
who harped on about their ailments.

'Phoned in sick,' said Lisa, who materialised beside
him. She was smirking – tactlessly, for someone who'd just
dumped him, he thought. He couldn't help wondering if
it was because of his bandy legs.

'Didn't you two go out last night?'

Clive hung up his coat and wrapped a large white apron
around his waist. He wore his longer than the other waiters, in the hope that it would cover up the worst of his

problem. Mick made a face at him behind Lisa's back, waving a thin but sharp vegetable knife in his direction, warning him not to get Burt into trouble. Everybody loved Burt. Clive couldn't imagine any of them sticking up for *him*, though.

'Yeah, we had a drink,' he replied, his fingers fumbling with the ties of his apron. 'Burt said he wasn't feeling great then – he went home soon after. Said he felt sick.'

Soon after had actually been six hours later but hey, Clive thought, it was all relative. And it earned him a wink from Mick.

'You look rough yourself,' said Lisa, fixing her unnaturally green eyes on his face. Clive was convinced that she wore coloured contact lenses, but had been unable to verify this, even on the occasions he'd stayed over at her place.

He stuck out his chin and ran a hand through his hair. 'Never felt better.'

'Good, because we need everyone to be on top form. We're packed tonight.'

By 7:30 the restaurant was already three-quarters full. Dido had been turned up from three to eight on the volume dial of the hidden stereo, and Lisa had dimmed the lights twice. Clive watched the bones in her wrist and hand flex beneath the thin covering of her skin as she twiddled the dimmer switch, and he felt nostalgic for what might have been. He didn't normally 'do' relationships, but there'd been something special about Lisa. Dammit, he even felt sad.

But by the time he had served sixteen portions of that evening's special – bream on a bed of pureed cauliflower with lemon-glaze carrots – any vestiges of sadness had been bludgeoned away by the pounding of his head. The chunks of bream, with their blackened scaly skin, were making him queasy. They looked like he felt: crispy with lifelessness.

Just then a group of four attractive women moved through the doors together, fluid as jellyfish, waving their arms, talking and laughing. Lisa showed them all to one of Clive's tables, where she distributed menus and wine lists.

Clive momentarily forgot his hangover and began making bets with himself as to which of these women he could score with. They were all a little bit older than him; early thirties, perhaps, and all sexy – although that black-haired one was a bit skinny. There were two short-haired blondes, one slim with glasses, and one more chunky, with a long nose. The last woman, a brunette, was particularly lovely; buxom, but not in an obvious way. Sparkly eyelids, but not overdone. Her, he thought. I want her.

'*Excuse* me,' said an irate middle-aged man with such a big stomach that his shirt buttons were almost popping. 'If you've *got a minute*, we'd like to order.' His girlfriend, an emaciated old bird in a miniskirt, tutted in agreement. She must have been at least forty-five, thought Clive with disdain. He didn't mind an older woman, but there came a time when females should admit defeat and cover up.

'Certainly, sir,' Clive said, whipping his order pad out of his apron pocket whilst simultaneously giving the customer's unattractive belly a hard stare, as if to say, *not that you need anything more to eat, fat boy*. He took the order, all the while straining his ears to try and eavesdrop on the table of women.

'He did what?' screeched the one with the glasses, her hand flying to her mouth. 'Oh, I'm sorry, but that man is just way too possessive of you.' She was addressing the gorgeous brunette.

Damn, thought Clive, she's already spoken for. Still, she hasn't met me yet, has she? He smirked faintly, noticing that his banging headache had subsided to a manageable throb.

'I *said*, what does that come with?' Fatboy was getting annoyed.

Clive checked his pad to see what he had automatically written down – the man's words having bypassed his brain completely and come straight out on the pad. Oh, right, he'd ordered the pheasant.

'It comes with sugarsnaps and baby new potatoes, sir,' he intoned, aware that his supercilious expression meant that he'd be kissing goodbye to a tip. Sometimes it was worth it, just to wind them up. Customers – he hated them. Unless there was something in it for him, such as a shag.

By the time Clive had taken the women's orders and poured their wine, he had gleaned that the brunette lived with her (possessive) husband in Camden; the black-haired one had recently become pregnant – she put her hand over the top of her empty wineglass when he approached with the bottle, and simpered, 'I wish I could drink for two as well as eat for two, but I'd better not,' and they all laughed; the blonde with glasses was celebrating a large bonus at work and would therefore treat them all tonight; and the tubby blonde had been feeling poorly earlier.

He thought he'd been doing pretty well on the flirtation

front. He met their eyes, smiled, nodded attentively, made sure he was standing underneath a spotlight so that it would give his hair a luxuriant sheen. And they were all responding beautifully; giggling and peering over their menus like geishas simpering behind fans. He was in there, definitely – but with which one? Any of them would do, frankly, even that pregnant one, at a push.

Just as he was walking away to get the women a new bottle of mineral water, it happened. His hypersensitive radar alerted him to the fact that they had all suddenly fallen silent; and then – then – there was a great, unanimous gale of uncontrollable but swiftly stifled *laughter*! He wheeled around to catch the pregnant one pointing towards him, quaking with hilarity.

Clive's bandy legs – the subject, he was sure, of the hilarity – almost buckled under the humiliation, and his hangover immediately returned at full blast.

How dare they? Those judgemental *bitches*! Had they no sensitivity? He felt his peaky skin warm into a flush. Risking a glance towards Lisa, he saw that she was biting the insides of her cheeks as if trying not to laugh too – oh God, this was terrible!

He stormed through the restaurant and out of the fire door at the back, crashing down the heavy metal bar with the heel of his hand to open it, and blundering outside. He leaned his head against the rough brick wall, breathing heavily. *Bitches, evil bitches.* He contemplated doing a runner, never coming back – but then he had a better idea . . .

Revenge was a dish best not served on a bed of pureed cauliflower, he thought, his mind racing through a rudimentary plan. The worm would turn. He was going to teach these women that you didn't laugh at Clive Sampson and get away with it.

Ten minutes later the plan was under way. He began with the pregnant one and the long-nosed blonde. Those two were easy to sort – pregnant women were always moaning about their ailments, and the blonde had already complained of feeling sick. So Clive crept back inside and sidled across to the pegs where the staff kept their coats. Glancing around to make sure no one was looking, he slipped his hand into the pocket of Mick's overcoat. Just as he'd anticipated, his fingers closed around a packet of laxatives – and, much to Clive's delight, Mick preferred his laxatives in powder form. It was no bother at all to surreptitiously empty all ten sachets of the medicine into two portions of mashed potato and mix it up.

His glee at the revenge plot almost made him forget the affliction which the women had been so cruelly mocking, but as he walked out with the two seasoned main courses, he was reminded again. It was almost beyond belief, the way that they appeared to find his unfortunate disability – for this is how Clive viewed his bandy legs – so hilarious.

He took a deep breath and forced his most beaming smile upon the women.

'Which of you beautiful ladies is having the sea bass?' he asked, inclining his head coquettishly, willing them to stop laughing. The long-nosed blonde and the skinny black-haired one put up their hands, still fighting back titters.

He slid their meals in front of them. 'Enjoy,' he said, before turning to gaze at the other two with rapturous attentiveness. 'Yours are just coming,' he murmured, his eyes flicking down the brunette's cleavage. She was delicious, creamy-skinned and perfect. Her husband really isn't going to be happy when he finds out she's been messing around with other men, thought Clive.

After he'd served a seafood risotto to the other blonde, and a skate wing to the brunette, he walked up to Lisa. Unbelievably, she too was still smirking.

'What's so damn funny?' he hissed at her.

'Nothing, Clive.'

He wanted to punch her. 'Right. Well. I'm just going on my break for ten minutes, okay?'

'Make sure you're back by the time table ten finish their mains, won't you?'

He nodded curtly and waited until she set off across the restaurant floor. Then he dived into the cloakroom. Coat, coat, what sort of coat had the brunette been wearing? Something big and red, he thought. There were only two red overcoats amongst all the tightly packed outerwear in there, and he found what he was looking for almost immediately.

Oh, this is too easy, he thought as he pulled her travel-card out of her coat pocket. Her name was Jayne Harmony. Very glamorous photo – she looked as if she was about to slide a tongue over her hot, glossy lips. He slipped the card out of the clear plastic folder and examined the back of it. *28a Mitchell Gardens, Camden*, it said in small neat black ink, and underneath, bingo! A telephone number, which he copied down on his pad, before replacing the card in her pocket.

'Fag break,' he said to the chef on his way past. The

chef glowered at him. He was arranging herbs around a steaming skate wing, white and terrifyingly skeletal on the plate.

Ponce, thought Clive, retrieving his mobile phone from his own coat pocket. Outside again, he lit a cigarette for appearance's sake, and took a deep drag. With the other hand, he dialled Jayne Harmony's telephone number.

'Hello?'

'Mr Harmony?'

'Who wants to know?'

'Jayne's husband?'

'Yes. Who is this?''

'I'm not telling you my name,' Clive paused. 'Perhaps you've already heard it, though. Perhaps when you're in bed with Jayne, she might have let it slip? Because she was always calling it out when *we* were together . . .' He let this sink in. 'Mr Harmony?'

'This is a wind-up . . .'

'No, Mr Harmony. Your wife was a great lay, by the way. She's decided it's time to move on to the next one, but that's her decision. I just thought you should know.'

The line went dead. Clive exhaled a plume of smoke, and smiled.

Back inside, he was unsurprised when the blonde with the glasses beckoned him over, a worried look on her face. She and Jayne Harmony were sitting alone at the table. Blimey, that was quick, he thought.

'Can we have the bill, please? One of our friends isn't feeling well.'

Only one of them? He had to bite his lip to stop himself saying it. Their plates both had pleasingly sizeable chunks of the mashed potato missing. 'Sorry to hear that, Madam. Nothing wrong with the food, was there?'

Jayne Harmony smiled. 'Oh no, it was lovely. Wish we could stay for dessert.'

He smiled back. 'You must come again.' Clearing the plates, he braced himself slightly as he turned away, waiting for more laughter, but none came. They must be too preoccupied with their sick friend, he thought. As he passed the Ladies, the long-nosed blonde emerged. She looked pale and shaken.

'Is everything all right, Madam?' he enquired.

'Can you call an ambulance, please? Our friend is very ill in there. She's in the early stages of pregnancy – it could be serious.'

'Right away, Madam. Sorry to hear it,' he lied, mentally tutting to himself. An ambulance! For a bit of diarrhoea! Women were such drama queens. Talk of the devil, he thought, as Lisa bustled over.

'This lady's friend is unwell.' He moved away, letting Lisa take over, and prepared their bill, which he handed to the woman with glasses. She flipped a gold Visa card onto the little tray without even looking at it. She was too busy gazing towards the door of the Ladies' and saying to Jayne, 'Should we go in and check?'

'No. We wouldn't be helping. We'll just let them know when the ambulance arrives.'

Both women looked upset. Good, thought Clive. He swiped the credit card through the machine – £120 – and then again – £400 – and took the first of the two printed receipts back out for the blond one to sign. Pity he couldn't keep the £400 – Lisa would notice if he removed any cash – and the woman would probably get it back eventually, but it would be a hell of a hassle for her.

He was already planning the Internet shopping he'd do when he got home. He could get anything delivered to that empty house next door – an iPod, perhaps. Maybe even a plane ticket to somewhere exotic. He'd had it with this dump.

Her name was Rebecca Murphy. She signed the slip in a flashy squiggle, adding only a measly ten pound tip. Clive was affronted as he peeled off the yellow copy and handed it back to her. The tight bitch! Still, it only took a minute to copy her card number and expiry date into his notepad.

A voice behind him made him jump. 'Could we have our coats please?' It was the other blonde, looking a bit green around the gills. Jayne Harmony came up beside her.

'You know, Jayne, I think I'm coming out in sympathy with Eileen. I don't feel at all well.'

'Is it the same thing you had yesterday?'

'Might be. I've just suddenly got a really bad stomach-ache. Is Liz okay going to hospital with Eileen?'

Jayne nodded. 'I think so. I'd go myself, only I promised Steve I wouldn't be late. You know what he's like.'

'Look after yourself, then. Let's meet for coffee on Saturday. Eleven o'clock at Sergios?'

'Oh God, I've got to go . . .' The blonde bolted into the disabled toilet, just as a blue swirl of ambulance lights lit the restaurant, and two ambulancemen rushed in, carrying a stretcher. The diners' eyes were out on stalks.

Clive quietly lifted his coat off the peg and, for the final time, slipped out of the fire exit and caught the tube home, dreaming of the extended holiday he'd have on Rebecca Murphy's credit card.

By Friday everything was organised. He rang Lisa and told her he'd broken his leg, and wouldn't be back at work for three weeks. As predicted, she told him not to bother coming back at all. He tutted to himself – talk about loyalty to your staff! It was a joke. Courtesy of Rebecca Murphy he had a one-way flight to Goa all booked and paid for, plus a mini iPod, a new rucksack, new trainers, and a small tent. They'd all arrived by Next Day Delivery at the empty house next door (which he entered via a back window, to wait for his purchases). He was due to leave on Saturday afternoon.

One thing, though, still nagged at him. He didn't feel guilty or anything – why should he? They'd been laughing at him. But he suddenly really wanted to know how it had all turned out. If Rebecca had stopped her card. How sick the others had been. What Jayne Harmony's husband had done . . .

Against his better judgement, he found himself pushing open the door of Sergio's coffee shop in Camden at 10:45 on Saturday morning, his rucksack on his back, shades hiding his eyes and a baseball cap rammed low on his head.

He ordered a cappuccino and pretended to read a newspaper. At 10:55 Jayne Harmony walked in. She too was wearing shades, but they didn't hide the livid violet bruise covering her cheekbone and eye socket. She sat down at a nearby table with her back to him.

Five minutes later, Rebecca arrived. The two women

greeted one another sombrely, their muted kisses so different from the exuberant entrance into the restaurant the week before. Rebecca cried when she saw her friend's face.

'He went mad,' Jayne said quietly. Clive had to strain to hear her. 'Called me a slag, accused me of having all kinds of affairs . . . I think he's schizophrenic. I've left him. I'm staying at my mother's. I'm glad, in a way, that I've found out what he's really like. I always did have my doubts – you know that.'

Good, thought Clive. He'd done her a favour after all, then. Perhaps when he came back from his trip, he might look Jayne up, see if she fancied a drink or two. Now that she was free.

'And how's Eileen?'

'She's going to be fine. They said she was very lucky not to have a miscarriage.'

Something unfamiliar prickled at the back of Clive's neck – guilt. He dismissed it. There had probably been something else wrong with her, not laxative-related at all.

'Guess what? They did a scan, and it turns out she's having twins! Can you believe it? She's over the moon.'

'That's incredible. Well, she always did want a big family. Did you know that Liz had a stomach upset too? She's better now, though. Actually she's quite chuffed – she lost six pounds in four days.'

Clive felt faintly annoyed. His big revenge plot was turning out to be a damp squib. Of course, he wouldn't have wanted the skinny one to lose her babies, but still, they all seemed a bit overly fine. And Rebecca obviously had no idea about her credit card's adventures, either. Oh well, he thought. No harm done. I taught them a lesson.

Now I'm off on a well-deserved holiday. He put down the newspaper and swung the heavy rucksack onto his back. Without leaving a tip, he began to walk towards the door. Rebecca opened her mouth as if to say something else, but Jayne interrupted her, her voice bright again.

'Still – we did have *one* good laugh,' she said.

Rebecca snorted into her coffee. 'How could I ever forget?'

They suddenly giggled, and both began to talk at the same time:

'That waiter . . .'

'That *prat* . . .'

'Thought he was God's gift . . .'

'Really fancied himself . . .'

'And all the time walking about—'

'*With last night's underpants sticking out the bottom of his trouser leg!*' they chorused hysterically.

Clive swallowed hard and walked past them, turning sideways to manoeuvre himself and his rucksack through the door. He headed for the tube to catch the Piccadilly Line to Heathrow Airport, unaware of the burly detective sergeant who'd be waiting for him at the check-in desk. Visa's computers had picked up certain irregularities on Rebecca Murphy's credit card, informed her, and she had told the police. If Clive had stayed in the coffee shop long enough to delve in his pockets for a tip, he'd have heard her telling Jayne all about it.

Fiona Walker

The Kato Lover

'How do I make Kate say "oh"?' he asked as he thrust away enthusiastically. 'How do I do that, baby? Make Kate say "oh, ohhhh, OHHHH!" Kate – oh!'

'Kato?'

'Yes, baby. I want to make Kate say "oh".'

Kate watched his face and fought giggles.

They were making love, she reminded herself. Think passion. Do *not* think Peter Sellers with a moustache, under attack.

'Oh!' she managed to squeak.

'Yes, Kate – oh! How do I make Kate say "oh" again – how, Kate – oh!'

She chewed back the delight. 'You could try hiding in the wardrobe, catching me unawares and then leaping on me.'

'Eh?' The tempo slowed briefly and then he plunged on. 'I was . . . thinking . . . Christ that's good . . . more along the lines of . . . you going on top.'

Kate, who had formed a very comfortable nest amongst the pillows, had no intention of moving. Tonight, she was on a missionary mission.

'You carry on like that, darling – it feels just great.' She tried to hurry him along. She had an early start in the morning. Her recent fight with the giggles was a fair second to the orgasm that would take forever to arrive. 'That feels great – *mmm*.'

Afterwards, she stared up at the ceiling in the dark and wondered if their sex life was ever going to get any better. It had been so wonderful once. She missed the laughter. She knew that she was guilty of becoming lazy and complacent, but Sandy was equally guilty of sameness. Their lovemaking had changed from bawdy five-act opera to predictable soap – three episodes a week with an omnibus repeat at weekends. And the storylines kept coming round again and again.

Rolling onto her side, she remembered how much they had giggled at first, white-hot passion and mirth seeming so natural together. As the years passed, sex had to be timetabled into the short gaps between his shift-work and her nine-to-five, and it had become a far more intermittent, serious business. The spark that had once ignited carnal firecrackers now lit faithful and sombre church candles – the flame yet to be snuffed out, but the dirge well under way.

'We could try something a bit different next time,' she suggested tentatively.

'Is that what all that hiding in the wardrobe stuff was about?' he asked sleepily, as he spooned his belly against her back in a post-coital moment of openness.

'Maybe,' she seized the togetherness second. 'You remember Kato, the character from the *Pink Panther* films who leaps on Inspector Clouseau when he least expects it?'

There was a long pause as post-coital openness closed its tired eyes.

'You want me to attack you when you least expect it?' he humoured her.

'Not attack – ravish.'

There was another pause and then he gave the nape of her neck a drowsy kiss. 'Leaping out from a confined space practising martial arts is hardly seductive, Kate.'

Put like that, he had a point. She tried to explain it better: 'I thought you pouncing on me without warning might spice things up a bit?'

A tired yawn almost unlocked his jaw but closed proceedings. 'I'm not into wife beating, baby. Let's go to sleep.'

You beat me in the race to an orgasm every time these days, Kate thought silently as he gave her a sluggish goodnight kiss on the ear, then rolled his spine to hers with a final slump and sigh.

Listening as his breath deepened in sleep, she imagined an athletic figure dressed in black hiding in the en suite and enjoyed a brief shiver at the thought. It was ages since she'd enjoyed a really good fantasy.

'You've done *what?*' her sister gasped the following week.

'I've taken a lover.'

'Good God, Kate. Does Sandy suspect anything?'

'This is a Kato lover. He's very discreet.'

Her sister studied her wisely and then laughed. 'Is this one of your imaginary friends?'

'I'm far too old for imaginary friends.' Kate winked.

He hid in the wardrobe the first time. Kate knew that he was in there – the fact that he had been forced to remove half her clothes and drape them over a chair in order to fit himself in gave the game away – but she still experienced a rare frisson of excitement and fear. Humming the tune to the *Pink Panther*, she moved around the bedroom as she undressed, helpfully indicating her whereabouts. When her back was turned, he stole out from his lair and kissed her throat.

'Don't look round,' he ordered, slipping a scarf around her eyes.

Kate almost fainted with anticipation.

'What exactly does this Kato lover *do*?' Kate's sister asked, taking in her bright eyes and beaming smile the next day.

'He catches me by surprise.'

'Isn't that rather alarming?'

'Not if you're hoping it will happen all the time.'

'What if Sandy catches you by surprise with your Kato lover?'

'That's the whole point.'

The next time, he hid beneath the bed and waited until she was almost asleep before rolling out and pouncing. Over the coming week, he holed up in the boxroom, the airing cupboard, the larder, the coal bunker, the garage and then the cupboard under the stairs – leaping out amid a clatter of ironing board crashing on vacuum cleaner. Whether hot-tank sweaty, coal-dust grubby or surrounded by domestic appliances, he was the most exciting thing in her life, and she thought about him night and day.

He hid beneath the dining room table, behind the sofa and in the garden shed. He leapt out from the most unexpected places, charging even mundane tasks with sexual anticipation. Foreplay had never been so much fun.

'Oh, Kate!' Sandy gasped as she bounced joyously around on top of him, facing his feet, his big hands on her waist.

She eyed the wardrobe dreamily, thinking about her Kato lover who had just been hiding there.

'I love you, baby!' he called out. 'Oh, Kate, oh, Kate, oh, OH!'

Moaning in delight as she rode him home, Kate couldn't agree more. 'Kato! Oh, Kato!'

'You're looking fantastic.' Kate's sister eyed her enviously. 'Are you on a new wonder drug?'

'I've told you. I have a Kato lover. He's the perfect tonic.'

'Well, yours has taken years off you. Can I borrow him?'

'Absolutely not.'

'Are you sure Sandy doesn't suspect anything?'

'Of course not,' Kate smiled. 'He's having a wonderful time. Which reminds me, he's on a late shift tonight. I want to cook a special meal. I know he'll want steak and I don't have a clue, so . . . ?'

'Hot pan, knob of butter, sizzle three minutes each

side – keep it very pink inside. Then take the meat out, swirl the butter in the pan, add red wine and peppercorns. Serve.'

'So I take them out when the middle's still pink, pan the butter and add the extras?'

Kate's sister nodded thoughtfully, eyes narrowing. 'Are you trying to tell me something?'

'Got to go!' Kate leapt up and aimed random kisses at two pale cheeks.

'Kate, I should tell you I'm meeting . . .' Her sister threw her hands up in despair as she was left alone. '. . . Sandy later,' she tutted under her breath. 'Oh, Kate.'

That evening there was a note on the kitchen table. '*Why not surprise me for once?*'

Kate's eyebrows shot up. The suggestion made her anxious and euphoric at the same time. She might have to wait in a confined space for hours, and he had already used the best hiding places in the house. Yet he would surely love the thrill that she had in store for him.

She went for a quick scout around, dismissing the wardrobes and under-stairs cupboard as too obvious. If she was going to lie in wait for him it had to be comfortable and it had to be somewhere he would never think to look.

Her eyes alighted on the loft-hatch in the ceiling above the bed. They had boarded the attic space last year. It was perfect, she realised as she hooked down the loft ladder and trotted up it to recce her lair beneath the eaves of the roof. Now all she had to do was dress for the occasion.

Kato always wore a black polo-neck and trousers – part jewel thief, part Milk Tray Man. Kate adopted the colour-scheme as she selected a lacy bodice, G-string and stockings – might as well go for the full impact. She sprayed herself liberally with scent, gathered a torch, high heels, a magazine, a big bar of chocolate and some breath fresheners before ascending the ladder and pulling it up behind her.

On closer inspection, it was very cold and cobwebby in the roof, and the duvet stored up there felt damp and clammy as she wrapped herself in it. She hoped he wouldn't be long.

'I'm worried about her,' Sandy told his sister-in-law as they settled in a corner table at the village pub. 'She's been acting very strangely.'

'In what way?'

He cleared his throat, editing the more graphic details. 'She gets agitated every time I open the wardrobe; she keeps taking everything out of the cupboards – and she asks me to check under the bed and in the garden shed all the time.'

'Well, there have been a lot of burglaries in your area.'

He sighed. 'Perhaps I'm over-reacting, but I love Kate – oh, believe me, I love her.'

Kate's sister's eyes twitched. 'Of course you do. Kate – oh, she's a diamond.'

'Absolutely. She thinks I'm on a late shift tonight and—'

'You think your diamond might get stolen while you're away?'

Sandy balked. 'Look, I hate to drag you into this, but you know her better than anyone. I need answers. You must have picked up on it. I think she might be—'

'Having an affair?' The eyes twitched again.

He looked up sharply from his pint. 'I was going to say "having a breakdown".'

'Oh . . . whoops. Freudian slip.'

'You mean she *is* having an affair?'

Kate's sister was fed up with the carry-on. With clues so blatant, she was amazed Sandy still hadn't twigged. It was time to throw some light upon the jewel that every thief wanted to steal and that dear, unwitting Sandy had firmly in his grasp. Her eyes were twitching uncontrollably now.

'You should know Kate by now, you fool. She has a very vivid imagination. She latches onto an idea and becomes obsessed. She used to have all these imaginary friends as a child and now she has 'dream' lovers in the same—'

'Who *is* the bastard?' Sandy raged. 'I'll kill him!'

His sister-in-law sighed and clasped a hand to her twitching eyes, knowing that he didn't understand what she was saying. 'She calls him Kato.'

At last! Kate could hear somebody crashing around below. She carefully laid her magazine and chocolate to one side, knocked back a breath freshener and straightened her suspenders. It was time to act.

He was moving about immediately below her now, making a surprising amount of noise. He appeared to be pulling out drawers and upending things. Why did Sandy always have to be so messy?

Kate pressed her hands to her lips to calm herself. This was supposed to be a sexual fantasy, not a domestic scrap. *She* was the Kato lover now. And she couldn't wait to get out of the chilly attic.

In her plans, she hadn't considered how best to lower herself from the roof hatch. Putting down the ladder and clambering out was hardly sexy – the sight of her white bottom dangling from above the bed wasn't her fantasy at all. She'd just have to dive out head-first and aim for a slick SAS landing on the mattress. Very Lara Croft.

She stealthily lifted the hatch and peered out.

It was dark in the room – strange, given that he appeared to be searching for something just out of her line of vision. Why look for it in the dark?

Still, it at least gave her much-needed cover. She licked her lips, crouched carefully by the hole beneath her, eyed her landing spot and sprang out.

Sandy spotted the white van parked just around the corner from his front drive, half-hidden in the trees. Bastard! He was in the house right now with Kate. Much as he longed to leap out of his own car and slash the van's tyres, he was in too much of a hurry.

The front door was ajar. He slipped silently inside.

The noise coming from upstairs was unmistakeable – grunts and groans and those little wails Kate let out when she was excited. God, they were going at it like animals!

Furiously, Sandy stormed up to confront them.

The sight of his wife in black lacy underwear, straddling a man dressed in black almost finished him off.

'You bitch!'

'Sandy!' She had the grace to look terrified.

'You harlot!' he bellowed.

She seemed to be trying to wrap a stocking around her lover's neck – auto-asphyxiation, Sandy registered in contempt. He'd never seen this side if her. What's more, she seemed to want him to join in:

'Quick, grab him!'

'Whoa!' He backed away, appalled.

'He's broken into the house!'

In the face of such overwhelming evidence to the contrary, Sandy snarled and stepped back further, punching out at a wall and then fighting tears as the pain from his smashed knuckles joined that from his broken heart.

'Don't think you can fool me with that one! You might be quick-witted, Kate, but it's bloody obvious what's going on here.'

There was a muffled groan from the man that Kate was still straddling. It was hard to make out what he was saying under his balaclava, but it sounded almost like '*please get her off me!*'

'How could you do this to me, Kate?' Sandy yelled. 'You were my life!'

'Call the police!' She looked up at him wildly as the man beneath her fought to struggle free.

'You were my life!' Sandy repeated.

Moments later, sixteen stone of balaclava-ed terror had crashed his way down the stairs to flee the house.

'You idiot!' Kate slumped back on her heels, her stockings shredded. 'You let him get away.'

'I'm so sorry,' Sandy muttered. 'I didn't realise you wanted him to hang around for a nightcap – and a threesome.'

'I'm calling the police.' She crawled to the phone.

'Good. Tell them someone stole my diamond from under my nose.'

The police tried hard to hide their smiles as they told Sandy and Kate that this was – *ahem* – not the first time a husband had mistaken an intruder for his adulterous wife's lover.

'I am not adulterous!' Kate wailed.

Sandy remained unconvinced. 'You have a lover – your sister told me.'

'I've never been unfaithful to you.'

'What about Kato?' he accused.

'He's a character in a film! I just used him as a fantasy.'

'You fantasised about *Burt Kwouk*?' He seemed appalled. 'Who?'

'He's the actor who played Kato.'

'No! He wasn't my fantasy. You were Kato. *You* were.'

'Liar!' He laughed disbelievingly. 'You're just trying to cover up a seedy affair —'

'Our sex life had become so mundane, Sandy.'

He cleared his throat, looking at the police inspectors who were swigging tea nearby. 'Not now, Kate – oh!'

She kicked him on the shin. 'Don't you dare accuse me of having an affair again! You thought my Kato idea was stupid, so I daydreamed about it instead. It was innocent fun. And tonight I thought I'd try it on you.'

'Well, I wish you'd warned me.'

'How was I to know someone would break into the house?'

'Yes, all too convenient an alibi!' Sandy might be as macho and compassionate as a fire-fighter hooking a kitten from a high branch, but he was hopeless at arguments. 'You're just making this up – you always were a pants-on-fire liar!'

Kate's temper ignited fully. 'My pants hadn't been on fire for months before the Kato idea came along – that's the point!'

'Liar!' Sandy roared, playing to the crowd. 'Arrest her for wasting police time!'

The police didn't stay for a second cup of tea. Politely asking Kate and Sandy to leave everything where it was until their SOC team arrived, they beat a hasty retreat.

The argument raged through the night and soon the mess created by the balaclava burglar was joined by the mess created when Sandy and Kate threw things at one another. Before long, the scene of the crime was beyond disturbed – it was demolished as they slung bra after belt after necklace after compact disc. Kate even tried for a couple of karate chops, but missed.

'How can you be jealous of something that was just a figment of my imagination?' she screamed at him.

'And how can you accuse me of being a boring lover? I'd do anything for you. You're the one who can never be bothered to make an effort.'

'*Hello?* I just hid in the roof for you and waited for hours!'

'Thanks, but I'd rather you dressed up as a French maid in future.'

'You sexist pig!'

'Cow!'

'Warthog.'

'Bitch.'

'Big pink panther.'

He was momentarily wrong-footed. '*Panther?*'

Realising that the animal analogies were used up, Kate fled, leaving the door swinging.

She begged temporary shelter with her sister. Not that the fighting ended there.

'I can't believe you told him I was having an affair!' Kate fumed on, picking out a new target over sauvignon and sympathy.

'I did point out that it was probably a figment of your imagination.'

'You *what?*'

'Well it was, wasn't it?'

Kate hung her head. Her sister always cut to the chase, unlike Sandy, who could cut heartstrings and arteries without ever getting to the point. She guiltily remembered all the delicious times Kato had leapt from his hiding place around the house, intent on carnal pleasure.

'I just liked to imagine – when Sandy and I made love – that he'd been, sort of hiding.'

'*Hiding?*'

'Like Kato.'

'You fool, Kate – oh, you are weird sometimes. I'll have another word with him,' her sister offered with a wry smile. 'Sometimes you hide your true feelings in the oddest of places. Sandy loves you very much, I have no doubt, but he needs help understanding you. Who can blame him? Lord knows, it's taken the rest of your family a lifetime to figure you out.'

Sandy polished off another scotch and looked at the scribbled reply he had left that morning to Kate's note asking what he wanted for supper.

Why not surprise me for once?

Well, she had done that, all right.

And then it hit him. His daft, dreamy Kate really had been telling the truth all along. She had wanted him to hide around the house waiting to seduce her unexpectedly, and he hadn't even noticed. When she had tried to be the Kato lover herself, she'd jumped on an unsuspecting burglar.

'Kate, oh, you fool – you gorgeous fool.'

He started to laugh. Poor, sweet Kate. He had to make it up to her.

And when he saw car headlights coming along the drive, he didn't hesitate. He slipped the back door off the latch and crept into the sitting room to hide.

'What do you mean, arrested?' Kate clutched her mobile to her ear in shock.

'The police had a patrol car cruising past our house. They guessed we might be targeted again – our burglar has been quite busy in the area, it seems. When they spotted me behaving suspiciously through the front window, they thought I was him.'

'What were you doing?'

'Trying to hide in the ottoman. I gave your sister a terrible shock. She fainted on the hearthrug when I jumped out. Then the police stormed in and arrested me.'

Kate started to giggle and then stopped herself. But the laughter that came down the opposite end of the line knew no such self-control. 'Oh, Kate! Kate, oh Kate. We will make love in every cupboard dressed as Ninjas from now on if it makes you happy. Just come and take me home. I love –' He couldn't speak for laughing.

Neither Kate nor Sandy tried to hide from one another for a long time after that. They didn't hide their bodies or their feelings. They made love far more often and with far more effort. Sandy tried hard to be more spontaneous and Kate tried to explain better what made her go '*oh*'.

Occasionally, Sandy dressed all in black and crept up behind her, but that was as far as it went. Kate bought a French maid's outfit that made them both laugh far too much for hot action.

It was almost six months later that they found themselves spending a lazy Sunday afternoon in bed watching *The Return of the Pink Panther*. When Kato leapt out of the fridge to attack Clouseau in his apartment, they exchanged a long, excited look.

'You're where?' Kate's sister asked as she received a crackly phone call the following evening. 'Casualty? Oh God, is it serious?'

She listened for a long time. 'Kate, it's the middle of summer. How on earth did you both get *frostbite*?'

Daisy Waugh

Breaking Away

She could have given up smoking, got married, started a family or come into some money. She could have decided that the grey old city she'd been living in all these years, as blissfully discontented as the rest of her acquaintances, was no longer the city for her, and that she was going to fuck off to live somewhere nicer. Where the sun shone. And the vegetables still tasted. And the houses were cheap and didn't all look the same. And the streets weren't clogged with cars, and the pavements weren't covered in gob and gum. And where keeping up with one's friends – their bank accounts, their careers and their impeccable bloody 'life-style choices' – wasn't quite so relentlessly disheartening.

Susie Hall, mid-thirties, professional, trundling through an averagely unpleasant West London life, with a nice boy-friend, plenty of successful friends and a well-decorated but nonetheless depressing – and absurdly overpriced – base-ment flat, had spent many evenings fantasising about all of the above. She dreamed of escape.

So it ought not to have come as a surprise when, one Tuesday night in early spring, she put in a call to her two oldest, closest, dearest friends, Poppy Starke and Travis Holby. Poppy and Travis lived and worked together, and had done since their adulthoods began. Susie rang them at the office.

'*Poppy!*' Susie said. There was a note of creamy triumph in her voice which might have been a little irritating. 'I've got – I mean *we*, Sylvester and I – *we've* got *so much* to tell you. Can you and Travis meet us in the Bush Bar later tonight? Early or late. It doesn't even matter. Any time. Only please say yes. We want you guys to be the first to know.' She laughed a little breathlessly, Susie did – Susie, who usually sounded so calm. 'We've got *so much* good news, I swear I'm not even going to know where to *start*!'

Now. Who could resist an invitation like that?

Poppy smiled. Broadly. Susie and Sylvester were broke (compared with Poppy and Travis) and rarely suggested meeting anywhere but Pizza Express. Drinks at the Bush Bar cost serious money. Or they did when you got glugging, as old friends like Poppy, Susie, Sylvester and Travis invariably did. So Poppy said, with sincerity, 'My God, how *exciting*. What are you going to tell us? Can't you tell me now?' Susie said she couldn't.

'Bloody hell. You're killing me, Snooze. I'm not sure I can wait!'

Susie (Snooze) Hall and her boyfriend Sylvester had been enjoying quite a run of good news recently, registered Poppy quietly, as she and her old friend chatted on. For example Ikea, having messed up with the delivery of a sofa and armchair, had sent them a gift token, virtually unsolicited, for

£150. Most people only got £50. Then Sylvester had found some deal to New York on lastminute.com, and they'd taken themselves off for a weekend of sex and shopping. Just like that. Which was fun for them. And then last week – this one had been a little harder to swallow – Susie, who worked quite low down at Radio 4, had somehow managed to find a small publisher willing to take on her collection of love poems. Which, for the record, Poppy had read and secretly told Travis she thought were *utter crap*.

Poppy and Travis worked in television, the way a lot of people do who can afford to live in nice big houses with solid oak floors in Shepherd's Bush. They owned their own production company, with offices in Soho, and currently had not one but *two* shows running on different UK cable channels. The first was a thing for young mothers, people stuck at home mid-morning with no sensible means of escape. It featured a group of leather-faced women 'pundits' curled onto comfy chairs, gusting coffee-breath at one another and laughing uproariously at each other's lady-jokes. The usual drivel.

The other show was not quite so good: a late-night sort of dating show, in which contestants had to guess one another's personalities by the shape of their naked bottoms. That one was bad. That one was devastating drivel. Poppy and Travis could laugh about it, and they did, for example with Susie and Sylvester. But at the same time it did pay the mortgage. And as anybody living in Shepherd's Bush would tell you, that is no mean feat.

Poppy and Travis weren't doing anything that Tuesday night, unusually enough, and the thought at four o'clock of getting pissed on the Bush Bar's caipirinhas almost made Poppy dribble, made her yearn for eight o'clock. Ditto Travis, when she put a hand over the mouthpiece and shouted across at him. Travis loved cocktails almost as much as Poppy did, and he was sufficiently metropolitan not even to be ashamed of it.

So they were in for the long haul. One long night of celebrating Susie and Sylvester's exciting surprises, whatever they may be. And it would be fine. It would be *fun*. Besides, Poppy and Travis had enjoyed their own fair share of good news over the years, and Susie and Sylvester had always been there for them. For example, when they won the *Bums Away!* contract, Susie and Sylvester had sent them a whole case of champagne, and a giant bunch of helium balloons in the shape of bottoms. Which, as Travis said to Sylvester, and Poppy said to Susie, must have cost them a fortune they could ill afford.

Poor-old-Sylvester, Travis had taken to calling him recently, as Sylvester's worldly fortunes waned (and Travis's restaurant-girth expanded). Sylvester had started life so full of ambition and promise. But then he'd dropped out of journalism for some quasi-ethical reason nobody had been much persuaded by, and last month he had completed a year-long course in landscape gardening. Very nice and everything, Poppy and Travis agreed. Nobody would ever argue that Sylvester wasn't nice. But how was that going to pay the mortgage, or the school fees, or whatever?

It was actually getting to the point now, Poppy and Travis also agreed, where it could be quite embarrassing going out with them. For example, when they were in restaurants together, Poppy sometimes felt quite self-conscious about ordering expensive items from the menu.

Anyway, none of that mattered. Not tonight. Poppy and Travis adored their old friends. Ever since university, they'd been getting high together, making plans together, drowning their sorrows together and doing a whole lot of other things, some of which they didn't even like to talk about. They knew each other inside and out. Literally. And Poppy loved Susie, and Susie loved Travis, and Sylvester loved Poppy, and Travis loved Susie, and everybody loved everybody, and that was that.

Susie and Sylvester were already into their second round of drinks by the time their friends arrived. They had their arms linked and their foreheads almost touching and they . . . glowed. It was unmissable. And astonishing, honestly. After twelve years together, they still looked like a couple newly in love.

They glimpsed Poppy and Travis making their way over – late, as usual. And they might have pulled apart, if they'd wanted to. But neither of them did. Just for a second or two they pretended not to notice.

Beside him, Travis felt Poppy tense a little; felt the tremor of failure travel through her, the tremor of resentment that she and Travis couldn't look at each other in the same way. And he simultaneously felt his own buttock muscles clenching, as they always did at moments of stress or emotional awkwardness. (It was how he had come up with the *Bums Away!* brainwave, needless to say.) Travis truly believed that the human arse held secrets to its owner's personality. His own was spotty but toned – and a lot less flabby than the rest of his body, because of all the clenching. But what does that really tell us? Anything much? Possibly not. The point is, some people look out and see only poetry in the world. Others may see only pretension, injustice, cowardice, conspiracy, and so on. Travis wasn't so limited. He saw the world – all of it, including his own bottom – entirely in terms of how it might work on low-budget television.

'Okay guys, break it up!' yelled Poppy merrily, swooping for the usual hugs. Susie and Sylvester did a mini-jump, as if they hadn't been expecting her. 'Sorry we're late,' Poppy said. *Kiss kiss.* 'Some sod in LA called just as we were leaving. I'm beginning to think they do it on purpose. Either that or they haven't yet clocked that the world is round and we work in a different time zone over here. *Oooph!*' She collapsed onto the banquette beside them. 'Well done getting a table,' she said over the general hubbub. 'Budge up, Sylv. Christ! I'm *gagging* for a drink. Travis, darling, be a love. Don't sit – please. It'll only waste precious drinking time. Go and fetch us some caipirinhas.'

Travis looked faintly pissed off. Hesitated.

'Ooooh. *Please-please-please-please,*' she cajoled him, sweetly. 'Get a round for all of us.'

'I think I'll have something soft, actually, Travis,' Susie said significantly. 'Maybe some elderflower juice.'

But Poppy wasn't listening. 'In fact, get six,' she ordered. 'Get eight. They always take so bloody long to make.'

Sylvester paled. Did the maths. Said nothing, since – though they maintained the Going Dutch charade right up until the end of every evening they ever spent together – Poppy and Travis always wound up footing the bill. Which was okay, Susie and Sylvester thought, because they were all such old friends, and because everybody knew Susie and Sylvester did lovely gardening and lovely poetry and cared about the environment and things and were therefore always broke. 'But be quick, mate,' Sylvester shouted after him. 'Or Poppy'll have got all our news out of us before you get back.'

Travis returned fifteen minutes later with a tray full of caipirinhas and nothing soft, having failed to register Susie's elderflower request.

'*Travis!*' Poppy exclaimed, her voice full of leaden excitement, her teeth grinding with difficult smiles, unspoken hurt, and all her untold reservations. 'You'll never guess. Remember that awful guy James Russell? Works at the *Guardian*?'

'Don't think so.'

'Anyway, he had dinner with Snooze and Sylv last week. He's put in a bid for two hundred thou for the flat! Cash bid. Wants to be in next month. Can you believe it?'

'Really?' Travis said comfortably, balancing the tray, looking for somewhere to rest it. 'I didn't even know it was for sale.'

'Well it wasn't,' Susie beamed. 'That's what's so amazing!'

'So – well, that's good news. Is it? I presume it is. Where are you going to live?'

Poppy grabbed a caipirinha from Travis's tray and sucked it up in a single gulp. 'The south of France, darling,' she said brightly. 'They're going to live in the south of France.'

'Oh—'

'*Mmm.* And Susie's given up smoking.'

'*Susie?*' Travis began to laugh. 'Not *smoking?* This is all a joke, right?'

Poppy slugged back a second drink, also in one. 'She's pregnant.'

'*Oh!*'

'Yes. Isn't it fab? Fabulous. Isn't it *fabulous?*' Poppy said.

'. . . I know it's a bit sudden,' Susie murmured, having finally peered through the haze of her own smugness and noticed the unhappy faces of her oldest friends. 'But you know . . . you get to a point in life . . . oh,' she giggled, unable to contain herself even that long. 'And we're going to get *married*, too! In Carcassonne, we thought. On one of the little turrets. Have you been to Carcassonne? I think it's the most romantic place in the—'

'*Married?*' interrupted Poppy in astonishment. '*Married?* I didn't think you believed in marriage. But you do!' she added quickly. 'Goodness. Well. All these surprises. Anyway, I'm so happy for you,' she said, really trying to be. Smiling at them. 'And I think you're both very, very *clever.*'

'Thank you,' Susie said.

And then Poppy turned to Travis. The smile on her face became a little more fixed. 'Sylvester says one of the main reasons they want to escape to rural France is because they can't stand any more British telly!'

Sylvester groaned. 'She's taking what I said out of context. *As usual.*'

'Most particularly,' Poppy continued, a glint in her eyes, 'British telly shows like ours.'

'It's not what he meant, Poppy, and you know it,' Susie

said. 'We just meant . . .' She reached across, more or less unconsciously, and took Sylvester's hand. 'After James put in his bid we got to thinking just how lovely it would be to get away from it all, lead a quieter, simpler life; one that isn't so career-focused. In a place where the pervading culture isn't so damn aggressive and so damn *dumb* . . .'

'See?' Poppy said.

'Oh, come on, Poppy. You know it as well as I do. The kind of telly shows you make are – I'm not saying it's your fault. We're not *blaming* you. It's what gets commissioned these days. But they're typical, aren't they? Of the way our culture is going? And we just don't want to be a part of that culture any more . . . You can understand that, can't you?'

'Absolutely,' Travis said lightly. '*Absolutely*. Well—'

'. . . and then I realised I was pregnant. And honestly – to bring a *child* up in this kind of sniping, sleazy, backbiting environment . . .' She shrugged. 'Plus it all seemed so incredibly auspicious. Such perfect timing, the baby and everything. It just seemed *perfect*.'

'Well, well, well!' Travis said – at last. He pulled himself up to his full height and slapped Sylvester hard on the back. Very hard. 'What can we say? Congratulations, mate. Really. And you, Suze. Snoozy Suze. We're bloody heartbroken you're leaving. But seriously – *congratulations!*' He glanced across at the array of expensive cocktails in front of him. 'I think we should forget about these, and get some champagne down us right away. Don't you?'

After that everyone – apart from Susie, of course, who ordered herself some grilled lobster, to make up, and then fresh figs and pasteurised cheeses, and pears poached in a rare pudding wine – got uproariously drunk. Appallingly, filthily, stinkily drunk. Travis and Poppy, who could drink more and faster than just about anyone, kept ordering more and more bottles of champagne. And delicious champagne it was too, Sylvester commented, glugging it back.

'C'mon,' slurred Travis again and again, and then again. 'It's not every day your best friends announce they're pissing off to the south of France. *Let'z-gedanuther-one!*'

'Actually, Travis,' Susie screwed up her face apologetically, 'I don't want to be a spoilsport, but I've really *got* to go to bed.'

'Me too,' Sylvester nodded. 'I'm wasted.'

They called for the bill, and a slightly sour silence fell. Suddenly Travis laughed. Not a particularly nice laugh, either. 'You're going to go bust,' he said. 'You do know that, don't you? Sixty-five per cent of English people who do what you're doing crawl back home with their tails between their legs within eighteen months. You're going to lose everything.'

'Don't be mean,' Poppy said vaguely, lighting herself one last cigarette. 'They've obviously thought it through.'

'Of course they haven't,' Travis snapped. He drained his glass. '. . . make a great TV series, though.'

'Shut up, Travis,' Susie and Sylvester said simultaneously, and smiled at one another.

'Seriously, though,' Travis persisted. 'We could call it *Breaking Away*. Or *Breaking Up*. Or *Going Broke*.' He chortled. '*Making a Prat of Yourself*. There are endless possibilities.'

'Piss off,' Sylvester said, more irritably this time. 'We don't want anything to do with your tacky TV shows. So forget it.'

And then the bill arrived. Travis pounced on it, as he always did. Slowly, he opened it up.

Sylvester belched. 'Nasty feeling about this one,' he said casually. 'We haven't exactly held back.'

Travis looked at the bottom line and whistled. It was usually at this point – it was always at this point – that Travis or Poppy shrugged, pulled out their platinum credit cards and told Susie and Sylvester the night was on them.

But this time nobody shrugged. Nobody pulled out anything.

'Jesus!' Travis muttered. 'You're bloody right, Sylvester. It's a biggie, all right.' Travis showed it to Poppy.

'*Travis!*' Poppy scowled. 'You ordered the most expensive – and *four* bottles of it! What the hell were you *thinking* of?'

Travis smiled. 'It was bloody good though, wasn't it?'

'Not £165-a-bottle good. No, it bloody wasn't. Idiot. *I'm* not paying for that. You can bloody well pay for it yourself.'

Sylvester swallowed, uncertain if he'd heard quite right. £165? Obviously not. 'Go on, then,' he said, making a good-natured show of reaching for his wallet. 'What's the damage?'

'You're not going to like it, I'm afraid,' Travis said, sliding the bill across the table. Susie and Sylvester craned forward to have a look.

Susie gasped.

Sylvester's eyes bulged.

Words failed.

'. . . but I only drank elderflower juice!' Susie said at last.

She and Sylvester glanced nervously up at Poppy and Travis, waiting for the nod, for the stay of execution. Still it didn't come.

'But we can't pay for this!' Susie panted. 'It's half my salary!'

'Should've thought of that before,' Travis grinned. He leaned towards them. 'Imagine, Suse,' he said softly. 'All that free publicity for your poems. How could it possibly be tacky?' He turned to Sylvester. 'And your gardening thing. You'll have clients flocking. You'd be celebrities!'

'Yuck!' said Susie, blushing.

Sylvester shuddered.

'Say you'll do it,' Travis fingered his credit card.

A pause. A long pause.

And while they waited Poppy Starke stretched across the happy couple and kissed Travis full on the lips.

Kris Webb & Kathy Wilson

Number 6 in Race 6

The two women silently contemplated the dark building across the road. Although there was a strip of bustling restaurants and bars less than fifty metres away, this part of the suburb was deathly quiet. Carolyn broke the uneasy silence.

'Are you sure you've got the right address? This place is creepy.'

Her friend held up the business card, although in the dim light Carolyn could barely see it, let alone read what it said.

'It says right here. Ambrose Walters, 22A Crown Lane, Carlton.'

Tracey had shown Carolyn the card the day before. Thick and creamy, with embossing, it had looked like it belonged to a doctor or a lawyer. But this was certainly no inner-city office block. Carolyn tapped a finger on the steering wheel as she chose her next words.

'Trace . . . you don't really believe this fortune teller is going to help you find true love, do you?'

Tracey straightened her shoulders defensively and looked at Carolyn.

'He's not a fortune teller, he's a—' she glanced back at the business card. 'He's a futurist. Two of the women at work say he's fantastic. He knew all kinds of personal information and saw things that have happened to both of them. They swear he's the real thing.' She paused. 'They did see him at lunchtime, though – I'm sure this place looks better in the daylight.'

Carolyn wasn't sure she shared Tracey's confidence. The ground floor of the building was a convenience store, which had needed a coat of paint five years ago. A metal roller door was pulled down over the entrance and secured by a large padlock. Another smaller door, off to the right of the building, stood ajar. Presumably that led upstairs to Ambrose Walters' home and office.

Carolyn looked at her friend's profile and wished she hadn't said anything. The fact that Tracey actually wanted to do this was just another sign of how much the breakup with Joel had affected her. Finally accepting he wouldn't leave his wife after four long years of empty promises had been a step most people had thought she couldn't take. What was the harm in having her future read if it made her feel better for a little while?

Okay, so they weren't exactly in Collins Street, but so what? Besides, it wasn't like she had anyone to rush home to. Gary was working late again and she'd given up waiting for him long ago.

'Fine then.' The interior light went on as Carolyn turned off the engine and opened the door.

'Let's do this.'

The stairwell was dimly lit and smelled faintly musty. They walked up two flights of concrete steps, pausing next to a freshly painted wooden door at the top. A small hand-written sign on the wall told them to come in and make themselves comfortable. The flowing lines of the black pen on the white cardboard lifted Carolyn's spirits temporarily. At least the guy had nice handwriting.

Unable to help herself, she muttered quietly, 'I guess if you can see the future you don't need to lock up much. Just when you know someone's planning on robbing you.'

Tracey ignored her and pushed open the door.

The room they entered was small, but surprisingly pleasant.

A deep-pile, olive-green rug covered a large part of the wooden floor, and a cream sofa and two overstuffed chairs were arranged in a rough circle. As they hesitated, the door opposite them opened and the fortune teller stepped into the room.

The first thing Carolyn noticed about him was his eyes, which were bright blue and unclouded by his fifty or so years. His grey-flecked hair was cropped short and with his tailored trousers and long-sleeved shirt, he looked rather like Sean Connery from twenty years ago. Tracey stepped towards him, extending her hand.

'Ambrose, I'm Tracey Cameron. And this is my friend Carolyn – she came along to keep me company.'

'Nice to meet you Tracey. You too, Carolyn.'

He smiled briefly.

'Sit down ladies, please.' He gestured at the armchairs and Carolyn took the one closest to the door, trying to be as inconspicuous as possible.

'So . . .' Ambrose turned his gaze to Tracey. 'Did you bring me the item we discussed?'

Tracey rummaged nervously in her bag. 'I had trouble deciding what was my most important possession, I hope I got it right.'

Carolyn was surprised at Tracey's discomfort. She was behaving like this man was doing her an enormous favour. Had she forgotten he was charging a hundred bucks for a ten-minute session?

Ambrose took the necklace that had once belonged to Tracey's mother and held it in his hand. Closing his eyes, he rubbed the emeralds between his fingers. 'Ah yes,' he murmured, 'I see . . .'

Just then Tracey's handbag started to play 'Amazing Grace'.

'Oh my God!' Tracey gasped. 'That's the song my mobile plays when Joel rings.' The man in front of her forgotten, Tracey dug desperately around in her handbag until she found her phone.

'Yes?' Her voice sounded shaky as she walked out the front door, closing it behind her.

Carolyn smiled at the fortune teller apologetically. 'Boy-friend,' she said, by way of explanation. 'Ex-boyfriend, actually,' she added.

Ambrose smiled back at her. 'I know,' he said calmly.

After considering and discarding several replies, Carolyn just nodded. Insulting Tracey's lifeline wasn't going to achieve anything.

'It will end in wedding bells.' He spoke as if he was reading a newspaper.

'What will?'

'Tracey and this man, Joel. They will have four children.'

Carolyn tried to keep a straight face. Bad luck for the wife he's already got, she thought. 'Uh-huh.' She nodded non-committedly.

'He has already left the other woman – that is what he is calling Tracey about.'

'Uh-huh,' she repeated, wondering how long Tracey was going to be.

'Your husband isn't your destiny.' Again the words were delivered without emotion.

Startled Carolyn looked at him, sure she'd misheard. 'I beg your pardon?'

'You married the wrong man.'

There was no room for misunderstanding now. Startled, Carolyn looked at him, searching for words.

'That's not true . . . he just – he works . . . a lot,' she finished weakly.

'Your true love is still waiting for you. He is the one who will make you happy.'

Anger overcame her surprise. 'Look, Mr Walters. I'm here just to keep an eye on my friend. I don't believe in this kind of stuff, so don't waste your time on me. My life is none of your business and I'm not even slightly interested in whatever stories you want to come up with. Save it for someone who might want to listen to you.' She bent down to pick up her handbag. 'I think I'll wait for Tracey outside.'

'You're going to the Melbourne Cup tomorrow,' Ambrose murmured as if she hadn't said a thing.

'Well, what a surprise,' Carolyn replied sarcastically. 'So is half of Melbourne, given that it's the biggest social day of the year.'

Once again Ambrose ignored her.

'Have a little wager on horse number six, race six. Oh, and keep your eyes open – no knowing who you'll meet.'

Carolyn strode out of the room and clattered down the stairs. Furious, she walked straight into Tracey on the footpath outside. Oblivious to the impact, Tracey murmured into her phone a few moments longer, before pressing the disconnect button. She turned toward Carolyn, eyes shining.

'You'll never believe what's happened. Joel has finally left his wife!'

The shadows were lengthening and the beautiful people weren't looking quite so beautiful any more. Blue skies and an unexpectedly high temperature for Melbourne Cup Day had raised hems and plunged necklines. Earlier, the path through the hospitality tents had resembled a catwalk as coiffed, designer-clad beauties of both sexes paraded past to see and be seen. But the glamour had been dissolved by the hot sun and too much champagne. Now rumpled women tottered along on spiked heels, past perspiring men with ties askew.

Realising she was frowning, Carolyn rearranged her features into a more festive expression. She'd begun the day full of optimism, but now her head itched under her hat and the pink straps of her shoes sliced into her toes. Something had come up at work and Gary hadn't made it at all, despite phone calls every couple of hours telling her he was on his way.

Even alcohol hadn't helped save the day. Despite her best efforts, she seemed only to be drinking herself sober.

Tracey was having a wonderful time, delighted at finally being out in public with Joel. But her happiness was only making Carolyn feel worse and her face ached from forcing a smile. She'd disappeared on the pretext of finding a toilet and had been wandering aimlessly for the last half-hour.

'Goddamn,' a man beside her muttered, dropping his ticket onto the stiletto-churned turf. She glanced up toward the big screen, the real horses being a hundred metres and a hundred thousand closely packed human beings away. The tote was paying 63 to 1 on the winner of the last race, which had just edged out the favourite.

Carolyn looked away, uninterested. Except for a dedicated few, the races were little more than a distraction from the associated revelry. But a number registered belatedly and her eyes flicked back to the screen. Horse number six had won – in race six. She stared at the horse, seeing instead the blue eyes of Ambrose Walters, the fortune teller.

'You lost too?' the man beside her asked.

She glanced over at him and nodded vaguely.

'Well, so much for my great tips from the tea lady at work. Now I know why she's still a tea lady.'

He smiled at Carolyn. 'What about you – hot tips from a friend?'

'Not exactly,' she replied. She pushed at a divot with the toe of her shoe, thoughts running wildly.

If the man noticed her confusion, he gave no indication.

'Ah well, maybe the next tip will be the one. Time for a drink, I think.' He paused. 'I don't suppose you feel like joining me?'

Carolyn looked around the room.

This was a city bar; its stark white walls reflected in the expanses of chrome. It was full of dark-suited men and women celebrating the end of the working day or perhaps, like her, delaying the inevitable return home. The friend she'd met after work had just left to catch a train, but Carolyn lingered over the dregs of her drink, in no rush to return to her silent apartment. She glanced at a man hunched over a corner table nursing what didn't look to be his first beer of the day. He turned in her direction and her heartbeat resounded in her ears.

Without any conscious thought, she picked up her drink and approached him. The flesh on his cheeks had sagged towards his jaw and a network of red lines marched across his nose. But when she saw his eyes, she was sure.

'Mr Walters?'

His answer was a laugh overtaken by a belch. 'That is a name I answer to,' he managed finally.

She pulled out a chair and sat down, attracting several curious gazes. The fortune teller looked terrible close up. The smart clothes she remembered from their one meeting were still there, but looked like they hadn't been washed or ironed in a long time. His eyes, while still a piercing blue, were dull. If she'd had a bad three years, his looked to have been worse.

Her fingers gripped the moisture-beaded glass, her bitten nails showing white. 'Mr Walters, I visited you with a friend three years ago.' It seemed a ridiculously formal way to address a drunk in a bar, but she couldn't bring herself to use his Christian name.

'Did you, now?' he muttered, seemingly more interested

in his beer than the conversation.

'You picked a winner on Melbourne Cup Day, at very long odds.'

'Uh-huh.'

Finally she understood and waved a waitress. 'I'd like another gin and tonic please and—' She looked over at him.

'Scotch and Coke,' he replied. 'Black Label,' he added, like a three-year-old testing his luck.

She nodded to the waitress and they waited until the drinks arrived.

'Did you see what was going to happen to me that day at the races?'

'Lady, I'm flat out remembering where I live. I've got no idea what you're talking about.'

What the hell was she sitting here with this derelict for? Carolyn knew she should just walk away, but not a day had gone by in the last three years without her wondering about what this man had told her.

'I came to see you with a friend. You didn't read my fortune, but you figured out I was going to the races the next day and told me about a horse that was going to win.'

'Big deal, I used to have a mate on the inside, got all kinds of tips. Sometimes they worked but not often enough, unfortunately. If I got it right you would have been happy, right?' He registered her silence. 'Not right, obviously.' She saw him hiding a smile and her mouth burned with the acidic taste of her anger. This man had changed her life, but couldn't even remember meeting her.

An image of the last time she had seen Gary flashed into her mind. Gary pushing a pram through Flinders Street

Station, smiling lovingly at the woman beside him. She had a sudden urge to reach across the table and slap the drunk in front of her. She spoke in a low voice.

'My marriage was going through a difficult stage, you told me –' She swallowed hard. 'You seemed to know and you told me I'd find my destiny. I met someone just as your tip won the race and I . . . well, it was the worst mistake of my life.'

His hands shook slightly and his breath stank of alcohol, but when he looked at her he seemed stone cold sober.

'Sweetheart, I've been telling fortunes for fifteen years. You wanna know what I've learned?' He didn't wait for her to respond. 'It's very simple. Most people do what they want to do. But if they can believe that they're powerless and just being carried along by fate they feel a whole lot less guilty about it all. That's where I come in.'

'No,' Carolyn shook her head. 'It wasn't like that.'

He laughed. 'It's always like that. I watch, I listen – hell, I go through handbags if I get the chance. People aren't very complicated when you get right down to it.'

'But you knew I was unhappy with my husband . . .'

'Sad lady wearing a wedding ring, it's not rocket science.'

'You knew my friend's boyfriend was going to come back to her.'

'Boyfriends often do. Even if they don't, it keeps the girls coming back to have their fortunes told. A fortune teller who predicts disaster and misery for his clients doesn't get much repeat business.' He took another sip of his drink and then continued. 'Anyone that believes in destiny is a fool. You want to blame me for your life, go right ahead.

Trust me, you won't be the first. But do you really think it could have been any different?'

The piercing scrape of Carolyn's chair on the polished floor seemed to echo in the air long after she'd left the room.

Isabel Wolff

In Agony

'Problems, problems,' Jane muttered as she opened her mailbag on Monday. 'Problems, problems,' she repeated testily. 'As if I don't have enough of my own.' The thirty or so letters seemed almost to vibrate with indignation, resentment and rage. There were brown envelopes and white ones, airmail and Basildon Bond. There were typed ones and hand-written ones, some strewn with smileys and hearts. Jane's practised eye had already identified from the writing the likely dilemmas within. Here were the large, childish loops of repression, and the backwards slope of the chronically depressed. There, the stabbings and scorings of schizophrenia and the cramped hand of the introvert. Jane fancied she could hear them, like childish voices, whining and pleading for help.

'*Dear Jane*,' she read, '*I have a problem . . . Dear Jane, I just can't sleep . . . Dear Jane, I'm so terribly lonely . . . Dear Jane, I feel so bad . . .*' *Dear Jane*, she thought to herself bitterly. Dear Jane. Dear, dear, DEAR. 'Oh dear,' she repeated testily as she turned on her computer. 'Off we go again.'

For Jane was neither an enthusiastic, nor even sympathetic, agony aunt. She had always regarded the *Post*'s problem page – she still did – with something close to contempt. 'But here I am – in AGONY,' she muttered. She longed for some anaesthetic to ease the pain. But '*Ask Jane*' was undeniably popular; more importantly, it paid the bills. Because for two years Gavin hadn't earned a penny, having given up his job in the City to write. He'd been 'trouble-shooter' at Debit Suisse. 'But I'm the real trouble-shooter now,' thought Jane. And it sometimes amused her to think that Gavin's literary career was subsidised by the co-dependent, the abandoned and the bald. Jane had been a journalist for ten years; but her spell as an agony aunt had never featured on the imagined trajectory of her career. She had visualised a seamless progression from the diary to the news desk, to signed interviews, to glamorous features (with photo byline) and thence to a highly visible – and frequently controversial – column in some respected broadsheet. Her readers would gasp at her erudition. No subject would elude her grasp. She would pontificate on Britain's entry to the Euro, on drugs and welfare and defence. Her trenchant opinions would be regurgitated at lively dinner parties in Islington and Notting Hill. She would be invited to appear on *Newsnight*, on *Today* and *Question Time*. Instead, she found herself dealing with premature ejaculation, nasty neighbours, infidelity, impotence and debt.

This unexpected professional detour had happened entirely by chance. Two and a half years previously, Jane had been doing a reporting shift on the news desk of the *Sunday Post*. As she put the finishing touches to what she thought was a rather good profile of Cherie Blair, she noticed a sudden commotion. People were running. Doors were slamming. An atmosphere of tension and panic prevailed. Enid Smugg, the *Post*'s ancient but hugely popular agony aunt, had gone face down in the trifle at lunch. Before Enid's stiffening body had even been stretchered out of the building, Jane had been deputed to complete her page. Keen, above all, to appear willing, she had gritted her teeth and agreed; and despite her lack of experience, or even natural sympathy, she'd acquitted herself pretty well. Too well, she now realised bitterly, because she'd been stuck in the job ever since. Still, forty grand was good money, she reminded herself, and God knows they needed the cash. Their flat in Regent's Park was gorgeous, but the mortgage on it was vast. But Jane adored her husband, Gavin – 'Gorgeous Gav' – and she believed that his boat would come in. Moreover, she was secretly quite happy to be the bread-winner – it placed Gavin firmly in her debt. And she especially liked the fact that he no longer went to work. Jane had been to Gavin's office a few times and had been disconcerted and demoralised by the sight of so many sweet-faced, lithe-limbed blondes. For Jane was a very plain Jane – tall, big-boned and rather flat-faced, and she knew she'd married out of her league. She quite liked having her handsome husband safely at home, out of harm's – and temptation's – way.

But above all, she luxuriated in the knowledge that it was her professional sacrifice that enabled him to write. He'd probably dedicate his book to her, she mused contentedly.

When it was published. Which it would be, quite soon. The phone would ring one day and it would be an editor from HarperCollins or Faber, begging Gavin to let them publish his intergalactic thriller, *Star-Quake!* Jane had to admit that Gav's books weren't quite her thing. But then she'd never really been a sci-fi fan. Gavin was an avid amateur astronomer and was aiming to become the new Arthur C. Clarke. Jane had a sudden, happy vision of them attending the Royal Premiere of *Star-Quake!* in Leicester Square. There they were, standing next to Nicolas Cage and Michelle Pfeiffer in the line-up to meet Prince Charles.

Gavin had not yet allowed Jane to see his manuscript. But a few nights before, when he'd left for his astronomy evening class, she'd gone into his study and sneaked a look. She'd found the story a little hard to follow, with its huge floating aliens, exploding supernovas and fur-clad talking snakes. But still, it was genre fiction, Jane reasoned, and there was a huge market for that. In any case, she supported Gavin unquestioningly, because she adored him. She always had. That's why she was prepared to be 'in agony' as she jokingly put it – so that Gav could fulfil his dream. And at least – and thank God for this – none of her friends knew that '*Ask Jane*' was her. For she had resolutely refused to have her surname or her photo on the page. '*Got a Problem? Ask Jane!*' it announced above a photo of a disembodied – and clearly female – ear.

Jane had assumed, when she first started doing the agony column, that her stewardship of it would be short-lived. She'd imagined that before long, some celebrity would be hired to take over, or some famously humiliated political wife. For a while there'd been talk of Trisha from daytime telly, and even of Carol Vorderman. But weeks had gone by, then months and here Jane still was, over two years on. But not for much longer, she thought to herself happily, because soon Gavin's writing career would take off.

'You're my rock, Jane,' he'd say with a smile that made her heart swell and tears prick the back of her eyes. 'You're my asteroid – no, my shooting star.'

Well, she certainly shot from the hip. Or rather, from the lip. But that's why people wrote to her. They wanted firm, robust advice. She turned back to the day's bundle of letters with a weary, regretful sigh. Christ, it was tedious – and it wasn't as though any of the problems were *new*. She had long since covered every conceivable dilemma: low libido, domestic violence, bad breath, bereavement, debt. Pregnancy, both wanted and unwanted, nasty neighbours and thinning hair. She'd helped *Divorcing of Dagenham*, *Paranoid of Petersham*, and *Borderline Bulimic of Bath*.

'Who have we got today?' she muttered. '*Phobic of Finchley? Suicidal of Solihull? Jealous of Jupiter* would make a nice change,' she added sardonically, 'or maybe *Miserable of Mars*.' Jane never felt guilty about her lack of sympathy for her readers. If these people wanted lovely, mumsy, kind Clare Rayner, then they could damn well write to her instead. But 'kind' simply wasn't Jane's style. Her advice was uncompromisingly tough. She prided herself on being as sharp and to the point as an assassin's blade. Oh yes, Jane like to tell it straight. She didn't mess about. First off was Sandra from Suffolk. Not getting on well with her husband's mum.

'*Dear Sandra*,' Jane typed. '*It's a GREAT pity you spoke to your mother-in-law like that. Let's face it, calling her a "twisted old battleaxe" is NOT going to make relations more cordial! May I respectfully suggest that you try and THINK a little before you open your big trap. In the meantime I enclose my leaflet on Tact.'*

Jane re-read her letter, sealed the envelope, tossed it into her out-tray, then turned to the next. Oh God – another fatso with low self-esteem.

'*Dear Terry,*' she wrote. '*I know you'd like me to tell you that looks don't matter, and that some nubile blonde is going to fall in love with your 'great personality'. But the fact is, poppet, that no self-respecting woman is going to be seen dead with a guy weighing eighteen stone. Here's the Weightwatchers number for your area. Ring it right now and lose the lard.*' On further consideration, she decided the letter might be a little harsh. So she scribbled, '*Do let me know how you get on*' at the bottom, to soften it a bit.

Not that anyone ever did 'let her know'. They never got back to her. Her replies went out into the void, like meteorites hurtling through space. In the two years she'd been 'in agony', she'd never heard from anyone again. Occasionally she would wonder why, but she had long since concluded that the brilliance of her advice obviated the need for further help.

Now she earmarked the four letters she would feature on this week's page – money trouble, transvestism, booze and menopause – then turned to the final letter in the pile. 'Oh God, *Betrayed of Barnes*,' she said irritably. 'You poor thing – boo hoo hoo!'

'*Dear Jane, I don't know what to do,*' she read. '*I've been married for seven years and love my wife dearly but fear she has started to stray. She is far more attractive than I am and*

I often feel insecure.' Jane felt a sudden pang of recognition which she did her best to suppress. '*I have no hard evidence,*' the writer went on, '*but I believe she's seeing a colleague at her TV company, because she talks about him a lot. It's 'Ronnie this' and 'Ronnie that' so I assume it must be him. What's more, she's been dressing particularly well lately, with a new hair-do, and once or twice I think I've detected alien aftershave on her clothes. I have never been possessive,*' the man continued. '*I've always encouraged my wife to see her friends, go to the gym, attend classes etc. but I'm now so anxious that I feel ill. Please, please advise me Jane. Yours in desperation, Alan.*'

'*Well Alan,*' Jane wrote back. '*It seems to me you've got three options. You can a) stick your head in the sand and hope the problem will go away. But the problem with having your head in the sand, sweetie, is that you leave your backside dangerously exposed. Or you can b) confront her. But if you do, you'd better prepare yourself to hear something you're not going to like. Or you can c) have her followed. Go to a private detective – just look one up in Yellow Pages – and get a Dick Tracy on the job. At least that way you'll know for sure. So bite the bullet, Alan, and best of luck.*'

Jane finished the letter with a sense of satisfaction. She'd given him the best advice she could. She wondered what the upshot would be, but knew that she'd never get to know. So she was rather surprised, a fortnight later, to hear from Alan again.

'*Dear Jane,*' he wrote. '*Thank you for the excellent advice you gave me recently. I had my wife followed, as you suggested, with surprising results. It turned out that her colleague, 'Ronnie', was in fact a woman – Ronnie is short for*

Veronica apparently.' Well then you're a lucky bunny Alan, thought Jane as she raised her coffee cup to her lips.

'*However*,' she read on, '*my suspicions about my wife were sadly proved right – in an unexpected way. The detective's dossier revealed that she HAS been having an affair, with a man who attends the same evening class. It appears they share a passion for amateur astronomy. He's a married man, very attractive, a former banker, who's trying to write a novel. I'm devastated, as you can imagine. But what I need to know NOW is, should I get in touch with this man's wife?'*

Deborah Wright

In Bed with Lord Byron

The day I broke up with my boyfriend was the day I decided to invest in a time machine.

Buying the time machine was relatively easy, as you can imagine: I just clicked onto eBay and discovered an auction ending in an hour's time. The seller, a man called Brian Pincher, described his machine as:

> Six months old and only used once. I took a quick trip back to lose my virginity to Dolly Parton but realised, to my dismay, that I am a nervous flier and ended up puking all over her guitar during a rendition of *I Will Always Love You*. The pain of this memory, which has since crippled my confidence with women, has put me off ever using the machine again. But I hope it can give someone else a little happiness.

Perfect, I thought.

The bidding was ferocious, and I ended up paying £900

for it. Another one to slap on my bulging Visa card. When the machine arrived, I was slightly alarmed to discover it came as a box of parts, all needing to be put together. I was just sweating over inserting tube A into circuit B, when suddenly my phone rang and the answer phone clicked on.

'Hi, Deborah, it's Anthony here. So, um, yeah, I can come along to the dinner party you're having on Wednesday . . .'

I sat up, a lock of sweaty hair falling into my face. I'd entirely forgotten that I'd suggested the dinner party, as a 'let's be friends' gesture.

'And I'd like to bring, um, my new girlfriend, um, Kerry.'

Kerry? We'd only been broken up a day and he had found someone new?

Then again, I had been the one to break off our relationship. It wasn't that there was anything wrong with Anthony. He was tall, dark and handsome. He had a good job, working in the City. But that was the *point*. We were so good together; and yet I felt bored. Call it the grass-is-greener syndrome if you will, but I always suffered this restless ache that Mr Perfect, someone who was just that little bit taller and darker and more handsome and funnier than Anthony, might be just round the corner. Now I was finally going to get it out of my system. I was about to woo one of the world's greatest lovers.

I couldn't help feeling that the machine, though a delightful shade of scarlet, was somewhat flimsy, though. Spotting the trademark MFI on one corner was perhaps a clue as to why.

My next question was: what date to put in? I wanted to meet Lord Byron when he was in his prime. Men are supposed to be the best lovers at the age of eighteen, but I had no wish to end up in Harrow, watching Byron caught up in a whirl of homosexual politics. My experiences at Oxford had also taught me that public school boys should always be avoided at all costs.

Finally, I decided to program in April 1813. Byron would have just been writing *Childe Harold*, and would be at the tender (but not too tender) age of twenty-five. I exchanged my jeans for a ball gown, slipped a copy of my own novel, *The Rebel Fairy*, into my pocket, along with Leslie Marchant's *Byron: A Biography* (all 3 volumes – bloody heavy), so that I could flatter Byron with a deep understanding of his childhood and ennui, and off I went . . .

DEBORAH'S DIARY: 2005 / 1813
Day One of the Seduction of Lord Byron: 3 p.m.,
5 July 1813
Thoughts before going into battle

Interviewers are always interested in whether books are autobiographical. But what's far more interesting is what happens to the author after the book is written – the way the book shapes the author's identity. As Oscar Wilde summed up: 'Does art mirror life or does life mirror art?'

I realised that there was probably a wide gap between Byron and his poetry. Obviously, it is the mark of a good author that they write with so much charisma that at the end of the book, the reader longs to meet them. The book seems to shine and scintillate with their personality. Hence – reading Jilly Cooper makes you long to walk with her in the Gloucestershire countryside; reading Jostein Gaarder makes you want to discuss life, the universe and everything with him for hours on end; and reading Will Self makes you want to take him to a Häagen-Dazs cafe and discuss whether his *Cock & Bull* is as impressive as his novels suggest. Whether or not there is a gap between the creators and the creations doesn't matter; we are seduced and sucked in. Byron, too, perfected the art of the literary image; in writing *Childe Harold*, he fashioned a caricature of himself. Women read the poem and fell in love with him, assuming that Byron was Childe Harold – the brooding, melancholic, world-weary libertine – aided by the fact that within the poem itself the narrator and hero blur together until finally they merge around Canto 13 and become one.

Who can tell which of Byron's facades, the various costumes he put on, are real or masquerade? Tonight, I was determined to try and find out.

3 a.m.: House of Tom Moore (a fellow poet and close friend of Byron)

I entered the ball *in media res* – entered to hear shrill banshee screams and breaking glass. A woman was led from the room leaving a trail of blood behind her. A thousand heads watched her go, mouths agape. I realised then that the lady was the famous Caroline Lamb – Byron's latest lover, whom he had clearly grown bored with. All very ominous. And then I saw him, across the crowded ballroom. The man himself. Mr Mad, Bad and Dangerous to Know.

I could hardly believe it when he came over and introduced himself. He was indeed beautiful. He was not as tall as I had imagined, nor was his limp as exaggerated. But he certainly had presence. I couldn't think of what to say to him. I was about to start debating the topic of whether he was really a Romantic poet or an Augustan at heart, when he started knocking back glass after glass of wine. He seemed shaken after the Caroline ordeal.

'Maybe you should lay off the booze,' I suggested nervously. I couldn't help remembering that when Byron died and his body was cut open, the sutures of his skull were found fused together – normally a sign of old age, though he was only thirty-six. 'You might end up in A.A.,' I slipped up. Byron had no idea what I meant, but he didn't seem to care. 'Can't!' he cried. 'I shall drink as I like!'

And with that he smashed his glass and pulled me out to his carriage, ordering the driver to take me home. I said I had no home, and he gentlemanly offered to take me to Tom Moore's house, declaring that I would not be refused accommodation. I told him that he was a gentleman and I could never repay him. He told me that I could repay him with a kiss.

I blushed and looked away. We sat in the carriage, him watching me, me staring out of the window watching his reflection, silvery against the blue landscape. Our knees were brushing. Even though the night air was freezing, tiny beads of sweat were breaking on my forehead. As the carriage wheels started to slow, he leaned forwards and took my wrist, stroking the veins delicately. We kissed the rest of the way home. At Tom Moore's, I staggered about in post-kiss bliss. Moore gave me a quizzical look and Byron steadied me with his hand on my back, making a joke about me being drunk. 'Drunk on love,' he whispered, as he kissed me goodnight.

The next morning, Byron paid me a visit and declared that he would do anything to make me happy. 'All right,' I said. 'Come back to 2005 with me. I think you'll enjoy it.'

Back in Surrey, England

For three nights in a row, I made Byron suffer. Determined not to become another Caroline Lamb, I inflicted The Rules on him. No matter how he tried to woo me – whether it was with flowers, verse, or chocolates, I refused to give him more than so much as a kiss. At first he was cajoling; then he began to get quite peevish and starting muttering remarks about going back to be with Augusta.

Then Wednesday came, and I woke up with a jolt. I had completely forgotten that tonight I was meant to be having a dinner party, with Anthony and his new girlfriend, Kerry. I went into the living room and found Byron on the Net, ego-surfing. Having typed his name into Google, he was delighted to discover he had 1,070,000 hits.

'God, this broadbent is so much fun,' Byron murmured.

'Broadband,' I corrected him. 'Look, I'm having a dinner party tonight and I really need you to be on your best behaviour. For one thing, I can't introduce you as Lord Byron.'

'But why not?'

'Because they'll think I'm mad.'

'But you are mad. Surely if they're your friends, they've already worked this out?'

'I'm just going to say you're George, all right? Look, just keep remembering this rhyme in your head,' I improvised wildly. '*I'm not a famous poet, I don't like lovemaking / My name is George and I work in computing.*'

'I don't think I'd care to remember such a frightful piece of poetry. The scansion doesn't work at all,' Byron's eyebrows knitted together in an elegant, faintly disdainful frown. 'Perhaps you ought to be dating Andrew Motion, not me.' He laughed as I threw a dishcloth at him and stormed out.

I wasn't quite sure why I felt so jittery about the dinner party. I spent two hours getting ready, and everything I tried on or took off was assessed in comparison to an imaginary Kerry. My picture of her began to escalate in my mind until I felt she could be no less beautiful than Aphrodite rising out of the ocean: hair aflame, face an oval of perfection, body a sea of curves. By the time I'd finally decided on my little black dress, I was nearly hysterical with nerves. Twice, I picked up my mobile and nearly called Anthony to pretend I was sick and wanted to call it all off. Then 7 p.m. came and the doorbell rang.

'Hi, Deborah,' said Anthony, giving me a kiss on the cheek. To my surprise, I felt a flutter in my stomach – I had forgotten how dark his eyes were. 'This is Kerry.'

Relief soothed the anxious grinding of my stomach muscles. She was pretty, but not *that* pretty. She had short hair, for a start – an autumnal haze of highlights – and Anthony had once confided in me that he hated short hair on women. I looked at Anthony, but he was gazing at Lord Byron. I groaned silently. Though Byron had put on a pair of jeans, they didn't really go with his eighteenth-century coat and cravat.

'Hi.' Anthony shook his hand. There was a slightly twisted smile on his lips. I felt a flutter of alarm. Could that smile mean something beginning with j . . . ?

'Hi,' Byron said, rising. For one moment, as he puffed up his chest and his chin, I saw the vulnerability beneath his arrogance. Then, seeing Kerry, he gave her a wolfish smile.

'Hi,' she said, as if sensing the ruffles of awkwardness and doing her best to smooth them over. 'Great to meet you! I'm Kerry.'

'I'm Byron,' he purred softly, ignoring the frantic look I gave him.

'Oh, Brian – oh cool, I once knew a Brian and he was great,' she enthused.

We sat down to eat.

'So, what do you do for a living?' Anthony asked.

'He's a—' I began to interject again, when Anthony said, smiling gently: 'I think Brian can answer by himself, Deborah.'

'Uh huh,' Kerry echoed under her breath, and I had to force myself not to give her an utterly monstrous look.

'I'm a poet,' said Byron importantly. At which point, about a hundred women would have collapsed at his feet. But this is the twenty-first century and if you announce at a dinner party that you're a poet, people will react with polite distress.

'Well,' said Anthony, 'good for you. But it must be tough trying to get recognition, right? I mean, I had a friend at uni who decided to become a poet and he spent years scraping by, sending things out to magazines and radio stations and never getting anywhere. By the time he finally managed to get something accepted by Bloodaxe, the bailiffs had taken away half his flat.'

By now Byron was nearly purple.

'He has had stuff published,' I said quickly. 'And it's been well received.'

'Oh wow, what about?' said Anthony, pointedly addressing the question to Lord B.

'He likes writing about nature,' I said. 'About birds and trees and that sort of thing.'

'Sounds very Wordsworthian,' said Kerry, and I saw Byron's fingers tighten around his knife as though he wanted to plunge it into someone's chest.

'I can assure you that Wordsworth has never been an influence on my work,' said Byron acidly. 'Blake – a fellow genius – once blamed a lifelong bowel complaint on reading Wordsworth's poetry.' We all laughed.

The dinner party came to an end. We waved them goodbye and I stood on my doorstep, watching them walk down the street. Anthony took off his coat and put it round Kerry's shoulders and I felt as though someone had stabbed an icicle into my heart. Then I felt a warm breath on the back of my neck. Byron had come up behind me. He took my hair, twisted it into a tight coil and pinned it up with his fingers. I watched Anthony again as he disappeared into the darkness. I felt Byron place a tender kiss on the back of my neck. And that was when I made the mistake.

Reader, I slept with him.

11:30 p.m.

A post-coital chat between me and Byron, on literature:

'So, what poetry are you reading?' he asked me.

'Uh?' I gasped, bumbling about. 'Er . . . Coleridge.'

'Coleridge! What an idiot! Coleridge, explaining metaphysics to the nation – I wish he would explain his explanation.'

I burst into fits of laughter and he smiled, kissing my shoulder.

'That's from *Don Juan*!' I cried eagerly, then realised: fuck, it's 1813, he hasn't written that one yet.

'Don Juan,' Byron frowned as if suffering from inverted déjà vu, sensing that title would one day be meaningful to him. 'Hmm. I like that. I must write it down.'

'I think it would make a good poem,' I added cheekily. 'The adventures of a rake, travelling all over Europe, a little quietly facetious about everything.'

'Not bad at all.' Byron kissed me again. 'I may well use that idea at some point.' 1818, to be exact, I thought.

'Deborah – you're more than just a pretty face.' And with this affectionate cliché, he promptly fell asleep.

I lay awake. I tried to analyse the feeling in my stomach. I felt empty, as though filled with smoke. I couldn't believe that, during our lovemaking, I had had to fake an orgasm. This was Byron, for goodness' sake. But all the way through, I had been unable to stop myself from thinking about Anthony, about the way he kissed me, the way he touched me, the way he used to enter me and stare deep into my eyes and whisper 'I love you'. Beside me, Byron snored loudly.

The Morning After

Byron woke me up the next morning with a gentle kiss. I blinked blearily, noticing that my own novel, *The Rebel Fairy*, was looking reassuringly dog-eared and well-read. He had obviously found it amongst my clothes and was now reading it.

'Did you like the book?' I asked, expecting bemusement rather than praise. Perhaps he might even think me a genius. Perhaps I ought to go back to 1813 and republish *The Rebel Fairy*. Perhaps Byron might pass it on to his publisher, Murray. It could be published as a sort of light-hearted *1984*, a look to the future. For a moment I pictured the reviews: '*The ability of this young novelist to predict affairs of the heart in future centuries is extraordinarily perceptive!*' Byron and I would become a famous literary couple; we would marry and produce children who won the Booker Prize.

'Well?' I repeated. 'Did you like *The Rebel Fairy*?'

'Load of tosh!' he said. 'The woman who wrote it was obviously a born-again virgin. And what's all this about *fairies*? I tell you, I knew *real* fairies when I was at Harrow, and they most certainly didn't have wings!'

And with that, he tore out the first few pages and pretended to eat them, flecks of paper spraying from his mouth, crying, 'Delicious!'

Over the following week, my relationship with Byron went from bad to worse. I hardly ever saw him at all, for history had repeated itself. Byronmania had swept the country. After Byron had gone out on the town to Chinawhite, the inevitable occurred: a brief love affair with Jordan had ensued. He was splashed over every tabloid in town, whilst the magnificent ode he published on her bosoms (not having heard of plastic surgery, he was convinced they were a divine miracle) was revered in every broadsheet.

Then, after penning a poem that was published in the *Guardian*, challenging Andrew Motion to a duel, Byron was invited onto *Celebrity Big Brother*. Eight million viewers fell in love with him all over again as they watched him bicker with Jeremy Edwards, flirt with Caprice and discuss the origins of his deep-set chauvinism with Germaine Greer. The night of the *BB* final, I sat on my sofa, the cat on my lap. To my horror, the camera zoomed in on Byron lying in bed beside Germaine Greer.

'Since arriving in 2005,' Byron whispered, 'I've slept with many a pretty face. But you, Germaine, are the first woman I have bedded who has *brains*.'

The telephone rang. Anthony's voice rippled out.

'Um, Deborah, I think you ought to switch on the TV,' he said.

'I'm watching,' I sobbed. 'I suppose you and Kerry think it's hilarious.'

'I haven't seen Kerry,' Anthony said quietly. 'The night I brought her over, she went on and on about bloody Byron all the way home. She just sits at home, masturbating over his poetry. So . . .'

'Oh,' I said, suddenly feeling deliriously happy.

'Shall I come and keep you company?' he asked gently.

'Yes, please.'

'And just ignore Byron. Everything he says is cant.'

The last thing I did before Anthony came over was to hack my machine to bits and put them in the bin. No more fantasies, I thought with a smile, as the doorbell rang. From now on, Mr Normal will do just fine . . .

Notes on the Contributors

Jessica Adams

Jessica Adams has worked on the editorial team of six books in aid of War Child, including this one. She is a trustee of No Strings, the astrologer for *Vogue*, *The Australian Women's Weekly* and *Cosmopolitan*, and the author of five novels including *The Summer Psychic*, out in 2006. Visit jessicaadams.com

Cecelia Ahern

Before emarking on her writing career, Cecelia Ahern completed a degree in journalism and media communications. Both her novels, *PS, I Love You* and *Where Rainbows End*, are international bestsellers. She lives in Dublin, Ireland, where she is working on her third novel.

Shalini Akhil

Shalini Akhil is a Melbourne-based writer who also dabbles in stand-up comedy. Her first novel, *The Bollywood*

Beauty, was published by Penguin Books in 2005. Shalini was a Raw Comedy National Finalist in 2003, and has had a love/hate relationship with Bollywood cinema since 1983. She eagerly awaits the DVD release of the complete series of *Beverly Hills 90210*. Her website address is www.kai-india.com

Maggie Alderson

Maggie Alderson was born in London a long time ago, and is the author of three bestselling novels, *Pants on Fire*, *Mad About the Boy* and *Handbags and Gladrags*, which have been translated into many languages. Moving to Sydney was the inspiration for the first two, while *Handbags and Gladrags* is set at the designer fashion shows of New York, London, Milan and Paris, which Maggie has been covering as a glossy magazine editor and newspaper fashion writer, for over 15 years. She has also published *Shoe Money* and *Handbag Heaven*, which are compilations of her 'Style Notes' column in *Good Weekend* magazine. This is the second anthology she has co-edited in aid of War Child.

Lisa Armstrong

Lisa Armstrong is Fashion Editor or *The Times*, London. She has written four novels, including *Front Row* and her latest, *Deja View* came out in 2005. She has never, to her knowledge, sold 'dirty eyelid' creams on cable TV.

Tilly Bagshawe

Tilly Bagshawe is a novelist and journalist. Her first novel, *Adored*, was published this year by Orion in the UK and Time Warner in the US where it went straight into the

New York Times top ten. A Cambridge graduate, and a single mother at eighteen, Tilly has contributed numerous articles to *The Sunday Times*, *Daily Mail* and *London Evening Standard*. Now thirty-one, she divides her time between London and Los Angeles.

Faith Bleasdale

Faith Bleasdale grew up in Devon, studied history at Bristol University, and then moved to London where she decided to put her passion for writing to good use. She now writes full time, and is currently based in Singapore although frequently returns to the UK to get her London fix. Her novels include *Deranged Marriage, Peep Show* and *Agent Provocateur*, the last of which was published this year.

Yasmin Boland

Yasmin Boland is a full-time author and astrologer. You can read her Stars and more of her stories on her website www.moonology.com

Elizabeth Buchan

Elizabeth Buchan began her career as a blurb writer for Penguin Books. She later became a fiction editor at Random House but decided after a couple of years that she should do what she wished to do: write. Her novels include *Daughters of the* Storm, *Light of the Moon, Consider the Lily, Perfect Love, Against Her Nature, Secrets of the Heart* and *Revenge of the Middle-Aged Woman*. The last has sold all over the world and has been made into a television film for CBS. Her latest novels are *The Good Wife* and *That Certain Age*. Elizabeth reviews for *The Sunday Times* and the *Daily Mail*. Her short stories have appeared in various magazines and have been broadcast on BBC Radio 4.

Meg Cabot

Meg Cabot is the number one *New York Times* bestselling author of the *Princess Diaries* series, as well as teen favourites such as *All American Girl*, *Teen Idol*, and the *Mediator* and *1-800-Where-R-You* series. She also writes books for older readers, such as *The Boy Next Door*, *Boy Meets Girl*, and *Every Boy's Got One*. Like the character in her story for this collection, Meg hates parties. She currently divides her time between New York City and Key West, Florida, with her husband and one-eyed cat, Henrietta.

Jill A. Davis

Jill A. Davis is the author of the bestselling novel, *Girls' Poker Night*. She is a former writer for *Late Show with David Letterman*, for which she received five Emmy nominations. Her next novel will be published by Harper Collins in 2006. She lives in New York with her husband and daughter.

Barbie (Barry) Divola

Barry Divola is the music critic at *Who* magazine, a senior writer for *Rolling Stone*, and a contributor to *Sunday Life*, *The Bulletin* and *Entertainment Weekly*. His first book, *Fanclub*, is about obsessive music fandom. His second book, *Searching for Kingly Critter*, is about obsessive toy collecting. Barry won the 2004 Banjo Paterson Award for short fiction for his story 'Nipple', and the 2005 award for 'Circada Boy'. He also spins discs as DJ, K-Tel, and once a year plays bass in The Fluffy Boys, who celebrated twenty years of ineptitude in 2005.

Stella Duffy

Stella Duffy has written ten novels, including *Parallel Lies* (Virago) and *Mouths of Babes* (Serpent's Tail), both published in 2005. She has written over twenty-five short stories, including 'Martha Grace' (Tart Noir), which won the 2002 CWA Short Story Dagger Award. She was born in the UK, grew up in New Zealand and now lives in London.

Nick(ola) Earls

The following was received from Nick(ola) Earls' agent.

Thank you for your inquiry concerning my client. The answers to your questions are as follows:

(i) She still has the pashminas and is a slave to no one's fashion sense

(ii) Her cat went over the fence of its own accord, and against advice

(iii) About six times. Certainly no more than seven

(iv) I can neither confirm nor deny any association between my client and Nick Earls, author of the bestsellers *Zigzag Street*, *Bachelor Kisses*, *Perfect Skin*, etc. and chair of War Child Australia.

Imogen Edwards-Jones

Imogen Edwards-Jones is a journalist and broadcaster and the author of four novels – *My Canape Hell*, *Shagpile*, *The Wendy House* and *Tuscany for Beginners*. She has written a travel book, *The Taming of Eagles – Exploring the New Russia*, and ghosted the best-selling exposé on the luxury hotel business – *Hotel Babylon*. She was co-editor of the previous War Child anthology, *Big Night Out*, and is currently working on the BBC TV drama series adaption of *Hotel Babylon*. Her new book, *Air Babylon*, is out this year.

Michaela (Mike) Gayle

Mike (Michaela) Gayle was born in 1970 in Birmingham. In that time he has (although not necessarily in this order): gained and lost several girlfriends; freelanced for the *Guardian*, *The Sunday Times*, *FHM* and *Cosmopolitan*; made a phone call from the loos at 11 Downing Street; been employed as an agony uncle for *Bliss* magazine; learned to walk; dyed his hair red for *Just Seventeen*; grown taller; gained O levels, A levels, a Bachelor of Science in sociology, and a post-graduate diploma in magazine journalism; been a false answer on a question on *Who Wants To Be a Millionaire*; got married; broken his leg playing football; and written five bestsellers – *My Legendary Girlfriend*, *Mr Commitment*, *Turning Thirty*, *Dinner For Two* and *His 'n' Hers*. His new novel, *Brand New Friend*, is out now. Mike can be contacted via his website: www.mikegayle.co.uk

Emily Giffin

Emily Giffin graduated from Wake Forest University and the University of Virginia School of Law. After practicing law in New York City for several years, she moved to London and began writing full time. She is the author of the *New York Times* bestselling novels *Something Borrowed* and *Something Blue*. She now lives in Atlanta with her husband and twin sons and is at work on her third novel. Please visit her at www.emilygiffin.com

Kristin Gore

Emmy-nominated comedy writer Kristin Gore was born in 1977. She graduated from Harvard, where she wrote for the *Harvard Lampoon*. She has written for several television shows, including *Saturday Night Live* and *Futurama*. Her first novel, *Sammy's Hill*, was published in September 2004 and became a *New York Times* and *Publishers' Weekly* bestseller. Kristin is currently writing the screenplay of *Sammy's Hill* for Columbia Pictures and working on her second novel.

Anita Heiss

Anita is a descendant of the Wiradjuri nation of western New South Wales. She is an author, poet, social commentator and cultural activist. Her publications include the satirical commentary *Sacred Cows*, historial novel *Who am I? The diary of Mary Talence, Sydney 1937* and nonfiction work *Dhuuluu-Yala: To Talk Straight: publishing Aboriginal literature*. Anita has performed her work throughout Australia, across the USA and Canada, and in Barcelona, Austria and Noumea. In 2003 she was awarded the inaugural ASA Medal for her contribution to Australian literature and community life. She is currently working on a new novel, *Not Meeting Mr Right*.

Lauren Henderson

Lauren Henderson was born in London. She worked there as a journalist before moving to Tuscany and then to Manhattan. She has written seven books in her Sam Jones mystery series, which has been optioned for American TV, and three romantic comedies – *My Lurid Past, Don't*

Even Think About It and *Exes Anonymous*. Her latest book is *Jane Austen's Guide to Dating*, which has also been optioned. Her books have been translated into fifteen languages. Together with Stella Duffy she has edited an anthology of women-behaving-badly crime stories, *Tart Noir*; their joint website is www.tartcity.com

Wendy Holden
Wendy Holden was a journalist before becoming an author. She has published six novels, all top-ten bestsellers, and is married with two young children.

Anna Johnson
Anna Johnson was born in London and her journalistic career started in Australia with *Stiletto* magazine in Sydney at the age of nineteen. She went on to serve as Fine Arts editor at *Interior Design* magazine, and art critic for the *Sydney Morning Herald*, Radio National and ABC TV, and a freelance writer for publications including *Vogue* Australia, *Vogue* UK, *Harper's Bazaar* Australia, the *Evening Standard*, Conde Nast *Traveler*, *Vanity Fair* and *Elle*. She has also worked for BBC Scotland, SBS TV and Foxtel's *By Design*. Her first book *Three Black Skirts*, is published in seventeen languages and her second book, the bestseller cult fashion title *Handbags: The power of the purse*, is now going into European translation. Currently she divides her time between New York and Sydney.

Belinda Jones
Belinda Jones is the author of four novels – *The Paradise Room*, *The California Club*, *I love Capri* and *Divas Las*

Vegas – and one real-life romp across America called *On the Road to Mr Right*, which made it onto the *Sunday Times'* list of top ten works of nonfiction in 2004. Belinda grew up in Oxford and Devon, dreams of owning an Italian villa and is currently renting an apartment in a mock southern plantation mansion in Los Angeles, California. For more information visit www.belindajones.com

Nicola Kraus & Emma McLaughlin

Nicola Kraus and Emma McLaughlin are the authors of the bestselling novels *The Nanny Diaries* and *Citizen Girl*. They live and write in New York City.

Melanie La'Brooy

Melanie La'Brooy studied at the University of Melbourne, majoring in art history and classics, which finally came in handy with the release of *Troy*. She spent five years working with art auction house Christie's in both Sydney and Melbourne, before becoming a full-time writer. She believes there are ten different ways to misspell and mispronounce her surname, but would be interested to hear any further suggestions. Melanie is the author of *Love Struck* and *The Wish List*, which have been published in Australia, New Zealand, Europe and the United States.

Kathy Lette

After several years as a singer in the Salami Sisters, a newspaper columnist in Sydney and New York (collected in the book *Hit and Ms*) and a television sitcom writer for Columbia Pictures in Los Angeles, Kathy Lette began writing novels, producing *Puberty Blues* (now a major motion picture), *Girls' Night Out*, *The Llama Parlour*, *Foetal Attraction*, *Mad Cows* (made into a movie starring Joanna Lumley and Anna Friel), *Altar Ego*, *Nip 'n' Tuck* and *Dead Sexy*, all of them international bestsellers. She is now published in 17 languages and over 100 countries. She lives in London with her husband and two children.

Louise Limerick

Louise Limerick is a Brisbane-born novelist and mother of three. Her first novel, *Dying for Cake*, was published by Pan Macmillan in 2003. In 2004, she was selected for a *Sydney Morning Herald*'s Best Young Australian Novelists' award. She is currently working on her second novel.

Gay Longworth

Gay Longworth was born in London in 1970. She lives there with her husband, a theatre producer, and their daughter. She has written four novels – *Bimba*, *Wicked Peace*, *Dead Alone* and *The Unquiet Dead* – and should currently be at work on her fifth. She also wrote 'Harvest' for *Big Night Out* and is delighted to have been asked to write for yet another impressive edition of *Girls' Night In*.

Mardi McConnochie

Mardi McConnochie is a novelist and scriptwriter. Her first novel, *Coldwater*, was shortlisted for the Commonwealth Writers' Prize (First Novel – Pacific Region) and translated into four languages. In 2004, she was named one of the *Sydney Morning Herald*'s Best Young Australian Novelists for her novel *The Snow Queen*. Her third novel, *Fivestar*, will be published in 2005.

Monica McInerney

Monica McInerney is the bestselling author of five novels, *Family Baggage*, *The Alphabet Sisters*, *A Taste for It*, *Upside Down Inside Out* and *Spin the Bottle*. Monica grew up in a family of seven children, in the Clare Valley wine region of South Australia, where her father was the railway stationmaster. She has worked in book publishing, arts marketing, children's television and the music industry, and has lived in many parts of Australia and in Ireland and England. She now lives in Dublin.

Chris Manby

In 1995 Chris Manby met a New York psychic who told her she would write seven novels. She has just published her ninth, which means she probably won't marry that millionaire either! Raised in Gloucestershire, Chris now lives in London. Her hobbies include Pilates and finding creative excuses for avoiding it. Her novels, *Flatmates, Second Prize, Deep Heat, Lizzie Jordan's Secret Life, Running Away From Richard, Getting Personal, Seven Sunny Days, Girl Meets Ape* and *Ready Or Not*, are all published by Hodder and Stoughton.

Lara Martin

Winner of the 2004 Dilmah *Women's Weekly* Short Story Competition, Lara Martin completed an arts degree at University of Western Australia, which included a creative writing unit. She has contributed to a poetry anthology and is currently working on a fantasy novel. She lives in a small coastal town in Western Australia.

Carole Matthews

Carole Matthews is the author of nine outstandingly successful romantic comedy novels. Her unique sense of humour has won her legions of fans and critical acclaim all over the world. Her books include *A Compromising Position*, *The Sweetest Taboo* and *With or Without You*. *For Better, For Worse* was selected by one of the United States' top TV book clubs, sending it straight onto the *USA Today* bestseller list. *A Minor Indiscretion* is in development in Hollywood. Her books are published in seventeen different countries. To find out more go to www.carole matthews.com

Anna Maxted

Anna Maxted is a freelance writer and the author of the international bestsellers *Behaving Like Adults*, *Getting Over It* and *Running in Heels*. Her latest novel, *Being Committed*, was published in 2004 by ReganBooks. She lives in London with her husband, novelist Phil Robinson, their sons and two cats.

Sarah Mlynowski

Twenty-something Sarah Mlynowski was born in Montreal, Canada. After receiving an honours degree in English literature from McGill University, Sarah moved to Toronto to work for a romance publisher. Unfortunately, she never met Fabio. But she did write her bestselling first novel, *Milkrun*, which has since been published in sixteen countries. Sarah is the author of *Fishbowl*, *As Seen on TV*, *Monkey Business*, and the teen novel *Bras & Broomsticks*, as well as co-editor of the American edition of *Girls' Night*

In. Currently a full-time writer, Sarah lives in New York. Say hello at www.sarahmlynowski.com

Santa Montefiore

Santa Montefiore was born in England. She is the author of *Meet Me Under the Ombu Tree*, *The Butterfly Box*, *The Forget-me-not Sonata*, *The Swallow and the Hummingbird* and *Last Voyage of the Valentina*. She lives with her husband, historian Simon Sebag-Montefiore, and their two children in London.

Liane Moriarty

The eldest of six children, Liane Moriarty grew up in Sydney and was one of those annoying little girls whose friends had to hide their books when she came to play. She became an advertising copywriter and has written everything from websites and catalogues to TV commercials and cereal boxes. Her first novel, *Three Wishes*, was published in 2003 and her second novel, *The Last Anniversary*, was published this year.

Elizabeth Noble

Elizabeth Noble is the author of two novels, *The Reading Group* and *The Tenko Club* (Hodder & Stoughton). Her third, *Alphabet Weekends*, will be out in January 2006. She lives in a haunted vicarage in Surrey with her incredibly tolerant husband, David, and her two young daughters, Tallulah and Ottilie, who are actually more frightening than the ghosts. As she careers towards forty, her girls' nights out have definitely become more womanly (and the more precious for it) – and, yes, said fabulous women were involved in a 'research' trip to Las Vegas for this story, and, no, she's not telling . . .

Adele Parks
Adele Parks lives in London. She has published five best-selling novels to date: *Playing Away, Game Over, Larger than Life, The Other Woman's Shoes* and *Still Thinking of You*. Her books are sold throughout the world. Her sixth novel, *Husbands*, will be published in June 2005.

Victoria Routledge
Victoria Routledge was born in the Lake District and she prefers it when it's raining. She also likes cars, strong coffee and spooky old houses. Victoria's latest novel, *Constance and Faith*, is published by Simon & Schuster.

Allison Rushby
Having failed at becoming a ballerina with pierced ears (her childhood dream), Allison Rushby became a novelist instead. Her first novel, *allmenarebastards.com*, was published in Australia in 2000. It has since been translated into Czech and published in the United States as *Friday Night Cocktails. It's Not You It's Me* followed and has been translated into Italian. Her new novel, *Hating Valentine's Day*, was released for Valentine's Day 2005. Visit Allison at www.allisonrushby.com, where you can vent about Valentine's Day and see Allison update her diary irregularly, mainly with sad-Mummy, baby and cat photos.

Tamara Sheward

Tamara Sheward is a journalist, occasional smut peddler and author of *Bad Karma: confessions of a reckless traveller in Southeast Asia* (Penguin Australia, Summersdale United Kingdom), the not entirely politically correct tale of two hapless Australians attempting to stagger off the backpacker trail. An aficionado of independent travel to the world's weirder places, Tamara has recently returned from a solo jaunt across Russia and Mongolia, where she bumbled through war-torn Chechnya, survived a railway inferno and learnt to love the taste of raw pig lard.

Rebecca Sparrow

Rebecca Sparrow's first novel, *The Girl Most Likely*, is about a travel writer who goes to Vegas, secretly marries her American boyfriend and winds up living in her childhood bedroom at her parents' house, nursing divorce papers. Coincidentally, Rebecca Sparrow was a travel writer who secretly married her American boyfriend in Vegas and wound up living in her childhood bedroom at her parents' house, nursing divorce papers. Aside from writing novels, Rebecca writes a weekly column for the *Courier-Mail* and volunteers as the national publicity co-ordinator of War Child Australia. Her second novel, *The Year Nick McGowan Came To Stay*, is due out in 2006. You can learn more about Rebecca at www.rebeccasparrow.com

Rachael Treasure

Rachael Treasure is the author of bestselling novels *Jillaroo* and *The Stockmen*, and the SBS Television screenplay *Albert's Chook Tractor*. A former rural journalist, Rachael now lives in Tasmania where she farms sheep and breeds kelpies, stockhorses and human babies with her husband. She has an addiction to the land, lanolin and writing. She is currently working on her second baby, third book and wool clip.

Alisa Valdes-Rodriguez

Alisa Valdes-Rodriguez is the *New York Times* bestselling author of the novel *The Dirty Girls Social Club*, which will be a television series on the Lifetime Network. Her second novel, *Playing with Boys*, was published in October 2004 and her third novel, *Make Him Look Good*, comes out in 2006. An award-winning print and broadcast journalist, Alisa was on-staff at the *Boston Goble* and *Los Angeles Times* and holds a master's in journalism from Columbia University. Alisa is a jazz saxophonist and is at work on her debut album, due out sometime this year. She lives in New Mexico.

Louise Voss

Louise Voss is the author of four novels for Black Swan/Transworld: *To Be Someone*, *Are You My Mother?*, *Lifesaver* and *Games People Play*. She lives near Hampton Court Palace in south-west London, with her seven-year-old daughter and their flatulent cat. Her website is www.louisevoss.com

Fiona Walker

Fiona Walker began her writing career at just twenty-one, and had instant success with her first novel. Since then she has written eight bestsellers, most recently, *Tongue in Cheek*. In her trademark 'bucolic frolics', larger-than-life characters enjoy sex and laughter, as well as tears and temptation, in action-packed rollercoaster plots with the best loved-up endings in the business. Fiona lives in cheerful chaos in the Cotswolds with her husband, four horses and two dogs.

Daisy Waugh

Daisy Waugh has written three bestselling novels, *The New You Survival Kit*, *Ten Steps to Happiness* and *A Bed of Roses* (watch out for the pricks). She is married with two children and lives in London and France.

Kris Webb & Kathy Wilson

Sisters Kris Webb and Kathy Wilson are the Brisbane-born authors of the novels *Sacking the Stork* and *Inheriting Jack*. They began writing together five years ago while living in different countries. 'Number 6 in Race 6' is their first joint project since being back in the same city.

Isabel Wolff

Isabel Wolff read English at Cambridge, and worked as a broadcaster and journalist before becoming a full-time writer. She is the author of six bestselling romantic comedies, including *Rescuing Rose*, *Behaving Badly* and *A Question of Love*, and is published in over twenty languages. She lives with her family in West London and spends most of her spare time playing table-football – at which she excels.

Deborah Wright

Deborah Wright is the author of the bestselling magical romantic comedies *The Rebel Fairy* and *Under My Spell.* Her new novel, *Love Eternally,* a ghostly love story, was published this year by Time Warner Books.